# *Portal Warriors*

THE COMPLETE DIVINITY WARRIORS SERIES

MICHELLE M. PILLOW

MICHELLEPILLOW.COM

ISBN: 978-1-62501-325-5

Published by The Raven Books LLC

Cover design by Silvana G. Sánchez / SP Designs

# Divinity Warriors Series

In a land forever at war, the Starian men are so busy fighting that their marriage ceremony has been reduced to a "will of the gods" event where they simply pick a woman out of a lineup and claim her as a wife. With women becoming scarce, it's necessary to trade the offworld Divinity Corporation for brides.

They live a very Medieval-like existence. Instead of medical advancement and technology, all of their focus has been on developing weaponry and battle strategy. With places named for war, such as Spearhead and Battlewar, these men have been left in charge way too long. They are in desperate need of a woman's touch.

# *Divinity Series*

**Divinity Warriors**
Lilith Enraptured
Fighting Lady Jayne
Keeping Paige
Taking Karre

**Divinity Healers**
Ariella's Keeper
Seducing Cecilia
Linnea's Arrangement

# Author Updates

Join the Reader Club Mailing List to stay informed about new books, sales, contests and preorders!

http://michellepillow.com/author-updates/

# *Lilith Enraptured*

BOOK ONE BY MICHELLE M. PILLOW

Second Electronic Printing January 2012, The Raven Books

First Electronic Printing March 2009

ISBN 9781452403717

# *About Lilith Enraptured*

DIVINITY WARRIORS BOOK ONE

**In a land forever at war, meeting women is the last thing they can think about, so what's a lonely alpha warrior to do?**

Sorin of Firewall lives in a land forever at war. In fact, the Starian men are so busy fighting, their marriage ceremony has been reduced to an alpha male "will of the gods" event where they simply pick a woman out of a lineup and claim her as a wife. With women becoming scarce, it's necessary to trade the offworld Divinity Corporation for brides. Duty-bound to attend the ceremony, he has no intention of picking a bride, let alone one from another dimension. That is, until he sees Lilith, the bewitching woman sent by the gods to reward—or punish?—him.

# CHAPTER 1

"The faster you make them come, the less time you must spend in their presence," Sera whispered, her words accented with an unfamiliar intonation. The tight fit of her white corset top squeezed her healthy waist and thrust up two very generous breasts. Long blue skirts billowed around her legs. She eyed the half dozen girls in the cell as she handed them loaves of bread. The need to be helpful shone from her sincere expression. "That is all they want—a vessel to find release in. Do not expect tenderness, but if you don't deny them, if you don't resist, you'll be treated fairly enough. And if you give them sons, you'll be greatly rewarded. Life here is not so bad."

Lilith Grian didn't move. She was still trying to get over the fact that she'd gone to bed in her own, lonely San LoFrancis apartment and awoke to find herself kidnapped and locked away in some small cell packed full of terrified women, with nothing but a long white robe over her body. The thick wool and shapeless design was a little too "sacrificial" for her tastes. A sniffle sounded next to her and Lilith glanced at the dark-haired woman crying next to her.

"This isn't happening, this isn't happening," the woman repeated, over and over. "Wake up, Edith, wake up."

Almost pleading, Sera shoved a loaf of bread toward Lilith. "I'm telling you how to best survive this place, please, listen. Spreading your thighs is an easy enough task for a decent life. Don't bring trouble upon yourself. Let them find release. They are not such boars when they get what they want."

Edith continued to rock herself, refusing bread and becoming more hysterical with every breath. Lilith wasn't sure who "they" were, but she sure as hell didn't like them already. Unlike Edith, she wasn't upset about the whole inter-dimensional travel scenario. As an historical and cultural analyst for the Divinity Corporation, it was her duty to jump from one plane of existence to another and collect intelligence on that world. She loved discovering the different intricate paths of the human experience, how one tiny event could change the course of humanity. What did concern Lilith was the fact that this jump wasn't assigned, and she was supposed to have two weeks off pending a board review of her last screwed-up mission.

Since Divinity had the only known source of top secret inter-dimensional travel technology on her plane, she guessed that maybe the review wasn't going her way. That or someone wanted her gone. Out of the four-hundred-thirty-six known dimensions, she didn't recognize this one as being charted, but to be fair it was difficult to determine much from inside a prison cell. As an analyst, Lilith had traveled to and studied most of the parallel planes. From what Sera described and the way everyone was dressed, this was new territory.

*They shipped me off to an uncharted dimension?*

Shock at her surroundings turned to outrage. This wasn't an accident. She would have had to have been drugged to be dressed in this outfit and sent through the portal unaware. Natural slips were extremely rare and completely predictable by the company. Sure as sunshine, a portal would not have opened up in her bedroom.

*How dare they! One fuck-up that wasn't even my fault and I'm suddenly exiled?*

She wondered how human this reality was. Some had vampires and werewolves, some had faeries and gnomes, and some had humanoids so alien her dimension's species were hardly compatible. Many of them had never even heard of dimensional travel or portals.

Some societies were obsessed to the point of compulsion, some with power, some with medical advancement and some with gladiator fights to the death.

"I can't be here," Edith whispered, shaking her head as if to make it all go away.

Partly taking pity on the frightened woman and partly desperate to get her to shut up, Lilith asked, "Where are you from?"

"San Francisco," Edith said. "What's going on here? Who are these people? Is this a reality show?"

Lilith ran through possibilities in her mind, trying to narrow down the geography to the right plane. "Is that the United States or Dominative Republic?"

"United States," Edith mumbled, sniffing loudly.

Lilith nodded. No wonder the woman was scared. Her dimension had only theorized alternative realities. They weren't even close to learning how to control them. This would be like time travel to her.

"First, you're not crazy. This is another plane of existence you've stepped into." When the woman only looked confused, Lilith explained, "Looking at a foreign dimension is like looking at your world if it had evolved in a different way. To a point there are many similarities. Languages, generally, are relatively similar. Some people will look the same, but not be the same people. Certain events like natural disasters will be shared. Weather is the same and this is still Earth. These people are still human-ish."

Lilith frowned, studying the iron bars keeping them locked in. Apparently, this particular dimension hadn't made it too far past the Middle Ages—if the trencher to hold the bread, serving wench and barbaric mentality of "just make him come and keep him happy" was any indication.

"You're as crazy as they are," Edith declared, backing away from her.

*So much for helping out my fellow humanoid.*

The other women in the cell held themselves quiet. Each wore the white, shapeless dress with bare feet. A blonde woman whimpered pathetically, watching as a tall, black-haired woman paced in front of her as if she might pounce. The dark-skinned beauty strode with amazing grace and poise, much like a dancer or martial artist.

A redhead merely sat, staring at the bars as if she knew exactly what was happening and where she was. Her fingers picked absentmindedly at the long sleeve of her gown. She hadn't moved since they woke up that morning. The last prisoner, a well-endowed brunette, had pulled a thin metal clip out of her upswept hair and thrust it into the outside lock, trying to work the door free.

Suddenly, the brunette jerked her hand back and thrust the clip into her hair. A burly man dressed in a hard leather jerkin and dark breeches approached the cells, standing between the bars and the blue-grey stone wall on the other side of the narrow hall. Metal diamonds plated the leather, creating a symmetrical pattern over his thick chest. The guard crossed his thick arms, creating a veritable blockade more effective than the iron.

Lilith knew how to defend herself if the need arose, but he would be a hard opponent to beat. Well, to be honest, she hadn't actually practiced her defensive moves like she should have been according to Divinity employee policy. Her punches would only do so much damage and he had the muscle mass to absorb her blows with ease. A long, thin scar traced down the side of his cheek, adding a dangerous appeal to his look. Edith and the blonde whimpered. Lilith couldn't help but note that maybe she was the only one who thought the man appealing.

The warrior guard studied them one by one, not appearing pleased with what he saw. Then, motioning to the side, he beckoned another warrior man to appear next to him. "The flaxen one and the crying one. They do not carry themselves well. Take them and give them the philter."

Lilith automatically touched a lock of her straight, blonde hair. Her heart jumped a little in her chest, until she saw the guard look at the other flaxen-headed woman.

"What?" Edith screamed. "No, wait! I'll be good. I swear I'll be good. Please, don't hurt me. Please, I'll do anything you want. Do you want me to make you come? I will. I swear I will. I'll do you all!"

To disprove her point, her body began to shake and she started bawling anew.

The guard looked disgusted by her display. Lilith couldn't say she blamed him. Where was the woman's honor? Her pride? If death was to come, there was nothing to be gained by tears. What she should be doing is analyzing their environment and calculating her escape.

The barred door opened and four men filed inside. Their massive warrior-like presence made her feel tiny in comparison as they crowded the cell. Two grabbed the now sobbing Edith and dragged her out. The blonde screamed, kicking and fighting as tears streamed down her face. The four remaining women held perfectly still. Lilith did not want to be grabbed next. The gods only knew what this "philter" was. It didn't sound pleasant.

As soon as the men were gone, the brunette went back to work, her face set as she tried to feel around the lock with her hairpin. The cell became eerily quiet now that the two women had been taken away.

"You won't be able to open it," the redhead said, staring at the lock picker. "Even if you did, there would be no escape. You'd have to fight through the warriors' hall, out of the guarded castle gates and run three strikes over open prairie until you reach the forest. Should you survive the wild beasts that live there, you'd soon find yourself prisoner to an even more vicious race of creatures—monsters so fierce and depraved they'll make you beg for death. Trust me, with the war going on in this forsaken place, we're in the better of the two sides."

"Who are you that we should trust what you say?" the brunette asked.

"Name's Paige," the redhead answered.

"Lilith," Lilith inserted, glad they'd finally started communicating. She didn't blame them for being cautious. All morning there had been a secret judging and assessing between them.

"What do they want with us?" The black-haired woman stopped pacing. All eyes turned to her. "Oh, I'm called Jayne."

"They want us to be their whores," Paige answered, bitterness seeping into her hard tone. "They don't call it that, but that's what they want—a subservient woman to rub their feet and spread her legs. If you don't, they get pissed and the whole lot of them stares at you like you are demon spawn incarnate and blames you for your chosen warrior's bad mood. It's either fuck them and suck them, or you're treated like the bottom rung of Starian society."

"Again, I ask, why should we trust you? We don't know you." The brunette continued to try to pick the lock. "You could be a plant sent here to make us behave with horror stories of what's beyond the tree line."

"I don't care if you trust me, but I know what I'm talking about. This isn't my first time in a cage." Paige tilted her head back and sighed. "They'll be coming to get us soon."

"What's your name, locksmith?" Jayne asked the brunette.

"Karre."

"Well, Karre," Jayne said, "I don't think we have much of a choice. If we all work together, maybe we stand a chance. Now, I don't know how we all got here and at this point I don't think it matters, but I do know I'm not staying to spend the rest of my life as some guy's sex toy."

"I agree." Lilith stood, hoping Jayne would have a logical solution they could use. "We need a plan."

"Fine," Karre grumbled.

Paige opened her eyes and shook her head. "Don't look to me to join your little band. You're only fooling yourselves. I've been to the Hanging Forest. I made it all the way to the Starian borders and I've seen the creatures that wait beyond."

"What about a dimension jump?" Lilith asked. "Does anyone know if this place has inter-dimensional travel technology?"

"A what?" Paige furrowed her brow in confusion.

"Staria? It's too primitive. They don't have the technology here," Karre said. "I got a glimpse of the castle when they brought me to this cell. Through a door I saw servants cart water from a well in buckets and the drive wasn't paved. No artificial lights or motorized vehicles. Though there were several large horses."

"I've never been here," Jayne contributed, "but I'm inclined to agree from what I've observed. These prisons don't use lasers or shocks."

"Someone's coming." Karre pulled her arms out from between the bars. She thrust her lock-picking tool back into her upswept hair.

A new guard arrived, dressed similar to the other men she'd seen. His nose had a crook across the bridge. He frowned. "Only three new ones?"

"It's all they sent us," said the man who'd ordered the other two women away.

"How's it going, Edward?" Paige taunted, her face hardening to hide all emotion. "I see the nose is healing nicely."

"Lady Paige," Edward growled, glaring at her as if he wanted to pull the sword from his waist and run her through.

"Open the door, Eddie," Paige taunted. "Let me break it again."

Edward grumbled, but didn't answer.

"I thought there were five new," another of Edward's fellow barbarians said, completely ignoring Paige.

"What's wrong, Brock? Don't I count anymore in your little ledger?" Paige taunted. Lilith kept quiet, observing as was her nature to do.

"You are not new," Brock stated, frowning at her in disapproval. "Your lord is waiting for you and I do hope his punishment is harsh."

Paige's smirk faltered. Brock grinned victoriously.

"You already have one of these guys?" Karre whispered, grabbing Paige's arm.

"Two were not suitable. They were taken away," Edward said, answering his companion. His nostrils flared in distaste. "Too weak."

"Three will have to do," Brock answered, sighing. As the two men walked off, he added, "I'll tell my Sera to make ready."

A long silence filled the cell, broken only when Paige whispered, "Ladies, welcome to Battlewar Castle."

If Lord Sorin hated anything, he hated waste—wasted resources, wasted hours, wasted lives. And, as far as he was concerned, these breeding ceremonies were a waste of time. Nothing in the process of prancing women before the warriors, who then picked them based on an urge, guaranteed a well-made match. Their ancestors had the right idea when they'd raided villages and took the women they wanted. At least the raids served three purposes—the need for men to find a woman to put into their bed, the need for men to have sons and the need for men to fight their wars. Besides, going on a raid would not take the warriors away from the battlefront, not like traveling back to Battlewar Castle in the northernmost part of their kingdom for a breeding ceremony.

Women were scarce in this hard land. Sons became a necessity and their natural evolution seemed to answer the call with more sons than daughters—when they did have children. Their low birthrate wasn't from lack of trying when the warriors were home, but war took them away all too often. Sometimes forever.

Sorin glanced around his castle chambers, the place he always stayed when he came to Battlewar. Ever since his own castle, Firewall, burned to the ground, this was as close to a stationary home as he had. Like all male rooms, the decorations were sparse—a large bed with a mammoth-wolf fur coverlet, a large wall filled with every weapon he'd ever owned in chronological order, a fireplace, comfortable chair, a trunk for his personal belongings and two doors.

The black stone walls pressed in on him. He shouldn't be here. He should be at the encampment with the other men. What did he care if tradition dictated he at least attempt to take a breeding partner, a mate, a bride, a whatever the women liked to call the joining nowadays. He had a bride once and it did him little good. Bianka, the accursed wench, was dead and it suited him just fine not to replace her.

Still moist from his recent bath, he adjusted his hips on the chair and wrapped his callused fingers around the semi-erect member between his thighs. Granted, self-satisfaction wasn't as gratifying as the real thing, but it would keep his head level during the ceremony. He would never forgive himself if he did something stupid. The longer his kind went without the exhausting pleasure of the bed, the more their moods were said to be altered. Sorin grunted. He thought he did just fine without a woman.

He gripped his cock hard, squeezing in irritation as he tried not to think of how he wanted to be far away from there. It didn't take long for his erection to reach full capacity and begin to ache. Veins strained along the firm flesh, leading a familiar trail over his shaft from thick base to smooth tip. The water dried and the rough texture of his war-hardened hand caused an insistent friction along his shaft. Nothing about the grip reminded him of the soft folds of a woman and that's the way he liked it—hard and empty.

He stroked fast and tight. The muscles in his stomach tightened. His body knew its part and didn't need to be romanced into climaxing. Closing his eyes, he let the end come. Physical release sated one hunger, the feast being prepared below stairs would take care of the other. By morn, he'd ride out with his brother to join the battlefront.

Sorin stood and stretched his hands over his head. The low fire had dried the water from his naked flesh. All this sitting around and reflecting didn't sit well on his mind. Completely comfortable in his nakedness, he strode to the trunk and flung it open. Tradition demanded he dress nicely this evening, even though he much preferred armor to silken threads.

But hate all this nonsense as he may, it was his turn to sit before the stage and watch the newest batch of women being paraded before them. And, like the several times before, he'd do nothing but sit and wait and curse the hours of his life that were being wasted.

# CHAPTER 2

"I say we make a fight of it," Jayne put forth, twisting her arms in an effort to be free of the ropes around her wrists. She'd already put up a good fight as the men came to restrain them in the prison cell. Karre had been no less defiant, though her moves seemed more calculated and her eyes ever watchful. Paige simply held out her hands and let them bind her, as if whatever fight she'd once had disappeared completely.

Lilith clearly wasn't the fighter Jayne was, nor was she the beaten pushover Paige had obviously become. If anything, she was like Karre, watching and waiting, analyzing as she always did on assignment. Only this time there were no safety protocols if she got into trouble. The fact terrified her. She knew self-defense and had been trained in basic survival, but in truth, she was just an analyst. She spent most of her field hours in libraries and tech labs, learning about the different dimensions' individual histories and political systems. Occasionally she'd attend banquets and celebrations, always observing, rarely participating. She collected intelligence, sometimes known by that particular plane's authorities, sometimes not. Her job was to observe and under no circumstances was she to interfere.

So what did all those years of training mean now? Did she fight?

Every instinct told her to stay calm and observe, to wait and learn. But was fear making her cling to the familiar? She had to remind herself that this wasn't a mission. This was her life, potentially the rest of her life if she didn't find a way out. There was no safety button hidden in a necklace that would alert the company to come and get her. She was on her own.

No, that wasn't true. She had four potential allies standing right next to her in the same sacrificial white gowns and rope chain accessories.

"Paige already tried fighting and running," Lilith whispered, automatically testing the tight ropes around her wrists. They bit into her flesh, seeming to get tighter the more she pulled at them. A guard stood at the end of a long hall, which passed rows of cells much like the one they'd been kept in. The women made no move to follow the man out of the prison area. "The way I see it, we don't have any choice but to join forces and pool our knowledge. I think we should gather intelligence. None of us seem to be from this world, so that means they had to get us all here somehow. If we keep our ears open, we'll find out how. There might be a way out of here yet."

"I've already looked for fairy rings when I was in the forest," Paige said. "I didn't even find evidence of fairies. Though, I'm not surprised. Fairies don't like wars and this place is nothing but one giant battlefield. I think my journey here was a one-way trip."

"Fairy rings?" Karre snorted with soft laughter.

"What?" Paige asked, looking around at the others. "Isn't that how you all got here?"

"No more talking. They're ready for you," the guard announced, motioning his fist forward. "Let's go. March."

Lilith didn't readily move. The prisons felt oddly safe. Once she stepped out into this world who knew what she'd encounter.

"March!" the guard yelled in irritation.

Lilith jolted, shivering.

"Let me help." Paige tugged on her arm, dragging Lilith forward a few steps before letting go. "Brock's ill-tempered and in the end you'll still be marching out there. Just be glad he's letting you keep the clothes. This is one group you don't want to greet naked."

The women filed out of the prison corridor into a blue-grey stone passageway. This time one of the guards did walk behind them as they followed Brock. Wooden doors with thick metal handles spread out on either side, lit by torches placed on the walls. Material whispered with each step and the sound of their bare feet padding across the cold floor created a steady beat to the harder clomping of the guards' boots. Otherwise, the castle was silent.

The long passageway turned into another, then into another, becoming an endless maze of twists and turns. As the sound of voices penetrated their march, Lilith stared past Karre's shoulder. A new light shone from ahead, brighter than the torches but still flickering like firelight. The nearer they walked toward the light, the louder the sounds became. Rowdy, gruff and very male, the voices caused Lilith to falter in her steps. Paige bumped into her back, only to forcefully push her forward.

Her breathing deepened and her heart raced. Each heavy thump brought her closer to passing out. The firelight began to dance in her vision.

*No!*

Lilith jerked her senses back from the threat of oblivion and steeled her nerves. She might be just an analyst, but she had been trained for tactical situations. She needed to focus. This was a mission. She wasn't being paid for it, but it was perhaps the most important mission she had ever been on.

Holding her head up high, she walked under the narrow archway into a crowded hall. First, she needed to survey her surroundings. Battlewar Castle appeared to be a beefy evolution of the medieval period, honed to perfection by centuries of care, and decorated by men. Lilith had seen castles before and, though they had distinctly different styles, the layouts were generally the same. If it stayed true to common form, there would be a town beyond the inner gate, spread out over the distance and leading to an outer gate.

Warriors watched the four women with interest from the long rows of tables in the main hall. Though gruff in appearance, most of them looked recently bathed. Some wore lightweight tunics, others leather jerkins like the guards, others light chainmail and pieces of armor, and still others wore no shirt at all. Big metal goblets had been set before them, next to matching pitchers. She'd thought the guards were scary, but some of these men were practically gigantic. Muscles bulged, littered with puckered scars and tattooed designs. Despite her best efforts, her heart hammered wildly and her throat became dry. She was expected to sexually satisfy one of these warrior knights? If their cocks were anything like the rest of them, they'd tear her apart.

The light came from a large fireplace along a far side of the room. Like most things in this place, it was immense and towering. Woven tapestries lined the walls in strips of material, showcasing coats-of-arms and various symbols she didn't yet recognize.

"Come on," the guard muttered, his voice not booming like before as he led them through a path made between the tables.

Lilith noticed women mixed in with some of the men. Though not so tight as Sera, they had corset tops clearly designed to entice and enflame their male leaders, and skirts for easy access. A bearded knight licked his lips as she passed, his eyes raking over her as if she were already naked and strapped to the table. She swallowed hard, realizing he wasn't the only one looking at her like that. Lilith wondered if the firelight revealed more of her naked body beneath the white gown than she would have liked. She pulled her arms close.

Sera's words echoed in her head, "The faster you make them come, the less time you must spend in their presence. That is all they want—a vessel to find release in."

Did they expect the women to please all these men? The hungry glances and deepened breathing didn't deny the idea. Tension filled the air and the talking had quieted by small degrees. The prisoners turned and were led forward to the front of the hall. A raised table, set high upon a platform of honor, awaited empty.

"Stand here," Brock ordered, pointing before the tables. Then yelling, he announced, "Bring in the firsts so they may make their choice."

Firsts? Did that mean her worst fear was correct? They would have to pleasure more than one of these giant, warrior men? However would she survive it?

The hall erupted into a crescendo of good-natured laughter and cheering. Six men walked into the main hall, fierce and proud. Their clothes gleamed in a way not seen in the others' clothing. A small detail, to be sure, but it did set these men apart from the others. Each wore a different colored long tunic, reaching to the knees, over tight brown breeches. Woven belts wound their waists, the end straps hanging along the right thighs.

A wave of foreboding washed over her. Lilith took in each man in turn. The first walked with a slight limp, though it didn't detract from the power of his stance. Next a dark-haired knight with softer set features and an easier gait followed. His gaze moved over each of the women in interest.

Suddenly, Lilith's eyes stopped and her body froze. The third man in line towered the others in breadth and height. A raw, potent energy radiated from him, hitting her in the chest. Every nerve tingled with awareness and warmth, creating a curious reaction between her legs.

Lilith didn't know what to make of him. His size frightened her even as it intrigued her—so large and thick, yet so purposeful in his movements. He walked with a stalking grace that came only from years of exercise and training. Dark hair framed his face in thick waves, not so long as to touch his shoulders, but long enough to make her want to sink her hands into its depths and pull. Silken blue clung to the sculpted valleys of his chest and arms.

Then he looked at her, intense dark brown eyes piercing hers, and she couldn't breathe. He didn't smile, didn't show any pleasure in what he saw. The hard line of his mouth tightened, as if he wanted nothing more than to jump over the table and strangle her. Fists clenched alongside his thighs, tight, hard balls of steel that could easily take her head off with one blow.

Terror filled her. What had she done to draw his notice or his anger? Had she stared too long? Did he simply hate blondes? She wrapped her arms around her waist, hugging tight. The man wouldn't stop staring at her, as if he knew he dominated her with just that one look. Was he going to be her "first"?

"We have to get out of here," she whispered, filled with the urge to run.

"There is nowhere to go," Paige said, just as quietly. "I already tried. Resign yourself for we will never escape this place. Survive or die, those are your options."

Sorin took several deep breaths, feeling as he did when about to go into battle. Heat filled him as tension worked its way into his limbs. With a single thought, he could will his body to spring into action. He could erase her from the world and end this before it started.

But it was too late. He was lost the moment he'd looked at her, had seen her big blue eyes staring at him in trepidation. No, he was lost before that, when he *felt* her looking at him, beckoning him with her unwavering gaze to find her in the crowd.

Temptress. Witch.

He willed the desire inside him to go away. It shouldn't have been so strong. He'd relieved himself like he always did, had spilled his seed to ease the lonely ache.

Light from the fireplace shone through the white of her gown, silhouetting the long length of her legs and arms. The linen clung to her shoulders, swooping gently along the curves of her breasts—breasts that would be bare beneath. The tied hands were a new addition to the ceremony, thanks to Sir Aidan's wayward woman, Lady Paige. Sorin's barbaric side found he liked the addition.

Hunger rushed into every limb, lifting his cock beneath the long tunic. He didn't think to hide the reaction. No one would care. It had been so long, so very long, since he'd had a woman in his bed. He suppressed a groan. Soft flesh. Round breasts. Taut nipples. Slick, warm vessel to catch his passion. That certain female smell when he pressed his nose to her sex.

A thought whispered in the back of his mind. *Maybe she's different. Maybe she'll be better. Maybe this one will stay.*

He cursed the thought. No. She wasn't different. She wasn't better. Sorin had made up his mind long ago. He'd come, he'd look, but he never, ever wanted to find someone. He wasn't meant to have this, or her, or any kind of peace. Sorin was born into a land of war. He was made for it, every piece of him. One of the bloodiest battles in their history happened the very hour his mother gave birth to him.

Some were lucky to find peace in marriage, but not him. Tradition and necessity dictated he come to these ceremonies and try to find someone. He came from a noble line, a position of power, one that demanded he have sons to carry on his family's name. But society could not make him choose. It could not make him step forward and lay claim.

"Mine."

Where did that word come from? It sounded like his voice, booming over the hall to quiet all who watched into stunned silence. It felt like his body refusing to go to his place at the table, instead moving forward with arm uplifted to point at the blonde-haired beauty. But it couldn't be his body or his voice. That would mean he'd just announced his claim. Everyone would have heard it. He couldn't back out once the word was said.

"Sorin?" his younger brother, Ronen, hissed. Like Sorin, Ronen led one of the more renowned armies in all of Staria. Very few would dare to challenge their word or honor and the fact made it even more impossible for Sorin to take back what he'd done.

"Mine," Sorin found himself repeating. Was he possessed? What madness was this? He kept walking toward her. She merely stared at him, those wide, gorgeous eyes capturing his. Straight blonde hair hung long down her back, just as a woman's should.

"Brother?" Ronen questioned. The shock was evident in his voice. Sorin couldn't blame him for the surprise because that very day he'd been instructing Ronen to stay strong and not fall for a woman's pretty face. And what did Sorin do? He claimed a woman with a pretty face.

The hall remained quiet. Sorin stopped before the woman, noting with pleasure that she didn't cringe and fall away from his looming presence. Her strength would serve her well. Years of frustrated desires surged inside him. He couldn't put them off any longer. Deny it as he might, he needed a woman. He would never admit the words out loud. The need was not just for physical release, but for the softness of her, the sweet smell and the temporary relief from the endless fighting that such a creature could bring.

*You tried this before, Sorin. Such things are not for you.*

*Fool.*

*Idiot.*

*Weak.*

His accusing thoughts infuriated. Reaching for her bound arms, he took hold of the ropes. Not even his condescending inner voice could stop his actions. Sorin held her gaze steady, stating so she couldn't mistake his claim, "You are mine."

---

*Did he say "mine"?*

If she could have forced her limbs to move, Lilith would have blazed a trail out of there so fast the castle would've exploded. She'd heard about people being petrified with fear, but she never realized it felt like this. Not even her heart seemed to beat in her chest. She opened her mouth only to close it. Her eyes stared at his, unable to blink. Sound wouldn't leave her throat. She tried again, working her lips several times before managing a very inaudible, "No."

Dark eyes narrowed. This wasn't a man used to being refused. All around her, the hall had silenced. She heard the gasps as he'd first spoken, followed by rushed whispers. But none of the others could have been as stunned as she.

*This man wants me? This impossibly strong, muscular man? This deadly warrior with the imposing features and angry eyes?*

"Ah." The man standing near the head table cleared his throat. "Rejoice, Lord Sorin has chosen!"

The statement came out more like a question than an announcement. Cheering erupted, jarring Lilith to her senses. She jerked her bound hands, trying to free them. Lord Sorin held tight, unaffected by her protests.

"No," she managed, loud enough to be heard by the women standing next to her.

A low growl escaped Sorin.

"Stop it." Lilith tugged harder, not caring who heard. "Let me go. This is a mistake. I did nothing wrong. I'm not supposed to be here. Contact Divinity Headquarters on dimensional plane 269. My employee number is 54367D. I don't belong here."

"Eh, my lord, if you wanted a woman, you should have waited to see their temperaments," a knight shouted, causing a round of laughter. "Methinks you found the shrew!"

"Ach, he's lucky to have a bit o' fire betwixt the sheets," another answered. A loud bang followed as people hit their goblets on the wooden tabletops.

"Are you saying my Bertha does not have fire?" the first man accused.

"Not as much as my Darla!" the second answered, the original playfulness no longer in his tone.

Fighting erupted behind her, but Lilith couldn't turn around. Sorin still stared at her, his dark eyes commanding.

"Come with me," Sorin ordered, tugging her behind him as he walked.

"Brother," the easy-going knight insisted from behind the table.

"It is done, Ronen," Sorin answered. "Tell Sera to send food to my chambers."

As he dragged her by her wrists from the crowded hall to a narrow archway next to the fireplace, Lilith tried to brace her feet against the floor. The fruitless effort caused her to stumble erratically so she gave it up. She glanced behind her. The other women appeared a shade paler as they watched her being carted away like a newly acquired sex slave. And as far as she knew, that's exactly what she was.

# CHAPTER 3

Lilith trembled as the giant man led her up a wide, spiraling stairwell. The noise of the hall faded behind her, insulated by the thick stone walls. The heavy thud of his boots echoed around her, encasing her in his ominous presence. He kept her wrists in his fist, but didn't look back at her.

She let her feet trip on the stairs, trying to make him stumble and let go. That's all she needed, for him to release her for just a second so she could run. Fleeing one man had to be better odds than fleeing from a packed hall. He didn't break stride, didn't let on that he felt her struggles. They passed a narrow slit in the wall, a thin window leading outside. They were getting high off the ground. She got a glimpse of an open field leading off into trees. Paige had told the truth.

"You have the wrong woman," Lilith broke the silence. Perhaps reason would work. Some primitive parallel cultures respected reasoning. "I'm an analyst."

Unexpectedly, he stopped and swung around to face her. "There is no mistake. The words were spoken, Lady Ann Anna List. It's done. You're mine."

She shook her head. He loomed over her, made all the taller by the higher step he stood upon. "I'm not—"

Sorin surged forward, tugging her into his chest at the same time. She crashed into him, gasping at the hard wall of his body. Not a measure of fat marred his thick frame. A shock of pure, sexual awareness poured over her flesh, enrapturing her nerves and turning her knees to weakened jelly.

"You are," he said.

"I'm not named Ann." Lilith's bound wrists were trapped between them, the sides pressed near the front of his thighs. If one of them moved, his cock would be squarely in her hands. "I-I'm Lilith Grian. I work for Divinity. Have you heard of them? I'm not supposed to be on this world. I'm not sanctioned to travel until after..." She paused, not wanting to say "my trial".

Sorin continued to stare at her, his brow slightly arched and his eyes cold.

"...after this thing. It's a mistake. Please, you appear very," she glanced at his chest, so close and powerful, "very reasonable. I'm sure you understand, I'm not—"

"You are," he answered, as if he hadn't heard a single thing she'd said.

Lilith gritted her teeth. Reason didn't work. Perhaps false bravado would. "I'm warning you. I'm trained to fight."

At that he grinned. The look did nothing to soften the hard lines of his face. He adjusted his hips and as she suspected, his cock pressed into her hands, letting her feel how very strong and powerful it really was. A hard knot formed in her stomach. Tears threatened her eyes as fear took hold. She held them back, feeling the burn in her nose. Her lips parted in shock and he took full advantage.

He didn't test her resolve or ask permission with a light brush of his lips. Instead, his mouth ordered her, commanding it to open wider with the probe of his tongue. The sweet, spicy taste of liquor flavored the hot kiss. It had been a very long time since a man kissed her like that.

Who the hell was she trying to fool? A man had never kissed her quite like that.

Pent-up desire and passion flowed through her, awakening nerves she'd long neglected. For a brief second, she thought of giving in. Who would know? This world was so far beyond the scope of hers. But when he had his way with her, would he pass her on to someone else? This man was a stranger on an uncharted world. She needed more facts. Lilith knew nothing about the true culture and laws of this place or of her place in it.

The taste of him burned into her mouth, combining with the very masculine smell of his body. She turned her head violently to the side, wrenching it back and forth to get her mouth away when his lips would follow. "No. Stop. Don't."

To her great surprise, Sorin let her go and stepped back. "You are right. This is not the place. Forgive me."

He hardly sounded contrite. Dizzy from the abrupt withdrawal, Lilith stumbled when he pulled her forward once more. The stone walls appeared to have darkened, not in reflected light but in color. "Where are you taking me?"

"The Black Tower," he answered, "our home. At least while we reside at Battlewar. When you come with me to the battlefront, we will stay in my tent."

"Our?" Lilith nearly collapsed in surprise. Did he just say she was going into battle? "Then you're not going to share me with the other men?"

"Share?" At that he almost looked offended. The blue tint of the stone faded into black, casting darker shadows over his face. Her heart raced and she backed away from the low tone of his voice. "I do not share what is mine. You are mine and you will not share yourself with others."

His possessive decree did not comfort her. Her breath sounded odd as it came out in rough pants. The end to this long stairwell had to be near.

"No, I'm not, Sorin," she said. "I don't belong here."

"You do now. I claimed you, you are mine. It is done. The decision is made." Coming to a door, he stopped and pushed it open. Without ceremony, he directed her inside.

Lilith's eyes went directly to the large bed covered with a fur pelt blanket. Firelight danced over the textured surface. She took a step away from him and then another, going the only direction she could —deeper into the chamber. The glint of metal caught her notice and she saw the weapons on the wall—gruesome, deadly instruments that would strike fear into anyone. The hilts were faded and worn, attesting to their frequent use.

Out of all the outcomes this day might bring, being tortured by deadly weapons hadn't crossed her mind. Lilith swallowed, realizing she'd held on to the idiotic idea that she'd be rescued if things went bad. But there was no safety feature hidden in her shapeless gown. Divinity would not be coming for her. This was real. Dark and twisted and real. If she refused, what would happen? If she gave in, what would he do? She'd never had a large warrior in her bed before, instead preferring to copulate with the tame, nonthreatening bookish types she met on assignment. There had been something safe and noncommittal to a man who lived on another plane—at least until now.

A warm hand touched the back of her neck and she gasped, jerking violently. She didn't dare move, but her eyes found a second door. It was only a few feet away, but it might as well have been a mile.

"Take this off," Sorin said. He brushed aside her hair and drew his mouth to her neck.

"Ah!" Lilith cried, running for the door. Her bound wrists made it impossible to pull the latch. She couldn't do this. Not with him. Selfishly, she wished he'd chosen one of the others. Jayne seemed tough. She'd know what to do with a guy like this. Even the quieter Karre could have handled the giant before her better than Lilith ever could.

Her escape ended as fast as it began. Sorin grabbed her arm and spun her around. Her back hit against the hard wood of the door. Lilith inhaled a deep, shaky breath.

"I do not feel like playing a teasing game. There is much I have to do." He stroked her cheek and looked meaningfully to the bed.

"Please." Lilith looked at the weapon-filled wall, quivering so badly she could no longer stand on her own. "Please, don't hurt me."

---

Sorin wasn't sure what exactly made him stop his pursuit. Her words were so soft and worried, and her body appeared so small and fragile trapped against the door. Her eyes stared at him in raw fear. He'd seen that look in battle—the wild, round gaze, the trepidation and terror. He did not want that look from her, not from the woman in his bed.

*Fool.*

*Idiot.*

*Weak.*

His body hummed with desire, reminding him how long it had been since he'd felt the softness of a female's touch. The painful arousal between his thighs annoyed him. Her resistance annoyed him. The wasted time he'd spend thinking about his new situation annoyed him. And the fact that he'd claimed her against all planning and better sense really annoyed him.

"Argh," he growled low in his throat. She jerked, closing her eyes tight. He could take her, make her want him. His desire begged him to. The taste of her mouth still lingered on his lips. She'd kissed him back in the stairwell. He'd felt her respond for the briefest of pleasurable seconds.

Why did she turn from him? Sorin didn't want her like this. He didn't want her scared of him, trembling like a fall leaf. Already he knew women were apprehensive of his size, but he was an accomplished lover. He could bring her to release. Even Bianka had given few complaints in that aspect of their marriage.

Sorin didn't need this aggravation. He needed someone who did her duty by him as he would by her. The Caniba tribes attacked further north than they ever had before, rising from the earth and disappearing like ghosts. That was where his concentration needed to be and he didn't have the time to explain it all to a stranger.

Frowning, he studied her tightly drawn face. He stepped back, pulling her away from the door so that he might open it. It had been a long time since he'd looked inside. The smell of dust wafted over him. Apparently, it had been a long time since any of the castle servants had gone in as well. It appeared they had listened to him when he ordered that the room should rot like the decay of his first marriage.

"You will live here," he instructed, feeling a slight twinge to think of another woman in Bianka's old quarters—even if Bianka only made use of it for one night. Light from his room cast into the dingy chamber, parting the shadows to reveal a dust-covered floor. Pale green cobwebs hung from the ceiling in withered strands, swinging gently and aimlessly. He hadn't thought to have the chamber prepared since he never planned on filling it. "Have it cleaned for it has seen little use. You should find whatever it is you females need for your daily routines."

"There's no other way out," Lilith observed, edging away from him. What happened to the proud woman who held her own in the main hall? He didn't like the protectiveness this fragile creature brought forth. "You're holding me prisoner?"

"There is no need to trap you, my lady. None of the others will touch you. They respect my claim." Sorin put distance between them. If she wasn't going to let him bed her, he wasn't sure what other need there was to be in her presence. His cock throbbed, so full and tight he could barely stand it. Every ounce of him pleaded for relief—the feel of her hand, the sucking kiss of her mouth, anything to end the suffering.

Striding to his fireplace, he grabbed an unlit torch and thrust it into the flames. Once lit, he went back into her room to find she hadn't moved. Sorin placed the torch in a sconce, casting the room with light.

He looked at the dirty bed. How easy it would be to bend her over the high edge. Growling low in his throat, he left her, slamming the door behind him. Once alone in his room, he paced the floor, tossing the front of his long tunic over his bent arm as he fumbled at the laces along his hip.

Sorin managed to free his sensitive cock from its painfully tight restraint. Every nerve in his body beseeched him to go to Lady Lilith. From the first moment, he wanted her. His body ached and his flesh burned.

"Witch," he whispered, trying to reason what had happened to make him claim her. "She's enraptured me in her spell."

He was lying to himself.

Starian men depended a lot on instinct. They made decisions fast and stuck by them. Sorin knew how to size up a person in a few seconds. In war, he had to know his opponent. Lilith held his most withering gaze when most men could not. She kept her arms close to her body when she moved and didn't wiggle and display herself for any man who cared to look in her direction. Her voice stayed soft, pleasingly so, even when she yelled. Well, "pleasingly" if he didn't take into account what she said. Hurt her? He'd never hurt a woman outside of battle, and then the heathen Caniba females could hardly be considered ladies on the same level as a Starian.

In one second, he knew. Lilith was for him. It did no good to deny it. He couldn't even explain it. But that was how their gods worked. He'd tried to force the ceremony before, thinking more of duty than fate. It had not worked out well for him. This time he acted on faith.

Then why in all of the burning forests was he standing alone in his bedchambers with his pants around his ankles about to grab his own cock?

Lilith caused his current affliction. It was her duty to take care of it. Why did she resist? The decision was made. She was his. Nothing would change that.

Gripping his erection hard, he began to stroke. This time, the vision of his new mistress filled his mind, fueling his passions. Sorin fell back onto his bed, into the soft fur of his coverlet. He cupped his balls, rolling them in his palm as he sought to bring himself relief.

Lilith paced the horrible bedroom, tugging at her bound wrists. A narrow window showed the impossible height of the tower she was supposed to call home. Even if she could squeeze through, it would be at least a nine-hundred-foot drop to her death. And falling was only a slightly worse option than going to face what awaited on the other side of the door.

Lord Sorin.

"Think, Lilith." She reached a dusty, spider-web-covered wall and turned to walk the other direction. This room was not acceptable. Sure, the amenities appeared to be fine, if she could dig them out from under the twenty thousand pounds of dust that covered almost every inch of the place. The only hint of the room's use before this night was a strange trail of footprints marring the blanket of dust on the floor. They started at Sorin's door and looked as though someone paced to the corner of the room, turned around and left, over and over again. "Forget the footprints. Forget the dust. Think, Lilith. Analyze the situation and come up with a plan. Academy might have been a long time ago, but you were trained to get out of sticky situations."

*Yeah,* her mind answered peevishly, *with the use of a Divinity emergency call-button hidden in my clothes.*

Now that she was out of Sorin's magnetically alluring presence, her mind seemed to come back from a foggy abyss. At the time, she hadn't realized the complete and utter effect he had on her. First, his eyes penetrated, causing every nerve to tingle. Then it was his smell, so masculine and erotic. He had the body of a gladiator, the grace of a martial artist and the face of a god of war. When he kissed her, raw passion washed across her body.

Lilith's breathing deepened and moisture pooled between her thighs. Each pacing step became a jolt to her system. She looked at the door. Who would know?

"I would," she answered her own question. "Think, Lilith."

Sorin's hands had been so strong and firm when they held her to the door, his tight body close to hers. And all he wanted was to throw her down on the bed and have his wicked, wicked way with her. With the way he moved and the very size of the rest of him, she just bet he knew how to work his well-endowed cock.

*Ah! Think of something else!*

"Um..." She looked around the room, desperate for a plan of escape. Just a few moments in Sorin's presence and she contemplated ways to separate him from his clothing. Men of war tended to have stamina. She bet he could last for hours.

*Stop it! I don't know anything about these kinds of men in bed. I'm no match for him. I don't like it rough, or painful, or... Stop it!*

He'd stopped when she'd told him to stop. Mr. Warrior Man had impulse control. Plus, he claimed no other man would touch her. He clearly was a man of power and, even if he wasn't, Lilith doubted any of the other knights would be stupid enough to cross such a formidable male.

"Escape." Lilith glanced at her bound wrists. First things first, she needed her wrists free from the ropes. Unlike Sorin's room, hers didn't have a wall teeming with weaponry.

Lilith walked to the door and leaned her ear against the wood. Inside silence greeted her. After several seconds, she became relatively sure he'd left. Lilith fumbled at the latch before pulling it open. Sorin's bedroom seemed an odd contrast to her dirty one as she stepped over the dirt-lined threshold. Not a speck marred his floor or the immaculately polished blades on the wall.

Lilith began to lift her arms, intent on grabbing the nearest blade to free herself, when a very peculiar noise stopped her. Friction? Rubbing?

She turned to the bed and froze. Sorin lay on his back, his tunic pulled aside and his pants open. One strong hand pumped the length of his very erect cock. Lilith inhaled a deep, shaky breath. Her earlier assumption had been right. The man was extremely well-endowed. His eyes met hers, completely unconcerned with the fact she reached for one of his blades, and he didn't stop pleasuring himself.

"Ah," Lilith stammered. "Um?"

"Have you come to finish me?" His lids fell heavy over his eyes, but he kept them on her as he quickened his pace.

Lilith glanced at the wall. He thought she came to kill him? She must be a laughable opponent indeed if he didn't bother to look concerned.

"Good. I want you to finish me. Straddle my waist and—"

"Hands," Lilith managed, "going to get...for the hands."

Straddle him? Her heart hammered out of control.

"Take off your gown and come here," he ordered. "I desire you to finish me."

Lilith didn't know how to respond. Did the well-proportioned, godlike man have no shame?

"It is too close for me to stop, but I will recover quickly to finish you." He panted hoarsely.

*No, apparently not.*

His body tightened and she could sense he was close to release. A part of her wanted to obey, to at least finish watching the erotic display before her. Her sex tingled, aching to be filled by the incredibly giant cock in front of her. The size of him would undoubtedly hurt, yet she couldn't convince her pussy it didn't want to take every inch of his hard, thick arousal.

*Maybe a little pain and a little rough wouldn't be so bad.*

Images flashed in her mind, thoughts of straddling those tight, perfect hips. Or maybe she could crawl onto her hands and knees as he stood at the end of the bed, his bronzed body outlined by firelight as he thrust behind her. Then again, what would it be like to lie on her back and let him worship her with that beautiful mouth? Did strong manly men like him go down on their women?

"Come. Put your mouth on me and taste." He grunted heavily, his breathing harsh.

"Hands," Lilith answered a little too loudly before running through the open door to her bedroom. She hit the hard wood with her hands, slamming it shut.

Sorin heard the door close. A second later, he came, releasing his warm seed over his tight fist. He pumped a few more times, milking every last drop from his body.

Just seeing her face had been enough to thrust his desire to the breaking point. The pleasure of release mingled with disappointment. She'd watched him, her wide eyes taking in every stroke of his hand with obvious interest. Yet, she didn't act on what had to be a mutual lust.

Grumbling, he slid out of bed and righted his clothing. If Lilith wasn't going to do her duty, then he'd go back down and join the celebration. Despite the release, his mood soured quickly.

*She just watched and did nothing!*

Sorin stomped out of the room, taking the long row of steps two at a time. Coming quickly around a corner, he almost bumped into Sera on her way up with a large tray of food.

"Oh!" Sera gasped in surprise, awkwardly trying to curtsey under the weight of his glare. "My lord, excuse me."

Sorin growled at her, low and dark, nearly knocking her over as he quickened his pace. He needed a drink. Now.

---

"I told you what you needed to do." Sera frowned as she sawed through Lilith's ropes. The serving women had tried untying them, but the men had bound the knots around her wrists too tight.

"Can you please hurry?" Lilith answered. "My fingers are numb."

"Your brain is numb," Sera insisted, sawing harder. The motion jiggled the serving woman's cleavage and Lilith looked away. "Keeping a happy bed is a simple enough task for the sake of the kingdom. I saw the look on his face. You did not do your duty by him."

"Easy, don't cut me!" Lilith jerked her arms when Sera sliced too close. She frowned on principal. "For your information, he did his own 'duty'. And I don't see what my sleeping with some overbearing lord has to do with the sake of the kingdom. If he wants to throw a temper tantrum, let him. It has nothing to do with me."

"Do you truly have no idea of by whom you have been chosen?" Sera asked, giving one last saw of the blade. The ropes fell free and Lilith moaned as she stretched her hands. Her fingers tingled sharply as blood rushed toward the tips. "Lord Sorin is one of the greatest warriors in the kingdom. It is a great honor to be his lover. None thought he'd ever claim a woman, not since his last one. It is your duty and honor to please him in all ways."

"Last one?" Lilith eyed the servant carefully. "What happened to the last one?"

"She did not please... Anyway, she's dead," Sera dismissed, clearly not wanting to get too far into it.

*Dead?!* Lilith gulped.

"Be Lord Sorin's vessel for release," Sera persisted. "Do not resist, do not deny and do not expect tenderness. In return, he will give you a noble life, my lady. Women would kill for the chance to be Lord Sorin's mate."

Lilith grimaced, reaching her arms over her head into a deep stretch. "I've heard this speech of yours before."

*Dead?!*

"Clearly, you did not or else you would have spread your thighs and drained the ill temper from him." Sera stood, huffing in irritation. She crossed to the tray of food she'd brought up with her and lifted it from a dressing table. "His mood affects the mood of his men, which in turn affects the moods of their women. Lord Sorin is not some lowly foot soldier. He's a hero."

"I don't care what you or the other women of this accursed dimension say." Lilith stood, facing the woman with her fists on her hips. Her hands ached but she ignored the discomfort. Even though she felt a very real attraction to Sorin, there was no way she could sleep with him. She refused on principal alone. "I am not and will not whore myself out to your precious Lord Sorin just because he is going to pout like a big baby who doesn't get his way."

"Well." Sera's mouth worked in anger. She set the tray down on the bed beside Lilith. The food slid around on the trencher and a small flurry of dust lifted around it. "I was going to order your bedchamber cleaned and gowns fitted, but now you can do it yourself, my lady."

Huffing, Sera marched out of the room, leaving Lilith alone.

Ignoring the tray on the bed, Lilith went to the pitcher Sera had put on the dressing table and poured herself a drink. The liquor burned, but she drank it gratefully. Under her breath she continued her fight with the now-absent servant, muttering, "Well, Sera, I've seen your outfit and I think I'll be better off if you didn't order my gowns for me."

# CHAPTER 4

Despite Sera's threat, two dozen maids arrived with buckets of hot water and fresh linens. Lilith watched in amazement as they made systematic work of the dirty room, scrubbing each stone and polishing each piece of furniture. A fire had been lit in the fireplace, casting a soft orange warmth over the interior.

The dark wood of the furniture gleamed in unsurpassed perfection. Simple engravings ringed the legs of the dressing table and matching chair. A cushioned seat rested near one wall paired with a small, circular table. For a society formed predominantly of warrior men, the slight delicateness of the furnishings surprised her.

Out of all the objects, she found the four-poster bed the most extravagant. The same rings wrapped the legs, matching it to the dressing table set. The dingy comforter was replaced with a richly embroidered red and gold. Lilith already knew from sitting on the mattress that it had been designed for comfort. Suddenly, the image of Sorin on his back, pleasuring himself, came to mind and she quickly looked away. Just thinking of his rock-hard body moving with warlike grace made her shiver.

She had to get out of Staria. Fast.

The servants nudged her out of their way, not deigning to speak to her as they whispered amongst themselves. She curled her toes against the damp stone beneath her feet, really missing her own clothes. Even though they ignored her, she didn't dare leave the tower for risk of facing Sorin and more angry Battlewar citizens. Thoughts of what Sera said filled her mind, not so much the "please him or he'll be in a bad mood" part, but the last woman he'd been with ending up dead.

Did Sorin kill his last lover for not pleasing him? She saw the danger in his gaze, the simmering emotions just below his hot surface. Would he kill her if she didn't sleep with him? And what if she slept with him but wasn't any good at it? How could she tell if she was any good at it? Would she be good at it if she was nervous about being good at it?

Lilith's stomach tightened and she felt as if she might be sick. She needed to think of something else, *anything* else. Eyeing a nearby maid, she said, "Excuse me, but what is philter? The guards said they were giving it to some of the women. Is it a poison?"

The woman waved a dismissing hand. "It's to make you forget things."

"So the other women, they weren't killed?" she insisted. The servants all stopped what they were doing to look at her in offense.

"The otherworlders were sent home," the maid ground out and they all went back to work with a renewed fury. Under her breath, the woman muttered, "They weren't suitable for this world." By the glance she gave Lilith, it became clear she didn't think her suitable either.

As the last of the withered cobwebs were wiped away, all but two of the women left the room. Placing their hands on the stone wall perpendicular the door, they pushed. Lilith watched in amazement as the women moved the wall. Stone scraped against stone and light streamed in from within the hidden room.

"What is it?" Lilith couldn't help her curiosity.

"Your bath, my lady," a giggly brunette named Nan answered. A row of stone steps led up to an inset tub, large enough to fit five of her comfortably. The servant stepped inside the tub and twisted a metal ring on the bottom to tighten the plug. Fresh air flowed from several narrow slits in the wall, giving a slight chill to the air.

"Unless you prefer a metal tub like my lord," Hannah added, her big green eyes looking more at the floor than directly at Lilith. Her bright red hair was piled high on her head.

"This is fine," Lilith said, a little uncomfortable with the way they spoke to her. She was used to fading into the background, not being treated like a princess about to give royal decree—albeit a despised princess being blamed for the ill fate of the entire kingdom.

"Yea, my lady." Hannah went to a hand pump and began to work the lever up and down, filling the bath with blue-tinted water. Nan climbed out of the tub, narrowly missing getting her shoes wet. To Lilith's surprise, steam rose around them. The water was heated.

Nan must have seen Lilith's amazement because she giggled and explained, "The blue minerals in the natural underground springs keep the water warm."

"Interesting," Lilith said more to herself as she reached to touch the water. Sapphire-blue droplets dripped off her fingertips. "I haven't seen this before on the other planes."

"Do you need assistance, my lady?" Nan asked.

"No," Lilith rushed. "I can do it myself."

The two women bowed and shuffled out of the bedrooms. The sound of their laughter could be heard, fading into the distance.

Lilith contemplated the water, wondering if it would stain her skin to an unnatural color. Then, deciding at this point she didn't care, she shrugged out of her shapeless gown and stepped into the bath.

*Did Sera really mean to say dead?*

---

Sorin's cock still ached. The desire he'd managed to keep at bay all these years flared its randy head now that it had a target. And what a lovely target she was, too. He longed to touch her pliant flesh, flesh that would mold to his will, and her velvety soft hair and even softer lips.

What in all the bloody battles happened? One look at a woman and suddenly a hole as wide as the castle punctured his neat and orderly world. As if his fate wasn't bad enough, his brother, Ronen, had also claimed a woman. What sort of witchery beset them this day? Two of the most confirmed bachelors in the land were now bound.

They'd been fools to enter into this agreement for women. When Divinity first approached them in the midst of battle, the Starians had almost slaughtered them where they stood, believing the oddly dressed creatures to be allies to the Caniba tribes. After much negotiation, investigation, a little bit of pleading by the Divinity scouts, and hours of council meetings, an alliance was formed with the alien beings.

Divinity wished for samples of the blue mineral water, water that stayed warm no matter how long it sat away from another heat source. The blue water springs ran deep and wide. There was no shortage of the mineral and giving some away was a little enough consideration. In return, the Divinity aliens provided a resource much needed by the Starians—women. Out of the women Divinity sent, three were chosen as being of the right temperaments to stay. The new blood was just one of the reasons all the "firsts" were of high military rank or distinction.

"Ronen, you fool," Sorin muttered, lifting a goblet to drink deeply. He stared at the woven banners along the wall, each depicting an important Starian religious and political symbol.

"I could well blame you, brother," Ronen answered, brooding next to him. None in the hall dared to break their dark mood. "You fell first. I had no choice."

A darkening bruise marred Ronen's cheek where his woman had struck him, and his clothes, though on, were exceedingly disheveled. At least his brother's woman fought him. Lilith cowered like she thought he might run her through with a blade.

Sorin growled low in the back of his throat. Curious eyes turned toward them from the hall floor, but none dared to approach. "I did not fall. These foreign women have bewitching powers. We should never have entered into an agreement with the otherworlders."

Ronen grumbled incoherently.

Eager for a more comfortable subject, Sorin turned his attention to Sir Rian. The knight had stood next to them during the ceremony as a first, but had luckily chosen no woman. If he had, he'd not be drinking with his fellow knights. Waving the soldier to the head table, he gestured that the man should sit. Rian didn't hesitate, despite the forbidding moods of the brothers, and took a seat next to Sorin. "Any word from Lord Serik's man? Do the Caniba armies march against the forces at Spearhead?"

"They do not march yet, but Lord Martin suspects it will be soon," Rian answered, keeping his tone low. "Sorceress Magda's scouts were captured in the southern marshes, but at the loss of two good men—Richard of Daggerpoint and Peeter of Fallenrock. They died well and were not taken by those cannibals. Sir Vidar goes to lead the interrogations. He has already left with his new bride."

"Vidar, too?" Ronen sighed before muttering again to himself. Sorin frowned, sorry for his friend's shared misfortune.

"Yea, Vidar, as well," Rian agreed. "Though he looked about as pleased as the two of..." The words tapered off and Rian gave the brothers a dismissing wave of his hand.

"And Aidan?" Sorin asked. All knew without question that the last woman, the infamous Lady Paige who'd been a gift from the fairies, would go home with her husband, Sir Aidan. "How did he fair?

"He did not look well when he left Battlewar." Rian leaned forward to grab an abandoned goblet and lifted it to a maid. She nodded, running to fetch him a clean one. "Nor did Lady Paige."

"This is a bad year for finding mates," Ronen asserted, his frown deepening. "Perhaps we should cancel the ceremonies, especially those involving the otherworlders."

"The decisions are made," Sorin broke in, knowing honor would not let them change their minds. He reached his goblet out as a maid appeared with a pitcher. He already felt the heady effects of the drink but didn't care. Right now he wanted to feel numb. Maybe liquor could take the terrible ache in his loins away. "There is no reason to contemplate them."

"Though, it does not mean we have to choose the women they send," Rian offered.

Sorin focused his attention on his brother. Ronen leaned to the side to address Rian. "What other news?"

"Not much else. Lines hold strong on both sides. Vidar hopes to discover where the Sorceress' encampment lies. We suspect she is in the Hanging Forest, but..." Rian didn't reveal anything they didn't already know. One of the self-proclaimed queens of the Caniba tribes, Sorceress Magda was as elusive as she was cruel. Over the last four years, she'd been one of the more aggressive Caniba factions attacking the borders.

"We should ride to the borderlands," Ronen said, drawing Sorin's wandering attentions back to the conversation. "We will be of more use there."

"We have not been summoned," Sorin lowered his voice to a whisper, "and unless the king orders otherwise, we will be forced to bring the women with us."

"Not if they become with child," Ronen reasoned.

Sorin tensed, reminded of how unlikely that possibility was at the moment. The accursed woman rejected him. Him!

How proud it would make him to have a child, whether it be a boy or girl. However, admittedly, his aim when it came to Lady Lilith wasn't so noble as perpetuating the family line. He wanted a lover first and a wife second. "We would do better to pray for war, brother."

---

Dead.

The word wouldn't leave her, no matter how hard Lilith tried to erase Sera's comment. The idea that a woman, a sex slave, would be killed for not performing wasn't totally unheard of in the histories of the parallel worlds. Staria was clearly a barbaric land, from their simple "mine" ceremony to the "lord and lady" structure of their undoubtedly feudal society. In what most places remembered as the medieval period, lords often took what they wanted with little effective protest from the masses. If Lord Sorin wanted her, she doubted any would stop him. None had tried so far and none had reason to do so.

And if Lord Sorin wanted her dead?

Lilith trembled, missing the safety of an old library and dusty books as she studied and recorded historical facts. By the time she got there, her assigned dimension had been cleared by a tactical team, usually several of them, and was deemed safe.

"I have to act," she determined. "Survival first."

Coming up with a plan was easier than implementing it. The maids had left behind a thin linen cloth for drying after her bath. As she wandered the room, looking for her white gown, she realized that the linen was all they had left her.

"Sera," Lilith muttered accusingly. The servant probably thought she'd be helping Lord Sorin by stealing his sex slave's clothes.

After digging through every drawer and small trunk in her room to no avail, Lilith decided to check Sorin's. She couldn't very well wear the bed sheet or the fur coverlet downstairs. Wet hair stuck to the back of her neck as she slowly opened the door to Sorin's room. All was silent, but she peeked in at the bed anyway. He wasn't there. Disappointment filled her and she wondered at it.

*Put your mouth on me and taste.*

Part of her had wanted to do just that, but fear held her back.

"Be brave," Lilith whispered, stepping into the empty chamber. She went first to his trunk at the end of his bed and pulled back the lid. Neatly stacked clothes lined one side and pieces of armor filled the other. Lifting a black tunic with a red patch on the chest, she brought it to her nose. It almost smelled like him, clean and fresh, but lacking that very masculine quality.

Not wanting to dig through his things, she decided the long tunic would work. She fitted it over her head, taking the first belt she saw to tie the waist like a dress. The shirt fell to her calves and bunched at the shoulders. She rolled the sleeves so her hands poked out of the bottom.

With bare feet, she made her way from the room and down the

tower steps. She took them two at a time. Confusion warred inside her and she doubted what she was about to do.

*Curse it! I need facts. How can anyone make a decision without all the facts?*

Her feet padded on the stone, making soft, steady noises as she quickened her pace. Then, seeing the end of her journey down the steps, she slowed. The sound of voices carried in from the main hall where the knights gathered. In the opposite direction, she heard the clang of metal and smelled the distinct aroma of baking bread.

"Hey!" the whispered hush caused Lilith to jolt in alarm. A hand slipped over her mouth and pulled her to the side. Jayne appeared next to her, pressing close as they hid inside a narrow alcove behind the tower stairwell. Glancing down, Jayne chuckled, "Looks like we shop at the same store."

As the woman let go of her mouth, Lilith looked at Jayne's clothes. She wore the exact same tunic, only Jayne had cut her sleeves to length instead of rolling them. Her hair had been pulled back into a single ponytail at the back of her head, tied with what seemed to be the excess sleeve material.

"I overheard the maids talking," Jayne said. "I was about to come up to the tower to get you." She looked at Lilith's bare feet. "Couldn't find any shoes to steal? Follow me, there's a laundry room this way. They have shoes."

Lilith didn't know what to say to her. Jayne stared at her with pity and determination, but there was something else behind her gaze—fear. What had happened to her to make her look like that? Though smoothed back, her hair had a disheveled appearance to it. Had the men hurt her? Had she been claimed by someone with less self-control than Sorin? Lilith tried to think of the right thing to say to comfort the poor woman, but couldn't come up with the right words.

Jayne leaned forward and kept her voice low. She tugged on Lilith's arm. "Come with me. I promise Lord Sorin won't touch you again, but you have to make a fight of it."

"Wait." Lilith refused to move. Jayne's words confirmed her

suspicions. Something terrible had happened to the woman. "What did they do to you? Did they hurt you?"

Jayne glanced everywhere but at Lilith's direct gaze. "No, they didn't touch me, but I don't want to give them the chance to."

"What are you planning to do?"

"Karre and Paige have been taken south by a couple of the barbarians. With any luck, we'll be able to find them. Paige seems to know her way around this backwater place." Jayne again tried to pull her. "The timing is perfect. They're in there having a party and getting drunk. It will be dark soon. We'll find a way out of the castle and wait until nightfall. If we travel by dark, we should make it through the prairie to the forest. From there, by the grace of some miracle, we'll find a trail to follow—"

"You're going to escape?" Lilith jerked Jayne back. She might not have known the woman all that long, but she was really the only friend Lilith had in the castle. Mutual circumstances made for a joint cause. "You can't, Jayne. I've talked to a few of the servants. If we displease them, I think they might kill us."

"They didn't kill Paige for running," Jayne reasoned.

"Yet," Lilith asserted. "How do you know that's not what they're taking her south for? You heard the guard. Her master might delve out a harsh punishment."

Jayne paled. "What would you have us do? We can't stay here forever, waiting for them to get tired of us. What if they try to philter us like the others—whatever that means. What if they make us take on more men? If you saw what I saw walking these hallways, you'd know we have to run. I can't stay here and be a whore and that's exactly what I think this place is. A whorehouse."

A whorehouse? Lilith wasn't so sure. "I was told the philter is a drug to make you forget you've been here. They said those women from the cell with us were sent home because they were unsuitable."

"I don't think that'll work for us. We've been chosen to stay." Jayne didn't make it sound like much of an honor. If she thought this place was a brothel, Lilith could understand why.

"I think we should stay in the castle for now. Sorin didn't seem too keen on passing me around to all the men." Lilith reached caringly toward her. "Are you sure you weren't hurt? Did your man…? Did he make you…?"

"Ronen? No. He didn't try to pass me out." Jayne shook her head in denial. "I would have ripped off his balls had he tried."

"I can learn more here in civilization than in the woods. If we keep our heads low and try to behave, maybe we'll find a way home. I think we'll have better luck here at a castle than in the wild. Besides, running is too big of a gamble. How will we survive in the wilderness? How will we eat? What kind of animals are in the forest? Poisons? Flora and fauna? Insects? What about the people the Starians are fighting? What's out there could be much, much worse than what is in here. Paige seemed really scared when she spoke of the monsters."

"Paige could be lying. This castle could be a theme place and beyond the compound is a thriving society with technological advances. Whatever it is, I can't stay here. I'm not scared of dying," Jayne stated grimly, "but I will never live as some man's slave. Please come with me."

Lilith looked to the main hall. The unknown outside these castle walls or Lord Sorin's property? With one she'd have freedom. With the other she'd have shelter, food, protection and access to the castle grounds to look for a way home.

"I can't go with you," Lilith decided. "I'm taking my chances here."

"Do you have a plan?"

Lilith nodded, trying to look confident. "I think so. If I find a way to escape, I'll do my best to let you know about it."

"And if I do, I'll try to send word," Jayne glanced down and smiled, "in a pair of shoes."

"Good luck to you then." Lilith held out her hand.

"And to you. Don't let them break you. One way or another, we're going home. I promise." Jayne shook it briefly before disappearing down the hall the way she'd come.

Lilith watched after Jayne feeling very alone. All her prison buddies were gone, leaving her at the castle. She felt confident in her decision to stay and only wished Jayne would have remained as well.

Traipsing across foreign countryside wasn't a logical plan of action, no matter how badly she wanted to run away from the powerful Lord Sorin. Still, she respected Jayne for taking the risk.

Lilith turned her attention to the main hall, trying to build up her nerve. She couldn't do this, even if just thinking of him made her entire body tingle. Sorin was too big, kissed with so much aggression. Of course, with him being the aggressor, she wouldn't have to do much by way of seduction.

*Be Lord Sorin's vessel for release, do not resist, do not deny...spread your thighs and drain the ill temper from him.*

As arousing as the idea was in the theoretical, Lilith was frightened by the idea of the actual. Sure, the thought of Sorin would fuel any woman's late night fantasies. Who wouldn't be attracted to a big warrior man with alpha tendencies and the body of sheer perfection? Even now she felt the impression of his large cock against her stomach. The man had been trained to move and knew his body.

"If his displeasure doesn't kill me, his body just might." Lilith took a deep, shaky breath. "By all the gods worshiped in all the parallel universes, please don't make me regret this."

# CHAPTER 5

Sorin stopped listening to his brother as all senses went on alert. Ronen didn't talk about anything important, just words to add fuel to their mutual drunkenness and gloom. Normally, if they were upset, they'd volunteer to ride out and face the enemy whether the enemy engaged them or not. There was nothing like a hard and vicious fight to drive the demons away. But because of their idiotic decisions, they couldn't even find the sanctuary of battle to leave them in exhaustion. No, instead they were stuck at Battlewar with seductresses sent to torment them.

"...pray for an attack..." Ronen was saying. Sorin nodded in agreement, not hearing the whole statement.

His skin tingled and the nerves pulled his attention toward the hall floor. Instinct told him Lady Lilith had to be near. Jealousy and mistrust caused his eyes to scan the main hall floor, searching every knight, every filled lap and busy pair of arms.

"...it is better to die in battle than..." his brother continued.

*I'll kill the wench before I let another woman embarrass me again*, Sorin swore. *I will not be cuckolded. I will not be dishonored.*

Bianka's faithlessness had been a huge blow to his masculine pride and reputation. His honor would not recover a second time.

Sorin's vision blurred slightly, as his gaze traveled once more over the main hall. It had been a long while since he'd drank to such excess. Seeing blonde hair, he stiffened, ready to pounce. The woman straddled Gregor's lap, wiggling brazenly as she kissed his neck. The man pulled on the blonde waves, jerking her face toward the ceiling. Sorin blinked hard, bringing her into sharp focus.

"Margaret," he muttered. The blonde was Gregor's wife.

"What of her?" Ronen inquired.

"What of who?" Sorin pretended not to understand.

"Margaret?" Ronen persisted.

"What of Margaret?" Sorin grumbled.

"I thought..." Ronen's words tapered off. "Never you mind. I'm drunk and hearing voices. The woman has ridden me mad."

There. Lilith.

Sorin caught his breath. He'd found her. Lilith waited in the doorway, watching the hall with a mixture of trepidation and determination. She gripped the stone, her body hidden from view—all but her lovely face, a black covered arm and one bare foot. Her eyes darted to his briefly before looking to the floor. Her foot pulled back, as if she would hide.

Sorin held still, watching to see what she'd do. Wide blue eyes captured his once more, looking nothing like the near black pits of Bianka's soulless gaze. From the very beginning, Bianka had an air to her. She charmed everyone, being exactly what they wanted her to be. Well, at least at first she had. All Sorin had wanted was a mate, someone to share life's journey with. Bianka had never been that.

His heartbeat quickened and he gripped the stem of his goblet tight. Was he mistaken or did Lilith try to smile at him? Her lips parted, drawing his full attention, and her fingers curled as if to call him toward her. Liquid heat swirled inside him, blazing down his chest to lift his cock in thick arousal. He forgot the hall and his chatty brother. Thoughts raced, but the hesitance of his mind didn't stop his body.

Sorin stood, leaving his goblet on the table. The cup was empty anyway. The more he consumed, the longer it took the maids to refill his drink. Or perhaps, he simply drank faster. It didn't matter now, with her standing there, staring at him, and beckoning him with her very presence.

Lilith stiffened, coming more into view as she faced him. He half expected her to run, but she held firm. Did she know how she affected him? Surely women were born with such knowledge. She had to know that licking her bottom lip only made him look at it with longing. She had to know that her eyes, wide and beautiful and clear, caused his chest to tighten with the urge to hold her against him and protect her from all things. Her loose hair made his fingers flex to run the entire silky length.

What was it about women that could make men fall to their knees and forget everything?

*Fool.*

*Idiot.*

*Weak.*

Only when he neared did he take note of her clothes. The dark red of his family crest stared out at him, branding her as his. She'd grabbed his battle tunic, the shirt he wore when he led men to war. It identified him as a leader, and her wearing it only publically declared she thought herself above him. Sorin glanced behind him, wondering if anyone else saw. A few of the knights frowned in her direction, shaking their heads.

"My lord," she said, her voice trembling.

Sorin grabbed her arm and pulled her out of the archway before anyone else noticed her clothes. "What are you doing, Lady Lilith?"

"I came down to..." She motioned weakly to the stairway, then to the hall. Her gestures made no logical sense. He let go of her arm, crossing his over his chest. She pulled back from him as he towered menacingly over her.

"What is the meaning of this?" He pointed at his tunic.

"I..." She looked down her body. "The servants..."

By all the bloody sword blades, if she didn't look sexy in his clothes!

"The maids took mine and I didn't have anything to wear and I wanted to come down here and..." She picked at the coat of arms on her chest, flicking the edge of the embroidery with her fingernail.

"And?" he prompted, aware of how hard he sounded.

"And," she repeated.

"Well?" He shifted his weight from one foot to the other, placing his hands on his hips.

"This." Lilith shot forward, arms rising toward his head. She brought her face quickly forward.

Sorin automatically defended himself, easily capturing her wrists and jerking them to the side. Her body slammed into his chest. When he looked at her face, her eyes were closed and her lips were puckered, as if she'd been about to kiss him. Her forehead bumped into his chin, knocking hard.

She made a small noise of pain. Lilith's eyes opened in shock at his rough hold and her lips pulled tight against her teeth. "Oh, I, ah, I'm not any good at... Okay, sorry, you can let me go now. Go back to drinking. Forget I came down."

She struggled to pull her hands free. Sorin tightened his grip. Without hesitating, he swooped in for a kiss. His lips met hers. She gasped and he took it as an invitation for more. Who was he to turn down such sweetness? Mindlessly he kissed her, delving his tongue into the very depths of her mouth.

Sorin let go of her wrists, only to wind his hands along the small of her back to hold her closer. The tunic slid beneath his touch, revealing a smooth texture underneath. She wore no undergarments to hamper his discovery. He rocked his hips, reveling in the pressing heat of her stomach. His cock ached, urging him on. With the way he felt, he could love her all night and all morning. Hard, soft, fast, slow, he didn't care how or where. He burned to be inside her.

Lilith lifted her hand to touch his jaw, sending light, feathery caresses across his cheek. The willing exploration threw brush on the dangerous inferno of his greedy passions. His kisses became aggressive as he nipped at her mouth, drawing her bottom lip between his teeth.

She made a weak noise and twisted her head to the side. The sound of her ragged breath beat against his ear. Sorin kept kissing, devouring her jaw and neck, nipping and licking wherever his mouth could reach. The feverish rhythm of her pulse drummed along his lips. She felt it too, this deep passion, she had to.

She tasted like honey and sweet berries. His hands worked along her back, urging the tunic up. Sorin groaned, not caring who heard him. The people of Staria were not shy about their passions. Why should they be? Having sex was as natural as breathing and infinitely more fun than war.

"Not here," she breathed heavily into his neck. "Please, not here. I can't if..."

Her words caused him to look around. His cock screamed in protest, declaring that here and now was perfect. Almost confused, he looked for a place to take her. The wall? The stairwell? The floor?

"I can't in front of the others. Please, don't make me. I don't want them watching." She shivered in his arms, glancing meaningfully at the main hall. Sorin studied her face, done in by the way she bit her lip.

*Anything my lady desires of me.*

Sorin stiffened. The thought wasn't like him. He was not a man to bend to the will of others. "Where would you have me take you?"

*Fool.*

*Idiot.*

*Weak.*

"May we go back upstairs?" She said the words, but her eyes didn't look as certain. He wondered at the change in her, but didn't ask. Her lush lips reeled him in and he captured them with his own. Moaning, he lifted her off the floor, letting her feet dangle as he carried her upright toward the stairwell of the Black Tower.

Her legs swayed and the natural rocking of her body hit against his already strained cock. Traveling up would be torture, but he was loath to put her down. Sorin pulled her closer, wishing she'd wrap her legs around his waist.

Lilith held on to his shoulders, gripping tight. He kissed her harder. She moved her lips, but her tongue didn't delve into his mouth. He sucked, trying to draw it forward to explore and taste.

Soft globes rubbed his chest through the material of their clothes. He needed to feel them. Quickening his pace, he carried her up the tower stairs. Her grip tightened, her legs pulling strangely to the sides as if looking for hold on the stone walls.

Nearing the halfway point, he stopped. Her nearness was agony. He couldn't wait. Later he would take her in a bed, but for now the privacy of the stairs would have to do.

Lilith's feet hit the floor and she swayed weakly, her knees giving out before she could catch herself. Sorin held her arm, keeping her from falling. "No one will happen upon us here, my lady."

*Here?*

Lilith gulped. Already she knew she had made a grave mistake in going to him. She was out of her league. At least in a bed she knew she'd had a little practice to back up her meager skills as a lover.

Sorin's intensity frightened her. Just the size of him, without the piercing force of his dark brown eyes, made her quiver. But when he stared at her, with the unmistakable look of a predator about to devour prey, she nearly fainted.

Sorin leaned in to her and Lilith leaned away. He stalked her until she sat on a step, perched along the uncomfortable ledge. How in the world did he plan on making this work? He braced an arm beside her, trapping her beneath with little air separating their bodies.

Sorin reached for her, touching her hair. The dark tan of his flesh contrasted the blonde. He fingered the strands, gripping them so that the roots pulled slightly. It didn't hurt, but she wondered at the greedy way he licked his lips.

The waves of his hair framed his face. Now that she could see him in finer detail, she noticed the scars that ran along his neck. One began at an ear and sliced down, just missing a vital artery. Another started at the base of his throat and disappeared beneath the neckline of his tunic.

Her breath caught, a phenomenon that seemed to happen a lot when she was around him. His hand left her hair for her chin, continuing downward, over her neck to glide over the material of her borrowed tunic.

To her surprise, when he reached a breast, his touch turned caressing and gentle. A light moan left his parted lips. A trail worked down her breast to the blazing heat of her sex. If he kept touching her like that, she wouldn't be able to control herself.

Lilith tilted her head back, closing her eyes. But as suddenly as the slow seduction started, it ended. Sorin's hand became firm, squeezing harder before letting go to unfasten her belt. A leg bumped into hers, and she opened her eyes to find him fumbling with the laces to his pants. He'd pulled his tunic aside, which revealed the unmistakable strength of his arousal beneath the barrier of clothing.

Harsh pants of air washed over her, zealous in Sorin's eagerness. Unsure of what to do, she began to back away. This wasn't what she imagined. The whole scene had been planned out in her mind. She'd go down and get him to come back up. She'd "please" him—in a bed —so he wouldn't be tempted to kill her. Then that would be that. Nowhere did her plan allow for passion-induced, near-crazed warrior man with a formidable weapon taking her on the uncomfortable stairwell with people milling just feet away.

"Pull up your skirts," Sorin ordered, his voice hoarse.

Lilith acted on instinct. Though every nerve inside her pussy yelled and screamed for him to touch it. Her confused, out-of-depth mind revolted. She needed to regroup and come up with a new plan. Oh, why hadn't she run away with Jayne?

*Run away. Good plan.*

Lilith turned, intent on running up the stairs until she could get her overheated body under control. Sorin's nearness only caused confusion and chaos. When he kissed her, she couldn't think straight. If she couldn't think straight, how was she to make sure she was any good in bed and thus avoid the whole "dead" scenario?

"Mm, yea, my clever lady," Sorin groaned in approval. He grabbed her hips before she could fully stand. Now her back was to him and she couldn't see what he was doing. "It will be easier to take you like this."

Lilith's fingers worked against the rough texture of the stone. His warm hand slid up her leg, boldly moving up her outer thigh. Emotions waged a confused battle over her. She wanted him. She'd just met him. It felt really good when he touched her like that. This wasn't logical or considered. This had to stop. She needed to think. What was she doing here? One little mistake on the job would not warrant banishment. But if it did? What would she do? What if she couldn't find a way home? And did he have to grab her ass like that?

The cool air of the stairwell hit her flesh as he bared her from behind. Lilith made a weak noise, the sound somewhere between panic and pleasure. Callused hands, strong and sure, explored at will. Fingers ran up her spine and down her ribs, teasing the sides of her breasts.

The bittersweet ache of his touch filled her, concentrating every part of her being on the needy ache in her sex. She closed her eyes tight, remembering the size of him, how rough he could be when he kissed her, held her. He touched her pussy and she jerked, knowing he found the betraying wetness of her arousal. A low, dangerous groan left him, loud and echoing against the stone.

Lilith opened her mouth to speak, unsure whether the words would be a protest or approval. His cock had been as large as him as she'd watched him pleasure himself. How did they get like this? She couldn't see his eyes. She wanted to see his eyes. What was he thinking? What was he looking at? What was he...?

And then it happened—an incredibly thick pressure, entering, probing. She couldn't help herself as she yelped in surprise, jerking away from him before his cock made it more than a half inch past the entrance. Lilith reached for the next step, ready to scurry away and regroup. Sorin's hold on her hips stopped her.

He brushed her again, his cock glancing along her inner thigh. Lilith tensed.

*I want this. I can't want this. I want this. I can't want this. Oh please, don't hurt me.*

For a long time his fingers worked, clenching and unclenching against her hips. She stayed rigid, waiting, anticipating, over-thinking every second. Her hand clutched the step, working violently into the hard stone.

"You act as if you don't want this." Sorin's words were low, harsh and unmistakably upset.

"No," she answered, trying to form a complete thought.

"No? Then why did you beckon me to you? Why did you summon me from the hall and put your lips to mine?" His grip tightened, painful now.

"Please," she begged. "I don't want to die."

"Die?" This time he let go. Without his support, Lilith fell against the steps. All too aware of her naked ass hanging out for him to see, she pushed frantically at her clothes to cover it. "Did the Divinity leaders tell you they would kill you if you didn't come here?"

"They didn't say anything," she answered, unsure if she should be pleased he finally seemed to listen to her about her erroneous presence.

"Then why would you die?" Sorin wasn't so modest as to cover himself. His pants clung to his large thighs, held up only by the sheer breadth of his muscles. The tunic had been pushed aside, catching now on the incredibly erect length of his cock.

"Because if I don't please you, you'll kill me like your last lover," she blurted, instantly wishing she could take it back.

Sorin's eyes darkened as he narrowed them in rage. A ripple washed over him, stiffening every muscle. Lilith cowered on the steps, trying to press her body into them until she faded into the hard stone. His chest rose and fell, panting heavily, and his fists clenched at his sides as if any second he could tear her apart.

"Who told you of Bianka?" he demanded.

Lilith shivered violently, managing a small shake of her head. No words would come out of her mouth.

"Argh!" He slammed his hand into the wall, and she screamed. Lilith backed away from him, knowing that the tower would only trap her, but unwilling to try to push past him. When he didn't stop her, she turned and ran, stumbling as her legs tangled in the skirt of her tunic.

Reaching his bedchamber door, she pushed inside and slammed it shut, not stopping until she was blockaded inside her new room with the vanity pushed tight against the door. Light from the open bathroom wall shone over the room, helping her to see as she made her way over to burrow under the covers. Turning her eyes to watch the bedroom door, Lilith doubted the barricade would keep him out if he wanted to get in, but the furniture line of defense gave her a small measure of comfort.

---

Sorin glared at his erection, hating that he still wanted Lady Lilith even after her words. A tiny voice whispered to take her anyway, to not stop. It was his right, after all. He couldn't. He was not the monster she thought him to be.

How did she know about Bianka or her death? Apparently, the servants gossiped and the fact only served to fuel his rage. He had ordered all talk of his late wife to cease. If he could have, he would have ordered all thoughts of her erased from the minds of Starian society.

How dare Lilith come to him like that? How dare she kiss him, let him kiss her? And how dare she show him her perfect ass, so smooth and unflawed, so unlike the hard scar-riddled length of his body. But, most of all, how dare she give him a glimpse of happiness only to rip it away?

Sorin braced his hand on the wall and gripped his cock hard, pouring all his anger into the yanking thrusts of his tight fist. She didn't want him. That much was clear. She only came to him because she thought he'd kill her if she didn't. Death or his bed? Those were the choices she believed she had?

And kill her? Kill her?! What was he? A dishonorable brute? A mindless Caniba? A beast who raped and pillaged? The insult cut deeply into his pride. Why did the gods of war curse him? He did all they demanded of him. He went into battle without hesitancy. He lived by the sword.

Sorin found no pleasure in the act of release, only a bitterness that was hard to contain. His seed spilled onto the steps but he didn't care. Twice he'd been cursed. The first was a cuckolding witch and the second was so afraid he might hurt her that she served herself up like a sacrifice.

Sorin tugged on his clothes, knotting the laces in his haste to be away from the Black Tower, from Battlewar Castle. He couldn't run away, the last shreds of his tattered pride wouldn't let him. Without cause, he couldn't go. Not yet.

"By all the fires of the afterlife, by the will of the gods, please bring Staria a great battle. Call me away from this place. I beg of you."

# CHAPTER 6

Perhaps all his years at the sword did not go completely unnoticed by the eyes of the gods. Sorin jarred against the back of his horse, feeling the pounding beat of the large animal's hooves carrying him away from Battlewar's outer wall. The familiar creak sounded behind him as sentinels lowered the large wood-and-iron gate. The heavy weight of it made for a slow decent, but in time of attack, if the rope were cut as a man rode under, it would impale him and his horse under the deadly weight of the reinforced metal crossbars. Everything about Battlewar Castle had been designed for war, just like everything else in their land—from the long battlements that stretched around the main castle and Battlewar Town to the secret passages and underground escape routes.

Lady Jayne had disappeared from the castle and, after an extensive search of the grounds, it was decided two small groups of knights would ride after the escaped woman. The others headed north to search for a trail, though it seemed unlikely she'd choose that treacherous route. Already word spread through the town in the outer bailey, and all the residents of Battlewar Town would be on the lookout if she hid within the city walls. Lucky for them, she did not know of the tunnels leading from the castle to outside the walls or how to reach them. It made their search easier. Ronen barely spoke as they looked, but to utter quietly, "My wife has run away. The gods truly frown upon me."

The full moon shone bright over the prairie grasses, giving the knights enough to see by as they rode hard over the fields. Sorin felt sorry for his brother, but couldn't help the selfish relief that he had an excuse to run away from his own torment. As the head of his family, capturing Lady Jayne demanded his attention. He had to go. They would find the woman, Sorin had no doubts about that. Many of the knights trained at Battlewar in their youth, and this prairie and the surrounding forests were extensions of that very education.

The wind hit hard upon his face, whipping Sorin's hair back. Once they crossed the prairie they would spread out into the forest, searching for a sign of her passing. She couldn't have gone far on foot, and most likely her screams would alert the men to her whereabouts. No matter how much or how little Divinity told them, these otherworlders didn't know this land or the dangers that waited in the forest at night.

Ronen rode beside him. Sorin lifted his hand. The trees were near and the ground more treacherous. The small contingency of knights slowed. Pointing first to the east and then to the west, he soundlessly ordered the men to spread out and begin their search. When they were alone, Ronen said, "She does not know what she faces, even with my knife to arm her."

"The forest at night can be a daunting thing," Sorin comforted. "Rest assured in that we are far away from the battlefront. The Caniba tribes will not have ventured this far. One look at a wild beast and she'll scream for us to save her."

"Let's ride," Ronen urged, nudging his horse toward the trees. He pulled his sword from his side, gripping it tight. Sorin followed, veering to the right as they spread out. Each man would remain within whistling distance should the lady be found.

"Keep the lady safe," Sorin whispered to the trees, "but don't let us find her too close to the castle. Let her lead us far away from here."

"He left me?" Lilith frowned, knowing she had no right or reason to be shocked at Sera's grumpy news. The servant glared at her, only taking her hateful eyes off Lilith long enough to glance at the dislodged furniture barrier and trail of trinkets that had fallen off the top when Lilith moved it to the door.

"You're surprised, my lady?" Sera demanded. "Did you expect him to stay when you bar him from your chambers like some kind of—?"

"Of what?" Lilith snapped. Late morning shone through the slit window, lighting the room in a softened glow. The night had been long and dark, as Lilith hovered beneath the covers. Several times she'd dozed, but never for long. Lack of rest made her waspish, and Sera's accusing tone only added to her ill temper. "Like some kind of sane person? You might like to sleep with complete strangers because they picked you out of the lineup, but I actually prefer to know the person. Maybe go out on a date. Have a conversation beyond, 'Take up your skirts for I will do you now'."

Sera gasped, her mouth hanging open. She sputtered before finally managing, "You would question the will of the gods?"

"Sorin is not a god," Lilith assured the woman, jerking at the long sleeve of the black tunic. It unrolled in the night and now hampered her fingers. "Trust me. Everywhere I go, there is some man claiming to be a god."

"No, Lord Sorin is a man of flesh and blood, but the gods choose you for him. You are his reward for great service in battle." Sera searched her face, as if she were a fool not to know about their gods and customs. "Men have needs, especially Starian men. They need passion for it keeps them strong in horrific times. Women are the vessel for release, a means to have children. That is our role. That is our duty. In return, we are protected and provided for."

"What of love?" Lilith asked, almost feeling sorry for the woman. She ran her fingers along the back of the cushioned chair. The small, fine stitching had been done by hand.

"What of it?" Sera waved her hand in dismissal of the idea.

"Should you come to care deeply for him that is up to you, but I would not encourage such affections. It makes losing them in battle harder. Do not expect tenderness or dwell on romantic emotions. It is not in their nature. It goes against everything they've been taught. They will care for you in their way and it is enough."

Enough? A life of mutual convenience was enough for these people? No love?

*How tragic.*

"You are lucky for your husband's station will provide better than others. You do not have to work. It's not so unreasonable a trade." Sera's first irritation lessened, though now she sounded a little annoyed.

"Husband?" Lilith weakened and she barely managed to fall into the chair. "Did you just say he's my... No, that can't be right. No one said anything about getting married. I sure as sunshine would have remembered hearing about that little gem. They said lover and I believe mate was used, but... No."

"Husband, breeding partner, mate, lover, master..." Sera picked up a few of the fallen boxes and bottles and piled them on the bed before going to push at the vanity. Between shoves, she added, "Call it what you will, it all amounts to the same thing. The ceremony is done and you belong to him. He chose you."

The woman had to be wrong. Maybe Sera didn't understand what she was talking about, or perhaps the word "husband" had a different meaning on this dimension. Lilith had run into such confusions before. Language tended to be the same, but it never evolved exactly on each plane. In some cases, a single word could take on a whole new social connotation. Maybe when they said "husband", they meant "man you were partnered up with until he got tired of you and decided to get rid of you".

"I don't belong here," Lilith said, more to herself.

"I don't understand you otherworlders," Sera grumbled. "You get the best of our men and then you complain. If you ask me, you don't deserve them."

*I didn't ask you.*

"Well, if you don't wish to be Lady Lilith, mate of the honorable

Lord Sorin, then you can just fend for yourself like any other unattached female. Meals are served below stairs in the main hall. I'll not be carrying up your trays. If you wish for a bath, draw it yourself. And as far as the gowns go, I was going to help you direct the seamstress today, but you can just do that, too." Sera gave the vanity one last push, setting it into place. Then, huffing, she stomped from the room and didn't look back.

"They're all crazy," Lilith whispered, standing to grab the items off the bed. She placed them on the vanity, randomly organizing them. "And they're going to make me crazy, too."

---

Lilith came to believe that Sera only gave idle threats. Sure, the servant never carried a tray back up to the Black Tower, but another maid did. The dry bread and cold meats was hardly a feast, but Lilith fashioned them into a decent enough sandwich. However, that had been hours ago and the pains of hunger were slowly creeping in. What she wouldn't do for a large fettuccine Alexus with crusted bread and garlic. Just thinking about it made her mouth water.

Soon after Sera's huffy departure, the seamstress, Fantine of Battlewar, arrived with an entourage of workers in tow. She'd been horrified to see the black tunic Lilith wore for a dress and instantly demanded the lady remove it. Lilith refused until another gown could be brought in to replace it, even then demanding they give her privacy. The people of Staria might like to walk around naked, but Lilith lived in San LoFrancis, and there people wore clothes. Lots of them.

Fantine worked with a mind of her own, asking questions but then deciding her own answers. She spoke in rapid half-sentences that her helpers appeared to translate, but that left Lilith with a slight headache.

"I told you, I'm not wearing a low neckline," Lilith tugged at the soft tan material of the tunic dress she tried on. The garments were readymade, just in need of a few alterations. Lilith placed her hand on her chest. "I want it to cover here."

"That is not the fashion." Fantine shook her head in disapproval, pointing at a dark blue corset. A soft-spoken brunette with short curls handed it to her. "What pleasure is that to...?" The words trailed off.

Precise, nimble fingers clipped material deftly into place as the seamstress fitted material around Lilith's slightly protesting body. She pulled the corset tight, constricting Lilith's waist and making her gasp.

"Eyes," one of the helpers said as she studied the outfit.

"Agreed." Fantine nodded. "More blues."

"Blues," the others repeated in unison.

"More here." Lilith again patted her bare chest. The corset thrust her breasts up, like it did on the other women. Glancing around, she grabbed a wide scrap of material off the bed and wrapped it around her shoulders before tucking the two ends into the front bodice to create the affect of a shirt. "See."

All the women tilted their heads to the side at once. Fantine frowned. The others bit their lips.

"We got what we require," the seamstress announced, waving her hand for the others to follow. They scurried to pick up their messes before rushing out the door.

Now that she was alone, she studied the quiet chamber. Lilith normally adapted to new surroundings and sounds. She had to with her job. This place was different. The silence pressed in on her, broken only by the occasional whisper of the wind against the window slits. The fireplace in both her and Sorin's room were barren, causing a chill to settle in the tower.

Dressed modestly in her new gown, shawl, and blue corset, Lilith found herself in Sorin's chamber. She thought it sad that so much of his life focused on war—from the beliefs of his people to the arsenal of blades attached to his wall. Where were the photographs? Or the paintings of loved ones and ancestors? Where were the books or games? Did the man do anything outside of battle? Nothing in the room told her about the man she now lived with. Did he have hobbies? Aspirations? Or perhaps the lack of personal belongings was more telling than not. Maybe a knight didn't have aspirations for the future because they didn't believe they would have a future.

When she carefully dug through his trunk, desperate for a hint of the man who lived there, she found a neat stack of clothing atop a folded blanket. Armor and chainmail dominated most of the space, some shiny with elaborate carvings and others tarnished and worn by time. A few of the chest plates had puncture holes in them.

Thinking about it made Lilith's head spin. She became desperate to discover something, *anything*, about Sorin's human side. So far, all she'd seen was a dominating warrior with questionable restraint when it came to sex.

"I don't belong here." Lilith closed the lid, leaving everything the way she'd found it. She wrapped her arms around her stomach. The idea of forever in Staria scared the hell out of her. She hadn't been bred for this life. Giving in to weakness, she leaned her head down and began to cry. "Please, Divinity, get me out of here. I didn't screw up this bad. I don't deserve this. I don't belong here."

Four days. Four very long, emotional days. And she spent them completely and utterly alone.

Lilith stared at her fingers, refusing to look around the main hall. She missed Jayne and Karre, even Paige. At any rate, she missed the idea of them. They would have understood her position, the stranger set on display before a group of very moody, very accusing knights and their women.

For the most part, no one talked to her. After the seamstress's visit, she hadn't had anywhere near a real conversation. The few who ventured the occasional words did so with disdain, some with open hostility. They made her feel like evil incarnate, and all because she wouldn't fuck their most beloved warrior.

They allowed her full access to the castle and she spent hours during the day exploring, analyzing her situation and searching for a way home. She even pressed against the walls, looking for secret rooms like her bathroom. She found none. Her natural curiosity made her perfect for her job. Torches, fireplaces and narrow windows remained the main sources of light wherever she went. She could only imagine that the Starians had spent so much time on perfecting war that they spent little effort on other technologies.

Inside the castle, a large kitchen buzzed with constant activity. If they weren't serving one of the two main meals of the day, the cooks stayed busy baking breads and pastries. Lilith loved the smell outside the kitchen and would have taken a closer look had her presence warranted more of a welcome. Accessible from the kitchen, castle gardens and a small fruit orchard spread out over an enclosure.

Below stairs, there were sewing chambers with enormous looms and sewing tables, a laundry room with a boiling pit of the dark blue water, quarters for servants, and walk-in linen closets. The shelves were filled with sheets carefully labeled with various coat-of-arms and symbols. Larders and dry storage overflowed with food and drink. Should there be a siege, Battlewar would definitely stand independent for many months.

Stairs led down to a dark dungeon, one she could only see through the barred window on the thick door. When she tried to get a better look, Brock chased her away. The accommodations were much worse than her initial holding cell.

Several private towers, like the one she lived in, lifted high over the castle. Then, directly above the hall, smaller apartments were set for the knights of lesser rank and their families. Her welcome there had been just as cold, as she walked the long hallway and peeked inquisitively inside any open doors.

One mother had even gone so far as to shield her smiling little boy, warning, "Stay away from the witch or she'll curse your sword hand." The cute smile faded to be replaced by instant fear.

*Harlot or witch.* Lilith gave a sardonic laugh. *Great options.*

If the days were bad, the nights were horrific. Lilith lay those long hours, alone in her tower, surrounded by darkness and plagued by her own mind. It became impossible not to think of Sorin, of how she was expected to give herself to him. Then she'd remember his kisses, passionate, demanding and completely overwhelming.

There, in the relative safety of her bed, surrounded by the

dancing firelight and shadows, she allowed herself to fantasize. She hadn't seen him naked, not even bare-chested, but her imagination could fill in what she didn't know. Many of the men had tattoos on their arms and flesh littered with scars.

"Sorin," she'd whisper, feeling foolish now that she thought about it in daylight. In her fantasy, he made love to her slowly, tenderly. His thick, strong body would stretch out on top of hers, their legs entwined. Hands ventured over every inch of flesh, tracing muscles and discovering secrets.

Lilith adjusted her hips, pressing her legs tightly together as she adjusted her skirt. A few of the knights stared at her as she reached for a drink. The maids thought it odd she insisted on juice for the evening meal instead of liquor. As appealing as drunken oblivion sounded, the last thing Lilith needed was to be inebriated.

Her mind wandered once more as she set the goblet down. Sorin's restraint surprised her and the more she thought about it, the more impressed she became. The feel of his cock, pressing at the entrance of her pussy as they lay in the stairwell, haunted her. There were so many other ways she could have handled that situation.

In reality, she doubted she'd ever fuck a man in the stairwell of a castle, but in her fantasies the idea was arousing. She closed her eyes and leaned her head against the high back of the chair. Part of her wished he would have just thrust and taken her, not giving her a choice but to let him ride her. She shivered, forcing the thought from her mind, sure she'd prefer the soft and gentle version of her dreams.

---

Battlewar loomed like a dark omen over Lord Sorin's head. His brother stayed behind with a few of the others, not ready to come back as he rode to tell the king about the Caniba spies they encountered in the forest. Seeing the blood staining his hand, Sorin wished he could have been the one to ride for the southern borders.

Seated upon his steed, Sorin waited in hopes that Ronen would send for him. The harsh lines of the castle stood firm against the streaked magenta-orange sky. The three knights who traveled back to the castle with him were already well into the outer bailey, and the sentinels guarding the wall stared at him in curiosity, holding the gate open.

Sorin didn't want to ride in. Lilith was in there, in his home, invading his life. His cock pulsed, never satisfied, always half erect, but he determined he couldn't touch her, no matter how much he wanted to. If he dared, he'd not be able to stop. Even in his dreams, he had no control with her. Each night when he closed his eyes, he'd picture himself behind her, thrusting like a madman, pounding violently into her until he came, only to do it again and again.

*Why have the gods cursed me?*

A sentinel lifted his arm, gesturing toward the open gate. Sorin blinked, needlessly looking back in hopes of an escape. No rider came for him, and he found himself nudging the horse forward before turning back around to face his fate. Ignoring the quizzical expressions of the guards, he kept his back straight and his eyes forward. He had to look a fright, covered in dirt and blood, but it wasn't anything the people of Battlewar Town hadn't seen before.

Through the corner of his eyes, he saw people in the town pointing at him from outside their closely set homes. Intermingled with the homes in the outer bailey were a couple of barns, many workshops, small breweries and a large marketplace where the commoners sold their wares. A few of the soldiers lifted their hands in greeting.

Sorin slowed his horse as a little girl ran after a chicken. Her pretty dress was covered in mud and she gave him an impish smile. All he could manage was a nod in return. Her smile fell somewhat. As one of the few female children, she'd be used to more attention.

"Curse the witch, my lord!" a peasant woman yelled, pointing her finger in the air. Dark, small eyes watched him from within a sea of hard wrinkles. "We'll sacrifice a goat to send her back to the otherworld!"

"Yea, my lord!" an old man next to her added, just as drunkenly. "Curse the witches that bring unhappiness to your home!"

Sorin's brow furrowed in surprise. It would seem rumors had spread while he was gone.

"Bless Lord Sorin! Bless Lord Ronen!" another voice added, calling over the distance. He couldn't see who screamed it. "Curse the witches!"

A round of agreement seemed to move over the street, traveling away from him throughout the town. "Curse the witches! Curse the witches!"

"Bless you as well," Sorin answered, hoping to quiet some of the whispers with words of his own. The king would not be pleased to hear the people of his most beloved city had revolted against the two brides of Firewall. "But they are merely foreign wives, not witches. They will learn our ways."

*One can only pray.*

"Wives are witches, my lord," the old man cackled. "You just haven't been married long enough to see it!"

"Eh!" the woman next to him screamed in protest, instantly throwing a tankard of ale at his head. "I have four men waiting in line to replace you. We're all just waiting for you to drop."

The man ducked and began to run down the muddy street. "See what I mean!"

Beyond the market, in the center of the city, a second, shorter wall encircled the inner bailey yard and castle. Contained within were the exercise yard where the knights trained, a small chapel, and the stables. Sorin found himself riding abnormally slow as he passed through the inner gate. Young pages ran for him, eager to take his reins so that he may dismount and go inside. Their eyes lit with boyish excitement to see the blood-stained tunic their lord wore.

The towheaded page nudged the darker one, prompting him to ask, "Did you slaughter Ronen's witch, my lord?"

*By all the bloody battleaxes in Staria.*

Sorin sighed heavily, swinging his leg over the back of the horse and tossing over his reins. "I did not see any witches, but my sword did meet Caniba spies."

The boys nodded in excitement, whispering fervently as they hurried to take care of his horse. He desperately wanted a drink, but didn't dare enter the main hall to face more curses or worse—his wife. Slipping around the side of the castle, he ducked under a narrow entryway mostly used by maids carrying wet laundry outside to dry.

"My lord," a servant gasped in surprise to see him. She gave a small curtsey. "Is there aught I can do for you?"

"Here." He pulled his tunic over his head, glad to be rid of it. Tossing it at her, he asked, "Where is Lady Lilith?"

"In the main hall for the evening meal, I believe, my lord," the woman answered. "Would you like me to fetch her?"

"No. Leave her. Have someone bring food to the Black Tower."

"And your bath?" she asked.

"I'll use the one in my lady's room," he answered, not wanting to wait for someone to cart up his usual metal tub.

# CHAPTER 7

"Lord Sorin beheaded four Caniba spies in the forest with no help from the others. Sir Traven said he is possessed and the men who rode with him are in a dark mood because of it. Sir Traven said they should have taken at least one of the Caniba men alive so they might discover what they were doing this far north. It's true what they say, that witch Lady Lilith cursed him into madness."

"Those in town say we should dunk her in the river. If she comes to the surface, she's a witch. It's the only way to be rid of that kind."

"Not true. There's always fire. Witches burn faster than humans."

"And the other? Lady Jayne? Did they find her?"

"Dead, too, for all I know. And good riddance for the poor Lord Ronen."

Lilith didn't know the maids who spoke, as she waited on the tower stairwell, just out of eyesight but close enough to eavesdrop on their conversation. She strained to hear more, but they walked off. A sick feeling curled in her stomach. Sorin decapitated four men in a fight and they blamed her for it?

"I don't belong here. I don't belong here," she repeated, whispering the mantra as if saying the words could make the land of Staria disappear.

Her legs ached, the muscles still adjusting to the endless progression of steps. By the time she made it to the top, she longed for nothing more than the warmth of her bed and the secret fantasies of her late night dreams, tucked away from the spiteful eyes of the hall.

The soft glow of firelight shone from her room. It wasn't unusual as someone usually lit it at night. For all its barbaric tendencies, Battlewar Castle flowed to a unique rhythm perfected by time and practice. Things were done, even when you didn't see someone doing them.

"I don't belong here," she said under her breath as she entered her room.

Lilith tugged at the scarf around her neck. Fantine had matching ones made for all her new gowns, though some were so fine and thin their transparency did little to provide cover. The material trailed behind her as she absently dropped it on the end of the bed and walked across the room to the window. She peered out the slit, seeing a few trees and plenty of darkening sky. Stars poked in from the heavens, just starting to shine through.

"Why did you send me here?" Lilith moaned. She'd worked so hard for the company, had done her job, gathered information and they were going to punish her like this for one, little, stupid accident? Feeling helpless, she hit her hand on the stone wall, slapping it. "I don't belong with these people."

"Is my lady too high for us?"

*No.* Lilith stiffened. *It can't be.*

Almost afraid to look, she slowly turned to face the room. Her eyes went to the doorway. He wasn't there. Her heart quickened and she fought to control the breathiness in her tone. "Lord Sorin?"

He didn't answer, but movement caught her attention and she turned to the tub. Sorin sat in the dark blue of the water, his arms stretched to the side. His wet hair slicked back from his face, revealing the stark lines of his features. She bit her lip and pressed her legs tightly together. Firelight danced over his flesh, molding to each and every dip and curve. A black tattoo wound his upper arm, the lines bold and confident just like the man.

Lilith shivered. She hadn't fantasized about him in there, but it was possible he wasn't real. Right?

"Leave me," Sorin closed his eyes and leaned his head back.

Wrong.

Lilith tried to make her legs move, but they kept her rooted to the floor. Curiosity urged her forward, to try to see beneath the water's surface. The brawny muscles of his chest and neck called to her hands. In her current situation it had been hard not to think of his naked body over hers. Those images came back to her now and a deep longing filled her. She parted her lips, almost feeling the wet glide of flesh against them as she imagined kissing his neck.

*He's a stranger*, her logical mind argued.

*He doesn't feel like a stranger*, her treacherous body replied.

Lilith tried to think of something to say to break the silence and slow her departure. "I'm not a witch."

His head lifted and he arched a brow.

"Apparently the people in town are under the impression I'm a witch and wish to drown or burn me to find out for sure. I can assure you, I'm not a witch." She dared a few steps closer, her eyes glancing down into the water. The darkness kept him from view. Not really paying attention to her words, she continued, "Not that there is anything wrong with witches. I've met some very nice ones on other planes. Then again, I've met some bad ones. Anyway, I'm not one."

He didn't move.

Lilith took another step forward. "So I guess what I'm saying is I'd like to know if you have a library I can look at. A records room? Scroll lock? Database?"

Still nothing. No response beyond the aggravatingly straightforward look.

"I'd like to read over your laws to know what my options are." Lilith was about to go closer when his words stopped her.

"Your option is to let me protect you," he stated. "As your husband, it is my duty."

She flinched. *There's that husband word again.*

"That's kind of you to offer, but I'd still like to read—"

"Please, drop the deceptions. You wish to find a way out of our joining. There is no way out, save death." Again he closed his eyes, looking very weary as he sighed. "Perhaps you will become lucky and I will perish in battle."

"Don't say that," she snapped. Lilith leaned against the opened bathroom wall and it moved under her weight, making her pull instantly back. "I never wished you dead. I have never wanted anyone dead. Well, there was this boy, Billy Holliday, who sat behind me in grammar school and used to flick eraser bits at me, but... Is it true you cut off four guys' heads because of me?"

"Did you send the Caniba spies into the Hanging Forest?"

"No."

"Then it was not because of you," he answered reasonably.

Somehow, without her realizing it, she'd come to stand beside the tub. The bathroom seemed small with both of them in it. Heat radiated from the water, contrasting the cooler air flow from a window. Lilith still hadn't figured out how to open and close the window slits. "Is your bad mood with the men because of me?"

His eyes opened and he surged to his feet. "By the teeth of the damned, woman, I asked you to leave."

Rivulets cascaded down his flesh, creating wet trails that her eyes delightedly followed. The scars continued from his neck down, attesting to a dangerous life. Firelight caught on the water, decorating his entire length with tiny dots and trails of light. His broad chest tapered to a thick, tight waist, which in turn molded into perfect hips. But it wasn't his hips that made her stop and stare. His cock stood tall and proud, so erect that veins had risen along the sides.

"Do not look at me like I am about to attack you," he growled.

"You're not?" Lilith wondered at the disappointment in her tone.

"Not if you go now. I am aware you do not wish for me in your bed, and I will not go where I'm not wanted." When she didn't move, he stepped over the tub's edge onto the stone step. "But if you think you can escape our dismal fate you are mistaken. The decision has been made. We are joined."

He appeared so forlorn that she couldn't help but reach for him. Her hand slid onto his arm. The muscle flexed.

"I don't mean to insult you, Sorin. It's not you, it's this place. I don't belong here. Normally if I travel to a new dimension it's for work. I go, gather information and then leave. But I was not assigned to come here. I simply went to bed one night and then woke up in your prison." She tried to pull him around to face her, a great feat considering how he towered over her.

"So you are a spy?" he concluded, clearly not pleased by the fact.

"No. I'm a data analyst. I read books and take notes. I analyze facts and create historical profiles of the parallel universe I'm assigned to and then input them into Divinity's central database. When I go to a place, the governments know about it—well, mostly they do. But I assure you, there's no spying involved." Lilith swayed on her feet. His body radiated warmth. The muscle beneath her hand didn't relax. She flexed her fingers, wanting him to look at her. "Why did you choose me? I heard some of the women talking and they said you weren't expected to choose anyone."

"The gods told me to." The words lacked passion, as if they were a simple truth. "If what you say is true about Divinity and they broke their word, we will renegotiate our position with them. As for us, it's too late to change what has happened. Honor forbids it."

Maybe it was the softness of his tone or the romantic cast of firelight against his naked body, but Lilith found herself not caring about freedom quite so much. She slid her hand down his arm to his wrist and leaned her face next to his bicep. He reached around her stomach to her hip, gently pulling her in front of him. Dark eyes bore into her questioningly.

"I'm not very experienced." Heat fanned her cheeks, but she forced her eyes to stay on his. Sorin tightened his grip. His strength radiated up her hip and spread like a spark throughout her body. Moisture gathered in the folds of her sex. "I mean, I know about it, but I haven't, you know, a lot, and you look like you might...uh, hurt."

*By all the weapon thingies they normally curse to, I did not just say that—and to him! How embarrassing. I couldn't sound more like a moron if I tried. Oh please, floor, open up and drop me.*

Lilith wanted to sink into the stone and hide. What was it about him tonight that turned her into a babbling idiot? And why did all her fantasies keep flashing in her mind as laughable examples of what this man was really like during sex?

*I know about it? You look like you might hurt? Oh, Lilith, don't say another thing ever, ever again. Vow of silence from this point on.*

"I mean, you're pretty aggressive." Why was her mouth still moving? And why in the world didn't he just say something to shut her up? Did he just have to stand there, staring at her? "Which I suppose is war training, or at least a side effect of being trained as a warrior. But I'm not a warrior, obviously." She glanced down, suddenly realizing she'd taken the scarf off, and her breasts were thrust together and up by the dark blue of her corset. Torn between acting like she didn't notice and covering up her displayed chest with her hands, she continued, "So I hope you understand what I'm saying."

When she looked up, she found him staring at her chest intently. His lips had parted in quickened breaths. All too aware of his naked body so close to hers and the telltale lift of his towering erection, she tried to take a step back. His hand on her hip tightened, not letting her go.

"Please tell me what you're thinking, Sorin," Lilith whispered. "I can't tell."

He chuckled and lifted a brow. "How incredibly sexy you are in that corset. How much my body aches to be inside of you. How I want nothing more at the moment than to throw you up against the wall and ravish you. How... That's pretty well it."

"Oh," she breathed in mild surprise, not expecting that answer.

He leaned his face toward hers, licking his lips. His hand moved to the small of her back, forcing her next to his taut body. The unmistakable length of his shaft dug into her skirts. He stroked her cheek before pulling her mouth softly to his lips. "Touch me."

Lilith took hold of his arms, using him for support as her legs weakened. The tip of his tongue traced the rim of her mouth, teasing her lips apart with their wet, probing insistence. She savored each movement, each new sensation. A soft moan escaped her. He tasted so good, like sweet wine, and smelled even better.

Sorin cupped her ass, massaging the cheeks firmly so that her thighs pressed forcefully to his. His hips rocked against her skirts. After several moments, he withdrew his lips and brushed them across her cheek to her ear. "Touch me." He took her hand and compelled it between their bodies so that she palmed his arousal. The thick appendage filled her hand. Then, the same guiding hand lifted to her mouth, and he pressed a finger between her moist lips, rubbing them meaningfully several times before hooking her teeth and urging her down. "Finish me."

Lilith's eyes rounded as she got his meaning. He wanted her on her knees so she could suck his cock. Her pussy protested the one-sided idea. Her mouth watered, tempted.

"Finish me, so that I do not lose myself and take you too hard." He rocked his erection into her hand and groaned. "It is not my wish to hurt."

No man had ever said such a thing to her. The finger slipped from her mouth, wetting her jaw as he reached for the top of her bodice. He grabbed hold, several fingers pushing down between the tight squeeze of her breasts. Her breathing became hard and choppy and her heart beat so hard against her chest, she knew he had to feel it. She waited, wanting his fingers to find their way to her aching nipples. The nubs were erect, puckered and waiting for him.

Lilith found her knees bending under the intensity of his gaze. This had to be a dream, no matter how real he felt. She wasn't like this. She didn't succumb to mindless lust. The erotic placement of his fingers only made her body all the hotter. Each movement stung, sending wave after wave of delicious warmth down to her stomach.

Her fingernails pressed into his sides, raking their way down as she knelt before him. Curse it all, but this man was in perfect shape! He let go of her bodice, reaching to grab his cock and angle it toward her mouth as if he couldn't wait for her to do it herself. He bent his knees to better position himself for pleasure.

Sorin tensed, his stomach tightening in front of her. Lilith licked the mushroomed tip and he jerked violently, gasping. She flicked her tongue several times to taste the warm, salty essence of him. The power of him flooded her. He was so strong, so virile, such a perfect specimen of masculinity. The feel of the smooth shaft overwhelmed her like a potent sex drug, making her want to take him deeper into her mouth until she choked on the length of him.

Lilith grabbed the extra length of his shaft and moved her lips to meet her fists. Sorin buried his hands in her hair. She sucked, twirling her tongue around the ridge while carefully gauging his response.

Sorin gasped and grunted, communicating his satisfaction in animalistic noises. He arched his back, thrusting into her. The saliva from her mouth wet him as he moved, creating a slick tunnel inside her fists. He worked his body, the full length of him covered in the orange glow of firelight, more so now that the sky outside had darkened.

His hold on her head tightened almost painfully. Lilith sucked harder. Sorin jerked, keeping her mouth locked on his shaft. Crying out, he thrust one last time and released a stream of hot cum into her mouth. He didn't release her, forcing her to swallow the salty essence. When finally he let go, he stumbled back. Lilith licked her lips, the erotic taste of him in her mouth.

"I feel weak," he said in surprise. Lilith's body stung with need, and she didn't feel too strong herself at the moment. She backed toward the bed, sitting the instant the mattress hit the back of her thighs.

Sorin followed her, crawling over her as she fell onto her back. His knees and hands pressed around her, trapping her down. Now that he'd met with release, an almost devious light entered his eyes. A slow, predatory smile curled the side of his mouth. "Where do you think you're going? We are not finished."

Now that he had her, he wasn't letting go. Sorin's body sang with the pleasure of her mouth, but he was only getting started. He sat back, keeping her under him as he tugged at her skirts, pulling them up to free her legs. He settled his knees between her bare thighs to better look at her. The mattress shifted under his weight. After her earlier plea, he promised himself he'd take it slow. His size clearly frightened her. The thought gave him more than a small measure of pride.

The smooth skin of her calves and thighs were unmarked by hardship. He stared openly at her, unashamed and immensely curious. How quickly things seemed to change. When he'd seen her from his place in the tub, he thought her a dream come to torment him. Now the dream had become real, flesh and blood, delicious and sweet.

Lilith brought her upper legs together and pushed her skirts down a few inches. He frowned, not liking the way she hid herself from him. He wanted to look and he intended to do just that.

Sorin again pushed at her skirt, lifting it higher. A narrow strip of shortly cut hair lined her pussy. She had her skirt covering it before he had a chance to really look.

He frowned, persistently endeavoring to uncover his new treasure. Sorin massaged her legs, hoping to relax them open. Breasts strained against her corset, lifting and falling in a mesmerizing rhythm. Everything about her entranced him. She smelled sweet. Her skin was so soft. When she kissed him, she made a small moaning noise that drove him to distraction. He doubted she was even aware that she did it.

Sorin wanted to explore, wanted to see and touch and taste, but she kept hiding herself from him. Lilith angled her hips, moving so the skirt fell back down to hide her pussy. He gave a low growl of frustration.

"You hide," he said, keeping his tone low. Sorin suppressed the animalistic urge to rip at her clothing so she couldn't do it again.

"You're staring," she defended.

Her words made no sense. Of course he stared. He wanted to see. A beautiful woman like her had no reason to hide. Actually, to the men of his country, no woman had a reason to hide.

Coming up with an idea, he grinned and reached for the scarf she'd discarded on the end of the bed. Sorin leaned over her, letting the material slide over her throat. He snaked it over her arm, winding it lightly before moving to the other one. Then, before she realized what he'd done, he pulled both ends and drew her wrists together. Lilith's eyes widened as he quickly bound her arms over her head.

She squirmed beneath him. "What are you doing? Sorin?"

He crawled down her body, stopping when his mouth reached her knee. Blowing against her flesh, he answered, "Kissing you."

"But..." She worked her legs restlessly against the bed.

"I'm taking you prisoner so you can't hide from me. I wish to look." He grinned, liking the idea of her being under his control. She tried to protest, the weak attempt of someone who didn't believe wholly in the cause they were fighting for. He tore at her gown, ripping the material of the skirt out of his way. The loud noise silenced her as rounded eyes stared at him. The corset held the dress tight to her chest and waist, but exposed the engaging sight of her sex to view.

Sorin took his time, lightly kissing every inch of revealed flesh. He licked along her inner thigh, before settling next to her pussy. Almost shaking with eager excitement, he kissed her sex, letting the taste of her cover his lips. He breathed deeply, intrigued by the very femaleness of her body. Soft, yet toned. Smooth and unscarred. Intoxicatingly sweet.

He licked her hard, moaning into her sex. Lilith arched, gasping as her legs tightened around his head. She pulled at her wrists, trying to break free. Experimenting with his tongue, he twirled it within her slick folds, testing her responses. But soon his tongue wasn't enough. He wanted to touch, too. He slipped a finger inside her, wiggling it as the tight hold of her body gripped him.

Sorin's cock strained, swollen with need, and he wondered if he'd ever get enough of her. She bucked against his mouth, trembling with release. Cream dripped from her sex, wetting him with her desire. He moaned, crawling up her body, pausing to kiss the tops of her breasts. She squirmed beneath him, her head rolling on the mattress as she blinked lazily in his direction.

Wondrous sensations filled him, ones he didn't care to look too deeply at. He needed to be inside her, to end the torment he'd felt since first feeling her in the hall. Sorin was not a man used to being controlled, but when she looked at him, her lips parted and her cheeks flushed, he felt himself desperate to please her, no matter what she would command of him.

Sorin's thighs forced hers apart. A light sheen of sweat covered their bodies. Lilith tensed as he drew his cock along her slickened folds.

*Easy. Slow. Do not frighten her or she will banish you from her bed.*

With more self-control than he'd ever thought possible, he slipped his hard cock along her yielding sex. Moist heat welcomed him and he gulped. Sorin brushed his mouth to hers, liking the way their tastes mingled in the kiss. He rocked his hips forward, entering her.

*Tight. Hot. Blessed night!*

*Go. Slow.*

Gradually, he eased into her, stretching the tight muscles to fit his girth. Bracing his elbows, he kept his body close, enjoying the contrast of the harder corset to softer flesh against his chest. Lilith accepted his easy pace, her legs relaxing along his waist to let him go deeper. Oh, but it was hard not to just pound into her, taking her rough and fast. Every primal urge inside him told him to ride her, to make her feel every inch, to let her know she'd been claimed.

*Slow. By all the stars in the sky, Sorin, go slow.*

He held his breath. He'd never known a woman to be so tight. Unable to take the torment, his hips flexed on their own accord, seating his cock to the hilt. She gasped and arched, her muscles gripping him.

Sorin worked his hips in shallow thrusts, panting for air as he slid in the wet heat of her pussy. He pushed up for leverage, watching her glorious body beneath his. Her breasts bobbed, and he wished he had a knife to cut them loose from the binding top.

When she didn't protest, he thrust harder. Her body met his. Soft moans of pleasure escaped her. Then, suddenly, she tensed, her entire body going rigid as she met her release. The tremors were too much. Sorin grunted, a loud, primitive noise of power and completion. With a jerk, he emptied himself into her before collapsing forward. He kept his weight on his elbow so as not to crush her.

After his heart slowed and he caught his breath, he reached to untie her hands. She made soft noises, her eyes closed as she cuddled into the bed. Sorin studied her for a moment, knowing if she demanded it he could rise again. But, when her eyes opened, they appeared tired and it was late in the evening. For the time being, his body would have to be sated.

Leaning over, he kissed her once and said, "Good eve, my lady." Rolling off the bed, he walked to his room to sleep.

---

Lilith watched Sorin walk away from her. The sexy muscles folded and flexed with each step, seductively revealed by firelight. As if they weighed a ton, she struggled to free her heavy limbs from the scarf. Every bone in her body felt as if it had melted. Her nerves tingled with a fantastic numbness and all he could say was good eve? Good freaking eve?! After what they just did he left her for his own bed?

Too tired to chase after him and unsure she'd have the courage to confront him if she did, she didn't move from her spot on the bed as she reached to pull the laces of her corset. The restrictive clothing made it hard to breathe. Finally free, she flung the material on the floor. The gown would have to do for nightclothes, even with the torn slit up the skirt, for she wasn't getting out of the bed to find something else.

If she hadn't been one hundred percent sure he'd orgasmed, she would have thought she'd done something wrong. In fact, it felt as if they'd done something very, very right. Turning her back on the door, she jerked the covers over her body and snuggled into the mattress, pretending the lump in the folded coverlet was really Sorin resting next to her. Tomorrow she'd analyze what happened. Tonight she just wanted to dream.

# CHAPTER 8

After their evening together and his abrupt departure from her bed, Lilith wasn't sure what to expect. Surprisingly, she slept better than she had since she woke up that first morning in Staria. She half expected to be sore after sex, but aside from a mild ache, she felt great.

Nevertheless, with the morning light came her overactive brain's logical demands. What did sex with Sorin mean? Would she be treated differently now by those in the castle? Would they stop calling her a witch? Would Sorin expect her to lift her skirts whenever the mood struck him? What if he did? What if he didn't? And what in the world did she say to him?

Confusion filled her. She felt connected to him now, but knew she couldn't stay. This wasn't her dimension. Sure, she didn't have much of a life in her own parallel, but it was hers. That's where she belonged. And someone at Divinity owed her an explanation.

With her only way out blocked by Sorin's room, Lilith listened for signs of movement and watched the door in hope that he'd walk in. All was silent.

She took her time getting dressed, bathing, then fussing over which of the dozen outfits to put on. Well, a dozen minus one. Her gown from the evening before had been ruined. She finally decided on a soft cream-colored tunic dress with burgundy corset. The cream material had simple embroidery around the edges, not nearly as decorative as she'd seen on similar garments from other planes. As she looked in the polished metal they had in place of a mirror, she contemplated leaving the scarf off. The thought only lasted a second before she crammed a sheer piece of burgundy material down the front of her bodice.

Still, no sounds came from Sorin's room.

Opening the little containers on the vanity, she found one that she'd determined to be kohl eyeliner. She smudged it lightly over her lids, giving them a smoky effect. Then, braiding her hair into two sections, she wound them at the base of her neck and fastened it with a decorative comb.

And still, no sign that Sorin stirred from his sleep.

Maybe if she tiptoed really quietly, she could sneak downstairs. It might be easier to face him if they weren't quite so isolated in their tower. Morning-afters always tended to be a little awkward, especially, she quickly discovered, when the man she'd slept with was the incredibly confident Lord Sorin.

Slowly pushing open the door, she peeked through the crack. The messy comforter at the end of his bed didn't move. She watched the folds carefully, leaning down to crawl across the floor. Keeping her eyes on the edge of the bed, she inched her way along the stone. When she reached the end, she couldn't stop herself from pushing onto her knees to see if he slept naked. The bed was empty.

Lilith gave a small laugh and stood from the floor. She'd been up since dawn so either he left really early or the insulation between their two rooms was better than she imagined. Recalling how he'd pleasured himself the first day they met, she knew the latter was exceedingly possible.

On her way down, the sounds of footsteps greeted her. Sera appeared, smiling as she balanced a giant tray of food on her shoulder. She again wore a corset that seemed two sizes too small for her generous chest. Steaming miniature bread loafs, red liquid sauce for dipping, sliced meats, fruits, a large bowl of green gelatinous substance, and the biggest flaky pastry she'd ever seen filled the serving tray to capacity.

"Lord Sorin is not in the tower," Lilith said, knowing all that food couldn't be hers. At most, they'd given her dry bread and cold meat trays when she was alone in her room.

"My lord ate below stairs with the men before going out to the exercise field to do mock battle with the squires," Sera explained. "Maray made this especially for my lady to break her fast."

"Really?" Lilith arched a brown in dubious surprise. Why was the woman being so nice to her? "What is it? Poison?"

Sera's smile didn't falter. The servant turned and began the long trek down. "Since you're coming down, I'll bring your tray to the hall. Most of the castle is finished with the morn meal, but I am sure someone will linger for conversation."

"Is there a particular reason you're...?" Lilith stopped. If Sorin went to the hall and announced that he'd gotten a piece of ass from her, she really didn't want to hear it from a gloating, I-told-you-to-listen-to-me Sera. Then again, Lilith had never been completely sure about this maidservant's sanity. "Never mind. Thank you, Sera, and I don't need conversation."

*Like I really want to start my day by being called a witch as people shield their children from me. I have enough to think about without a posse trying to drag me into the courtyard.*

Sera led the way into the main hall. Loud bouts of laughter, not unlike the day Sorin chose her, sounded from within. Lilith approached cautiously, half expecting another group of unwitting females waiting before the crowd. A pang of jealousy hit her as she imagined Sorin choosing another to take her place.

"My lady," a servant greeted, smiling brightly. She carried an empty pitcher in her hands. "Good morn."

"Good..." Lilith didn't finish the thought. What was going on here?

"Good morn, my lady," another woman said, coming from the kitchen with a full tray of food.

"My lady," still a third greeted, nodding her head.

*Welcome to Crazyville, please be sure to wear your padded suit.*

When the fourth maid tried to hurry past with the same happy greeting, Lilith grabbed her arm to stop her. "I'm not being burned alive today, am I?"

"My lady?" the young woman inquired, perplexed. Her brown eyes reminded Lilith of a fuzzy baby animal begging to be picked up. Lilith had noticed the maid before, hanging back from the others when the hall became too boisterous.

"The villagers wanted to burn me as a witch," Lilith explained. "That's not happening today, is it?"

"Oh, you knew about...?" The maid cleared her throat. "No one really thought you were a witch, my lady. I do not think we would have burned you. Lord Sorin made it clear this morning you were not to be touched."

"He made an announcement?" She gave a weak, disbelieving laugh. Well, he did promise to protect her.

"Yea, my lady, he decreed that he inspected you quite thoroughly and you were most assuredly not a witch, and there was to be no drowning or burning of his wife." Her grin widened knowingly. "We all thank you for taking the fire out of his temper."

Lilith made a weak noise by way of an answer, unsure whatever she said was a coherent series of words. Sorin made an announcement? Sure, she assumed people might suspect something, eventually, but she didn't expect a formal decree of her bedding.

Hurrying inside, she kept her head down in hopes that she wouldn't be noticed making her way to the head table. She always hated being the center of attention, set high above the others as if on display. The crowd was abnormally large for so late in the morning. At her glances, several of the women stood to wave at her. Many of them wore scarves draped over their necks, just as Lilith had been doing.

"My lady!" a loud knight called, lifting his goblet toward her. She flinched as the loud sound turned every pair of eyes to her. She lifted her hand, giving a halfhearted wave of acknowledgement. She scanned the hall for Sorin, relieved when she didn't see him.

Lilith sat at the table in front of the food Sera laid out for her, all too aware of being the center of attention. She'd seen societies, especially ones where people lived in such close proximity, where everyday happenings of the individual were common knowledge throughout the population. But she'd always watched from the edge of their social circles, taking her notes. Now it would seem she was one of the top celebrities. If the negative attention made her uncomfortable before, constant stares and waves made her want to jump up and scream.

Her hand shook as she reached for the bread. The crowd stared openly at her, taking in her every move with wide smiles and avid attention. She much preferred the moody accusations as they refused to acknowledge her. Tearing off a bit of the crust, she stuck the dry morsel in her mouth. The staring didn't stop.

*Is this some kind of new torture? Attention me to death?*

A group of women stood from one of the front tables and slowly made their way forward. The same group had gone out of their way to snub her in the halls a few days before. Whispering and giggling, they pushed a tall, thin blonde to the front. Greta curtsied, saying meekly, "My lady."

Lilith didn't move as she fingered her bread. Greta looked to her companions. They shook their heads and motioned her to speak.

Greta cleared her throat. "We wish an audience."

Lilith looked behind them to the full hall and stated dryly, "You have one."

Greta relaxed. "It is our wish to welcome you properly to Battlewar."

"All right," Lilith began. "Thank—"

"With a fire celebration," Alana asserted, jumping a little in excitement.

Lilith didn't move, as she thought dryly, *They want to set me on fire. I knew it.*

"May we?" Karima asked when Lilith didn't answer.

Refusing to agree to anything she didn't know about, she shook her head in denial. "No."

As if they were all struck by the same magical gale, their expressions fell. Losing all gaiety as they slumped back to their table, the women rejoined their men. Alana went so far as to pull the scarf from her neck and throw it down in an open display of pouting.

Feeling somewhat vindicated for the snubbing, Lilith tore off another piece of bread and dipped it into the red sauce. Maybe this celebrity thing wouldn't be too bad.

---

Being a celebrity blew like the geysers on dimensional plane 237.

The small fire celebration victory lasted all of two minutes before the staring and waving resumed. Lilith could barely force herself to swallow, feeling like they counted every bite. By the time a loud ruckus came from the back of the hall, she was ready to kiss the feet of whoever took the attention from her.

Sorin.

The name caught on her lips. Towering over a group of shirtless men, he strode boldly into the main hall, dominating everything around him. In the light of day he appeared handsomer than before —his sweat-glistened chest, the tight fit of his breeches, the thick line of his tattooed arm.

Wet heat pooled between her thighs. Her pussy was all too ready to remind her of the night before. Thick, tight muscles. Strong, sure hands. Firm, smooth ass. Hard, delicious cock. Being tied at his mercy as he ripped her clothing.

Unlike other times, he actually smiled. The expression lit up his entire face, gentling the harsh, disapproving lines. She struggled for breath, drawing in raspy gasps of air through her parted lips. This couldn't be the same man who randomly chose her from a line of women. He appeared too...happy.

The knights made slow progression, filtering through the crowd, stopping to talk and laugh. A warrior with a missing hand spoke to Sorin, pointing his wrist toward the front of the hall. Sorin's smile dropped some as he looked at her over the crowd only to resume the second his gaze met hers. Heat flooded her features.

Sorin strode through the hall, heading in a straight line to where she waited. She bit her lip, trying to think of something clever to say and all too aware of their audience. He came around the table, practically leaping up the platform steps. Dipping his finger into the green substance she had yet to touch, he brought it to his mouth and sucked lightly.

"Good morn, my lady," he said quietly, leaning to kiss her. His eyes glowed with an inner light, drawing her toward him.

Lilith almost let him, but her eyes drifted over the watchful eyes. On instinct, she jerked away, denying him. A low murmur started over the crowd. Sorin stiffened, hurt flitting across his expression before his mouth dropped into the impassable mask she was used to seeing.

"I understand." The flat statement landed on her like a death sentence, hard and condemning. All around the main hall, smiles faded into irritated frowns, as if the whole lot of Starians were joined emotionally to Sorin's moods.

"Sorin, I—" Lilith peered over the watchful faces. "We need to talk."

He crossed his arms over his chest and arched a brow. The motion yanked her gaze down to his thick, tan chest. She flexed her fingers, aching to touch him.

"Not here," she answered, standing. Her feet couldn't carry her fast enough.

Once out of the hall, she started to go to the stairs only to turn around, start for the kitchen, stop and finally decide on the hall she'd last seen Jayne disappear down. She paced nervously, feeling Sorin before he rounded the corner. The man had an energy about him.

Her stomach fluttered. Perhaps alone wasn't such a great idea. Crossing his arms over that mammoth chest, he said nothing. She went to him, closing the distance. Heat wrapped round her, like a million tiny fingers pulling her into him.

"This isn't going to work for me." Lilith moaned softly. That didn't exactly come out right. "I mean to say, we should discuss—"

"I do not see what there is to discuss. You changed your mind about us." His features were as hard as ice and his eyes just as cold. The man was like a broken faucet, hot and cold, cold and hot.

"That's just it," Lilith exclaimed. "This whole 'us' idea. We just met, Sorin."

"The gods willed—"

"No." She held up her hand. It pressed against the hard flank of muscle over his heart. The steady beat drummed against her fingers, contrasting the erratic rhythm in her own chest. "Not the gods, not the knights or their women, you. I don't know you."

"You knew me well enough last night." Was she mistaken or did some of the sparkle come back to his gaze at that statement? He reached for her hip, jerking her against him. Her hand crushed between their bodies. With a swift turn, he had her pinned to the wall. "Should I remind you?"

"That's different. That's..." Lilith struggled to define what last night was. She pushed at his chest, but wasn't able to push him away. His heartbeat quickened as the length of his cock grew thick against her stomach. "It was sex."

"Good sex," he offered, rocking into her.

"Ah, fine." Lilith suppressed a moan. Did he not realize someone could walk around the corner and see them? Starians really had no sense of modesty. None. "However, that's not the issue."

"So you admit that it was good between us." The side of his mouth curled in self-satisfaction. He licked his mouth, his tongue taking a leisurely route along the supple lips.

"I admit that...that is not the issue," she tried to focus. Why couldn't he just listen to her? Why did he have to look at her with those piercing eyes? Press that gorgeous body still bulging from a workout against her? She swallowed, her mouth suddenly dry. "Sex is sex. Strangers have it all the time, but people are acting like we're a couple."

"We are a couple," he said, his tone aggravatingly certain. "You are my wife."

"Please, Sorin, not here. This is the kind of thing I wanted to talk to you about. I don't want to sit up at the high table. I don't want people watching me all the time."

"You pulled me aside to tell me you don't like your chair?" He chuckled, the sound low and incredibly seductive. "Very well. You will receive a new one."

"It's not the chair. It's the staring and waving and watching and people trying to talk to me and..." She didn't want to move. When he was next to her, she didn't think about freedom or escaping. She couldn't see past his eyes. "Do marriages last forever in Staria?"

To her surprise, he let her go. She stayed against the wall, watching him put distance between them. "You cannot end the marriage."

"This is what I'm talking about. This whole 'us' issue. You make these definite decrees but you don't tell me why. You don't even answer my questions. I didn't ask how to get out of our arrangement." Calling what they had a marriage seemed strange. "I just asked if marriages, here in Staria, lasted forever."

"Until death." He gritted his teeth. "Women especially are expected to find another mate. So you do not wish to end the marriage?"

It was her turn to refuse to answer outright. "We don't know each other. We skipped a lot of important steps here. I just want to get to know you. Is that such an outlandish request?"

"What 'steps'?" The ice melted by small degrees from his face, and she got the distinct impression that he chuckled inwardly at her. "What is it you want to know?"

"Like, why me? Why did you pick me? Be honest and don't say the gods." She held up a finger in warning. "Unless they walk in the front door and say, 'hey, it's us, the gods, I don't want to hear their opinion in the matter."

He sighed, nodding once. "Very well. I did not plan to take a wife but realized it was time. Duty demands I lead by example and that I have sons to carry on my name and position. Should I die and Ronen as well, there will be none left to lead in our places. The Firewall armies will fall to another, and the hope and sacrifice of our noble ancestors will be forever buried in the past. Staria's defenses could weaken and the Caniba tribes could finally make their way across our borders in full force. Plus, by taking you, I do not have to continue to go to the marriage ceremonies. I can stay on the battlefront with my men."

War. She asked why she was chosen and the answer was war.

Lilith bit her lips and looked to the floor. Well, she had wanted honesty. It wasn't exactly a profession of love at first sight.

Sorin leaned over, forcing her to once again meet his gaze. "You are disappointed in my answer. You asked for honesty."

"I know I did. It's not like I expected you to profess love or break into song or anything." She gave a nervous laugh, almost wishing she hadn't asked to learn more. "That would be ridiculous."

"Love?" His arms dropped to his sides, tilting his head in question.

"You don't know what that is?" How sad. "A man and woman meet, over time they have feelings that aren't just physical..."

"I understand the concept. Many of the women brought to us by the fairies speak of romantic love and it is written in our legends. Most marriages even foster genuine affection over time, but our ways do not give consequence to such notions. Marriages are unions. Women need men to protect them, to fight so they do not have to. Men need children and physical release. We stay faithful because the gods demand discipline. War demands discipline."

No wonder the man left her bed with hardly a word. She was pretty much a concubine with privileges of his station. Whatever girlish hope she'd refused to acknowledge died a little. Sorin offered sex, which admittedly was a great checkmark in the plus category. He offered protection so long as he lived. But what if he died? The thought caused tears to well in her eyes. She blinked them back. In this war torn land it was a great possibility that a solider would parish in battle. Then what? She had to go "marry" the next guy who grabbed her arm and said, "mine"? What if the next guy wasn't so restrained? Or smelled funny? Or happened to be a pig farmer who lived forever and condemned her to an eternity of mucking pens?

*I really don't belong here.*

Lilith trembled. She didn't want anyone else to claim her. Out of all the men in this dimension, Sorin definitely ranked as a top catch, if she ignored the fact that he'd never come to love her and she'd been chosen on impulse more than emotion.

"You do not speak." He pulled her attention back to him by slipping a finger under her chin. "Is that all you wished to know?"

Lilith thought about lying, but he'd been honest with her. She could at least return the gesture. "No."

"What else?" He inched closer.

"I'm not sure. Some things can't be learned from a series of questions, Sorin, but from time. Perhaps we could do something together."

His eyes lit with interest. "Something?"

"Not that something, something else." Even as she denied it, the idea had great merit. "Something fun."

"I need to bathe, you may join me." He grinned, unmistakably aroused.

"Like doing something outside, fully clothed."

"A ride?" he offered. "Treacherous Pass should be dry."

"I don't ride," she said.

"You wish to," he thought for a moment before finishing, "practice with blades?"

Lilith shook her head in denial. "I don't blade."

"No blades?" Sorin questioned in disbelief. "Not even a knife? Dagger? Short sword?"

"I'm a fair aim with a gun, but that's it." Shooting had been a required course in her academy training before hiring on with Divinity.

"Gun?"

"Never mind." The last thing Lilith was going to do was add to their arsenal of war implements. They could find their own ways to hurt each other. She frowned. What had Divinity been thinking? Sending her here with all she knew of the other planes. What if she introduced nuclear science or showed them how to make gunpowder? And not just her, but the other women as well. They could really injure a whole society by helping it to advance too quickly.

"What do you think about when you look like that?" His finger slid over her jaw in a light caress. He furrowed his brow and scrunched his nose, mimicking her.

Lilith gave a halfhearted shrug. "I analyze and take mental notes of things. It's how I process...it's not interesting."

"You are female," he declared as if it was a great discovery. "I will take you to Battlewar market. Women like the market."

Lilith smiled at his expectant look and nodded. The man seemed very proud of himself. She envisioned rows of sword blades and battle axes with matching sheathes. They'd probably throw in inducements like free blade sharpeners with every sword purchase. "Sounds perfect."

*Okay, so one lie won't hurt.*

"I must bathe first." Sorin began to back away. "Lady Alana has requested a private audience with you. She is waiting—"

"Audiences, by nature, are public," Lilith broke in, not wanting to talk to the woman.

"It means they wish permission to speak to you. I believe they desire to have a fire ceremony. As the highest-ranking lady in the castle, you must approve."

"Permission?" Lilith frowned. "They didn't need permission to call me a witch and hurl insults. I don't see why I should give them permission to talk."

"That was before we—"

"Don't say it!" Lilith held up her hands. "I'll go audience them and tell them no."

"Fire ceremonies are well received by the townsfolk. It would be a nice gesture, a gift if you will from their new lady." Sorin gave a small bow and hurried from the hall. She detected his feet hitting hard on the stone as he rushed up the tower steps.

How fitting would that be? A fire ceremony for the people who wanted to burn her as a witch.

"My lady?" Lady Alana came around the corner, as if she'd been waiting for Sorin to leave. Lilith thought it a good thing she didn't give in to the desire to kiss him. It might not have stopped there. Sorin already proved himself to be a man willing to pleasure her no matter where they were at.

"I'll give you an audience, Lady Alana," Lilith lifted her chin up in the air and brushed past the woman. "Tomorrow."

# CHAPTER 9

The bright day brought with it a perfect mixture of sunny warmth and cool breeze. Battlewar market teemed with activity. Permanent booths of the local tradesmen clustered together to form narrow walkways impossible to pass through on horse. They butted against the inner bailey wall, packed tight with merchandise. To the south, off the main road through town, traveling merchants set up horse-drawn carts, side by side, and sold wares out of the back. They decorated them with brightly colored strips of material to draw the eye.

A woman with flowers sang loudly, not the songs of Staria but from whatever land the fairies brought her. She paused long enough to lean over to a group of men and receive a kiss from each of them.

"So not everyone is a warrior," Lilith observed from his side. "Inside the castle they made it sound like every man went to war."

Sorin tried to act nonchalant, but it was hard not to reach over and lift Lilith from the ground to twirl her about. She was light enough. He could carry her for miles and never get tired. The breeze caused the scarf around her neck to flutter, lifting just enough for him to get a glimpse of a lifted breast. "Not by daily trade, but most have fought in battle and would answer the call to arms should the king command it."

He escorted her past the booths, enjoying the way she tried not to get excited about a stack of scrolls and giant silver-edged books, yet completely glanced over a stack of lace and ribbons. When she accepted his offer to take her to market, he'd been ecstatic to know she would let him show her as his wife for the whole town to see. And see they did. Wherever Lilith walked people stared and pointed and tried to get her attention with a smile. She acknowledged everyone with a little wave, but didn't seem pleased by it. More often than not, Lilith would try to hide in the shadows or turn his direction down the less crowded path. Being born into his position, Sorin thought nothing of the attention.

At first, it seemed odd that she wanted to "know him" and he had a difficult time making conversation flow. Bianka had never tried to know him. She just took what she wanted and left him with a tattered reputation. Normally, with the other knights, he would discuss battles, training, wenching, tournaments, duty and honor, or generally cursed the Caniba tribes. Lilith wanted to know about him—what he thought about living in a castle surrounded by so many people, if he liked a particular shade of blue, if he read books or sang or played games or did any number of un-knightly type things. But the more she talked, the more he realized he didn't have much of these other things in his life. Castles were acceptable, but he'd lived most of his life in an encampment inside a tent and surrounded by nature. Blue was a fine enough color, but he preferred the red of his family crest. He read missives from the king, sang drinking songs around a campfire and he played games, but they were tournaments designed to enhance battle skills.

With each answer he gave, he saw a pitying wave cross over her eyes. He didn't like it. Any other woman would be proud of his accomplishments and life. Lilith appeared sad for him, but she never said anything about it beyond a nod of her head and a thoughtful, "Oh."

"Can I ask you something else?" Lilith paused near the end of a cart selling raw leather and touched a couple of pieces.

"Yea." Sorin suppressed a smile. She'd been asking him questions all day. Seeing the merchant, he pointed down to a stack of leather strips, held up two fingers and pointed toward the castle. The man nodded, not moving from his place next to the cart. Like always, Lilith didn't seem to notice his purchase.

"Is Jayne dead? And the others who were in the cell with me? Are they all right?" She turned her eyes to him and he hated the frightened expression in their depths. "Sera said you sent the two who had philter home, is that true?"

"I did not," he stated. "It's not my duty to see to it, but they were sent back to Divinity unharmed. They were not suitable."

"And I am?" She gave a small laugh. "They didn't exactly interview us. They just looked in a cell and pointed at the two who were crying."

A measure of pride filled him. "You carried yourself well."

"So the others? Karre, Paige and Jayne?"

"Jayne we shall see in a few months and you can ask her yourself, but my brother would not harm her." Sorin silently added, *Unless he had to.* "Sir Aiden has taken Lady Paige to their home. Sir Vidar and Lady Karre reside near the battlefront at Spearhead. I am sure both ladies are well. We do not beat our women..." He lowered his voice and slipped his hand along her hip, daring to touch her and hoping she didn't shy away like in the hall. "Unless they ask us to."

She shivered but didn't jerk away. "I've been watching, listening, since I've arrived. I know you need women because you don't have a lot of your own. I know you made a deal with Divinity."

"Yea, we did. They approached us during battle. We almost slew them as allies to the Caniba."

Lilith slipped away from his touch and he felt an acute disappointment. Sorin followed her past the next cart of animal pelts, pointed at two soft furs, and motioned to the merchant. Not wanting the conversation to die, he told her about the first meeting with Divinity, the otherworlders' proposal for trade and assurance that they could find willing women who'd love to come to live at Staria.

The light clanking of a blacksmith drew Lilith's attention as she watched the man forge a blade. Sorin knew him well. Helmut produced some of the finest swords in all of Staria. He had several hanging on his weapons' wall.

"But they didn't tell us about it. They kidnapped us and sent us here." Lilith motioned toward the center of the market. Peasants continued to mill about, the busy sounds of their daily lives oddly comforting in their familiarity. "I've seen plenty of women who appear unattached. Why not marry one of them?"

"Unattached?" Sorin frowned, following her gaze. "Where?" He'd only seen three unattached females, but it would be years before any man thought of marrying them.

"Everywhere," she stated. Lilith looked around, finding a willowy sprite of a woman next to a group of five men. "There. She looks single and she's pretty. No wonder all five men are fighting for her attention. Why not seduce her with your power and rank? Or there, the dancing flower lady, I've seen her kiss three different men."

"They were her husbands," Sorin explained.

Lilith paled and she gasped. "You mean, I could have more than one husband?" She hugged her arms around her waist. "They could just come up and choose me?" Her eyes darted around the market, as if waiting.

Sorin tensed. "You wish for more—?"

"No!" she instantly denied. "I didn't ask for one husband. Is that why everyone keeps staring at me? Am I on the market, in," she gestured around, "the market? We have to go. I don't want some pig farmer jumping up and grabbing me. I highly doubt he has a high-tech facility like where I'm from. If you think I'm a wreck living in a castle, you don't want to see me on a farm. I don't do dirt or dung."

He relaxed somewhat amused by her reaction. "It's different with the peasants. The men choose, but are encouraged by the women who often take two or more husbands and never from the same family. Once a family is formed, they all have to agree before another man is let in."

"And there isn't jealousy?" Lilith bit her lip and scrunched her nose, instantly fascinated now that she wasn't being hunted by pig farmers. Sorin recognized her expression. She was analyzing and thinking again. What did she call it? Taking mental notes? Her constant curiosity didn't go unnoticed. The few times she'd talked to merchants it had been to ask detailed questions about their trade and their wares—how they were made, how long it took, how they liked living in a village towered over by a castle.

"It is necessity. The men need wives and poorer families can live and work in larger numbers. This way, no one starves, everyone has shelter and families are protected. Those women who do not wish to marry choose a life of service following the armies. They're well taken care of and treated like queens."

"You mean whores." She nodded in understanding.

Seeing a knife with a pretty silver hilt carved with pictures of the forest, he picked it up and waved his hand to get Helmut's attention. The man kept working, hammering without watching his hands. Sorin indicated he planned on taking the blade. Helmut smiled and turned his attention back to what he was doing. Sorin handed the knife to Lilith. "I'll teach you to use it. Every woman should know how to protect herself."

"What? Running and hiding behind you isn't an option?" She laughed, taking the weapon from him. She pulled it from its sheath and examined the sharp blade. "I don't think my money works here."

"Why not? Mine does and what I have is now yours."

"Thank you. It's sweet." She glanced up and graced him with a faint smile before turning her attention to the gift.

By all the gods, he wanted to kiss her. Just looking at her made his body tight from head to foot. Why wouldn't she reach for him? Didn't she want him as he wanted her? Even now he burned.

*Fool.*

*Idiot.*

*Weak.*

Sunlight illuminated the back of her long neck, as wisps of blonde hair escaped her upswept locks. He hesitated, but finally slid his arm around her waist to walk next to her. She didn't pull away. He clung to each sign of her acceptance of him.

"Tell me about Bianka."

Sorin dropped his arm from her, feeling as if she'd struck him. "There is nothing to tell."

"You know that's not true. What happened to her?"

"She's dead and her death is on my head. It was my duty to protect her, but I couldn't get to her in time." Sorin quickened his pace, forcing her to keep up.

"Did you care for her?"

"I told you, we don't give weight to such notions." Why couldn't she just leave the topic be? He didn't want to talk about Bianka, or think about her, or even remember her.

"Curse it, Sorin, you had to feel something. I can tell you cared for her by the way you react. Call it what you like, but I think you loved her." She tried to grab at his arm. Peasants stopped what they were doing to watch the noble couple.

Sorin came to an abrupt halt. Glancing around, he saw they were close to the main road leading up to the inner bailey. He hooked her arm with his and guided her toward the gate. When they were relatively alone, he said, "You wish to know what I felt for her? Hate. Disappointment. Disenchantment. Her own people shoved her into a fairy ring to get rid of her. When I first saw her, I felt sorry for her. She looked like she needed protection."

"Sorin—"

He cut her off, continuing toward the gate. He kept his voice low so only she could hear and plastered a fake smile on his face for those who watched them. "Then her true nature was revealed. She was a selfish, cruel wench who demanded everything and gave nothing. When I left for war she tried to seduce the whole of my castle. When none would touch her, she burned down my home and ran away with every valuable she could fit onto her stolen horses. Nevertheless, she was my wife, and it was my duty to rescue her and keep her safe. I should have locked her in a tower. By the time I found her, she'd crossed over the Caniba border and propositioned one of their raiding parties. First, they took what she offered, then they took her valuables and her horses, and then they took her for food."

"Oh, Sorin, no."

He decided to take her to the brewery, knowing it would be

empty and they'd have privacy. "I see the look on your face when I speak of fighting and my life, but there is a reason we are always at war. There is no peace with the Caniba. They are dishonorable, disgusting creatures. So as long as there is a Caniba and so long as there is a Staria, we will be at war. That is the role our gods have given us."

Though still brusque in nature, Sorin at least spoke. Lilith didn't know how to answer his tirade. When she thought his hesitance to talk about his late wife was due to emotional pain, it had been strangely imperative that she confront him. She had to make him face the truth of his loss if there was to be any hope of deepening their relationship. But this? His hard features and flat tone revealed not how much he could love, but how he could hate.

As they'd walked the marketplace, his hair dried into soft waves. Cotton fabric molded to his strong body, stretching over his thick chest and muscular back. All day she did her best not to look at him too long. It had taken all her willpower not to touch him. But now, as he dragged her behind him, stiff and angry, a large part of her thought of running away and hiding in the surrounding town.

The market had been a wonderful experience, aside from the constant stares from the villagers. She did her best to pretend she didn't notice. Lilith loved studying their social interactions. It told a lot about the society to see their poor. Though, in truth, the poor didn't appear so poor. Everyone seemed to prosper. They were well fed, gave the impression they were happy, children ran around freely and not one beggar lined the streets in need of alms.

Sorin led her through the gate. Inside the inner bailey, soldiers practiced in the exercise field. They threw spears at distant targets, cheering good-naturedly when someone hit their aim, which apparently was often. Hurrying to catch up to Sorin as he strode toward a wide building constructed of wood, she tried to change the subject back to when he'd been talking to her without scowling. "So, none of the noblewomen take more than one husband? Is it illegal? Mind you, I don't wish for multiples, just asking."

He quirked a brow and directed her to follow him inside. The strong, stifling odor of fermenting liquor instantly filled her lungs. She blinked heavily, adjusting to the dim light as she coughed.

"Try not to breathe too deeply. They're malting the grain." He motioned to the side, but all she saw was a long stretch of material covered in what appeared to be dark sand over a smoker. Sorin took her hand and guided her through the first room. In the back, a narrow row of stairs led into the ground. The second room contained barrels of stored liquor, didn't smell as strong and had a chill to it. He turned a sharp corner, pushing into a third room. Light shone from a row of holes in the ceiling. Muffled noise from the exercise field filtered in. Despite the dirt floor and a single pale cobweb in the far ceiling corner, the place was empty.

"Where are you taking me?" The words barely escaped her when he tugged her into his arms.

"Right here." He stepped assertively forward, forcing her against an uneven stone wall. "I'm going to take you right here. No one will think to look for us in the cellar and I know you wish not to be seen."

Lilith saw the intent in his impassioned expression, felt it pressing unmistakably against her stomach. A shiver erupted along her flesh. The memory of his kiss caused her lips to tingle.

Deft fingers tugged at the scarf around her neck, parting it to expose the tops of her breasts. He squeezed her through the corset, moaning as eager hands worked a breast free from the top. Sorin pinched her nipple, following the hard caress with the softer suck of his mouth.

Lilith let out a weak cry. He devoured her with his hands and mouth, tugging at her skirt to lift it, slipping fingers next to his tongue so both could play with her nipple. Desire wet her pussy in anticipation. She helplessly explored his neck and shoulders, unable to do much else as he pinned her to the wall.

"I need to be inside you," he growled in animalistic urgency. "I've been hard since I woke up this morn, and your kiss in the hall only made the ache worse. All day I've pictured throwing you over the booths, taking you in the silky ribbons, on the fur pelts, over the hard iron latches."

It wasn't public and she knew no one could see them, but the sounds coming from outside, knowing so many people were close, caused her heart to quicken in what wasn't exactly repulsion. Sorin ran his hand up her bare thigh to her sex. He thrust a finger into the moist folds of her pussy.

"A-ah," he breathed hotly against her chest. "Please, do not deny me, my lady. I need you. If I don't find release soon inside your sweet body, I'll explode. Lift your legs around my waist. Let me inside you."

Lilith slid a leg to settle next to his waist. Sorin grabbed the other, hoisting her easily from the floor. She held onto his shoulders, gripping his tunic. Like a spear finding its target, he moved his shaft up her thigh. The thick tip of his cock head hit against her pussy, an instant reminder of how large of a man he was. His grip tightened on her hips and his eyes bore deeply into hers, as if to silently beg permission.

Lilith wiggled, circling her hips so she teased his arousal with the inviting wetness of her pussy. It must have been all the answer he needed, because Sorin lunged into her. Unlike the night before, he didn't ease his way into her depths. Instead, the full length of him glided to the root, burying itself in the tight sheath of her sex.

"Ah, I need to have you." As he said it, he pulled back and thrust again, hard and deep. "You're still so tight around me. I want to pound you until your pussy's the shape of my cock. I'm going to make you come so hard you'll never want another man between these soft thighs."

Lilith couldn't find the words to respond to his possessive decree. She'd never been taken so forcefully, so desperately, as if he'd die if he couldn't stake fast and hard claim to what he considered his. And as he jabbed wildly in and out, she couldn't think of one good reason why he shouldn't think that way. She was his, marked to her very core. Even if she left him, she'd never forget a single detail.

Sorin wasn't the only one whose desires had been building all day. Lilith met her release fast and hard, just like he promised. She tensed, panting and shaking as he thrust a few more times. Her legs went limp, the bones turning to tingling liquid. Sorin grunted, pressing her hard against the stone as he climaxed. He nuzzled her neck before letting her go. Her skirts fell about her unstable legs, and she stayed against the cool stones while she adjusted her bodice. Sorin pulled up his breeches, lacing them along the side of his hip.

"The hall should be ready to dine," he said, opening the door for her. She nodded, not meeting his gaze. He sounded so nonchalant. "It would be good for us to be there, together."

Lilith wound her hair back into the braids as she left the ventilated room for the stifling brewery. As she stepped past, she expected Sorin to pull her into his arms and maybe kiss her temple, some sign of affection beyond the sex. His hand brushed the small of her back, guiding her along, but that was all.

"Have you considered the fire ceremony?" he inquired. "The weather is perfect for it, and it would be a nice gesture from the new noblewoman."

Lilith closed her eyes briefly. She didn't want to talk about a fire ceremony. She wanted him to kiss her head and say he cared for her. She wanted tenderness, affection. Hell, she wanted a hint at the possibility of love.

"I told Alana I'd speak with her tomorrow," she said flatly, not ready to give in to the bitch brigade who'd treated her like dirt before Sorin's public announcement.

"And tomorrow, what will you tell her?"

Lilith gave a small smile. "I'll probably tell her that I'll talk to her tomorrow."

# CHAPTER 10

Lilith stared in amazement at her bed. Piles upon piles of trinkets from the market filled every corner until she realized that somehow each and every item she'd given so much as a sidelong glance at had been delivered to her room. There were bolts of fancy material, a wooden chair with a forest carved over the back, a sewing kit, woven baskets, ribbons and perfumes. A thick, silver-embossed book caught her eye and a tiny flutter went across her stomach.

Setting the knife Sorin had given her on the vanity, she walked around the bed. Pieces of leather rested atop fluffy white pelts. A wooden box filled with white candles butted up against a tall stack of blank parchment with feathery writing utensils and pots of colorful ink. There were silver goblets and chained necklaces such as she'd seen some of the women wear around the castle but had never really looked too closely at.

"Sorin?" she called, hearing someone move on the other side of the opened door. They'd just finished the eve meal and she'd come up before him—mainly to avoid more audience requests from the seemingly endless stream of women making their way to the head table. "I think there's been a mistake." She couldn't resist touching the book. Tracing the cover's edge, she lifted it open to peek inside. The language was nothing she could read without a translator unit and weeks of time. "I must have ordered things by accident when I was at the market. I didn't realize if you touched it you had to buy it."

"Accident?" Sorin appeared at her doorway, his heated gaze glancing over her before turning to the bed. She shivered at the unmistakably aroused attention. All through the meal he'd stared at her, touching his leg to hers under the table, pretending to bump into her hand whenever she reached for her goblet. "No, no accident. It looks like everything I ordered for you. If I missed something, let me know. Though, the maids should have put it away when I had them fill the tub. I'll send for Sera. They can work while we bathe."

He was out the door before she could protest his idea. Unwittingly, her gaze traveled to the bath and her skin began to tingle. His wet, gliding hands would feel pretty good against her flesh.

*It's not like everyone doesn't know what we're doing,* she reasoned, only to argue, *but that doesn't mean I have to flaunt it.*

When she heard the unmistakably steady beat of his footfall as he came back, she said, "You didn't have to get me all this stuff. I don't really need any of it. Well, I really like the paper and ink. And did you see inside this book? I think it's handwritten. I've never had a book like this." She continued leafing through the pages, desperately wanting to keep it. "Oh, and the perfume does smell really nice, but I have no idea what do to with iron hinges and raw leather."

"Ach, you are still clothed." Sorin stood in the doorway, naked. Her mouth fell open in surprise, not expecting it. He must have taken his tunic and breeches off in the speed of light as he crossed his room to get to her. "I had hoped to find you already in the bath." He strode to her, reaching to pull the scarf from her neck. "It is easily resolved. Unlace your corset. I have yet to look upon you naked and I plan to correct that without delay."

"The maids are coming," she said by way of denial.

Sorin groaned and leaned his mouth to claim hers, not caring that maids were on their way up and he was naked before the opened door to her room. He slanted his mouth to hers in a wondrously talented assault. When he pulled away, he rubbed his thumb between her eyes, smoothing out her wrinkle of concentration. "No, stop thinking about everything and just feel. No one cares what we do but us. I want to see you now. I want to feel every inch of you and give you pleasure."

Lilith found herself nodding, despite her logical judgment. His hands went to her bodice and pulled the stiffer material free. He pushed the corset down her hips, tugging it down to the floor. Outside the sky had darkened with late evening and firelight hit her from behind, casting her shadow across the floor. Next, he reached to pull the laces along her shoulder, unfastening the gown but not pushing it down her body. Warm hands ventured over her hair, undoing the braids so that the length fell free down her back.

"So lovely," he murmured. He stepped away, openly looking at her as he backed toward the fireplace. Taking an unlit torch from a basket on the floor, he pushed it into the fire and carried the flame toward the bathroom. All the while, he kept his eyes on her. His cock towered over his hips, already fully aroused and cast into stark detail under the bright torchlight. "Soft and sweet."

Lilith followed him to the bathing chamber. When she cleared the wall, he pushed on it, closing them in the smaller room and giving them privacy from the maids. Sorin hooked the end of the torch into a sconce carved in the wall. He stepped into the water and sat.

"Take off your gown. I want to see you." His arms spread over the back of the tub, as he watched intently.

She trembled under his full attention, but did as he commanded. Tugging at her shoulder, she let the material slip down her arms to reveal her chest and stomach. She pulled out of the sleeves and pushed the gown over her hips. Almost nervous, she stood, feet buried in her discarded gown. The chilled tower breeze hit her naked flesh and her nipples tightened in protest to the cold.

"Turn in a circle," Sorin ordered. "Slowly."

Lilith resisted the impulse to cover herself. Sorin's lids fell heavy over his eyes as she spun in a circle. When she made a complete rotation, she found Sorin with his hand on his cock stroking gently beneath the dancing orange surface.

"Come here," he beckoned.

Lilith stepped into the warm water, watching it ripple around her legs. Before she could sink into the tub, Sorin surged forward. Droplets trickled over his chest in captivating rivulets. He started at her toes, working up over her ankles, before his hands glided up the back of her legs to wet her skin. She sucked her bottom lip between her teeth, biting down.

She panted, a ripple of need coursing over her. His hands dipped down only to glide back up with the aid of the water. When he looked at her, she fell under his powerful trance. His will overtook hers and she knew she'd do anything he asked of her.

Sorin touched her flesh, rubbing delicately. His face was only a millimeter away from her stomach, his nose very close to nuzzling into her sex. She swayed on her feet, focused on the contact. Lilith welcomed the rush of sensations that his nearness brought. Hands moved along the intimate curve of her knee, tickling her with the lightness of their caress. Nestling his face intimately against the apex of her thighs, he inhaled, shamelessly reveling in her scent.

Lilith met his eyes, unable to fight the spell he wove over her. She trembled. Her pussy became very wet in a way that had nothing to do with the warm bath and everything to do with the sexy man currently worshiping her with his hands.

The torch reflected in his gaze, giving the piercing dark depths a mythical glow. Dark waves framed his face and she reached to brush the locks from his face. He closed his eyes and leaned into her palm, stroking her with his whiskered cheek. The thick muscles of his neck and shoulders shifted erotically with each subtle movement. He caressed her hips, squeezed her ass, licked a hot trail around her navel.

Then he did something completely shocking. He wrapped his arms around her and hugged her. The action was completely out of character for the great knight. Sorin's head pressed to her stomach and his hand splayed across her back as if he'd never let her go. Lilith trembled, about to stroke his hair when he released, continuing as if the moment never happened.

Throaty and raw, he whispered, "I want to bathe you."

He pulled back and she felt a chill without his touch. Lilith dipped down into the water, letting it lap against her shoulders. Nothing in this world seemed like it could be real, and she pictured herself strapped to a scientist's table somewhere being fed dreams while they probed her mind. The dark water reflecting torchlight, the handsome man who looked at her as if she were the most beautiful thing in all the dimensions, all of it had to be a dream.

"I don't want to wake up," she whispered. He looked at her questioningly and she blushed, realizing she'd said it out loud.

Sorin dipped his hands into a small jar left near the bath and rubbed them sensually together. Soap lathered between his palms. He stayed crouched in the water as he came for her with predatory grace. "Stand up."

Lilith obeyed. The long strands of her hair clung to her shoulders, glued in place as the water ran down her body. His firm lips set in concentration as he soaped her skin, gliding easily over her upper thighs, hips, ass and finally her breasts. She closed her eyes, enjoying the sensation of his touch. When she was alone with Sorin, she couldn't think or reason. All the dimensions faded away and there was only the two of them.

He stood, slithering along her flesh. The soap glided between them, an erotic caress, and she couldn't resist running lathered fingers over his arms and chest, washing him as he had her. They slid together, each caress a heady sensation. She liked the feel of him, the strength. He closed his eyes, moaning softly.

Sorin kissed her, working his mouth gently to hers. His hard cock pressed to her stomach. Fire shot through her senses, centering over her breasts and pussy. He tightened his hold and they sank into the bathwater. Sorin sat on the underwater stone ledge and tugged her onto his lap. Lilith straddled his thighs.

He looked deep into her eyes, forcing her to hold his gaze as he lifted her by her hips. The hard tip of his arousal, unyielding in its size, brushed her sex. She lowered herself onto him, impaling her pussy on the thick shaft. Sorin groaned, burying his face against her chest.

Lilith set the pace, tentatively at first, as she lifted up and down, up and down. He leaned back, giving her control. She grabbed his neck, holding onto his hair. The glow of firelight caressed every nuance of his bronzed flesh, giving texture to the many scars. Lilith didn't mind them, except for the hard life they represented. She felt bad for him and a little proud.

The slow, deep rhythm felt so good and weak noises of pleasure escaped her throat. Her breasts bobbed before his face, drawing his avid interest. Lilith tried to make the feelings last, not wanting the terrific build of sexual tension to find release quite yet. But the more she rode him, the faster desire made her go until she found herself bucking wildly on his lap. Water splashed out of the tub, sloshing over the sides and onto the floor.

Lilith gasped, crying out as her climax hit her. She tensed, unable to continue moving as she stayed impaled on his cock. Sorin grabbed her hips, forcing her in shallow thrusts as he worked for his own release. He came soon after, joining her cry with an open-mouth yell of his own. For a long moment, she stayed on his lap with her head resting on his shoulder, breathing hard and willing her heartbeat to slow.

When finally she pulled back, insecurity filled her. Not because of what they did or how he was looking at her with a self-satisfied gleam to his gaze, but because as she looked at him her heart actually, physically ached. For the first time since waking up in Staria, she allowed herself to truly consider what it would be like to stay here, as his wife, for better or for worse, forever. The better would be these moments together. The worse would be the day the news of his death in battle would be delivered, and she would be expected to go to another husband.

Sorin moved beneath her and she slipped off his lap. Lilith dipped under the surface, rinsing off all remnants of soap. Sorin did the same before going to push at the wall.

"Wait," Lilith stopped him, brushing the wet locks from her face. "Are they still here?"

He glanced out into her room and shook his head in denial. "They are done."

Lilith stepped from the tub and reached to grab a folded linen. Their loveplay had wet the drying cloths. Before she could wrap the damp material around her body, Sorin lifted her into his arms. One hand wound around her thighs and the other behind her back. His fingers grazed the sides of her breast, skimming close to the nipple. The cloth dropped forgotten to the floor. He kissed her jaw as he walked her toward her bed. The maids had put everything he'd bought her at market away.

"Why the stone wall? Why not build a door?" Lilith asked.

"The builder claimed that in the winter it would provide better insulation in such a high tower." Sorin gave a small chuckle. "We all think he made a mistake of judgment, but couldn't admit to it because it is not the Starian way to rethink decisions."

Lilith had seen that Starian trait first hand. They definitely were a decisive people.

"That, or he wanted a place to please his wife and hoped the others wouldn't find out about it and think him weak. We were not always such a gentle people. Men did not always lavish their wives with gifts so openly, until someone discovered there were rewards to be had from a pleased mate."

Gentle? Lilith tried not to giggle at the concept. Lord Sorin might touch her gently, but she'd be hard pressed to call a warrior like him gentle.

He laid her on the warm, dry coverlet and stood by the bed. His eyes devoured her hungrily. "I should like to have you again, if you will allow me."

Lilith didn't know what to say, so she nodded in approval.

Sorin grinned, crawling next to her on the bed. Lying on his side, he cupped a breast, massaging leisurely before making a trail down her stomach. "So soft."

Lilith traced a long scar along his stomach. "So hurt."

Sorin glanced down the length of his body to what held her attention. "It healed fast. I was only off a horse for two months."

Lilith found another scar and began tracing an oblong path

around it. "I've been to these dimensions that are so medically advanced they can treat wounds like these in about two weeks, maybe even faster. They have lasers that do everything."

"Lasers?" He watched her finger find its next scar.

"Machines run with electricity." She frowned. How to explain?

"Ah, electricity." He nodded. "Divinity offered it to us when they saw our fires, but we have such knowledge. We find the torches better suited. Torchlight cannot be cut off by enemy spies."

That surprised her. She'd just assumed since they lived in the "Middle Ages", they *were* the Middle Ages. "But there is so much more than lights."

"What else do we need?"

"Medical lasers." She tapped his scarred chest.

"And who will make these lasers?" He leaned over kissing her neck. "You?"

"I don't know how." She shivered under his touch.

Sorin laughed. His fingers lightly brushed over the soft curls guarding the slick folds of her pussy. The touch stayed light and teasing. "Nor do we."

She closed her eyes enjoying his exploring hands. Lilith tried to anticipate his movements, but it became impossible. His fingertips skated over her stomach, creating haphazard designs along her pelvic bone and up her chest. Tweaking a nipple, he made it erect.

Warm lips found her shoulder as he breathed against her. He encircled her clit, wetting himself in her cream. Lilith ran the back of her hand against his chest as she adjusted her hips on the bed to give him better access. The thick probe of his finger ran along her slit before thrusting inside.

"Oh," Lilith breathed, turning her face toward him. Her lips met with his forehead. The damp locks of his hair tickled her cheek.

One finger became two. Sorin moved within her, working in and out, faster and faster with each pass. Tension built. Lilith clutched at his hand, wiggling her hips as he brought her to climax.

Breathing heavily, she squirmed restlessly as he climbed on top of her. Sorin's body joined with hers. She wrapped her legs around the backs of his as he rocked inside her. Lilith moaned in encouragement. As his cock conquered her sex, his finger rubbed the hard bud of her clit. Wondrous sensations washed through her, and she couldn't believe she was coming again so soon.

Sorin's primeval grunt reverberated around her. His mouth opened wide and they both tensed in perfect unison. For a long moment they stared into each other's eyes.

Lilith yawned, every part of her relaxed. "I think I could sleep forever."

Sorin gave a small smile and nodded. He brushed his nose against hers. "Rest you well, my lady."

His weight left her. Lilith reached for him. But instead of lying down next to her, he stood beside the bed. Her hand fell short, hitting the air. Sorin strode from the bedchamber, going to his own bed. As he reached the door, he glanced back the second before disappearing.

Lilith sighed, a little hurt that he didn't stay. Was this what it was going to be like, a half marriage with a man who connected physically, but in no other way?

"Goodnight, my lord," she whispered, moving to hug her blankets.

# CHAPTER 11

Lilith strung Lady Alana and her bunch of elitist snobs along for exactly eight days before finally allowing them to plan the festival. She still had no idea of what happened during the fire ceremony beyond the fact that there was fire, but Sorin insisted it would be good for her position as his wife to host it.

Now that people wanted to talk to her, she learned quite a bit about their lives at the castle—from how it ran so smoothly to the social hierarchy of the Staria system. Underneath the tough, war-focused exterior, it really was an impressive set up. They had a very "this is the way it is" attitude. Everyone had a job to do and they did it with little complaint.

Somehow, over the course of four weeks following her trip to the market, more and more duties were given her. First, it was the audience—normally women seeking favors of some sort or wanting scarf-wearing fashion advice. Once, it was a knight trying to convince her to stop wearing the scarves so his wife would quit covering up her bosom. The old man's plea was so genuine that Lilith almost gave in to the request. Half the time Lilith got the impression they just wanted to talk to her so they made up excuses.

Next, they came to her with disputes—petty stuff that only

required a mediator to announce the logical conclusion. Then they came to her for household decisions—what color to dye the next batch of bed linens, the upcoming week's menu approval—none of which she was properly trained to do. When she mentioned this, they brought her inventory of the larder and cold storage to help her decide. By the time Lilith realized she'd been systematically assimilated into the position of power she "married" into, it was too late to stop it. According to Sera, until a higher-ranking noblewoman came to the king's castle, Lady Lilith was in charge of all feminine concerns.

But then, there was her time with Sorin. Just looking at him made her forget whatever annoyances she had with her day. In the mornings, he'd take her out to the practice field to throw the knife he bought her. He wanted her to have a means to protect herself. Lilith was the first to admit knives were not her biggest talent.

After—and occasionally during—the lessons, he'd sneak her away to some private spot in the inner bailey and they'd make love. Sometimes he was hard and desperate, other times sweet and slow. Their evenings were spent in her bedchamber and her nights were spent alone. Sorin never once fell asleep by her side.

"Tell me about your home." Lilith glanced at Sorin next to her at the head table. He'd been quiet for days, even during sex, not that he was ever very talkative.

She still didn't like the watchful eyes of the others, but she'd gotten used to it. Poking at a strange brown and orange leafy salad, she pushed it aside. She wasn't the only one not eating it.

"Firewall?" He stiffened. She'd avoided talking about anything that hinted at Bianka, but it had been a month and her patience wore thin when it came to waiting for Sorin to volunteer information. "It is ash and rubble. Many of the villagers have moved away."

"Tell me about it before," she insisted. Lilith was relatively sure he wouldn't yell at her in front of everyone.

"It was a fortress halfway between here and the borderland marshes, a last defense before Caniba armies storm Battlewar." Sorin dipped a piece of his bread and chewed.

"Was it a castle?" Did she have to stick a knife to his throat to get him to talk?

"Yea."

"Was it like Battlewar?"

"Smaller."

"Will you rebuild it?"

"Perhaps. Ronen wishes me to."

"Do you want me to finish you tonight?" Lilith put her hand on his thigh. Sorin tensed, his eyes rounding as he nodded once. It was the first time she'd ever taken such a bold initiative. "Then get used to having a conversation, my lord, or I'll lock my bedchamber door tonight. If you don't wish to talk about Firewall, then talk about something else. Just talk."

"The king sends for me to join the battlefront," he answered. "Sorceress Magda plans to lead her minions against Spearhead, a fortress near the marshland. Sir Vidar discovered her plot, and the king has sent for my army to reinforce Spearhead's knights."

"Is she really a sorceress?" Lilith trembled, seeing the serious line of his face.

"Yea. It is said she studies the black arts. Her followers dance with the serpent and are made to endure its poison before joining her army. Only those who live, the toughest of the Caniba, are allowed into her ranks, and those men live only to serve her with blind, obsessive loyalty." Sorin pushed his trencher of food away and grabbed a goblet of ale. "It's impossible to tell her numbers. Her armies live in the ground, hibernating like snakes. Most of our men who try to infiltrate her camp never come back. The others are never the same."

Lilith glanced out into the hall, noticing that several of the knights were just as stoic. It wasn't the ugly salad that put them off their appetites. They all knew what was happening. "I apologize for threatening you. I didn't realize you had so much on your mind. Why didn't you tell me?"

"You do not like hearing of war, and I do not like the disapproval on your face when I mention it. You always ask me about castles and people and food, but you never wish to hear about the realities of my life." Stormy eyes met hers.

"When do you have to go?" Lilith knew this day would come, but she'd always found ways to distract herself from thinking about the reality of it.

"We march in the morning."

"The morning?" she gasped. "When were you going to tell me you were going?"

"Tonight." He set his goblet down and slipped his hand on her knee. "Or perhaps in the morning."

"How long have you known?"

"The king sent a missive."

Lilith jerked her leg away. "That doesn't answer my question."

"For some time." He didn't try touching her again.

"And you weren't going to tell me until you were practically riding out the castle gate?" She leaned into him, keeping her words low. "How long will you be gone? What if you don't come back? What am I supposed to do? I don't want to sit here and run a castle with nothing better to do than pine away for a man who may never return."

"What would you have me do, my lady?" His voice was calm, but the underlying current of anger was unmistakable. "Hide beneath your skirts like a coward? Send a missive to the king declaring I cannot fight because my woman disapproves and I shall forevermore be a farmer?"

"Excuse me, my lord." She stood from the table, trying to remain calm. "Please don't follow me. If you do, you'll not like the scene."

She strode from the room, fighting the nausea rising in her throat. Tomorrow? Not even twelve hours from now? What if he didn't come back? What if this was their last night together? Why in all the bloody Starian mace weapon things didn't he tell her this sooner? Because she made some kind of strange expression when she thought about him marching off to battle?

Lilith pulled at the red scarf around her neck, gasping for air. Her lungs constricted, as if she couldn't get enough oxygen. She'd seen the change in him, but only now did it make sense. He'd known he was leaving for days, possibly longer. The fantasy was coming to a swift end. She'd allowed herself to be swept into his gaze, telling herself that she still looked for a way home, but she hadn't really been looking. Not really. Not fully. Not like a woman who wanted her freedom.

She did want to leave, right?

Lilith took another deep breath. It didn't help. Did she go back to Sorin? Did she run? How long would he be gone? How dare he not tell her he was leaving her behind, in charge of a castle. Alone.

The sound of footsteps echoed on the Black Tower steps and voices carried from within the kitchen. Not wishing to see anyone, she ignored the stairwell and turned away from the kitchen. By now she knew her way around Battlewar Castle. Everyone would be at the eve meal leaving the sewing and laundry rooms abandoned. No one would think to look for her there.

Hurrying past the dungeon steps, she glanced down. Lilith stopped, taking a step back so she could get a better look. The door at the bottom had been left open a crack. Aside from each individual home above the hall, it was the only part of the castle she hadn't explored. She'd even been back to her old holding cell, though now it was empty.

Lilith ran her hand along the wall. The cold hard texture scratched her fingertips as she went to the thick door at the bottom. Expecting to see the surly Brock, she peeked through the barred window. The long, shadowed hall was empty.

Lilith glanced up the stairwell before hooking her finger around the edge of the door. She opened it slowly, trying to make sure it didn't squeak on its hinges. Rows of doors lined the long corridor. The first six on either side had bars, but the ones beyond that looked older with thick metal strips riveted across the front.

Her heartbeat quickened, so loud it echoed in the caverns of her ears, and she wondered what or who they had locked inside. Surely the Caniba people wouldn't be here, not the creatures whose name the Starians whispered like curses. Snake people who lived in the ground. Eaters of men. Monsters. Her natural curiosity forced her to move. Lilith took a deep breath, holding it as she crept up to the first door. There was only one way to find out.

---

Sorin nodded once as Brock appeared in the doorway to the main hall. The man's grim face told him everything he needed to know. Taking up his goblet, he couldn't bring himself to take a drink. A hard knot tightened inside his throat and his guts twisted, the sensation not unlike the moments before an unfavorable battle.

He'd agonized over his decision for days, but Lilith had to be tested. In the end, getting her to the dungeon door had been easy. Sorin was a master at strategy. Lilith wouldn't be able to resist exploring the unseen parts of the castle and an opened door to a sealed area would be all the invitation she needed.

The king needed him to march at Spearhead. Sorin needed to trust Lilith. He'd trusted Bianka and, the second he'd left her, she'd dishonored him and burned down his ancestral home. He could not make that mistake again. Already Lilith's reaction proved she wasn't happy about being left behind. Though, with her, he wasn't worried about her seducing other men so much as her leaving him forever. Two wives who didn't wish to be claimed by him? He shuddered to think on it.

The last few fortnights had been unlike anything he'd ever known. When he touched Lilith, he forgot everything but the feel of her skin and the look in her eyes. But not once did he imagine her to be content. He saw the way she thoughtfully looked over the distance. He heard reports of her endless questions to the servants. Had they seen any peculiar objects in the castle? Did they know how Divinity transported her there? No one told her anything and Lilith didn't yet have a clear picture of Starian loyalty, but that didn't stop her from trying to discover the truth.

What Sorin didn't know was, did her desire to know mean she'd leave him if she had the chance, or was it just her natural curiosity? He was sure he wouldn't like the answer.

*Fool.*

*Idiot.*

*Weak.*

Sorin watched the stoical nature of the hall. The men didn't know of his plan to test his wife and would think his mood due to upcoming battle. Tearing off a piece of bread, he forced himself to take a bite. Tonight, Lilith's true intentions would be revealed.

Lilith edged up to the door from her crouched position to peek through the bars. Tension rolled over her as she expected someone to reach out and grab her head the second it came into view. When nothing stirred inside the empty cell, she frowned and went to look inside the next ones. They, too, were empty.

*Who guards empty prison cells?*

Lilith wondered if they'd transported everyone out of there, or if perhaps they hid a more important secret. Her breathing deepened and she couldn't stop her legs from hurrying down the corridor in excitement. She tried the thick, metal doors, pulling them open. Some were weapon storage, crammed full of swords and shields, crossbows and maces. Others contained mining instruments and warm pipes that led up from the ground.

*There has to be more.*

As she neared the end of the corridor, she reached for the second to the last door and pulled. A soft blue glow came from within, very unlike anything else she'd seen at Battlewar Castle.

*Divinity.*

Lilith knew that light. She'd found the way home.

Inside, the blue glow lit her way as she hurried down a long row of stairs. They led deeper into the earth before opening into a large underground clearing. The cave's dirt matched what she'd seen on the mining instruments in the other room. At the end of the clearing, a large domed vault had been constructed to reflect the architecture of the castle. Every Divinity portal had a different look to it, but the main construct remained the same. A domed arch with a back and two side walls covered a center platform, their mass deceptively dense as to increase its own gravitational field and draw objects to it. The stone hid a complex configuration of liquid crystals, electrical currents, mirrors and vacuums. It was held in check by the wavelength of a specific blue light, which kept the portal inactive. Should the light change, a dimensional shift would occur taking whoever stood on the platform to a new parallel universe. In the early days, before the platforms, travel had been a haphazard affair, and many of the testers died by materializing inside solid objects. Now Divinity sent out microscopic probes first.

Once she found the controls, getting home would be easy. She'd simply send a long pulse of light color coded to her dimension and jump in. Though, on the other side, she'd find herself at Divinity headquarters in front of a team of their scientists. They might not be too happy with her return, but at least there would be plenty of witnesses there to see it. Maybe then she could get some answers. Maybe then she could help Jayne and the others and keep countless other women from being thrust into a strange world against their will.

Following the concentration of blue light to its source, a high beam shot from a high corner, she found the main controls mounted into the stone wall. Twelve turn dials indicated the color coding, including intensity and saturation.

Lilith hesitated as she stared at the dial. If she left Staria, she'd never be able to come back. Even if she got access to a portal, she didn't know the right code, and it was unlikely Divinity's directors would share the information once they authorized an origin reversal scan. She could portal jump for an eternity and never find her way back to Sorin. He'd be lost to her, forever. She didn't plan to make this discovery today, and it might be years before she could find her way back down the dungeon steps. She didn't even say goodbye.

How could she go?

How could she stay?

"I don't belong here," she whispered, trying to steel her nerves as she reached for the first dial. Turning them to the right settings was easy. She'd done it many times.

*Sorin's going off to battle. These people are not my people. I can't spend the rest of my life in this castle. After I learn all there is to learn, I'll have nothing to do but waste away. I can't live in one place, not knowing all the unexplored worlds that are out there. And I can't make this decision for just myself. The others need me to get help, to tell what Divinity has done.*

So many reasons to go—logical, good reasons. One reason to stay. She turned the seventh dial into position and reached for the next one.

"You chose to leave." Sorin didn't sound pleased as his voice echoed over the enclosure.

Lilith stiffened, making herself turn around to face him. "There is no choice, Sorin. I don't belong here."

"Somehow I knew you'd fail this test." An emotionless face stared at her, caressed by Divinity blue.

"You let me find this place." Lilith shouldn't have been surprised. It had been too easy—open dungeon door, empty cages, missing guards. She'd been so focused on discovery.

"Yea. I had to know if I could trust you when I was away or if you'd try to leave." He looked at the portal. "I see I have my answer."

"Let me go, Sorin. Let the others go. We don't belong here. We weren't given a choice. Please." She didn't try to finish dialing in the coordinates. There was no point. If he wanted he could easily stop her. The only way she was getting out of there now was by his good graces.

"You can choose to stay, my lady," he stated. After the intimacy they'd shared she hated to see that cold expression and tense body.

"No. I can't." She shook her head in denial.

"So be it." He sighed, his shoulder lifting under the effort. "Then I shall decide for you. You will stay. Come."

"No," she said louder, praying she sounded brave and feeling incredibly weak. "I won't."

"I didn't ask." Sorin marched away from her toward the stairs, each movement taut with rage. Lilith reached for the eighth dial. Only five more to go. She clicked the next one into place. Sorin growled, spinning around to face her. He stormed across the clearing. Lilith flinched. He grabbed her arm and dragged her behind him. "I will not be betrayed again, Bianka."

"My name is Lilith, not Bianka," she corrected, noting the shaking in his hands and the fire in his eyes.

He blinked heavily when he looked at her and she saw the sway to his steps. He was drunk. "I will not be betrayed, Lilith."

"Is it so wrong to seek my freedom, my lord?" She tried to yank her arm from his grasp, but he only tightened his grip. Rage filled her at his heavy-handed treatment. "You claim Starians to be this noble race, so much better than the people you fight, but you kidnap women and force them to your will. What nobility is there in that?"

"I did not steal you, I chose you. You are my wife. My honor could not take it if you left me." He quickened his steps, not saying another word as he met several of the guards at the top of the stairs. He nodded once at the group before hauling her back to the main floor of the castle.

---

*You are my wife.* I *could not take it if you left me.*

Sorin's fingers molded around the soft flesh of Lilith's arm, but she didn't cry out in pain so he didn't release her. He knew he drank too much ale at the eve meal. He felt the liquor flushing his face and heating his veins. Every thought echoed in his numbed head, forcing him to act on his most primal of instincts.

*Fool.*

*Idiot.*

*Weak.*

*Do not let her go. Force her to stay. She will be the ruination of me.*

Words tried to form in his throat, unfamiliar words, ones he would never allow to be spoken. He wanted to hurt her as she hurt him. His free hand balled into a tight fist, clenching and unclenching at his side. He wanted to reach into her chest and rip out her heart. He wanted to kiss her and touch her until she felt the passion he felt, the burning ache to be near her. He wanted her to think of him as he did of her, all the time, until the maddening need to just see her face and hear her voice were too much to take.

But she didn't feel that way. Her desire to leave him proved it. She didn't ache or burn or have a maddening need. Sorin couldn't imagine life without her, and Lilith didn't even care enough to tell him goodbye.

The pain hurt so badly he screamed, letting his voice roar over the hall as he pulled her to the Black Tower stairwell. He had to get her away from Divinity's portal, far away where she could never reach it.

"Sorin," Lilith said behind him, panicked. "You're scaring me. Let me go."

He stopped on the stairs, not even halfway up. With a swift pull, he brought her to his chest and held her tight. For all his pain and torment, he had to kiss her.

Lilith stiffened for a moment and he softened his touch. Her lips became pliable beneath his as she moaned softly into his mouth. With a hard push, she slammed him into the stairwell wall. His head banged against the stone but he barely felt it.

Like a woman possessed, she clawed at his clothing, scratching his flesh with her nails in her attempt to free him from his breeches. He enveloped her breasts in his palm, rubbing the globe until it slipped up and out of the corset top. Pinching the nipple, he liked the way it hardened between his fingers.

Lilith forced her hand down the front of his breeches, locking her fingers around his cock. She drove her hand up and down, fervently stroking him. Sorin couldn't focus beyond the taste of her lips or the feel of her hand. He wanted to shove himself inside her and slam his hips until he filled her with his seed.

Their bodies warred for dominance, continuing their earlier battle. She cupped his balls, rolling them. He inhaled a deep, ragged breath.

Sorin spun her around so her back was to him. Lilith gasped at the sudden movement as her hand was pulled from his erection. Clamping onto her hips, he forced her ass against his cock and groaned to feel the soft folds her gown padded by the firm line of her cheeks. He ground into her, undulating as she bucked beneath his hold.

Already she'd partially freed his cock and he made quick work of finishing the job. He clutched at her bodice, using the tight laces to control her. The length of her blonde hair tickled his fingers. Bending her forward so her ass arched toward him, he welcomed the vulnerability of her position. With his free hand he worked at her gown, lifting the skirts.

"You will feel me," he swore, desperate to make her understand his claim.

The smooth skin of her ass tempted his fingers and he splayed his hand over the warm flesh and squeezed. He rocked against her, letting the dry heat capture his shaft. Needing a wet ride, Sorin reached around to tweak the nub buried in the soft folds of her pussy. He knew how to rub her, how to make her instantly wet and ready. It didn't take much before the cream flowed freely between her thighs.

"You will feel my claim. You will know you belong to me." He barely heard the words, didn't care that they escaped his mouth. All that mattered was plunging inside her silken core.

Sorin pulled her over by her bodice so she had to support herself on the stairs. Then, taking her hips, he angled them up. Already the tip of his cock was wet with pre-cum.

The pink lips of her sex glistened with moisture. The erotic vision of his cock being swallowed into the folds made him bite his lip hard. He buried himself to the hilt. The tight muscles of her sex quivered and squeezed. Sorin took hold of the back of the corset to control her movements as he brought her back and forth on his cock, riding hard.

Lilith moaned, not fighting their passion. She let him have control, let him conquer with forceful thrusts. He let out an animalistic growl. Even in his anger over her betrayal, he couldn't get enough of her.

The sensations built. He wanted all of her, not just her body. Why in all the bloody wars of Starian history did she try to leave him?

Lilith tensed, her pussy clamping down on him as she came. Sorin answered her call, spilling his seed into her, hoping it took root. He wanted to fold her tight into his chest and never let go. Instead, he released her hips and fell back against the wall. The stairwell spun around him, and he had to close his eyes as he endeavored to slow his breathing.

"You will ride with us in the morn to Spearhead Fortress." Sorin couldn't let her stay behind. To give orders to have her watched would be humiliating, and he couldn't leave her unattended so close to Divinity's portal.

"You're never going to let me leave, are you?" Lilith asked, her soft voice hurting him worse than a dagger to the gut.

When he opened his eyes, she sat on the stairs, looking up at him with her damning blue eyes. She'd righted her clothing, but the tousled hair and flushed cheeks showed all signs of their shared passion. Sorin answered the only way he could. "No, my lady, I will never let you leave."

# CHAPTER 12

Lilith didn't speak as they rode from Battlewar. When she told Sorin she couldn't ride, she hadn't lied. Straddling a giant horse as it nervously pawed the earth, she'd spent all of one minute on the creature's back before Sorin ordered a cart with blankets so that she may be pulled behind the traveling band of knights.

The cart suited her better than the animal, as she rested in the back, curled around a blanket and praying the bumpy trip would be a fast one. She hugged her hands to her chest, cuddling beneath the covers. Her palms were raw from gripping the stairwell. At the time, she hadn't noticed, too caught up in Sorin's violent possession.

How could she have thought of leaving him?

How could she think of staying?

The sound of pounding horse hooves echoed on the prairie, trampling the tall grasses as they made their way to a forest path. Lilith moaned, pulling the blanket over her head to block the sunlight. When Sorin said they'd leave in the morning, he hadn't been lying. He had her awake and packed before the sun even rose.

"So close," she whispered, thinking of the portal. If she hadn't hesitated, she would be home demanding answers. The "why" bothered Lilith more than anything else. Part of Divinity's creed was never to play god.

"Are you ill?"

Lilith pulled the blanket off her face. Sorin rode beside her cart and from her angle he seemed a giant, towering beast of a man. "I didn't sleep well."

His mouth pulled into a straight line and he turned his eyes forward. "Signal if you have needs."

He rode off and Lilith pulled the covers over her head once more. Right now her most pressing need was sleep.

---

After three horrible days inside the jerking cart, suffering from aching muscles, stomping horses and a husband who barely said more than ten words to her, Lilith had never been so happy to see a castle in her life. Though nothing compared to the great city of Battlewar, Spearhead had a quaint charm—for a fortress on the brink of a vicious Caniba attack.

A single tall watchtower lifted into the sky, lording over the square-shaped castle beneath. Thorn hedges formed a perimeter around the outside wall, surrounded by the murky waters of a moat. As they passed over a bridge to the opened front gates, Lilith swore she saw something swimming in the water. The raised stone of the bailey wall surrounded the courtyard, looping about from one side of the main castle to the other in an oval shape. Atop the wall that stood several feet wide was the walkway surrounded by battlements with corner spiral stairwells leading from the ground to the battlements. Next to the tower, the main part of Spearhead Fortress sprawled along the backside of the wall.

Shadows fell heavy over the wide courtyard and a gentle evening breeze flitted over them. Spearhead guards pushed the oversized doors of the main gate closed and latched them with a thick timber. A couple of women hauled baskets heaped with laundry, while others carried water buckets from the well.

"I see you've survived," a female voice yelled as Lilith's cart came to a stop. "I had my doubts."

Lilith crawled out of the cart, rubbing her aching back as she tried to force her numbed legs to stand. A loud, ear-splitting whistle resounded over the yard. Lilith jerked, turning to the noise. Karre stood bound to a t-shaped post in the middle of the courtyard. A chain ran along the top, binding her wrists over her head and a large shackle held her waist to the post, leaving her feet free to kick at the dirt. Smiling, the woman waved her fingers, causing her chains to jingle at the movement.

"Great weather we're having," Karre said conversationally, smiling as if she sat down for a fancy evening with the ladies. Lilith glanced around the yard. Sorin's dirt-covered knights and equally caked horses hardly qualified as fancy.

Seeing her husband talking to a group of men, Lilith walked toward the woman, wondering if anyone was going to stop her. No one did. She lowered her voice to ask, "Karre? Are you all right? What's happened here?"

"Small misunderstanding." The woman gave a derisive laugh. "Nothing to be concerned about. How's your guy been treating you?" Karre leaned to the side, studying the newcomers. "Which one was he again? The big guy?"

"I found the way out. It's at Battlewar Castle in the dungeons," Lilith whispered. Karre's easy smile dropped and her eyes narrowed. "I tried to leave to bring back help, but it's too guarded."

Okay, so it wasn't a complete lie. There was no reason to say she hesitated and got caught in Sorin's trap, that he let her find it to test her.

When Karre didn't answer, Lilith continued, "Have you seen Jayne or Paige?"

"No. You're the first." Karre's smile lifted somewhat, though her eyes stayed focused in concentration. The expression appeared to be more for show than a real emotion.

"I promised Jayne I'd try to get word to everyone. I'll draw you a map and write down the code to my home dimension. I'll find a way to get it to you, just check your chambers. Someone at Divinity headquarters should help anyone who comes through the portal if you tell them what happened. If you see Jay—"

"Sh." The single, quick syllable cut her off. Louder, Karre announced, "Yep, beautiful weather for a ride into battle."

"My lady," Sorin said behind Lilith. She wasn't sure which "lady" he spoke to, so she didn't answer.

"My lord." Karre bowed her head, the action mocking when done with rattling chains. Lilith opened her mouth to speak, hoping to reassure the poor woman. Karre cut her off when she began to hum a playful tune as if she hadn't a care in the universe.

Sorin took her arm and led her from Karre. The knee-length flaps of his black long tunic brushed against her. His faster gait caused her to stumble and swing back as he held her tight. He stopped and she caught herself.

"You look pale." Sorin placed a finger beneath her chin and lifted her head.

"Just tired. The horses didn't stop and I'm not accustomed to sleeping in moving carts." Her neck muscles twinged and she turned away from his touch to get more comfortable. Though, in a way, she was happy for the aching muscles. They had distracted her from the ache in her chest and loins. Seeing Sorin, so thick and proud, astride his giant horse did things to a woman. Had they been alone she might have jumped from the cart and knocked him to the ground to have her way with him.

"The speed was necessary," he said. "Sir Vidar sent word that we were to hurry."

They stood in the courtyard, surrounded by the bustle of the newly arrived guests. Horses were led away by young boys. Servants welcomed the men, ushering them inside. Friends greeted friends.

"Was that the rider we met two days ago?" Lilith remembered seeing the rider, but no one had told her anything. As the only woman on the voyage, she'd been lacking in conversation. Though she did overhear a very inappropriate conversation about hanging genitals and severed heads.

"It was." He nodded.

"I wondered." She hoped to keep him talking, but already she felt him slipping away.

"You should have asked." Sorin took her arm, gentler than before, and led her inside the keep. Though like Battlewar in concept, the main hall was smaller and lacked all decorations.

"What's happening to Karre? Why is she tied up?" Lilith asked when they found seats at the high table.

"A misunderstanding," a deep, resonate voice answered, leaving no room for further questioning. The knight bowed toward Sorin, acknowledging him before doing the same to Lilith. She nodded once, struck by the strangeness of his hazel eyes. Flecks of gold gave them an animalistic property.

"Lady Lilith, may I introduce Sir Vidar." Sorin motioned to the man. "This is his home."

"Only until the king assigns it to another," Vidar answered. "My lord, if you would come with me?"

Sorin looked as if he'd touch her, but instead he merely turned to follow Vidar, leaving her alone at the head table. Feeling a whole new set of curious eyes examining her, she tried to smile for the people of Spearhead. They did not smile back.

"Did you find out why Karre's been chained?" Lilith sat on Sorin's bed in the small guest chamber, her eyes on him the second he opened the door as if she'd been waiting for him to arrive. "Sorin?"

He sighed at Lilith's panicked question. When would she learn that the Starian men did not harm their women? What business was it of his if Lady Karre enjoyed being tied in the courtyard? Had she actually been abused, most likely the people of Spearhead would have revolted against Sir Vidar in protest.

"I did not ask," he said honestly. Weary from a long evening pouring over maps and organizing the armies, all Sorin wanted to do was rest. Well, resting wasn't *all* he wanted to do. He could think of at least a dozen other things that all included his wife naked and impaled on his cock. However, after his drunken blundering in the stairwell, he couldn't bring himself to touch her. "It is between Vidar and his wife."

"What did you talk about, then?" Lilith made no move to go to her own adjoining room. "Your war?"

Sorin pulled at his boot, flinging it aside in frustration. It wasn't *his* exclusive war. He didn't lie in bed at night thinking of ways to start battles—at least not often. "It's been decided that we ride south at dawn to join an encampment of soldiers not far from the borderland marshes."

Lilith moaned, rubbing her neck. "Do we have to leave so soon? I haven't recovered from the last journey."

"You will remain here." He tossed the second boot and rolled back on the bed, his feet planted on the floor. "It is too dangerous. Sorceress Magda has yet to show herself, but they found tracks near the marshes. It's not safe for you at the encampment."

"You want me to stay here alone?" She crawled to sit close to his head and look down at him. Blonde hair framed her, cocooning his vision so all he could see was her face.

"A small contingency of soldiers will be left behind to guard the fortress. They will protect you."

"You can't leave me here," she insisted, her eyes widening. "I don't belong here. These—"

"You keep saying that, Lilith, but you do belong here. I'm here. You're my wife and I want you close." He closed his eyes, unable to keep looking at her without touching her. Three days without her body next to his had been too long.

"Don't you mean you want me prisoner?" The bed shifted and he felt her pulling away from him.

"No," he stated flatly. "You made your choice. You cannot be trusted to remain at Battlewar. Had you not tried to leave, I would have let you remain there."

"Sorin, can't you understand? I've spent the last three days trying to think of how to explain it to you. It's not that I want to leave you." She pushed up from the bed and began to pace. "You have your job, your war, your life here. I'm nothing. I hate approving menus. I hate being asked which color of linen to put on the beds. My idea of a décor is leaving stacks of books on the floor next to my bed. I can't stand listening to two women fight over who saw a trinket first at market, and I definitely don't want to be the one to decide who should get it." He watched her agitation grow, not knowing what to say. "I want to learn things. I want travel to other dimensions. I love my job. I love the books and the scrolls and the meticulous research. I love observing other cultures. I miss pasta and pizza and room temperature controls. I miss pullovers and cotton pants. I miss," she shrugged helplessly, tossing her hands to the side, "so much."

He clenched his teeth, not liking her words but respecting their truth.

"And I'm sure it's the same for the others. If you force us to stay, then we're nothing more than slaves you traded minerals for." She stopped pacing and stood before him.

Sorin hated the look in her eyes, the desperate pleading for him to understand. He understood, but how could she ask it of him? How could he let her go? Forget what it would do to his reputation and honor. How could she expect him to go on without her? Every instinct told him to cling to her, to force her to care for him. He was a man of action and power. He bent men to his will with the force of his reputation proven in battle. His reputation didn't impress her. Nothing about him impressed her. So, how could he make her stay without force? Never before had he been so conflicted. He knew right, but every part of him begged for wrong.

"Don't say anything now." She came back to the bed and sat next to him. "I know what I ask conflicts with your culture, but please consider it."

He nodded once, not speaking.

Lounging beside him, she ran her hand over his heart, first tracing the red crest on his chest before following the valleys of his muscles down to his flat stomach. "Thank you, Sorin."

He refused to move as she pulled at his tunic, working it up over his thighs. Then, dipping her hand beneath the thick black fabric, she continued her teasing caress along the flesh of his abdomen. Her fingers felt cool compared to his body heat.

Lilith concentrated on the movement of her hand, watching the bump it made under his tunic. Sorin drew his hands behind his head, eager to see what she'd do next. Normally he was the one to touch her, seduce her. His breathing deepened. A delicate fingertip traced his navel before sliding up the center of his stomach. His tunic stopped her progress and she had to change routes, moving along his side to his hip.

"You're always so warm," she whispered thoughtfully. "It's like you burn a couple degrees hotter than everyone else."

His cock pressed against his breeches, lifting them visibly.

"Maybe you do," she continued, her fingers becoming heavier against him as they glided down to cup his growing erection.

---

Lilith held his tunic as she brushed feathery kisses across his stomach. The familiar smell of him filled her head, potent and raw and so very male. Everything about the way he moved, looked and tasted bespoke of something primal. Unable to resist, she drew her tongue over his flesh, eliciting a small groan from Sorin.

She held his cock in her hand, marveling that it could already be so hard and ready for her. Her body became wet in response. Small, animalistic noises escaped him as she continued to stroke and kiss. He shifted as he reached for his waist to tug at the laces along his hip. The material beneath her massaging hand loosened to give her a better feel of his shape.

Sorin put his hand back behind his head, letting her have her way. She kissed harder, biting and licking along his hipbone. The faster she rubbed his heavy arousal, the more his breeches bunched. They pulled down to expose the tip of his cock. The mushroomed head was so close, so smooth and tempting. Her lips willingly answered the call, opening wide so her tongue could lick a torturous trail along the ridge joining salty tip to thick shaft.

His body shifted and his hips rose from the bed. She kissed the tip, rolling her tongue down the length of his shaft. He jerked and moaned, clearly past the point of going slow. Hands delved into her hair, pushing her down to take him deeper.

Lilith braced her hands on the bed to keep him from pushing her down too far. As she sucked, his grip lessened and he let go. She rolled his balls in her palm gently. Her entire body tingled and ached. She didn't want to think about anything beyond this moment.

"Come here." Sorin groaned. Taking her by the arm, he pulled her off his arousal and up his body.

Lilith lifted her skirts and straddled his waist, as Sorin made quick work of her corset top. Warm hands slid up her gown to cup her breasts, pinching and rubbing the nipples until she writhed on top of him. Her pussy ached, wet and needy, ready to be dominated by the handsome warrior beneath her. There was an urgency to their touches, a desperation that hadn't been there before. She couldn't help thinking this might be the last time they were together. What if he didn't come back from battle? What if she never felt the touch of his hands? Saw the steamy glaze to his passion-laden eyes? Or felt the confident thrust of his body in hers?

Lilith gasped, torn between the momentary pleasure and the unexpectedly deep pain that racked her heart. How could she have thought of leaving him? Just the thought of never seeing him again tore at her chest until she wanted to scream with the agony of it. She closed her eyes tight, fighting back the bittersweet tears, not wanting him to see her cry.

*I love him.*

The thought she'd been trying to suppress since first she saw him came surging forth.

*I love him. I love Sorin. Don't go tomorrow. I won't be able to take your leaving.*

There was no point in saying the words out loud. He didn't put stock in love. He was a warrior. Her warrior.

She lifted up, all inhibitions gone. She wanted him inside her, needed to feel their connection. All thoughts left her at the intimate brush of his arousal. Three days had been too long a time to go without him.

Lilith pushed down, impaling herself on his length. The thick probe stretched her wide, forcing her to go slow as she fitted him inside her. Once deep, she moved her hips in small circles, rocking around and around, hitting that sweet spot of pleasure inside her pussy.

Sorin grabbed her thighs beneath the gown and held on tight. He lifted her up, controlling her as he slammed her down hard only to let her lift up once more. Lilith rose above him only to have him jerk her down as he arched off the bed to meet her thrust for thrust.

She gripped his hands through the material, enjoying the wild ride. Suddenly, she tensed and fell forward, shaking with release. Tremors erupted all over her body, making her limbs weak. Her heart raced, pounding so loud it echoed in her ears. Sorin bucked beneath her, growling as he held her flush against his cock. He jerked in violent climax.

When he let go, she fell next to him. Neither of them moved, as they lay with disheveled clothing and limbs sprawled at odd angles. Sorin breathed heavily next to her, the harsh sound holding her attention.

Lilith didn't want to love him. What did she know about loving a warrior in a primitive land? This place wasn't her place. She hadn't lied to him about that. She hated directing servants and all the other things a Lady of Staria was supposed to do.

*But Sorin is here,* her heart argued. *What does all the rest matter if you get to have him?*

Sorin's hand brushed her cheek softly, drawing her gaze to meet his. "Good eve, my lady. You rest. I will take the other bed."

Lilith reached out, grabbing hold of him to keep him from leaving. "Don't go."

Surprise filtered over his face. "You wish to do it again. I thought you were exhausted from our journey." Though obviously tired, he looked willing.

"No, you need rest."

Sorin's surprise turned to confusion and he nodded before starting to sit up once more. "Very well."

"Stay," Lilith said when he would leave. She pulled on his arm.

"I wish for you to stay with me." He lay back down. Lilith let go and climbed up the bed to crawl under the covers. He turned his head, angling his neck so he could watch her. She patted the pillow next to her. "Sleep."

"Together?"

"Yes, my lord, together. Sleep." She again patted the bed. He pulled out of his clothes, tossing them aside before joining her under the covers. Lilith tried to close her eyes, but felt his attention on her and finally opened them.

Resting on his side, his arm bent under his head, he studied her. "I have never slept with another in my bed." Lilith would have giggled at the admission, except that he looked so serious telling it. "It is not done except in poor homes."

"And what is the reasoning for that?" She ran her hand over the bulges in his arm.

"Women normally demand their own space, so that we husbands do not take too many of our husband rights. Additionally, if there is an attack, the ladies will be safer away from the main door to the bedchambers."

Lilith did giggle that time. She couldn't help it. "That has to be the sweetest reasoning, though I think I am safe enough next to you." She laughed harder. "I thought it was because I snored that you kept leaving my side."

"I have never heard you," he assured her. "So, where you come from, is a shared bed the custom?"

"Yes, it is." Lilith felt giddy. This was perhaps one of the very rare times he asked about where she came from.

"I cannot do anything about our station, Lilith, but I will speak to the servants. I do not want you to hate your life here, but please understand, I can't let you go." He didn't touch her and she let her hand slide from his body.

"Why?" Lilith held her breath. *Say you love me.*

"You know that answer. Honor. Duty. Tradition. Reputation. You are my wife. We belong to each other."

*Say you love me.*

He didn't.

"We should sleep," Lilith said, trying not to choke on the words. "You have to ride in the morning."

"I will do right by you," he persisted.

"Good night, Sorin." Lilith closed her eyes and pretended to go to sleep, telling herself that at least this time he stayed.

Sorin did not want to leave his wife. Her gentle presence throughout the night had soothed him, and he'd slept deeper than he could ever remember. Perhaps it was knowing she was so close at hand, that all he had to do was reach out and touch her to assure himself that she hadn't left him.

However, as he looked down at her sleeping form, over the flushed warmth of her cheeks, the long line of her neck exposed by tousled blonde hair, he shivered. In the early morning hours he couldn't fool himself with dreams. She didn't want to be here. If he hadn't stopped her, she would have left him. She would leave him still.

He didn't like the fear he felt in going off to fight. Never had he hesitated when riding off into battle, not even the cold wintry morn of his first bloody fray as an untried youth. It wasn't the sword or even death that frightened him. It was the thought of Lilith finding a way to leave him and never coming back.

How could he live without her?

How could he breathe?

Even now his chest constricted. Damn honor and reputation and pride. He wanted her to stay. Sorin reached out to touch her, intent on shaking her awake and demanding she never go. His knee hit the bed and she sighed, her head turning. The soft action stopped him. Everything about her seemed so fragile. He clutched his hand into a fist and backed away.

"I will fight well. I will make you proud, my lady," he whispered. It was the only thing he could think to say. Everything else jumbled in his mind, unable to find the right words or expression. "Upon my death, I will honor you."

# CHAPTER 13

Sorin lifted his sword, slashing and hacking his way through the throng of hairy, man-eating beasts. The Caniba warriors all looked the same to him—smelly, pelt-covered monsters with sunken eyes and sharpened teeth. Their hair hadn't seen a comb, ever, and he highly doubted any of them had heard of bathing.

Rumors flew that these creatures weren't men, but beasts created from the fornication of people and ancient wolves. Sorin had killed plenty of them to know that they were of flesh and blood. They had the bodies of men, but were the basest example of what men could become. He doubted the noble wolf sired them, but he did not doubt for a second that they were truly beasts.

Three days earlier, Sorceress Magda's army had come up from the ground right through the middle of their encampment. Like a giant serpent of dirt snaking through the ground, the topsoil had sucked into a pit taking a few of their men with it. Caniba warriors rose up, splitting the Starian army in half. Sorin's half was surrounded and fighting an army twice their dwindling size with little reprieve.

Sorin thrust his sword into the stomach of his enemy, watching the beast's gnarled face remain impassioned as if he didn't feel death. He'd seen the same look many times. The Caniba felt nothing beyond a driving need. Sorin spun on his heels and withdrew his blade just as quickly as it went in. Yelling to release the tension of battle, he swung once more and beheaded a blood-soaked figure.

The smell of sweat and dirt and death filled his nose. Metal clanged, men screamed and moaned and died all around him. Sorin knew these horrors well, but this battle was different. Try as he may, he couldn't keep Lilith out of his head. He saw her disappointed gaze staring at him from the corner of his eyes. Her face appeared in swirls of kicked up dust and her tears in droplets of blood. She would not be pleased with what he did. His honorable deeds would not make her proud.

Sorin fought harder, driving through the throng. He needed to get to her and hide her from the truth. If she discovered his deeds, if one of the men sang his praises not knowing her heart, Lilith would run.

*Just like Bianka. No, never like Bianka.*

"Argh!" Sorin swung his arm, the movements as natural and practiced as walking.

"To Lord Sorin!" a cry went out over the field, only to be repeated. "Follow my lord, he's going for the Sorceress!"

Sorin glanced over the battlefield, his vision hampered by dust. Before him he saw the makeshift throne of Sorceress Magda. Eerily pristine in her gown of sparkling white, she sat on a carved wood platform, lifted up so that she might watch the carnage she'd created with the pride of a goddess. Dark, smooth hair fell about her shoulders to her waist, and the inky depths of her eyes became even more so by the black lines drawn thick around them. Right now, that bloodthirsty gaze was on him. Her evil children swarmed around her, a thick, living wall of protection.

He realized he'd fought his way close to her, closer than they'd been the entire battle. Sorin had been so distracted by thoughts of Lilith that he'd broken rank, leaving the tightly formed unit of knights behind him. Caniba soldiers turned their attentions to him.

"To Sorin!" the men shouted. "To a good death!"

"Forgive me, my lady," Sorin whispered in response to their cries. There was no way he could fight his way to kill the Sorceress, and by the gleaming pleasure of her expression she knew it as well. He had one chance and he was going to take it. For Staria, for Ronen, for family honor and for Lilith, though she would not appreciate the deed, he arched back and threw his main line of defense. The sword flew through the air, singing toward Magda.

A swarm fell on him, blocking his view. Teeth bit into his forearm, as he grabbed the knife from his waist. The weight of thronged bodies pushed him to the ground, and all his strength and training couldn't stop it. Burning, white heat filled his arms while sharp, metal-tipped nails clawed into flesh. The foul Caniba smell encased him.

*I fought well, my lady, take pride in that.* Sorin thought, hacking the best he could with restrained arms. *Upon my death, I honor you.*

The sound of the gate caused Lilith to jump from her seat in Spearhead Fortress' main hall. She'd grown to know it well in the two weeks she spent waiting for Sorin's return from battle, and each time it drove the stake of fear deeper into her chest. How could he go without waking her? Why didn't he send word?

*I should have made him promise to come back. He would have kept his word.*

Panicked, she tried to act nonchalant as she walked through the aisle of tables to the door. Karre had disappeared that first morning, and someone told Lilith the lady rode to battle with her husband. It had been an easy enough task to find Karre's chambers and hide directions to the portal. She only hoped a servant didn't find it first.

Knights came and went, always armed and covered in blood as they rode into the castle, always grim-faced and determined when they rode out. A few times she'd seen them walk to a random woman in the yard to present the sword of a fallen husband. Most accepted the dark gift with a nod and stiff retreat. One woman screamed and fell to her knees, shaking and grasping the blade as if she'd end her own suffering. No one moved to stop her, but in the end she merely curled into a ball and lay in the muddy earth. Lilith had stayed back at the glare of a guard warning her not to interfere.

What if she was next? What if it was Sorin's blade they presented to her?

*I can't take this. Please, make it stop. I can't take it.*

As she stepped into the evening sunlight, she pressed a fist to her chest. The unknown was slowly killing her. She'd barely eaten. The smallest of sounds would cause her to jump out of her skin, and every moment became a worry-filled piece of hellish agony.

The sound of horse hooves greeted her as a single rider passed through the gate. Guards hurried to close it as soon as he'd cleared the large doors. Lilith stumbled to a halt, instantly seeing the extra sword sticking from the pack on the man's horse. She knew that hilt, that blade. She'd seen Sorin clean it after their morning knife-throwing lessons.

"No." Lilith shook her head, backing away from the man, willing him to disappear, to not see her. If he didn't hand it to her, it wouldn't be true.

The knight's eyes scanned the courtyard before finding Lilith. She froze. He didn't look away. Why didn't he look away? The sword had to be a replica of Sorin's. It couldn't be his.

Tears filled her eyes, blurring her vision. She blinked hard, trying to keep her world from spinning in circles. The hall behind her had gotten eerily quiet. People no longer moved about the yard. Why were they looking at her?

*Look away! All of you. Stop it.*

The rider dismounted, his actions seeming both fast and slow at the same time. By the heavy breathing of his mount, he'd ridden hard to get to Spearhead Fortress. His brown hair slicked back from his head, plastered into place by sweat, and his face carried the same grimness the others bore. She didn't recognize him.

Lilith grabbed her stomach. Taking the sword from the pack, he revealed the broken blade. The metal had been snapped in two.

Hot tears spilled down her cheeks, sliding down her chin to drip onto her scarf. As the knight neared, she clutched her stomach harder, grinding her fingers into the hard corset to stop its ache. She tried to break the connection of their gaze, but his eyes kept her steady. Hands lifted to give her the sword, and she saw dried blood still caking the remaining blade. Lilith shook her head in denial.

"No," she whispered, barely able to make the word leave her throat.

"My lady, I—"

Lilith didn't give him a chance to finish. Bile rose, making its way up her body and out her mouth. The knight jumped in surprise as she threw up on the front of his tunic. The broken sword fell from his hand, hitting Lilith's skirt and snagging the dark blue material.

"By the rotting marshes, my lady," the man swore.

"Cedric!" a stern voice charged. Sir Oskar had command of the fortress in the absence of Sir Vidar. "You will not swear at Lady Lilith or upset her."

Cedric's brow furrowed as he looked at his stained clothes.

"All know she is with child," Oskar announced.

That brought her head around. "What?"

"It is quite all right, my lady. We noticed your pallor, refusal to eat aught but pieces of bread, the restless wandering at night, and your nausea confirms it." Sir Oskar gentled his look as he spoke to her. "Cedric should not have alarmed you with news of war without talking to me first. Lord Sorin asked us to look after you, to make sure you were comfortable and not bothered with talk of battle. We came to understand quickly his reasons."

Lilith shook her head, utterly confused. She wasn't pregnant. She couldn't be. Turning to the more horrific matter of the sword at her feet, she asked, "What happened? Can I see him?"

At the news of her "condition", Cedric calmed his temper and he began tugging out of his tunic. "Lord Sorin honored your family name, my lady. He fought well against the Sorceress's army."

She touched her stomach. A baby? A piece of her husband to carry with her? If only...

At their expectant looks, she nodded weakly. Inside, she felt numb. "I'm sure he did. He's a very good soldier."

Cedric dropped his tunic on the ground before reaching to take the broken sword. He again tried to give it to her. Lifting his voice so all those gathered could hear, he announced, "With this blade Lord Sorin injured the Sorceress Queen, proving she's mortal and bleeds like the rest of them."

Cheers erupted. Lilith flinched, wanting desperately for them to shut up. The sound echoed in her head.

"I present it to you, my lady, to honor you and your child." Cedric bounced it in his hands.

How could she touch it? "Where is he?"

"At the encampment. He asked that I bring you to him," Cedric answered.

"Bring me...?" she repeated, breathless. "But, how could he ask? Are you saying he's not...?" Lilith didn't dare hope.

"My lady?" Cedric prompted.

"He's not dead?" Lilith looked at the broken weapon.

"No, my lady."

"Then why in the blasted stars are you bringing me this?" Lilith slapped at the hand holding the sword, making him drop it. She screamed in anger, releasing some of the pain he'd caused her with his little show of presenting the sword. The weapon dropped and Lilith swung at the man's chest, landing a loud smack against his flesh. "I thought he was dead, you imbecile!"

"But, why would you think that?" Cedric blocked her very unladylike attack of slapping hands and backed away. Lilith followed him, enraged all the more when he chuckled at her efforts. "My lady, halt, I beg you. I did not bow down when I took the sword. I know you saw me. I—"

"Bow down?" She stopped hitting, breathing hard. "No one told me you had to bow down—*argh*! These stupid customs should be written down somewhere so they can be read by newcomers like me. How in all the accursed dimensions am I supposed to know these things if I'm not told? If I brought you to my home dimension, do you think you'd get on with no help?"

"Lady makes a good argument," Oskar put forth.

"Why didn't Sorin come himself?" she inquired.

Cedric glanced at Oskar who nodded his permission to answer. "He's been injured."

"Take me to the encampment. Now," she ordered, determined to see Sorin for herself. The fear she felt when she'd thought him dead didn't leave her, and it wouldn't until she could touch him and feel the warmth of his flesh.

"I'm assured he will recover. There is no reason to take you into the marshland in your delicate condition, my lady. Lord Sorin has recovered well in the past. He is strong and a hero. We have great hope—"

"You can tell me everything on the way," Lilith interrupted.

"It will be night before we get—" Cedric again tried to talk her out of her plan.

"Take me to my husband. Now." Lilith turned and strode into the castle to get a blanket for the cart.

"Everything" might have been the wrong command to give. Cedric obeyed, explaining in full detail every gory, horrible second of the attack on the first encampment. By the tone of his voice, it was clear he had no idea how close he was to being thrown up on again.

Lilith's cart ambled toward the newly set up second camp where Starian forces had combined. She'd refused to get on a horse. Thinking it was because of her baby, Cedric agreed to the slower pace of the cart. Lilith did not correct him. What did she care if he thought her pregnant? It's not like she'd started the rumor. And if their misunderstanding made them a tad more accommodating, so be it.

The air became almost stagnant the farther south they traveled, making it hard to breathe. Moss-covered trees lined the wetlands, before spreading into an opened space of shallow waters covered with oddly shaped patches of vegetation. Cedric led her horse right into the marsh, splashing them through the shallow waters before reaching higher ground.

Lilith saw the tops of rectangular tents outlined by firelight, dusk and the large moon, before she heard the gentle murmur of voices coming from the encampment. The smell of burning wood from the bonfires mingled with nature's perfume. Tiny sparks from the flames danced in the evening sky before dying out.

"Do not worry, my lady," Cedric assured her. "The Caniba cannot rise up from the marshes. You will be safe."

The tents, varying in sizes, spread out over the high clearing on an orderly grid to create pathways. The larger tents were in the middle with progressively smaller ones fanning round them. Banners hung from the tent flaps, pinned to the opened entryways. Their brilliant colors stuck out against the light caramel of the canvas.

Lilith searched the gathering crowd for her husband, but didn't see him. Curious eyes stared at her, a few of them familiar, most not. Then, seeing Sorin's crest hanging from a flap, she jumped from the slowing cart and ran for it.

"Sorin?" she called, not stopping to knock. "Are you in here? They said you'd been injured. Cedric wouldn't tell me how badly. What happened? Are you all right?"

Her eyes adjusted to the dim light and no one answered. A pitcher had been placed on a small wooden table. The steady rise and fall of breathing drew her attention to a fur-covered bed. Sorin rested with his hands at his sides, above the fur coverlet. Someone had bandaged his arms from wrist to shoulder with cloth strips.

"Sorin?" she asked, quieter as she made her way to him. She touched his head, trembling to feel the feverish heat.

"He fought well."

Lilith turned, about to tell whoever spoke that she really hated that saying. Out of respect for Sorin and knowing that "fighting well" was something he took pride in, she stayed quiet. "You're one of his men. Lance, right?"

"Yea, my lady," the redheaded warrior nodded. "I tend to the injured. My family has a gift for it." He crossed to his patient. "His wounds are clean, but his fever won't break. I've given him every herb I know, but now it is up to the gods."

Lilith nodded. After all the emotions that run through her, she now had to face losing him all over again? She wasn't sure she could stand it a second time.

"He's been asking for you. Because he can't travel, I sent for you." Lance touched her shoulder lightly. "Steel yourself. Don't let him see that pity on your face. In his state he might think you are not proud of him. He is a hero, the gods will favor him."

"It's not pity." She rolled her arm away from Lance's touch. "It's determination. He's not going to die. If he did, I'd die with him and he promised to always protect me. His stubborn pride won't let him go back on his word." She stood next to the bed, looking down at Sorin's pale face. "Do you hear me, my lord? If you don't fight, I'll be right behind you and I'll make your afterlife a living hell. There is no way you're leaving me alone in this forsaken dimension to be claimed by some other man."

Sorin didn't move. Lilith pretended to be brave, hoping that her actions would convince her terrified heart. She reached for a bandage, peeling it back. Long deep gashes created crosshatched patterns over the flesh. What had they done to him?

Lance peered over her shoulder. "I still need to cauterize the wounds on this arm. I did not wish to overtire his body. He's lucky he wore armor. The Caniba tribesmen could not bite through the metal plates."

"How soon until I can take him to Battlewar?" Lilith asked. She couldn't leave him in the marshes. He needed medical care—real medical care—and she knew just the people who had it.

"Why would you wish to move him? If it is supplies you seek, we can send for anything you need."

"I need a handheld medical laser from dimensional plane 187." Lilith redressed the wound, careful not to press too hard. "He appears stable enough if we travel slowly. There is no reason we should risk his life when I can obtain the treatment he needs."

"I cannot allow you to use the Divinity portal." Lance shook his head. "We don't trade off-plane."

She arched a brow. "I'm here, aren't I?"

"Yea, but Lord Ronen spoke to the king and asked him to cease all trades because the women didn't know they were being transported." Lance frowned. "It's been some cause for disappointment amongst the unmarried men."

"Listen to me, Lance. You see a lot of wounds, don't you?"

Lance nodded. "Yea, too many."

"What if I told you I knew of a device that could repair the flesh better than fire and iron? And that these wounds could be healed in two weeks time, possibly faster?"

"This handheld medical laser can do that?"

"Oh, yea, it can do that." She nodded. It took all her willpower not to jump on him and shake him until he came to his senses. Her husband was in pain and she knew how to save him. "I have a cart outside. If we can load him up and take him to Battlewar, I can get that laser."

"No, I'll go. I cannot let you—"

"Have you been to 187? Have you ever traded with another plane directly?"

Lance frowned, shaking his head in denial.

"I know them. I lived there for two months. I know their customs, their weaknesses. I know how to get that laser." Lilith motioned to Sorin. "Do you wish to see your great war hero suffer like this? He did injure the Sorceress, after all."

Lance nodded. "I'll ready the cart and assemble the men. We'll ride at first light."

"We'll ride now," Lilith corrected.

Lance nodded, hurrying to go.

Lilith sat precariously near Sorin's head. Shaking, she touched his cheek, feeling the heat. "I wish I was as brave as I sounded, but until I am, I'm going to fake it. I know you'd want me to do you proud. I won't dishonor you." She kissed between his eyes, holding her lips against him. "Damn you, my lord, you're not allowed to die on me. Do you hear me, Sorin? I can't live without you. I love you. I need you. Just don't leave me."

# CHAPTER 14

"I want you to know, my lady, you will be taken care of. We all admire how brave you are and how you honor your husband. You do not have to worry about your babe should—"

Lilith glared up at the man on the horse, cutting him off. After four days, she knew all the men by name. They were pleasant enough for the most part, though she was not in a mood to be social. Every inch of her body ached, she'd barely slept, stress and worry filled her waking moments and Sorin's condition didn't improve. She walked next to Sorin's cart to stretch her legs as they neared Battlewar. Fatigue settled in her shoulders, stiffening her muscles, but she refused to stop. "Do me a favor, Rodrick."

"Anything."

"Spread the word. If any man tries to claim me, ever, he'll wake up a woman." Her meaning wasn't lost. Rodrick gulped and leaned forward on his steed as if to protect his balls. Realizing how mean she sounded, she felt instantly sorry and opened her mouth to apologize, but the knight nudged his horse, riding ahead of her.

Sorin groaned as the cart jerked. Lilith instantly crawled next to him and put her hand gingerly over his heart. The gesture always seemed to calm him. Throughout the journey, he didn't wake up or open his eyes. His fever lifted for a few hours only to come back. She was extremely glad she decided to take him back to Battlewar Castle. If he didn't improve soon, she wasn't sure he ever would.

"We're almost there, my love," she whispered, talking to him softly as she had throughout the journey. Lilith tried to keep the fear out of her voice, even as tears welled in her eyes. It couldn't end like this. She didn't know if he could hear her, but she still tried. "Just a little farther."

To her surprise, he blinked. Glazed eyes found her. Hoarsely, he ground out, "I saw you on the battlefield watching me."

"What do you mean? I wasn't there." Excitement filled her voice. He spoke!

"Don't use the portal."

"I have to. I already told you why." She cupped his whiskered cheek. The scruff of growth scratched her hand. She willed his eyes to clear, to really see her. They didn't.

"Then I forgive you." His eyes closed once more.

"Sorin, for what? You forgive me for what?" She tried to keep him talking, but he passed out. Dismissing his feverish words, she clung to the hope that they weren't too late.

---

His body hurt so badly he wasn't sure he still lived. Every inch of him ached—his back from lying down, his wounded arms and legs, his broken heart. Through his dreams he heard Lilith's voice calling to him. Like when he fought on the battlefield, she haunted him.

Not knowing whether he was awake or asleep, he tried to grasp onto the ghostly figure always inches from his tattered hand. She stood, watching him, those big blue eyes tearing into his soul.

"I saw you on the battlefield watching me," he tried to tell her. *I always see you.*

Lilith didn't answer, but he'd heard her words before. She took him to Battlewar, to the Divinity portal. He knew she wanted to leave him. As much as it was his, this life was not hers.

"Don't use the portal." Sorin hated his weak body. Why didn't he move? *Please, stay with me.*

This time, her ghostly lips parted and he heard her voice. "I have to. I already told you why."

She had told him. Her misery etched itself into his heart. Why didn't the gods just let him die in heroic glory? He was nothing without her. "Then I forgive you."

*If you must go, I will no longer stop you. I forgive you for finding your happiness, lady wife, and for taking my heart. But, please, I beg you to choose me. Stay. Forever. All I am is yours. I am undone by you. You have conquered me.*

---

Lilith stared at the dials, her hand shaking. No one would know if she dialed home until it was too late. Someone at Divinity could bring a medical laser back. They had plenty of them in the store room. She could leave Staria and find justice for what had been done to her and the others.

She could leave. Forever.

"If my lady hesitates, I will go in her place. Instruct me." Rodrick placed a hand on her shoulder. His boyish crush was harmless enough, and she knew it was because he met very few women out on the battlefield. She understood why the Starians bartered for brides, but that didn't make it right, at least not when the women had been kidnapped.

"No. There's no time." She turned a couple of the dials. Dimensional plane 187's coordinates were memorized by all Divinity employees in case of an emergency. The doctors on the other side would help her with little question, so long as she gave them the clearance codes and a little incentive. "Did you bring it?"

"Here," Rodrick handed her a vial. Hopefully it would be enough.

"But the child..."

"Rodrick, there is no child," Lilith answered, wondering why it hurt so much to say the words out loud. She'd let everyone believe she was pregnant, never once correcting their assumption. "It was only a rumor. No one thought to ask me if it were true."

She thought of Sorin and her decision was simple. She couldn't go. Not yet. He may never come to love her, but his presence would be enough. She might never adjust, she might grow bored and bitter, but right now, she knew what must be done.

"Stay back from the light!" Lilith ordered. She didn't hesitate again as she set the dials. Then, pushing a button, she turned to the domed arch over the innocuous-looking center platform. The blue light shifted to pale green as she walked toward the portal. The closer she got, the more the light lured her in.

Suddenly, the strong gravitational field pulled her off her feet, hurling her toward the back of the platform. Defensively, she curled her arms over her head and closed her eyes tight, braced for impact. She clenched the vial tight, careful not to let go. The concentrated light burned and every cell in her body felt heavy. She couldn't move as her head hit the back wall. But what should have been a hard crash was only a moderate brush across her scalp.

No matter how many times she went through, she would never get used to the sensation of being pulled apart at a molecular level. Like riding on a bad carnival ride, she kept still and stiff and waited for the second it would be over. The pull stopped and her body dropped with a hard thud on a metal platform.

"Ugh," she moaned, coughing as her body adjusted to the abrupt freedom. The blue light shone from above in a less primitive version of the Starian portal. A loud alarm blared overhead, buzzing annoyingly. The smell of metal and 187's air-filtering sterilizer wafted over her.

"Sterilization commencing. Please stand and move away from the platform."

Lilith trembled weakly, but pushed to her feet to obey the male, automated voice. If she didn't let them sweep her for other dimensional parasites and viruses, they'd stick her in quarantine for a year. A shield came down, blocking the platform from the scan as a series of lights flashed over her.

"Sterilization complete. Please state your clearance code."

"Lilith Grian. Divinity Corporation Analyst. Employee number 54367D."

"Accepted. Please move to the orange door."

The door was actually metallic gray with a series of numbers and letters written in orange across the front. It opened automatically and she passed through. It might have been awhile, but she remembered the layout well enough. Every facility on 187 had the same architectural design. The citizens were obsessed with immortality, and each worked for the central hospital government in some capacity.

"Sans Grian," Dr. Lu greeted. His long blue coat with red trim was standard issue for the facility, as was his shortly cropped hair, his perfectly groomed eyebrows and his manicured nails. "Welcome back to our facility." He looked at an orange electronic clipboard and frowned. "Your scans show no injury or illness and you're not due for a physical. I do see low levels of homytobin and plytomikin. Not threatening to life, but known to cause fatigue." He reached into his pocket and took out a syringe. Like everything else it was electronic. He pressed the tip to the clipboard, waited for a beep and then leaned forward to press it to her bare neck. "That boost should take care of the deficiency. Good day, Sans Grian. I will send a copy of your record to Divinity Corporation Headquarters."

She wasn't surprised by the dismissal. If anything, 187 was efficient. "Wait, Dr. Lu. I'm not here for me. I'm here to barter for a handheld unit."

He turned, again looking to his clipboard. "Divinity has several in working order. I don't see why—"

"I have trade." She lifted the vial. "Blue mineral water from an underground spring. It has very unique properties. I doubt Divinity's shown it to you yet. They'll want to wait until they need a big favor."

His eyes lit with interest as he looked at it. "What kind of properties?"

"Feel it for yourself." She tossed it at him. He dropped his clipboard, not even seeming to notice as he studied the vial. "It stays warm, even when not exposed to a heat source. Just think of the possibilities. Deaths by freezing will be eliminated. Mountain climbers, deep sea divers, all your medical expedition teams can go longer and farther."

"Where...?"

"I'm not sure of the dimensions coordinates, but if you give me a handheld and reverse the portal I just came from, it's all yours." She smiled, knowing she had him. Scientists couldn't resist such temptations.

"I will have to get the proper clearance." Dr. Lu didn't take his eyes from the mineral water.

"I'll need you to hurry. A friend of mine doesn't have much time." She thought of Sorin in so much pain. His condition seemed steady, but she couldn't help the urge to hurry. Before, traveling to a new dimension, even one she'd been to before, would have thrilled her. Now, she found herself annoyed by the hum of the overhead lights and the sterile smell of air.

He reached for his clipboard, refusing to let go of the new find. Pushing the clipboard's surface a couple times, he lifted it up and began to speak. Lilith watched in silence as he transmitted his image to other doctors in the facility, telling them of her arrival and of her proposal. Finishing, he said, "I call for a vote."

*Just a few more seconds... Come on, hurry.*

Lilith tapped her foot, eager to leave but understanding their protocol in such matters. By the light in Dr. Lu's eyes, the trade would be a done deal. The sound of footfalls echoed along the hall, and she automatically moved to the side to let a couple of the doctors pass.

"Denied," an authoritative voice answered through the clipboard. "Please escort Sans Grian to Security Observation Five. She is to be detained in accordance with treaty law..."

"What?" Lilith screamed, ready to bolt. The two doctors she'd moved over for had stopped. They grabbed her arms. Dr. Lu held the vial in his palm as he led the way to the security wing. Kicking her feet, she jerked violently. "What are you doing? I came for a simple, peaceful trade. Stop at once!"

They didn't listen and they didn't let go.

"Please, I have to get back. Please..."

---

Warm, soft hands touched him, gliding over every inch of Sorin's flesh. He knew those hands, the way they dipped and explored every curve as if mesmerized by his form. Every part of him felt on fire, burning in agony as if he'd been set on fire.

*Lower.*

His cock ached, so hard and tortured. He couldn't move his limbs to take it. In fact, his body didn't seem to work at all, except for the hard mass surging painfully between his thighs. He couldn't move, couldn't look to see Lilith's face. Oh, how he wanted to look at her! It was one of his great pleasures to watch her move.

*By all the gods, lower.*

After what seemed to be an eternity, she finally complied, running a tormenting trail over his stomach and hips. Every part of him tensed. What would it be? Her mouth? Her hand? The sweet creamy heat of her sex? Sorin didn't care, so long as she released the pain her nearness caused.

*Finish me. Oh, blessed night, finish me.*

Random images filtered through his mind, thoughts of her bent over on her bed as he took her from behind, of her pressed against the bumpy stone wall in the brewery cellar, of how she'd sucked his cock after knife-throwing practice in a small alcove behind the castle.

Mmm, those lips, soft pink disconcerting lips. How he'd liked the way her hair appeared to radiate sunlight even in the shadows. Her breasts bobbed, only giving him a teasing peek through the scarf. At first he wasn't sure, but now he liked that she hid her charms from others. They were his. She was his.

Sorin shifted his hips at the memory, finally breaking free of the paralysis. He remembered clearly how it looked to watch his cock slide in and out of her mouth, going in dry only to come out glistening and wet. Lilith seemed to enjoy it as well. She moaned into him, sucking as if she'd drain the essence from him and leave him for dead. Her hand rolled his balls and she gripped his hip tight. Sorin groaned. The memory so vivid he felt the graze of her teeth, the press of her lips, the lick of her tongue.

*Yea, Lilith, finish me. Oh, by the gods, finish me. I need you to...*

Sorin tensed, his hips jerking so hard it shook his entire body. Moisture flooded his stomach and he jolted awake, glancing down to see wet cum gleaming on his flesh. Dazed from release, he blinked heavily and looked around. His head felt light and dampened by a strange, cool sweat.

"Lilith?" The word came out in a stranger's voice, croaking and hoarse. He cleared his throat, coughing before trying again. "My lady?" The sound was little better.

"My lord? Are you awake?"

Sorin frowned, turning his head to the doorway. This wasn't his chamber—not the tent or the Black Tower. Seeing Sera, he deduced he was at Battlewar Castle. He must have been in common quarters above the main hall.

"How...?" He frowned, feeling a burning along his arms. He looked at the bandages, noticing the pain in them for the first time upon waking.

"Shh." Sera rushed in and grabbed his coverlet, pulling the fur over his naked body. He barely registered the fact that the evidence of his desire for his wife lay across his stomach. The servant touched his head. "You were wounded at battle, my lord, but you did honor to your family name. You wounded the Sorceress, proving she is mortal. All of Staria sings your praises."

"Where...?" His muscles ached and his head pounded violently from the effort to sit up.

Sera pushed him down. "No, my lord, do not. Lance said we should not move you after so hard a journey."

"Why am I here? Why not leave me at the camp?" He frowned. This time he knocked Sera's hand aside when she tried to hold him down.

The servant refused to answer as she stood to retrieve a pitcher from the table. Pouring him a goblet of water, she brought it back to him. "I've been by your side, tending you, my lord. You have not been the easiest of patients. You need to drink and eat more."

"Why have you tended me? Where is...?" He stopped mid-drink and lowered the goblet before it touched his lips. "Where is my wife?"

"My lord, you shouldn't upset yourself. Lance said—"

"I do not care what Lance said, Sera," Sorin yelled. "Where is my wife?"

"She's not here, my lord." The servant eyed him fearfully as she backed toward the door.

"What do you mean she's not here?" Sorin gripped the goblet. The soreness of his throat and dryness of his mouth forced him to drink its contents. Even so, he didn't take his deadly eyes off Sera.

"She left, my lord."

"Left?" Fear gripped him. *No.* "Where?"

He knew the answer before she said it. "Through the portal. Please, my lord, do not get up. You must rest."

"When?"

"Five days ago. The same day you arrived here." At his dangerous look, she rushed on to explain. "She said she was going to get a medical device to cure you and would be right back. Rodrick took responsibility for her and brought her to the portal. He waited for her return, but when it became clear she would not he had himself locked in the dungeon to await your punishment for losing her. I'm sorry, my lord, but she has—"

Sorin yelled, throwing the goblet at the wall. The metal clanged on the blue-grey stone, but the loud noise did not satisfy him. Sera yelped, jumping in alarm as she ran for the door. Enraged, he tried to get out of bed, making it to his feet. The second he stood, his world spun in fast circles around him, and he felt himself falling backward as darkness consumed his mind.

---

The only advantage to being held against her will by a dimension obsessed with health was she'd never felt physically better in her life. They forced her to exercise for a precisely calculated amount of time. They took her "not optimal for total health" clothing to be destroyed, replacing the Starian outfit with a pair of slacks and loose long shirt in the red and blue facility colors. Every meal, though bland, was perfectly balanced with her body's dietary needs for the day. And whenever her stomach started to churn with stress and worry, someone came to give her a shot in the neck to take the symptoms away. But no shot in all the worlds could end how she felt about Sorin.

Did he worsen? Had he awakened? Did he know she'd left? She could only imagine what everyone thought when she didn't return.

"Sans Grian," the automated voice said, "your lidic levels are rising again. A medic has been dispatched..."

"...to blah blah blah blah blah," she mocked loudly, not stopping her restless pacing around the small room. White walls and metal accoutrements surrounded her—precise, clean and irritatingly lacking in craftsmanship. She missed her thick cushiony bed and the carved detail of her furniture. She missed banners and towering castles. She missed her warrior husband. "If you really want to cure me, robot, send me home."

The automated voice didn't answer.

The door slid open and Lilith didn't bother looking to see who'd come to shoot her in the neck this time. She turned on her heels, walking away from the door.

*Sorin, please be all right. I'm sorry I couldn't get the handheld to you. I tried to escape. I tried to get back to you. I—*

"Lilith, how surprising to see you here."

Lilith stiffened. She knew that voice. "Director Carretta?"

"I admit to being a little stunned when the Medical Supreme contacted us as to your detainment, especially when you had no apparent injuries and thus no reason to seek this dimension," the director answered. "I rather like to think there was a certain man friend you wanted to look up, but your profile doesn't sustain the theory."

"I didn't realize I needed to be detained." Lilith slowly turned, facing the woman.

Samanta Carretta smiled politely, but the look couldn't be trusted. The mission director always wore that expression. Slim and gorgeous, with smooth dark skin and short black hair, Carretta could turn any man's head. However, that gorgeous innocence was her most dangerous weapon. Carretta could kill a man twice her size in under three moves, before he even realized she planned to attack.

"Of course we put a detainment bulletin out for you. What did you think would happen when you disappeared with a sacred artifact from 228?" Carretta clicked her tongue, coming all the way into the room. The door slid shut behind her. "Very naughty, Miss Grian. I have to admit, we never suspected you for a thief. Had we known your predilection, we'd have put your talents to better use instead of having you waste away doing cultural analyses."

"I didn't take the book," Lilith defended.

"Then how do you explain the traces of the text found in your crate. Your thumbprint was on the seal."

"It's a mistake," Lilith said, defensively holding up her hands. "I packed that crate myself. I didn't steal any sacred book. I only took the copies they said I could have for the Divinity archive. When I got back, I found the book stuffed in the bottom. The magistrate on 228 showed me the book when I took a tour of their archives. They had it locked up. There is no way I'd take it on accident."

"Hm," Carretta hummed thoughtfully. She reached into her pocket and pulled out a black box and fingered it gingerly. "So you admit you took it on purpose. Who did you sell it to?"

"I didn't take it." Lilith backed away from the box. Fear gripped her. The director didn't believe her. "When I discovered what had happened, I followed protocol. I turned the item over to Director Tomes. He sent me home and said I'd be contacted after an investigation to give my report of the events. The next thing I know I'd been transported to an uncharted dimension filled with barbarians."

"Director Tomes? That's an interesting story, Miss Grian, but there's no need for you to explain. I think we'll have our answers soon enough." Carretta tapped the top and long thin blades shot out of both sides. Lilith flinched, her back hitting the wall. The director's smile stayed perfectly intact. "Don't look so worried. Over half the people we use this on survive without brain damage."

# CHAPTER 15

"Show me what she did," Sorin ordered, shoving the unresisting Rodrick at the control panel. It took two days for him to gather enough strength to walk down the stairs and, as sure as battles were bloody, he was not going to stop now. The castle didn't stir at such a late hour, and he'd gotten no resistance from the sleeping guard who watched over Rodrick.

"My lord, your wounds," Rodrick pleaded. "I know what you plan. The king ordered that none should go through the portal, but if you insist on following her, let me go in your stead."

Sorin knew the man's fear. It was an emotion they all shared. None of them liked the idea of traveling to different worlds, their bodies sucked into nothingness and disappearing into the unknown. The king had ordered they take their dealing with Divinity slowly and cautiously. Besides, none of them knew how to navigate the system. Divinity warned them that if they were to try, they might end up in the middle of some dark ocean a thousand feet down or worse.

"She is my wife. I will go." Sorin gave him another shove. His limbs hurt but he'd bound them tightly. "Show me."

"The dials have not been moved." Rodrick flattened his hands to motion over the controls. "All she did was press this button and then walked there." He pointed to the platform Divinity built them. "It carried her off her feet and swallowed her into the light."

Sorin limped to the platform and stood in the center. He'd seen others leave and knew what he had to do. "If I do not return, tell Ronen the family honor rests with him. Tell him I do what duty demands I do."

Rodrick nodded. "Fight well, my lord."

Sorin touched the sword at his waist. It wasn't his blade, but the weapon would work just as well. Inside he was bound into knots, knowing he might never see his homeland again. He got a sense of what Lilith must have felt, waking up in his world with no idea of how she got there. Part of him believed it to be the will of the gods. Why else would they bring her to him? The rest of him didn't know what to believe.

"Press it." The hard command sounded confident and brave, nothing like what he felt inside. Who knew what kind of place he'd find on the other end of this thing?

Rodrick pushed the button and the light began to change. Sorin stood at the ready, gripping the hilt of the sword. He ignored the weakness of his body as his limbs pulled toward the ground. The brightening light burned into his eyes, forcing them to close.

He tensed. The force against his body increased, pulling at his wounds until it felt as if they ripped open beneath the bandages. Sorin suppressed a scream of agony. Then it was over. The pain lessened and he stood, breathing heavily, covered in sweat and shaking like he'd just run from Battlewar to the borderlands.

Opening his eyes, he steeled his nerves. The strange silver box of a chamber appeared to be carved into metal. His nose wrinkled as he tasted the sickeningly sweet air. Stumbling forward, he tried to get his bearings. Metal room. Three doors painted with colored numbers. Portal. Loud buzzing. He flinched, cupping his ears.

"Sterilization commencing. Please remain away from the platform."

Sorin jolted, spinning in circles with his sword raised, as he looked for the owner of the docile male voice. A wall slid down from the ceiling, blocking the portal. Sorin charged it, banging his fist to the metal. The action jolted his arm, but he barely noticed. Lights began to flash all around him, disorienting him with their random pattern.

"Sterilization complete. Multiple unclosed injuries and fluid detected. Please state your clearance code."

"I'm here for my wife," Sorin yelled, menacingly. "Bring her to me."

"Please repeat, clearance code not accepted."

"I am Lord Sorin of Firewall and I demand you bring me my wife!" He lifted his sword, searching for the origin of the voice.

"Unauthorized entry detected." The buzzing grew to an awful earsplitting pitch, pulsing rhythmically. The ceiling opened and an oblong sphere attached to a skinny pole lowered. "Containment orders commencing."

"Give me my wife!" Sorin glared at the speaking sphere as it tried to blind him with a flash. He growled, swinging at with his sword. The weapon sliced through the pole, killing the talking orb with a giant, showering spark.

He rushed the door with green writing. Not finding a handle, he thrust his sword along the edge to open it. Within he found an open area with several tiny beds spread out before him. Each bed held a sleeping person while people in blue and red uniforms walked around them. At the sound of the crashing door, eyes widened in panic as several faces turned to him.

*What in all the burning forests is this place?*

A nearby woman screamed, nearly tripping over a bed to get away from him. When several of the males charged forward, Sorin slammed the door and ran to open the orange one. He kicked the dead sphere out of his way so he could thrust his sword along the edge.

"Unauthorized entry orange hall. Please cease your progress. Sealing for detainment." The voice was back.

Sorin searched the metal corridor for the sphere, expecting it to be on the floor, rolling after him. His heart beat heavily in his chest. This was nothing like he'd imagined. How could this world be a version of his? He stumbled on the smoothed floor, tripping through the endless tunnel, unable to see aught by walls that wound around forever.

*Lilith, where are you?*

Was this her world? No wonder she felt so out of place in his.

"Lilith!" he yelled, quickening his pace. "Bring me Lilith!"

---

"Hmm, interesting." Director Carretta stared at the medical clipboard she held. Lilith heard and saw everything, but she couldn't react. The truth box had been fastened to her head. It projected her memories in painful reality as a holographic image and forced the truth from her mouth. She'd heard the devices hurt, but nothing could prepare her for the slow, agonizing sensation of her brain being stabbed and probed without numbing. "It seems we have a visitor."

Lilith tried to moan, but only a trickle of drool made its way over her chin. Her body stayed slumped against the wall. Internally connected to the machine on her head, she knew exactly which images it pried from her thoughts. A picture of Director Tomes appeared.

"No, not Tomes. I've already contacted headquarters about him. It seems you've been telling the truth." Carretta knelt on the floor and held up her clipboard in front of Lilith's face. "Recognize this man?"

Sorin!

He charged though the halls, screaming like a crazed warrior and brandishing a sword. Her heart filled with longing and surprise. What was he doing on 187? How? Why? Thoughts of him were forced from her mind and a rush of images flashed overhead. Carretta stood up in surprise, her eyes rounding as she watched incredibly intimate memories.

"Stop there," Carretta commanded. The memory of holding down Sorin's arms as she rode him came to the forefront of her thoughts. Firelight illuminated his thick muscles and shone on her bouncing breasts. The director's breathing deepened and she slammed the clipboard face down, shutting it off. "I had no idea you were so..."

Lilith tried to think of something else, but she couldn't. The memory aroused her, as real as if she still lived it. Her pussy moistened and she wanted to feel the thick length of her husband conquering her.

Carretta leaned closer, staring above Lilith's head to the projection. Whispering, she ordered, "Show me his cock." The scene changed to one of Lilith about to take him into her mouth, freezing like a snapshot. Carretta licked her lips. "He's huge. I'll bet he knows how to take a woman."

"Yes," Lilith answered, unable to control it.

Carretta's hand brushed her thigh and she leaned into Lilith's ear. "Show me. I want to watch him come."

The scene played in all its realistic detail. Lilith tasted his flesh, felt the probe of his cock as it pushed past her teeth.

Carretta walked out of her eye line. "I'll bet he tastes good."

"Yes," Lilith answered. "Unlike anything you've ever savored."

"Will you let me taste him?" Carretta's breathing had become ragged and harsh. "I don't care if you watch. I just want that cock in my mouth."

"You touch him and I'll rip out your heart, you fucking cunt bitch," Lilith threatened, though she was in no position to follow through with it.

"Well, at least I know you're not lying," Carretta chuckled. "I don't blame you. I'd be possessive too."

Sorin's body tensed in the memory, becoming tight as he jerked his release into her mouth. She tasted his cum. Carretta moaned softly, making a strange noise.

After a moment, the woman asked, "Are all these Starians like that? When you said primitive, I didn't think to look at them. I thought cavemen, or dirty barbaric..." A scene of the main hall, of the first time Lilith had walked into the crowd of lusty knights, formed.

"Yes, they are all well formed."

"Tell me about them," she ordered.

"They lack inhibitions and women," Lilith began, before going into a detailed analysis of Starian culture. By the time she'd finished, Carretta was sitting in front of her with sparkling eyes.

"I must have one for my collection," she said. "Tell me, do you want to go back there?"

"Yes, with all my heart."

"Even though they don't fall in love?"

The fact hurt, but she answered, "Yes. I love him."

"Here's where we stand, Miss Grian. Director Tomes will be arrested and tried for the theft of the sacred text. I'm supposed to bring you back to headquarters for reassignment," Carretta scratched her manicured nails against her palm. "But clearly there's some explaining to be done to the Starian government, and we're going to need someone to mediate this mess he made. I didn't know about Tomes' trade agreement. Kidnapped women are bad business, but we can't very well go back on a deal, can we? I swear, for a smart man, Tomes is an idiot. If he needed volunteers all he had to do was market the product. Plenty of women would sign on to be the wife of such virile specimens."

Lilith couldn't move or speak.

"Besides, that blue water you brought does show potential. The doctors thought the vial was our stolen artifact and they're salivating to get their hands on it. There's some trade to be done here." Carretta glanced at the hall filled with warriors. "I also have a personal interest in assuring trades continue. Someone's going to have to go to Staria as an ambassador and such trips do have their perks." Her catlike smile gave full meaning to the perks she planned on partaking in. "I'll make you a deal. I'll send you back with lover boy and instate you as our official liaison with the Starian people. You'll integrate yourself into their customs, live there, become an expert in Starian politics and in return we'll continue the trade—only this time with willing women. I'll also expect there to be a plethora of willing men of a certain stamina to choose from when I arrive. I have appetites, but I'm not a monster. I like my participants enthusiastic."

"Yes," Lilith agreed. She highly doubted finding lonely men eager for a romp would be hard. "Deal."

"Oh, but there's one last thing. You are never, ever, not under pain of torture, allowed to tell the folks at headquarters about the nature of my visits. Who I plan to fuck or how many at one time is none of their business. You keep my secret and I'll make sure your dimension is listed as an uninteresting trade plane and buried in a back file."

"Deal," Lilith repeated. Her heart began to race.

"Let's get this off you." Carretta tapped the box once. The thin blades retracted. "I believe there's a crazed maniac on the loose screaming your name, and the good doctors are frantic that he needs medical attention. Apparently, he's dripping blood all over their halls." She picked up her clipboard, the motion turning it back on. "The man looks fine to me."

As soon as the box released control, Lilith screamed, gripping her head.

Carretta flinched at the sound. "Yeah, sorry about the inconvenience, but we had to know the truth. Dimensional harmony is a delicate thing."

*Lilith!*

Her scream echoed all around him and Sorin pressed on through the endless maze of halls. They didn't go anywhere, just looped around. His drops of blood marked his fruitless path. He couldn't find a door and, except for the occasionally annoying male voice announcing a "lock down", he didn't hear anything.

Until now.

Lilith's screams propelled him on. He grabbed his thigh, pressing into a bite wound. Sweat beaded his brow at the effort it took to move. His strength depleted fast and he hadn't even fought. But he couldn't stop. Not now. Lilith needed him.

"Lilith?" he yelled, the tip of his sword dragging behind him.

He shouldn't be so weak. Even when he'd been gouged in the

stomach he'd managed better than this. He blinked heavily. The corridor wall slid up and the screams became louder. Just a few more steps.

Sorin wavered on his feet as he stumbled to the door. The sword became heavy and dropped with a loud clang. Lilith writhed on the floor, clutching her face as a black creature with silver legs attacked her head. Another woman stood next to her, arms crossed and expression calm.

Sorin fell to his knees in the doorway. Why couldn't he stand? His vision swam, causing Lilith's form to dance before him. He dropped to the floor, rolling onto his back.

"Sorin," Lilith called his name, but he couldn't reach her.

The dark-haired woman stepped to him, peering down. "Perhaps the Medical Supreme should reconsider the security dosage in his hallways. You breathed in enough sleeping dust to take down twelve normal men. But then, you're not a normal man, are you?" She knelt beside his prone body and gave a secretive laugh. "I think I'm going to like this arrangement we have with your dimension, Lord Sorin. Yes, indeed."

---

Lilith stretched her neck as she turned on her side. Sorin lay on the cot next to her. It took a little convincing on Carretta's part, but the woman knew how to manipulate, and she soon had Sorin under the best medical treatment in all the dimensions. Even in her irritation over being put through the truth box hell, Lilith couldn't help but be grateful for the help. How could she hate Carretta when with each passing second Sorin's color darkened to a healthy glow?

He was there in front of her. She nearly squealed with excitement. In her darkest times, she feared she'd never see him again, feared his death.

The doctors had made some advances since Lilith visited last. One painted muscle tissue into Sorin's wounds, healing them from within before another sprayed skin regenerate. Almost visibly the gashes healed and the old scars lessened. Several medical students were even brought by to witness the progress. It was rare they had such a broken specimen to work with.

Lilith had to hide her amusement when one of the doctors, a short, slender man, said with obvious disdain, “Look at the primitive display of muscular tissue due to excessive exercise and improper diet.” The female students all glanced at each other, staring at the “primitive display” of Sorin on the bed, but obviously not as disgusted by the look of him as the instructor.

*Let them stare,* she thought. *They can't have him. He's all mine.*

“Can we examine the specimen more closely?” a woman asked, leaning over to pull at Sorin's covers. Her eyes were unmistakably on his cock.

“Back off, Red,” Lilith warned, stiffening, “or your classmates will learn about limb reattachment.”

The woman yelped and ran. The other students trailed behind her at a slower pace. Lilith smiled victoriously.

“Scan,” a medic said, coming to the bed with a handheld. Lilith didn't move as the man worked. He pressed his syringe to the unit before leaning over to give Lilith whatever medicine she required. The tension in her head lessened.

“I am glad to see you have a fighting spirit.”

“Sorin?” Lilith's eyes rounded and she pushed up. He didn't look at her, but that was definitely his voice.

“No, do not move. I hear three others on the far side of the room. As soon as they're gone, we're getting out of here.” He definitely spoke, but his lips barely moved, and his chest rose and fell in even breath.

“But—”

“I won't let them hurt you anymore,” he swore. His eyes opened a sliver so he could look at her. “I won't fail you.”

“Sorin, I'm fine. They didn't hurt me. Well, it hurt, but it was just a mind probe. I had to clear my name.” There was so much she needed to explain, but the sound of his voice flustered her and she couldn't think of all she wanted to say to him.

“Then this is your home.”

“No, it's not. It's 187, a medical dimension.”

"You were not coming back to me." He frowned, his eyes opening further. Lilith slid off the bed and went to sit next to him. He gave up the pretense of sleep and looked at her in confusion.

"I tried," she whispered, not wanting the doctors to overhear. "I came here to get medicine to help you heal. Your wounds were so bad and Lance said you'd recover, but I saw the uncertainty in him. Everyone kept telling me to trust in the gods, they'd reward a hero, and maybe they did. You're here and you're healed. But before, you were in so much pain and your fever wouldn't break. Then you started mumbling incoherent thoughts. I had to come."

His frown deepened.

"I did plan on returning to help you, but Divinity had a bulletin out on me and my arrival set off the security systems. They wouldn't let me leave until Director Carretta cleared me of all charges. It seems I was sent to your world to cover up a theft." She touched his face. "What are you doing here? Why did you jump into a portal? You had no way of knowing what awaited you on the other side or if you'd even make it back."

"I came for you," he stated, his expression softening. "I knew you wanted to leave my world, but I had to check on you. You are my wife. I would jump through a million portals to look for you."

"Sorin, I—"

"No, do not say it. Let me speak." He pushed up. The covers dropped around his waist, revealing a smooth, naked chest. She couldn't resist touching him, as she ran her hand down the center of his chest to rest between his pectorals. His warmth worked its way into her fingertips, spreading awareness down her arm. "I understand that coming to me was not of your choice, but I believe it happened for a reason. If you cannot stay in my world, then let me stay in yours. I will learn your ways. I will live within these unnatural walls and breathe this sweet air, if it pleases you to have me do so."

"What about your home? Your family?"

"Ronen will carry on the family name," he stated. Cupping her face, he said, "You bewitched me from the moment I first saw you. I swore after Bianka that I would never take another wife but one look and I was yours. In battle, I could not concentrate for fear you would not be there when I came home. I cannot survive without you, my lady wife. When Sera said you went through the portal, I died inside. So I beg you, go seek your happiness in whatever world you choose, only take me with you."

Lilith gasped and a hot tear rolled over her cheek, hitting his hand. "I want to go home."

"Then we'll go home," he assured her, leaning in to press his lips to hers. "What is this world of yours like?"

She gave a teary laugh. "It's filled with stubborn men with strange customs and noble battles. There are castles made of stone and torchlight and were clearly named by men for no woman would ever name a home after a weapon. The air smells of earth and flowers. The servants are annoying, but it's all worth it at the end of the day because I have you."

"You would choose a life with me?" He looked around the metal room.

"There is no choice, Sorin. I love you." She ran her hands into his hair, thoroughly kissing him. His tongue slid into her mouth, deep and sure. Lilith shivered, forgetting everything but his touch.

"You were telling the truth. They are uninhibited." Carretta chuckled from the end of the bed. "Please, don't stop on my account. I don't mind taking in a good show now and again."

Sorin stiffened, pulling Lilith into his protective embrace. She put her hands on her husband's chest and pushed gently so she could look at him. "Everything's fine. I'll explain it to you once we're back home."

"I see you're healed, Lord Sorin." Carretta nodded in satisfaction. "Unfortunately though, they don't carry shirts in your size and they burned your clothes—a strange custom here. Fear of parasites and natural fibers, you understand. You'll have to wear the blanket home."

Sorin looked at his arms, his eyes rounding as if he'd noticed them for the first time. "How long did I sleep?"

"A few hours," Lilith said. "This is why I wanted a handheld. Think of the lives we can save with it."

"Ah, speaking of..." Carretta reached down to pick up a canvas bag. "As part of the mineral water trade agreement I just signed, Staria is presented with its own medical unit with complete accessories and enough injectible meds to cure ten thousand big beefy warriors for hundreds of years. Instruction manual and your very own Divinity translation guide included."

"You negotiated a hand-held for Staria?" Lilith asked in surprise, reaching to take the offering.

"Don't tell management." Carretta winked. "Besides, we can't have them getting sick. Be sure they get the booster pack. Hurry up. I'm expected back at headquarters tomorrow morning."

"We need to talk about a few things first," Lilith said. "Not only must the females you bring be willing, but they will come awake and aware, with full health screens and documentation."

"Yes, yes." Carretta waved her hand in dismissal. "Of course, all that."

"And I want my belongings delivered, a data unit with a copy of the recipe database in a language readable by the castle's kitchen staff. I want a—"

"Write it all down," the director interrupted. "I'm sure everything you want can be met. Now, about my wants... Let's go. I believe you promised to introduce me to unattached men."

"Is she a..." Sorin studied Carretta as she sauntered away, "camp follower?"

Lilith snorted with laughter, covering her mouth. "She's one of the top people at Divinity. I've only talked to her a handful of times."

"Come here." Sorin made a small noise in the back of his throat as he leaned in to kiss her. "I wish to finish what we began."

"Sorin!" Lilith said under her breath, blushing profusely. "We can't do that here."

He grinned. "I meant the talking, but I assure you I feel well enough for the other."

Lilith glanced to where the redheaded student stared at them from across the room. Hefting the canvas bag onto her shoulder, she said, "Let's go home, my lord husband. We have the rest of our lives to talk."

"You're sure this will make you happy?"

"You will make me happy." She slugged his arm lightly. "At least you better."

He grinned, a completely saucy look filled with promise. Standing from the bed, he pulled the covers with him, holding them at his waist. Lilith walked beside him toward the portal.

She moaned softly, twining her fingers around his muscular arm. "I won't feel right until I'm safely tucked away in our bed."

"Our bed?" He lifted a brow.

"Yep, I decided you're never leaving my side, my lord." She smiled happily, leaning her head next to him.

"Then I feel duty bound to tell you, my lady." He untangled himself from her hold and slid his hands over her shoulders. They made their way through the hall, both eager to get to their dimension. "You do snore. Loudly."

Lilith gasped, hitting him in mock affront. "You will pay for your insults."

"Warriors are not frightened by torture." He paused as they reached the orange door. The lock had been scraped and broken. Sorin chuckled at his handiwork, the sound filled with masculine warrior pride.

"About time. I've set the coordinates," Carretta stated. "I'll let you go through first. I'd hate to cause alarm arriving unannounced."

Lilith led Sorin to the platform. Her heart fluttered inside her chest when she looked into his eyes. "I meant it when I said I love you. I know you don't put much faith in the emotion, but everything I am belongs to you."

"You are my heart, Lilith." He brought her hand and pressed it to his chest. "I am nothing without you. If that is not love, then I do not understand the meaning."

She lifted up on her toes to kiss him, but a brilliant red light washed over them, pulling them through the portal.

# CHAPTER 16

"Lord Sorin!" Rodrick shouted in excitement.

Lilith gasped as she materialized next to her husband. They both stumbled apart as gravity released them from its clutches.

"Lady Lilith! Blessed night, you made it!" Rodrick continued.

The couple grinned. Lilith pulled Sorin out of the way before Carretta came through and landed on their heads.

"And you're healed!" Rodrick hurried forward, lifting Sorin's arm to examine it in amazement, as if he looked at a god himself. Suddenly, he snickered, "And soft as a newborn's backside."

Sorin frowned, looking down as if seeing his body for the first time. He grabbed his stomach, dropping the covers from his waist. "They took my scars." Lifting his arm, he shouted in disbelief, "My mark of manhood. Those accursed gnomes took my mark."

"Ah," Lilith mouthed in surprise. Out of all the things to get upset over, she hadn't expected that.

"Now it looks as if I've never seen a battle!" Sorin proceeded to examine his perfectly smooth skin for old war wounds. He touched his thigh. "The lance Ronen hit me with as a child. It's gone." Sorin began to charge the platform, completely naked. "We're going back and demanding they return—"

"Sorin." Lilith hurried after him, pulling him back. The platform flashed and Carretta appeared, wobbling on her feet. She'd mussed up her hair and had put on makeup before coming through.

"Mm, I like it, very dungeonesque." Carretta's eyes found Rodrick. "Please tell me you're not married."

"Rodrick, consider her your punishment for losing my wife," Sorin muttered.

"Oh, punishment, I like that." Carretta batted her lashes, walking around the stunned Rodrick like he was a piece of meat and she was the butcher. The poor knight didn't stand a chance. His round eyes stared at her and his breathing deepened. Lilith was pretty sure his boyish crush on her was over the second Carretta grabbed him by the front of his tunic and pulled. "Come on, you naughty boy. Show me where you keep the prisoners."

"Wow, around headquarters I had no idea she was like that," Lilith whispered. "You do realize what you just ordered Rodrick to do, don't you?"

"He can handle himself in battle, he can handle that witch." Sorin grunted. "She will make him a man."

"Rodrick's a virgin?" Lilith really felt sorry for the guy. When she turned back to her husband, he had started examining himself again. Licking her lips, she let herself enjoy the sight of his naked body cast in blue light. She ran her hand over his firm ass, raking it with her nails. "You know, if you're really upset about how the doctors healed you..."

Sorin's head snapped up as she gripped his butt cheek hard. "Yea?"

"I can think of a few ways to mar that pretty flesh of yours that doesn't include bloody battlefields." Lilith nipped at his back. She'd never really hurt him, but it was fun to play. Now that she knew his true feelings, every last hesitation flittered away. She was his, completely and forever. Sliding her hand around, she pressed to his back and grabbed his cock. "And when we're done, you won't need a tattoo to remind you that you are a man."

Sorin growled, spinning on his heels to face her. He caught her up easily, tossing her over his shoulder. The canvas bag remained on the floor, forgotten.

"Sorin, wait, you're naked! The hall..." Lilith kicked her feet, laughing as he hurried to the stairs. He didn't stop, merely walked faster as he made his way through the prison hall.

"Whoa, um, Carretta," Rodrick stammered through one of the doors with a barred window.

"I said take off your clothes and get on your knees, prisoner!" Carretta commanded.

"Y-yea..." Rodrick's answer was lost as Sorin took the stairs two at a time.

Lilith watched the firm line of her husband's ass, enjoying the play of muscles. Sorin had a firm hold on her and she let go of him only to playfully scratch at his flesh.

"Oh, Lord Sorin!" Nan and a couple other servants jumped out of the nobleman's way as he strode past.

Lilith lifted her head and gave the gawking Nan a superior grin, calling, "You act as though you've never seen a naked god before."

He flung around the corners to the climb to the Black Tower. His fingers dug into her upper thigh, holding her steady. Cream already infused her pussy, making wet and ready for his touch. It had been too long since he made love to her. Her heart ached as she thought of everything she could have lost.

By the time he kicked open the door to his chambers and lowered her to her feet, Lilith's arousal hit full force. She tore at her clothing, pulling the patient issue off her skin. Before the last piece of clothing fell, Sorin lunged forward, tackling her onto the bed. His body pinned hers. Flesh molded to perfect, hot flesh.

"A god?" He grinned at her, his face cast in shadows as there was no fire in the fireplace. "That must make you my goddess." He slid up, then down, forcing her nipples to rub against him. "How should I best worship you, my lady goddess?"

"Love me."

Lilith arched against him as he obeyed. Sorin sucked a breast into his mouth, moaning so loud, vibrations moved over her chest.

His tongue swirled the nipple, forcing it to peak between his lips. A hand slipped between her thighs to tantalize the aroused clit he found there.

She undulated her hips against him, trying to tempt his finger to press inside her slick pussy. How could he have so much control? Her body felt like it was on fire. She gripped his arms, digging her nails into his flesh, unsure if she tried to pull his body up or push his mouth down.

"I need you inside me," she begged. "Please, Sorin, take me, finish me."

---

Sorin groaned, trying to keep his head as he moved to the other perfect breast. His finger glided between the velvety folds of her sex and he traced the length of it, refusing to dip inside. Lilith gripped him tighter, gasping and panting as she writhed beneath him.

*Not yet...*

Sorin wanted to make sure she never forgot this moment. He bit at her breast, unable to get enough of the soft mound. She opened her legs wider and he pinched the small bud of her sex.

"Ah, please, I'll do anything you want, just finish me." Desperately she bucked against his hand, searching for release.

How could he resist her?

*Fool.*

*Idiot.*

*Weak.*

Sorin grinned, the words not bothering him as they once had. So what if he was a fool for her? Or an idiot to give in to her every demand? What did he care if she, his beautiful goddess, his wife, was his one weakness? She loved him. Nothing else mattered.

Sorin buried himself in the sweet glide of her pussy, giving her what they both wanted. She squeezed his cock with her sex, the muscles surrounding him like a tight sheath. He rocked his hips in a shallow thrust.

"More," she groaned, clawing at his ass. "Hard."

Sorin let loose an animalistic growl as he pulled back only to slam forward. She moaned in loud pleasure. He did it again and again, pausing with each forceful thrust.

"More," she commanded, her hands roaming his body in haphazard, nail-scratching patterns. "Fast. Take me. Finish me."

He lifted up, bracing his weight on his arms. His knee slid up to settle beneath her thigh. Sorin pounded his hips, giving her what she begged for. She inched along the bed but he merely followed her with his hips, driving in and out at a frantic pace. Whatever the doctors had given him worked. He felt strong and alive. With each joining of their hips, he grunted. Her sweet warmth took every inch, so soft and wet against his hard size. Sweat beaded his flesh and his stomach muscles began to burn from the frantic excursion, but he couldn't stop.

Lilith cried out, tensing in beautiful release. Her pussy quivered and gripped his shaft. The sensations were too much. His yell muffled hers as he came, spending his seed deep inside her. He jerked uncontrollably as she milked every last bit of it.

Weak, he fell onto the bed next to her, careful not to crush her with his weight. Lilith rolled onto her side, breathing hard. After a long moment passed and his heart began to slow, she said, "I demand that you finish me like that every night."

He chuckled in contentment. Tapping the end of her nose with his finger, he said, "Yea, my lady, an order I will gladly follow. I shall also finish you in the morn." He drew his finger over her parted lips, tracing her delicate features. "Twice in the afternoon. Before the evening meal. Whenever I see you across the courtyard. Whenever I think of you and must seek you out."

"Maybe we should never leave the bed," she giggled, the sound the sweetest music he'd ever heard.

"Mm." He cupped a breast, lazily weighing it in his palm. "Perhaps that would be best. I will just have to figure out how to do my duty while I'm trapped in your bed, doing my, ah, *duty*."

She gripped his hair, forcing him to look at her. His hand paused on her chest at her serious expression. "I want a life with you, a long, long life. I know you must fight, but no more rushing off into battle on your own. You have earned your honor, my lord, and you have earned the right to be happy. I want to give you that happiness and I want you around to share in mine. I want a family and a home."

"Family?" His knee nudged her thigh and his brow lifted in question.

"No, I'm not." She blushed and he found it endearing. "Divinity issued me a BCP ring to prevent pregnancy, but I had the doctors dissolve it. They said the ring's effect should be reversed fully in a month's time."

"Then I'd better hurry." He massaged the globe beneath his hand. "We do not have much time."

"Hurry?" Her round eyes looked up at him, confused. "Do you want me to have the ring put back? If you don't want children—"

"Of course I wish for children, I merely wish to practice more." He grabbed her hip and slid her next to him. "And it will take me time to have a castle built. My lady wishes for her own home and I intend to give her one. I will have Firewall rebuilt and it can be any way you wish it to be."

"But, the portal is here and I'm supposed to—"

"Sh." He silenced her with his lips. "You think too much, wife. I can see your mind working behind those bewitching eyes of yours. But now is not the time for thinking, now is the time for feeling."

Lilith opened her mouth to speak, but he didn't give her a chance. Sorin crawled down her body and pushed her legs apart. Her sex still glistened from her release and he grinned in anticipation.

# Epilogue

"By all the bloody, mace-wielding wenches! I told you they were going to set me afire!" Lilith cursed, hitting at her skirts. Her favorite gown was ruined, burnt by the torch a drunk Lady Alana had dropped during her spin around the center bonfire. Sorin pulled her away from the giant flames. They grew taller as the townsfolk threw wood onto the inferno, rising above the prairie outside the gates of Battlewar Town. "I knew a fire ceremony would include fire, but—"

"My lady," Sorin laughed. "It's a small singe."

"This plane is dangerous, my lord." Lilith gave up on her skirts and poked at his chest, only to walk her finger across a naked pectoral to slide lightly along his arm next to a fresh tattoo. "I see you have regained your manhood."

"And a scar!" He turned, showing her a cut along his back. The superficial wound was only one of the very few marring his smooth flesh.

"You fell off the balancing beam, didn't you?" She laughed.

"It is still fairly won." Sorin pretended to frown at her teasing.

"And a beautiful one at that." She smiled, kissing his back, away from the small cut.

"I have news of Karre, Paige and Jayne," he said, yelling louder as music rose over the earth.

"Tell me later for I know in my heart they are well." Grabbing his hand, she bounced as a musical beat rained over them. Lilith had never been so happy. She had the excitement of talking about other planes with Divinity employees and a life with Sorin that made her complete. "Twirl with me around the fire, my love."

Sorin complied. The motion wasn't really dancing, but more of a lively spin in the firelight that wouldn't stop until they couldn't breathe and their hearts beat wildly in their chests. Lifting her off the ground, Sorin held her to his chest, carrying her as he twirled. "It would seem the gods were not set on punishing me after all."

The End

# *Fighting Lady Jayne*

BOOK TWO BY MICHELLE M. PILLOW

Second Electronic Printing February 2012, The Raven Books

First Electronic Printing May 2009

ISBN 9781452447353

# *About Fighting Lady Jayne*

DIVINITY WARRIORS BOOK TWO

**In a land forever at war, meeting women is the last thing they can think about, so what's a lonely alpha warrior to do?**

Jayne Hart has earned her independence by becoming Divinity Corporation's inter-dimensional boxing champion. Life is great, until a dirty fighter knocks her unconscious and she loses everything. Now, abandoned by the corporation in an alternate reality filled with alpha male warriors and strange marriage customs, Jayne will use every weapon she has. Even if it means running from her sexy new "husband" and spending the rest of her life in a primitive forest.

Ronen of Firewall longs for a woman to warm his bed and his home, but he had no intention of choosing a bride. In an unprecedented move, one chooses him. Never in the history of the marriage ceremony has a woman dared to lay claim. How can he resist the alluring Lady Jayne? She's confident and sure in her decision to be with him—until their wedding night when she's nowhere to be found. But, Ronen is not one to shy from a battle. He will find Jayne and, when he does, he will do everything he can to tame the heart of his wayward wife.

# *Prologue*

Getting her teeth knocked around in her head hurt like hell, but being able to spit blood into the face of her opponent more than made up for the discomfort. Jayne "The Sweet" Hart laughed as Big Bobby Bishop sputtered in anger. She knew he expected her to cry at the landed blow. Truth was, part of Jayne did want to cry. She wasn't a glutton for a beating, and that last hit had left blood running out of her mouth at a steady flow. They'd been going at it for nearly a half hour, bare-knuckle boxing —no protective gear beyond any sanctioned bioengineering, no referees, not like some of the other dimensions had. No, here on dimensional plane 241 almost anything was legal. That's why the gladiator ring paid such big money and drew the notice of rich, inter-dimensional travelers who could afford a private plane jump through Divinity Corporation. It's also why Jayne agreed to travel from her own world to this alternate reality where laws were more of a suggestion and killing someone in a fight was considered a good thing.

In many ways, each alternate reality was like drifting through time on her own home plane, had a singular event on the timeline been changed. Each dimension seemed to be a different outcome to a similar historical start. Some were so technologically advanced everything was done for them, and they'd found a worldwide peace and understanding. Jayne generally stayed away from those levels of existence. There wasn't much employment for fighters in such realities.

Other planes hadn't even developed a means of fast communication beyond throwing a bird into the air with a tiny letter tied to its leg. Still others had just installed their first aqueducts or invented their first vehicles to run without horses or oxen. Or, like 241, they had every technological comfort and yet somehow managed to maintain their barbarian sensibilities.

Any way you looked at it, Earth was Earth, just different versions of itself—same languages, matching natural events, some people looked the same but weren't. Humans, for the most part, still resembled humans. And those with power were still greedy bastards trying to tell her how to do her job.

Big Bobby watched her expectantly, his mouth opened as if to scream in victory at any second. Jayne knew he expected her to fall with that punch. She watched as the excitement slowly died from his eyes, replaced by shock, then confusion, until finally a boiling rage. His eyes scanned the crowd before moving toward the large balcony to where his daddy sat watching. Big Bobby's father and known gangster boss had undoubtedly assured his halfwit-of-a-lug-nut son that he was a sure winner. It wouldn't have been so bad if Big Bobby had been an admirable opponent, but after a half hour, she could still see out of one of her eyes, and he only managed to knock her off her feet twice.

And Bossman Bishop wanted her to take a dive to this chump?

Jayne snorted. Not bloody likely. She'd never work as a boxer again—not that she had to. In her home dimension, she had plenty of money to bide her twelve lifetimes.

Divinity Corp paid her big for this fight. They were her ticket home and had the only known source of inter-dimensional travel technology on this plane. Natural slips were extremely rare and the timing of them completely predictable by the company, even if they didn't know where the slip would go. If they didn't take her home, she'd be stuck until the end of time. Besides, there was no way she was taking a dive just because the local gangsters had promised to...

What had Bossman said again? Oh, yeah. They were going to gang rape her grandma while she watched. It had hardly been a threat. Jayne was an orphan. Still, a part of her was up in arms for the hypothetical grandmother they'd threatened.

There was no way Bossman could know about her lack of family. The publicity put out by Divinity Corp's entertainment division fostered the wholesome image of their Sweetheart Jayne. Of course, it was all a lie. They hired a family to take pictures with her at a rented country home—the devoted mother, the fake twin sister with a poor health condition, the baby brother and suit 'n' cravat dad.

The loud, almost fanatical cheering of the crowd grew. They surrounded on all sides, lining the rows upon rows of rotating theater seats. Every few minutes, the seats would shift, changing the angle from which a person watched. Lights flashed all around her. Floating cameras zipped by her head, but she ignored them. Most of the bets were on her and she never lost a fight. Never. And she would be damned if she gave this guy the reputation of being the one person who could take her down. He didn't deserve the title or her respect. Rage grew within her that he even dared to presume he was worthy of taking her down.

*Do it for your family, Jayne*, she thought sardonically.

Jayne decided to teach him and Bossman a lesson. She drew her body around, preparing to kick him upside the head in a move she knew he wouldn't see coming. Big Bobby swung again. She dodged the blow, and this time his hand merely grazed her cheek, stinging the cut she had there. She didn't hesitate. Whipping her leg around, she swung for his head. Suddenly, every nerve in her body exploded with pain. There was no stopping her body's momentum as it lifted off the hard mat. The noise of the crowd faded and grew until stopping altogether. Big Bobby caught her suddenly slowed foot and pushed her backward. Nothing was as it should be. Lights streaked in her vision before her body was abruptly stopped by a metal pole slamming into her back. Then, darkness clouded her mind and she could only think one thing.

*Boxers' Poison.*

# CHAPTER 1

Jayne perceived the exact moment her mind became aware that something wasn't right. Her body didn't ache and her body always ached—if not from a fight, then from her workouts. The second hint that all was not well came in the form of her mattress. The thing was much too soft. She didn't sleep on soft things, *couldn't* sleep on soft things. Jayne had grown up in an orphanage. Where she came from that meant hard floor beds and a high pain tolerance from the daily obedience beatings.

Where in the bloody fucking misery was she?

She listened first, not moving, not changing her breathing. The soft whispers of others filled the space around her. People slept. The even tempo gave it away. Opening an eye, she glanced around and took quick inventory—dim light, stone wall, barred door, five sleeping women, not counting herself, on mattresses placed in various positions around the room.

*Prison.*

Jayne frowned. Her tank top and exercise pants must have been confiscated, replaced by a shapeless white, very one-size-fits-all, dress. She'd been arrested before, usually for disorderly conduct. Surely she'd remember celebrating her victory. Nothing to worry about.

Divinity Corp always sent someone to get her out of jail. Ah, the perks of being a champ.

*Wait, victory?* Jayne shot up on her mattress. *Boxers' Poison.*

"Bloody fucking misery, son of a whoring cat..." Jayne cursed under her breath. A blonde head moved nearby, followed by a light whimper.

Jayne didn't care if she interrupted her neighbor's beauty sleep. How could that father of a monkey do this to her? Big Bobby had drugged her. His last hit had been tainted with Boxers' Poison. One punch to an open wound and down went your opponent. All fighters were supposed to have been tested for such tricks, as was protocol. Even on 241 it was illegal. What fun was a drugged fight to the crowds? Well, except for the drugged fights on plane 23.

"That flying piece of monkey dung," Jayne swore again, feeling the familiar urge to hit something ball up inside her. She wasn't sure what was worse—being cheated or having nearly four hundred dimensions that participated in the underground entertainment division of Divinity Corp think she lost to such a whoreson.

"Keep it down," someone mumbled. "I'm trying to sleep."

"You keep it down," Jayne muttered under her breath, unafraid of the warning in the woman's tone. Where was George, the Divinity Corp entertainment lawyer? He should be getting her out of there already.

A sinking feeling came over Jayne. What if George wasn't coming? Technically, she'd lost the fight. If Divinity believed her to have lost a fortune in assets, they'd...

"Oh, misery." Jayne reached for her face, not feeling a single swollen eyelid or bruised cheekbone. She'd been healed. That meant she'd been out for at least a couple weeks. Boxers' Poison didn't last that long, so someone had deliberately kept her under while they transported her to this cell. Management always joked that they'd make her disappear if she ever lost a match. She'd thought they were teasing. Someone always had to lose. Sure, it was never her, but someone had to. "Oh, bloody misery. They shipped me off. They made me disappear."

"I said to keep it down!" A dark-haired woman sat up, blinking hard. "What the...? Where?" Her gaze darted around the room in surprise, and she let loose a loud, long, hairsplitting scream. The prison cell instantly became a blur of jolting movements as the other women awoke. Jayne covered her ears, glaring at the woman who refused to stop her incessant yelling.

"Eh, what's all this noise?" A gruff voice yelled. A man who could only be their prison guard appeared in front of the bars. A burly man dressed in a hard leather jerkin and dark breeches stood between the bars and the stone wall on the other side of the narrow hall. Metal diamonds plated the leather of his clothes. He clanked a heavy metal weapon against the bars to make them ring. "Stop that. You woke me from a dead sleep. No talking. No waking. Lie down until it's time to break our fast. The next one to make a sound, I swear to the fire goddess I will run you through with my sword."

The woman stopped screaming, but her wide eyes still yelled in silent terror. Jayne looked around at the rest of her companions. None were as silly as the screamer, but nearly all looked just as confused. All except a redhead who hugged her arms around her legs and rolled back down onto her mattress bed.

One of the two blondes whimpered and did as she was told, sniffling noisily. Jayne realized it was the same woman who'd been sniveling as the others slept. The second blonde appeared much calmer as her eyes met Jayne's. She didn't say a word as she took in their surroundings. The last prisoner, the brunette, scratched thoughtfully at the back of her head as she eyed the retreating guard.

"We'd better do as he says," the brunette said, only to add to herself, "for now."

Jayne silently, though reluctantly, agreed. There was no point in causing trouble until she knew what was happening. Pressing her hand against the hard stone of the floor, she slid the mattress aside. Though bumpy, the stiff bed was a cool relief to the softness. Threading her hands under her head, she closed her eyes. The only thing left to do was wait, for all would unfold itself in time.

"The faster you make them come, the less time you must spend in their presence."

Was this whore serious?

Jayne eyed the servant who'd introduced herself as Sera. At least, the woman said she was a servant. What kind of servant, Jayne wasn't sure. The woman had a white corset top, laced so tight it made her generous bosom nearly pop over the top of her shirt. Long blue skirts, a favorite accessory of most of the whores Jayne had met in her travels, billowed around her legs. They made for easy access to the professional tools.

"I'll make them do something, all right, but it won't be making them come," Jayne muttered under her breath, as she accepted a loaf of bread from the woman. The other women in the cell did nothing to acknowledge they'd heard what she said. Of course, none of them were really talking, not since the guard had come in the middle of the night to threaten them. Maybe if she yelled the guard would open the door to give her the fight she was brewing for.

*Calm down, Jayne. It's like Coach Wagner used to tell you. Not everything is settled with fists.*

To which she always replied, *Yeah, there's kicking, too.*

"That is all they want—a vessel to find release in," Sera continued softly, her rounded eyes trying to convey her sincerity. Jayne didn't trust her. In fact, she didn't trust anyone, not completely. "Do not expect tenderness, but if you don't deny them, if you don't resist, you'll be treated fairly enough. And if you give them sons, you'll be greatly rewarded. Life here is not so bad."

"This isn't happening, this isn't happening," a dark-haired woman repeated, over and over. She only became more hysterical with each passing moment. "Wake up, Edith, wake up."

Jayne blocked the sniveling woman out of her mind and bit into her bread. There had to be a way out of the prison. If only she had something besides a white, shapeless gown to bribe the guards with.

"I'm telling you how to best survive this place. Please, listen," Sera insisted. "Spreading your thighs is easy enough a task for a decent life. Don't bring trouble upon yourself. Let them find release. They are not such boars when they get what they want."

Jayne hummed softly as the servant woman left them. Perhaps bribing with coin wasn't the way. Escape might be much easier. Edith became louder still and Jayne thought about knocking her out to put them all out of their misery. One of the blondes tried to soothe the hysterical one's fears while the other blonde whimpered. The redhead picked imaginary dust particles off her long sleeve, ignoring everyone.

Jayne turned her attention to the brunette, watching as she pulled a hairpin out of her hair. The woman didn't hesitate as she knelt down by the bars. Reaching through, she closed her eyes and slipped the tip of the hairpin into the lock and began to work it in small circles. Jayne bit her lip, leaning in to stand watch without having to be asked.

"Put it up," Jayne whispered, seeing a wooden door open at the end of the long corridor. Two burly men dressed in dark breeches and hard leather jerkins with the metal diamond-shaped plates strode toward them. Jayne slowly backed away from the bars as they came to stand in front of her. A warrior studied them one by one, not appearing pleased with what he saw. Jayne knew the feeling. She wasn't too pleased with him either. To the other guard, he said, "The flaxen one and the crying one. They do not carry themselves well. Take them and give them the philter."

"What?" Edith screamed. "No, wait! I'll be good. I swear I'll be good. Please, don't hurt me. Please, I'll do anything you want. Do you want me to make you come? I will. I swear I will. I'll do you all!"

Both guards snorted in disgust. Jayne resisted the urge to thank them. With the two crybabies out of the cell, she might be able to come up with a plan. One motioned to the door and soon four men were crowding into the small place. Two grabbed the now-sobbing Edith and dragged her out. The blonde screamed, kicking and fighting as tears streamed down her face. The four remaining women held perfectly still.

After the men passed through the door, the brunette set back to work, her face set as she tried to feel around the lock.

"You won't be able to open it," the redhead said, staring at the lock picker. "Even if you did, there would be no escape. You'd have to fight through the warriors' hall, out of the guarded castle gates and run three strikes over open prairie until you reach the forest. Should you survive the wild beasts that live there, you'd soon find yourself prisoner to an even more vicious race of creatures—monsters so fierce and depraved they'll make you beg for death. Trust me, with the war going on in this forsaken place, we're in the better of the two sides."

"Who are you that we should trust what you say?" the brunette asked.

"Name's Paige," the redhead answered.

"Lilith," the remaining blonde put forth.

"What do they want with us?" Jayne inquired. All eyes turned to her. "Oh, I'm called Jayne."

"They want us to be their whores," Paige said bitterly. "They don't call it that, but that's what they want—a subservient woman to rub their feet and spread her legs. If you don't, they get pissed and the whole lot of them stares at you like you are demon spawn incarnate and blames you for your chosen warrior's bad mood. It's either fuck them or suck them or you're treated like the bottom rung of Starian society."

"Again, I ask, why should we trust you? We don't know you." The brunette continued to try to pick the lock. "You could be a plant sent here to make us behave with horror stories of what's beyond the tree line."

"I don't care if you trust me, but I know what I'm talking about. This isn't my first time in a cage." Paige tilted her head back and sighed. "They'll be coming to get us soon."

"What's your name, locksmith?" Jayne asked the brunette.

"Karre."

"Well, Karre," Jayne said. "I don't think we have much of a choice. If we all work together, maybe we stand a chance. Now, I don't know how we all got here, and at this point I don't think it matters, but I do know I'm not staying to spend the rest of my life as some guy's sex toy."

"I agree." Lilith stood. "We need a plan."

"Fine," Karre grumbled.

Paige opened her eyes and shook her head. "Don't look to me to join your little band. You're only fooling yourselves. I've been to the Hanging Forest. I made it all the way to the Starian borders and I've seen the creatures that wait beyond."

"What about a dimension jump?" Lilith inquired. "Does anyone know if this place has inter-dimensional travel technology?"

"A what?" Paige asked.

"Staria? It's too primitive. They don't have the technology here," Karre said. "I got a glimpse of the castle when they brought me to this cell. Through a door I saw servants cart water from a well in buckets and the drive wasn't paved. No artificial lights or motorized vehicles. Though there were several large horses."

"I've never been here," Jayne put forth, "but I'm inclined to agree from what I've seen. These prisons don't use lasers or shocks."

"Someone's coming." Karre pulled her arms out from between the bars. She thrust her lock picking tool back into her upswept hair.

A new guard arrived, dressed similarly to the other men she'd seen. His nose had a crook across the bridge. "Only three new ones?"

"It's all they sent us," said the man who'd ordered the other two women away.

"How's it going, Edward?" Paige taunted, her face hardening to hide all emotion. Jayne watched in surprise, liking this version of Paige much better than the sulky one. "I see the nose is healing nicely."

"Lady Paige," Edward growled, glaring at her as if he wanted to pull the sword from his waist and run her through.

"Open the door, Eddie," Paige pouted her lower lip. "Let me break it again."

Edward grumbled, but didn't answer.

"I thought there were five new." Another of Edward's fellow barbarians joined them, completely ignoring Paige's comment.

"What's wrong, Brock? Don't I count anymore in your little ledger?" Paige asked.

"You are not new," Brock frowned. "Your lord is waiting for you and I do hope his punishment is harsh."

Paige's smirk wavered. Brock grinned.

"You already have one of these guys?" Karre whispered, grabbing Paige's arm.

"Two were not suitable. They were taken away," Edward answered Brock. His nostrils flared in distaste. "Too weak."

"Three will have to do," Brock said to Edward. As the two men walked off, he added, "I'll tell my Sera to make ready."

"Ladies," Paige whispered. "Welcome to Battlewar Castle."

---

Lord Ronen eyed his older brother as Lord Sorin lifted his arm toward the guard atop the castle wall, showing the bright red crest on his arm as he silently ordered the knight to lift the outer castle gate. The balding knight motioned down in understanding, disappearing over the side.

Like his brother, Ronen wore the red crest on his sleeve. The family symbol marked their respected ranks as leaders to two of the best armies in all of Staria. Very few would dare to challenge their word or honor.

Behind them, a small contingent of warriors rode in single file, followed by young valets and pages on foot. The boys led pack horses carrying the brothers' armor. It was a rare occasion that the warriors went without it.

Ronen rolled his shoulders. His simple, linen undertunic had been made from the naturally dark brown fibers of local plants. It fell loose and long over his tightly fitted black breeches with a long slit up the sides to ease the movements of the upper thighs. The warm day made an overtunic and cloak unnecessary. A woven belt wrapped loosely around his waist, holding a sheathed knife. Opposite the short blade, his sword hung from a shoulder scabbard that crossed his chest.

The steady clop of horses' hooves slowed while the oversized gate creaked its way up. The wooden crossbars were reinforced with iron and formed into giant spikes at the bottom. If the rope to the gate were cut as a man rode under, it would impale him and his horse under the deadly weight.

Everything about Battlewar Castle had been designed for war, just like all else in their land—from the long battlements that stretched around the main castle and Battlewar Town, to the secret passages and underground escape routes. This was the world Ronen had been born into. It was a world he knew well.

Yet, somehow, he always found it odd that on these occasions they rode not into the familiarity of battle, but to the only soft thing in a warrior's life. A woman.

Always before these ceremonies, something happened to his insides. As desperately as he wanted a woman to fill his bed and give him children, he was terrified that he'd actually find one. After what happened to Lord Sorin, Ronen wasn't in a hurry to find a mate.

"Relieve yourself beforehand. That was my mistake," Sorin said under his breath. It was the same advice he gave his younger brother each time they rode to the castle for a breeding ceremony. Since the loss of his first wife, Sorin's heart had been surrounded with bitterness. Well, loss was putting it lightly. The harlot Bianka had tried to seduce the whole of Firewall Castle before setting into motion the events that burned their ancestral home to the ground. When no one at Firewall would sate her, she ran away and threw herself at the enemy.

"There is no need to worry about me, Brother. I have better things to think of than binding myself to a woman," Ronen answered. A flurry of movement surrounded them as they rode into town. Women went about their work, busily preparing for the festival, ignoring the well-known sight of the warriors riding in. "At least coming here we'll get to feast on something other than dried meat and stale mead."

Intermingled with the peasants' homes in the outer bailey were a couple of barns, many workshops, small breweries and a large marketplace where the commoners sold their wares. Beyond the market, in the center of the city, a second, shorter wall encircled the inner bailey yard and castle. Contained within were the exercise yard where the knights trained, a small chapel, and the stables.

"Yea, there is that," Sorin agreed. Neither brother hurried to ride through town, instead occupying themselves with watching a group of children play. Five boys showed off for the attentions of a pretty girl. As one of the few female children, she'd be used to the notice. Even at a young age, the child would know how to manipulate the opposite sex to her whims. All females did.

Finally making it to the inner gate, Ronen sighed. A few of the soldiers glanced up, lifting their hands in greeting. The brothers nodded in unison, not needing to say another word as they solemnly made their way up the incline to the castle. It would all be over soon, and they'd be riding off to the battlefront at dawn.

# CHAPTER 2

Jayne glared at the guard's back, hating him with every fiber of her being. All four women prisoners stood in the corridor outside the cell, but down the hall from the guards. Jayne found it odd that they didn't escort them properly, one in front and one in back, but it wasn't like they could run anywhere.

Jerking hard at her bound wrists, she ignored the burn of the rope against her skin. The longer she struggled, the tighter the binds became. She'd already put up a fight when they first tried to restrain her. Lilith and Karre made a proper show of struggling as they were tied, but Paige merely lifted her arms and let them work.

"The way I see it," Lilith said, "we don't have any choice but to join forces and pool our knowledge. I think we should gather intelligence. None of us seem to be from this world, so that means they had to get us all here somehow. If we keep our ears open, we'll find out how. There might be a way out of here yet."

"I've already looked for fairy rings when I was in the forest," Paige said. "I didn't even find evidence of fairies. Though, I'm not surprised. Fairies don't like wars and this place is nothing but one giant battlefield. I think my journey here was a one-way trip."

"Fairy rings?" Karre snorted with soft laughter.

"What?" Paige asked, looking around at the others. "Isn't that how you all got here?"

Jayne frowned. Fairies? Those things actually existed? She remembered vague tales of them from childhood. They were said to be horrible little creatures who, unlike Paige described, liked war, had supernatural powers and were to be avoided at all costs. If those mortal hellions were their only hope for escape, they were all in trouble.

"No more talking. They're ready for you," the guard announced, motioning his fist forward. "Let's go. March."

---

"Bring in the firsts so they may make their choice." As the guard, Brock, made the announcement, Ronen looked up from where he'd been staring at the tips of his boots. A crescendo of laughter and cheering washed into the passageway from those gathered in the great hall to watch the ceremony. Being one of the six "firsts", it was Ronen's privilege to have first choice of the women awaiting them. He didn't plan on taking the honor.

"Any word from the front?" Ronen asked Sorin, who stood behind him in line. He fell into step behind a limping Sir Aidan, as they made their way forward. Behind Sorin, Sir Rian, Sir Vidar and Lord Serik awaited their chance to find a mate. Each man wore a different colored long tunic, reaching to the knees, over tight brown breeches. Woven belts wound their waists, the end straps hanging along the right thighs. "The scouts should have reported back by now."

"No, they must be delayed." Sorin kept his voice quiet.

"I have a man on the gate watching," Lord Serik put forth. "He's to notify me at once."

"I head for the battlefront near Spearhead as soon as this is finished," Sir Vidar said. "If any of you have messages..."

His words tapered off as they walked into the main hall. A high table had been set with metal goblets and pitchers of mead and ale. Like the rest of the castle, the hall had been designed over centuries of careful planning and fine tuning. The large fireplace along a far wall radiated enough heat to warm the hall. The immensely thick stone insulated loud noises from the outside. Woven tapestries lined the walls in strips of material, showcasing coats-of-arms and important religious and political symbols.

Ronen first saw the other warriors, as they watched from the rows of tables spread out over the hall's floor. Some wore lightweight tunics, others leather jerkins like the guards, others light chainmail and pieces of armor, and still others wore no shirt at all. The effects of battle could be seen proudly displayed on their flesh—gruesome scars and tattoos of honor. Mixed in with the men were their women. Tight corset tops and flowing skirts had been designed to tease the Starian male's overactive senses.

When the Divinity otherworlders first approached them in the midst of battle, the Starians had almost slain the foreigners where they stood. They believed the oddly dressed creatures to be allies to the Caniba tribes. After much negotiation, investigation, a little bit of pleading by the Divinity scouts, and hours of council meetings, an alliance was formed with the otherworld beings. Divinity wished for samples of the blue mineral water, water that stayed warm no matter how long it sat away from another heat source. The blue water springs ran deep and wide, and there was no shortage of the mineral. Giving some away was a little enough consideration. In return, the Divinity leaders provided a resource much needed by the Starians—women.

As the firsts walked in, all gazes were focused in a single direction, toward the four women who'd been brought to Battlewar Castle's main hall. Out of the women Divinity sent, three were chosen as being of the right temperaments to stay. The new blood was just one of the reasons all the firsts were of high military rank or distinction.

Despite the fact that he'd relieved himself twice before coming down to banquet, Ronen found his body stirring with the thought of softer company. Denial wasn't easy for men as hot blooded as they were, and the mortality of war tended to make every second count.

His eyes turned to the women in curiosity. He hid a smile. The firelight shone through the white of their gowns, outlining their bodies in perfect temptation. He glanced over all of them, not really seeing their faces. His cock stirred, begging him to reconsider his decision. What was he fighting? A soft vessel in his bed? Someone to please his every decadent whim? A woman to service his member in any way he chose—sucking him, finishing him, offering every inch of herself to him? Ah, but to wake up in the morning and be able to go to the adjoining bedroom to have his morning arousal sucked out with soft, wet lips. To have a woman bathe him, using her hands to cleanse every inch of his body. Oh, the nights! To be able to bend her over and pound away in a tight, wet sheath. Ronen nearly came just thinking about it.

No. He had to stop thinking about sex. Ronen knew he had to stick with his decision. Like Sorin, he could stay strong. The men of Firewall would not take brides. Never.

"Mine."

*What?*

Ronen glanced around in surprise. The voice sounded like his brother's, booming over the hall. Surely, no. It couldn't be...

"Sorin?" Ronen whispered, glancing at the place next to him behind the table. His brother had stopped walking before reaching his seat.

"Mine," Sorin repeated.

Ronen couldn't believe his ears. He followed Sorin's line of vision to the women. His brother ignored those in the stunned hall as he made his way to a pretty blonde with wide, frightened eyes. At least the woman wasn't a fool. With Sorin looming over her, she should be scared.

"Brother?" Ronen questioned, knowing the shock had to be evident in his voice. How could it be? That very day Sorin instructed him to stay strong and not fall for a woman's enchanting ways.

The skin at the back of his neck prickled. Someone watched him. Ronen glanced away from his brother only to find sinfully dark eyes studying him. His breath caught. Before when he'd looked at the women, he'd stared lustfully at their bodies. How could he have missed those bewitching eyes? That lush mouth parted in steady breath?

"You are mine." Sorin grabbed the blonde woman's ropes and held them tight, laying unmistakable claim.

Ronen barely noted the sounds of shock as murmurs ran over the crowd. His heart beat loud in his ears. Every nerve in his body shot with awareness. He'd seen women, but never had one struck him with such potent sexual awareness. Never had one made him want to throw her down, draw his tunic aside and begin wildly thrusting into her at the high table, not caring who watched.

What bewitching spell was this? He must fight it.

The herald made a weak noise, finally breaking the hushed tones of the crowd as he announced, "Rejoice, Lord Sorin has chosen!"

The statement came out more like a question than an announcement. Cheering erupted and still Ronen barely noted anything but the dark woman's steadfast gaze. She was tall and slender with flawless bronzed skin. Though she didn't move, he guessed she'd be graceful by the way she held her shoulders back and her neck long. She blinked, glancing to Sorin and the blonde before her gaze swept back to him.

Ronen smiled, hoping she'd return his lustful look. She didn't, but she didn't frown either. Commotion erupted and the woman turned her back to him to watch a fight in the crowd. It was as he suspected. She moved with poise and grace. This woman knew her body and how to use it.

"Come with me," Sorin ordered loudly, tugging his new wife behind him as he led the way from the main hall. He didn't even stay to feast with the others.

"Brother," Ronen insisted one last time, still not believing his own eyes. The mighty Lord Sorin, his respected brother, had fallen. Again.

*Women will be the death of us, Brother. You said so yourself.*

"It is done, Ronen," Sorin answered before disappearing completely. "Tell Sera to send food to my chambers."

*Ronen, hmm...*

Jayne glanced between the two brothers, feeling sorry for poor Lilith. Lord Sorin was a giant amongst men, at least physically, and his ill humor left much to be desired. By the look on his face, it was quite possible Lilith was in for a beating. Feeling something akin to her days in the orphanage, a kind of helpless longing to join arms with her sisters and fight oppression, she took a deep breath. There was nothing she could do for Lilith. Childhood taught her that harsh lesson. The woman would have to survive whatever was coming to her and get past it. Jayne had her own problems.

She turned her attention forward. Sorin's brother seemed much more malleable. Plus, he already seemed to take an interest in her. The knight had stopped just short of drooling all over the hall floor as he looked at her chest.

*Ronen. Easy target. Not at all hard like his brother.*

Jayne had watched the firsts as they walked into the hall. The first one seemed too bitter and more interested in pointedly ignoring them. Sorin chose Lilith. Guess the man had a thing for blondes. Ronen's interest was obvious. By the way he eyed all the women's forms, he was just horny and looking for a place to find release. The fact annoyed her a little, but she assured herself she had no reason to care. Men got horny. It was the way of things. Besides, he meant nothing to her. Then there were the last three knights—two of whom seemed more interested in each other than the women and one who appeared disinterested in everything.

*Ronen it is. Besides, handling one is better than taking on many.*

Horny she could work with, perhaps even enjoy, especially when the man had the body of a warrior. Thick muscles held a tightly constructed frame, forming the perfect specimen of masculine beauty. But unlike the others, he had an ease to his movements. Dark waves framed his face, falling to his shoulders. He looked a lot like his brother, only shorter and less menacing. Then there were his eyes, dark and deep and expressive. She'd have to be careful of those eyes.

Jayne preferred to fight with her fists, but feminine wiles could work just as well. She let a small smile curl her lips. People around her talked, but she ignored them, focusing all her concentration on what she was doing. She kept her sights on her target. Ronen made a move to sit, but froze mid-action at her look.

*That's right, sunbeam, I'm looking at you.*

Stepping out of line, she walked right for him. Jayne let her hips sway, being sure to keep her back to the firelight. The action wasn't lost on Ronen. His eyes went straight to her waist.

Jayne felt the gaze of the crowd on her, but that didn't make her nervous. She was used to an audience. Still watching him, she stepped up the two stairs to reach the high table and lifted his goblet of liquor. With her hands bound, it was hard to hold on to the goblet, but she managed. Ronen practically fell into his chair. Closing her eyes, she drank deeply, purposefully letting little trails of liquid slide down her neck and into the ugly white gown's bodice. Jayne ignored the burning sensation that numbed her tongue and heated her throat and stomach.

When she finished, she set the goblet back down and licked her lips. Ronen's eyes followed the gesture, his mouth agape. Jayne put her bound hands on the table, leaned across the wooden top and stated, "Mine."

A round of gasps met her declaration. She was pretty sure by the look on Ronen's face that no woman had pulled this little stunt before. Well, they were sorely mistaken if they thought she was just going to stand there and be a timid little creature awaiting the first guy who decided he wanted to fuck her.

"Pardon me?" the man managed weakly, glancing back and forth as if he couldn't believe what he'd heard and needed outside confirmation.

She'd shocked him. Good. She would twirl his mind around in so many circles he wouldn't be able to see straight. By the time she was done with him, he'd try to conquer the entire country of Staria if she demanded it.

"Mine," she declared even louder.

He looked down at her chest before drawing his gaze back to her eyes. Ronen shook his head in denial. "It does not work—"

"Sunbeam, I'm sure it works just fine," she whispered, giving a meaningful glance down to his crotch. Was she mistaken or was Mr. Happy poking his head up to play?

"What?" He looked at his lap, jumping a little. "Of course that works—"

Laughter broke out at the head table, cutting him off. His lips pressed tightly together.

Jayne pointed at the man who'd made Sorin's announcement. "Say it."

"My lady?" the man asked in surprise. Jayne rolled her eyes. Had none of these men ever seen a strong-willed woman before? "Lord Ronen, shall I...?"

"Say mine, Lord Ronen." Jayne leaned closer, parting her lips. Keeping her tone sultry and filled with erotic promise, she panted, "Say it. Say Jayne is mine."

She waited. His lips parted, as if he would answer but couldn't. He stared at her, stunned into obvious silence.

Without giving him warning as to her intentions, Jayne grabbed Ronen's face and jerked him to her. Her body fell across the tabletop and her elbows banged into the hard wood a little too firmly, but she ignored the little hints of pain. She'd expected the kiss to be a cold, calculated form of seduction. What she didn't expect was the rush of warm pleasure that started where their mouths met and ended in her toes. It was meant to be a quick, playful kiss, but it soon turned into more.

Jayne opened her mouth, sucking his bottom lip between hers. He tasted like liquor and something else she couldn't quite name. At first, he remained stunned, not kissing her back, but then his tongue slid into her mouth, rubbing and exploring. Their lips sawed together, rough and just a little awkward as they learned each other's rhythm.

Jayne gripped him tighter, becoming aware of her awkward position as she tried to hold onto his face for support. A utensil of some sort poked her ribs, digging in uncomfortably. The sound of cheering rushed over them, as the men from the lower tables went crazy with good-natured laughter and approval. Jayne was used to the crowds, to discomforts and pain. But she wasn't used to a mouth that tasted like his, or lips that felt so firm and good.

Her body tingled, each nerve ending seeming to fight for attention. But he didn't touch her, didn't grab her back, only returned the heated kiss she'd initiated. Well aware that her plan was quickly backfiring and she'd soon be lost to his touch and begging for things she didn't want to beg for, she pushed back. Breathing hard, she whispered to him, "Mine. Say mine. Say Jayne is mine."

"Mine," Ronen mouthed, as if entranced. He licked his lips slowly before he cleared his throat. Nodding, he repeated with more force so the cheering hall could hear, "Mine. Lady Jayne is mine."

"Good boy," Jayne blew him a quick kiss and stood, hoping she effectively put on a playful, unconcerned air. Inside, she still trembled. His taste was still on her tongue, teasing her with the promise of more.

*Get control, Jayne,* she ordered herself harshly. *It is time to perform. It is time to fight.*

Years of fighting in the ring and living as she did, trained her to quickly get all her emotions under control. He took her by surprise once with his taste, but now that she knew it, she would not let it happen again. Jayne turned to the announcer and arched a brow. Forcing a smile she didn't feel, she said, "Well? Get on with it."

"Rejoice!" the man called. "Lord Ronen has also chosen. The house of Firewall is complete. This is truly a day blessed by the gods!"

The hall broke out in a mixture of cheering and encouragement. Jayne winked at the crowd, waving audaciously to give them the performance they wanted. Just like her fans, none of these men really cared about her or the other brides. They wanted a show, something to gossip about later. And Jayne was always good at giving the crowd exactly what they paid for. Jayne suppressed a mocking laugh as she lowered her hand and turned to Ronen. *Poor, poor, Ronen. You're so out of your league.*

Ronen endeavored to slow his racing heart. Never in the history of his people had a woman stood up and announced her choice. But today, at this ceremony, it had happened to him. Lady Jayne chose to be his wife. She chose him. She wanted him. And she didn't hesitate, or doubt, or hold back. She sang her desire to the world, stroking his masculine pride for all to see, laying claim to him with her lips. Ah, those lips, so full, so pleasurable. Perhaps the gods knew he'd hesitate to say the words himself and gave her voice to initiate the claim. Either way, she belonged to him.

Ronen grinned. *Mine.*

The war gods smiled upon him for his deeds in battle and rewarded him with a gorgeous woman with an animalistic appetite to fuel his. He'd felt the envious eyes of the others as he whisked his new bride away to his chambers in the Mace Tower. None would dare to touch her, no matter how much they wanted to.

He breathed deeply, panting as if it had taken all his strength to walk the winding stairwell. Already he could envision tearing the clothes from her body, finding the soft womanly flesh, those secret crevices and gentle slopes only a lover could touch. He tried not to let his eagerness show, but he found himself slamming the door shut behind him.

"I hope this meets with my lady's approval." Ronen motioned around his tower room. None of the Starian men took pains to decorate their chambers and he was no different. A few necessary staples graced the room—a large bed with thick fur blankets, a weapons' wall to display and hold the majority of his belongings, the fireplace, a thickly cushioned chair and a trunk for the rest of his belongings. He motioned toward the far door next to his bed. "That door leads to your room."

"You live here?" she asked, her voice losing some of the smoky seduction of before.

"When I am here," he answered, wondering how long until she kissed him again. This time, she wouldn't stop. He wouldn't let her. "Normally I live at the battlefront or at Firewall Castle, my family home, before it burned to the ground."

"Firewall burned down?" Her mouth twisted slightly, and he

wasn't sure he appreciated the humor she seemed to find at the irony.

He stiffened defensively. "It will be rebuilt when the resources can be spared."

Jayne's face sobered and she nodded, guarding her expression from him. Instantly, the playfulness came back, and he realized it was a practiced look, a defense, a way to hide her true emotions from the world around her. He wondered at it and opened his mouth to speak, but her words stopped him.

"This will do, I've stayed in worse." She made a show of walking around his room, touching his things with the delicate tips of her fingers. Each seductive brush sent an erotic shiver over his flesh, as if she marked all he was as her own. She ran her index finger over the long center indent of a sword. When she reached the end, she jerked her finger away, making a small noise of surprise. She stuck the digit between her lips and sucked. Ronen nearly came undone at the sight.

"Sharp," she whispered around her finger, indicating she'd cut herself.

Firelight caressed her every move, casting shadows in stark relief across her face. The orange glow caught up in her eyes, giving them a temptress's gleam. He swallowed over the hard lump in his throat. She didn't look away, and for the first time in Ronen's life he felt helpless.

"You have a lot of weapons." Jayne let the finger slip from her lips as she stepped brazenly toward him. Ronen couldn't move, could barely breathe. "Are they decoration or do you know how to use them?"

"Men must be..." His breathing deepened, and he could barely concentrate to answer as her eyes glanced to the bed and back again. It had been so long since he'd been with a woman. The camp followers were few and the number of men they serviced were many. "Must be prepared for battle."

"That doesn't answer my question, Lord Ronen. I asked if you knew how to wield your weapons." She smiled, an achingly seductive look. The white material of her gown clung to her breasts, teasing him as it hid her body from view. A strand of inky black hair fell over her smooth cheek. Every thought in his head centered on the hard heat of his cock. Never had it felt so full and thick, practically throbbing for attention.

Ronen nodded. "Yea, of course. I have held a sword since the night I was born and..."

Sanity left him. How could he think with her lips so close, so full and lush? How could he concentrate when every breath brought him the scent of a clean field, untouched by bloodshed? Never had a woman chosen him above all others. Sure, the camp followers enjoyed his bed on those rare moments he'd been in their company, but he was one of many to them. Lady Jayne chose him to be her one and the very idea of it spun his brain around in his head.

She touched the middle of his chest. It was just a gentle fingertip but enough to send a shiver over his entire frame. Jayne ran the caress down his tunic, just like she had with the sword blade. Reaching his waist, she stopped right next to his erection. "All your weapons?"

He tilted his jaw down in affirmation, realizing what she'd meant. Her hand cupped his cock, wrapping it tight through the material of his tunic and breeches. Ronen balled his hands into fists, curious to see what she'd do next.

"Yea," he managed, completely disarmed.

Jayne licked her lips and tugged at her gown. She pulled the material over her head, inching it up slowly. Strong, tan calves grew into perfect thighs. Tradition dictated that she'd be naked under the gown, and he waited with bated breath to see the apex revealed. Naked, shaved flesh or soft black curls?

Absently, he tugged at the laces on his shoulder to loosen his tunic. The gown moved higher and his fingers stopped. Short curls formed into a strip to guard her sex, greeting him. Sleek muscles and rounded hips tapered to a flat stomach. With a deft swoop, she jerked the gown over her head. Breasts bobbed at the motion, a perfect handful. Dusky, round nipples puckered in the firelight, erect and begging for attention.

"Prove it," she ordered.

Ronen sprung into action, happy to obey. As he shoved his long tunic aside and tore at the laces to his breeches, she backed into the bed. He followed her, his pants falling over his boots to trap his feet. Jayne gasped, her eyes going to his full arousal.

No thoughts beyond the driving need to feel the warmth of her wet pussy passed through his mind. He needed her. He wanted her. He had to be inside her. Now.

Ronen pushed her shoulder and she landed on her back, her legs dangling over the side. The long strands of her hair spilled around her head, framing her gorgeous face. Her willingness was all the invitation he needed. Eagerly, he grabbed her legs, thrusting them open. Jayne's eyes widened in surprise. He wanted to take her then, hard and fast, but the bounce of her breasts caught his eyes. Leaning over, he buried his face between the soft mounds and groaned in pleasure. Her clean smell consumed him, scented by the distinct hint of her femininity.

He ran his hands over her sides, trying to explore everywhere at once. The urgency inside him wouldn't let him slow. Not yet. Not now.

Ronen pulled a taut nipple between his lips and sucked. She arched and moaned, grabbing his hair and tugging hard. The sound of her pleasure drove his aggressive lips on.

"Ah, in all the bloody battles of Staria," he cursed in frustration. His lips wanted more, but his cock refused to wait. The heat of her sex radiated onto his stomach. The call was too much for his libido to handle. Roughly, he grabbed her hips and dislodged his mouth from her breast. The wet nipple glistened, scorched with the orange firelight.

Ronen fumbled with his tunic, growling when he couldn't move the front of it fast enough. Mindless with passion, he brought himself to her sex. Jayne said something, but he couldn't hear her through the rushing sound of blood in his ears. The thick tip of his cock head slid along her moist heat, parting the curls. She felt so right, so slick and hot and ready.

He surged forward, pressing his cock into the velvet length of her sex. Ronen grunted, slowing in astonishment as the tight muscles of her pussy clamped down on him. Withdrawing, he worked his hips in easier thrusts, going deeper with each pass, not wanting to hurt her.

Jayne wrapped her legs around Ronen's waist, hooking her feet behind his ass. She forced him into her deep, making a strange noise as he penetrated her completely. His feet braced on the ground for leverage as he began to thrust. Her pussy clamped around him, giving the perfect amount of resistance.

Ronen felt like an untried youth, fumbling his way through his first time. A voice inside his head screamed at him to take his time, to enjoy the moment, but the desire raged and demanded satisfaction.

Jayne held onto his arm with one hand and rubbed her sex with the other. All the while, her legs controlled his movements. Ronen gripped the fur bedding, rocking wildly. He slammed into her, making her perfect breasts bounce. There was so much more he wanted to do to her. He tried to hold off, to stop the inevitable surge of release.

Muscles trembled and clamped down. He lost himself, spilling his seed with a hard jerk inside her body. His mouth opened wide and he groaned hoarsely. The loud sound echoed around them.

Jayne gulped for breath. As they had sex, her mind strayed from her purpose and she'd actually enjoyed herself. She refused to believe the fact meant anything, reasoning that it had been a very long time since she'd been with a man. And so what if she enjoyed it? Sex was meant to be pleasurable. It didn't mean she couldn't manipulate the man on top of her afterward.

"I would do that again and slower," Lord Ronen said, pushing up from her, "but I am expecting a report from the front lines."

*What?*

Jayne sat up in surprise.

"Your every comfort should be met next door. Look around and make it your own. If you've brought any personal items with you, they'll be delivered by the maids. A seamstress will come around. Please, direct her to make any gowns you'd like. I can well afford to clothe you." Ronen leaned over to grab his pants, pulling them up so he could re-lace them at his waist. His businesslike tone annoyed her.

*What?! Where do you think you are going?*

"But..." Jayne frowned, pushing up from the bed. Her first instinct was to cover her nakedness, but she refrained.

His eyes moved over her. "You wish for more? I will come back after my meeting to attend you."

"Wait, I think we need to talk." Jayne crossed in front of him, blocking his path to the door. This wasn't happening. *He* was dismissing *her*? Men did not dismiss her. She was Jayne Hart.

Ronen tilted his head. "I see nothing to discuss. If you have questions, the maids will help you find your way."

"I mean about this," Jayne waved around the room, "and us."

Did she just say that? Why in the world was she sounding all girly and clingy? What did she care if he didn't want to stay and cuddle in the aftermath? It's not as if they meant anything to each other.

"The choice was made." He tried to walk around her. Jayne again blocked him, forgetting her plan to manipulate him in her irritation. So what if she'd been planning on leaving him? His actions were unacceptable. "I see nothing to discuss. You are mine."

"Then I change my mind. There is no decision." Jayne put her hands on her hips, trying to rankle him. "I unchoose you."

Ronen's eyes narrowed in instant rage, the easy expression in his gaze fizzling out like water under fire. His shoulders tensed as he inhaled a deep, ragged breath. One very important fact became clear to her in that instant. Jayne underestimated the man before her. She'd seen him as the weakest of the pack, the one she could manipulate and push over. But she'd mistaken his easy manner for vulnerability. How could she have been so off in her assessment of her chosen opponent?

"You cannot change your mind," he growled, stalking her as she darted out of his way. "Law forbids it."

"I don't recognize your laws," she answered, just as loudly. Subtlety was not her strong suit and there was no point in searching for the trait now. With a forced laugh, she said, "I really don't recognize any dimension's laws."

"Tradition forbids it!"

"Curse your traditions. I don't recognize them either."

"*I* forbid it!" Ronen declared, his arms rising to the sides.

Jayne reacted on pure instinct, doing the only thing she knew to do. She drew back her hand and swung, saying more with her fist than she could with flustered words. How dare he treat her like property? Like some prisoner he could command? She was not some child to be locked away in an orphanage, kept like a dog to be beaten into obedience at the whim of her keepers.

Jayne had refused to think that there might be no escape until that moment, when his eyes flashed and his voice lifted. She didn't like being helpless. Plan one seduction-manipulation had been a complete failure.

*Then it is time for a new plan. I'll go with what I know best.*

Shock filtered over his expression for a millisecond before contact. Ronen didn't try to stop her as fist met flesh. His head snapped back, but he didn't stumble. Jayne leapt onto the bed, expecting him to make a fight of it. Once she subdued him, if she subdued him, she'd make a run for it. Giant prairies and Paige's monster-filled forest wouldn't stop her from trying to escape. Even if she had to live in the dirt for the rest of her days, she'd do it on her own terms. Free.

As she reached for a knife on his wall, his soft words stopped her. "You signed your deal. You cannot escape it and neither can I. We are together in this."

Wondering at the way he phrased his words, she turned. Already his eyes swelled with the red of her hit. Why wasn't he fighting back? She knew the punch had to hurt. The bioengineered, metal "boxing gloves" Divinity had grafted beneath her skin would see to that. He should have been raging in anger at her attack. Jayne's hand again automatically started to reach for the wall of weapons, but halted midair, unsure how to proceed. Why wasn't he fighting?

"Perhaps you should stay here in the room while your temper cools." Ronen grabbed her white gown from the floor and left, gripping it tight in his palm. As the door shut with a decisive thud, she stared after him in confusion.

"I've really underestimated you, Lord Ronen." Jayne bit her lip thoughtfully. Instead of grabbing a weapon, she went to look inside the room he said was for her. The furnishings were nice, if a person was into the domestic scene. Dark wood, simply carved, made up the furniture. The bed looked to be the same size as Ronen's, with white fur on the coverlet instead of gray. Jayne would never sleep in such a fluffy concoction. A dressing table arranged with little colorful bottles stretched along one wall next to a circular inlet with tiny slit windows and an oversized chair. The only way in or out was through Ronen's chamber.

Having no desire to go inside and explore, she shut the door. Air stirred around her naked body. If he thought stealing her clothes was going to keep her locked in her tower, then he'd sorely misjudged her. Striding to the trunk at the end of his bed, she flipped it open and began to dig.

*How dare he walk out on me!*

# CHAPTER 3

"These foreign women have bewitching powers. We should never have entered into an agreement with the other-worlders."

Ronen listened to his brother's bitter tone and nodded in agreement. Sorin fared little better in his choice of mate, already regretting his hasty actions as he glared at those gathered in the hall. Tension rolled from the lord's shoulders and Ronen knew better than to ask for details. When Sorin was angry, it was best to leave him be. One irritating move and he'd rip a man's head from his body. But, for all that rage, he would never lay a rough hand on his new bride. Even with Bianka, he'd never struck her and that woman deserved it.

Ronen related to the feeling and practically growled at the shadowy reflection in his pale yellow drink. His desire had been sated, somewhat, and replaced by fury. She tried to get out of their arrangement. How dare Jayne choose him, kiss him like that in front of everyone at the breeding ceremony and then try to leave him. This was his life, not a game. His stomach tightened into big knots. Only one thing had changed from her decision to take him as a mate. They'd had sex. By the teeth of the damned, it had been awhile. Had he truly been such a bad, clumsy lover? The idea that he'd failed kept him from repeating the act a second time, no matter how enthusiastically his cock wished for him to run back up the Mace Tower stairs. He needed to calm the lust running rampant in his blood so he could concentrate and do it right.

"Witches," Ronen muttered, waving to a maid to refill his goblet. As the woman dared to make her way to the ill-tempered brothers, Sorin motioned Sir Rian to join them at the table. By the un-tortured look of his expression, Ronen assumed the man hadn't chosen a woman.

*Lucky knight. Would that we had been so smart.*

"Any word from Lord Serik's man? Do the Caniba armies march against the forces at Spearhead?" Sorin asked.

"They do not march yet, but Lord Martin suspects it will be soon." Rian took a seat next to Sorin, his steady brown gaze meeting both men briefly. "Sorceress Magda's scouts were captured in the southern marshes, but at the loss of two good men—Richard of Daggerpoint and Peeter of Fallenrock. They died well and were not taken by those cannibals. Sir Vidar goes to lead the interrogations. He has already left with his new bride."

"Vidar, too?" Ronen let loose a long breath. It would seem all three of the foreign women had been claimed, not that it surprised him. Women were scarce and men were lonely. The fourth, Lady Paige, had been an arguably spiteful gift from the fairies and would go home with her husband, Sir Aidan, to be punished as he saw fit. Perhaps the foreign women were defective and should be sent back to their worlds. Surely Divinity only gave away those they needed to be rid of. The Starians should have known the deal was too sweet an offer. Blue mineral water for willing wives? More like water for witches.

"Yea, Vidar, as well." Rian agreed. "Though he looked about as pleased as the two of..." The words tapered off and Rian gave the brothers a sheepish look.

"And Aidan?" Sorin asked.

"He did not look well when he left Battlewar." Rian sighed, leaning forward to grab an abandoned goblet at the head table and lift it to a maid. She nodded, running to fetch him a clean one. "Nor did Lady Paige."

"This is a bad year for finding mates," Ronen put forth grimly. "Perhaps we should cancel the ceremonies, especially those involving the otherworlders."

"The decisions are made," Sorin broke in, giving Ronen a look of warning. He would not like any hint of dishonorable thoughts, especially not in front of witnesses. As the oldest brother, he took their familial duty very seriously. "There is no reason to contemplate them."

Rian nodded once in agreement. "Though, it does not mean we have to choose the women they send."

"What other news?" Ronen inquired.

"Not much else. Lines hold strong on both sides. Vidar hopes to discover where the Sorceress's encampment lies. We suspect she is in the Hanging Forest, but we can't find any who will speak of her. All they say is she lives in the ground like a serpent, rising up from the earth to feed. It's impossible to tell her numbers, and Sir Fredrick is still not the same since being held her prisoner. We must leave him in a room lined with mattresses to keep him from bashing his own skull against the stone walls of his chambers. He must eat without trencher or knife and a guard watches him at all times." Rian didn't reveal anything they didn't already know, more or less, and the news of Fredrick saddened Ronen's heart.

One of the self-proclaimed queens of the Caniba tribes, Sorceress Magda was as elusive as she was cruel. It was whispered that she studied the black arts and her followers, before being allowed to bear the mark of her soldiers, were made to dance with the serpent. Whoever endured the serpent's poison and lived was allowed to serve and they did so with blind obedience and obsession. Over the last four years, she'd been one of the more aggressive Caniba factions attacking the borders.

"We should ride to the borderlands," Ronen said, lightly touching his bruised eye. He'd had worse injuries in battle, but somehow this one stung more. "We will be of more use there."

"We have not been summoned," Sorin lowered his voice to a

whisper, "and, unless the king orders otherwise, we will be forced to bring the women with us."

"Not if they become with child," Ronen reasoned, suddenly sorry he'd spoken the idea out loud. He wanted children, many of them, but he was certain the woman abovestairs wouldn't be so inclined.

Sorin tensed, a severe frown crossing his features. "We would do better to pray for war, Brother."

"Witches," Ronen grumbled, falling into the comfort of his foul mood. "The gods have cursed us with witches."

---

"Yea, these be a poor lot of women," a brunette maid grouched as she lifted her arms over her head to hang a fresh tapestry in the long corridor. Jayne stayed crouched beside a door inset into the stone, shaded from their view. A large metal urn on the floor reflected the blurry figures just enough that Jayne could watch what they were doing.

"What do you expect, Nan? I told you foreigners wouldn't suit our men as well as we." A second servant laughed with pride. Her thick red hair was piled high on her head. "Only Starian women know how to properly please Starian men."

"It's too bad Lord Sorin and Lord Ronen didn't take their two south like the others," Nan said. "I wonder if Ronen's wench is anything like Lady Lilith."

"That one thinks she's the Princess of the Black Tower, or my name isn't Hannah. Barely said a word to us while we were up there. Princess Lilith, that one. Well, I will show her princess." Hannah lifted her foot and pretended to kick.

"Barely did a thing to poor Lord Sorin," Nan giggled. "Did you see the poor knight walking funny like his serpent was still full of venom? How hard is it to lie back and let a man have his way? I daresay I looked forward to an ease in that nobleman's temper. Now she's gone and made him worse. He practically strangled Sera in the stairwell. She was lucky those stairs are so close to the kitchen so we would have been able to hear her screams."

Hannah gave a dark laugh, stepping back to eye the tapestry on the wall. She nodded once in approval of it. "Don't you worry about that. I took her clothes out with the old bedding. One look at her naked body, even one as skinny as hers, and Lord Sorin will take what he needs from her, willing or no. That will cool his beast."

"Should we check on Ronen's wench?" Nan asked, as the women walked away.

"He's drinking with his brother and did not order us up to his tower. Let his wench fend for herself. If his dark mood is any sign, she knows nothing of spreading her legs either." Hannah laughed, prompting Nan to join her. They lifted up the rolled tapestry they'd just replaced and carted it off down the hall under their arms. "In some ways it serves the lords right for choosing otherworlders from the Divinity deal. It's not what the gods intended for our people. Had they been patient and waited for a blessing, they'd have been given a woman who knows how to move her hips."

*Like you're some prize to have in bed, miserable cat.* Jayne frowned after the women, as she pushed to her feet. *I know how to please a man. Lord Ronen wasn't complaining when I got done with him.*

Thinking of how desperate Ronen had been only made her eager to turn around and return to his bed. The fear of being trapped stopped her. She could not stay here and be some man's love slave—even if the mere thought of him caused her legs to tremble. The fact that she wanted him made her fear him all the more. Thankfully, in such a world as this, the man would never come to care for her. He probably wouldn't even bother searching for her should she run. Or, if he did, he'd soon give up.

Since Ronen confiscated her gown, she simply took one of his tunics—a long black affair with a red patch on the chest. The sleeves were too long so she cut them off to uncover her hands. Then she used one of the strips to tie her hair back away from her face and the other to sheathe the blade she had tied to her upper thigh with a piece of belt. The decorative jewel hilt of the knife would make for good barter should she have a need to trade it. The short boots she'd stolen from a laundry room pinched her toes but were better suited to running through a prairie than bare feet.

She resisted the urge to follow after the servants to give them a piece of her mind. Then again, she could always thank them for their gossiping help. With Karre and Paige out of the castle, it would mean she only had to find Lilith. Sure, she didn't really owe the woman anything and, by all reasoning, she could have left Lilith to fend for herself, but Jayne wasn't like that. When a child slipped through the orphanage's bars, they helped all they could through behind them. Besides, she didn't want to go it alone. Regardless of her strength and bravery, this was still a strange land and a strange people. Jayne could use all the friends she could get. Nothing made faster friends than two people fighting for the same cause—freedom.

Already she'd made slow progress through the castle. It would seem most of the occupants were in the main hall drinking in celebration, so she stuck to the narrow passageways and mazelike tunnels that wound around the central room. The blue-gray stone walls and minimal decorations made it hard to navigate—especially if the maids continued to change the tapestries.

Jayne had run into more than a few amorous couples in the act of "taking the venom out of the serpent". One pair, a knight and his busty mistress, went at it on a stairway leading down to utter darkness. Their clothes were simply pushed aside while they fucked hard and desperate, grunting like wild beasts. Another man found pleasure by his mistress's lips as she busied herself beneath the front flap of his long tunic. He kept his eyes closed, moaning softly as the shape of her head bobbed up and down beneath the green material.

By far the most salacious was the servant who took two men at once, sandwiched between them as one pressed his back into the wall. Jayne saw them through a cracked door, perfectly positioned as if they invited others to watch what they did. When she crawled past, she noticed that was exactly what was happening. A third man sat on a chair, stroking himself as he enjoyed the sexual exploits of the performers.

Jayne had been to wild parties before, but never on such a grand scale as this. There were more couples locked in various ways and not a one noticed her as she passed. Maybe this castle was a brothel of some sort and these soldiers were here on leave from their home dimension. Is that what happened? They paid the castle Madame to claim a woman in some strange custom in the front hall, took their fill of them and then left the woman for the next man? Did they know who she was? Was getting a chance to fuck the famous Jayne "The Sweet" Hart some sort of high-dollar draw? Rich men had offered her a lot of money in the past—not that she'd ever taken it. She'd seen women on the street who fell into such a life for the sake of survival. Jayne was surviving on her own. She didn't need to be a man's paid whore. But, with losing so much money in the last fight for Divinity, had they come up with a way for her to pay them back? She wondered how much Ronen paid for her. Was that why he hesitated when she lay claim? The whore wasn't supposed to pick her patron? Or had he been calculating the worth of her cost? Is that why he got mad? He'd paid for her and she was trying to renege on a deal she hadn't realized she'd made?

*I'm going to throw up.*

"All the more reason to find Lilith and get out of here," she said under her breath. Never having played the part of the prude, Jayne didn't relish the idea of being any man's permanent or temporary plaything. If luck were on her side, she'd find that kitchen and the Black Tower steps soon.

She hurried down several corridors, doing her best to navigate through the halls unseen. Slowing as she neared a sharp corner, she listened first and peeked second. The faint sound of padded footsteps caught her attention before being drowned out by a boisterous laughter from the main hall. She'd traveled along the back wall of the main hall, ending up on the opposite end of the castle. Jayne tensed, inching back, her legs ready to make a run for it should a boisterous knight happen upon her.

A woman appeared, dressed in a black tunic similar to the one Jayne now wore, only the sleeves were rolled instead of cut, and the lady had wrapped a belt around her midsection. Seeing the long, straight blonde hair, Jayne nearly laughed with relief. Lilith. It would seem luck did favor her. She suppressed the urge to make a sound and bit her lip.

Lilith appeared to be alone, as she glanced first at the noisy hall and then back the other direction. With no way to call out to her for fear of drawing attention, Jayne crept up behind her and slid her hand over the woman's mouth.

"Hey," Jayne whispered in her ear, pulling her back past the stairwell she'd emerged from into a hidden inlet.

Lilith tensed, jerking in alarm at the sudden attack. She began to claw at the hand over her mouth, but Jayne turned her around so they faced each other. Lilith instantly relaxed, though her eyes remained wary.

Pressing close in the tight space of the narrow alcove, Jayne glanced down meaningfully and gave a light laugh. "Looks like we shop at the same store."

Lilith followed Jayne's gaze downward, but didn't answer.

"I overheard the maids talking. I was about to come up to the tower to get you." She looked at Lilith's bare feet. "Couldn't find any shoes to steal? Follow me, there's a laundry room this way. They have shoes."

Still Lilith didn't answer. The poor thing looked terrified and completely out of her element. She almost felt sorry for those wide blue eyes. What had that giant of a man Lord Sorin done to her? Surely, he didn't break her spirit already? The maid said nothing happened between Lilith and Sorin, but seeing the woman's pale face, Jayne wasn't so sure. Some men had strange tastes.

Deciding scared company was better than none, she hoped to spur the woman into action and put her at ease. Jayne leaned forward and kept her voice low. She tugged on Lilith's arm. "Come with me. I promise Lord Sorin won't touch you again, but you have to make a fight of it."

"Wait." Lilith refused to move.

Damn those almost innocent blue eyes. They instantly drummed up protective, big-sister feelings inside of her. She'd seen that look on the faces of children as they came to the orphanage—scared, confused, hopeful and still capable of love. And then the years would hit them and Jayne would watch those eyes fade and the hope die. The death of the soul was worse than physical death and hurt a lot more.

"What did they do to you?" Lilith whispered, as if scared to hear the answer. "Did they hurt you?"

Jayne tried not to think about how great Ronen's body felt inside hers and lied, "No, they didn't touch me, but I don't want to give them the chance to."

How could she admit to what she'd done? Especially if someone had gotten paid for her to do it?

"What are you planning to do?" Lilith asked with a tinge of desperation.

"Karre and Paige have been taken south by a couple of the barbarians. With any luck, we'll be able to find them. Paige seems to know her way around this backwater place." Jayne again tried to pull her. "The timing is perfect. They're in there having a party and getting drunk. It will be dark soon. We'll find a way out of the castle and wait until nightfall. If we travel by dark, we should make it through the prairie to the forest. From there, by the grace of some miracle, we'll find a trail to follow—"

"You're going to escape?" Lilith jerked Jayne back, keeping her from leaving. "You can't, Jayne. I've talked to a few of the servants. If we displease them, I think they might kill us."

"They didn't kill Paige for running," Jayne reasoned.

"Yet," Lilith asserted. "How do you know that's not what they're taking her south for? You heard the guard. Her master might delve out a harsh punishment."

Jayne felt the color draining from her face. "What would you have us do? We can't stay here forever, waiting for them to get tired of us. What if they try to philter us like the others—whatever that means. What if they make us take on more men? If you saw what I saw walking these hallways, you'd know we have to run. I can't stay here and be a whore and that's exactly what I think this place is. A whorehouse."

"I was told the philter is a drug to make you forget you've been here. They said those women from the cell with us were sent home because they were unsuitable."

"I don't think that'll work for us. We've been chosen to stay," Jayne drawled mockingly. Though, it did sting that those whiny bitches from the cell got to go home and they were stuck here. Maybe she should learn to cry and pout more. Perhaps then Ronen would ship her off to be rid of her. Jayne wondered if she even had it in her to muster up fake tears. Fists were much more her thing.

"I think we should stay in the castle for now. Sorin didn't seem too keen on passing me around to all the men." Lilith reached to touch her shoulder lightly. "Are you sure you weren't hurt? Did your man...? Did he make you...?"

"Ronen? No. He didn't try to pass me out." Jayne said, only to add silently, *yet*. "I would have ripped off his balls had he tried."

Lilith's eyebrows lowered in thought as she reasoned, "I can learn more here in civilization than in the woods. If we keep our heads low and try to behave, maybe we'll find a way home. I think we'll have better luck here at a castle than in the wild. Besides, running is too big of a gamble. How will we survive in the wilderness? How will we eat? What kind of animals are in the forest? Poisons? Flora and fauna? Insects? What about the people the Starians are fighting? What's out there could be much, much worse than what is in here. Paige seemed really scared when she spoke of the monsters."

"Paige could be lying. This castle could be a theme place and beyond the compound is a thriving society with technological advances. Whatever it is, I can't stay here. I'm not scared of dying," Jayne put forth grimly. "But I will never live as some man's slave. Please come with me."

Jayne followed Lilith's contemplative gaze as she looked to the main hall. They heard a low murmur of conversation with the random bouts of laughter filtering in. If they were going to leave, they needed to go now while the men were distracted with their party. Maids or knights could happen upon them at any moment.

"I can't go with you," Lilith decided. "I'm taking my chances here."

"Do you have a plan?"

Lilith nodded, not looking too sure of herself. "I think so. If I find a way to escape, I'll do my best to let you know about it."

"And if I do, I'll try to send word," Jayne glanced down and smiled, "in a pair of shoes."

"Good luck to you then." Lilith looked as if she might hug her, but stopped and instead held out her hand.

"And to you." Jayne clasped it briefly. "Don't let them break you. One way or another, we're going home. I promise."

---

"She is my wife." Ronen stumbled into the wall and frowned at the stone. How did that get so close? He pushed away, continuing up the Mace Tower stairwell, only to hit the other side. When did the stairwell become so narrow? "I will grab her, shake her and tell her, 'you are my wife, my lady, um, my Lady Jayne'."

It was a plan. A great plan. A brilliant plan. She'd have to listen to his decree. He was a lord after all and a great leader. Men had to listen to him, why not his bride?

"Ugh," Ronen grabbed his head as his vision swam. He would declare his position and then to bed. Tomorrow he'd talk to Sera about the mead. It should not have been so strong. He'd only had...

Ronen frowned. How much did he drink? He started to sit down on the stairs only to catch himself. Why didn't Sera insist he eat something? Or had she? He vaguely remembered throwing a tray of food onto the hall floor.

"Jayne." He'd forgotten in all his irritation to order food sent to their room for her. Hopefully, Sera remembered. The servant was usually good about those things. It's why she held the position of honor in Battlewar Castle. "Jayne will be rested and fed, and now it will be time for her to listen as I explain her role as my wife. Starting with my bed."

The thought quickened his steps as he hurried the rest of the way to his chambers. Desire heated his liquored blood, causing his skin to tingle and his cock to lift high and proud. He opened the door, his eyes eagerly seeking the bed. She wasn't there. Then again, why would she be? This was not her room. Crossing over the floor with purpose, he opened the door to where she would be sleeping.

"Jayne," he announced, pointing his finger into the darkness. "You are my wife and that means something."

She didn't answer. The fireplace in her room had not been lit so he couldn't see beyond the soft glow coming from his own chamber.

"Jayne," he continued, holding onto the door frame. "You are a Lady of Firewall and there will be no more talk of you leaving me. The decision is made. I understand that there is nothing in the tradition of warriors choosing women from a group they just met that ensures a great, great, ah..." He frowned, blinking hard. "A great joining of two households, er, people. What I mean to say is at least I didn't raid your village like my ancestors used to do, grab you and cart you off to my bed. And you chose me for a husband without having ever met me. That must mean something. I didn't ask for a wife, didn't pray to the gods for one. You just happened."

Still she said nothing. It was just as well she listened. He had much he wanted to get straight with her.

"Though, many of us agree the raids were easier. That way we did not have to leave the battlefront to bother with a ceremony so far north in the kingdom." He paused, shaking his head. What was he talking about? Oh, his wife. "You are my wife and the gods chose you for me as a reward to my great service in battle. They brought you from your otherworld and we will have sons and if so blessed daughters when I am not at war. I will take care of you and protect you."

Still nothing.

"I realize earlier I might have been overeager, but I should like to make that up now." Desire at the idea of bedding her curled within him, stirring his lust to settle heavy in the already thick mass of his cock. "We Starian men have needs and I would not have you turning me away from your bed, but, if you command it, I will leave you be. I am not a monster."

She didn't answer. Did that mean she accepted him? He took a step toward where the bed would be hidden in the darkness.

Reaching out, his fingers bumped into the mattress. Excitement pumped in his veins and he prayed to all his gods that he'd be able to satisfy her this time. His hands remembered the feel of her skin. His mind conjured the silk of her flesh, the softness of her breasts, the athletic perfection of her form.

Pulling out of his tunic, he tossed it aside. Ronen crawled onto the bed, feeling around for her. Whispering, his hands shook, as he admitted, "I would have happiness between us, Jayne, and perhaps, in time, affection. I know it's not required in a marriage, or even sought, but I would have us come to care for each other."

Why wouldn't she speak? He'd laid bare his soul, a feat harder than facing a hundred Caniba warriors in battle.

"Jayne?" His hand slid over the bed. The coverlet hadn't been ruffled. In disbelief, he kept searching. If she wasn't in here and she wasn't in his chambers, then...

The realization sobered him greatly. She wasn't there. He leapt from her bed. Running to his room, he grabbed an unlit torch and thrust it into the fire. Once lit, he went back to search for her. Torchlight cast over her unruffled bed and revealed the unused chair and vanity.

"Jayne?" he called, knowing he wouldn't receive an answer from the empty space. He checked his own room again, his gaze scanning over the bed and trunk. Finally, they landed on this weapons' wall to the spot where the jeweled blade he'd had since childhood should have been.

Ronen's first thought was the Caniba had snuck in and stolen her away. He quickly dismissed it. That was not how the Caniba fought. They attacked in the open, crazed man-eating beasts without reason or thought, driven by their primal needs. There was no way they'd slip through the gates, pass through town and a castle filled with knights and servants. Not looking and acting as they did —smelly, pelt-covered monsters with sunken eyes and sharpened teeth.

But if not their enemies, then it would mean she'd left him on her own. Hoping that she'd gone in search of food, or to explore, he rushed down the stairs still carrying his torch. He turned away from the main hall's entrance, going to the maze of halls running behind it. Seeing a servant, he handed her the torch. "Have you seen Lady Jayne?" At the woman's blank look, he clarified, "My wife. Have you seen her?"

The maid shook her head in denial. "No, my lord."

Ronen's heart beat heavily in his chest, echoing in the caverns of his ears. With each person who told him they hadn't seen her, the more panicked he became. The servants and guards joined in the search, spreading from inside the castle to the inner bailey.

Sera brought him herbs to help clear his head of the liquor, but clarity of thought only convinced him that Jayne had run away. Thoughts of his brother's first wife, Bianka, filled him with fear. What if he was cursed to relive Sorin's pain? Seeing the torture the evil woman had put Sorin through had torn at Ronen's heart. His brother had never been the same. A vital part of him had died, leaving a hard shell.

What if Jayne did to him what Bianka had done? What if she suffered the same fate?

In the very short time he'd been in her presence, Ronen didn't suspect the lady to be a selfish witch who drained the very life force from those around her. But then, Sorin had thought Bianka a tender heart in need of protection. Only later did her true, cruel nature come out. Her own people had shoved her into a fairy ring to be rid of her.

Ronen thought of what he'd been prepared to confess to his new bride, of his desire for something more, deeper, in their lives together. If the men were to find out it would be an embarrassment, let alone if word reached his older brother. How could he have been so stupid? How could he have bared his soul like that? It was a small blessing she hadn't heard, and he would not be making the same mistake twice.

"Ronen!" Sorin stormed across the torch lit bailey. Tension radiated from his stiff movements and he looked like he'd crawled through the very heart of Caniba. "What news is this?"

"Jayne is gone." Ronen took a deep breath, trying to hide the pain he felt at admitting the words out loud. "You were right. I should have stayed strong and not allowed her to influence my choice. Now I have dishonored—"

"No," Sorin stated, cutting him off. He put his hand on Ronen's shoulder, drawing him near as he quietly stated, "We will find her before she dishonors you or our family. Are any horses missing?"

"No." Ronen shook his head.

"Then she is on foot. With the celebration tonight it would have been easy for her to slip through town and out the gate without being noticed. None of us thought another bride would run from her wedding night so soon after Lady Paige. It will not happen a third time. Precautions will be made in the future." Sorin motioned his hand to a nearby page. "Our horses!"

Several of the men heard the command and hurried to order their mounts as well, without having to be asked to ride out.

"We will find her, Brother," Sorin assured him. "Feet cannot outrun horses, even if she has hours upon us. And, if you have to, you will lock her away in a tower to keep her safe. This will be made right."

Ronen didn't answer. He knew Sorin also thought of Bianka's escape. Only, with Bianka, they'd not found her in time. Firewall Castle had been closer to the borderlands and all who lived there were busy with the fire. By the time Sorin and Ronen were told of her disappearance, it was too late. She'd crossed over the Caniba border and propositioned one of their raiding parties. First, they took what she offered, then they took her valuables and her horses, and then they took her for food. It was a nightmarish day they would never forget.

"She is not Bianka," Sorin hissed, willing it to be so with the hard tone of his voice. Even so, his gaze wavered in its certainty. Turning, he yelled, "Twenty men. We ride!"

Ronen blinked, spurred into action as he strode to take his horse. Two pages arrived, carrying weapons from the armory for the brothers. Another handed Ronen a tunic shirt.

*By all the bloody battlefields, do not let the Caniba take her.*

“Good ride, my lords!” the young boys yelled, unable to hide their excitement. How little they understood what happened.

Ronen ignored them, grabbing the reins and swinging up before slipping on his shirt. Then, taking the weapons, he rode for the gate, letting the horse guide the way as he tightened the cross strap of the scabbard over his shoulder and across his chest to his waist. To himself, he cursed, trying to forget his fears as he held onto his anger. “My wife has run away. The gods truly frown upon me.”

# CHAPTER 4

As they rode through town, word spread about the missing bride and, with the peasants searching to find Jayne, she wouldn't be able to hide within the city walls. Ronen ordered six of the men to ride north to investigate the only trail leading away from Battlewar Castle. The treacherous route was an unlikely escape, but he would not leave ground uncovered. The underground tunnels and secret passages were locked away and too hard to get to without knowledge of the castle.

Ronen didn't speak as he led the remaining knights in the most logical direction—south to the Hanging Forest. The full moon shone bright over the prairie grasses, giving the knights enough to see by as they rode hard over the fields. So many people had passed that way over the years it was hard to distinguish fresh tracks in the night.

Sorin rode next to him, equally as quiet. He gripped his reins, forcing the animal faster as if he couldn't run from the castle fast enough. Ronen knew his brother well and could easily gather he ran from Lady Lilith. As head of the family, Sorin would be duty bound to capture the wayward Jayne, but he didn't have to look so inclined to do it.

The wind hit him hard, causing his hair to slap across his face. All the knights riding with them had trained at Battlewar as children. They knew the prairie and the forest. They would find her.

*I will find her.*

"She could not have gotten far on foot," Sorin yelled over the noisy wind. The horses naturally slowed as they neared the tree line. If they rode too fast, the horses could lose their footing and break a leg. "No matter how much Divinity told them, these women cannot know what lies in our forests. With luck a bird will frighten her and we'll find her soon enough."

The words were hardly comforting. There was more to the forest than birds and innocuous insects. Wolves, wild boar, bucks, any number of creatures could attack her. He touched his sore eye. Though she threw a decent punch, he doubted she'd survive a pack of hungry wolves. What if he couldn't get to her before something bad happened?

Sorin lifted his hand and pointed to the east then west, ordering the knights to spread out over the distance and begin their search. Each man would remain within whistling distance, should the lady be found. When he finished, Ronen finally answered, "She does not know what she faces, even with my knife to arm her."

"The forest at night can be a daunting thing," Sorin comforted. "Rest assured in that we are far away from the battlefront. The Caniba tribes will not have ventured this far. One look at a wild beast and she'll scream for us to save her."

"Let's ride," Ronen urged his horse left, away from his brother. Pulling his sword, he gripped it tight, feeling some comfort in the weapon's weight.

*By all the blood-soaked fields of my ancestors, when I find you, lady wife, I will follow Sorin's advice to lock you away where you will be safe.*

In less than a day his life had changed drastically. It hardly seemed real. Maybe she had bewitched him or used a poisoned fragrance brought from her alien world. Whatever the cause, duty demanded he find her and honor their joining—whether she wanted to or not.

---

Jayne refused to stop running. The burn in her thighs was nothing new and actually comforted her in its familiarity. Physical exertion she could handle, even if the path was rocky to nonexistent, littered with forest trash and blocked by dense trees. She tried to stay in the moonlight, avoiding the darkest part of the forest, using a stick to swipe spider webs out of her way. The more distance she put between herself and the castle, the less chance she'd have of being found. Of course, Lord Ronen might not even look for her. Why should he? They technically just met.

Maybe she could negotiate a portal jump with the Caniba "monsters". In fights, there were always two sides and Jayne knew nothing about the Starian enemy. The Caniba might be a technologically advanced race whose use of electricity made the Starian people think of them as witches. Such superstitious nonsense wasn't unheard of.

She hated having so many theories in her head, not knowing which were real. Brothel dimension? Otherworld filled with beasts? A role-playing plane?

Suddenly, she stopped, gasping for air as she came face-to-face with a sharp cliff of dirt. The forest had shifted long ago, leaving a precipice filled with random plant shoots and a strange pink-tinted moss. Feeling along the darkened wall, she dug her fingers into the dirt. It crumbled, tumbling down to her feet. Though unsteady, she grabbed the knife and began to scoop out small footholds in the cliff. It wasn't so high she couldn't manage to climb up.

She breathed hard, the harsh sound drowning out the quiet chirps of insects singing in the forest. Jayne tried not to think about the isolation, putting the uneasy fear from her mind. It was for the best. Lilith would have slowed her down.

Jayne was used to being alone, but alone with other people. In the orphanage she'd slept in a room filled with other children—probably the closest thing to a family she'd ever had and she never talked to any of them anymore. After she ran away, it was a city filled with other homeless. Then, when Coach Wagner caught her fighting one of his students for pocket change, she'd lived in the boxer dorms. From there, she entered Divinity's entertainment circuit. Never really connected to the masses around her, but surrounded all the same.

"Don't think of the past," she whispered, trying to urge her tiring body on. She pulled the longer pieces of the stolen tunic shirt through her legs and fastened them into short pants with her belt and sheathed the knife at the back of her waist. "Concentrate on the now. Come on, Jayne, let's do this. Climb the wall."

Jayne took a deep breath and held it, thrusting her foot into a carved step before launching her body up the side. Silence surrounded her. The insects had quieted. She ignored the stab of hunger in her stomach. The castle's kitchen had been too busy for her to sneak in. It didn't matter, this wasn't the first time she'd gone hungry and she knew she could push through it.

"Just a little more, Jayne," she whispered, grunting as she slipped her hand over the top ledge. She pushed up and her foot slipped. A small noise escaped her, but she soon righted her hold. "Don't quit."

She pulled her torso over the top to firmer ground and gave a breathless smile of victory. After crawling over the ledge, she rolled onto her back and breathed heavily as she let her muscles rest. The large moon peeked through overhead tree limbs, the leaves crashing in a naturally musical rhythm.

So was this it? The next phase in her life? Were her days as a boxer over? What if the Caniba couldn't help her? What if she could never leave? What would she do?

Ronen instantly came to mind—his strong body and willful charm. For a moment, when he'd touched her, she'd forgotten to think. Even now, in all her tiredness, she felt desire for him. If ever she were to spend a lifetime with a man, he would be a contender. Strength and sexual prowess alone made him a frontrunner. Dominant attitude, while amusing, knocked off a few points.

*You are mine.*

Had he actually said that? Like she was a piece of property to be owned? The orphanage had thought that way about their charges until one of the kids shoved a metal bar through the workhouse manager's heart.

"Enough dwelling," she scolded her mind. "No weakness. No fear."

The shape of the knife pressed uncomfortably at the small of her back, and she rolled to her hands and knees. He'd never catch her. No one could. She was Jayne "The Sweet" Hart, inter-dimensional boxing champion. She was a fighter and she belonged to no man.

"You belong to me and I would take what's mine."

Jayne shivered, knowing something wasn't right but not caring. Ronen's soft words washed over her and a hand ran along her calf. The massaging motion felt good after her long run. How had he found her, hidden under thick undergrowth? She'd made sure to brush away her nearby tracks before burrowing into her makeshift bed as the early morning sun peeked through the trees.

"Come back to me."

Jayne moaned. The hand slid up her thigh, firm and confident. She shivered, instantly entranced. Cream wet the folds of her sex and sensational vibrations tingled every inch of her flesh. She found herself wiggling and parting her legs.

Ronen jerked her legs, pulling her roughly from her hiding place. Jayne gasped, reaching to grab the brush to stop herself. Ronen let go. He was alone, kneeling beside her. Sunlight haloed his head, framing his face with light.

"I will have you."

Jayne still didn't speak. She automatically reached for the knife under the brush, but couldn't quite grab it. Ronen's hands were at his waist, fumbling in their eagerness to unlace his breeches. When she tried to move, he grabbed her foot and pulled, sliding her on the forest floor to be close to him.

Ronen managed to free the turgid length of his cock and swallowed it with a strong fist, pumping lightly. With the other hand, he tugged at her tunic to expose her hips. Cool morning air caressed her pussy.

Ronen crawled over her. He grabbed at her neckline, ripping the front of her tunic open. Rough and eager, he feasted on her breasts, licking and sucking the mounds as his hand tested the wetness between her thighs.

Jayne panted and squirmed, gripping his hair. Small twigs and leaves ground into her back, dirtying her hair. His mouth slid from a taut nipple, leaving it wet and suddenly cold. He bit his way to her neck, nipping at her flesh, making her feel his hard kiss.

Urgently, he brought his cock to her sex, finding quick aim before ramming the full length deep into her core. She moaned in pleasure at the almost painful stretching of her muscles. Ronen growled, lifting up so he could pull out only to slam into her like a wild animal. His hips crashed into her, forcing her ass to slide in the dirt.

Jayne liked his vigorous claiming, the swiftness of his thrusts, the confident drive of his passion. She thrust her hand between them, letting his hips bump her fingers against her clit. The stroke sent shivers over her stomach.

Ronen's hair bounced around his tense face with each movement. His neck stretched long and he closed his eyes. Jayne made a weak noise as her orgasm hit. Her body jerked beneath him. He only became more impassioned, pounding her with his cock as she seized and shuddered. Then, suddenly, he made a loud grunt and sheathed himself to the hilt. Release hit and he practically convulsed as he ejaculated inside her.

"You can't hide, my lady, I'm coming for you."

Jayne gasped and blinked, still panting from their joining. She looked around, trying to get a sense of what happened. Ronen was gone, but her body lay soaked in sweat on the forest floor. Though untorn, her tunic was bunched at her waist, revealing the wet evidence of her recent orgasm. Whatever happened, it had been too real to be a dream. Yet here she was, alone.

Ronen gasped for breath, not getting up from where he'd fallen against a tree. Pumping both fists over his exposed cock, he met his climax with a violent jerk. Cum slid over his hands, wetting him as he milked every ounce of pleasure from his body.

He knew the sensations racking him were not a dream. He'd been fully awake when they'd started. But somehow it was more than a fantasy, taking control of his mind, grabbing onto what would have been a fleeting thought about finding Jayne and taking her wildly on the forest floor.

The smell of her surrounded him. He felt the soft globes of her breasts in his mouth when he enveloped them with kisses. He saw her face, felt her body, tasted her flesh.

Witchcraft. Spells. It was the only explanation that made sense. Somehow, Jayne enchanted him. But why? To delay him? Confuse him? Tempt him or drive him mad?

"Ronen, come!" Sorin's voice called. "Kar found her trail going up Boar Ledge."

Springing into action, he fastened his breeches before the others saw what he'd done and went to grab his fallen sword. He'd been searching the ground for her lost trail when the passion struck him. Now, having once again picked up her trail, he leapt onto his horse.

"Stupid woman," he cursed. Why in the name of the gods would she climb up there? The natural jutting of dirt kept the sounder of wild boars that lived on the high plain away from the rest of the forest. Young knights would go there to hunt and practice their survival skills, but it was no place for a woman with only a knife to protect her. The animals grew thick and fat without other natural predators to dwindle their numbers and to kill one would only mean you had a whole pack of them left to go. Even the wolves seemed to avoid it unless desperate during a harsh winter.

When he arrived, Kar already stood on the ledge with Sorin. Ronen reined his horse next to the cliff and climbed onto the animal's back to give him the leverage he needed to reach up. He took his brother's offered hand and jumped off the horse onto the higher ledge. They never brought the horses with them onto the ledge. There was no practical way to get the animals up.

"It leads that way." Kar pointed a scarred finger toward an opened path. He was one of the best trackers in Staria.

"Divide and ride around the ledge," Ronen ordered the knights below them. With luck, she'd have jumped off and continued along a safer route. "We'll meet on the other side."

The men instantly obeyed, splitting into two groups. Three of them grabbed the unused horses' reins to lead them away. Ronen placed his hand on his sheathed weapon and hurried to find Jayne's trail.

---

*Son of a whoring cat!*

Jayne leapt over a fallen log, running full tilt through the open forest. The thunder of many small hooves echoed behind her, punctuated by grunts. She'd sprinted into an open clearing of red bristled boars as they routed around in the earth during the morning hours. At least, she was pretty sure that was what they were. She'd slept near an animal collective for a few months when she lived on the streets, and there was a version of the creature kept there in a cage. Only that creature had been much, much smaller than the thirty six-hundred-plus pound hunters behind her.

At first, she hoped to back away slowly from the compact beasts, but her rapid appearance had gotten notice and beady eyes turned toward her in interest. If she weren't mistaken, they actually started salivating. Next, she hoped to startle them by screaming and waving her arms. It had been a mistake. They answered her flailing attempts with loud grunts as they worked their large tusks up and down.

*Cursed piglets from the underworld!*

The demonic creatures ran pretty fast for their short legs. Jayne leapt, trying to grab a branch to pull herself into a tree. The limb gave under her weight, cracking and refusing to support her. A boar crashed through the brush next to her, trying to ram her thigh. Jayne dodged the attack, but the animal managed to hook her tunic with his tusk. The material ripped. The boar grunted in short, noisy bursts and the sound of hooves shifted in the distance, growing instantly louder.

Jayne reached behind her back to grab the knife, tugging at the hilt. She'd bound it tight so it wouldn't fall or cut her, but now she struggled to free it as she inched away from the boar. Not wanting to face down all of them at once, she again took her chances in fleeing. She gave up on the knife, pumping her arms to propel her body forward. Seeing a formation in the ground, she ran for it and found it led to a steep drop in the forest floor. Looking down over the side, she saw the steep edge looked much like the cliff she had climbed up. The sound of hooves again grew closer.

"Here's hoping you can't fly." Jayne jumped, aiming for a flat spot of earth. But then, a tingling erupted inside her temple and her vision blanked out, replaced the ground with the image of a knight kneeling as he pointed into the distance. She stopped moving, feeling as if she stood perfectly still in the forest even though somewhere in her brain she knew she still fell. Inexplicably, she felt Ronen was close, so close he was almost inside her body, or maybe she was in his.

Suddenly, a hard thud jarred her from her thoughts, bringing her mind back to the present. A sharp pain radiated from where the knife's hilt slammed into her spine. Whatever vision had overtaken her during the fall was now gone.

Jayne moaned, rolling on the ground in agony. Through the corner of her eye she saw the boar, its feet digging into the earth to stop its progress. It was too late. The animal slid right off the side, soaring though the air with a squeal. Forgetting the pain, she jumped to her feet. The animal slammed into the ground, slid several feet before hitting a tree, jerked violently and then held perfectly still.

Reaching for the blade, she tore at the back of her tunic, gasping from her exertions as she finally managed to free the knife. She held it in her trembling hand. Her body throbbed from the fall. Jayne stumbled away from the creature, scanning along the top of the cliff for more. A few boars appeared, grunting in anger, but none followed their friend over the side.

Jayne grabbed the side of her head and pressed down hard. The tingling sensation had lessened, but left her dizzy. Something was very wrong. This was the second time she'd connected to Ronen when he wasn't around.

Then realization hit her. Jayne looked at her fingertip, where she'd poked it with the sword from his bedchamber wall. That's how it must have happened. She'd jabbed her finger, sucked it between her lips and then kissed him. She'd been warned something like this might happen when the Divinity scientists fitted her with the corporation's standard boxer's biogenetics package. But they also said it was a one in a billion chance.

*Son of a whoring cat!*

Ronen was her one in a billion and she didn't like it one bit.

# CHAPTER 5

Wild boar tasted about as good as it looked running around trying to kill her. Jayne had sliced off the chunk of meat, carried it into the forest and started a small fire in a hand-dug hole. It took a while to get the fire to light, because it had been a long time since she'd used the skill.

"These Caniba better be technological geniuses," she muttered, biting into the overdone meal, trying not to taste it. "I can't live in this forest."

Maybe Lilith had the right idea in staying at the castle. Then again, every ounce of Jayne rebelled at the idea of captivity. She had no choice but to run. Her head began to tingle and she dropped her meat, quickly turning to stare at the ground away from the fire. If Ronen switched sight with her, she'd not let him see anything that would help him track her.

*"...lock her away in a tower,"* Ronen's voice filled her head.

*"We lost her tracks, my lords,"* an unknown voice broke in, *"but I found evidence of a stampede."*

*"They found prey,"* Lord Sorin answered. *"We follow the stampede."*

Jayne grabbed her head, shaking it to get the voices out of her mind. She needed to get off this plane. Only then could she be rid of her one-night mistake.

---

"Caniba," Ronen whispered. The stampede tracks had led them back to the ledge with no sign of Jayne. What they did find horrified him. The Caniba should not be so far north, but only they would devour raw meat. The gnawed boar carcass had been bitten, the bites too round and short to be anything but human.

"Perhaps they are lost," Kar offered. Ronen grabbed his sword, prompting the other two knights to do the same. They scanned the forest in search of their enemy.

"They do not leave their encampments without orders," Sorin said, grimly. "They are spies."

"Lady Jayne is in this forest." Ronen frowned, ignoring the twinge he felt in his gut. He didn't need to look at his brother to know what Sorin was thinking. The Caniba did not treat their female prisoners well. He had to find her, save her, protect her. His arms ached to pull her to his chest and hold her. Why had she run? So soon after choosing to be with him? This was not how he imagined a marriage or a wife.

Already he was connected to her. He felt her like he'd never felt anyone. He detected her lips near his neck and heard her breathing in his ear, or what he imagined to be her breath. The sensation of her body pressed to his, and his cock stayed semi-erect, begging to be called into action. Why hadn't he stayed and made love to her again and again? If he had, maybe she would have been too tired to leave him. If he had, they wouldn't be in the forest looking at evidence of Caniba activity.

*The gods have their reasons.*

"Here, blood," Kar said, pushing to his feet as he rubbed the found droplet between two fingers. "It has been well over an hour since they passed, perhaps two or three."

"Ronen?" Sorin asked, deferring to him.

"Leave a sign for the others to follow," Ronen ordered. "We follow the Caniba. Nothing else in this forest is as dangerous."

---

The night sky didn't give much light as dark clouds drifted over the moon and stars. Jayne saw peeks of moonlight through the treetops and wished she'd brought her fire with her. But, it was better not to signal any surrounding knights. There was no doubt Ronen chased her. What? Did she hurt his male pride? Embarrass him? Why else would he pursue her so far away from the castle?

Whenever she felt Ronen invading her mind, she concentrated on blocking him out. For the most part, it worked. Though, the visions did continue—flashes of forest trees and knights, sounds of voices and running feet.

Darkness and little sleep forced her to find a place to hide for the night. Twice, she almost twisted her ankle because she couldn't see the ground beneath her. Unable to force herself into a tight corner for fear of what would be lurking there, she rolled beneath an overhang of low branches and spread out on her stomach. She laid the knife at her side within easy reach.

Tension rolled through her and she closed her eyes, willing her dreams to be filled with shadows and not sexually fueled fantasies of Ronen. She let the exhaustion have her, slipping easily to sleep.

At first, it was the hands stirring against her naked body that drew her from her slumber. His touch pulled her mind to awareness. Understanding what was happening, she knew she didn't really lie naked, only felt the sensations in her mind as if they were real.

Jayne fought her budding desires, not wanting to give in, but his touch was like a drug. The more she felt, the more she had to have him. Their connection became real, as if he stood in front of her, their minds joining. She actively pushed him from her thoughts, not wanting to let him into her secrets.

She tried to peek into his mind, but all she discovered were random thoughts. *Soft, sweet, mine...*

Jayne felt his possessiveness of her, his drive to capture her. She would never be his prisoner. Never.

Even as she thought it, knowing it to be true, she couldn't resist him. He touched her with such worshiping passion. Palms cupped her breasts, rubbing softly. They ran over her sides, across her hips, down her legs and up her inner thighs. She moaned in torment. How could she resist?

"Please let me go. I can't live as a whore," she whispered. "I wish I'd never met you."

She couldn't see anything, but the darkness only enhanced her other senses. Jayne smelled the freshness of the forest, felt it's coolness on her shoulders and feet. Beneath her, the hard ground pressed into her sore back, but it didn't hurt quite as badly as before. Her nerves focused on Ronen's hands, wanting more of him. He answered her silent plea with his lips, brushing soft kisses over her flesh along the same path his fingers had traveled. Soft breathing washed over her like a gentle breeze.

The moist heat of his mouth enclosed a nipple, sucking the taut peak. She lifted her hands to touch him, but her limbs were heavy as if paralyzed by her sleepy state. Ronen's tight stomach pushed at her thighs, urging them to part as he moved over her. He kissed a trail up her neck, stopping close to her lips.

"Touch me," he said, so softly she barely heard him. Or maybe he didn't speak at all, merely directed the thought into her mind.

Any hint of her resistance left her, and she stopped concentrating on blocking him from her. Almost instantly, her vision began to clear and a moonlit face appeared before her. Thick shadows contrasted the strength of his features and the cords of his neck. The low branches pressed over them, cocooning them in.

Jayne reached for him, grabbing his face to pull his mouth to hers. She gripped him tight, forcing him against her rough kiss. His lips tasted sweet, like fresh water from a spring and she drank thirstily. Her hands acted on their own accord, venturing over the peaks and valleys of his muscles. Restless legs moved along his hips, inviting him to conquer her completely.

Ronen flexed, surging forward. The turgid length of his cock probed the silken heat of her pussy. For a moment, he paused, letting her muscles adjust around him. He worked his body back and forth, going deep with each pass. It felt so good that she wanted to scream with the pleasure of it. Maybe she did scream, but she couldn't be sure.

He thrust hard and fast, as if desperate to mark her as his own. Jayne met his passion, silently battling him for control. The enclosure was too tight for her to roll him onto his back. She raked her nails over his back. Tree limbs scratched at her hands, but she didn't care. Ronen groaned, propelling his body onward.

Jayne gasped, tensing as she met with release. Her quivering muscles gripped his cock and he soon followed, grunting like a wild animal as he came inside her. The sound of their harsh breath joined in a frantic rhythm.

Ronen looked deeply into her eyes, his face still a heavy contrast. "I'm coming for you, Lady Jayne."

Within a blink, his body was gone, leaving her fully clothed and incredibly sated. She panted, wondering how much of her he'd read. Did he know where she hid? Did he understand what happened between them? Just as she started to calm herself, determined to come up with a new plan, her hair was yanked from above and an unknown hand pulled her from beneath her hiding place. Jayne reached for her knife, barely grabbing it only to have it slide from her fingers to be lost in the darkness.

He'd found her.

---

*Blessed night.*

Ronen shifted on his horse, glad for the cover of darkness to hide the passion he'd just shared with his wife. Spell or not, the woman knew how to sate him. What he didn't understand was why let him join with her as she tried to escape. Several times he thought of telling Sorin, only to refrain. If it was truly believed she was a witch, Jayne would be tried as such. He didn't relish the idea of his wife being burned alive or drowned in a river because of peasant fear. And if it wasn't a spell but the hopeful madness of his own mind, he didn't exactly want the lunacy known.

Automatically, Ronen searched the low branches, remembering the tight fit of Jayne's body to his in the tight enclosure. Sir Traven and Sir Walter had found the mark Ronen and his brother left near the boar's carcass and followed their trail into the forest. Walter rode back to get their horses and now they made good time through the trees. The other knights were deployed to look for signs of Lady Jayne around the ledge.

"Perhaps we should wait for morning light," Traven suggested. "It's too hard to find a trail in such darkness."

Though sensible, it didn't mean Ronen liked the advice.

"You haven't slept, my lord," Kar put forth. "Perhaps you should rest. I will look for a trail by foot."

How could he sleep knowing she was out there? That the Caniba were out there?

"No. I ride. Kar, you three rest and look at first light." Ronen's order ended all discussion from the men. To his brother, he said, "Make up your own mind, but I cannot stop searching."

"You are my blood. I go where you go," Sorin answered. "I ride with you, Brother."

Ronen nodded, having pretty much known Sorin would.

*By the wrath of the gods, I have to find her.*

---

Jayne expected to see Ronen as moonlight shone over her attacker, but instead she found a wild, furry beast. Light shone through the uncombed nest of its hair. The creature grunted like an evil gorilla that crawled from the depths of a nightmare.

Jayne sprung into action, pushing her legs off the ground to kick at the creature's head. The flat of her foot landed with a hard thud against its neck. Instantly, it let her go. She rolled onto her side, flinching as her back protested the movement. The last kick had irritated the already sore muscles.

Hands gripped her leg and arm, the clawed nails digging into her flesh. They pulled her across the littered forest, sliding her through leaves and twigs. The debris dug into her stomach, scratching and poking her through the long tunic shirt. The grunts got louder as another beast found hold on her bare calf and began pulling her in the opposite direction.

Jayne didn't make a sound, even as they lifted her from the ground and the pain surged through her body. They tried to rip her in half. She bit her lip, focusing all her energy on jerking her legs together. The two creatures were thrown into each other, hitting their heads. She fell the few inches down onto the ground. Once free, she pushed up, ready to run. More creatures blocked her path, making her stop short of escape.

Blood trickled down her leg and ankle. She hopped lightly, trying not to put weight on her injured limb. Jayne studied her attackers, seeing them more clearly from her new vantage point. They stood like men, only covered in fur. What were they? Wolf-men? Some other kind of creature from the stories told to scare children?

"Back away," she ordered, keeping a deadly calm to her voice. There were eight in all, counting the men she'd hit on the head who still lay unmoving on the ground.

"Fighter," one of the creatures ground out, his voice so gravelly she could barely make out the words. "We will feed her strength to the queen and be rewarded."

Jayne scanned the ground for her knife, but didn't see it. The shadowed figured moved in. She lifted her hands, hopping on one foot as she readied for a death match.

One of the men leapt, claws extended. Jayne pulled to the side, catching his head. She slammed her injured knee up into his face, hearing a crack. He dropped to the ground. Jayne spun, counting down their numbers in her head.

*Five remain.*

She turned to the side, putting them in front of her. How could she have been caught off guard with the foul stench of them filling her nostrils? The odor was almost unbearable and she tried not to gag.

Two surged at once, wielding long blades. Jayne swung her arms, but they anticipated her move and she missed. A sword bit into her forearm, slicing deep. She yelped in pain. Though she willed her body to keep fighting, it couldn't take much more abuse. She grabbed her arm, falling to her knees. She half expected the creatures to converge upon her with swords. Instead, one grabbed her by her hair and jerked her completely to the ground. He dragged her unceremoniously behind him. The others grabbed their fallen comrades and hoisted them up onto their shoulders to carry them from the forest.

---

Somewhere between the banging of Jayne's head against a log and the blurry vision of her awakening mind, the smelly men brought her to their encampment. Her entire body itched as it tried to repair itself. The cut on her arm ached terribly, but she knew it would be the first to heal.

A thick leather collar wrapped her neck and another held her waist, keeping her tight against the pole and making it hard to breathe when she moved. Jayne's hands were free and she felt behind her head. They'd hooked her to a low pole, her back straight and her legs sprawled out before her. She shivered, almost dreading the fact they'd kept her alive when first they acted as though they'd tear her apart.

Jayne twisted, trying to discover the source of shuffling feet. She found a pelt-covered man standing with his back to her. Her hands continued to search for an escape, but found no relief from the pole prison.

Taking a deep breath, she held it, endeavoring to ignore her injuries. The beastly man turned to her, whipping his head about. Sunlight illuminated his gruesome features. Jayne gave a loud inhale of surprise, the noise shrill. Sunken eyes stared at her, filled with hatred and something more she couldn't name. Then, he smiled, a horrific look that shook her to the bone. Teeth had been filed into sharp points, creating a mouthful of yellowed fangs. Scars lined his face, not like the Starian men, but purposeful scars that ran deep, as if he cut upon himself in a fit of madness. Some had yet to heal.

Upon seeing her awake, he strode toward her. Jayne tensed, bending her legs. It might break her neck to kick up at him, but she'd rather die fighting than be at this ungodly creature's mercy. The man laughed, grunting low in the back of his throat, keeping well away from her legs. Coming at her from the side, where she could just see him along the edge of her vision, he grabbed her injured arm and began sniffing at the wound. Metal-tipped fingers dug into her skin, drawing fresh blood. Jayne tried to pull away, but it only caused him to twist it at an awkward angle.

"Leave her!" another of the men yelled. His right nostril had been sliced off. By the way the sniffer dropped her arm and backed away, she guessed him to be the leader. "She is for the queen. Sorceress Magda will feed on her strength and she will reward us well."

"Sorceress Magda," they all murmured in reverent unison, revealing there to be more of these men out of her eye line.

Feed?

Jayne gulped. For the first time since running from Battlewar Castle, she hoped Ronen would catch her. Closing her eyes, she concentrated on connecting to him. Unfortunately, with her injuries, it would be nearly impossible. Her energy would be used to heal herself.

*Bloody fucking misery! I give up. You want me, Ronen, well come and save my ass.*

---

Ronen clutched the jeweled knife Jayne had stolen from him, swearing to himself that he'd find the Caniba and rip them of their hearts. He'd found the weapon in the dirt, surrounded by signs of a struggle. The trail had been easy enough to find. They simply followed the drag marks and droplets of blood leading away from the original fray south through the woods.

It always amazed him that the Caniba could survive as a race for as long as they had. They had little by way of tactical skill, not bothering to hide their tracks or plot intricate battles. If not for their leaders, they'd be a mindless army running haphazard across the countryside. Only by killing the leaders would the Caniba tribes fall. Unfortunately, it was not so easily done. The sheer number of the tribe kept anyone from getting too close.

Ronen lifted his hand, hearing a noise in the distance. The distinctive grunts confirmed his worst fears. His enemy had captured his wife. He listened for signs of her screams, but only met with silence. Closing his eyes, he tried to connect with her as he had before. Nothing.

Almost desperate, he gripped the reins of his horse. Pain stung him, seizing hold of his heart. He'd only had one night with her before she ran off, and it seemed strange that he'd already feel so connected to her. Looking at his brother, he thought of Bianka. Why had the gods cursed the brothers of Firewall? They fought every battle put before them, as had their ancestors. Why take their wives in such a cruel way?

Ronen refused to analyze the emotions whirling around inside of him, telling himself that it was merely duty and honor that made him feel anything for Jayne. Despite his hopes, he knew that it was unlikely she lived. The Caniba rarely took prisoners and a scouting party would be less likely to, for they would never see the tactical advantage in doing so.

Ronen grabbed his sword, silently prompting Sorin and Kar to do the same. The others had not caught up with them, but it didn't matter. The Caniba spies had taken his wife and his honor demanded blood. His rage demanded it. He needed to fight, to kill the ache burning his chest and pounding inside his head.

Sorin gave him a stiff nod, agreeing to battle. Kar swung off his horse and inched in front of them, disappearing into the forest. Seconds later, a soft chirp sounded, blending in with the forest noise. It pulsed six times indicating six enemies.

Ronen nudged his steed, ducking under a branch as he surged toward the Caniba encampment. Seeing movement, he rode for the first man he found, hollering to get his attention. The man-creature drew his sword to fight, but Ronen was too enraged to make much sport of it. He sliced the man up the chest, killing him instantly. The others sprung into action, leaping up from their spots on the ground.

"Ronen!" Sorin yelled, drawing his notice. "Your wife!"

Ronen stiffened, searching the campground. Sorin pointed at a low pole. Jayne's back was to him, but he could see her feet kicking at the ground as if she'd push the pole over. It didn't budge but she kept trying.

*She lives!* He couldn't believe it.

"Take her out of here!" Sorin ordered, his desperation to save his sister-by-marriage a mere droplet compared to Ronen's desire to save his wife. Sorin slashed at an attacker, beheading him. Ronen knew his brother could handle himself and did as he instructed, turning his mount toward the post. Kar appeared from the forest on foot, meeting swords. The clang of metal against metal echoed around them.

Ronen jumped from his horse, landing with a thud next to Jayne. Her entire body jerked at the sound. His eyes went first to the blood and dirt marring her flesh, searching for injuries. Her body was covered with them.

Light brown eyes met his. He expected there to be terror in her gaze, or even tears. Instead, she looked incredibly annoyed at having been captured.

"My lady, did they…?"

"Took you long enough," she muttered, struggling anew. "Mind cutting me free?"

"You wished for me to find you? Is that why you ran? Because of a game?" He frowned. Though the idea gave him hope. Ronen pulled the jeweled knife from his waist and began sawing at the leather straps keeping her to the post. The collar around her neck would have to come later.

"You really want to discuss this now?" she snapped. "Here?" Jayne reached for his hands to take over freeing herself. He swatted her away.

Ronen glanced up at the fight. All but one Caniba had fallen.

Sorin faced him on foot. Kar stood back, turning in circles as he searched the trees for more.

"Finally," Jayne said as she broke free. She pushed the leather band from her waist as she stood, ready to charge into battle. The action came too fast and she swayed on her feet, nearly collapsing on top of him. Ronen stood, catching her. "Let go. I'm fine!"

"Never," he growled, forcing her to walk with him as he hurried to his horse. "Get on."

"No," she denied. Though the sound was hard, there was a deep terror in her eyes that he'd never seen before. His wife was a fighter. He already knew that. But now, when she looked at him, it was almost as if he terrified her more than the idea of facing the forest alone. "I will not be told what to do. I can take care of myself."

"Is that what you call this? Taking care of yourself?" Ronen snorted in disbelief. She looked at him, her eyes wide. If he didn't know better, he would have thought he'd deeply hurt her feelings by pointing out her capture.

"I..." Jayne looked at the pole where she'd been tied. He could practically see her mind ticking away in her skull, trying to decide what to do, how to react.

"Get on the horse, my lady." He lowered his tone to a deadly pitch, hoping to jar her into action. Men would not disobey such a harsh command. This lady did.

"No," she stated loudly. Her eyes moved from him to the dead bodies on the ground. He'd seen that look before in young soldiers —the shock, the disbelief. Dazed, she said, "I can walk."

"Do not refuse help for the sake of being stubborn. Get on the —" Ronen jerked her hard, trying to get her to focus, needing her to snap back to her senses.

Jayne pulled her arm roughly from his grasp. Her voice rose as she yelled at him, "Stop telling me what to do. I'm tired of people telling me what to do. Because I'll tell you right now, I don't take kindly to being commanded or tied up or made to..."

"Ronen!" Sorin yelled. "Get her out of here. Now! We scout the forest and will meet you at Widowrock."

"I am not commanding you, I am protecting you." All right, so that was half true.

Jayne frowned. Despite her bruised and bloodied body, and the fact she stood in the aftermath of a miniature battlefield, she managed to look defiant. "I'm not yours to protect. I'm not your mate."

"Fine, breeding partner, wife, whatever you wish to call yourself." How was it he wanted to pull her to his chest and strangle her at the same time? Why did she fight him so hard when all he wanted was to hold her? Protect her? Emotions warred within him. He'd searched for her with little rest, and all he wanted to do was lock her away in a room with him where she would be safe. Maybe he'd leave the collar around her neck and tie her to a bed until she saw reason. "You are mine. I am yours. We are together."

"You can hang yourself." She began clawing at her neck, trying to get the leather off. It was then he realized what was truly happening. She fought with him because she didn't know how else to react. It was as if accepting his help admitted some kind of failure on her part. The reasoning wasn't logical, not by Starian standards. It was then Ronen also realized he knew so very little about his wife's past. He trusted the gods, trusted fate, but there was something more, something deeper to Jayne.

Was it possible he'd found a woman whose instinct to fight was stronger than any Starian man's? Ronen wouldn't pretend to understand tender, romantic feelings, but he knew women by nature were not usually so unwilling to accept friendship. But with the way Jayne was looking at him, it appeared she would be much more comfortable facing death than being with him as a wife.

"I belong to no one and the only thing we'll be doing together is—"

Ronen refused to listen to any more. Understanding her nature a little bit better did not lessen the danger of their situation. He grabbed her and tossed her across the back of his horse so her stomach lay over the saddle. The animal pawed the ground, snorting softly. Until Kar and Sorin had a chance to secure the surrounding woods, he couldn't risk keeping her out in the open.

He swung up behind her, perched uncomfortably on the saddle's edge. Jayne growled in protest, trying to push up with her one good arm. Pressing his hand to her back, he kept her down as he spurred the mount into action. It was a short ride to Widowrock and, so long as she didn't struggle, she wouldn't be dangling for too long.

"Let me up, you son of a whoring cat!" she screamed.

"We ride to safety." He kept his hand on her. "And my mother was a gracious and good lady. You'd do well not to insult her again."

Jayne mumbled an answer, but he didn't make out the words.

# CHAPTER 6

"Tell me something. Battlewar Castle, it's not a brothel, is it? A whorehouse? Gathering place for prostitutes?" Jayne stared at Ronen, willing him to fight with her. She could handle fighting. Being weak was another story. Besides, if he fought her, she wouldn't have to face that protective, almost gentle look on his face. How was a woman supposed to react to that? No one in her entire life looked at her the way he did. No one made her feel the way he did. Death she could manage and face. But this tenderness? It terrified her like nothing else had.

Ronen frowned, pausing as he swung from the back of his horse to look down at her. "No. It's the king's castle. The king doesn't stay there as there is always too much to do by the borderlands, but we use it for ceremonies and such."

*So much for that theory. I think I might prefer a brothel to marriage.* When Jayne looked at Ronen, she wasn't so sure she really believed that.

"You know, where I come from a man goes through certain rituals before asking a woman to marry him, and then they only cohabitate for ten years. If, at the end of that time, they want to file for another ten they can." Jayne hated feeling weak, but she'd pushed her body hard the last several days on little food. She could take the pain, even the hunger, but she couldn't take the fact that it had all been for nothing. Ronen had caught up to her. So what if he'd saved her life in the process. It didn't mean he planned on letting her go.

No, he thought she belonged to him. What was worse, he didn't consider her to be a slave or prisoner. No, to him she was a mate, a breeding partner, a wife. Out of all those names, wife scared her the most. Though, breeding partner did take a close second. Too bad for him, the biogeneticist assured her she would never have children. Divinity wouldn't want a pregnant boxer waddling around the ring.

"Here we mate until death," he answered. He turned his back on her and busied himself clearing a spot on the forest floor. He wore a different tunic than she'd last seen him in, but his eyes belied his exhaustion. The barest hint of whiskers textured his jaw, darkening the already tanned flesh. Bloody misery, the man knew how to move —from the strength in his chest and arms to the almost graceful rhythm of his walk.

Jayne went to a big boulder standing by itself in the middle of the forest, completely isolated from other rocks. Widowrock, they'd called it. On impulse, she braced her shoulder against it and tried to push it in his direction, grunting, "If you insist."

The boulder didn't budge. Ronen gave her a bemused glance, dismissing her idle threat. "Come sit before you hurt yourself. Let me take that collar off your neck."

"Shouldn't you go check on your brother? What if he is hurt?" She stayed against the rock, leaning against it. Even with tired eyes, Ronen was a stunning man. Their joined fantasies were never far from her thoughts. Though unreal, they felt quite the opposite. Funny how she'd made love to him more in her dreams than in real life. "Don't worry, I'll be sure to wait right here."

"For me to consider his defeat would be a dishonor," Ronen answered, crossing to her.

*Argh!* She hated his calm tone. She wished he would scream, yell, punch. That language she understood.

"Turn. I'll free you." He urged her head to the side with a gentle shove before taking the knife to her neck. The sharp blade soon had her free.

Jayne grabbed her neck, stretching the muscles. He stepped back and she watched in silence as he gathered dried leaves, branches and twigs to build a fire. Within minutes, a soft firelight cast over them.

"Let me see your arm." He stood, reaching his hand out for her to join him.

"It's fine." Jayne didn't like the softness in his gaze. Why wasn't he yelling at her for running away?

"You're wounded. I should bind it."

"It's already healing." She refused his comfort.

"Why must you make a battle of this?" he muttered, more to himself.

Jayne answered anyway. "If you don't like it, let me go."

"What is it that makes you want to fight and face death rather than accept me? You chose me. I was content to not claim a woman. It was you who bewitched me with your kiss." He strode toward her, closing the distance. Placing his hand on the rock, he leaned into her. "It is you who has been plaguing my mind with thoughts of taking you. We are connected. We are meant to be."

"We are joined by defective nanobots." She sighed heavily, letting him hear her frustration. "When I cut my finger on your sword and stuck it between my lips—"

"I remember," he interrupted needlessly. His tone dropped to a low whisper.

Jayne continued, trying to ignore the sultry dip of his lashes and the parting of his firm lips. "When we kissed—"

"Yea." His breath fanned over her cheek.

"One of them left my bloodstream and somehow took up residence in you. Since they're programmed to work as a team with my body, they've decided to talk to each other from inside our bodies." She leaned away from him, but the small distance did nothing to quell her growing arousal. "I was warned it might happen, but it was supposed to be a one in a million chance. Bloody misery, perhaps even one in a trillion."

Jayne frowned. It was why boxers took a special supplement before a fight so they didn't risk transferring their technologies.

"See, we are blessed by the gods." He tried to press his lips to hers.

Jayne jerked back another inch. Her resistance didn't seem to faze him. "How is it you hear about a scientific catastrophe and think it's a sign of true love?"

"I confess, I have no idea what manner of spell a nanobot is or what purpose they serve. But if it proves my point that we are meant to be, then I agree with them."

She scowled. "I've got news for you, warrior man, true love doesn't exist. It's an illusion."

"I agree."

That surprised her. With all his "mine" mentality, she just thought he'd be a romantic of sorts. He spoke of the "will of the gods" and "meant to be". She wondered why she felt disappointment at his cold, logical admission—an admission she said first.

"It is not in our nature to seek romantic love. Marriages are unions, partnerships. Women must be cared for and protected, provided for. Men need sons and," he brushed his finger over her cheek, "the pleasure of a woman's bed."

Jayne swallowed nervously. She didn't necessarily like the life he laid out before them. What if she couldn't escape it? Or him? Or this barbaric place? What if she didn't want to?

"It is my hope we will find a mutual affection in time," he continued, not taking his eyes from hers. "Marriages seem the better for it."

"I want you to listen to me, Ronen," she said, quietly, reasonably. Mutual affection? How could she make him understand that everyone who felt any kind of affection for her was dead? That it was better for both of them if they went their separate ways? "Do you really want a woman who was sent here as a punishment?"

"Punishment?" He dropped his hand. "You are a criminal? Traitor?"

"I'm a loser," she stated flatly. For all Divinity cared, it was the truth. She'd lost her fight, even if it was fixed.

"What did you lose? Something important? A king's missive?" He furrowed his brow, as if trying to think of all the lost things that warranted a punishment.

"My championship title to the cheating, son of an ape, Big Bobby Bishop in the gladiator rings on dimensional plane 241." Jayne felt angry all over again and pushed off the rock. "His gangster father tried to make me throw the fight, but there is no way I could take a dive to that no-talent buffoon." She paced across the forest floor. "They threatened to kill my family if I didn't fall. Well, my nonexistent family but they didn't know that. And the son of a whoring cat hits me with a whammy?! I let him beat on me for a half an hour to make a good show and to let him have a little dignity when he lost, and he drugs me. Me! Jayne 'The Sweet' Hart."

"I do not understand what this has to do with you as my wife." Ronen hadn't moved.

"I don't lose. I never lose. Divinity Corporation banks on that, and they've paid a lot of doctors a lot of money to make sure of it. When Big Bobby hit me with his drugged fist, a lot of money was lost by a lot of powerful people. Divinity would not have been happy about it and they were my way home. But instead of hearing my side, they packed me up and shipped me off to this forsaken..." She paused, trying to think of a description that wasn't as mean as the ones filtering through her head. "Ah, place."

"So you fight for money?" He looked over her in disbelief. "You do not look like a warrior. I have seen your body. The skin is smooth. There are no scars."

"Bare-knuckle boxing." Jayne looked down at her arm where the deep gash already began to heal. She held it up to show him. "I've been bioengineered to heal fast and not to scar. It keeps my face pretty for the fans."

He looked down at his body. "I have that thing. I will no longer scar?"

"Nano-robots are these tiny, microscopic, self-sufficient army of machines designed to replicate and act on a specific level of function while they travel around my bloodstream to heal my body. They're engineered to only work on me. But somehow one of my nanobots jumped ship and is inside of you. It should have deactivated."

"But the gods willed that we—"

"Ah," Jayne held up her hand stopping him from saying it. "Scientific mishap. With any luck you'll bleed the bugger out and the air will deactivate it. Then it's bye-bye shared thoughts. Or your own immune system will attack it and shut it down."

"No part of me could attack you, Lady Jayne."

Jayne got the distinct feeling he didn't understand half of what she said.

Ronen grabbed her hand and jerked her forward into his chest. The hard press of his muscles formed a solid wall. He turned her back against the boulder, trapping her. The unmistakable press of his erection made itself known. "I enjoy the shared thoughts." He rocked his hips. "And when I feel your sex clutching my cock as you finish, I know you enjoy them as well."

"I don't deny that there is, ah," she chose her words carefully, "sexual lust."

"We have time before the others arrive." He rocked again, swaying his hips back and forth. "And it is said any lady who makes love to her husband against Widowrock will never be named a widow."

"I don't believe in legends." Her breathing deepened. Every part of her body tingled, from the top of her head, the pointed buds of her nipples, the tight pearl of her clit, the slick folds of her sex, to the very tips of her toes. She couldn't think or reason, not when his delicious mouth was so close. Sex wouldn't change anything between them. He'd still demand she was his wife. She'd still try to find a way to escape.

Jayne grabbed his face and roughly pulled his mouth down to slam against hers. She bit at his lips, kissing him with a potent force. Ronen didn't seem to mind when she raked her hands over his tunic, jerking it up so she could free his thick cock. When she couldn't figure out how to unfasten his breeches, he helped her, tugging them so they loosened enough for her to reach down the front. She grabbed his rigid shaft, pumping it in a tight fist.

Ronen groaned, squeezing a breast. He whispered hotly against her throat, "Lift your skirts, my lady. I would take you now."

Jayne wanted to be in control. She let go of his cock and pushed him down. "On your back so I can mount you, Knight."

"Yea, my lady, whatever you wish." He scurried to obey, his breathing deepening in his eagerness to be ridden. Ronen pulled his breeches down, exposing his cock in readiness for her.

"My wish is to ride you." Jayne was hardly embarrassed by such admissions. She climbed over him, lifting the long tunic to bare her pussy. "Hard and rough until you beg me for mercy."

"I am not accustomed to begging." He gripped her bare hips, forcing her up against his cock. "But my lady is welcome to try."

Jayne grabbed him by the hair and lifted him up to meet her mouth. She kissed him hard, sawing her lips against his. The heat of his thighs teased her sex and she squirmed, undulating her hips.

Something about him drove her to distraction and she lost all logical thought. Knowing this was real this time and not just an overactive fantasy, spurred Jayne on. She needed him. Now.

Jayne dropped his head, lifting her body over him. Ronen took his cock in hand, guiding it to her as her fingernails dug into his tunic. She impaled herself on him, gasping at the pleasure of his thick probe. Warm, strong hands skimmed her thighs and hips, touching but not controlling.

Ronen moaned. Jayne found herself going slow despite her earlier decree. She savored each thrust, each sway. Rocking her hips in small circles, she found the perfect rhythm. She ran her fingers along his chiseled face, across the rough texture of a whiskered jaw. He trapped one between his lips, sucking gently.

Tension built, propelling her onward. Ronen managed to find her naked breasts beneath the shirt and cupped her so her erect nipples flattened against his palms. Jayne quickened her tempo until she slammed into him. Pleasure crashed over her, making her tense and shake. She inhaled deeply, her pussy quivering violently around his cock. Ronen still moved beneath her, taking shallow thrusts before finally exploding to join his release with hers.

Jayne rolled off him, falling onto her back. Her muscles still ached, but sex had done wonders to relax them. Inside, it felt as if her bones turned to water and every nerve was numbed with the euphoria of the aftermath.

Ronen tugged at his breeches next to her, lacing them along the hip. "I am glad you have accepted your role as my wife. I promise you will not regret it."

His words caused an ache deep in her chest. Didn't he understand what this was?

"I don't need a man's protection," she whispered. "I can take care of myself."

"You are strong," he agreed, "and will bring much honor to our family name, my Lady of Firewall."

"I don't think you understand. I have no need of a husband. I never wanted one." She didn't move beyond tugging her tunic over her exposed hips to hide them from view. "As for your reasons, I cannot fulfill them. I can't give you children. I won't keep your house. I hate cleaning up after other people. I won't feed you. All that leaves you with is a whore to see to your needs. Surely paying a prostitute is cheaper than keeping a wife."

Ronen visibly paled. Weakly, he said, "We have servants."

Jayne turned away from him, rolling her eyes in disbelief. Really? That's all he had to say? Servants? As if that solved all her issues and would suddenly make her want to be with him forever. She decided long ago that she wasn't one for marriage and family. Sitting on the ground, she gingerly pushed at her wounded arm, resisting the urge to scratch the healing tissue.

"I hear my brother," Ronen said, breaking the uneasy silence. He pushed up from the ground, hitting the dust from his clothes. Seconds later she heard the sound of horses' hooves. Lord Sorin wasn't alone, and when he rode into the clearing around Widowrock, fourteen knights came with him.

Moody eyes turned toward her. She arched a brow, forcing all emotion from her face as she stared back. Why were they mad at her? She didn't ask them to hunt her down.

"Maps," Sorin stated, looking at his brother. He held up a fur pouch. His hand was covered with blood.

"Watch my lady," Ronen told the men, automatically following his brother without a backward glance.

Jayne sighed heavily, letting the knights see her irritation. Muttering to herself, she turned her back on them and sat down by the boulder. "Fourteen guards, my lord? Do you really think that will stop me?"

---

Ronen was grateful for his brother's interruption. He still didn't know what to say to his wife. No children? It would be a lie to say the news wasn't disappointing. He wanted children very much—sons to carry on the family name and tradition, a daughter to bless their home. When she talked it was clear Divinity had done some diabolical things to her—nanobots and bioengineering? He didn't fully understand what those things were, but the way her arm healed was not natural. Is that why she couldn't give them children?

"Ronen?" Sorin frowned. "Do I have your mind?"

"Yea," Ronen lied. He hadn't been listening.

Sorin held up the pouch. "We found this on the Caniba spies. They are mapping routes through the forest originating at Spearhead."

"Magda," Ronen ground out.

"The Sorceress plans something." Sorin pulled out a piece of parchment and dropped the Caniba pouch on the ground. "We must warn King Wilhelm so he can order troops to reinforce the borderland marshes. His personal army should be camped near Daggerpoint Castle."

"I will go," Ronen stated. "You must go back to your wife."

Sorin's face darkened. "Be sure the king knows I'm ready to march."

"Is the choice so bad?" Ronen grabbed the parchment and slid it beneath his tunic, holding it in place beneath his belt.

"Battles are nothing compared to what she puts me through," Sorin answered. Ronen knew it was all the explanation he'd receive. But, he really didn't need words. By the look in his brother's face,

Lady Lilith denied him her company and her bed. Should it continue, it would make for a hard marriage and a miserable life for his brother.

Ronen thought of Jayne. It would seem the Lords of Firewall both had problems. "Trust in the gods, my brother. They do not give us trial without reason."

"Yea." Sorin instantly changed the subject. "I'll take most of the men back to Battlewar and leave four to scour the forest to ensure no more spies linger. I'll spread word in the village that Lady Jayne's departure was the will of the gods and she led us to the spies."

"Yea, and I'll take Kar and Lance. There might be need of a healer on the battlefront." Ronen held out his hand. "Journey smooth and swift."

"Fight well," Sorin answered, grasping his hand before striding back to where the men awaited their orders.

Ronen was glad for an excuse to avoid Battlewar Castle. Not only would the battlefront distract his mind, but it was far away from the only Divinity portal in the land and Jayne's only way out of his dimensional plane. By the will of the fire goddess, she would never have the chance to leave him again.

---

Jayne watched in surprise as the knights rode off after Lord Sorin. They'd only left her with two guards—albeit large, disapproving, intimidating guards. She interlaced her fingers, cracking her knuckles. Yeah, she was pretty sure she could take them.

Jayne made no move to leave the boulder. The guards had horses and trying to outrun them would be a futile effort, even if she were to knock them unconscious first. They'd already proved apt at tracking through the forest, and if her recent beastly captors were any indication, she couldn't rely on help from the Caniba.

*Technologically advanced race?*

Jayne chuckled at the thought. The knights frowned in her direction at the sound. She laughed harder.

"What has happened?" Ronen strode through the forest.

"She's gone mad," a knight answered. He was the one from her joined vision with Ronen who'd been hunting her in the forest.

"Methinks she is overtired," the third knight said, a redheaded man with steady eyes and a thoughtful expression. "Do we ride back to Battlewar?"

"No. We go to Daggerpoint to seek an audience with the king." Ronen strode to his horse and swung up into the saddle. Then, walking the animal toward her, he held out his hand. Jayne hesitated, gauging the jump up. Finally, too exhausted to argue, she grabbed his wrist. Ronen jerked, pulling her up. It wasn't her most graceful landing, but she managed to slide behind him on the saddle. It didn't seem to take much for her body to respond to his nearness. With her legs apart and the tight space holding them firmly together, her sex molded to his ass as her thighs pressed into his. He spurred the horse into a gait and her breasts bounced against his back. Jayne closed her eyes, trying not to get aroused.

*This ride is already too long.*

# CHAPTER 7

One long night of travel had been made even more so by the way her body rubbed up against Ronen's. The horse rocked in a steady, yet somewhat dizzying rhythm. Jayne tried to stay awake, but the forest was endless and the warmth of Ronen's back so inviting. Before she realized it, she had her arms lazily wrapped around his hips and her cheek pressed into him in sleep.

By the time she awoke, dawn streaked the horizon, illuminating a valley filled with caramel-colored square tents. They varied in sizes, spread out over the distance and towered over by a dark gray castle. The larger tents were closest to the castle gate with progressively smaller ones fanning away. Bright banners hung from the tent flaps, pinned to the opened entryways.

Daggerpoint Castle lived up to its name. Tall, smooth spires pointed into the magenta heavens, reaching into sharp points. Banners fluttered in the wind, and Jayne felt sorry for the person who had to climb up that daunting height to affix the things.

"Is this where the king lives?" Jayne asked, forced to grab Ronen's hips as he steered the horse down an incline.

"This is his camp, but he'll be staying inside the castle." Ronen tensed as she held him, and remained stiff. "Battlewar is his home, but he spends more time near the borderlands."

"Will we stay in the camp?" Jayne hoped so. The soft clang of sword practice echoed around the shouts of laughter coming from a group of men surrounding a couple of bare-chested brutes wrestling in the dirt. The fresh air and unrestrictive prison of tent canvas seemed a far cry better than a dark stone tower.

"If there is a castle nearby, noble ladies stay within." Ronen kept riding, taking a cleared path toward the castle gate. Several men lifted their hands in greeting, shouting welcome and inquiring after Lord Sorin. They didn't speak to her, but they watched her curiously.

"My lord?" Kar appeared at their side.

"Yea," Ronen answered, apparently already knowing what the man wanted. "Take your leave, clean up, drink. Find me after you have rested."

Kar and Lance, the redhead, turned to ride down into the center of camp. They disappeared behind a blue-bannered tent.

"Is there a queen?" Jayne craned her neck to look up at the highest dagger spire. Pointed lancet windows were much wider than the narrow slits of Battlewar Castle. An orange glow shone from within a few of them.

"Why?"

"Because I'm hoping he's without a mate. I wish for more power," she drawled wryly.

"Yea, there is a queen." Ronen grunted. "Besides, noblewomen do not take multiple husbands, only peasants."

Jayne almost said, "lucky them", but refrained. She doubted the moody Lord Ronen would appreciate her dry humor. "I don't see why they'd want more than one."

"Because you don't even want one?" he filled in.

*Yeah, Lord Moody all right.*

"Can we have a conversation or do I have to shove your ill-tempered ass off this horse?" Jayne gave him a small push. "Tell me about the peasants. Do they get into fights over whose turn it is to do the wife? Because from what I saw of their behavior in Battlewar's many hallways, husbands appear to be very, ah, what's a delicate way of putting this? Hornier than a sex-crazed maniac on hormones." Just to mess with him and amuse herself, she lowered her tone ever so slightly to a sultry, breathy whisper. "Or do the other husbands watch as they each take turns?"

Ronen shifted on his horse. Jayne tried not to laugh.

"I do not know what happens in their bedchambers. I suppose each marriage pact is different," he answered. Then, before she could plant more deliciously inappropriate images into his head, he rushed on, "The arrangement is necessary for poorer families."

"Why?" she whispered against the back of his ear. If everyone insisted on staring at her, she'd give them something to look at—Lord Ronen squirming in his seat while she smiled innocently behind him. "Are peasant women insatiable? Ravenous?"

"Poorer families n-need," he stuttered, "to work together so no one starves and all, um, in the family trade."

She squeezed his hip. "Have you ever wanted to be a peasant? Just throw away the restrictions of your position and join in the naughty group games?"

"Honor forbids I give up my title." The words were final.

"But you don't even fantasize that you're someone else?" She brushed her breasts to his back, unsure why she tried to exasperate him. "I don't see a lot of women in this camp. Those long winter nights have to get pretty lonely. It would only be natural if you—"

"I understand what you are asking." His back relaxed some. "Men who chose the solitary path are not looked down upon, but I am not one of them. I enjoy the company of women. During campaigns, the camp followers make their rounds to see to the needs of the men."

It was Jayne's turn to stiffen. That was *not* what she'd been asking.

"They are more than willing to play out the fantasies of—"

"Hey, just because they're royalty, I won't be expected to bow, will I?" she broke in, changing the suddenly irritating subject. If she wasn't mistaken, he chuckled softly. A jealous wave of possessiveness washed over her. She did not want to hear about him and other women. Sure, she didn't think he came to her bed an untried virgin, but that didn't mean she wanted full details of his past.

"No, women curtsey."

Jayne put space between them. "Maybe you shouldn't introduce me then. I don't do too well with authority. Besides, I'd rather take a bath."

---

It had taken Ronen a moment to figure out what Jayne meant to do with her questioning about peasants. Her obvious jealousy amused as it assuaged his male vanity. If she thought trying to poke at him until he exploded was wise, then he'd just have to show her that he could poke back.

At first, he nearly jerked her around the front of the horse for a sound, hard spanking. How dare she indicate she wanted more lovers? Ronen refused to share what was his.

He shifted his hips, trying to adjust his heavy erection into a more comfortable position. Even in his initial aggravation, her sultry voice had stirred his blood to boiling. Having those soft breasts bouncing against him had been agony, and it didn't take much to convince his knight to prepare for battle.

Ronen mentally felt for the map at his hip. Duty demanded he hand it over first thing, before bathing or eating. However, after that, he'd be free to whisk his pretty bride to a bedchamber for the rest of the day.

Ronen passed through the low gates of Daggerpoint before motioning to a page. The young boy ran to gather the lord's horse as Ronen hopped down. He reached for Jayne, noting how very unsuitable she was for a formal introduction. The king would understand, but the queen tended to expect more of her noble ladies—regardless of the circumstances.

"I wasn't joking," Jayne said as her feet hit the dirt. "If you make me meet anyone right now, I will embarrass you."

"Your absence will be understood," he promised her, unsure whether her threat should entertain or anger him. "I will have the servants bring you to a sleeping chamber where you can bathe and eat. It would be better for you if you greet the queen with a fresh face."

"Whatever," she dismissed, unimpressed by the fact that royalty was so close. He'd seen women freeze up and faint at the sight of His and Her Majesty. "I just want to lie down."

---

Jayne groaned for the thirteenth time in one minute as she pushed an overly soapy washcloth along her arms. Steam rolled around her from the stone tub, clinging to the warped lead plate windows surrounding three sides of the raised platform of the bath. She'd slicked her damp hair back on her head while keeping all but her face submerged in liquid heat. The dark blue of the water trailed her skin like wet sapphires whenever she lifted her arms from their depths.

"If I never leave this bath again, it will be too soon," she said more to herself than the two servants watching her from where they put fresh linens on the large bed. She felt their eyes on her when they thought she wasn't paying attention. "If you two don't stop staring, I'll order you both to strip naked and await my lord's punishment. He seems the type to be fond of spankings."

Both women gasped in unison and ran from the room. Jayne pushed up far enough to peek at the bed. They'd left the top coverlet halfway off the side. Laughing hard, she sank into the water once more to enjoy the fact she was finally alone.

Closing her eyes, she debated whether or not to fall asleep right where she lay. Or maybe she'd stir the remnants of desire still lingering from being pressed to Ronen all night. Before she could decide if the risk of drowning outweighed comfort, a small tingling erupted along her temple. She opened her eyes, recognizing the sensation. Her mind was trying to connect her thoughts with Ronen's.

Still irritated by the idea of him and other women, Jayne decided to let it. Unless his meeting with the king only lasted a few short minutes, he'd still be talking to His Majesty. Smiling mischievously, she saw a flash of Ronen's hands around a drink. Instead of exploring his mind, she opened hers.

Grabbing the soapy cloth, she pushed to her knees so she could kneel in the water. Cooler air surrounded her, causing her nipples to harden into two erect points. She ran the cloth up the center of her chest, squeezing it so soap ran over her breasts as she watched. Suds clung to peaks before dripping into the water.

---

"The map does not go too deeply into the forest. The beasts could not have been exploring long," King Wilhelm said, scratching his short blond beard. The main hall was empty except for the occasional servant. Queen Patricia had left them to attend the duties of lady of the castle. She liked her world to be organized in a particular way, and Daggerpoint had no official mistress to see to its daily demands.

"My brother has sent men to scout the forest to make sure none live to tell the Sorceress of their discoveries." Ronen didn't move in his seat, well aware of how dirty he must have appeared, covered in dirt and sweat. He needed a bath and a bed, desperately.

"And you're sure it is Sorceress Magda who sends the spies?"

Ronen curled his nose in disgust. "Yea, when they died they shouted the praises of their queen. It is Sorin's and my opinion that we should order troops to reinforce the borderland marshes at Spearhead. He says his men are ready to march at your command."

"We'll increase the forest patrols," Wilhelm said. "I will write to Lord Sorin and have him arrange it from Battlewar. And I will send a messenger to Spearhead for a report."

Ronen nodded, seconds away from pushing up from his chair to take his leave when the king's words stopped him.

"I am pleased to hear the brothers of Firewall have taken brides."

Ronen didn't answer. He didn't want to speak of his wife. Talking about her would make him think about her. Thinking about her would make him want her. Wanting her would only add fire to his already heavy cock, and the last thing he felt like wearing before the king was a giant erection.

"I know there were many who were hesitant with the alliance, but your example will go far in encouraging other men to take these otherworlders as brides." The king motioned a servant to refill their drinks. "How are the foreign women? Are they of good stock? Are they all Divinity promised?"

"No," he stated flatly. It served no purpose to lie to the king. Wilhelm's eyes rounded in surprise.

"Are they uncomely?"

Ronen drew his eyes to the far side of the hall in the direction of Jayne. "They are most beautiful, but the agreement was for willing brides."

"Is the Lady Jayne not willing?" The king gave him a wry look. "It would explain your dark mood."

"I believe the foreign women might not have known about coming here. They were not awake when they arrived, and Divinity transport insisted we put them into a cell while they adjusted to the new dimension. Two of the five had to be sent back as unsuitable. They were crying hysterically and dishonoring themselves before they even made it to the ceremony. They were given the philter and unhappily returned." Ronen wrinkled his nose in distaste. "It is said one offered to pleasure anyone we put in front of her without consideration in return."

"They sent a camp follower as a bride? That was not in the agreement. They were to be agreeable to monogamy." The king paused while the maid filled his cup. He gave her an absent smile.

When the maid finished with his goblet, Ronen reached to take a drink. He blinked, seeing a flash of soft, wet flesh reflected back at him. Shaking his head, he thought it to be his imagination. Riding with the tantalizing Jayne at his back all night was sure to invoke sexual thoughts. He tried to calculate how long it would be before he could finish with a bath and go to her. The king interrupted his thoughts.

"And the other three?"

"I don't think they knew either. They seemed shocked by our

ways. At the time we thought it nervousness from traveling to a new land, now I'm not so sure." He took another drink, trying to ignore the strange tingling all over his body. A flash of a soft breast covered with trailing soap filtered through his vision. Heat instantly surged through him, centering over his cock. He cleared his throat, coughing as he forced the image from his mind. "Lady Jayne said she woke up here with no clue as to how or why."

"But, you have explained it to her. She understands she must stay as your wife." The king's frown deepened. "I do not want marital chaos in my kingdom, especially amongst my noblemen. We need this trade agreement to work. More brides mean more children. Within a generation we'll have more knights to defend this kingdom. Already the Caniba outnumber us by at least threefold. Then, who knows, maybe this war will end and we'll wipe the beastly scourge from existence. I should like to be remembered as the king whose actions started the downfall of our enemy."

"The decision was made," Ronen stated. This time it was a feminine hand pushing between narrow hips. Its direction unmistakable as a finger glided to the top arch of his wife's pussy. "I will make it work."

*Ronen, come to me in the bath. I want you.* Ronen grunted softly, mentally trying to lessen the pressure between his thighs as Jayne's voice filled his head. *I know you can hear me, my lord. I can feel that you do. My body is all wet for you.*

"Good, good." Wilhelm nodded.

*Ronen, please...*

"You are a man of great honor," the king continued.

Though hard to concentrate with images of his self-pleasuring wife in his head, he managed to focus enough on the conversation at hand to say, "But before there are more problems, methinks we should postpone trading with Divinity until the terms can be clarified. Sorin and I will find a way to convince our wives, and Sir Vidar is a good man, but if there are others who are not willing..."

*Ronen! Mm, I feel so hot.* The words were accompanied by the vision of Jayne's hand gliding between her thighs, long fingers disappearing between the soft folds of her sex only to come out wetter than before. *Why won't you come? I want to feel you inside me.*

"Chaos could ensue," the king finished. "It would not do to have a country of discontented wives. I will give this matter more thought."

*Ronen, I'm about to explode.*

"Oh, yea," he whispered, seeing her hand moving faster. Ronen rubbed his thumb over his fingertips. It was almost as if he could feel her against his flesh.

"My lord?" the king questioned, staring strangely at him.

"Um," Ronen coughed. By all the blood-covered battleaxes in Staria, his cock hurt and his balls ached. "Yea, a wise decision, Your Majesty. Very wise."

The king gave a small chuckle. "Well, my lord, it's the only kind I make. Now, let's have another drink."

*Ah, Ronen, you're missing it. You'd better hurry or I will finish without you.*

Ronen grunted in pain, before clearing his throat. "Yea, a drink."

---

*By all the gods of war!*

Ronen tugged at his belt as he raced through the passageway leading to the guest chambers he shared with Jayne. Holding the belt tightly in his fist, he pressed his hand to the wall of a narrow stairwell as he took the steps three at a time. Why did the queen have to put them so far away from the main hall?

It had been nearly impossible to concentrate while the king talked. Images of Jayne's wet, naked flesh haunted him. After he managed to breathe past the increasingly painful press of his erection to his breeches, he realized she teased him on purpose. He could practically hear her giggling in his head.

Ronen pushed through the thick wood door without pause, grabbing the edge and slamming it shut behind him. Jayne stood in the bath, the light from the outside windows illuminating her from behind. She let him look, posing perfectly still.

The belt slipped from his fingers and he jerked his tunic over his head, throwing it aside. It felt great to have the dirty material off his skin. He walked toward her, kicking his boots off with more speed than grace. Jayne's arms lifted as she put her hand on her hip, turning slightly to the side. The light caressed her breast. Ronen nearly tripped over his own feet, unable to stare, walk and unlace the ties holding his breeches up at the same time.

"How was your meeting with the king?" Jayne laughed and he saw her body shake ever so slightly.

"That was a devilish game, my lady." Ronen finally freed his hips, pushing down the material. His cock only seemed to ache more now that it didn't have the pressure of his clothes to keep it down. "And now you will relieve the pains you've caused."

Eagerly, he climbed into the bath, splashing as his feet broke surface. The warm water lapped his calves. Without thought, he reached for her, pulling her clean, naked body hard against his chest.

Jayne threw back her head and chuckled. "Into the water, Ronen. You smell like your horse."

He growled in frustration. She was right, of course. Instead of letting her go, he forced her into the bathwater with him. A gentle current rushed by his knee as the tub filtered the mineral water. "And you smell like a wood nymph."

"I have no clue what that is." Jayne wrapped her arms around his neck, bringing him to her lips. "But I assume it's a compliment."

Ronen couldn't deny himself. He had to kiss her. His lips pressed hard against her mouth, staking fervent claim. She'd teased his libido to the point of breaking, made him feebleminded before the king, unable to concentrate. The driving need of his cock took over, telling his hands to spin her away from him, urging his hips to force her to the edge of the tub, making his hands reach under the water to spread her thighs from behind. He took his shaft in hand, guiding it like a sword into its sheath. The warmth of the blue mineral water heated his way, allowing him to glide into the sweet cavern of her sex.

Desperately, he thrust, groaning loudly to feel the tight muscles of her pussy gripping him. Friction and mineral water added an element of pleasure. The force between them became hot, enflaming his already warm cock. He couldn't stop, couldn't let go, though he desperately wanted to reach around to cup her breasts. But if he released her, their bodies might slide apart and he needed to finish too badly.

Ronen slammed into her, taking her rough and hard. The sound of flesh smacking flesh mixed with the splashing water. Jayne didn't protest. He wasn't sure what he'd do if she did.

And then, finally, blessed release. His balls tightened as he jerked to a stop. A harsh cry escaped his lips as he pumped his seed into her. For a moment, he held still, his heart hammering and his breathing ragged. Ronen's cock slid from inside her as he fell back into the tub, letting the warm water caress him like her pussy did his shaft.

Jayne turned and he expected to see a sated smile on her mouth. Instead, she grinned impishly. That's when he realized he hadn't felt her finish. He'd been so driven by her self-pleasuring torment, he'd gone temporarily mad.

"I will do right by you, my lady," he managed. A small fear wrapped around him. What if she discarded him as an inept lover? "You will find your pleasure many times this night."

"Once or twice will do," she laughed. "It's been a long couple of days and I'm exhausted."

"If you would not have run—"

"Don't, Ronen." She held up her hand. "Not today for there is no agreement to be made on the subject. It is in me to run and it is in you to capture."

Simple and matter of fact. Ronen sighed. "Very well, my lady. We will not discuss it now."

Jayne pushed up from the tub. She gestured to a door. "Why do all these castle bedchambers have two rooms in them like a his and hers suite at some fancy hotel?"

"I do not know what a hotel is, but all noble quarters have two chambers—one for the lady and one for the lord."

"Let me guess." She grabbed a drying linen from where it had been left on the bed and wrapped it around her body. "The ladies get stuck in the room with no outside door."

"Of course." Ronen took soap and began lathering his skin and hair.

"All wives are prisoners?"

"All wives are protected," he corrected. Why did she insist on seeing life with him as a prison? He would give her anything, all she had to do was ask. He'd slay an army for her, climb the northern mountains, give his own life to save hers. "Women need their own room so that husbands do not take too great advantage of the marriage bed. And I've been told there are rituals a lady performs that men are not allowed to see."

Jayne picked up a comb and began trailing it through her damp locks. He watched her from the corner of his eye, transfixed by the feminine scene. "What if I told you I wanted the room next to the main door?"

"I would know you wished to slip out in the middle of the night again." Ronen dipped under the water, rinsing the soap from his flesh.

"So it is a prison."

Ronen brushed his hands over his hair, wringing the water from the length. He sighed in exasperation. "It is necessary for protection, especially since we are so close to the borderlands here. If there were to be an attack, ladies would be the very last thing the Caniba creatures would find. It is for your safety."

---

Jayne shivered, holding her bathing linen tighter as she watched Ronen step from the tub. Rivulets of water glided down his skin, running onto the stone floor. Thick, bulging muscles sculpted into the perfect specimen. From the tight cords of his neck to the defined lines of his stomach, the tapering of his hips and the strength of his thighs, she couldn't help but look. His penis lay nestled between his thighs, and she wanted to touch it and watch it grow.

She automatically grabbed the other thin towel and tossed it at him. Seeing his naked body teased her senses and her pussy already begged for more. She knew she'd tortured him to the brink of sanity with her images, pushing him to take her hard and fast. Though she enjoyed it, she hadn't met with the earth-shattering climax her body craved.

"Are all the Caniba like those who took me?" Jayne didn't want to think of the beastly men who'd had her tied to a pole.

"Yea."

To her disappointment, he wrapped the linen about his waist, hiding his lower half from view. "I guess I owe you thanks for freeing me. I should have said something at the time, but I..." She gestured weakly. "I don't do well with help."

"Then I guess I accept." The corner of his mouth twitched up.

"I've been to a lot of dimensions and dealt with a lot of dark characters, but there was something about those guys that froze my insides." Jayne shivered, remembering their eyes. Paige hadn't been lying. "They had dead gazes. I remember seeing that glassy look when I lived on the streets. All the residents of drug alley had that unaware sheen to them. The Caniba had the glassiness but with complete awareness. It's hard to explain. It's like a force drives them to act, but they're mindless at the same time."

"That force would be Sorceress Magda," Ronen said. Jayne lifted the comb, absently handing it to him to use. He turned his back to her as he walked to a trunk in the corner. She watched the muscles of his back swimming beneath the tight flesh. "She wields control over her followers like a goddess. Many believe her to be immortal."

"Do you?"

"Logically, I want to say no, but there are times..." He tossed the comb into the trunk and let the lid fall shut. Waving his hand in dismissal, he said, "You do not wish to hear of war."

She stiffened. "Why? Because I'm a woman? I'll have you know war doesn't bother me. I've seen more violence than—"

"I only meant that you wished for..." He grinned. "Was it to be finished two times?"

Jayne's breathing deepened. If her pussy could scream in approval, it would have. Moisture flooded her sex, wetting the folds in welcome. "I'm pretty sure you said three."

"Did I?" He grinned.

"Perhaps four, five," she paused, biting her lip as she pretended to think. "No, it was fifteen that you said."

Ronen smiled even as he groaned. "You will be the death of me, but what a way to die."

Jayne laughed, unable to help herself.

"Remove the bathing linen and lie on the bed with your legs apart," he ordered, plucking at his waist. His towel slithered to the floor. "I wish to taste you and feel you come against my lips."

Jayne didn't try to resist as she dropped the towel and crawled onto the soft bed. Though she was in his possession once more, she assured herself nothing had changed. She'd find a way to leave him. Until then, she would enjoy her prison and manipulate her captor. Why should she deny herself something she wanted?

His fingers started at her foot, massaging slowly. Ronen's gaze focused on her, watching intently as he moved up her ankle to her calf. He explored her, taking in every inch of her legs, pausing to place random kisses to her flesh. Jayne closed her eyes to the pleasure, her mind focused on his touch.

A warm tongue darted along her inner thigh and she jerked, liking the way his breath cooled the wet trail he'd just made. She parted her lips, trembling in an effort not to force his head between her legs and smother him with her sex. Ronen nipped at her flesh, biting the tender crease where leg met pussy.

He groaned softly, the sound vibrating against her. She panted for breath, gripping the coverlet into tight fists. His mouth passed her center fire and moved over her hips, giving them the same attention he'd given her legs. He kissed her navel, swirling it with his tongue. He licked and bit over her stomach and ribs, massaged her sides, cupped her breasts but denied the hard nipples.

Before Jayne realized she'd let go of the covers, her hands were in his hair, urging his mouth to a taut nipple. It ached for stimulation, for the biting kisses he so generously gave the rest of her. Ronen chuckled, obeying her needy directions. He sucked the nipple hard, rolling it with his tongue.

Jayne parted her thighs wider, rubbing her legs along his hard flesh. She tried to grab his cock, but he turned his hip, denying her reach. So instead, she scratched at his waist, dragging her nails so they left red streaks in their wake.

"Ah," she gasped, pushing his head, "down."

The short plea was all she could manage.

Ronen chuckled, not moved by her strength as he took his time. Instead of obeying, he kissed his way to her neck, clearly not stopping until he'd touched and explored every inch of her.

"It is your turn to be teased, my devilish lady," he whispered before sucking the lobe of her ear.

Jayne became more aggressive, scratching at his arms and back, mindlessly trying to push him where she wanted him. Ronen resisted all her silent efforts as he made his leisurely way back down, reversing the path he'd first taken. Lips wrapped her nipples. His tongue flicked its way down her abdomen. Fingers gripped hips and ass.

"Please, Ronen." Jayne went from commanding to begging. There wasn't an inch of her flesh that didn't tingle, and she worried he'd make her turn over so he could journey up and down her backside. She couldn't take the torture if he did.

The bright light of late morning washed over them. To her relief, he merely ran his hands over her legs, not following with his slow moving mouth. Harsh breath hit against her sex, cooling and heating it at the same time. She felt the moisture gathered there, ready to ease his way.

Finally, he dipped his tongue into her folds, parting her sex as he tasted her. She grabbed his hair, doing her best to keep him there as she wrapped her legs around his shoulders. Ronen gave her pussy the same attention he'd given the rest of her. He probed her clit with his mouth until she cried out in sheer ecstasy. She watched the top of his head bob gently. Jayne squirmed, rocking into his mouth. He ran his hands up her stomach to rub her breasts. Her legs tightened, forcing him harder against her sex.

A sensual chuckle escaped him and he braced himself on the bed to push up. He inhaled deeply. "I will be no good to you passed out between your thighs."

Jayne was too close to completion. She moaned, tightening her grip to slam his face back into her sex. He bumped her clit and she jerked, nearly coming off the bed. Her leg slipped off his shoulder. She came hard, violently shuddering.

Her limbs sprawled on the mattress. She couldn't move and wasn't sure she wanted to. Ronen crawled next to her, grinning with pride as he lay on his side.

"You look proud." Jayne laughed weakly.

"That is one, my lady," Ronen answered. "Catch your breath, I owe you fourteen more."

Jayne rolled to face him, searching his face to see if he was serious. There was no way her body could take that another fourteen times in one evening. He merely smiled at her like a man who was very willing to try. She placed her hand on his neck, tracing his cheek with her thumb. "When did you shave?"

"On the horse last night while you slept. Soldiers learn to do what we can on the move."

"What else do you do on the move?" She continued to trace his cheek before moving to brush past his lips.

"We eat."

"Uh-huh." Jayne lazily swiped along the seam of his mouth when his lips closed.

Ronen nipped at her thumb, sucking it between his lips and biting gently. His lids lowered over his eyes. "We drink."

Now wet from his mouth, she again ran her finger around his lips. Her heart quickened. "And?"

"When we are alone, traveling those dark nights, we occasionally find our release." He turned his face into her palm, licking it. "And, when we are fortunate enough to have a woman, we fuck."

"While riding?"

"Yea, my lady."

Jayne furrowed her brow, trying to picture them doing such a thing.

As if reading her thoughts, he said, "Here, I will show you."

"You want to go for a ride now?" she inquired in disbelief. Jayne glanced at the lighted window. It still looked early in the day. Even so, she doubted she'd have the energy to make it out of the castle, let alone to the stables and onto a horse.

"No, my lady." He moved up on the bed so his upper back was pressed against the headboard. His cock was full and she realized whereas she had found release, he had not. He absently rubbed his stiff erection. "I wish for you to ride now."

Jayne licked her lips, eyeing his cock. "What if I don't want to ride? What if I'm hungry instead?" She lifted her leg, straddling his calves before leaning over. "What if I want to..."

Jayne flicked her tongue over the mushroomed tip, tracing the small indention she found there. His hips jerked and he reached over his head to grab hold of the headboard. She continued to tease him as he had her, flicking and licking, kissing and tasting. His legs worked against the bed, bumping up into her moistening pussy. Her breasts brushed along his muscled thighs until her own teasing began to torture her as well.

"Either take me fully into your mouth or mount up, my lady," he grunted. "For if you don't, I cannot promise to control my actions."

"Oh?" She sucked lightly on the tip, but only taking him as deep as the top ridge of his penis. Jayne wanted to ride him, but she also wanted to hear what else he had in mind. "What will you do when you lose control, warrior?"

"I will either grab you by the hair to forcibly fuck that temptress mouth of yours until I come down the back of your throat, or I will turn you around so that I may pound into you from behind like a wild beast in heat." The words came out harsh and panted, and he looked almost as if he didn't want to say them. "I have no desire to treat you so roughly and am ashamed I am so close to losing control."

Jayne had a very big desire for him to treat her so roughly. She crawled up onto his lap. Grabbing the headboard for support, she lifted up. Ronen grabbed her hips, as he maneuvered his cock along her slit. Quickly finding what he sought, he pulled her down onto him. A loud moan sounded over her as he buried himself deep.

Jayne lifted up and let her weight carry her back down, keeping it slow and steady as she impaled herself on his cock. Ronen gripped her tight, digging his fingers into her flesh as he tried to make her go faster. His face buried between her breasts as he made animalistic noises along her flesh.

"This is my ride, Lord Ronen," Jayne said, nipping at his ear. He groaned, finally giving over all control. As a reward, Jayne moved faster, slamming onto him. The pleasure built and she had to throw back her head in order to catch her breath. She gasped and panted, both fighting and accepting the rush of tremors that overtook her body, radiating from her sex.

Stiffening, she couldn't move. She came hard. Ronen cried out, his stomach tensing as his hips jerked up. He spilled his seed inside her, not letting go of his tight hold on her until every last ounce of their climax was spent. Jayne's forehead fell against his shoulder.

"There are so many ways my mind wishes me to take you," he said into her hair. "But my body needs to recover."

Jayne suppressed a yawn, too spent to move. "Now that you mention it, I am a little tired. We might have to hold off on numbers three through fifteen until later."

"As my lady wishes." He kissed her temple as he rolled her onto her back. "Would you like me to carry you to your bed?"

He really was going to kick her out of his bed? Jayne stretched her arms over her head. It was just as well. She couldn't sleep on the soft mattress anyway. Closing her eyes, she yawned, not in any hurry to move. "No, I can do it."

When she made no move to get up, she felt his arms slip under her back and legs. Ronen lifted her, carrying her naked across the chamber to her room. She didn't open her eyes, too tired to demand he put her down.

"Rest you well, my lady," he said, laying her on a different but equally soft bed. His hand brushed over her hair before the sound of his footfall faded across the chamber floor.

The cool mattress was an odd contrast to her heated body as he let her go. Mumbling, she answered, "Goodnight, Ronen."

# CHAPTER 8

She did it again. She left him.

Ronen stared at Jayne's empty bed in disbelief. He'd awoken rested and ready to make good on his promise to give her pleasure. Almost eagerly he went to her chambers, hoping to slip into her bed and pull her from sleep with his kisses. But she wasn't there. The bed was made, untouched.

Outside, the telltale streaks of evening encroached upon the land. How long had she been gone? How did she sneak past him without rousing him? He was a trained knight. No one was supposed to enter his sleeping quarters without him knowing. Men could tiptoe across the dirt outside his tent and he would notice. But somehow his wife went right by him and he didn't know it.

She left him.

Ronen felt a panic rise inside him causing his hands to shake. How could she do it? Here? The same day Ronen assured the king he'd make his marriage work.

Maybe she didn't leave. Maybe she went below stairs and even now sat with the queen, dining and talking of the secret things women discussed.

Going to the trunk in his room, he found a loose tunic and

breeches. The soft linen material wasn't cut to fit him but, considering he didn't have his own clothes, he couldn't complain. He grabbed his boots, tugging them on before hurrying toward the main hall.

*Be there, Jayne. Be in the main hall. Do not leave me.*

He paused, hidden around the corner as he tried to center himself. His hands still shook and his heart pounded hard. Anxiety gripped him, tightening his chest and throat.

*Be there, Jayne.*

He strode into the hall, seeking the head table. Queen Patricia sat by herself, her hands folded in her lap, her chin lifted regally as she watched the hall. Occasionally, she would motion a silent command to a servant. Much of the evidence of the eve meal had been removed from the tables, but knights still sat, drinking and talking. King Wilhelm joined his men at a lower table, drawing his finger over the wood to illustrate his point. The knights around him laughed, pounding their fists on the tabletop.

Seeing Ronen, the king's expression dropped and he stood, leaving his companions to watch after him. When he was within speaking range, he said, "Is there news from the forest?"

"No, Majesty," Ronen answered. "It is my wife."

"Is she injured? Did the Caniba violate her?" The king took his arm, leading him to the privacy of the passageway beyond the main hall.

"Methinks she has run off again. I woke up and she was gone." Admitting as much pained him, but he would not dishonor himself more by lying to the king. "Has she been to the hall?"

"No," the king shook his head in denial. "The queen would have demanded her presence at the head table had she arrived."

"I will ask about the encampment and see if any have seen her pass. With your permission, I ride at once."

"Yea, in a moment." The king made a low noise of irritation. "You are right, Lord Ronen. If a bride of Firewall, with all its power and glory, cannot be convinced to stay, then we cannot risk others coming here under the present agreement. I will suspend trade with Divinity, but we will keep this between us. I have no wish to dampen the spirits of the men with Sorceress Magda threatening our borders. The knights need a reason to fight, and the hope of a lady always seems to be the best motivation. Moreover, I am not ready to give up on this alliance. I will not have the trade agreement tarnished by rumors of the gods being angered with us for trying to take more brides than they readily bestow."

"Agreed." Ronen itched to be dismissed so he could run for his horse. Hopefully someone in the encampment stopped her. Surely news of her first attempt to escape him had made the rounds amongst the men. Just the thought made him tense. The embarrassment to his honor was unbearable. First, she chose him for all to see, and then she ran from him—twice. Any way a man analyzed the situation, it looked bad for Ronen.

Then there was his private torment, the insecurities he'd never felt before. Ronen had no instinct as to how to deal with them. Show him a battle and his instinct was to fight. Show him a sword and his instinct was to swing. Show him a wife and his instinct was to make love to her and protect her from all harm. Jayne didn't want him to protect her.

Why did she run? He didn't mistreat her. He had money and power. She would never want for anything. What more could she want from him? Was facing the Caniba in the forest so much better than staying as his wife? What had he done? And the most humiliating question of all, was he a bad lover? The women in his past never complained, though he knew he wasn't as experienced as a man who'd been wed for several years. It's not like women lined every street yearning for a man to take them. When women of trade were available, he had to wait his turn like everyone else.

"When you find her, Lord Ronen, the queen would like to speak with Lady Jayne. She will ensure the new bride knows her place." The king motioned that Ronen should go.

As he hurried through the passageway, avoiding those gathered in the main hall, his irritation only deepened. Now the queen wished to interfere in his marriage?

Ronen's fists tightened and he fought the urge to scream. This was too much. It was beyond anything a knight of his station and training should have to deal with. Jayne embarrassed him in front of his king and his people. She humiliated him, tormented him and worried him. All he wanted was a wife he could take care of and do his duty by. He wanted ease in his home and happiness.

Why did the gods curse him?

---

Jayne stretched her arms over her head and yawned. The fur pelt beneath her naked body tickled her flesh, padding it from the cool stone floor. She felt as if she'd slept for a year, glad for a bed that wasn't a pile of dirt beneath a shrub.

Grabbing the side of the bed, she pulled herself up from the floor. On the opposite side of the thick mattress, the door to Ronen's room was closed. The fire that burned when she walked into the room had died down to a soft glow. Combined with the darkened skies outside her windows, it made for heavy shadows. Jayne crossed to the fireplace and tossed in a log. The wood had been soaked in a sticky substance that instantly ignited but apparently caused the wood to burn slower and last longer.

Light crept brighter over the walls. The room was smaller than the one originally provided for her at Battlewar Castle. Two windows dominated one wall on either side of a thick chair. A small table, trunk and the box of firewood took up the other. The centerpiece of the room was the large bed whose thick mattress forced Jayne to sleep on the floor atop the fur rug.

A basin of water had been left on the small table and Jayne washed her hands. Next to it, she found a white, shapeless gown and a red corset top. A pair of short boots had been placed nearby on the floor. She'd seen how the women of this dimension dressed but refused to wear a corset tightened to the point she couldn't breathe for the sake of her cleavage. Before putting the clothes on, she tiptoed to the door leading to Ronen's room. He had promised to make her come, what was it? Fifteen times? Her rested body eagerly wanted to make good on the claim. Cracking open the door, she found the bedcovers messed up and the room empty.

She sighed in disappointment. So much for the idea of a quick romp before searching for food. Her stomach growled loudly. The maid who'd shown her to the guest chambers when they first arrived had offered to bring her food. Jayne should have said yes but, at the time, conceding she needed anything from Ronen or his people had been too much of a sting to her pride.

Slipping into her clothes, she left the corset loose and headed toward the passageways outside the chamber door. The castle was quiet. Each step sounded on the floor with a decisive hit. Jayne itched at her arm, pulling up her sleeve to check the wound. It had healed to a light pink, the skin only slightly textured.

The castle's layout was relatively simple compared to the maze of Battlewar. All passageways seemed to converge on one center spot—the main hall. Thick tapestries lined the walls, covering the stone with bright blues, reds and golds. They depicted bloody battles against legions of hairy Caniba warriors. From what she could decipher of the stories, they rarely ended happily for the hero.

Jayne understood fighting and the images didn't bother her as it might a more delicate lady. She might not go into battle, but each time she went into the ring she risked her life. Matches where death was a possibility paid more. Sure, she never actually killed someone in the ring, and the thought of killing for sport made her stomach curl, but she would if she had to. That's what some people didn't seem to get. Life wasn't some pretty day at the park, picnicking and laughing. Life was dirty and raw and filled with things she'd rather not think of. Jayne touched a tapestry, running her finger over a thick Starian hero marred with the horrors of war. The Starians seemed to have the concept down, though. Maybe she and Ronen were more alike than she first imagined.

What was she thinking? Ronen was her captor and every good prisoner knew there were only two options—live and die under the will of another or escape. It wasn't in her nature not to fight and, if she died, it would be her own doing.

"I must be delirious. I need food," she mumbled to herself, swatting aimlessly at the embroidered hero before walking toward a narrow patch of light coming from the direction of the main hall.

Though remnants of a crowd remained, giving evidence through scattered goblets and pitchers of liquor, the hall was nearly empty. A few servants cleared the remaining trenchers of mostly eaten food. Jayne's gaze swept over the hall, landing on a long table set high above the others on a stone platform. For a moment she thought the lady staring back at her was a statue. The woman didn't move, merely sitting with her chin imperially in the air and eyes narrowed in irritation.

"Lady Jayne, I presume," the woman said, coming slowly to her feet. Each movement was slow and steady. Her red gown and perfectly matched corset contrasted the drab color of the stone behind her and the muted brown and cream of her tablecloth. It set her apart from the hall. Her hair had been pulled up high on her head, piled in curls, and she wore a thick band of gold around the base of her throat. "You may approach."

Jayne arched a brow but stepped forward. It didn't take a genius to deduce that this was the queen. Only royalty would carry such a self-deserving, pompous look on their face. Stopping below the table, she stood, staring up as the other woman stared down.

"We are displeased with you," the queen said.

"Uh, thanks?" Jayne drawled, giving minimal effort to keep the dryness from her tone. She didn't think it possible, but the queen's face tightened even more.

"We would like an explanation." The woman walked very slowly around the table, not taking her eyes off the new "subject".

"We don't know what you're talking about," Jayne mocked. This woman didn't scare her. If Bossman Bishop and his goons couldn't make her throw a fight with intimidation, this slender thing hardly inspired alarm. Besides, Lady of Red here might be a queen, but she wasn't Jayne's queen—despite the royal's supposed assumptions otherwise. The woman's lip curled slightly, and Jayne found some amusement in watching her try to retain her composure. As she stepped onto the lower floor, the queen made a wide arch around Jayne, studying her.

"Margaret," the queen ordered, "send someone to find Lord

Ronen. Tell him I've taken his wife to my chambers. And tell Renell she is needed."

"Yea, Queen Patricia," the servant said, putting a trencher back down on the table. She curtsied before rushing out the door.

"Huh, I wouldn't have taken you for a Patricia," Jayne mumbled. Okay, so now she was just finding an excuse to be insolent. But really, the woman made it too easy. "You seem much too fun for such a serious name. How about we call you Patry? Or Trix?"

*More like Prunella or Prudence.* Jayne tried her best not to smirk. Hair of the smelly dog, she hated women like this! They were always so haughty and condescending. She bet the queen didn't know the first thing about taking care of herself.

"I do not like your tone." The words were low and hard.

"What happened to we? Did your other personality leave? Couldn't take your attitude either?"

"We is myself and my husband, King Wilhelm, but I am sure he wouldn't appreciate how you speak to me." Patricia gave Jayne a displeased once-over with her eyes, before ordering, "Follow me."

"No." Jayne didn't move.

"Follow me," the queen turned to stare Jayne down, "or I will have you paraded naked through the encampment below before being drawn and quartered. The knights have been a long time without an entertainment."

Jayne couldn't help herself, she smiled. Maybe this woman wasn't so bad after all.

"You don't believe me?" Patricia stiffened, appearing inches away from issuing the threat.

"No, I believe you," Jayne said, giving a small laugh. "Actually, I'm impressed. I have no idea what drawn and quartered means, but you made it sound very terrifying. Let me guess? You have an artist sew the event of my naked parade into a tapestry and lock me in my quarters?"

"You are tied to horses and your limbs pulled from your body."

That gave Jayne pause and she didn't relish the prospect. "So, your chamber is where, your, ah, queen?"

"Your Majesty will do," Patricia corrected. "This way."

Jayne followed the woman from the hall. When they were alone in the passageway, she said, "Uh, I feel I should tell you. I'm not really 'into' women. I mean, I'm flattered you'd like some alone time with me, but—"

"And if I was," the queen interrupted, "a disrespectful, unkempt, dishonorable woman who does not deserve the title of lady would be my last choice. In this dimension, women know how to look like women."

Jayne looked down the front of her dress and pulled at her corset, twisting the loose garment back into place. For some reason she couldn't explain, the words hurt. She knew she wasn't exactly the most feminine woman in all the dimensions, but in her world—the underground fighting world—she was Jayne "The Sweet" Hart, lady of boxing.

"Are you coming?" The queen's words broke into her thoughts and Jayne realized she'd stopped walking.

"What exactly are we doing?" Jayne asked. "If you just wanted to speak to me, we could have spoken in the hall."

"You might be accustomed to talking in front of gossiping servants, not caring about the uneducated impression you make upon others, but I know my place in society. With my station comes obligation and I take my honor and that of my husband very seriously."

*Now I'm uneducated? Ouch. The queen really knows how to throw a punch.*

The queen opened a door, leading the way into a room. The lavish bedchamber was clearly decorated for a woman. Delicate gold flowers embroidered the thick red curtains hanging over the bed and windows, matching the cushioned chairs. A small sword and an assortment of knives dominated one wall. Jayne closed the door, but stood near the doorway, not stepping too deeply into the luxurious chamber.

"It is apparent to me that you are a woman well used to control, and you gain that control by either fighting, arguing or acting contrary to expectations." The queen took a seat on one of the chairs, not once losing her solid composure. She gestured that Jayne should sit. "You ran from a Starian nobleman. Not just any nobleman but a brother of Firewall. You braved an unknown forest in an unknown land. You were kidnapped by the Caniba and kept yourself well. And, you stood up to me. Foolish, all these things, but brave."

Jayne sat but didn't relax. The queen appeared very reasonable, and she felt a little bad for her initial reaction to the woman in the hall. Patricia was right. Jayne's first instinct in any situation was to either antagonize or fight. It's what her childhood had trained her to do. When you lived in an orphanage or out on the streets, you learned to keep your emotions buried until they became habit to ignore.

"Did I leave anything out?"

"Only that Divinity more or less kidnapped me first and abandoned me here without my knowledge," Jayne answered. "Oh, and I was chased by a pack of wild boars."

"Lord Ronen spoke of Divinity to the king," Patricia acknowledged. "It is not in the Starian nature to rethink any decision once it's made. To do so negates the fact you made a decision in the first place. Indecisiveness is looked at as weak, and we are well used to making decisions at a moment's notice. But rest assured, we will be negotiating with Divinity again. They clearly do not understand the terms we set."

"Oh, I'm sure they understood," Jayne said. "The others that came with me didn't know what they were in for either."

"This is distressing information." The queen frowned. "Our ancestors would raid villages and claim the women they wanted with force. Centuries of war breeds such actions out of necessity, but we have progressed since then. The breeding ceremonies are an evolution of those raids, symbolizing the old ways and showing how we've changed as a people. But the women know why they are there and participate out of willingness or necessity—like those the gods send through the fairy rings. Like you, such women have no family or home in Staria and must seek protection."

"But I have a life off this dimension." Jayne felt a ray of hope.

The queen appeared very astute. Maybe she would help her. "I have means to protect and take care of myself. I don't need or want a husband. All I want is an inter-dimensional jump home."

The queen nodded, but didn't speak.

"Will you help me?"

"You showed honor in coming back here after running a second time. That gives me hope," the queen answered.

*A second time?*

"So you will help me?" Jayne implored.

"Yea, I will help you." The queen paused and Jayne almost broke into a grin, only the next words stopped her. "I will help you adjust to your new station as Lord Ronen's wife and a noblewoman of Firewall."

"But..." Jayne jumped up from her chair. "You don't believe me?"

"I believe you," the queen said, not getting up from her chair, "but there is nothing to be done for it. You are Lord Ronen's bride. It is done and cannot be undone. All I can do is to ensure your situation does not happen to others in the future. We will speak to Divinity and try to come to a better arrangement. Unfortunately, women are a scarce resource and Divinity gives us what our men so desperately need."

"What if I dishonor my husband?" Jayne asked, feeling trapped and desperate. "What if I keep running? Or cheat on him? Or, or..."

"I think you bluff. You must feel something for him. You came back this second time, why?"

"Second time?" Jayne threw her hands into the air. Had the whole universe gone mad? "What are you talking about?"

"Lord Ronen searches the forest for you even now. I sent a man to bring him back so he could call off the search." A knock sounded on the door, light and fast. The queen stood to answer.

"But, why? I was sleeping in my chambers. Is he blind? I was right there on the floor in front of the fire."

Pausing at the door, Patricia gave a slight frown. "The floor? Hm, this is unfortunate. If you didn't run, then Ronen's humiliation will be twofold. He will be seen as insecure in his marriage and rash in his actions. Perhaps we should say you ran and came back to him. The fact you tried to escape once is bad enough." Before Jayne could answer, the queen let in a servant. "Renell, attend to the lady's clothes and hair. We do not wish for her to look like she crawled from the forest. When you are finished, send for the seamstress so gowns may be fitted immediately for Lady Jayne. She will also need a lady's maid assigned to her. Pick one from the staff until the lady finds another more suited to her tastes."

"Yea, my queen." Renell, a short, squat redhead with pale skin and a smattering of freckles, curtsied.

"Lady Jayne, I look forward to helping you understand the Starian ways." The queen left Jayne and Renell alone.

"Ach, my lady, let's get a comb through that wild hair of yours. Come, sit, Renell will take good care of you."

# CHAPTER 9

Jayne felt strange, almost afraid to move. The tight corset, the same one she'd sworn never to wear like the other women, pulled against her ribs. She'd been poked, prodded, measured and pulled. Renell had called in a team of women to help her. They piled Jayne's hair on her head, much like the queen's. Margaret scrubbed her fingernails and toenails and shaped them into rounded tips. Another woman rubbed her shoulders and neck. Okay, so that last part of the pampering treatment wasn't too bad and almost made her forget someone poked annoyingly at her toes. And at least they fed her. She'd devoured an entire tray of fruits and bread.

"So if women are scarce, why do I see so many working in the castles?" Jayne inquired.

"It is an honored position granted to the women of knights, my lady," Margaret answered. "Residing in a castle we are more protected than the villages, and we receive word from or about our husbands sooner."

"Does anything here happen that has nothing to do with protection and war?" Jayne eyed each of them in turn, noting their somewhat confused expressions. "Didn't think so."

"The traveling markets come here more often, as well." Renell giggled.

"Wonderful," Jayne drawled. "Nothing we girls like better than shopping."

The sarcasm was lost on them as they nodded in excited agreement. Renell held out her hand. "I bought this pretty ring last time the silversmith came."

"Pretty," Jayne said, barely looking. The maids continued talking about the marketplace, of what they would buy and what they already had. She really didn't pay much mind to jewels—though she'd been given a few to wear as advertisement. That homeless woman had been ecstatic the day Jayne decided to clean out some of her promotional clutter. It wasn't like Jayne Hart could be seen publicly selling the stuff.

"What do you think, my lady?" Margaret asked.

What had they been babbling on about? Jayne pulled at her tight bodice, about to mumble something incoherently when the door swung open, saving her. Ronen appeared, windblown and stiff with rage.

"My lord," the servants greeted, almost in unison. Their giggling instantly died with his appearance.

"Leave us," Ronen ordered. The women practically ran from the room, and he kicked the door shut behind them. "What do you have to say for yourself?"

Jayne lifted her bare foot. "That Margaret wasn't done with my toes. See, two left."

"I am not amused, Wife." His fists clenched at his sides. Was that supposed to scare her?

"Well, that's your problem, Knight." She mimicked his tone, knowing all the while it probably wasn't the best thing to do. Prudence was never one of her strengths. "You have only yourself to blame for running off to the forest and alarming the king's army. I was asleep in my chambers. In fact, it is I who should yell at you. I had to sit and listen to the queen lecture me about honor, duty and my lack of education. And what's worse, she is just as bad as the rest of you. She knows I don't belong here and yet she, with all her queenly powers, does nothing to right the wrong."

"Keep your voice down, Jayne," Ronen warned. "You do not speak of Queen Patricia in such a way. She has earned the respect of our people, risking her life in battle to save her husband. She even had this chamber built so that if the Caniba attacked, she would be the first lady to fight and fall, giving others time to escape in the tunnels."

"Don't get mad at me. You embarrassed yourself." She crossed her arms over her chest, only to become aware of how exposed her chest was. Her breasts pushed up, showcased by the fit of the corset and low cut of her gown. Ronen noticed, too. His eyes went to her breasts and stayed. Jayne tried to pull at the laces along her back to loosen the corset's hold. "I already told you, I was asleep when you went running off. Maybe don't act so rash next time."

Steely eyes darted back up to meet hers. His voice a little hoarse, but no less angry than before, he said, "I checked your bed. It was not slept in."

"That's because I don't sleep in beds. I don't like the softness. I was on the floor." Jayne became aware of how alone they were in the queen's room. Ronen captured her attention whenever he was around, and her pussy chose that moment to remind her of the promise he'd made to make her come again. Cream instantly pooled along her folds, slickening her sex.

His brow arched in disbelief. "No lady chooses the floor to a castle bed."

"I've been trying to tell you, I'm no lady." Giving up on loosening the corset, she placed her hands on her hips and faced him down. The statement wasn't a lie. At the moment, very unladylike thoughts were traveling through her mind, and all of them had to do with freeing Ronen's cock from his breeches and making him take her right there in the queen's chamber. Oh, how his sensible honor would rebel at the suggestion. Knowing he'd resist only made Jayne want to seduce him more. She liked the dangerous excitement of fucking him in such a forbidden place, of making him so crazy he forgot himself.

Suddenly, the tight corset's constriction became pleasurable. It pressed into her aching nipples, rubbing them with each rushed breath. His eyes drifted over her length to again land on her chest. "You look very much like a lady to me."

"That's because they dressed me up." Jayne lowered her voice to a sultry whisper. She batted her lashes, keeping her eyes wide. "You should see what is underneath."

Ronen opened his mouth but no sound came out. Jayne trailed her hand over the back of a chair. She smiled innocently, inching away from him to round the side of the bed. He disappeared from view behind the bed curtain.

"Come, my lady."

Jayne smiled to herself, recognizing the barely contained passion in his words. *How quickly rage turns to lust, my lord.*

She appeared from behind the curtain, looking at him from over the large bed. "That is exactly what I plan to do, Lord Ronen." She licked her lips, moaning, "Come."

"I will take you back to our rooms."

Jayne pulled at her skirt, lifting only to let go as she crawled forward onto the bed. With her ass wiggling slightly in the air, she said, "But I want you to take me right here."

Ronen glanced around, as if they stood before a crowd of people. As his body shifted, she saw the unmistakable outline of his arousal poking at the material of his long tunic.

"Haven't you ever wanted to be bad?" She licked her lips, keeping them parted. "Naughty?"

"You should not be on the queen's bed," he insisted, reaching a hand to her as if he'd help her off. Jayne maneuvered back, forcing him to lean forward over the mattress if he wanted to grab her.

"What's wrong, Ronen?" She pouted. "Don't you want me? Undo your laces and let me see. If you need help rising to the occasion, I'd be happy to lend you a hand, or a mouth."

Instead of coming onto the bed, he marched around to the other side. Jayne pulled at her skirt, baring the back of her thighs before he got there. She spread her legs, pressing her elbows into the bed and her pussy up into the air. Moaning, she demanded, "Take me, Ronen. I'm burning for you."

*Just let him try to refuse me.*

He made a strange noise, reaching for her as if he'd pull her from the bed, but he was powerless against her seduction. His hand slid over her thigh. Jayne grew heady with control.

"We should not be doing this here." Ronen tossed her skirt up, baring her ass. Jayne heard the rustling of material behind her. When she glanced over her shoulder, she saw him tugging frantically at his breeches. His cock protruded, already tall and eager.

"You think too much about the rules." She gripped the covers, wrinkling the pristine bed.

"I think too much about you." Ronen jerked her hips, forcing her back. Her chest dipped as her arms slid out from under her, angling her body even more. His cock brushed across her ass. "I cannot get you out of my head."

Though sweet, she knew the sentiment only reflected the connection they shared. She was, literally, in his head as he was in hers. Jayne couldn't stop thinking of him. She knew the reason, but still found the fact disconcerting.

Her body heated, each nerve tingling with need. Her pussy felt so wet and desperate. The thick cock head probed her sex, gliding along her slit before finding its target as he stood beside the bed. Some of her control slipped but she didn't care. How could she? Now, in this moment?

The soft covers slid beneath her arms, as she tried to push back onto her elbows. Warm hands massaged her legs, holding her where he wanted her. Her heart quickened, seeming to pound violently in protest of the corset. She inhaled deeply, already breathless. Everything about the man intoxicated her.

Then he thrust, adding to the bittersweet torment brewing inside her sex. She gasped, her pussy stretching to accommodate him. Jayne squirmed, needing him to take her hard. The rich, lush chamber danced before her as she bobbed back and forth on the bed. She had full view of the door and she watched it in excitement, her ears straining past her lover's hard pants for a sign of an intruder.

Ronen drove forward, giving her what she wanted. She closed her eyes, feeling the size of him as he moved within her, pounding, plunging, faster and harder with each stab of his cock. Desperation surrounded them—to meet release, to finish before getting caught.

Jayne bit her lip, fighting the effort not to moan as release hit her. Her pussy quivered, gripping his cock in the primal effort to make him join her. Ronen buried himself deep and shuddered. He let loose a low groan, his hold on her weakening as he shook under the force of his climax.

Ronen's hands landed on the bed on either side of her body as he leaned over her backside. Gravity pulled her skirt over her ass. Jayne gave a small laugh, feeling powerful once more. He'd given in to her desires, going against everything to have sex with her.

"We should go." He breathed hard.

Jayne didn't deny it. She loved the thrill, but she didn't want to get caught. Half the fun of sneaking a quick bout in secret places was getting away with it. "Help me straighten the bed."

Jayne crawled forward, going to the other side. They pulled the covers straight, hiding all evidence of their lovemaking. Ronen's gaze met hers and he gave her a sated half smile. It would appear she'd discovered the way to cool his anger, and she made a mental note to remember it in the future. Ronen might be one of the most worthy opponents she had ever gone up against, but in the end she would win this battle. She would have her freedom.

---

Ronen had no idea what had come over him. Well, that was a lie. He had an idea, and it was a sexy, dark-haired vixen who made his blood boil and his fists clench.

When she crawled onto the bed and swayed her ass in invitation, how could he refuse? And even though he wasn't sure he believed her when she claimed to be sleeping on the floor, he couldn't deny her physically. Jayne had a control over him that he didn't understand.

Ronen felt the eyes of the main hall on them as he led Jayne through, intent on taking her back to their room. The knights had returned to their drinking after being interrupted to search for a lady who wasn't actually missing. The queen gently spread rumors through her servants that Lady Jayne ran away but had a change of heart and came back, the pull of her handsome husband too strong. By the time Patricia finished dropping clues, most would believe running to be a cultural custom from Jayne's homeland to entice her mate. Ronen hated lying, but he couldn't naysay the queen in front of the castle so he kept his mouth shut.

Jayne suddenly turned toward the lower tables, sliding into an empty seat. Smiling at the couple of knights who sat there, she reached for their pitcher of mead and poured herself a goblet. Ronen watched, unsure if she would merely take her drink and continue on with him. When she didn't, he slowly sat across from her, aware of the awkward glances the men gave him.

"I saw you fighting out by the tents, didn't I? You have a killer left hook." Jayne motioned to Dersly's scarred left hand before giving a small punch through the air to indicate what she talked about.

Dersly followed her gaze, examining his hand as if he'd never seen it before. The big warrior grunted softly.

"My lady?" Ronen tried to stand, hoping to prompt her to do the same. "Perhaps we should retire."

"I'm not tired. I slept most of the day," she answered. If he didn't already know her so well, he would have believed that look of innocence on her face.

Ronen frowned, not wanting to pursue the conversation and draw attention to the fact he'd sent the king's army into the forest to find a woman who might not have been missing to begin with. He lowered himself down once more, tensing with dread of what might happen next. He remembered all too well the way his brother's first wife flirted with the men of the castle.

"I bet you knocked out a few teeth in your time, too." Jayne lifted her cup to Gerald. Compared to Dersly's vast fighting experience, Gerald was an untried youth.

"My lady," Gerald nodded in affirmation, not as hesitant to return the lady's smile. "A fair few."

Jayne laid her hand out on the table. "I once hit a guy so hard his tooth became lodged between my knuckles," she paused, pointing at her hand, "right there. Let me tell you, Handsome Larry Turner wasn't so handsome after that."

It wasn't exactly what she said, but the animated way in which she said it. Suddenly, the stoic Dersly laughed. The deep brusque sound echoed over the hall. Ronen could barely believe it.

"My lady likes to tell tales, Dersly," Gerald said, chuckling and nodding, and he took a long drink.

"It's the truth!" Jayne gasped in unconvincing affront. "I never lie about a fight."

"A delicate thing like you," Dersly managed in between laughing gasps of air, "hitting..." He pounded the table, unable to finish.

"You have no scars, my lady," Gerald said, as if that explained away her claim.

"I don't get scars," Jayne answered.

"Was he a wee man?" Dersly grabbed his stomach.

Ronen watched the scene unfolding before him in amazement. In the course of two seconds, Jayne had integrated herself with the knights. Watching her closely, he said, "It is the truth. I have seen for myself how she heals."

Knights began to gather around them, moving from across the room to hear what made the mighty Dersly so amused. As Gerald explained what happened, Jayne slapped her hands together.

"So, Dersly, you don't think I can hit a big man like you?" Jayne kept her face composed, the almost innocent half smile on her lips.

"I welcome you to try, my lady." Dersly stood. "And I offer my face to the cause."

Laughter grew around the hall and fists began to pound in a steady, encouraging rhythm.

"Lady Jayne," Ronen began, intent on stopping her. The rambunctious noise surrounding them drowned out his reasoning.

"It hardly seems fair to hit a still target, but your face it is!" Jayne yelled, slamming her goblet down. The knights only cheered louder.

She pushed up from the table and made her way to Dersly. Ronen didn't worry about the man. Not a one of them would dare hit the Lady Jayne. Besides, she had claimed to be a fighter. Leaning forward, he silently admitted to being a little curious as to what his wife could do.

Dersly still chuckled as he turned his face. Jayne lifted her balled fists, keeping her arms tight to her body. As fast as a striking serpent, her fist struck, hitting the knight square on the jaw. The cheering instantly died into a palpable silence. Dersly's head snapped back and he swayed slightly before righting himself. Then, very slowly, he reached to touch his face, rubbing the wound.

"This one isn't a lady, she's a warrior in a lady's form," Dersly announced. "Methinks she could knock a man's tooth from his head."

The cheering erupted again.

"She hits harder than you, Gerald, to be sure," Dersly teased, inciting more laughter. "Bring the Lady Warrior of Firewall a drink. Let's see if she can hold her liquor like she holds her fist. Tonight, she celebrates like a true Starian knight!"

Finally, Jayne turned her gaze to him. She grinned, looking very pleased with herself, as if some strange plan she'd set into motion had come to fruition.

"A toast," Gerald called out, "to the Lady Warrior!"

Ronen had no choice but to grab his goblet as the men continued to cheer his wife. "To the Lady Warrior."

---

"I said I could fight, but I never said I could drink," Jayne mumbled, swaying into Ronen's side as he helped her to their chambers. "Good think, thing, think, drink..."

His wife was drunk. No, she had ridden well past the border of drunk and into the oblivion of nonsense.

"Good think I have the nanos. I would not want to feel my head tomorrow without them." Jayne giggled and draped her arm around his shoulders. She leaned her head onto his shoulder. Her breath a whisper against his neck, she said, "Mission accomplished."

"Mission?" Ronen stiffened and stopped walking. When he looked at her, she had closed her eyes.

"Mm, are we there?" Jayne asked.

He bumped her with his arm. "What mission, Jayne?"

Her lashes fluttered over her beautiful eyes. "What? Why are you glaring at me? You are the one who seemed all worried about what those men would think about me running away a second time, or not running away but you thinking I ran away. It's not my fault you didn't look on the floor. I hate soft beds, they're too soft."

He tried to take a step, but her feet didn't move with him. Sighing, he swept her up into his arms. Jayne gave a light moan and wrapped her arms around his neck.

"You were worried. The queen was worried. Margaret was worried. Renell was...well, Renell was chatty." Jayne moved in his arms, pressing her body against his chest. "You smell nice."

Ronen walked faster. Her lips brushed his neck, sending chills over his body.

"So I took care of it." Her hair tickled his chin. "I gave the knights something more entertaining to talk about."

"I don't think the queen would approve of your actions." Ronen had seen Queen Patricia pass by the hall. She had been far from pleased.

"I don't care. I much prefer the company of fighters. Men are easy, especially warrior types. Make a few jokes about fighting, prove you know what you're talking about by manipulating the biggest guy in the room into baiting you, take a punch or two with a smile and they'll let you glide right into their ranks. So much easier than dealing with women." She snorted. "Though I am kind of glad Dersly didn't hit me. He has really big fists."

"None of the men would dare to touch you." Ronen held her tighter, realizing there was a lot he didn't know about his wife. Just by watching her tonight with the others, he knew she was smart. She read people and fed off their reactions.

"That's not true."

Ronen stopped, tightening his grip as he got ready to turn back.

"Fredrick slapped me on the back and made mead go up my nose. It burned bad."

Ronen relaxed. Fredrick had been slapped himself and was knocked into Jayne.

"By the looks of the women around here, they are not the fighting kind. Now, when news spreads about me, I will be called Lady Warrior not Lady Runs-a-lot. And the men will speak of how I hit Dersly and held my liquor." Jayne moaned. "Well, almost held my liquor."

Ronen didn't want to tell her that after the first cupful, he'd ordered the servants to water hers down in secret. The mead had been strong and Jayne too slender. If he hadn't, she would have dropped dead on him.

"Mm, you feel nice. I love your hands. They're so strong." She wiggled again and he realized he'd begun massaging her as he carried her, kneading his hands on her thigh and near her breast. Jayne bit his ear. "Stop walking. Let's have sex right here."

"In the hall? But someone could walk by."

"It's late. No one is about." She bit harder, instantly licking the wound. "Come on, take me against the wall." Her hand glided up his arm. "You're so strong. I know you can lift me."

"You are far into your cups, my lady." He tried to reason, but it was hard to hold onto sanity when her breathy whisper begged him. "I will not take advantage of you."

"Why?" She chuckled. "I would take advantage of you if our roles were reversed."

His cock lurched to attention, very willing to be taken advantage of. Ronen's brain tried to resist.

"It will be quick, I promise." Her kisses hit his throat and hair, wherever her mouth could reach while he held her. "Just unlace your pants. I'll lift my skirt." She groaned into him, dragging her tongue over flesh. "Please, Ronen, I'm already wet for you. Put me down and take me against the wall."

"We're almost to our chambers." His words were hoarse and he walked faster. Having sex in such a place wasn't unheard of, but usually not where the queen resided. She had strict rules when she was in residence.

"No, here," she pouted. "Now."

Ronen couldn't take it any longer. His cock ached for the slick warmth of her body. How could he resist? His wife begged for him to take her and he wished for nothing more.

Ronen lowered her and she backed up against the wall, stumbling slightly. He eagerly reached to untie his laces, his fingers feeling thick in his urgency. Jayne pulled at her skirt in invitation. Finally managing to push his breeches from his hips, he went to her, crushing her against the wall.

Jayne gripped his shoulders, running a leg up his hip. Ronen pushed her up the wall, holding her thighs. Bracing her against the wall, he mindlessly pushed forward. The soft heat of her sex greeted the tip of his cock, enveloping it.

"Take me," she ordered, squirming.

Ronen plunged deep, enjoying the way her pussy clung to him. He ground his hips, rocking within her. Her cleavage bobbed with each push of his body, causing the tops of her breasts to dance erotically for his pleasure. "You will be the death of me."

"Ah," she gasped as he thrust harder. "No, I have no intentions of killing you."

"Just of leaving me." He quickened his pace, ramming into her as if he could make her want to be with him forever. Emotions warred inside him—fear that she'd leave him, the desire to hold her like this forever, anticipation of what she'd do next. Life with Jayne would never be boring.

Her sex began to quiver along his shaft. She dug her fingers into his muscles, squeezing tight. Suddenly, she made a weak noise of release, her pussy engulfing him in jerking waves. Ronen thrust a few more times before meeting his own climax. He kept her pinned to the wall, his cock deep inside her.

"You don't have to go, Jayne. I will be good to you. I promise." He smoothed back her hair and her foot fell to the floor without his support. His shaft pulled free.

"I can't stay. This world isn't for me." She closed her eyes, refusing to look at him.

"How can you believe that? It's a war filled with fighters. You said it yourself, you understand our ways."

"Ronen, don't." She shook her head. "I'm not a wife. I can't give you a family."

"I have given the matter thought and we can help raise my brother's future children. They are blood and will be like our own. Or there are plenty of boys who have lost their parents. They need good homes."

"Orphans?" Jayne finally looked at him, her eyes glassy. "I can't take care of children, Ronen. All I want is to be free to travel the dimensions and to live on my own terms. Alone." Her head fell forward and she sighed. "I'm so tired. I don't want to talk anymore."

Ronen stepped from her just enough to grab his breeches and tug them up his hips. He tried to force her words from his mind, hoping that by not thinking about it, the pain inside his chest wouldn't hurt so much. Not bothering to pull the laces tight, he lifted her into his arms once more and carried her to her own bed.

# CHAPTER 10

"Bloody fucking misery." Jayne's back felt as if someone stabbed her repeatedly along her spine. Moaning, she tried to move, managing to make it to her side to stare at the stone wall. She was all too aware of the fluffy softness surrounding her limbs. Why in all the dimensions was she in a bed? Naked?

She recalled hitting Dersly and bracing herself for a return punch before the man broke into laughter. The drinking she remembered. Singing drunken war ballads at the top of her lungs with a room full of inebriated knights was a little fuzzier.

Behind her a door creaked, but she didn't turn to see who it was. She must have spent the whole night in the same, unmoving position. Now her neck paid the price. Jayne groaned.

"Are you feeling the effects of drink?" Ronen inquired, as the bed subtly shifted.

"No. My head is fine." She groaned again as his weight jiggled her.

"See, the bed is not so bad, is it?" A warm hand slid along the small of her back and she focused on that heat. "The queen demands the best where she stays."

"Yes, it is bad. Horrible," she pouted. Jayne still didn't move, not even to squirm when he withdrew his hand. "It's like I have been thrown into the pits of hell and tiny demons with sharp feet are running up and down my spine."

"You did not mind it so much last night." Ronen kissed her neck.

"So, in the passageway? That was real?" Jayne summoned the cloudy memory, but only got vague impressions.

"Yea, my lady, very real."

"And the singing in the main hall?"

He chuckled. "Yea, my lady, you were very robust."

Desire stirred within her, making her forget her sore back. "And my taking you into my mouth against your chamber door?" Jayne licked her lips, confident she could remember the taste of him as he came into her mouth.

"Yea, my lady, you were very insistent." He began to massage her spine, rubbing his thumb in hard circles to loosen the knotted muscles.

"What about you bending me over the side of your bed? I have a vague memory of that." Jayne closed her eyes. Ronen's body gravitated closer and she thought to have felt the brush of his cock against her ass. Apparently, Ronen had a few ideas when he came to her room that morning.

Jayne glanced over the wall. Was it morning? The light shining from outside did appear bright.

"Yea, my lady." He kissed her shoulder and his erection grew bolder along her cleft. His heat radiated around her from behind, as he drew her to his chest. He pressed his body along her back, his hands skating up her body to cup her breasts. Ronen rubbed them gently and moaned. The naked, hard length of his desire for her was unmistakable. Licking her neck from pulse to earlobe, he whispered, "And once you held me down and rode me like I was a wild stallion you were trying to break. By the time you finished with me, methought you had drained my serpent dry." He rocked into her, causing her to instinctively arch. Fingers ran down her stomach, holding her flush against him so she couldn't wiggle away. "But it would seem I am eager to be tamed by you once more."

Pleasure coursed through her. He pressed his hand lower while nudging his leg from behind. He parted her with his thigh, holding her legs open so he could explore the naked line of her moistening sex.

"So sweet," he murmured, his words vibrating against her.

Jayne gasped as his finger grazed over her clit. "What about that thing where you poured wine all over my feet and sucked on my toes for an hour?"

"I..." Ronen pulled back. His hands slid from between her legs, leaving her pussy aching desperately. "I did not do that."

She pressed her lips tightly together to keep from laughing. "Are you positive?"

"I did not drink and had my wits about me," he assured her. Then, sounding unsure as if he should be angry, he began, "Did someone—"

Jayne couldn't hold her amusement. Laughter escaped her. "Huh, it must have been a dream."

He relaxed some. "You wish for me to dine on your toes?"

"No, my lord." She turned around to face him, running the back of her hand over his thick chest. Jayne loved touching his flesh, tracing his scars and exploring the muscular valleys. "I wish for you to not be so serious."

"If I am serious, it is your doing." He brushed the tip of his nose to hers. "If you would but promise to stay as my wife, I could relax."

Jayne couldn't meet his gaze, even though it was so close. A part of her actually considered what he offered until the logical part of her brain reminded her that the only thing she'd ever really, desperately wanted since those years in the orphanage was her freedom. How could she give that up now for a tight ass and delicious sex? What would happen when the flames between them died and they grew bored? The longer she stayed, the harder it would be to go. Already she found herself thinking positively about Staria and its people. She liked the knights, with their gruff, fighter ways and easy-going banter. She didn't care much for the clothes, but they could always be changed so it wasn't a big issue. The castle food tasted better than some of the finer dimensions she'd stayed in. Then there was Ronen—sexy, beautiful, masculine Ronen. Just thinking his name sent a shiver over her.

She looked at his chin, seeing the roughened texture of his whiskers sprinkling over his flesh. Instantly changing the suddenly uncomfortable subject, she grabbed his cock and squeezed along the base. With a firm pull from root to tip, she felt it rise even more in her hand. Mimicking the slight accent of his people, she said, "Methinks there be other ways to relax you, Lord Ronen."

At her touch, his lids drifted lazily over his eyes. "You twist my head, Lady Jayne, until I cannot think. You fight me, but then touch me like this."

"Trust me, for what I have in mind, you don't really need to think." Jayne pushed him so he rolled onto his back. Ronen's arms sprawled to his sides.

Jayne crawled on top of him, holding his strong body down with her smaller one. Her muscles twinged, but she ignored the pain. Leaning into him, she nuzzled her face against his rough cheek. Her nipples brushed across his chest, already hard from when he massaged them, and her pussy slid along his hard stomach.

Ronen moaned softly. "You are so beautiful. I could look at you forever."

Jayne gave a small laugh. "Forever's a long time."

Ronen pushed up from the bed, causing her to slide back onto his lap. His hard cock pressed against her ass as she became seated on his lap. "Stop."

"Stop?" Jayne's mouth fell open in shock before she could hide the expression behind an uncaring mask. The truth was she found she cared very much. Stop? He wanted her to stop?

"Stop forestalling a true conversation." Ronen's hands braced his weight, but his eyes pierced into hers, holding her captive more effectively than any hands could. "If I try to speak of something real, you dismiss it or you start kissing me so I forget what I wish to say."

Jayne didn't move. How could she? His irritation washed over her. Instinct told her to do one of two things, seduce him or fight with him. Naked on a bed, his cock pressed intimately against her cleft, she didn't really feel like fighting him. And his expression forbade any attempt at seduction.

"You have nothing to say, do you?" He frowned, though a deep vulnerability shone through his gaze.

Jayne opened her mouth, but nothing came out. A real conversation? That wasn't necessarily fair. They'd had real conversations. She'd told him some about her past. He spoke of his homeland, duty and family. Even as she tried to rationalize, she knew what he meant. She refused to talk about them, their situation. Sure, she'd dismiss or ignore any attempt he made at convincing her to stay. A deep realization hit her. The reason she refused to discuss it was because she was terrified he'd succeed.

"Methought not." The moment passed with his flat words and hardening eyes.

"I don't know what you want from me," she whispered.

"Then I suppose what I want is not there for you to give." Ronen rolled her roughly onto her back. "I will have to settle for giving you what you want."

His kiss ground at her mouth, as if he would punish her. Jayne resisted for a brief moment, before the passion in him drugged her senses. She grabbed his hair, accepting his forceful handling, not minding the hard grip of his roaming hands or the bite of his teeth.

Their lovemaking became a battle. Hands gripped, nails raked, lips fought and bodies rolled. Jayne forced him over, reaching between her legs to grab his cock. She squeezed and Ronen grunted. Before she could impale her body on his, he had her on her back once more. His strong thighs forced hers apart. Her body buzzed with sensations. What had started as punishment turned into a mutual, frantic desperation.

Ronen grabbed her legs, lifting them over his shoulders, using her own body to keep distance between them. "Is this what you want from me? A hard cock?" he demanded, as if punishing her with the physical pleasure he offered.

Sweat beaded their flesh. As he drew his erection along her wet slit, she bucked off the bed. His hands braced next to her shoulders while hers roamed aimlessly over his chest—pinching nipples and scratching pinkened trails.

Ronen propelled his hips forward, sinking deep inside her willing body only to pull back out. The position allowed him to go deeper and rougher than ever before. Jayne met his hard rhythm, punctuating each slam of their bodies with an audible gasp for air, only to be outdone by his louder grunts. He didn't go slow or easy, instead plunging in and out at a wild pace.

"Ronen," she panted, clawing at his neck and shoulders. He kept his gaze steadily on her, forcing her to look at him. His eyes seemed almost chilled, having lost the soft light they normally carried when they made love. She hated the coldness in them, but couldn't look away, couldn't think of how to ask for the softer Ronen back. She'd pushed for this with her words and deeds and fears. Even as her body enjoyed the rough coupling, her heart revolted.

She began to tense, but he did not slow his pace. Bittersweet pleasure erupted along her body. Her pussy tried to cling to him as she found release. Ronen thrust several more times, taking longer to find his end. Then, suddenly, he stopped, his hips flush against her. He growled, loud and long, screaming the gruff sound into the chamber. As soon as he finished, he rolled off her.

Sated and somewhat stunned, Jayne let her legs fall onto the bed. He breathed hard, not moving to pull her into his arms as he lay beside her. Gone was the considerate lover, replaced by the hard warrior who had just fucked her.

Before Ronen, sex had just been sex—a means to find selfish, momentary pleasure and nothing more. She hadn't realized just how different Ronen was, how tender and thoughtful he could be until he took that part of himself away. Now, as he took all emotion out of sex, she became all too aware of what she was losing. With Ronen, there had always been an intensity, uncalculated, unplanned, just there. But how did she get something like that back?

Jayne made no move to touch him, even though her fingers twitched and her hand lifted. She glanced at him but had to look away. She hated the cold chill in his eyes, despised herself for forcing it to be there. Maybe she wasn't meant to be loved or cared for. She wasn't any good at expressing such emotions, let alone asking for them from someone else.

Jayne opened her mouth, willing words to come out. She didn't know what they would be or what they would mean. But then he spoke, stopping her from trying.

"The king sent men to scout the borderlands," he said. "I'm going to ride out and join them. If I leave soon, I should be able to find them before they spread out."

Jayne didn't say anything, though questions formed inside her head begging to be asked. *You're leaving me? When will you be back? What if I try to run again? Do you even care? Why won't my voice work?*

Jayne frowned. She should be happy that he left her alone at the castle. Only now where would she run to? The Caniba had been a mistake. The portal wasn't anywhere to be found. But escape was what she wanted, wasn't it? Especially now after what sex with him had been reduced to. Could she really have a purely sexual relationship after she'd seen more from him?

Ronen rolled out of bed, striding naked across the room. She watched him, unsure what she should say or do, or of what she even wanted.

Stopping at the door, he refused to look at her as he said quietly, "My people do not put much faith in loving a woman, Jayne. It goes against everything it takes to be a hardened warrior. But what I feel for you has to be as close to that emotion as any knight of Staria can get."

Jayne didn't move, didn't act or speak. She lay stunned as he walked out of the chamber. Tears sprang into her eyes and a red-hot panic washed over every inch of her being. Instinct yelled for her to run away from any tenderness, said that it didn't matter if she ran to the Caniba or to live in the forest or to some unknown destination way beyond Ronen's reach.

*Run, Jayne. Freedom.*

Without thought, she jerked into her clothing, not caring that the blue corset with black laces didn't exactly match the red of the gown. She placed a strip of cloth between her teeth and brushed her hair away from her face with her fingers as she walked toward the door. Pausing before opening it, she tied her hair at her nape so the locks fell long down her back.

Touching the knob, she stopped. She heard Ronen on the other side. Her eyes swept over the chamber, knowing before she even looked there was no way out. The stone was too thick and if the windows opened, she didn't know how.

*Trapped.*

*"What I feel for you has to be as close to that emotion as any knight of Staria can get."*

*Run, Jayne. Run far.*

"Why did you have to say that? You could have said anything but that." She backed away from the door, bumping into the corner of the bed. Jayne didn't stop until she reached the far corner. Sliding onto the floor, she pulled her knees into her chest and hugged them tight. A tear slid over her cheek. "Goodbye, Ronen. I'm sorry. Now I really can't stay with you. Trust me when I say it is for the best."

---

Ronen took a long time getting dressed, partly because his hands shook and partly because he watched the bedchamber door in hopes that Jayne would burst through and say something—anything—to him. He waited and she didn't.

What possessed him to speak those words? Had he really expected to be met with anything but the silence she'd given him? Jayne made her position very clear. She wanted nothing to do with him beyond what his body could give.

Ronen paused on his way out the door, giving her one last chance to come after him. If only she'd ask him not to go to the borderlands, to stay with her for whatever reason she chose to present. If only she would give him a glimmer of hope that what he felt wouldn't always be one-sided.

The woman twisted him up inside, made him feel things he never imagined possible. She toyed with his mind, dominated his thoughts and drove his body wild. Ronen had fought many foes in his life, but none so defeating as his fighting Lady Jayne.

"So be it," he said to himself, doing his best to steel his nerves as he marched from their shared rooms.

---

Guards? He left her with guards?

Jayne frowned, staring at the two men standing outside Ronen's chamber door. They blocked her from leaving as she tried to make her way to the hall to get something to eat before exploring her options for escape from within the castle. Recognizing them as a couple of her singing companions from the night before, she forced a fake smile. "Why hello there, boys. Come to take a lady to lunch?"

The knights shared confused glances.

"To break my fast in the main hall," she explained, wondering why they didn't smile at her.

"Our orders are to escort you to the queen's chambers," Sir Harol answered. "This way, my lady."

"What if I order you, as a lady, to let me do what I want?" She batted her lashes and Harol looked as if he might waver.

"You do not have the authority to supersede our orders, my lady," the stoic Richard explained.

"Even if I promise to go to the queen's chambers after I eat?" Jayne kept her attention on Harol, the younger and more malleable of the two.

"We will see that a tray is brought to the queen's chambers for my lady." Richard motioned that she was to walk. Jayne stepped in front of him, feeling more like a prisoner than a guest.

"Did Ronen send you to guard me while he's gone?" Jayne asked. Even though the fact annoyed her, it also gave her a small sense of pleasure to know he cared enough to try to hold onto her.

"Turn right," Harol said.

Instead, Jayne walked straight into the main hall. Several of the tables were filled with knights. A couple bent over papers, drawing their fingers across maps. Others sat in deep conversation, slapping their hands to make a point. At her entrance, they turned to her and nodded in greeting. Jayne smiled back, unable to help herself.

"My lady," Richard insisted.

"What are you going to do?" Jayne arched a brow, shooting him with her most withering look. "Carry me?"

"If I must," he blustered.

Jayne laughed. She'd like to see him try. Noticing Dersly, she called to the man, "If you get these two sons of a whoring cat off my back, I'll owe you one!"

Dersly chuckled, but shook his head in denial. "Methinks my lady can handle her own cats well enough."

"Some champion you are," she teased, before sighing heavily. "Very well then, at least throw me the bread before they march me away."

Dersly obeyed, grabbing a loaf from the basket next to him and tossing in her direction. Jayne caught it and lifted it up in thanks.

"My lady," Richard insisted.

"Quit crowding me," Jayne warned him, growing more and more annoyed with each passing second. The pleasure she felt in Ronen caring about her staying soon faded into irritation at her personal guards' doggedness. "I'll go, but I'm walking at my own pace."

She took a deliberate bite of her bread, ripping it from her mouth. A few of the watching knights chuckled. Richard said nothing, but his face tightened in irritation. Harol tried to hide his smirk and failed.

"Well then, let's get moving," she ordered playfully, leading the way to the queen's chambers. "That way you boys can be on your merry ways."

"You are our merry way, my lady," Harol said.

When Jayne frowned in confusion, Richard explained, "We've been assigned as your personal guards until after Lord Ronen returns."

It was her turn to harden. Not saying another word, her pace quickened. *That whoreson! He's going to need to assign more than two men if he expects to keep me prisoner.*

# CHAPTER 11

"Lady Jayne, it's been nearly two weeks." Queen Patricia frowned, staring at the noblewoman who'd been bound and gagged and now lay protesting on her bed. "Do you not think the time for these mischiefs has come to an end?"

Jayne glared at her and growled, "Mrumpinumph."

The queen sighed, sitting delicately on a chair to rub her temples. "I didn't think so."

"Murmamer." Jayne struggled to be free, but the knots binding her only tightened. It was probably a good thing no one could understand what she was saying. The sensitively feminine queen would undoubtedly have her drawn and quartered for her language. "Mumonmofamaf."

Jayne snorted. *Yeah, like I'm going to wax bloody poetic just to sound like some sort of flowery lady. I should have punched her when I had the chance. Damn you, Ronen, for leaving me here. Couldn't you have picked a nice, damp, dark prison cell? Surely being tortured on some sort of rack is better than this agony.*

"Fine." The queen dropped her hands into her lap as if coming to a decision. "I will just have to give you your lessons like this.

Perhaps with a gag in your mouth you'll be able to actually listen to what I tell you and not aggravate me."

*Oh, bloody misery, no!* Jayne struggled harder, kicking and bucking on the bed. *Anything but this! Help! Ronen, remember the Caniba who held me prisoner? This is worse.*

"Let us speak about hair," the queen said, reaching to the table to pick up a comb. Jayne thought about crying. "A lady must never leave her chambers without first combing and styling her hair, preferably with the help of a servant. This also goes for when a lady finds herself staying in the encampments in her husband's tent near the battlefront. It gives the warriors a sense of pride and duty to have a visual of what they are fighting for. It is also a great honor to your family name to take pride in your appearance and manners." Putting the comb on her lap, the queen lifted her hands to pull at the fine clips holding her locks into place. "Should you find yourself without a servant, or mirror, it is up to you to still look your best." Long hair spilled over her shoulders. "I will now demonstrate a few simple techniques you can practice later. After today, I do not want to see your hair about your shoulders."

Jayne's eyes widened in horror and she tried to roll over so she didn't have to watch. This was worse than jumping into a portal right after a tough fight. In fact, she'd rather have the sensation of her bloody body being torn apart than sit through a full day of hair-styling lessons.

"If you look away, I'll only repeat myself," the queen warned. "I have no place to be. The king has ridden out to hunt with the men. The larders needed filling for winter."

Jayne growled but settled onto the bed, lying the best she could in her bound state.

"As with all rules there are exceptions," the queen continued, as if Jayne hadn't interrupted her. "In this case, if a lady finds herself under attack at night, whether it be in castle or encampment, there is clearly no time to attend personal matters. That would be selfish and vain and set a poor example for the women who will come after us. Only then is it acceptable to be seen undone. Oh, which brings me to the point of traveling by horseback overnight."

*Oh, please, someone, anyone, kill me now.*

---

"All clear, my lord," Stephans said, reining his horse near Ronen's. "No fresh tracks along the west section and the ground is undisturbed. None of the Caniba people have risen from the earth."

Ronen nodded. With Stephans' arrival, all of the men had now reported in. The borderlands of Daggerpoint were secured. The Caniba queen concentrated her efforts further west at Spearhead.

"Double the patrol anyway," Ronen ordered, rubbing the back of his neck. He'd ridden hard, searching the forest in hopes of a battle—not that he wanted the Caniba to attack so close to the queen's and his wife's current residence. He just longed for an outlet to his pent-up frustrations. "I will not trust Sorceress Magda to leave these borders alone. She could be trying to focus our efforts at Spearhead only to attack here when our guard is down. It is possible she wanted us to find her spies in the forest."

"Yea, my lord," Stephans agreed. "I'll see to it."

As the knight rode off, leaving him alone, Ronen sighed. His body ached, not so much from being on his horse, but from the long, empty hours he spent pining for Jayne. How could he have been such a fool to tell her he cared for her when it was clear she wanted nothing from him? Each night that scene played in his head. What didn't play was a repeat of their connection. He waited for those moments when he would feel what she felt or see what she saw. Whatever the connection had been, it was gone now. As much as he longed to see her, he wasn't ready to go back.

"Those who are not staying, we ride for Daggerpoint Castle," Ronen ordered the small group. *I cannot avoid my lady wife forever.*

---

"Any word?" Jayne rubbed her sore wrists absently as she slid in the seat next to Dersly. She peered over her shoulder to make sure they were alone. Her two guards sat three tables away as she commanded them to do whenever she was in the hall. If she had to be escorted by them all day and locked in her chambers at night, then she didn't want to have to eat with them too.

Dersly looked up at her upswept hair and pressed his lips tightly together to hold back his amusement. "Lessons going well, my lady?"

Jayne grunted.

"You are a vision of womanly—"

"Don't make me punch you again," Jayne grumbled, stealing Dersly's goblet to take a drink. She'd already confessed to him how miserable the queen's lessons on ladyhood made her. Dersly, being of a fighting mentality himself, well understood her pain. "Tell me, any news?"

She didn't have to explain what she inquired about. It was the same question she asked him every time she saw him.

"No word from Lord Ronen or his men," Dersly answered just as softly, lifting his hand to a servant to motion for another goblet. "Your husband is a great knight and leader. You should not let the men see you worrying about him."

"Do not give me the honor and duty lecture," Jayne warned. She scratched at her head, hating the way the weight was distributed toward her brow. It made her feel like she was about to fall face first onto the table. "I have had enough lessons and lectures to last a lifetime. I have half a mind to shave all the hair from my head after today. Let's see the queen try to test me on hairstyles tomorrow when I am bald."

Dersly frowned. "No, my lady, do not. I am sure Ronen would not—"

"I was jesting," Jayne drawled. "Besides, I tried it once. Easy to manage, but not pretty."

"My lady is always beautiful," Gerald announced, appearing across from her. He grinned and winked, taking a seat.

"Thank you, good sir," Jayne laughed, not taking anything the man said seriously. Gerald was a charmer, delightful and funny, but a charmer nonetheless.

"What were we discussing?" Gerald asked, glancing expectantly between Dersly and Lady Jayne.

"My lady wished to challenge me to another drinking game," Dersly said.

Jayne laughed, appreciating his discretion. As far as she knew, he'd not told a soul about her inquiries into Ronen's health. For that she was grateful. After what Ronen said to her, she couldn't help but worry endlessly about him. People who cared for her never lasted long. "That is not true. I have had enough of this mead to last a lifetime. Besides, I have already proven myself capable."

"Is this when we tell her Lord Ronen ordered her cups watered down, and she does not hold her liquor as well as she thinks?" Gerald smiled innocently at Dersly.

"What?" Jayne gasped, looking to Dersly for confirmation. "He did not!"

Dersly merely took the goblet offered by a servant and chuckled into it as he drank.

"Oh! I can't believe that miserable lout did that!" she exclaimed, a little peeved at having her victory taken away.

"I can only assume you're talking about me."

Jayne tensed, her heart suddenly quickening. As many times as she imagined his voice, she didn't expect to hear it now. "Ronen?"

"My lord," Gerald greeted.

"Lord," Dersly repeated, nodding his head slightly.

Jayne turned to see Ronen standing behind her. Tired half-circles marred the flesh beneath his eyes, darkening them. Exhaustion radiated off him like heat. Almost stunned, she said to Dersly, "I thought you said there was no news."

"Methought there wasn't." Dersly shrugged. Then to Ronen, added, "Is all well at the borderlands?"

"Yea. Nothing to be alarmed about," Ronen answered, not taking his eyes from Jayne's face. The exhausted depths bore into her, but she wasn't sure what they were trying to express. Anger? Rage? Exhaustion? Nothingness?

Jayne grew uncomfortable under his scrutiny and automatically became defensive. "Are you worried that I'm without my guards?

Don't. They're over there taking a break." She motioned behind him.

"Guards?" Ronen frowned. He started to speak, then shook his head as if it wasn't worth the effort to continue.

"My lord?" Jayne asked, wondering what was wrong with him. Maybe he was injured in a way she couldn't see. Well aware of how people stared, she refrained from asking. The truth was, she didn't know how to act. She'd put on a tough front for so long, she didn't know how else to be. Jumping up and hugging him was too out of character, even if every part of her being wanted to do just that. Then there was the fear—fear of what would happen to him if she allowed herself to get close.

"I go to rest." With that, he left her, walking around the table toward their chambers.

"I go to greet the riders. Since ordered to stay at the castle, I am starved for entertainment," Gerald said, pushing up from the table. He bowed, wishing them a good day before leaving.

"You are more like the people here than you know, my lady," Dersly commented when they were alone. "You have our hardness."

"What do you mean?" She looked at him in shock.

"You ask me fifty times a day about Lord Ronen's health, and when he appears, you show nothing of your emotions when I know you care for him deeply."

Jayne stared at her drink, as she contemplated denying it.

"What you do not have is our Starian sense," Dersly continued. "Life is to be lived, for it is a short time on this earth for a warrior. Go after your lord husband and give him some peace in this world. He should not have to wonder about your heart when he has the responsibilities of this country resting on him. If you truly care for him, you will be his constant. A man needs that, even if he doesn't say it."

"I thought I told you no lectures," Jayne mumbled, hating the wisdom in his words. "What makes you think you know anything about it? I see no constant in your life, unless Gerald—"

"My wife, stubborn wench that she was, never told me until it was too late. Had I known she cared before her deathbed, I would have done things much differently. But I was young and foolish and still believed the honored teachings of the war gods I'd grown up hearing. It never occurred to me to confess an emotion I could not name. Warriors were not supposed to love, not romantically, not wholly. Now, methinks our people would do well to look at the other deities of our ancestors for guidance. It is why I find hope in you otherworlders. Perhaps you can reawaken our spirits and give us more to live for than war and death. Staria needs more love in its veins to go with the fire in its heart." Dersly stared at her until she was forced to meet his eyes. "Do not make the same mistake I made in my marriage, and do not wait for him to confess what he feels for you first. Most likely, he won't. He won't know how. None of us really do."

Jayne started to deny her feelings when the knight stood, cutting her off.

"I do not ask you to do anything that is not in you, but it would be good for this land if you could make your marriage work. Rumor has it Lord Ronen asked the king to stop all otherworld marriages through Divinity. I suspect it has something to do with you, otherwise he would not have urged a decision to be remade. There are several versions of the story, but the disheartened result is the same. Without Divinity, we'll have to go back to praying for women to fall through the fairy rings as gifts from the gods. Many men will die childless and without knowing the pleasure of a wife." Dersly cleared his throat, all sentiment falling behind the warrior mask. "Methinks I will find Gerald and see what news from the borders. Good day, Lady Jayne."

Dersly walked in the opposite direction Gerald had left from. Jayne watched him in silence until a servant appeared to clear the man's goblet. "Margaret, have food sent to Lord Ronen's chamber. He looked half starved."

"That would be the hard beef and bread they live on while riding. Horrible stuff, but it does its duty." Margaret nodded knowingly. "And for you as well?"

"No, thank you, just Lord Ronen." When she was again alone, Jayne's eyes trailed toward her bedchamber. She respected Dersly as a fellow fighter and they'd become friends over the last couple of weeks. But his words didn't change the fear she carried. He couldn't expect her to try to give hope to a country of knights. She barely got by for herself.

*Run, Jayne,* her thoughts whispered.

She didn't move. What if she ignored instinct and stayed? What if she gave Ronen a try—a real try? If she were honest with herself, she did miss him while he was gone and had begun to miss the boxing ring even less. How did one compare what she did, fighting for money, to what these men did? They fought for honor and right. They didn't get paid an obscene amount of gold or get splashed across magazine covers. Their fame was earned by valor, not a well-paid camera man and creative biographer who invented a fake family for their little orphan street urchin.

*Stay, Jayne,* she consciously chanted. *Stay.*

Determined, and a little nervous, she finished her stout drink and stood from the table. Barely aware of her two guards right behind her, she forced her shaking legs to carry her across the main hall, through the passageway that seemed suddenly very long, and to the bedchamber door. Glancing behind her, she said, "Ronen is home now, you can stop following me."

"Not until the queen gives her order," Harol answered. "She was very specific, especially since you kept getting caught trying to leave the castle."

*I was trying to hide from her lessons.*

"The queen ordered me followed? Not Lord Ronen?" Jayne asked. Harol nodded. "Why didn't you say?"

"My lady did not ask." Richard shrugged.

Jayne arched a brow, but refrained from arguing with him again. To do so would only be a way to run from what she needed to do. Pointing down the hall, she ordered, "Stay twenty paces away."

The men nodded, backing out of eavesdropping distance, but close enough to see her door should she try to come through it. Satisfied they wouldn't be listening, she slipped inside. Her eyes went hungrily to the bath, instantly finding Ronen amidst the curling steam.

"You were gone a long time," Jayne said, trying to figure out what exactly she wanted to say to him. *You were gone too long, Ronen. I missed having you in my bed. I thought about you. I fantasized about you. I'm glad you are safe. I worried about you. I sound like an idiot.*

"Not so long," he answered, not looking at her. Didn't he care she was there? She couldn't force her eyes off him as they devoured every visible inch. Her fingers flexed, itching to feel his flesh. Moisture pooled between her thighs, her sex aching to the point she adjusted her weight from one foot to the other in hopes of relieving some of the pressure.

"Did you," she paused, trying to think of anything that might get him talking, "fight?"

"No." Again, flat and emotionless.

"So, no Caniba?"

"No."

Jayne glanced over her shoulder at the door. It wasn't too late. She could run. Maybe this time Richard and Harol would be off their guard. Whatever sentiment Ronen had professed as he left her bed seemed to have dissipated like the steam rising above him. Hot one second, gone the next. "So, nothing happened?"

"I am exhausted, Jayne. What is it you wish to ask?" He still didn't look at her. She thought of taking her fingers through his damp hair and jerking his head back to force him to.

"I'm just making small talk." Then, cringing, she added, "The queen says that it's a lady's duty to inquire after her husband, I mean her man's, um, wartime activities."

Ronen gave a derisive laugh. "Since when do you care about being a lady?"

"I don't," she answered honestly before she could catch herself. "I mean, I've been taking lessons. Did you see my hair? I did it with only my fingers and touch of water."

"It's lovely." The words hardly sounded like a compliment.

"Yeah, I know I need some work. I keep feeling like my face is being pulled toward the ground." Jayne tugged at the locks, roughly pulling them down. He didn't seem to care either way, and there was no reason for her to be uncomfortable if he wasn't going to notice her efforts.

"Then take it down." Calm, logical and still not looking at her. One of her clips fell on the ground and she wanted to throw it at his head. Maybe violence would get his attention. She picked it up, bouncing it in her palm.

"Dersly promised to show me how to wield a sword if you said it was all right." Jayne sat on the bed, keeping her eyes on him. "He says it's well and good that a lady can throw a punch, but to truly be effective against an attack, she should be able to wield a blade."

"There is no reason. I will protect you," Ronen said. Finally, he moved to look at her and she felt a hopeful leap inside her chest. She held her breath. He arched a brow, drawling, "Unless it is me you wish to attack?"

"Why would I try to kill you?"

He turned his back on her once more, sitting as if he hadn't moved. "To escape me because that is the only way I will let you out of our arrangement."

Jayne began to smile.

He continued, "The gods willed it for whatever reason and now it is our misfortune to bear."

Her smile dropped into a grimace. This conversation wasn't anything close to what she'd hoped. Sure, she didn't have clear plan for what she aspired to have happen between them, but if she did, this definitely wasn't it.

"That's a little harsh," she mumbled. "Clearly someone had a few weeks to brood."

"What?"

She didn't repeat the comment. Making a none-too-graceful transition, she rushed, "For the longest time I wasn't allowed to talk about my past because of the contract I signed with Divinity Entertainment. It had to do with the Public Appearance clause. Since my past was a bloody misery, I really didn't care if it stayed buried."

"What are you talking about?"

"The P.A. Department at Divinity. They wouldn't let me talk about my past until it became second nature not to say anything about who I was. But I suppose now if they kidnapped me and shipped me here, I'm probably no longer in contract. There are things in my life that I—"

He held up the back of his hand, cutting her off. "Jayne, if this is an attempt to leave me, please stop talking. As unfortunate as it is, I did not kidnap you and bring you here. You chose me at the ceremony. After witnessing the pain of my brother's first marriage, I had no plans to marry, ever, but you chose me and I accepted. Please, I'm exhausted and do not have the energy to fight with you tonight."

"No, I wanted to explain something, not fight. Would you just shut your mouth and listen? When I was little..." she paused in agitation. She hadn't intended to yell at him. Words jumbled in her head. Why did he have to interrupt her? She wasn't any good at this stuff. Calming her tone, she continued, "There was this girl, Clariah, and we entered the orphanage around the same time. After the first year, we both came to realize that we would never be adopted, which was for the best since the boys normally got taken to a workhouse and the girls became..." she grimaced, "used goods."

Ronen moved slowly along the edge of the tub, stopping when he was seated facing her. He looked at her, but said nothing. With those steady eyes on her, she now wished he'd turn around once more so she could talk to his back. Jayne found it ironic she wanted his full attention one minute only to dread it the next.

"Clariah was smart. Really smart." She pushed up from the bed and began to pace, moving her hands nervously before her as she spoke. "She could keep these complicated facts stored in her brain. She knew the exact time a guard would make their rounds on what day without even looking at a timepiece. She'd look at a new girl for two seconds and deduce what kind of person she'd be. She knew how the weather would affect Madam Gary's mood down to the degree. She calculated the number of days each month we'd go without food dependent on how many times Madam Timms smiled." Jayne stopped her story, explaining, "Madam Timms had a lot of male friends and when she met someone new, she always took the food money to buy a new dress and get her hair done."

"So you went without," he stated.

Jayne nodded. "We were rationed anyway and the food was terrible, so it wasn't so bad not to eat it."

His look said he didn't believe her. "You speak Clariah's name as if she is no longer. I take it you lost her?"

"It turned out she wasn't smart enough. After we'd been there for three years, she planned an escape. It was supposed to be the two of us, but after seeing a new girl get beaten, we decided we had to take her with us. However, in our empathy, we misjudged her. Susan changed her mind and told Madam Gary in return for favors. That daughter of a whoring dog ended up becoming the child guard six months later. She'd sell out her own dead mother for an extra bit of bread and grog."

"Did you make it far when you escaped?"

"Oh, they let us crawl through air ducts, choke and burn ourselves in the smoke room, before scaling a snow-covered wall. Just as our bare feet touched free ground, they caught us. They could have stopped us before we started, but they wanted to teach us a lesson." Jayne gripped her hands tight. "Punishment for runaway orphans on my dimension was harsh. From the first day we arrived, we were told we were property of the central government, which was afraid we'd ruin their clean city streets. So instead we were swept away into these giant cement homes and kept out of society's eyepiece."

"What did they do to you?" His hand balled into a fist along the back of the bath, but he showed no other emotion.

"They beat us until the snow turned red, and then they dragged us by our hair into a cell. They left us there for what had to be days. Clariah died the second night. One of the Madams had kicked her in the head. By the time the doctor arrived, an infection had set into my insides, and they had to scoop them out or I'd die as well. I often wondered why they bothered to save me. I would much rather have died. Clariah was like a sister. Without her, the place truly was hell."

"I'm sorry you lost her." His eyes softened, but she thankfully didn't see pity on his face.

"Thank you for not looking at me with sympathy. I don't tell you this to make you feel sorry for me."

"You only wished to explain how you cannot give me children," he concluded. "The robots cannot fix it?"

"The children thing is part of it," she admitted, "and no, the nanobots cannot fix what was not there when they were implanted. All they did was take away the surgery scars on my flesh. The biogeneticists confirmed it."

"And the other part?"

"I'm trying to explain it to you." She rushed on before he could interrupt. "After Clariah's death, I tried to escape every chance I got. I think I wanted to either be free or die trying. It's how I learned how to fight and take a punch. When finally I made it, I found the city streets weren't as clean as we'd been led to believe. An old woman found me and took me in. Having been an escaped orphan herself, Lotta understood there was little I could do to integrate myself into mainstream society. Everyone in my world is documented and scanned. For me to even try to get a job would mean I'd be captured and dragged back."

Jayne took a deep breath. Did he have to look at her like that? So intense and unmoving?

"Lotta came to care for me as a daughter and for a short time we were happy. But soon after I met her, she died from the cold. I took over her home until a couple of ruffians kicked me out. It really was just a small inlet in a delivery alley. I was alone and kept mostly to myself, though I did find a nice little spot near the animal collective for a few months. The older orphans had taught the younger ones to read, so I spent my time memorizing the plaques. This kind guy found me reciting the information without looking and took me in. I don't know that I ever knew his real name, but I called him Mr. Bear. He was arrested that very week and I never saw him again—though I did walk by his place from time to time to see if he came back." She waved her hand at Ronen, shooing his eyesight away. "Can you not stare at me? It's hard enough thinking of these things without your eyes... Can you just not?"

His brow arched and he reached to dip his hand into some soap. Watching him lather suds over his tight flesh did little to improve her concentration. She pressed her legs tightly together, trying to end the throbbing ache of desire building there.

"Then there was Coach Wagner, the boxing trainer who discovered me..." Her gaze focused on his hands, gliding over strong, hard muscles. They moved over his arms and shoulders, across the expanse of his chest, up the hard cords of his neck. She swallowed, panting softly for breath. "...found me on the..."

*Oh, bloody misery.* She bit her lip. Ronen circled a hard nipple with the tip of his finger. She opened her mouth, wanting to bite his flesh. Jayne stepped toward the bath, her eyes sweeping down to look into the blue tinted water.

"Found you?" Ronen prompted, smiling slightly but still not looking directly at her, as she'd requested.

"I fought, I mean I learned to fight for pocket change and table scraps. They let me live in the boxer dorms. I kept my mouth shut and they put me on..." Jayne swallowed, wondering if he was at all hard beneath the surface. She wanted to take his cock deep as she rode his lap. "Divinity's entertainment circuit. Coach Wagner saw I could take a hit and took me under his training. Then..."

"Then?"

Jayne stiffened, frowning as she tried to get a hold of herself. She'd come to talk to him with a purpose and his sensual bathing movements were distracting her from it. Quite aware that her story was taking a long time to tell, she again tried to rush through. "He died, too. His heart gave out when he was out running the Animal Pass. Coaches aren't considered worthy of the expense of a full-body bioengineered upgrade, and he didn't have any nanobots inside him to repair the damage. Because of him I've earned a great living, more than anyone thought an orphan could amount to. I have money and fame and a place to live that I don't have to share. I even had that damned orphanage torn to the ground and Susan turned out into the streets. It was easier to do than I thought. I simply paid off dirty politicians to change the laws for better child treatment. They loved having something to campaign about."

"I do not think I would like your dimension," he stated, his hands stalling on his chest. "I'm sorry you have suffered, but—"

"Wagner said he thought of me as family the night before he passed." She inched closer.

"But, here, there is no reason for you to suffer," he continued as if she hadn't interrupted. "You will be taken care of and, should I die, there are plenty of men who would seek you as a bride to ensure you are never without home or food. If you haven't noticed, women are prized treasures."

"Haven't you heard a thing I've said?" She came to the edge of the bath and couldn't help peeking down. His cock towered beneath the surface, erect and ready. "I can't stay here, Ronen. I'm not good for you or this country. I fight for money."

"Then try to run if you must, Fighting Lady Jayne." He surged forward, his hands striking out to grab her by her hips. He jerked her body forward, so his cheek pressed against her corset. "But I will follow you wherever you go. You will not escape me. Honor forbids it."

# CHAPTER 12

Ronen did not know what she meant to explain by telling her story. Why would anyone want to run back to a life that had caused her so much obvious loss and pain? Did she like to suffer? The look on her face when she spoke of her past belied the fact. Or did she seek comfort in the familiar?

His wet fingers dried against her thick skirts. Queen Patricia must have ordered his wife clothes, because her skirts had never felt so full. He didn't like it. The material kept his hands from molding along her thighs and ass. "I will confess that it amazes me how you claim to fight with your fists and yet your flesh is so beautifully unmarred. Methinks I would not like to see my battle scars healed. The length of a warrior's life is written on his body and scars are to be worn with honor." He reached over the bath, pulling at her skirts to lift them. Touching the back of her knee, he moaned. "But I find your smooth flesh very fitting for a lady, even one who can stand up to knights without fear."

Jayne leaned into him. Her hands grazed over his shoulders in light acceptance of his touch.

"Come." Ronen held her tight and pushed to his feet, lifting her up. "Let me see more of it. It has been too many days since I've felt your flesh around me, and my mood has soured because of it."

Jayne gave a surprised laugh and bent her knees so he could pull her over the edge. Then, letting her slide down his body, he lowered her into the water. Her gown pooled around her calves, engulfing his legs in the heavy material.

Pressing against him, she ran her hand through his hair and gazed into his eyes. "I'm glad you're unharmed."

It didn't appear that she tried to insult him, but the words cut. If she worried about him riding out to scout the borderlands, a rather unexciting task, what would she think of him riding off into battle? He'd led men into more than he could count, clearly always making it home alive, albeit sometimes with serious injuries. Then, as a thought occurred to him, he couldn't help giving her a lopsided grin. Did her concern mean she cared for him just a little? It was a small sign, to be sure, but he'd take it and gladly.

"Do not say such things in front of the men lest they think you worry. It would not do for them to believe that I am too soft to lead into battle." He found laces along her back and began following them with his fingertips to discover where they tied together.

"Soft?" She reached between them and grabbed his erection. "I don't think any part of you could be mistaken for soft."

Ronen groaned. He kissed her, feeling like a man possessed. There was comfort in avoiding the emotional and focusing on the physical. Every part of him needed more—more of her taste, her touch, her breath against his mouth. She'd gotten into his soul, entangling herself without even trying. He needed her like air and food, sure he would die without her. Words tried to form, but he didn't know how to say what he felt or if he even should. She made her position in his life clear.

*I can't let you go, Jayne. I know I should let you choose your own fate, but I can't even consider it.*

"I thought you were exhausted." Jayne walked him back and pushed him down into the water, completely unaware of the turmoil of thoughts warring inside him. His hands slid from her back, unable to find an opening to the corset.

*I want to pull you into my chest and never let go. I want to lock you in a tower so I'll always know where you are. I want to see you smile. I want your happiness.*

"How can a man sleep with you in his arms?" Ronen bit back the emotions, swallowing them deep and focusing on something he knew they got right—sex. The fatigue of his hard ride and sleepless nights seeped into nothingness. Her nearness gave him energy, fueling his passions and driving his need. She lifted her skirt so the ends floated over his thighs, tickling his flesh.

His heart beat a little faster as she took his face in her hands, angling his mouth for a kiss. Smooth legs brushed against him, sliding easily along his skin beneath the water. Jayne ran her hands wherever she could reach, exploring and massaging each muscle she came into contact with. He liked the feel of her soft skin, even though it covered a very athletic body.

Ronen closed his eyes and groaned as she rubbed his neck. Her kiss intensified, demanding he part his lips to allow her full access. He obeyed the silent command of her pressing mouth and probing tongue. His hard erection tangled in her skirts and he reached to free himself.

Everything faded by the woman straddling his lap. His thoughts focused on her lips, the pants of her breath, her wet thighs. Heat centered over him as she lifted up. Her mouth slipped from his with a heavy sigh. As she maneuvered her body over his, he took hold of her hips, waiting for the glorious second he could impale her on his shaft.

Jayne made a weak noise of pleasure as the head of his cock found entrance. Ronen needed no more invitation. A fortnight had been one fortnight too long. He pulled her down as he angled his hips up. Her weight pushed him back down onto his seat and he groaned loudly.

His gaze met hers, holding it steady. There was a new softness to their depths, something he was sure he hadn't seen before when she looked at him. What had happened while he was gone? The expression gave him a hope he dare not feel.

Jayne moved slowly, as if treasuring each moment. He knew he was. Holding her waist, he let her have control. Her fingers ran through his hair, pulling lightly so he was forced to look up at her fully. Golden firelight illuminated her face. Their open mouths panted in unison, almost touching with each down thrust.

Time stood still for them, cocooning them in a single moment when nothing else mattered or even entered into his mind. It was just Jayne, just him, together as one.

As the tension built, her movements became fast and shallow. Her head rolled back on her shoulders, breaking the eye contact in her rapture. He felt her pussy quivering over his cock, gripping him tight and releasing. She let loose a short, high-pitched cry as she jerked with release. Ronen couldn't resist answering her call and came soon after, jetting his seed deep inside her.

Her forehead lowered, pressing into his. She didn't move from his lap, keeping his cock imbedded deep inside her sex. Harsh breath mingled between them. Ronen held her, not wanting to let go.

"Ronen?" She breathed against his neck. "I don't like the idea of someone else trying to claim me if you died."

Ronen frowned, unsure whether or not he'd actually heard the quiet words or if his pleasure-numbed mind invented them to soothe the desperate need inside his chest. She didn't move, didn't indicate she had spoken at all so he said nothing.

After a long moment, she pushed off his lap and stood. Wobbling as she gained her footing, she moved for the edge of the tub. When she stepped out, water dripped from her gown, pooling loudly onto the stone floor.

"Then I must try not to die," he said, trying to make her smile while trying to find the words to make her stay. But tender words only seemed to make her uncomfortable and he wanted so much to please her. When she spoke, Ronen saw that it had taken a lot for her to tell him of her past. However, her words didn't tell him what he needed most to know—what she was thinking. Did she feel anything for him? Or did his tired mind just imagine it in her, grabbing onto any reason to hope? Or perhaps it was his needy heart that saw what it had to see? Then again, maybe she only thought of escape, of leaving him, of freedom from Staria.

How could he hold onto her when she didn't want to be with him? How could he force her to accept what she didn't want? And, most tragically, how could he even think of letting her go?

As if she hadn't heard his words over the swishing of her heavy skirt across the floor, she said, "I should find something dry to put on and fix my hair. Queen Patricia threatened to draw and quarter me, or chop off my hands, or some such nonsense if I ever showed up 'unladylike' in her hall again. Though, I wonder what she'd do if I paraded around naked. Perhaps it would give her a very delicate attack and she'd never bother me again."

She closed the door without a backward glance, leaving a trail of wet stone behind her. Ronen didn't move from the tub, too exhausted at the moment to even think of a reply.

---

Jayne took a deep breath, pressing her back against the door. She hoped her parting words appeared light and carefree because inside she felt like she'd been stabbed a thousand times. She'd opened herself to him and he said nothing. Now that it was over, her hands shook violently and she balled them into fists.

Though, to be fair, her mind seemed to run in circles until she couldn't remember exactly what she said to Ronen. She told him her story, but did she make her point? Did she say what she needed to say? Did he understand why she needed to leave him?

It was no wonder the man was confused. She tried to explain that she was no good for him even as she tried seducing him. He'd been naked and so incredibly alluring in his bath. How could she resist going to him? How could she think?

People who cared for her never lasted long. Sure, some carried on for a few years, but she didn't want to wait around to learn he died in battle. Then, what? Another man would take hold of her and say, "mine"? She'd thought that at least here, in a war-hardened land filled with warriors, a man like Ronen would never come to have feelings for her. Or had those feelings gone away? She wasn't sure which answer was worse. Had she known she'd end up here, confused and tearful, she'd never have chosen her original plan of claiming him and seducing him. It was never supposed to go like this.

"I rambled," she whispered, trying to make sense of the rush of words she'd thrown at him before resorting to sex to avoid saying more. "I didn't say it right. I need to go back and make sure he understands."

Her wet gown stuck to her legs, but instead of changing, she went back into his chamber. She looked at the bath, but it was empty. Scanning the room, she found him stomach down on the bed, naked.

"I'm afraid if I stay here, you'll die," she blurted, her voice soft. "Logically, I know it's stupid and that there is no such thing as a person being cursed, but I can't help it. I'm really confused. I don't want to lose more people and I think losing you might hurt unbearably. I hate you for making me feel anything. I was doing fine on my own. I had a life and security. But you see Dersly said I should come tell you, but I'm not convinced it's such a great idea. So..."

Jayne inched closer to the bed. He hadn't moved.

"Ronen?" Jayne leaned over, seeing his closed eyes lined with the purple of exhaustion. She gave a derisive laugh and backed toward her chamber and shut the door between them. "Oh, of course, you're asleep. I finally get the nerve to tell you I love you and you're sleeping. Maybe it's a sign that this isn't meant to be. Maybe here your gods really do have a plan and I ruined it by speaking up at the ceremony. I'm sure they have a nice, wholesome ladylike woman for you, Ronen, someone who can make you proud and be your constant. You deserve that much."

Jayne pulled at her corset laces, pushing the tight bodice over her hips to the floor. In irritation, she kicked at the stiff material so it flew into a wall with a splat. "For a place that's so sexual, they make it impossible to get out of their dresses."

Her hands fumbled on her gown and, with each effort to undress, she became more incensed, focusing her anger on the clothing so she didn't have to feel anything else. She flung her limbs wildly, clawing and cursing to get out of her wet gown. It stuck to her legs, itching uncomfortably.

"This dimension has messed with my head. I have to get out of here. Once I leave, it'll all go back to the way it should be." She heard a rip and pulled harder. The back split open and her gown gaped along the bodice. Tugging and kicking, she finally managed to free herself. She gasped for breath, panting from her tirade. "When I find the son of a whoring Divinity cat who did this to me, I'm going to rip him apart. He's going to discover just how tough Fighting Lady Jayne can be. I don't need Ronen. I don't need anyone."

As if all the energy was suddenly drained out of her, she sank to the chilled stone floor. A tear slipped over her cheek and then another.

*Please just let me go home. I don't want to feel, not this. I don't like being scared or out of control. Please, Divinity, just let me come home.*

---

The ache that settled inside of her chest didn't fully go away. Jayne had given herself the chance to say how she felt, and she doubted she'd work up the nerve again. The more she thought about Ronen's attitude in the bath, the more she was able to convince herself that his two weeks away from her had purged whatever feelings he thought to have. That or she'd dreamt the words in the first place.

Thinking about it made the pain worsen until the unusual threat of tears burned her nose and moistened her eyes. Jayne didn't want to cry, or feel, or be in Staria. She wanted the cold, lonely, fighting existence she'd built for herself. Adored by many, known by none.

*Quit lying to yourself,* her heart scolded. *You know as well as I that we don't want to leave him.*

*Stuff it, you bloody miserable, overactive, overemotional, treacherous organ,* her brain screamed back. *Home is where we belong.*

*He is where we belong. He is home.* Damn her feeling heart.

*He is not safe. We cannot take losing him. We cannot go through the pain of losing again. You know as well as I that everything we love dies in the end.* Damn her logical brain.

*For something that's supposed to think, you're a very stupid brain. Everything eventually dies. It doesn't mean we can't live.*

"Great, I've truly gone mad," Jayne mumbled.

"I should say. You're wearing down the stone floor like a woman possessed."

Jayne frowned, turning a rueful mask to the queen. The lady stood watching her pace the narrow side passage from the archway. She was immaculate in dress and regal in manners as always. Eager for an outlet and knowing a fight to be her easiest release, she said, "You better have your goons with you because I'm not coming to another lesson right now willingly."

Patricia chuckled softly, not giving her the argument Jayne was brewing for. "Seeing your hair and dress, I would say my lessons are doing you no good. But, hearing your argument with yourself, I would say you have much more on your mind than hair and dress. I forgot what it was like to be newlywed and unsure of your place."

"I don't know what you mean," Jayne lied. Had she been having her brain and heart argument out loud? How humiliating. Could this day get any worse?

"I'll send you back," the queen said.

"Excuse me?" Jayne stiffened in disbelief.

"To your dimension." Patricia tilted her head to the side, her eyes steady. "I have the power to send you back."

*No.*

"Why would you do that?" Jayne didn't dare move.

"To save you from the insanity that threatens. To protect the House of Firewall from another unhappy marriage. To replace you with a lady who wishes to be a lady and will not embarrass the proud tradition of Starian nobility." The queen walked slowly around Jayne, eyeing her. Jayne turned in a circle, returning the stare with an unpleasant one of her own. "Or perhaps it is because I simply do not want you here."

Jayne clenched her fists.

"Relax," the queen laughed, unaffected by the posturing. "The last reason was a jest. In truth, I find you amusing in your willfulness and the knights respect your strength. If you stayed, wholeheartedly stayed, methinks you could be a fine lady wife. But, if this dimension will take your sanity, then you should leave and spare Lord Ronen the agony of watching you deteriorate."

*No. And you can't make me.*

"What about your traditions? The ceremony? The whole mentality of not rethinking a decision once it is made?" Jayne waited, silently begging the woman to force her to stay.

"The choice is yours, my lady," the queen said instead, walking out the way she'd come. "Stay or go back through the portal."

Jayne stared after her. Then, the slight tap of footfall sounded behind her, firm yet soft, drawing her attention. Ronen crossed his arms. He looked rested but for the turbulent storm churning in his gaze.

"The queen is wrong," Ronen stated. "I do not know what game she plays, but I suspect she thinks to jolt you into a decision. However, she does not have the power to end our marriage. Only death or the gods can do such a thing."

"Or you," Jayne said. "But you will never let me go."

"You chose me. No woman has ever stated her claim to a man." Ronen studied her, as if searching for something he couldn't find. "Perhaps there is a reason for that. So be it. You win."

When he turned to leave with those cryptic words, she rushed forward to stop him. "So be what?"

"You can go home. Perhaps the House of Firewall was not meant for happy marriages. Perhaps the gods have been speaking and I've just been too stubborn to listen." He refused to look at her, even as she tried pulling on his arm to make him. "Go home, Jayne. Go back to your life and forget this place ever existed."

*Just like that he changes his mind? He is giving up?*

"Ronen," Jayne stated, desperate to get his attention. He tried to step forward, but she blocked his path. Fear gripped her and she wanted to shake him until he took the words back. He was giving her what she'd wanted but Jayne hardly felt victorious. If he wouldn't look at her, she'd get in his face and make him. His hard gaze stared over her shoulder. "Are you... What I mean to say is—"

"Sorceress Magda's warriors press upon our borders. She's the strongest leader we've seen in tens of years. I do not have time to fight with a bride, Jayne." He glanced at her before quickly staring down the hall once more. His jaw tight, he continued, "I do not have time to chase you all over the countryside. If I were but some foot soldier, such a luxury might be mine, but I'm a leader. Men look to me as an example, and it is better for my family name to have you gone than to have you constantly embarrassing me. It was a mistake to try and force you to stay. The whole trade agreement with Divinity was a mistake. Go home. It's what you want. When my men ride tonight, I ride with them and we will never see each other again."

"I thought the Starians didn't second-guess decisions." Why wouldn't he look at her?

*Great going, you stupid brain! You over thought and now it is too late*, her heart yelled.

*Bloody fucking misery*, her brain mumbled.

"We are not so foolish as to force a decision out of pride," he answered. "Besides, your presence proves Divinity cannot be trusted. I will not put others through a false marriage."

"What about you?"

"I'm a warrior. It's time I got back to being just that."

Jayne refused to move. Well, refused was a lie. The truth was she couldn't move. The weight of her limbs became impossible to lift. Ronen's words stung. She'd begged endlessly for him to let her go home, to give her freedom. She'd fought for this moment, and now that she had everything she'd pleaded for, she wanted to scream in agony at having received it.

"Ronen," she tried to speak. Her throat tightened and it became hard to breathe. Her brain seemed to spin in dizzying circles inside her head.

"The king orders that I ride at once," he said. "I will have Dersly escort you back to Battlewar Castle where the Divinity portal is kept. We were left with instruction as to how to contact them should the need arise. I'll send orders that you are not to be stopped. All I ask is you act with dignity before you go. Once through that portal, your life is your own and what happened here will be a distant memory."

"Ronen," she whispered, trying again to put into words what she felt. The problem was, she wasn't sure how to. "What will you tell people?"

"That's my concern."

"But—"

"Good journey, Lady Jayne." He lifted his hand as if he might touch her but then let it drop to his side. "And may you fight with honor."

He stepped around her and left. She stood, frozen, as his footfall echoed behind her before disappearing completely. Ronen set her free. No, he did more than that. He practically shoved her through the portal toward her freedom.

"Ronen, stop, I don't want to go," she whispered. But her throat was too tight and no sound came out. He'd just given up. Jayne knew she couldn't blame him. She'd fought him since that first day out of pride and stupidity. Part of her had never thought he'd give in.

Her mind raced, but she had no solution. The queen wouldn't stop her. Ronen wouldn't stop her. If royalty and her husband sent her back, no one would think to stand in her way.

*Husband.*

Jayne shivered. She'd never allowed herself to think of Ronen as a husband. Sure, others said it, but never her. She felt the walls inside her begin to crumble, but it was too late.

"Oh, bloody misery, Ronen." Jayne sank to her knees, trembling violently as tears rolled over her cheeks. How could she have been so blind? "I have truly made a mess of my life this time."

# CHAPTER 13

Ronen had faced terrible odds in battle. He'd seen death and made hard decisions. He'd been wounded and had nearly died on numerous occasions. Yet, none of those life experiences had come close to using the reserve of strength it took to say good journey to Jayne.

When he heard the queen's offer to set her free, he'd thought to deny it and never let her go. That is what his instinct told him to do. Queen Patricia had no authority to end his marriage, and Ronen had no clue as to why she said as much. Such things were the matters of gods, above men and royalty. But then he looked into Jayne's face, so full of emotions he'd never seen there before, ones he couldn't read. In that moment, he knew he'd lost the most important battle of his life. Somehow, he'd always known she'd win, that he'd give in to her and let her go, even if the act ripped out his heart.

*I am a leader of men. A warrior. A knight. The battlefield is my life. War is my mistress. I am not meant for softer things.*

His heart was one wound that would never stop aching, but hopefully with enough time it would harden and scar. Already he felt a fine rage settling inside his chest, urging him to strike out, to fight, to scream, to ride into Sorceress Magda's encampment and die a hero.

Unfortunately, the location of Magda's encampment was unknown, and any battles to be fought were days away from where he now rode through the forest with the small contingency of knights. The only enemy his sword could face was the bark of a tree, and his men might look at him strange were he to jump off his mount and attack yet a fourth hapless trunk.

"This clearing is as good as any other, my lord. A stream is nearby," Sir Thomas said, venturing next to him. "Should we make camp?"

"Further," Ronen grunted. Thomas slowed and backed away, not arguing. Ronen nudged his horse, urging it to run. If he couldn't fight his demons with a sword, he would try to run them ragged.

---

"It proves you can never predict the actions of a Starian warrior." Queen Patricia placed her hand on Jayne's shoulder. "Methought my decree would have a different effect on you two, but I see you are just as stubborn as he."

Jayne eyed the woman. Part of her wanted to hate Patricia for prompting the end of her marriage. Whatever the queen intended with her offer to send Jayne home clearly had not worked.

"Dersly is waiting," Jayne mumbled, purposefully turning her attention to where the big knight stood by two horses. His blank expression stared back at her, but she didn't need to see his emotions to know he was disappointed with her. "Thank you for your hospitality."

The queen arched a brow, but Jayne didn't correct her statement. Ronen's last request had been for Jayne to act with dignity and she intended to do just that.

"Your hair looks very nice swept off your shoulders. It's the first time I've seen you looking the part of a true Starian noblewoman. I'm proud to see my lessons were not all ignored. Safe travels,

Fighting Lady Jayne." The queen backed away several steps before turning to go inside the castle.

Jayne strode over the hard dirt path through the courtyard, trying not to break down again. She'd cried when Ronen left her in the hallway and as she'd watched him ride out of the main gate the night before. She'd wept through most of the night, curled on the hard floor and only falling asleep from pure emotional exhaustion. Never had she felt so miserable. Never had she felt so helpless and alone.

How was she going to live the rest of her life without him?

"I'm a fool," she whispered to herself.

Dersly grunted. "I will not disagree, my lady." He handed her the reins to her horse and cupped his hand to help her up. Jayne eyed the animal wearily. "It's a sweet mare. She'll not throw you and I'll ride slowly."

Jayne placed her foot on Dersly's cupped hands and considered asking for a wild, untamed mare that would trample her the second she tried to climb on its back. "Thank you, Dersly."

"Do you hear singing?" Jayne frowned, tilting her head to the side as the faint hint of voices roused her from her depressed thoughts. She hadn't said a word as they rode from Daggerpoint Castle, through the quiet encampment of solemnly and somewhat accusatory gazes of the knights. The forest even seemed dead to her, even though the soft hum of insects and the infrequent call of a distant bird interrupted the solitude.

Dersly glanced at her and she half expected him to be surprised that she spoke. Instead, his steady gaze met hers and he nodded once. "It is most likely travelers engaged in a little merriment on their way through the forest, but I will have to check it out. You should stay back."

Jayne laughed dryly. "Last time I was alone in this forest, I was chased by crazed boars and captured by man-eaters. Not that I can't take care of myself, mind you, but I think I'll come with you all the same."

Dersly grunted, nudging his horse to move faster. Her mare automatically kept pace without having to be directed. It was a good thing. Though she could keep her ass planted firmly in the saddle and hold on, she really didn't know much of the nuances of riding. If the beast were to take off at a dead run, she'd most likely take her chances jumping off the side.

The singing became louder and evidently more drunken in tone. Mismatched pitches rose and fell, some of the voices pausing at odd moments as if to take another drink. The lyrics, barely recognizable, were about some magical lady riding into battle and ending the war with her magical...

Jayne strained, trying to hear, but the uncontrolled laughter muddled the ending. If it made these burly sounding men so giddy, it had to be something dirty. Just as she was about to ask about it, one voice rose high above the others.

*Ronen!*

The instant rush of pleasure she felt instantly became replaced by rage. Unsure what she was doing, but too mad to care, she nudged the horse's side as she'd seen others do and held on tight as it shot forward past a startled Dersly. He reined to the side, letting her by.

Jayne wasn't sure how she managed, but after a few heart-thumping seconds, she broke into a clearing. Rounded eyes turned toward her. A few of the men grabbed their swords and dropped their jugs, ready to do battle.

"Stop!" Jayne yelled at the horse. She jerked on its reins and it slowed. Seeing she was riding past, she whipped her leg over the side and leapt off the animal's back. She hit the ground with a hard thud and the wind rushed from her lungs.

"What? Jayne?"

Inhaling deeply, she surged to her feet, running more on adrenaline than anything else. The skirt of the gown wrapped her legs, causing her to stumble as her foot caught on a leaf-covered branch.

Jayne cursed it, righting herself as she scanned the clearing for Ronen.

"Battle?" She swept her arm over the stunned group of men. "You had to go fight in battle?"

"Jayne," he stammered as her eyes finally found him. He held up his hands defensively in front of him, as if to stop whatever it was she was going to do to him. Bloody misery, he looked great, handsomer than that moment she first saw him in the hall. How could he have thought to send her home? How could she have thought to leave him?

She ignored the sound of Dersly's voice and the drunken murmurings of the knights. Ronen didn't move, though his lips stayed parted as if he would speak. Dark waves framed his face, falling to his shoulders. His black tunic molded the thick muscles of his chest and waist, muscles she could picture as easily as if she looked at him naked. She knew the location of every scar, could bring to mind the exact feel of his heartbeat beneath her hand and the sound of his voice catching the second before he met with climax.

In the short time she'd been there, she knew this man better than she'd really known anyone. He'd broken through her guard, pierced her soul. Perhaps she'd always known he would, from that first moment she saw his eyes, dark and deep and expressive. She knew then that she'd have to be careful of those eyes.

Well, now he'd have to be careful of her!

"You miserable son of a..." Jayne didn't stop as she stormed across the small encampment. Desperately needing to kiss him, she instead balled her fist and punched. It snapped against his jaw hard, throwing his head back. "That's fighting." She kept after him, hitting him in the gut. "This is fighting!"

"Jayne!" he ordered, catching her fist in his hand before she could land a third blow.

She tore her hand away from his touch. "You miserable coward! How dare you think you can just send me away and come hide in the forest?"

“I’m not hiding,” he defended, his initial shock replaced by a frown.

“Please, you’re drunk in the middle of the woods having a sing-along with the all-boys choir over there.” In disgust, she waved her hands over the group of knights. “And all the while, I’m in agony because I’ve been banished.”

“Banish—”

“I can’t believe you’re out here in the woods.” Her words lost some of the venom as she looked to the trees. The steady trunks and dancing limbs held no answers.

“What are you doing here, Jayne? Methought you wanted to go home. Methought I was giving you everything you’d asked for.”

“I did want to go home. I do.” She growled. Anger she could do, but it would seem she still wasn’t great at this part. “But only to gather my belongings, and for the selfish reason of avenging my name by kicking Big Bobby and his father’s asses. After that, I want to go home with you. I want to do the thing with the orphans and the rebuilding of Firewall Castle so I don’t have to live with the queen. I want one bed, no more of this two rooms nonsense. On my side, I want a hard, stiff mattress and on your side you can have your fluffy softness. And I don’t want to style my hair every morning and I want my own clothes. I’ve had enough of these corsets. I can’t run in a skirt.”

At the last bit, he smirked. “You can’t dismount either. I saw your landing from the horse. And I like your hair.”

“Well, tough,” she blustered. “I like it down or pulled back, not up.”

“Are we fighting about your hair now?” Ronen crossed his arms, but any menacing in the stance was taken away by the subtle shifting of light in his eyes. “What is it you want, Jayne? You ran from me, endlessly. You begged me to send you back to your dimension. You fought me at every turn.”

“I fought out of pride because I never thought you’d let go, but I was wrong. You let go and I hate it.” The more she spoke, the more she realized she did know what she wanted. “I want you, Ronen.

Just you. Well, you and that other stuff, but mostly you, my lord husband. I want a life here."

Ronen took a hesitant step forward. Jayne heard snickering and glanced to where their audience watched, captivated and amused. Dersly was the only one grinning openly, as he nodded his head in approval.

"I want you, too, Jayne," he whispered, drawing her gaze back to him with a gentle hand to her cheek. "But I refuse to spend any part of our marriage with one of us chasing after the other. I need to know you're sure, that you won't change your mind. I can't have doubts in my head when I'm away at battle."

At his admission, a rush of pleasure flooded her, carrying with it the barely suppressed desire that always simmered near the surface. "I don't want you to have doubts about my loyalty to you. I want you to be safe and careful so that you'll always come home to me. Because, if you don't, I swear I'll kill myself and come after you into the next life before I let another man claim me."

The pleasure in his gaze warred with concern. "You will never harm yourself." The words left no room for argument.

"Then you had better always come home. You promised to protect me, my lord, and I'll hold you to it." Knowing if she kissed him, she'd not be able to stop, she gave him a meaningful smile and leaned closer, dropping her tone to whisper, "Are you sure there will be no chasing in our marriage, my lord?"

When she pulled back, he watched her intently, not answering. Jayne backed toward the trees, keeping her eyes on him as she led him away from the group. The second her meaning became clear, he sprang into action, darting after her.

"We'll leave you to it, Lord Ronen," one of the drunken knights called after them.

"Unless you need help capturing the Fighting Lady," another added, which caused a fit of drunken laughter and a stern scolding from Dersly about respect.

Jayne chuckled, not bothered by the men's good-natured teasing. She ran faster, absentmindedly dodging through the trees, leaping over logs and ducking low-hanging limbs. Realizing she didn't hear Ronen's pounding feet chasing after her, she began to slow, her smile slowly dying on her lips.

"Captured," Ronen exclaimed as he emerged from the trees to grab her by the arms and pull her tight to his chest. Her heart pounded, more from the excitement than from the run. He'd barely broken a sweat and his breath was steady, but she felt the beat of his heart hammering in time with hers.

Pleasure erupted every place their bodies touched. Jayne focused on him and only him. When she looked into his eyes, the rest of the world didn't matter—not Divinity or her boxing career, not Bossman or his oaf of a son, not the Starian war or her past. All that mattered was Ronen and the life they would have together. And Jayne planned on fighting to her very last breath to keep it.

"Captured," she repeated, nodding her head. "Always."

Ronen grinned, his captivating eyes keeping hers locked in their magical pull. The hard length of him pressed against her, leading to the unmistakably thick outline of his cock. He kissed her and she moaned, wrapping her arms around him. Ronen knelt, pulling her down with him so that their knees pressed into the damp earth below. Leaves rustled in the treetops, as the forest seemed to enclose them in its private hold.

Their lips joined in a soft, exploring embrace. Jayne sighed. "You taste like mead." When he would stop, she moaned in protest. "No, I like it."

His kiss instantly deepened as his lips devoured hers. Ronen pulled at her corset, loosening it so she could pull it over her head and toss it aside. Without the constricting material, she breathed deeper. He gripped the gown at the small of her back, tugging but unable to pull it all the way up with her knees trapping the skirt. Giving up with a grunt of frustration, he instead found hold on her clothed breasts, massaging them through the bodice of her gown. The strong fingers rubbed in firm strokes, budding her nipples into his palms.

Jayne swayed back and forth, pulling at her skirt until it was finally free from her knees. With his fumbling help, she managed to wiggle out of it. Ronen snapped it in the air, laying it over the ground behind her. Now that she was naked, she set to work on the laces of his black tunic. It was the same warrior style she'd stolen from him the night they met and she had to admit, the outfit looked much better on him.

The hem of his shirt tickled her breasts as he lifted it over his head. Jayne eagerly explored his chest with her hands and mouth, trying to touch every muscle and trace every scar. She wanted to feel all of him at once, needed him to feel her. Ronen unfastened the laces at his waist, loosening his breeches. A twinge of anticipation worked over her, centering on her sex. Her pussy ached to be filled.

Jayne gripped his hair, forcing their mouths to join. She thrust her tongue into the warmth of his mouth, tasting the delicious flavor of his mead-laden tongue. She'd been so worried she'd never see him again as she rode from Daggerpoint, and now poured all that emotion into her touch. Panting against his mouth, she whispered, "I love you, Ronen."

He moaned into her, leaning so she was forced back onto the ground. The cool breeze was no match for the heat of his body. Her gown, padded by fallen leaves, crackled beneath her as she moved, creating the perfect bed.

Jayne hooked her legs around his waist, rubbing her thighs along his hips to push down his loosened pants. She loved the strong texture of his skin as muscles bulged in all the right places. He reached between them, cupping her sex with his warm palm. Ronen stroked the clit he found buried within the slick folds. Each stroke of a calloused finger made her jolt a little inside until she was moving restlessly against him in desperation.

"Methought I would never feel you again." He drew his lips along her jawline, nipping and licking a hot trail from her chin to her ear. Sucking on the lobe, he groaned and forced a finger up into her sex. Wiggling it inside her, he continued, "I was sure I'd die from wanting you."

"Then why did you send me away." Jayne gasped and arched, trying to hear his words but torn between the pleasure and need for concentration.

"To make you happy. My pain is nothing compared to your

happiness." He moved his finger faster, adding a second to the first while his thumb pressed over her clit. She jerked, squirming frantically for release. Ronen had found that sweet spot and worked it mercilessly.

"Ronen, I..." She gasped, unable to say what she meant as a long incoherent mumbling sounded from her throat. *Ronen, I'm happiest when I'm with you.*

Jayne clawed at his back with one hand as she reached for his wrist with the other. She forced his fingers from inside her before grabbing his cock and guiding it to the mouth of her sex. With a pant, she thrust up, urging him inside her. He obeyed, thrusting to the hilt.

As if unable to hold back his own desires, Ronen rocked wildly on top of her. He braced his arms on either side of her, slamming his hips in a primal rhythm. Jayne took everything he gave and returned it. Sunlight framed his body from above, slightly shaded by the treetops. The sweet smells of nature, pure and perfect, infused with the masculine scent of his flesh.

"Jayne." Her name sounded rough and loud from his lips as his body tensed. She came a second later, trembling violently in release. Ronen's body strained as he jerked a few more times. Then, with a shortened yell of victory, he too found his end.

When the tremors subsided, he fell to her side and cradled her against him.

"I could do that forever." Jayne yawned, closing her eyes. The stress of their fight had ebbed from her body. That, combined with sexual pleasure, left her spent.

"I told you the gods knew what they were doing." Ronen held her close, not looking as if he planned on moving to rejoin the encampment anytime soon.

Jayne merely smiled, perfectly content. "Perhaps they did."

# Epilogue

"I know I said we could raise a houseful of orphans, but don't you think we should rebuild Firewall first so we have somewhere to put them?" Ronen eyed the three little boys his wife had collected on their journey through Staria. She'd insisted on rerouting the drunken party of knights, taking a trip to every village between Daggerpoint and Battlewar, even if that village was a half-day's ride out of the way. A journey that should have been a matter of days, took weeks.

"What?" Jayne demanded, turning to look at him from where she stood next to the controls to the Divinity portal. She appeared to know what she was doing as she pressed the buttons and turned the many dials.

Turning her attention to the three dark-headed brothers, she asked, "You all don't care that we don't have a castle yet, do you? Hughe? William? Tree?"

The three boys quickly shook their heads in denial. They didn't say much, especially the youngest, Tree, who wasn't much older than three. After the tragedy they'd witnessed while living in the isolation of the forest borderlands, Ronen couldn't blame them. After their parents were murdered in front of them, they'd been shipped from family to family. None of the borderland peasants had the resources to care for three young ones for very long periods of time, though they'd done their best.

"See, they're fine. I'm fine. Are you fine?" She arched a meaningful brow, and he knew she wanted him to reassure the children they were wanted.

Ronen cleared his throat, still not completely used to the affections his wife wanted him to express toward the children. "Yea. I'm pleased to have such fine boys."

They merely stared back at him in confusion that he'd say such an unmanly thing. Oh, the things a man would do to please a wife.

"Why don't you take them out to the fire ceremony we saw them building outside? Or help them get settled into the spare room in the Mace Tower while I handle this." She turned her attention back to what she'd been doing.

"I'm not leaving you alone," Ronen stated. Jayne smiled, but didn't argue.

The portal was kept hidden in a special room beyond the old iron-door prisons, very unlike the cell Jayne had been kept in upon her arrival. Ronen almost laughed at himself for believing Divinity's lies about keeping the women locked up while they adjusted to the new dimension.

The room was more of a cave, hand dug especially for the portal to keep it hidden beneath the castle in an underground clearing. At the end of the clearing, a large domed vault had been constructed by Divinity to reflect the architecture of the castle. A soft blue glow shone onto the portal from the far, high corner of the cave.

"How does it work?" William, the middle child asked his oldest brother softly.

"Magic," Hughe responded, confident in his answer.

"That's right," Jayne said. "Magic."

Ronen suppressed a laugh. For someone who fought really hard not to be part of a family, she took to mothering better than any woman he'd ever seen—especially to children who were not her own blood.

"That should do it," she announced, pressing one last button before backing away from the controls to stand beside Ronen. She wore a pair of breeches and a tunic shirt tailored for her smaller frame. Even a small knife graced her waist, at his insistence. Though she swore she didn't need it and that her fists would do just fine.

"How do you know it will work?" he asked.

She angled her body so she stood before the boys. "I used the secure code for Divinity's head of entertainment and offered to let him hold a warriors' battle challenge here in Staria with the promise of so much money he'd not be able to refuse coming himself to seal the offer."

Ronen covered his mouth and coughed loudly, warning the soldiers he'd ordered to hide in the stairwell to be on alert. Jayne might think she could take on all of Divinity with her fists, but he wasn't taking any chances with her life. After a few minutes, the light on the portal began to shift from blue to a light gold.

Ronen saw his wife grin. "We're just going to talk to them, right, Jayne?"

"He's coming." Jayne lifted her hands to her hips and stared at the center light. A dark shadow began to appear.

"Uh, Jayne, right?" Ronen persisted, wondering why he hadn't demanded she promise to behave when he had the chance.

*Oh yea, she started kissing my stomach and I forgot.*

He swallowed hard, refusing to listen to his suddenly very interested cock.

Jayne's grin widened as a smiling figure emerged. "Go hide in the stairwell, boys, and see how your new mom kicks a little otherworlder ass."

The End

# *Keeping Paige*

BOOK THREE BY MICHELLE M. PILLOW

Second Electronic Printing March 2012, The Raven Books

First Electronic Printing July 2009

ISBN 9781452467696

# *About Keeping Paige*

DIVINITY WARRIORS BOOK THREE

**In a land forever at war, meeting women is the last thing they can think about, so what's a lonely alpha warrior to do?**

An outcast because of her psychic abilities, Paige doesn't expect her people to rescue her when a zealous sect of Faerians (fairy worshippers) sacrifices her to their gods. Thrown through a fairy ring to an alternate reality, drugged on ambrosia, she is compelled to claim the first man she meets. Only when the effects wear off and she's left with a husband expecting more than she's willing to give, does Paige discover the true extent of what the fairies have done.

Ordered by the king to marry, the warrior Sir Aidan of Fallenrock is dead set against taking a bartered bride from a parallel plane. He believes his people should be patient and wait for the gods to bless them. When the beautiful Lady Paige comes through the sacred rings, kissing him like she knows their joined fate, Aidan's sure he's being rewarded—until his new bride tries to back out of their marriage.

# *Prologue*

## GREAT FOREST, FAERIAN TERRITORY, PARALLEL UNIVERSE

"Oh, blessed fairies of the great forest, givers of spring, and givers of life after the cold! Take our autumn offering to grant us safe winter and bring life after the snow. Take our offered sister and make her a queen of your realm."

"Let me go, you crazed heretics!" Paige screamed, kicking and jerking her limbs to be free of the hands that held her high over a sea of ivy-crowned heads. Outrage pumped hard and fast through her veins until she felt as if her heart might burst from her chest in little pieces. "You don't want me. I'm not a believer. I will curse you with dead trees and wilted flowers. My father's people will not stand for this!"

All right, so the last part was a lie. Her father's people wouldn't care what the Faerians did to her. In fact, she half expected they traded her to the crazed women to be rid of the last of her cursed family. How else would the heretics have known where her hunting ground was located? Or that she'd be there following the buck migration?

The Faerians ignored her pleas and threats, answering the priestess's words with random exclamations of, "Oh, blessed fairies!" and "Take our Forestter sister. Grant us life!"

Long, drifting branches passed over her, the yellowed leaves falling with each push of the breeze. They hit her chest and hips, and fluttered onto the female heads surrounding her only to tangle in their flowing locks. A tiny giggle mingled amongst the swaying treetops and Paige stiffened in horror. Soon the first laugh was followed by more mischievous sounds, as if a choir of fairies watched the procession. She couldn't see them, but that didn't mean they weren't there and very real.

Paige didn't need to see the ground or the pathway in which they traveled to know what was happening. They took her to the sacred circle, to the fairy ring of the great forest to be sacrificed. The trees gave way to a grassy clearing. A ring of stone pillars created a large circle, each roughly carved and three times as tall as the women. Their towering height imposed as it impressed. The believers carried Paige between two of the pillars.

"At least give me back the clothes you stole from me. Don't send me like this!" she screamed, shaking now that they were drawing to the end of the journey. Everyone knew about the fairy rings, had been warned as children to avoid stepping within the fairy playground. Paige's own grandmother claimed to have come through them when she was a young girl. "At least give me my bow. Have some compassion. Don't send me to the fairy world unarmed."

Paige believed in the possibility of fairies, though she had never seen one for herself. From what she had been told as a child, they were mischievous, somewhat vengeful creatures and they liked nothing more than to play tricks on non-worshippers.

"Oh, blessed fairies, here is our sister!" the priestess called. The woman ordered her lowered and Paige felt the cold chill of a stone altar at her naked back. The flimsy gauze they'd wrapped around her waist like a belt hardly counted as clothing. As the material snagged on the rock, the pin holding it close to her hips dug into her flesh.

Paige struggled to be free. A ring of mushrooms grew in the center of the stones, so innocuous in appearance that if a person didn't know about their hidden magic they might be tempted to step inside. Was this truly the fairy ring, supposed doorway to fairy realm? The truth was Paige didn't know where the ring would lead.

No one did. She doubted even the Faerian priestess knew all the fairy secrets. Her grandmother came through and it wasn't the fairy world she had been living in.

The priestess stood over her as countless hands pinned Paige down. The woman's white gown formed tight to her bodice only to flow in long waves along her waist and hips. The skirt trailed behind her in a long train. Tiny gold flowers were embroidered along the hem. Her followers wore the same outfit, minus the embroidery and train. Long, straight black hair seemed to stir around the priestess's oval face, the thin strands dancing like snakes. The woman lifted a wooden cup she had carried with her from the village.

"Drink of the ambrosia," the priestess urged, her gorgeous brown eyes round and filled with promise. "Taste the nectar of the fairy goddess and feel the pleasures of old magic. Let it take you. Let it show you."

Paige clenched her mouth tight, struggling violently as fingers pressed into her cheeks to force her teeth apart. The priestess's expression didn't change as she leaned over and slowly poured the cup's contents into her prisoner's mouth. Wherever the liquid touched, tingling erupted, almost burning in its intensity.

Paige tried to resist, spitting the liquid out over her face, but it was too much. She was forced to choke down several gulps or drown. The tingling spread down her throat into her stomach and over her cheeks from where trails of discarded liquid touched her flesh. She tried to resist the alluring magic, but it was as useless as resisting the falling rain.

The instant the cup was empty the Faerian women let go, leaving her free to run. Paige shot up on the altar, ready to bolt into the woods to hide, only to be brought short by a transparent winged creature flying in front of her face. Paige jerked back in fright, sliding her ass on the rough stone. The fairy's gown matched that of the priestess, with the train trailing down past her feet as she fluttered about in the air. The creature's eyes looked too big for her face and her skin glimmered, tinged with pale blues and silvers. Silver threads wove in delicate patterns over her wings. Soon more small beings began to appear to her, each tinted with different shades of nature.

Paige couldn't move. The strange sensation of the ambrosia traveled through her blood, leaving her stomach to conquer her limbs. Even her fingernails and hair seemed to prickle. With each passing second, the fairies became clearer. They flew around the gathered worshipers, perching on their shoulders and heads, completely unseen by those who did not drink. Several pulled at the priestess's hair, combing the locks with their fingers to create the snakelike effect she had noticed earlier.

They buzzed around her and Paige jerked, trying to follow them with her eyes. But, when she looked too quickly, the forest blurred into streaks of impossible colors. The Faerians became excited at Paige's apparent visions.

"What madness is this," Paige whispered, swatting at the pests. The flat of her hand managed to smack one across the body and send it flying. Instantly, the others became enraged and attacked. Though Paige tried to fight them off, they swarmed her, pinching her flesh, pulling the long locks of her red hair and the gauze of her belt, pushing wherever they could touch—along the soles of her feet, her exposed sex, her nose and breasts. Paige grunted, flailing about in an effort to be free. With surprising strength, the fairies slid her ass over the coarse surface of stone toward the center ring. For a moment they held her suspended in the air before tossing her at the ground into the ring of mushrooms.

Paige screamed for salvation, but the only answer she received was the high-pitched screech of fairy laughter and the incessant droning of, "Oh, blessed fairies! Take our sister, grant us life!"

# CHAPTER 1

## HANGING FOREST, OUTSIDE FALLENROCK VILLAGE, PARALLEL UNIVERSE

Sir Aidan of Fallenrock grinned at his good friend Peeter's cherub-faced daughter. When Ileen had blinked her big brown eyes at him and begged him to let her decorate his long blond hair, he had known he would give in to her. The four-year-old had known it as well, for Sir Aidan could never deny one of her requests.

That is why he now found his hair pulled into a messy array of knotted braids and tied with yellow and pink ribbons. He was even sure she had stuck a few flowers and leaves in there for good measure. At her look of pride in her creation, he didn't have the heart to take it down until he was well away from the cottage. Even then, he would need a comb and about three hours of hard tugging.

"Pretty Dandan." Ileen had the look of her mother, dark skinned and eyes with tightly curled hair that bounced as much as she did. Only her nose took after Peeter.

"Beautiful Leenie," he answered, kissing the top of her head before moving to untie his horse's reins from a low tree branch.

"You should wear those ribbons to the breeding ceremony," Peeter teased, doing a horrific job of hiding his amusement. "How could any bride resist you? You'll be sure to fulfill the oracle's prophecy."

Aidan frowned, glanced at Ileen and bit his tongue. What he felt like saying to his friend was not fit for young female ears. Peeter laughed heartily.

"The town oracles have been wrong before. They don't know everything. There's no proof I must take a bride, let alone a bartered one. Besides, the old crones only said they strongly encouraged a marriage." Aidan wasn't sure who he was trying to convince more. The truth was, the oracles had been fairly certain of the signs, but he hadn't told anyone that part of the prediction.

"They have been right, too." Peeter grinned at his pregnant wife. She sat near the front door to their modest home, rubbing her swollen belly. "They said Shana would bear two daughters."

Women were scarce in Staria. With their endless wars, boys had become a necessity and their natural evolution answered the call with more sons than daughters—when they did have children. Their low birthrate wasn't from lack of trying when the warriors were home, but war took them away all too often. Sometimes forever. The fact that Shana gave birth first to a daughter was a miracle and a blessing.

"With enough tries, any man can give two daughters," Aidan teased, hoping to turn the conversation away. King Wilhelm already ordered him to Battlewar Castle in a little over a fortnight to attend the next breeding ceremony. It seemed all of Staria plotted to see him wed.

"So you have decided? You're not going to choose a bride?" Peeter's pity was almost too much to bear. His friend didn't want him to end up alone. "Won't you at least look at the women the king has bartered for?"

"Yea. I've been ordered to do as much." Aidan grimaced. "What if these otherworlders are misshapen or strange in the head? Or worse, cowards? I do not trust this Divinity Corporation to choose women who are right for Starian men. You've heard the tales of how the Divinity man-aliens looked—weak and simpering and endlessly talking. They depend on their technologies more than duty and responsibility and the power of a full day's work. They do not earn a trip through the fairy rings with the gods' blessings, they build contraptions to force their way where they do not belong. The gods would never bless such overstepping people. Here in Staria we know what is important—duty in battle, meeting your responsibilities as a warrior, as a husband, and as a man."

Peeter suppressed his laughter. "You do not speak of anything I do not know. Are you trying to remind yourself?"

"It is easy for you to be smug. The fairies brought you Shana long ago. If only I had seen her first, then perhaps it would be me laughing at you."

"Ach, she would not have you," Peeter dismissed, his amusement only growing in strength. "Besides, I am much better looking. She would have found her way to me either way."

"Pretty Dandan!" Ileen pouted, pushing her bottom lip out in defense of Aidan as she looked at her father.

"Only because you made him so," Peeter answered. The child giggled and began skipping around the yard in a random pattern.

Aidan scratched at his knotted hair, watching the child briefly before stating the biggest affront, "Not a single one of those otherworlders carried a sword when they appeared in the midst of battle. What fool doesn't take a sword to a fight?"

"Perhaps the women will be grateful to be away from such weak men. They'll be enamored of our warriors and very willing to—" Peeter stopped talking, giving a conscious glance to his playful child.

Aidan sighed. Every belief he carried since childhood told him it was wrong to barter for otherworld brides, especially when the cost wasn't too high. Nothing good came without some sacrifice. The gods of war taught them that much. Besides, what woman agreed to travel to an unknown world just for a little blue mineral water? The stuff ran in springs beneath the earth. It would be like bartering for dirt or handfuls of grass. "The king should not have meddled in the will of the gods. If they wished for me to find a bride, they would have sent one through the fairy rings as is tradition. Since they have not, I can only assume I have yet to earn one."

"You? Not earn one? You have fought more battles than anyone in the village. The fact the king wishes you to be amongst the firsts to choose from the new blood means you are honored." Peeter firmly gripped Aidan's arm. "The king only wishes to ensure happiness for his people. Is it so wrong for men to want softer company? I don't want you to end up alone, not after all the loss you have suffered."

"Peeter," Shana scolded, not standing from her seat. "Leave Aidan be. His heart will choose what it must. Whether these brides are gifts from the gods or an abomination of Starian beliefs, it is for each man to decide for himself. You have your bride. Leave Aidan to choose his wife in his own way."

"Yea, my lady." Peeter instantly gave in to his wife's command. "As you so desire."

"Thank you, most wise Shana," Aidan said, bowing his head toward her.

"Though, you'd do well to find someone who can cook," Shana said, laughing, "or who doesn't mind that you make bread as hard as rocks."

"Ugh, won't let me forget it, will you?" Aidan swung onto the back of his horse, naturally adjusting into the saddle. He barely had to give the animal directions as it turned from the small cottage on the outer edge of Fallenrock Village. "How do you know I didn't cook like that on purpose, so you would take pity on me while my mother is at sea?"

"That is perhaps the saddest thing you have ever said to me." Shana suppressed a smile. "Very well. Come back as often as you must, good sir, and you will be fed."

"Now we will never be rid of him," Peeter protested good-naturedly. "He will be at our door like a stray wolf begging for scraps."

"Too late, my friend. you cannot rescind the offer now." Aidan grinned. He said his final farewells before riding into the solitude of the forest. The hairstyle had to be the most unmanly look for a serious soldier of Starian's army and he couldn't ride through town during the daylight hours lest it be seen. It didn't matter if he whiled away the hours in the forest. No one waited for him at home. The pang of loneliness settled once more in his chest, only having been temporarily lifted by the company of his friends.

"Despite what the oracles say, I will stay strong and wait for the gods to bless me. I will not take a bartered bride from another world who I have not earned. When it is time, the fairies will bring her to me." Aidan drew little comfort from the sound of his own voice. Convictions were good and well, but they did not fill his arms or his home. And until after the breeding ceremony, the king commanded him home to get his house in order. Without the thrill of the battlefront, he had nothing to fill his hours but the aching loneliness of his heart and the empty rooms of his home. Regardless, he had made his decision to honor tradition and, once made, a true Starian did not change his mind.

Spring. It was spring.

Paige stared at the treetops, entranced by the way the sun shone through the limbs to backlight the leaves to a lighter shade of glowing green. Almost dazed, she breathed deeply, taking in the smell of moss and dirt, of bark and fresh air. The warmer hint of a breeze caressed her skin, even though she stood in the shade of the forest. It looked like the great forest, but it couldn't be. It was spring and the great forest was in the throes of fall.

"The fairy realm," she whispered, blinking but unable to see any flying pests.

*The fairies must always live in spring. Those crazy Faerians were right. The fairies keep the spring season and only let it loose once a year in my home world. The priestess did it. She sent me to the land of the fairies.*

The ambrosia tingled through her senses, making it impossible to feel much of anything beyond the euphoric spell that grew deeper with each passing moment. Perhaps it was a blessing, otherwise she would be screaming in fright at what had been done. Her flesh itched and she rubbed her hands over her arms to make it stop. Unfortunately, touching only made the sensations worse until her heart hammered in her chest and the not-so-curious sensation of desire flooded her thighs. Even the simple act of breathing seemed to incite a wild, uncontrollable lust.

Her nipples hardened, yearning like never before. Paige knew desire, but she rarely acted on it and never had she felt it to this strong of a degree. This must be what the people of her village referred to as the madness of passion. She had never understood how simple lust could make people witless and imprudent or how they could use it as an excuse for their idiotic actions.

When she couldn't run her hands over her chest, shoulders and neck fast enough, her flesh went from itching to burning. The colors of nature became brighter, more vibrant, as if kissed by a light that did not exist. Leaves crunched under her feet, untouched forest litter that tickled her senses and caused her to stare at the ground in wonderment as she half danced, half marched in a noisy circle.

A green spider caught her attention and she pressed her face close to its back and wondered at the odd shade of its man-size web. Paige lifted her hand and reached to pet the insect's back. "Good day, small creature. So lovely to see you."

"Halt! When they are that shade of green it means they are filled with poison."

Paige blinked as the loud voice boomed over her forest playground. She pulled her hand away from the web, despite the fact she still wanted to touch the spider's fascinating back. How could something so wondrous and beautiful be filled with poison?

"Who are you? Come out from there. What are you doing in this part of the forest?"

Paige leaned around the spider's tree, touching the opposite side to peek at the person who spoke. Her hand caressed the rough bark, gripping it as she pressed her weight forward. She worked her fingers against the bark, liking the pressure against her tingling nerves. His voice was strange, accented in a way she had never heard. But, what did that matter? She understood his words easily enough. Unnaturally shy, she watched him with wide eyes.

"Come out. I will not hurt you. I promise." He gentled his voice and swung down from his mighty horse. She had never seen a creature so big and thick with muscles. The Forestter men were lean and tall, like the trees that filled her homeland. His horse was huge too. Paige guessed it would have to be to carry such a man as this.

He wore a loose shirt over tighter breeches. Boots laced up his calves, over the pants. A sprinkling of hair exposed through the opened laces of his shirt caught her attention, as did the puckering of a scar. Her eyes lifted to his hair, messed up and accented with bits of the forest. Bright ribbons caught her attention. They fluttered in the breeze like small flags.

"Fairy," she whispered, realizing this must be what the flying pests looked like in their own world, all big and tall. She looked down at her arms. Was she little now? Would she grow wings?

The fairy man lifted his hand to her, drawing her flighty attention back to him. A hint of dark black design showed on his wrist. His fingers curled as if to order her gently from her hiding place.

But nothing about this man appeared to be a fairy pest, beyond his ribboned hair. No, he looked...

Big. Muscled. Strong. Extraordinary. Delectable.

"Fairy?" he repeated, the word softer than the others. "Are you new to my world, my lady?"

Paige nodded, entranced by his lips and the way they opened and closed each time he spoke. Even from the distance she could see the fine texture of their fullness. She wondered if he would let her touch them. Her fingers tapped lightly against the bark. The scent of nature became heady as her breathing deepened.

His beckoning fingers stopped moving and his hand dropped somewhat. Huskier than before, he asked, "Did you come to Fallenrock through the fairy rings?"

*Fallenrock? What a curious name.*

Again, she nodded. Heat churned inside her, melting her insides and causing her to shake. Every instinct told her she was safe, that he wouldn't hurt her, that she could go to him, that she should go to him.

*Go to him.*

"I am Sir Aidan of Fallenrock. I promise you, no one will harm you here. You are most welcome, my lady. You are—"

Paige stepped from behind the tree and stood naked before him. Well, naked except for the gauze belt whose ends tickled her thighs when she moved. His words ended abruptly, dying on his still parted lips, as his eyes swooped down and up only to finally land on her breasts. The brown-green orbs lit with an inner magic. She could see it in the way the light reflected in the pools of his eyes. This proved it. He was a fairy after all. It made sense that she would fall for his magic.

She stared back just as intently, taking in the thick cords of his neck, the texture of his skin, the breadth of his shoulders, the tapering line of his waist, the thickness of his legs. That's where her eyes stopped. His weight shifted just enough so she could see the bulge of his erection hinted beneath his shirt. Her desires only increased, as did her curiosity to see more, until she couldn't think or reason beyond the feelings of lust churning inside her. She wanted him. No, she needed him. He was air and food and water and shelter. He was every base need she had ever experienced and she could no more stop her feet from walking toward him than she could give up all those other things.

*Go to him. Touch him. Feel him. Breathe him in.*

Words were beyond her. He hadn't moved, his hand still unmoving between them, his lips still parted as if frozen in time. Paige didn't try to make sense of what was happening. She went to him, drawn to the texture of his skin, the strength of his body and finally into the heat of his chest. Selfishly, she studied his features up close, not stopping to wonder what he thought or what he wanted. He smelled of fallen leaves and she pressed her cheek along his jaw to breathe him in. As her skin brushed his for the first time, she moaned.

*Touch. Feel. More. Breathe.*

Paige reached for his neck, running her hands over his tense muscles. He didn't stop her. In fact, he still didn't move. Her fingers traced the scar on his neck before twining in the laces of his shirt.

*Touch more.*

She ran her fingertips over him. Reaching his waist, she thrust her hands beneath the hem of his shirt, driving them upward onto the naked flesh of his stomach and chest. Paige felt small next to him and she was considered tall for her people. Moaning, she explored the defined valleys of his upper body. Every nerve stung with desperation and it showed in the growing roughness of her touch.

"Were you sent for me?" he asked.

Paige barely heard him. But at his expectant look, she nodded—anything to get him to touch her the way she needed him to. Her sex ached, radiating hot desire. He lifted his shirt and tossed it aside, revealing the muscles she had been so apt to explore. Scars marred his skin and the black designs ringing his wrists were repeated higher on his biceps.

*More.*

He lowered his mouth and kissed her, hard. Paige let him, parting her lips to allow him complete access. The taste of him filled her mouth. His chest pushed fully into her breasts, rubbing the taut nipples. It was unlike anything she had ever felt. Even in her euphoric state, she let him take the lead, bending to the obvious confidence of his embrace. Strong, firm hands slid down her sides, cupping her hips and ass. She was still a little sore from where the fairies slid her ass over the coarse stone, but the pain seemed far away and unimportant. Aidan pressed her against his arousal, rocking so she felt every inch. At any other time she would have been afraid, but the ambrosia didn't allow for fear or prudence.

*Must have more. Feel him. Touch him. Breathe him. More.*

Paige reached her arms around him and held tight. He walked her back into a tree, holding her up by her ass when she would stumble. The bark scratched her skin, but not so bad she wanted to stop. She clawed frantically at his flesh, scratching in her haste.

Aidan's hands were between them now, jerking at the laces along his hip. When he couldn't free himself fast enough, he growled. The animalistic sound gave her chills. He was as desperate as she.

Even before the pants slid around his hips, he lifted her legs and surged forward. With little effort, he found the entrance to her sex with the thick tip of his cock. Paige's eyes opened wide at the innumerable sensations the touch caused. She looked at Aidan's face, but his eyes were closed tight and his mouth open. Her hands had tangled into his hair, dislodging a ribbon.

*More?*

She trembled, shaken from the euphoria as her confidence wavered. The intimate press became firm as he thrust up into her. A tiny glint of pain struck her, but the ambrosia-induced tingling soon replaced it, urging her back into the sexual trance until every part of her concentrated on the heat between her thighs. Her body's moisture welcomed him, but the muscles were not so accommodating as they pulsed tightly against the thick intruder. If Aidan noticed, he didn't let on. A light tickle erupted along her clit as Aidan moved. He pumped himself into her, pushing deeper with each pass.

"Ah, this feels so..." His words faded as he moaned in low tones, the sounds almost like words but nothing she could understand.

Paige let it happen, back pressed into a tree and all her senses on fire, not wanting him to stop but unable to do much more than hold on while he claimed her. She clawed at his neck, the ache too much, too hot, too deep. If it didn't end soon, she just knew she would die. Surely no mortal could survive such bittersweet agony.

And then, finally, she found blessed release. Tremors racked over her stomach, sending a burst of energy over her form. Aidan grunted, jabbing a couple more times before going still.

The energy dissipated into the nature around them. Paige felt it go, leaving her relaxed and tired and incredibly warm. The flutter of a bright ribbon caught her attention and she mumbled, "Lovely, lovely fairy, breathe in the beautiful fairy," before falling into a dreamless sleep.

* * *

Aidan caught the woman up in his arms and held tight as her head rolled back on her shoulders. Her chest rose and fell against him in even breaths. Stunned that he had acted with little thought to the consequences, he looked around the forest. They were alone. He lifted her up and carried her around the tree where he had first seen her hand reaching out toward the spider. By the delicate wrist bone, he had known her to be female, but never could he have expected just how womanly she was.

When she stepped in front of him, naked and unashamed, his heart nearly leapt from his chest. One look at her pale skin and he had been bewitched. The supple flesh was completely unmarred but for a long, trailing scar that wound from beneath her armpit to her navel. The scar would be of much envy and reverence, for this woman was a survivor and a great addition to Starian's proud society.

And she was his. All his. A blessing from the gods.

Rich, red waves flowed wildly around her shoulders, as if combed by the wind. And those eyes, so wide and curious, so confident and alluring, deeply green like the fresh grasses of springtime. His cock had lifted as he looked her over and he couldn't turn away. Oh, and how tight she had been, squeezing him in a way he had never felt before with the camp followers who serviced the armies.

He had wished for a wife to come through the fairy rings, had begged the gods to make him worthy of a real bride, not a bartered one. As if by divine intervention, here she was, in his arms, so sweet and accepting, agreeing to be his.

All his.

Aidan grinned and hugged her tighter. He was sure he had never felt so happy—at least not since childhood when he had been entrusted with his first real sword.

The forest ground was clear with no evidence of a fairy ring beyond a flattened circle of grass. He supposed that could be it. Though he had never actually seen a fairy portal, he had always heard the rings were made of mushrooms.

Wherever the woman came from, it was clear she was not from Staria. Women from his world might dress provocatively, but they'd never run around the forest in nothing but a sheer belt. Feeling her warmth, his sated body began to stir once more. The gods had indeed blessed him. With the breeding ceremony so close, the king expecting him to choose a wife and the Oracles of Fallenrock warning he must quickly take a bride or be forever alone, Aidan knew it was none too soon.

Hugging her close, he fought the urge to shout his happiness to the whole village. He couldn't carry her through town for all to see —naked and unconscious. Feeling the tickle of ribbon at his neck, he realized his hair was still ridiculously braided. It only confirmed what he already knew—she was not Starian. A Starian woman would never have ignored such a humorous sight.

Aidan adjusted her in his arms and set to work dressing her in his tunic shirt before angling her limp body over his shoulder to mount his horse. The trained animal stayed steady while he slid her before him. The softness of her pressed tightly to him and when the horse took a step, rocking her gently against his hips, he groaned in pleasure-pain. His desire was far from sated and he thanked the gods the king sent him home to await the breeding ceremony. If he kept her in his house, away from everyone, at least for a while, he would have time to fulfill his passions and hers. Pulling her close, he buried his face in her hair and whispered, "Mine."

# CHAPTER 2

Paige tried to open her eyes, but her vision blurred and she was forced to close them to block out the dizzying sight. The smell of the forest engulfed her, warm and earthy, yet sweet as if she lay on a bed of flowers. The sensations that racked her before had yet to wear off and the more aware her mind became of her surroundings, the more the magic of the fairy ambrosia seemed to once more work its way over her flesh.

Was this what it felt like to live in the fairy realm? Sexual need every waking moment? Fiery passions and desperate need?

She moaned, wiggling on the ground. Petals tickled her naked legs though material covered her sensitive breasts and stomach. With the movement, the smell of Aidan replaced the forest. The desire she felt bubbling beneath the surface intensified.

*Aidan of Fallenrock. Aidan.*

A flood of memory came back to her. Aidan's kiss. His touch. His body inside hers.

*Aidan, surely is a prince amongst fairies. Prince Aidan. Handsome prince of the fairies.*

Did he give her the shirt she now wore? Would he be there if she opened her eyes? Or would her desires lead her to the next man she saw, fading Aidan as another took his place? Did sex with any man, or rather fairy, feel the same as it had with him? She couldn't imagine how. Then again, from her very limited sexual experiences, she couldn't imagine much.

"I'm here. Methought to wait until the cover of darkness before riding close to town. Methought you might like privacy to—"

"Aidan?" That voice! It sent delicious chills over her. Had she called out to him? She couldn't remember and barely processed anything he said. Things did not seem to move the same in the fairy world. Blindly, her hand searched in the direction of his voice, easily finding warm flesh. She slid her fingers over his naked chest, skimming the hard, small buds of his nipples. He trembled beneath her touch and she smiled. "My prince."

"Hardly a prince." His hand slipped over hers and he lifted a wrist to his mouth. "Merely a knight."

His tongue flickered over her pulse, causing it to race. When she opened her eyes, she saw evening had darkened in the fairy forest. She sought Aidan's face, finding him bent over her arm. The ribbons were gone from his hair and it had been combed and smoothed about his shoulders. A damp lock tickled her arm and she realized he had bathed.

"I did not mean to injure you, my lady." He kissed the tips of her fingers, saying in between caresses, "I found blood. Had I known you were untouched by men I would have been—"

Paige moaned, finding hold in his hair to draw his face down to hers. She parted her lips, unable to think or talk, unable to listen to his words. All she could do was feel and touch. The tingling came back, not as fiery as before, but insistent and very real. The closer Aidan leaned, the hotter she became until cream flooded her sex and the ache of her desire shook her to the bone.

He braced his weight on either side of her, as he gave her the kiss she craved. His tongue dove into her mouth, exploring and tempting. When she moved to return the kiss, he sucked her tongue between his lips. Every movement became a desperate, thoughtless search for completion. She had tasted release once and her body demanded she do so again and again.

Paige clawed at his flesh as her legs sought to entangle his. She found the smooth material of his breeches and wanted to scream in disappointment. She extended her leg until her foot bumped his naked one. Frantic with the ever-growing need, she worked her toes along his calf, trying to grab the tight material of his pants to tug them off.

Heat centered on her breasts, which seemed to radiate and pulse with the sensitive fairy magic. It was the only way to describe the dull pain that settled there. Squirming like a madwoman, she tore at her shirt, finally managing to work it up so that her stomach and breasts were exposed. Aidan grabbed on to her, molding his hand to her chest as he rubbed an aching globe.

Her toes weren't making progress and she groaned. With a strength she didn't know she possessed, she rolled Aidan over onto his back. He gasped in surprise, but didn't stop her from tugging at the laces along his hip. She jerked at his pants, trying to get them off.

"Ow, my lady, hold a moment," he exclaimed, as the tightly fitted material caught on his erection. He took over, pulling the laces free with practiced ease and pushing the material down without doing further injury to his cock.

Paige tossed her shirt aside. Without apology, she lifted above him with a single-minded purpose. She needed him, had to have him. When she guided his stiff arousal to her sex, she nearly screamed at the explosion of pleasure that racked through her entire being.

Paige impaled herself on his thick shaft, ignoring the sore muscles and tight fit as she finally got what she wanted. She kept him deep and circled her hips, exploring the fullness of the penetration.

"You will be the death of me," Aidan exclaimed, gripping her hips tight. He lifted her up only to slam her back down. Paige yelped in surprise at the plethora of sensations the action caused. Pleasure rippled over her, coupled with a driving need for more. When he would stop, she lifted herself back up and did it again.

She braced herself on his chest and her knees on the ground, riding him without thought or care. Nothing mattered beyond the burning desire low in her belly, the deep ache needing to be filled, the instinct to find completion. When she felt her climax nearing, she rocked harder, leaning closer to his chest.

"Ah, ah, oh," Aidan breathed, punctuating each slam of her body to his.

He tensed beneath her, jerking violently as his mouth opened wide. She kept going, closing her eyes tight until finally the tension exploded into a wave of perfect release. Only the tense quivering of her muscles kept her upright. When finally, the tremors lessened, she collapsed onto Aidan's chest. Arms caught her, but she still felt as if she were falling through the very earth beneath them. And before she could utter a single word, sleep claimed her once more.

* * *

Aidan breathed hard, weak from the intensity of his climax. He had never seen a woman ride him quite like...

He frowned. He still hadn't gotten her name. In fact, he hadn't gotten much at all beyond her seemingly insatiable cravings.

She lay against his chest, unmoving, with his cock still imbedded inside her. Had she not so fully slaked his lust, he would have been curious about her behavior. Maybe she had orgasmed so hard she passed out. He knew he had never come quite like that. Then again, maybe the trip through the fairy ring had been rough. Whatever the reason, it didn't matter. They had the rest of their lives to get to know each other and he looked forward to discovering everything. As he ran his hand over her naked back, he groaned.

*Everything.*

Rolling her over, he gently laid her on the ground. His body slipped from hers and he couldn't help but look at her naked form sprawled beneath him. The ever-darkening sky shadowed them in their own little alcove. Red hair wisped over her face, as if pointing his attention down to her breasts. Cupping one gently, he drew his hand lower, tracing the scar over her stomach to her navel before detouring down to the darker red curls guarding her sex.

By the way she acted, it was quite possible he had been wrong about her maidenhead. It wasn't like he had been with an untouched woman before. Either way, it didn't matter to him. She was his now. No man would ever dare to touch her. He would make sure of it.

*Mine.*

With the late hour, it would be safe to ride by town under the cover of darkness. Most of the villagers would be finishing their evening meals and settling in for the night. There was little risk of them being seen.

"Rest well, my lady," he whispered, stroking her hair from her face to reveal her delicate features. She made no indication that she heard him. "I will have you home soon enough and there we can properly start our life together. I will honor you and make you proud to be my wife. Together we will have many sons, and if the gods so bless us, a daughter."

---

*Accursed, hateful, spiteful Faerians.*

Paige's head throbbed, each pulse sending a sharp pain down her spine to dissipate throughout her limbs. Once as a young child she had picked a bad mushroom in the forest and chopped it onto the family meal, thinking to be helpful. The hallucinations of dancing tree rats and singing grass blades were nothing compared to what she had just experienced at the hands of those spiteful, fairy-worshiping wenches.

Thankfully, whatever they drugged her with had run its course and her brain was again her own—even if it pounded like the maydrums of festival. Like she would willingly believe she had fallen through a fairy ring and met up with a handsome, sexy fairy prince lover without first being poisoned. Well, those ladies had their little fun. It was Paige's turn—as soon as she felt up to it. It wasn't like she had anything better to do with her upcoming winter. By the time she finished with the Faerians, they'd think the forest was overrun with ghosts and the priestess would have no choice but to move the fairy worshiping village north, far away from Paige's home.

*They drugged the wrong Forestter and they will pay for what they did. I'll make sure of it.*

Paige moaned, stretching against the softness cradling her body. She didn't remember grabbing the winter furs for her bed, but she must have because she was lying on them. How exactly did she get home? The Faerians kidnapped her in the hunting forest and didn't necessarily know where she kept her home. She had made a point of cloaking her cabin with trees, rocks and bushes. As a woman living alone, separated from her people, she couldn't be too careful.

And why in the world did her lower stomach feel as if it had been ripped open and crudely sewn back shut? Paige reached for her side, running her hand along the old scar, half expecting her stomach to be ripped apart. Wrenching open one eye and praying the light wouldn't hurt her already pounding head, she frowned. This wasn't her cabin. In fact, this wasn't any place she recognized.

Even in the dark shadows cast with a dying fire, she could see the clay walls were nothing like her wooden ones. It seemed strange to put a fire in the wall. Where she came from, her people had center pits that rose through a hole in the ceiling. Then again, their homes were made of wood and a fire wall would have burned them down.

*Where have they taken me? I need to escape.*

A small slit on the wall served as a window. There was no way she could slip through the narrow space. Her other option was a door, but who knew what awaited her on the other side?

Did the Faerians keep her?

Finding a wall filled with weapons, her concern deepened. No, this wasn't the Faerians. Fairies were reported to hate all things war and a self-respecting Faerian would never keep a weapon in her home—let alone two dozen displayed on her bedroom wall like trophies of honor.

Had the Faerians sold her?

Paige sat up and her stomach twinged. She pressed the flat of her hand against it, massaging the muscles in tight circles. Forget ripping her apart, she felt as if someone had punched her repeatedly in the gut. A fleeting image of her body being pressed into a tree filtered through her.

"No, surely..." She reached over her shoulder, trying to feel her back. When that didn't work, she lowered her arm and tried reaching behind her waist. The backs of her fingers grazed over a light, burning scrape. "No. That was a dream. It couldn't be real."

Reality hit her hard. Her first time with a man and she did it drugged, with a stranger? Her whole adult life she wondered what it would be like, but none of the men from her tribe would touch her. They thought her cursed like the rest of her family and perhaps they were right. Sure, she pleasured herself whenever the mood struck and had even seen couples in the forest when they thought no one watched.

Was this the man's home? Had he helped her? Decided to keep her? What tribe was he from? She closed her eyes, trying to remember what he looked like—strong muscles, hard skin, scars. "Ribbons."

Ribbons? Paige shivered. No warrior man would dare to wear ribbons unless he hailed from the south. The Carvers were reportedly insane from years spent deep in caves. But, no, surely not one of them. No one had seen a Carver for decades.

It only left one plausible option. She really did travel through the fairy ring. She followed the memory of his face, forcing her brain to concentrate. As recollections trickled to the forefront of her thoughts, she remembered him mentioning the rings.

A creak sounded and she jolted in alarm, tugging the fur up to cover her naked body. The man fairy appeared in the doorway, though he had no ribbons or wild braids. His long, blond hair had been combed smooth and left to hang about his shoulders. In fact, he wore nothing at all.

Paige clamped her legs together, almost unable to breathe. The memory of her release was not lost to her, but the pounding, wanton acts to get there came with it. Her eyes rounded and she looked at his naked cock. By its aroused state it became clear what he thought she would do for him. But the wanton, ambrosia-laced Paige was gone. She hugged the fur tighter.

"You are awake, my lady." The husky tone sent a shiver down her spine. What she wouldn't give for her bow and quiver of arrows.

He glanced down his body before giving her a lopsided grin. "Methought to make it easier for us this time."

This time? Paige opened her mouth to speak, but only a squeak came out. How did she answer such an assumption? How did she answer a naked man at all? She tried to push the fur into her skin until it became so lodged he would never be able to rip it off.

"I wish to take you slower, so that I may touch and taste every inch of your body. It will be a pleasure to explore you." He stepped closer and his erection only grew.

Paige lifted up her hand, finally managing to eek out, "One moment, there, Sir, ah, Fairy. Whatever you think is going to happen is, ah, well, not going to happen."

"Sir Fairy?" His smile fell and the playful light died in his eyes. "I am Sir Aidan of Fallenrock. Do you not remember me? I am the man you came through the rings to find."

"I somewhat remember you," she offered weakly. "It's been a really long, strange, *very* strange day. I'm afraid I haven't been myself and you might have gotten the wrong impression about me."

"No, I understand perfectly, my lady. You have no reason to worry. I will honor you and make you proud. I officially spoke the word. I chose you for mine."

"For your what?"

"The gods had the fairies send you to me to be my bride. When you arrived, you said it was so and I have claimed you as my wife, my lady. Do not worry. It is done."

*Wife? My lady? Done?*

*I'm in trouble.*

*Danger, Paige. The man fairy is delusional.*

"I am not a lady," she said, her voice not as strong as she would have liked. "I am not of noble birth."

"All women in Staria are ladies, from the fisherman's wife to Queen Patricia," he assured her. "And you are *my* lady."

"I might have been fairy drugged, but I'm pretty sure I'd remember two fortnights filled with no-touch intention courting and the exchanging of blood to seal a union." Just in case, she looked at her arm to be sure it wasn't cut. The skin was smooth. Even if it wasn't, she definitely remembered there being a lot of touching going on. If it would have been possible, she would have clamped her legs even tighter.

"That must have been the custom from your world." He nodded and seemed to relax, as if understanding her confusion over their shared situation. "Here, in Staria, the man simply has to state it is so and a woman becomes his bride. Because we are always at war, it is necessary to make the most of the life we have. Often, there is no time for so much stating of intentions before marrying." Then he laughed. "And we definitely would not go two full fortnights without touching our wives should they be near enough to touch."

"You're always at war?" What the devil was happening here? She looked at the weapons wall. How could he be a fairy if he went to war and had knives in his home? "You're not a fairy, are you?"

"I am mortal. We do not have fairies in our land. It is said they do not appreciate wars and so stay away." He stepped closer, so close she could have touched him had she felt the need to reach out. She gripped the fur tighter still. "We only find the gifts they send us from the gods to reward us for serving well in battle. You are my gift."

Paige tried to inch her way toward the wall without being too noticeable. It was hard with his brown-green eyes piercing into her, watching her every breath. With the intent of keeping him talking and distracted, she asked, "And who exactly are you at battle with?"

"The Caniba, a horrible race of snake people who live in the ground and eat the flesh of men. We have fought with them since the beginning of written time and we will always fight until the last one is dead." His gaze narrowed in distraction.

"Sounds more like a tale to scare children," she mused. *That's it, just a little more, almost there. Keep him talking. Get a weapon.*

"They are no child's tale. The Caniba are very real," he assured her. "It is told to children that our enemies are beasts, a race born of the unholy fornications of people and wolves. I have killed many to know they are of flesh and blood, but the Caniba are the lowest possible form a man can become."

Aidan reached for the wall and took down a knife. Flipping it around in his palm with practiced ease, he offered her the hilt. "You may have it and others if it makes you feel better, but we are far north of the borderlands. And I promise you I will protect you with my life. You have no reason to fear. You are safe."

Paige's hand trembled. She had not distracted him for a moment. He knew she reached for a weapon and offered it freely, completely unconcerned with what she might do with it. She reached to take the short knife, feeling only slightly better now that she held it in her grasp.

Paige did her best to look at his face, consciously keeping her gaze from wandering down his body. A small tingle erupted inside her, not like the rush of ambrosia but a normal, feminine reaction to a handsome man—who just happened to be standing naked and aroused before her as if any second she would stop talking and invite him into her bed. For the life of her, she didn't even know how to do such a thing without dying of embarrassment. Heat rushed over her face at the very idea. "So... what? The gods send you a woman and you just decide to love and marry her just like that? No conversation? No careful consideration?"

*That's right, Paige, keep him talking until you can think of how to get out of this.*

"Love?" He arched a brow. "I do not believe I said anything about such nonsense. I have heard it told that many of the women sent to us by the fairies speak of romantic love being a reason to join. Such is not our way. It is hoped a union will produce affection and, more importantly, a vessel for sexual release and pleasure."

"Why marry at all?" She fingered the blade gingerly. Her jaw tightened at the idea of being called a mere vessel to fuck, as she uttered, "If all you need is a vessel then why not find a willing woman of low morals? Or have they all been claimed by other men?"

"The gods smile at our unions and once we marry, we do not seek another. We stay faithful because the gods demand discipline. War demands discipline. Marriage is not based on love. It is need. A man needs a woman to give him children, to cook and look after his home when he is gone to battle. And, in return, the woman is given a place to live, food and protection."

*How romantic*, she thought sarcastically.

"I see." Paige should have been shouting to the heavens in relief at his words. It would have been much worse, and a little creepy, if this stranger professed to love her unconditionally. Instead, his logic was calm and reasonable. Marriage out of necessity. It wasn't an unheard of concept. Many people married because they didn't have much of a choice, though it was usually ill-tempered men who no one else wanted and useless women who were bad with tools and couldn't survive on their own. "But I think I'm going to have to decline your generous offer. New world or not, I can take care of myself. The forest will provide everything I need. It feels like spring, so that gives me what? At least a full season before winter sets in? I can have an adequate home built by then and, so long as the hunting is good, enough food stocked to last me. In the end, I suppose one forest is as good as any other to call home. So, I unspeak the words. This marriage is undone."

*There. That should take care of it.*

It wasn't like she had a bunch of friends or family waiting for her. Paige bit her lips. She might have to "borrow" a few tools to get the job done, but she would make it work.

His jaw stiffened visibly for a long moment, but then he began to laugh. "My lady likes to play games." Aidan pressed his knee onto the bed. The angle of his body gave her full view of his naked form and showcased the towering member between his legs. "You wish for me to convince you I am man enough to keep you. I am ready to meet your challenge."

"Ah no, I really don't." She tugged at the fur, but his knee had pressed into it and held it tight to the bed. "You said we are away from the battlefront. My people are Forestters. I will be fine on my own. I have been for years."

"That is your name, my lady? Forestter?"

"Paige of the Forestters," she answered absently. Paige tugged harder on the covers.

"Now that you are mine you are to be called Lady Paige of Fallenrock." The playful light didn't leave his handsome gaze. He thought she jested. Aidan slowly licked his bottom lip, drawing her eyes to it. "My very beautiful lady wife."

"Thank you, but no thank you." She tried to sound firm, but with him on the bed the room suddenly felt too small and devoid of air. Paige was running out of ideas. She had never been in this situation before. Sure, she had fought off men who'd invaded her hunting ground, and argued with the old hags who came to purify her of her curse until they left crying and screaming. But this man hunted her body and, by the look on his face and the sexual memories becoming ever clearer in her head, what he had in mind definitely wasn't pure.

"I invoke the law of tribal council and demand my plea be heard," she blurted, desperate.

"We have no such law or council." He licked his lip again. Curse him.

*Keep him talking. Make him concentrate on something else until that look is out of his eyes.*

"Then what laws do you have for the settlement of disputes?" Was the room getting hotter? Did he lean closer? She resisted the urge to fan her flushed cheeks.

"The highest-ranking man hears the complaint and passes a binding judgment." When he leaned closer, she could smell the subtle hint of what had to be soap on his skin. "With my position in the military, I am the highest-ranking man. Lord Valt of Fallenrock leads armies against the Caniba and has not been home for many, many years."

"Then I demand a second decision! It is not fair for you to judge a situation you are in." Paige's tone rose, not out of anger so much as desperation and a touch of fear.

"No one will dispute my claim. Here in Staria, once a decision is made, it is done. There is no point in making a decision if only to rethink it. You have no Starian husband and, even if you did, I would only have to seek his permission to be a second husband. With my standing, I would not be denied. If you had a husband before coming to this world, he does not matter anymore. The gods knew he was not the one for you. You didn't have a husband, did you?"

"No," she dismissed following with a question of her own. "You said second husband?" Paige gulped. Was this day getting worse? "I'm going to be plagued with more of you, running around and claiming I'm married to them?" Then, under her breath, she muttered, "I'd be better off being a woman of low morals, for at least then I'd be paid and then left alone."

*Cursed Faerians!*

That statement killed some of his good humor. Paige wondered if he realized he was talking to her naked. Then she wondered if he walked around naked in his home all the time. There was talk of a tribe far, far south of her homeland that never wore clothing. Ever. Her eyes began to trail down his chest once more, but she caught herself and again stared at his intense eyes. She wasn't sure which direction was worse.

"Multiple husbands are only out of necessity. I have land, property, rank and honor. There is no need for us to allow another into our marriage. I can provide for you on my own." Was that jealousy in his voice? He had only known her what? One day at best? With the fairy euphoria, it was a little hard to tell for sure how much time exactly had passed since coming through the ring.

"And I can provide for myself," she insisted. "Whatever you think happened between us, you need to know I was drugged by the fairies—well, by the fairy-worshiping wenches who kidnapped me. If I said or did anything that made you think I agreed to be your wife, I am sorry, but surely even you with your stern 'decisions are decisions' speech can understand that I am not—"

Aidan surged forward and kissed her. For a second, her fingers loosened on the fur and she gasped at the hard yet gentle way he consumed her mouth. Her lips parted. However she didn't return the kiss—not because she didn't want it, but because she had never wanted anything more. Without the ambrosia urging her uncontrollably on, she had time to think and feel, to savor and fear.

When he stopped, he didn't pull away and his lips brushed hers as he spoke. "You did much to convince me and I would have you do much again. We are a good match. The gods chose well."

Her stomach tensed, reminding her just how sore it was. Even if she was brave enough to give in and act the wanton fool, her body wouldn't be able to take it. Mumbling the first thing she could think of, she said, "You hurt my belly. I cannot."

His eyes narrowed and he instantly let go of her. He sat back on the bed, his face paling at her words as if she had slapped him. For a long moment, he didn't move, barely breathed. Aidan looked to her stomach and then down at his cock, clearly understanding what she meant. To her great surprise, he stood and strode to the door. He nodded once, not meeting her eyes again as he stared past her to the wall. "I will leave you to rest."

Stunned, Paige didn't move from her place on the bed as the door shut firmly behind him. Her words had actually stopped him. "Kiss my toes, that really worked."

# CHAPTER 3

Aidan didn't come back that night. Though tired, Paige's mind wouldn't let her sleep as she stared at the bedroom door. She wasn't so foolish as to run away in the middle of the night without a stitch of clothing, into unknown woods with unknown creatures. Besides, that would require her to run naked through an unknown house first. After seeing the heat blazing in Aidan's eyes, she knew dashing about naked in front of him was the worst possible plan.

Strange that she should leave her homeland where no man wanted her, to a place where she could potentially have several husbands. Paige supposed she should have been more shaken by her trip through the ring, but it's not like magic was unheard of in her life. She herself was "cursed". Paige always thought her grandmother exaggerated the stories she told of falling through the fairy ring, coming from a land filled with giant square homes called apartments and men who shifted into cats and back again as easy as breathing. It was from her grandmother that Paige and her father had gotten their gifts, or rather her family curse.

When her eyes did wander from the door, she had time to study the room. The firelight died slowly in the square fire box, fading the walls from a brighter orange to a darker brown. The weapons on the wall were well crafted and clearly dominated the room's décor. A few personal toiletries lined a low table in the corner—a comb, an empty bowl and pitcher. All were plain, made more for function than beauty. The last piece of furniture was a wooden trunk at the end of the bed. It was small and she hadn't noticed it when she awoke to find the naked man striding into her room ready to copulate.

A chill worked over Paige each time she thought of it. Aidan had been so proud and carefree in his nakedness without the burden of modesty. And why should he be modest? A man like him, so strong and defined, would know his body and his beauty. By the scars, she believed him when he said he was a fighter. The warrior aspect made her nervous. She had met plenty of fighting men in her forest and they were a stubborn, self-assured lot to deal with. And the men who had a cause? They were the worst. Killing Canibas and following the will of his gods apparently were Aidan's causes in life. If he believed something to be true, for example his marriage to a preordained bride, he would be hard pressed to change his mind about it and even harder pressed to let her go.

Logic told her there was only one way out of this situation. She would have to run, preferably out of Staria to the Caniba side of things. In war, each side hated the other and said nasty things. Paige wondered if the Caniba were so bad as the man-eating beasts Aidan described. If she stayed in this new world, she definitely wanted to see for herself.

If she stayed? Paige laughed wryly. Unless she found a fairy ring to jump through, she was staying. Even then, there was no way of telling where the fairy ring she found would take her. She might end up in a boiling lake or in the world of demons.

As the sun peeked through the window, Paige pushed up from the bed and tried to look out over the land. Not surprising, she only saw trees beyond an empty clearing. She went to the trunk. A few pieces of clothing filled it, all clearly meant for Aidan. They smelled of him, which only brought back the sexual rush she had been trying hard to suppress.

*Cursed fairy magic. Cursed Faerians.*

Out of the whole situation, her loss of control upset her most. Had she had her wits about her, she could have faced Aidan logically and reasonably, stopping him before he came to the conclusion they were destined to be together.

Knowing a stolen shirt was better than a fur blanket, Paige slipped it over her head. The pants were too big, even with the laces on the sides pulled tight. But after a few triangular cuts along the waist, combined with holes poked with the blade tip, she was able to add two more rows of laces in the front and back.

Quite pleased with her handiwork, Paige "borrowed" a knife and tiptoed barefoot from the room. Outside the door she encountered only silence. Window slits in the wall illuminated the sparsely decorated room, revealing a large wooden table and chairs. A barren fire box dominated the wall on the far side of the large rectangular room.

One direction appeared to lead deeper into the house to a row of closed doors. In the other, she saw a narrow stroke of pale, outside light peeking along the bottom seam of a doorway. Paige instantly chose to walk in the direction of freedom, eagerly breathing in the fresh air as she slipped from the house.

A narrow rock-lined path disappeared into the woods beyond the clearing. Paige ignored it, opting for a more rugged escape where she could disappear into the trees. Snaking around the front of the house, she noted how big it was, stretching a half-pacing strike in front of her. Paige's own home barely took up an eight of a strike.

"Come for your morn exercise?"

Paige stiffened, her breath catching in her throat. The sound came from the back of the house and for a moment she could pretend the question wasn't for her.

Aidan slid around the back corner, confronting her. His naked chest glistened from whatever exercise he had found himself engaged in. Hair slicked back from his face, revealing each hard plane of his face, from the bold set of his nose to the shiver-inducing pierce of his eyes. Firm lips brought up the all-too-recent memory of his kiss.

"I see you brought a knife." He glanced meaningfully toward her hand where she gripped the hilt, holding the blade in front of her in a protective gesture. "Do you wish to join me in training? Or are you off to the Hanging Forest to hunt?"

"Hanging Forest?" Paige glanced at the trees.

Seeing her apprehension, he said, "It is only a name—nowadays anyway."

"Oh."

"You have come to train with me, then?" He stopped walking when the blade tip neared his stomach. With one thrust, she could have killed him but he was completely unafraid.

"No. I—I..." Paige shook her head in denial. She lifted the hilt and offered it to him. He took it, tossing it toward the ground without looking to make sure it landed. It did, poking from the earth at a sharp angle.

"Or are you too sore?" He didn't move, didn't flinch. Somehow, Paige knew he had suspected her attempt to leave him and wasn't worried by it.

"Sore? No, the bed was comfortable enough—*oh*." She grabbed her stomach, looking down as if something might suddenly jump out of it. "Um."

Suddenly, he was close, shadowing the light as he towered over her. Aidan placed a hand on the side of the house, leaning so her back was forced against the hard stone. He reached, as if to touch her cheek, and then paused. "Your passion overwhelmed me, but I will be much gentler next time. It had been a long time for me, but I will not lose my head again."

"Next time?" The words squeaked awkwardly out of her throat. Paige knew how he could make her feel, but without the fairy magic urging her on, how did she give or accept such an offer?

Her heart sped and she wondered if perhaps he planned on that time being now. His eyes definitely said he wanted her, as they boiled with hot emotions. His restrained fingers flexed, so close to her face she felt their heat tingling into her nerves. Through the corner of her vision, she saw the designs etched into his flesh, as much a part of him as his skin. Paige didn't move. Whatever he expected, she could not be the wanton temptress who jumped at the very sight of him. The fairy magic was gone, leaving Paige embarrassed and nervous with memories of what she would never be able to be again. "The fairy magic wasn't me. I was drugged with ambrosia."

"It felt like you." Aidan's fingers glanced along her neck, skating a direct path from her ear to her shoulder, only to stop when he reached the edge of the stolen shirt. "Firm yet soft, warm and wet, so sweet."

The words sent chills over her, creating a liquid warmth between her thighs. She clamped her legs tight. How did she respond to such a thing? Men never talked to her like that. Sure, a few looked, but none dared to touch her.

"You don't want to be with me." She swallowed, hard. "I am cursed."

"Cursed?" He arched a brow, looking more amused than scared. Apparently, the word didn't hold the same meaning here as it did back home. "Tell me, can I help with that affliction, my lady?"

"It is not a game." Paige frowned at his lighthearted treatment of her family shame. Trying to make him understand, she said, "It is going to rain tonight."

Aidan glanced at the clear sky, unconcerned. "This is Fallenrock. We're near the sea cliffs. It rains almost every night." Then, lowering his voice, he leaned closer still. "It is said that the night is when the sea gods come out to play, throwing the waves up over the sides of the cliffs."

Paige felt the whisper of his breath on her lips, caressing her and causing her mind to focus on each unsettled nerve. Fine, if he wasn't impressed with that prediction, she would look for something else. Then see how fast he took back his words about their intertwined fates.

Closing her eyes, she tried to focus even as a large part of her resisted. She didn't want to see, had worked hard to block out what she could never help or control. The cold chill of water splashed over her skin, shivering her to the core. She felt the rocks more than saw them as the wind carried her along the cliffs, past a quickly changing sky. Light turned to darkness and rain. A sea storm raged and her mind became pinned to the rocks before getting sucked into the water. The image of a watercraft being tumbled against the waves hit her and she felt sickened by the turbulent motion. Moonlight caressed an old, weathered hand as it latched onto a rope. The water lurched, tossing the craft onto its side. Wood cracked and splintered, instantly swallowed by the angry ocean.

She opened her eyes, ignoring the discomfort of saying what she saw out loud in the hopes that it would scare him away as it had others. "The storm over the water will be rough. An older man from a coastal village will be taken by the waves tonight when his watercraft is smashed into rocks within ten strikes from here."

Aidan frowned, withdrawing. There. That was the reaction she was used to.

"Did you see his face? What did the boat look like?" he asked.

Now it was Paige's turn to frown. That was *not* the reaction she was used to getting. "No face, just an older hand with a jagged scar across the back." She drew her finger over her hand to show where the mark had been. "And on the boat, there were long beams with rope, but no sides to the craft, just a flat bottom. That craft never had a chance against the sea's wrath."

"That is an old fisherman's boat. It shouldn't be hard to find the owner. Not too many are made like that anymore," Aidan stated. "I had planned on keeping you to myself for a while, but if what you see is true, we must ride to the village center and warn the fisherman. What he does with the knowledge will be his decision."

"You want me to go to the village right now?" Paige began to shake her head in denial. She did not want to face a town full of people, all those eyes on her, judging her for what she saw and for the fact she could see the future at all. "I do not, ah—"

"Not at this exact moment." His tone lowered, drawing her attention back to him. "We have time before we must ride. The rains will not come for many, many hours and the fisherman won't leave port until evening. It will be easier to find him when the village is ripe with activity. With a distinct scar and old boat, it will only take a few moments to locate who you saw."

She found herself nodding in agreement with him, all of her senses reaching out to him. He smelled of power and strength—an intoxicatingly raw scent of man. It called to her on the most primal of levels. Her nerves tingled with the overwhelming potency of his nearness. The look in his eyes was unmistakable, as was the way his breathing deepened. Paige could think of nothing else, but the virile man growing more dangerous and alluring by the moment.

She tried to tell herself to run, far and long, to escape the passion snapping the air between them like lightning. It connected them somehow, a strange feeling she didn't care to explore. Paige tried to blame the fairies' ambrosia, but she knew that poison had already left her. Whatever happened now was all her.

There was something about him that made her want to throw caution to the wind and act the part of the animal, surviving on pure instinct, fulfilling each animalistic need as it arose.

"I wish to kiss you, my sweet lady," he whispered, the words hoarse and low and incredibly alluring. Paige parted her lips, unable to stop herself. Logic and reason left her and all the excuses in the world couldn't make her stop what they were doing. "I want to taste you."

She panted and his lips caught her breath into him. The soft kiss sent a thick wave of awareness throughout her body, arousing her until she wanted to scream with desperate need. His tongue circled her lips, tracing around the outer edge, just as her body wanted his cock to trace her most intimate opening. With her eyes closed, she could practically imagine what it would feel like to have him there, thrusting hard into her wet pussy.

"Feel how ready I am for you. Feel how hard my cock is." Aidan moaned, the sound begging her to let him fuck her. To prove his words, he rocked his hips forward, bending his knees to rub his cock into her sensitive stomach. Her back fell against the side of the house, keeping her from falling. "I promise to go slow, to not take you too hard. But I must be inside you, my lady. I ache to find my release, to feel your release as you ride me."

Paige tried to speak, but she couldn't force much more than a squeak from her tight throat. How did she say yes to such a thing? How did she tell this man, this delusional man who claimed they were married, that she wanted him to take her right then and there?

What kind of a message would that send? Already he thought she was his wife. What would happen if she said yes to his lust? To her lust? To the very delicious way his cock rubbed into her stomach?

He moaned, as if he could hear every one of her thoughts and was frustrated by them. As if to convince her, his hands began to move, pressing her hard to the side of the house while they explored everywhere they could reach. Fingers tangled in her hair, gripped her waist, glided along her arms and hips, before finally reaching to make quick work of ridding her of her breeches. He tugged at her shirt, lifting it just enough so his breeches pressed into her naked flesh.

"Ah," Paige gasped as the breeze hit her naked thighs. The word "yes" threatened to escape and she pressed her lips tightly together. She prayed she was able to maintain some sort of decency, but the thought was met with a deep, mocking, inner laughter. How was standing alongside a house, trying not to moan, while the most delectable man she had ever seen said he wanted to fuck her, even close to decent?

Before she knew what she was doing, her hips moved forward to meet his, feeling the intimate outline of his arousal along her exposed sex. Her fingers glided around his waist to squeeze his muscular ass and pull him closer. It felt too good and she found herself controlling his hips in her desperation, forcing them forward. She freed her foot from the fallen pants and lifted a leg to rub along his, spreading her thighs to him.

"This is wrong." She tried to be reasonable, but it was hard. "We should stop. We're strangers. You cannot really think we're married."

"You know you were meant for me. The gods sent you to me." He breathed into her ear, the sound raw with desire. "This is not wrong. It is natural and right. You are my wife."

He seemed so sure and his confidence made her less so. She would never be able to justify what she was feeling out loud, but a deep sense of understanding washed through her. Or perhaps it was just a deep sense of lust. Either way, it overpowered her and she found herself nodding in agreement.

Every nerve reached for him, tingling for contact. She couldn't fight it any longer. She needed release. Her fingers became frantic as she clawed at his clothes. Aidan reached for his breeches, undoing them to free his cock.

Leaning into her, he devoured her neck with kisses before licking a hot trail over her throat to nibble at her ear. He gripped her hips, lifting both of her legs as he pressed her into the wall. Paige cried out in pleasure at the show of strength. The man overwhelmed her. His muscles bulged beneath her hands, flexing and moving with each jerky movement.

Tiny eruptions worked from her pussy through her stomach to her breasts, hardening her nipples beneath her shirt until every little stroke felt like pure torture. Her hands fumbled to touch him, eager to discover if he was as big as she remembered. She took his hard shaft in her hand to feel his enormous length. Even as her pussy grew impossibly moist, she whispered, "This is insanity. This isn't happening."

"Do you want me to stop?" He pulled back, his eyes tortured by the very idea. "I would never force you."

Paige shook her head in denial. She let go of his cock and clung to his shoulders as he adjusted her hips to find aim. If he stopped now, she really would go crazy. Her body was on fire for him, her sex drenched. Maybe her reaction to him wasn't all of the fairies' doing.

Low, primal noises escaped him as he drew the mushroomed tip of his cock along her slick folds. He bumped her clit, causing her to buck up. The side of the house scratched at her back but she didn't care. His cock glided to her moist center, finding her pussy soaked with the cream of her body. He buried his face close to her neck as he thrust up.

Aidan rocked. Her pussy convulsed with pleasure, tightening around him. He leaned back to study her face. A relieved grin crossed over his devilish features. The long length of his hair blew back from his shoulders, adding a wild appeal to the warrior before her.

Holding her with ease, he did not ask permission again as he moved within her. He went slowly at first, in and out, in and out. Her legs wrapped him, urging him to go harder with each pass. As he obeyed the silent command, she cried out in pleasure. The natural rhythm of his hips quickened.

Aidan answered her with a loud grunt. Losing all control, he drove himself forward, only to pull out and do it again, conquering her fully. Tension worked its way over her, centering on her hips. With each thrust he pounded deeper and she was sure he might rip her in half.

But oh, what a way to go.

She held onto him, helpless to do anything but ride out the bittersweet ecstasy of pleasure. Paige gasped loudly several times before softly moaning as an orgasm racked her body. Aidan slowed but didn't stop. He rode out her release. As the tremors subsided, he groaned and seated himself deep. He jerked violently, his body exploding inside her.

Their trembling aftermath continued for what felt like both an eternity and an instant. Slowly, he lowered her to the ground. Her legs felt like they were weighted with steel cuffs. Kissing her gently, he looked into her eyes as if he would never let go.

But he did let go. The tenderness she saw vanished as quickly as it came. Paige eyed him, insecurely searching for a sign of something —of what exactly she wasn't sure. It wasn't as if she expected words of love or even mild affection. When he didn't readily speak, she said awkwardly, "We should leave."

*Not that I really want to go to the village.*

"Of course. I will be but a moment." Aidan patted her arm, appearing distracted, before rushing toward the front of the house.

Paige watched him, stunned. Though she wasn't sure what shocked her more—the fact they'd just had sex and he acted as if nothing transpired, or that when she told him about her vision, he didn't look at her like she had lost her wits. Aidan accepted what she said, no questioning or fear, and acted. She turned her attention to the nearby forest. If she ran, she could hide in the trees. He would never find her, not if she didn't want to be found.

She couldn't move her feet. What if this vision was different? What if the fisherman was saved?

"Do you ride?" Aidan asked.

Paige blinked, realizing he had come back while she was lost in thought. He had put on a fresh tunic shirt and had slicked back his hair with water. Frantically, she reached to the ground to pull on her pants. When he approached, she detected the faint hint of forest herbs on him. "I run. Where I live I can't afford to keep a horse through winter. You do mean a horse, right? Or did you mean a cart?"

Aidan smiled slightly, striding toward the back of the house, motioning her to follow him. She did, lacing her pants as she walked. He reached down to grab the knife, wiping it on the inside of his tunic before slipping it into a sheath along his upper thigh. "Methinks our worlds were not so different. I am very glad. It means you will be comfortable here. Some women who have come through the rings speak of strange contraptions that, for all I can understand, only encourage laziness. They take longer to find their happiness in Staria for they are not used to doing for themselves. I have heard tales of a woman who stared at a fire pit yelling at it to feed her because in her world she merely had to demand her needs from a magical cooking box."

"How many worlds are there?"

"Countless. We have no way of knowing the number, though there are those who say the worlds go on forever. For all I know, you came from across the ocean, from a land I've never heard of right on this planet." Aidan led her across the back clearing, toward a long, stone building. From the width and height of the doorway, she deduced it was his stables. "To tell the truth, other than waiting for you to fall through the fairy rings, I have not pondered the other worlds too much. The only reality that matters is this one—ours."

Paige waited for him outside as he disappeared into the building. Aidan seemed so sure of their shared fate. He truly believed the fairies sent her to him and that they would live the rest of their lives together. Sure, today the thought might be tempting, even tomorrow—especially when her bones still felt like liquid and her heart still fluttered in remembrance of his touch. But what about after the newness of discovery wore off when he learned she kept to her own schedule? When she disappeared for days, beholden to none, just so she could sleep beneath the trees and stars? Even if she could recapture the passionate confidence of the fairy magic, reality would find its way in.

He returned, leading a horse to where she stood. "This is not how I would spend your first day in our home."

*Our home.* Paige couldn't meet his gaze. This wasn't her home. She had no home thanks to the Faerians.

"But if you have the gift of the oracles, we cannot ignore what you saw." He touched her cheek, forcing her to look at him. "Now, more than ever, I am confident the fairies sent you to the right place. Fallenrock is home to all oracles and I vow to protect that gift, lady wife."

*Lady wife. Oracles. Gift.* Paige screamed silently at herself for not running when she had the chance.

"Come, you'll ride with me until we can get you your own mount." He cupped his hands, indicating she should hop up onto the large animal's back.

She did, swinging her leg up and over as she grabbed the beast's mane. On instinct, she nudged its side, trying to race it forward and away. The horse lurched, but a quick command and tug of the reins by Aidan stopped the animal from darting off.

"We will have to teach you to ride as well." Seating himself behind her, he wrapped an arm about her waist and pulled her tight to his chest. Fire erupted along her back, trailing its flame through her blood to center over her chest and thighs. Lowering his voice, he whispered along her neck. "You're shivering. There is no reason to be frightened of the villagers. They will rejoice in your coming as I have."

---

Aidan was glad that his wife's face was turned from him because he couldn't quit grinning like a fool. As easily as he could accept the will of the gods, he still found amazement in the fact that they'd so thoroughly answered his prayers. Not only was Lady Paige beautiful and soft and full of passion for him, she had the gift of sight. As an oracle, she was exactly where she belonged—away from the borderlands and the reach of the Caniba. Here, the people of Fallenrock would guard her secret with their lives. In fact, they guarded all oracles so fiercely that a large part of Starian society didn't even know the seers existed.

The steady gait of his horse rocked the couple as they took the easiest path through the forest. Trees surrounded them, the leaves crashing their music as the limbs protected the travelers from the high breeze. He hugged her tighter and she stiffened.

"Do you worry for the fisherman?" He worked his fingers along her stomach, massaging her while keeping her close. Her words about his hurting her stung. He hadn't meant to treat her roughly. Women were to be protected, not harmed. In fact, he wasn't sure it was exactly his doing. Hadn't she been the aggressor those first times?

*Still, I should have resisted her. I should have taken better care with such a delicate creature.*

Ignoring what he thought might be her resistance to him as the paranoia of a new husband, he stayed on course. Naturally, there would be an adjustment as they learned each other's moods, but this marriage was meant to be, ordained by the gods in reward of his loyalty, valor and sacrifice. He had lost his family to the battlefield, leaving him with little more than an empty house, old memories and a mother who'd taken to the sea to both escape suitors and reality.

But Paige would change that. She represented the future. Together they would fill their house with sons and the walls would no longer echo the deafening silence. With her arrival, he felt hope. She saved him from facing the Divinity otherworlders and she would save him from the lonely emptiness. The gods decreed it. How could it be any other way? Their joined destiny was as sure to him as the surrounding trees and rocks.

Aidan took a deep breath, trying not to smell her hair as it tickled his face. His cock had been half aroused since sliding behind her on the horse, even after she allowed him to take her against the house. Surely she felt it, knew how he wanted her again, how he ached to carry her off into the forest and make love to her under the dancing shade of the trees.

Finally, after a long silence, she answered, "I don't hold out much hope of saving the people I see, any more than I can control the weather that's coming to take them away."

The sound of waves crashing over rocks could be heard long before Paige saw the expansive ocean reaching out over the distance near the bottom of a steep incline. At first, it was hard to block out the water, even as the sounds of Fallenrock Village grew in volume. A long dirt and rock street led through the center of town, flat and well looked after. On either side, small homes sprawled out into the distance. They were constructed from the same material as Aidan's but were much smaller in design.

Young boys played in the yards and along the street, swinging sticks, knocking over planters and yelling words of mock battle. No one paid the lads any attention, as if their mischief were part of any regular day. Only when they started calling out to Sir Aidan, inquiring about the woman on his horse, did the townsfolk actually look up to see what the commotion was about.

The farther they rode, the more houses gave way to tightly set structures. Strange smells wafted over what Aidan called the center square, flavoring the air with odd herb combinations as they passed cooking meats and breads. A large, carved hole in the middle of the square had steps winding down into the earth. People appeared from within carrying pitchers of water. They stopped to look at her, joining the growing crowd that now blocked the road.

The women eyed her clothing and frowned, whispering amongst themselves. They all wore dresses—long skirts and bodices so tight they nearly squeezed their womanly charms up and out of the low-cut necklines. How a woman could work, let alone breathe in such a contraption, was beyond Paige's imagination.

The men, though rough in appearance, wore clean clothes much like the ones Aidan donned. Tunic shirts in light-colored fabrics hung loose over tighter breeches. Many wore no shirt at all, instead showing off bare chests bronzed by the sun. From young to old, they appeared healthy and muscled and some of them were practically gigantic. Scars lined their bodies, attesting to a hard life. All but the boys and women had black bands around their upper arms and a few even had wrist markings like Aidan.

If she had doubts, this town confirmed she wasn't home. The men of her village were tall and slender, made for running through the trees while shooting a bow. Only the tales of the Carvers could match the breadth and height of these men, though Starians clearly lacked the wild lunacy of that race.

"Tell them what you saw," Aidan urged her, his breath tickling the back of her ear.

Paige stiffened fully, if that was even possible since she had been rigid from the moment he had slid behind her on the horse. She shook her head in jerky denial. The last time she had been in front of a crowd of villagers there had been talk of stoning her for "bringing on the wrath of Sister Nature".

"This is my bride, Lady Paige, sent by the fairies to Fallenrock because she is an oracle," Aidan announced. The words were met with a rush of excited chatter. A group of young boys lifted their stick swords, pumping them in the air.

"Hand me your knife, Aidan," she whispered out of the side of her mouth, reaching around to Aidan's thigh. He placed his hand over hers, stopping her from finding it. Apparently, the townsfolk weren't so keen on the idea of another oracle. She twisted her hand in the horse's mane, ready to ride—with or without Aidan on the back.

"Rejoice!" an old man with a weathered face and raspy voice called from the crowd, the word lifting above the others. Paige jolted in alarm. "Rejoice! Sir Aidan has chosen."

"Rejoice! Rejoice!" Shouts joined the first, growing and floating over the distance. "Sir Aidan has chosen a wife! The new oracle is his wife!"

A sudden panic filtered through Paige. Her eyes darted over the crowd, seeing their smiling faces looking up at them. They stepped forward, moving as one mass to press in upon the new couple. A hand brushed her calf and she automatically lifted her knee to get away. She pressed into Aidan's chest, trying to climb up onto the horse's back. His hand snaked around her waist, holding her steadily to his hard frame. A shiver worked over her, but the sensation barely registered. After living in the forest by herself, she didn't like all this direct attention.

"Back," Aidan commanded. He was met with instant obedience. "The oracle needs space." Then, to her, he whispered, "At ease, my lady, they mean you no harm. They only wish to welcome you."

Paige relaxed by small degrees, but still kept a wary eye on the crowd. Aidan didn't let go of her waist and she squirmed, uncomfortable with the public claim. Every part of her wanted to run away into the trees and hide. What was she doing here? In a town filled with strangers who would undoubtedly blame her when her prediction came true and a life was lost.

When Paige didn't speak to the expectant onlookers, Aidan cleared his throat. "Lady Paige has foreseen a terrible storm on the water tonight. All fishermen should be called in."

"And lose a day of work while the blugin run?" a man with short black hair yelled. "We only have two nights to pull the supplies we need to last a year. Who will feed our children when the food runs out next winter?"

"The rest of the season's catch won't compare to the blugin run," said a blonde woman with a small boy huddled into her skirts.

Paige looked at the young boy's face. Her voice soft and a little too high for normal, she said, "There is no reason you all have to stay ashore, so long as you come back when you feel the storm. We are only concerned about one man in particular. We're searching for a man with a scar."

"She doesn't act like the other oracles. Have her powers been tested?" someone asked.

"You expect us to stay out of the water on an untested prediction?" another added.

"Some prediction!" a woman cackled sarcastically. The tight pull of her laced bodice squeezed a pair of very generous breasts to the point they looked as if they might burst. "A man with a scar in Staria? If that's a prediction, I can do you one better. I predict I have five husbands."

A round of laughter instantly filled the center square.

"We are all oracles. I predict trees are growing in the forest," a voice mocked. "And those trees have leaves."

"I predict my wife will slap me," another man added, "for saying she's got a large—"

Sure enough, a woman slapped the man upside the head, stopping the rest of the comment.

"Is this the scar you are looking for, Lady Paige?" The black-haired man showed a red, puffy gash across his stomach before turning to let her see rounded marks on his back. "Or these?"

Instantly trying to outdo each other, the men lifted their shirts and pulled at their sleeves, pointing out their many scars. Even the boys joined in the teasing.

"I have nigh twenty, my lady, if you count the ones run together," someone hollered.

"And I nigh thirty," another voice chimed.

"Forty here!"

"Forty-one!"

"I have one, my lady," a child yelled, shoving his stick under his arm to hold it in place as he struggled with his neckline.

Behind her she felt Aidan shake as if holding back his own laughter. In her ear he whispered, "They are only teasing. They must like you."

This was how they greeted people they liked? Paige didn't say a word.

"I have got a scar to show you, but it's on my arse." This response got a solid thump in the chest from the man's wife and more laughter from the crowd.

That was it! Prying at his arm, she got him to loosen his hold on her waist. Swinging her leg around the side, she slid from the horse. Her legs wobbled as they hit the ground. If they only wanted to mock her, then the lot of them could rot for all she cared.

"We're looking for an older man with a scar across the back of his hand. Jagged," Aidan said. She heard him land on the ground behind her. Paige inched away from him, eyeing the crowd for her easiest escape. As the new woman wearing unsuitable attire, she knew it wouldn't be easy to blend. No, her best bet was slipping notice while Aidan was distracted. Then she would head for the trees.

"Do you speak of Callum?" someone offered. "He has such a scar."

"Aye, I have a scar on my hand."

Paige turned to find the man from her vision staring at her. Instantly, she sought his hand, finding the exact scar she had pictured. All thoughts left her as she whispered, "That scar. It's you. You're the man I saw."

Callum rubbed the back of his hand with his thumb, but the gruff lines of his weathered face didn't flinch. "A barbed hook caught it during blugin season when I was a boy. We had no choice but to rip it out and bandage it up." He flexed his hand.

"Don't go to the water tonight. Stay inside." Almost desperate, she rushed forward. Never had she been so close to saving a life before. The Forestters didn't want to hear about her visions, didn't want her help. They threatened and blamed her for whatever misfortune came if she tried. "If you take to the sea, you'll be killed when the waves destroy your boat. Try to stay away from all water, just to be safe."

Again, Callum didn't flinch. Worry didn't enter his steady gaze, but neither did doubt. He dropped his hand. Nodding once, he said, "Thank you for the warning, oracle."

Then, turning, he picked up a bucket of water from the ground and carried it down the road as if nothing in his life had changed. Paige lifted her hand, thinking to stop him. "But..."

"Rejoice, the oracle has spoken!" someone yelled causing her to jump in surprise. The cry was followed with shouts of, "Rejoice! Rejoice!"

Even Aidan uttered a very low, "Rejoice," while looking at her with his hot, seductive eyes. There was something else in his gaze—

pride. She trembled, overwhelmed by the crowd's acceptance and excitement.

"Come on then, we have duties to attend to." A plump woman waved her hand, ushering a couple boys into one of the nearby shops. The crowd followed her lead and began to disperse. A few even paused to congratulate her on her marriage.

"But..." Paige jerked as Aidan touched her elbow.

"Are you hungry, my lady? The Axe Hitter Tavern will gladly take our coin."

"I don't have coin," Paige answered without thinking. She lifted her hand to point down the road Callum was quickly disappearing. "Did he not believe me? I'm not teasing him. I really did see his fate on the water."

"I'm sure he believes you. Had he not, Callum would have laughed at you and denounced your claim. See, all is well. He goes home. You have done what you've come to the village to do." This time he grabbed her arm and forcibly made her turn toward the horse. "Callum will make his decision."

Not wanting to sit close to him again and subject herself to another round of agonizingly unfulfilled desires, she shook her head. "I think I would rather walk."

"As you wish," he answered. His low voice sent an animalistic thrill over her.

Heat curled in her stomach and she realized she didn't have to sit next to him to feel the pain of hunger and need. Just knowing Aidan was near caused her body to respond with wet passion. Her throat dry, she managed to inquire, "Which way to the tavern?"

# CHAPTER 4

By all the bloody swords in Staria, Aidan wanted her like he'd never wanted anything in his life. Everything about her caused his blood to boil in his veins until he had to actively focus his thoughts to keep from fantasizing. He suppressed a groan. Everywhere he looked, he thought of ways to take her against him—behind cottages, against trees, over the table that now stood between them. It was madness and he wasn't sure he wanted to find a cure for it.

Aidan found it hard to swallow his meal as he watched Paige's tongue trail across her bottom lip to sweep a small bread crumb into her mouth. The tavern was empty, which wasn't unusual for that time of morning. Many would have had their morn meal before the sun rose over the earth.

Set along the edge of town, the Axe Hitter Tavern brewed most of the town's ale and became a natural gathering place for the locals. A sweet tinge of liquor always flavored the air, seeping into the main building from the stone structure around back.

Rough-hewn boards held together with plaster formed the tavern building walls. According to the owner, Merrit, the design came from her homeland. Inside, wooden tables and equally plain chairs lined up like soldiers in orderly rows. Strips of material, bright and festive like a lady's skirts, covered abnormally large windows. Because of the large oven, the room was warmer than outside, but a pleasant breeze through the opened door made it agreeable. Having Paige as his company made it even more so. Even if she didn't say much, the growing gleam in her eyes said more than words ever could.

"How is your mother, Sir Aidan?" Merrit asked him, sauntering to the table. Though tall and slender, there was a seedy coarseness to the inviting sway of her hips. Wherever the fairies had sent this woman from had been a hard place. She ran the Axe Hitter with her husbands.

"Still at sea," Aidan answered. "I don't imagine she will be back before midsummer."

"Still swimming away from the suitors is what you mean to say," Merrit chuckled. "Hasn't Martin caught her yet?"

"No, not yet. Though I doubt she is worried. With you in town there are no men left without a bride. How many do you have now? Thirty-seven?"

"Eleven. Poor Tomm died last winter." Merrit clicked her tongue, lightly running her hand over her red curls. "It is a shame. He was a good man, if not a little bit of a stinker. I hated to lose one of my collection. I don't suppose you want to replace him? Come on, Sir Aidan, be the first Starian man to take two wives. We will change the world, the three of us."

To Aidan's pleasure, he saw Paige's fist tighten over her bread. She stopped eating but didn't interrupt Merrit's banter.

Aidan laughed at the very absurdity of the idea, thoughtlessly giving her a small grin. "I am not sure that would work or that it would have the gods' blessing, for to do so I would be taking on eleven husbands and you a wife. I will have to decline."

"I don't know about your gods, Sir Aidan, but mine heartily approve." Merrit swiped the two nearly empty trenchers of food from their table. "Help yourself to the rooms in back. They're not all clean but they are all empty." With a wink she left, leaving them with only themselves and a couple of goblets of slightly soured ale.

"You have a mother?" Paige asked, her eyes steadily on his face.

"Doesn't every man?" he chuckled, his mind instantly taking his gaze to the hall leading back to where Merrit put up travelers for the night.

"I meant alive. You have family?" She licked her bottom lip. By the teeth of the damned, did she have to keep doing that? His cock lurched in his pants, demanding the full focus of his brain.

"Ah," he took a drink, gulping down the liquor. When he could again think, he said, "My mother, Lady Carrina, is at sea."

Paige glanced at Merrit. "I heard."

"Yea, I suppose you did. My mother spends most of her life at sea these days. Ocean life agrees with her, or so she says. She was born here in Fallenrock Village to a fisherman."

"And this Martin?" she prompted.

"Martin wishes to claim my mother, but he cannot seem to catch her." Aidan shook his head, amused and a little sorry for the old warrior. "She left after my father died and only sneaks back at night in the middle of summer to avoid being claimed a second time."

"And is she an oracle too? Is that why you don't question what I say?"

"No. She is not, though I sometimes think she wishes she'd been so blessed. And why would I question you? You have no reason to deceive me." Aidan leaned closer, reaching out to touch her hand as it lay on the table. She pulled it just out of reach.

"Do you have brothers or sisters?"

"No sisters. My family was not blessed with girls." Aidan went on to explain the Starian's lack of daughters and need for wives. He wasn't sure why, but he felt himself rambling, anything to bring forth hints of interest to her green eyes. "I had brothers but they were killed in battle. And you?"

"Everyone I had is dead." Short. Simple. That was all the answer she would give him.

"Did your family possess gifts?" he asked.

"Just my grandmother and my father. I suppose I'll pass it to some of my children." She paused, not meeting his eyes at that last comment about children. Clearing her throat uncomfortably, she continued, "But the Forestters don't call them gifts."

"Ah, that's right. You said you were cursed." Aidan again reached to touch her, more quickly this time so she didn't have a chance to pull back. He held her small hand easily under his larger one, conscious of the delicate fingers curling against the tabletop. "I don't think I'd ever understand people who look at such a blessing as a curse. Without you, Callum would take to the sea, unknowing of his fate, unable to do what he must."

She visibly swallowed. "Do you really think I saved him?"

The need in her expression was tinged with fear. He wondered exactly how badly she had been treated by her people because of her "curse". Smiling, he held her hand tighter. "You did well, my lady. Do not worry yourself about Callum. You did what you could by him."

* * *

Paige's heart raced until she was sure it would explode. Inside the tavern, hidden in the dim light away from the crowd, she had begun to relax, but now Aidan's hand on hers made her all too aware of his touch. A nervous, excited tremble began at the contact and radiated up her arm and throughout her body. No man looked at her the way he did, hot and liquid and unafraid. His passion intrigued and frightened her. She was scared to want him as much as she did, scared of what it could mean, of what could be won and lost in his embrace. A small whisper in the back of her mind told her to run away until she could reason out what was happening, but that whisper was drowned out by the thumping of her heartbeat echoing in her ears.

Out of all the times she had tried, she had never been able to save a life before. Her grandmother had spoken of it several times, of how some man in their family lineage had kept his entire planet from being destroyed. Though, Paige's visions were nowhere near as powerful as those. Her sight was tied to the weather. She saw death by water or air or earth, but never by a human hand. Her grandmother always told her to be patient, that more visions would come. Paige didn't want them to get stronger.

"Tell me about you, my lady. You have listened to me talk, but you have said little about your life beyond short, necessary answers." He looked so sincere, so eager to know her. "I would know more."

Paige opened her mouth, but an answer didn't readily come. Living alone for the last several years had only taught her to talk to herself and the trees. "I hate crowds."

"I gathered as much," he chuckled. "You looked as if you couldn't run away fast enough. What else do you hate?"

*I hate seeing visions of people dying. I hate being treated like an outsider. I hate that fear people get in their eyes when they get too close to me. I hate the Faerians, but perhaps just a little less than I did this morning. I hate the way you're looking at me now, like you know a secret that I should know too. And I hate Merrit for disregarding me while she tried to make you a twelfth husband—even though that doesn't mean I want you for my husband. Because I don't.*

Paige frowned. Was it possible that her brain actually started laughing at her?

"This ale tastes off. I don't like it very much," she whispered so Merrit couldn't hear her. Paige touched the rim of the goblet.

"It is a little past its time," he agreed. "What else don't you like?"

She gestured helplessly, trying to pull her hand from his. The warmth tingled up her arm and she took a deep breath as she stared at his larger palm engulfing hers.

"Then, what do you like?" His fingers moved. She couldn't see it, but she could feel it, a tiny vibration along her flesh.

"Rain," she said simply. "When it falls all around me, my head is quiet. It washes my thoughts and I don't have to see anything. Sometimes I wish it always rained."

"Then I was right, you are where you belong. It rains almost nightly in Fallenrock." This time she did see his finger move. His thumb brushed along her wrist, as if strumming an invisible thread from her hand to her chest. A second hand captured her free one, pressing it to the tabletop. Her heart pounded, beating a rhythm in her ears.

"I like music and hearing people sing. Sometimes I would sneak to the edge of the village and listen to the festivals from the trees. Music always sounds better over a distance. I always wished there was a way to capture the music and replay it back later. Silly, huh? Like we'd ever be able to capture something as fleeting as sound." Paige sighed, closing her eyes slightly. Her limbs felt heavy and energetic at the same time. Her breasts ached and she clamped her legs together to keep the sensation from spreading downward. It didn't work. Her sex dampened with desire.

"What else?" he whispered, the sound a little hoarse.

The room appeared to blur as she looked at his face. Had he leaned closer? "I like, ah..." Paige let loose a shaky breath.

*I like your forest-colored eyes? I like your slightly crooked smile? I like you, your...*

"I like your fire boxes." If he wasn't holding her hands down she would have smacked herself across the cheek.

*Fire boxes?!*

"Fire boxes?" He turned, his hands slipping somewhat as he looked at the wall. "You mean the fireplace?"

Paige nodded.

"You don't have..."

"Our place for fire is in pits in the center of a home." Was she a complete imbecile? What was she even talking about? And why couldn't she concentrate?

"I like your soft skin." His fingers massaged deeper into her flesh. "Your deep, green eyes so full of mysteries I can't wait to unravel. Your red hair that—"

"Aidan," she tried to stop him. "You're..."

"I'm?" There was that crooked smile again—utterly charming and completely devastating.

"I'm," she started a second time, struggling with the words.

"You're?" How did he get so close, leaning into her from across the table? When she didn't find the words, he stood, pulling her with him.

Paige couldn't think of what to do, so she followed him, letting him lead her through the main room of the tavern toward a back hallway. The faint sound of Merrit's laughter penetrated the fog in her brain but it wasn't enough to draw her out of the trance Aidan placed over her senses.

Wood walls striped with white passed along either side of them. Aidan led her to the back before opening a door and pulling her inside. She got the briefest glimpse of a trunk and bed before Aidan jerked her into his chest. Fiery heat exploded where he touched, spreading throughout her with a mind-swirling speed. She gasped and he drew his lips down to devour hers.

*What is happening to me?*

Aidan's tongue slid over her mouth, translating the desperation of his body. Before she could react, he turned, pressing her back into the rough-hewn wall. The unmistakable outline of his arousal dug into her stomach. She had felt hints of it as they rode but had forced herself to ignore it. Now, with the evidence of his desire so blatant, she couldn't think of anything else.

"Such softness beneath these clothes," he groaned into her mouth as a hand cupped her breast through the shirt she had taken from his trunk.

*Such hardness beneath yours*, she thought.

Tentatively, she touched his arms, sliding her fingers down his biceps to his elbows, only to let them drop to his waist and continue along his thighs. The hilt of the knife bumped her hand and she thought about taking it. Paige hesitated too long because Aidan grabbed it first, broke the kiss and turned to throw it at the wall. It stuck into the wood plank above the bed, vibrating before coming to rest.

His actions became more aggressive. He delved his hand beneath her shirt, instantly grabbing a naked breast. His hips ground into hers, forcing her ass hard against the wall. Paige turned her head before he could kiss her, gasping for air. He didn't stop. His lips found her neck only to bite and lick a trail along her jaw to her earlobe. Heavy breath surrounded her, cocooning her inside the rapid sensations.

"Aidan," she panted, fighting in a sea of desire and fear. Her body ached for him, but already he reached between them to free his cock from his breeches. "Aidan, no."

He groaned into her neck, a sound of pain and frustration. When she expected him to yell or ignore her, he asked, "Do you still hurt? Was this morning too soon?"

"It's not that. I..." She swallowed nervously, her fingers digging into his upper arms. "I don't..."

"You don't want this?" The sound in his voice tore at her, but he didn't back away.

"I don't know what I'm doing."

That brought him back. "But, before—"

"Fairy magic. They poisoned me. I haven't..." She couldn't look at his eyes. They were too penetrating. She felt a slight flush heating her cheeks with embarrassment. "Men in my village are afraid of me. After I told them of the earth opening up and they didn't listen, they blamed me for causing the deaths with my curse since I'd spoken the words out loud. I was eleven when it happened and every man has been too afraid to come near me."

*Not that I wanted them near me. Not like this.*

"So I haven't, I mean I don't know... I'm really bad at this." Paige let go of him to fan her face. Every nerve in her body had been brought to stinging life. "I think I need air."

"Methinks you need a husband who is gentler." He cupped her cheek and turned her jaw so she looked at him. "Forgive me. It is not in a warrior's nature to be tender, but I see the fear in your eyes when you look at me now and I do not like it. I will try harder to please you."

When he moved away, she expected him to lead her back out into the main part of the tavern. Instead, he pulled her toward the bed. When he let go of her, he tugged at his tunic shirt and tossed it aside. He eyed her expectantly, as if waiting for her to do the same.

Without the same grace of movement he displayed, she obeyed the silent command. She pulled the shirt over her head and let it drop on the floor by her feet. Paige watched his face, not moving to cover herself.

Aidan drew his finger over her stomach, tracing the long scar from her navel to beneath her armpit. "Any warrior would be proud to wear this."

Proud? She should be proud about being flayed alive?

"To survive such a wound shows you have strength. I would happily show it to the others, but I don't think I want them looking at you so intimately." He traced it back down and up again, the finger an odd contrast to her cooling skin. "How did you receive it?"

"Some of the children were not happy when their parents were swallowed by the ground," she answered. Paige could still see their childhood faces, contorted with hate and nightmares. "They came for me convinced if they killed me they could trade my life for their parents'. My father stopped them, but was almost too late."

Aidan sank to his knees slowly. He leaned over, brushing his lips against her flesh. He traced the scar with light, feathery kisses before his knees finally reached the floor. He knelt before her, his hands on her waist. Tugging at the laces along her hips, he loosened her waistband.

"You do not have to worry about such things anymore. Here you will be protected. I will let no harm come to you," he said.

"What about when you leave for war?" She touched the top of his head, running her hand over the silken texture of his blond hair.

"Should there be an attack this far north you'd be taken to the castle with the other oracles. Every man in Fallenrock would die protecting you." The laces at her waist loosened and he tugged at her pant legs. He kissed her exposed hip.

"I don't want that, Aidan." She pulled his hair, turning his face away from her stomach to look at her. "I can take care of myself. I've been doing it for a long time now. Please understand I don't want people dying for me."

"But you're a woman." Aidan's hands splayed over her hips, bringing her body closer so he could rub his cheek against her. The subtle hint of whiskers scratched her, but the sensation was hardly unpleasant. "Women are to be protected and cared for. What better cause to fight for than in protection of the fairer sex?"

The way he said it—simple, factual, indisputable—made her tremble.

"You are my wife. I would be a disgrace as a soldier if I did not lay down my life for you." His hands slid down her hips, pushing the pants down to spill around her ankles. He squeezed her ass, drawing her body closer still as he turned his mouth to brush over the soft red curls. Her legs shook, instantly weak as warm breath fanned across her sex.

If what he was doing didn't feel so good, she would have run from the room to calm the emotions running rampant inside of her. "Aidan, you don't know me."

"I know the gods sent you to me. I asked them for a bride and they gave me you." A low moan escaped him and he became more aggressive with his kisses—biting and licking a hot trail over her lower stomach and thighs. The little nips teased her, making her hot for a more intimate contact.

Paige never held out much realistic hope that she would someday find a husband, but in her unspoken fantasies she was like any woman. Who didn't want a man strong enough to protect his woman? But she didn't just want a man who'd die fighting for her. She wanted a man who loved her, adored her and needed to be near her. Aidan offered half of the fantasy. Could she really complain if he didn't offer it all? It's not like she had men lining up at her door in her realm. Wasn't something better than nothing? She wouldn't have to be alone the rest of her life, and when he went off to war she would be left to live in the forest just as she liked.

Unsure if she had actually come to a decision, Paige closed her eyes and let the sensations of his kiss wash over her. He massaged her ass and the backs of her thighs, only to caress up her lower back and down her legs. She had never been touched so completely before and her flesh was starved for the contact. Her fingers slipped from his head to rest on his shoulders for support.

Aidan reached for her breasts, but when he moved his hands from behind her, she stumbled back and bumped into the bed, immediately falling to sit on the stiff mattress. He walked on his knees, coming to her. With a firm shove, he spread her thighs. Paige stared at him, wide-eyed as he lowered his face between her legs. A loud moan sounded seconds before his mouth captured her clit in a deep kiss. His tongue lapped up her slick folds, kissing and sucking and tasting.

She gasped, falling back with the intention of lying on the bed. Her head bumped into the wall and she jerked. "Ow!"

Aidan chuckled, lifting his head from her. "Turn."

Paige wrinkled her nose at his amusement, rubbing her sore scalp, even as she obeyed. Stretching out on the mattress, she forgot all about her injury as Aidan crawled on top of her.

"It is taking every ounce of my control not to wildly take you as we did in the forest." He nuzzled her neck while palming a breast. "But if I have to be tortured, I would have it at your hand, my lady."

"This is madness," Paige whispered as she touched his cheek. He didn't answer but to bite at her earlobe.

Aidan reached between them and she felt his hand working at his laces, bumping along her pussy and thighs. The clarity of the moment was a stark contrast to the times before. Her brain registered every little detail and captured it. She moved restlessly beneath him, her entire being growing hotter with each passing moment.

Aidan's hot breath fanned her neck with warmth. His chest teased her hardened nipples, tickling them as she moved. The back of his hand stroked her sex, sending a delicious sensation over her clit. Paige couldn't help herself. She arched her hips so they again rubbed against each other. A light moan of pleasure escaped her and she closed her eyes.

When Aidan freed himself from his pants, he removed his hand and braced his weight on the bed. Lifting up, he untangled his legs and fitted them between hers, holding her open. Their bodies moved restlessly against each other. The stiff bed pressed into her back, but she didn't notice it. How could she when he looked at her the way he was? His lids fell over his eyes, shading them as he studied her face. They moved over her, as if memorizing every detail. Had she been standing, she would have run from his deep perusal—not because she didn't like it, but because the intensity frightened her.

The strands of his hair framed his face as he maneuvered his hips. The first brush of his cock along the wet folds of her sex made her jolt involuntarily. She remembered what it felt like, his thick body pushing roughly into hers, stretching, pounding, claiming.

But instead of the hard thrust, he took her gently, easing his way in with a controlled push of his hips. Aidan bit his lip, sighing even as he tensed. The thick splay of muscles across his chest moved erotically beneath the skin. Paige held onto his arms as her body accepted him.

The intensity of his eyes burned into her, capturing her until she couldn't look away. Aidan took his time, slowly pulling out and thrusting in a seamless, perfect motion. His scent surrounded her, fresh and clean yet tinged with the herbs of the forest.

Paige worked her legs against the bed, digging her heels into the mattress. Her hands glided restlessly over his body, touching everywhere she could reach. Leaning slightly to the side, he grabbed her thigh, lifting it high along his hip while he continued to thrust. The new position brought him deeper and her entire being shuddered in response.

She moaned, suddenly clawing at his firm ass. The pleasure built into a frenzied tension. She couldn't catch her breath, couldn't stop moving her hips. Aidan grunted, his movements becoming harder as he quickened his pace. He grabbed her breast, massaging it briefly before again bracing his weight on the bed.

"Ah," he groaned. "By all the sword blades in Staria, you feel like a fresh victory."

Paige didn't know how to respond to the strange compliment so she moaned incoherently instead. Tremors took hold of her stomach, shaking their way from her sex to the rest of her body. She tensed only to jerk several times as she met with release. Aidan looked down at her like a man who'd just conquered his world, joining her with his own heavy climax.

# CHAPTER 5

Rain pelted her face and chest, but Paige made no move to get out of the foul weather. Even cold and hard, the droplets felt as close to heaven as she had ever been. Each one hit her flesh like a tiny blade, sharp and poignant, leaving behind a shard of numbness that slowly spread over her limbs.

With little effort, her head cleared until no thoughts flowed but her own. She breathed deeply, loving the absence of emotions. Normally her body felt like a breeding ground for strange feelings, but now, in the rain, she felt only herself. It was only in these moments she had any kind of real clarity.

*What in the green of the forest am I doing here?*

After the rush of sexual release in the tavern—and again in the forest on the way back to Aidan's home, and pressed up against the stables after stalling the horse, oh, and lest she forget the side of the house because they didn't make it inside after the stables—she had felt the call of the oncoming rain.

The storm from her vision started with a few gentle drops snaking down Aidan's strong face as the magenta light of evening darkened his features. Hope and excitement warred with the fear of disappointment. She couldn't keep kissing Aidan, exploring his touches and his embrace, with the reminder that a life might end on the sea. When Aidan led her inside with the offer of sleep and food, she had followed only to slip away the second his attention turned from her to slice strips of meat on a cutting table.

*What do I do? Stay? Go? This is not my homeland.*

Paige turned to look at the looming house cast in blue moonlight.

*This is not my home.*

"But it could be," she whispered.

The cold water stuck the borrowed tunic to her flesh and the wind blew it tight to her chest. Strands of her hair plastered against her neck and cheeks. She didn't bother to pull them off.

"I could live here," she continued, "as an oracle. I could save lives."

Did she dare to hope?

The frigid water combined with the rush of chilly air coming off the sea became almost unbearable, but she was hesitant to leave the clarity of the rain. Inside, she would have to work to keep the visions from rushing back in—not as hard as when the skies were clear, but she would have to work all the same—and she still didn't know what she wanted to do about Aidan. She did not share his confidence in their joined futures.

Paige turned into the trees. Now that was a life she did understand—uncomplicated, peaceful, free. The building smile faded before it had a chance to grow. And that life was very, very lonely.

Hands wrapped her waist from behind, drawing a startled gasp from her. Aidan's voice rose above the pounding rhythm of the raindrops hitting the earth. "I understand your need for silence, but I worry about you in this weather. The cold sea rain can cause a breathing sickness."

Even after the day they'd spent having sex, she still felt the quivering temptation of his touch. The heat of his body chased away the chilly rain and Paige found she didn't mind the jumbling of her thoughts as her focus turned from the weather to Aidan's strength. When he hugged her tighter, she dropped her head back against his chest. Aidan's chin moved down along her ear, coming to rest near her cheek as he curled around her. The now very familiar rub of his growing erection brushed along her ass.

"Come inside." Aidan gently pulled her with him a couple steps before sweeping her up into his arms. Cradling her against his body, he hurried to the opened door of his house. He kissed the corner of her mouth before dropping her legs to set her down on the floor. "If you desire a bath to warm yourself, the bathing room is at the end of the hallway. Lift and push the pump handle and the water will flow. I will finish cooking."

"You have bathing water in the house?" Curious, she turned from him. Water dripped from her clothes and the smell of cooking food followed her as she made her way down the hall. Pushing open the door, she found a large, smooth stone hole in the floor. Lidded jars lined the far edge and a hand pump rose from the ground. Though the design differed from what she was used to seeing, she could determine its function easily enough.

As she lifted and pumped the handle, a stream of dark blue water poured from the spigot into the bathing pool. Paige watched, mesmerized, and lifted her hand to watch the gemlike water trail over her skin in sparkling rivulets. Why hadn't the Forestters thought of indoor water pumps? They had to cart water from the outside brooks to a giant storage bin.

Standing, she peeled off her wet clothes. Warm water tickled her legs, lapping gently as she moved into the bathing pool. Sinking into the depths, she perched her ass on the edge of an underwater seat and sighed with relief as heat enveloped her. Tension eased out of her shoulders and neck, causing a tingling sensation on her scalp.

Paige rubbed her shoulder, liking the way her fingers slipped over flesh with aid of the water. Watching the door for signs of movement, she wondered if Aidan would follow. When he didn't she moved her hands to her breasts, massaging them gently. In light of the pleasure Aidan had shown her, her sensitive body was only too willing to find release again.

Paige ran her hand down her stomach, tracing the scar that led to her parted thighs. The warm bath made her sex so wet and hot and rubbing along the slit was both easy and highly pleasurable. She kept her eyes on the door, not wanting him to catch her as she slipped a finger inside. Wiggling the digit in small circles, she tried to mimic his touch. She clamped her thighs tight against her hand, holding it in place. Her hips rocked so that her clit brushed up against her palm.

She suppressed a moan. The heated water lapped against the top of her breasts and neck, the surface rippling with her movements. Her lids fell heavy over her eyes, but she didn't look away from the door. Thoughts of Aidan swam in her brain. Paige panted, biting her lip hard as her hand worked harder and faster. She grabbed a breast, pinching the nipple between two fingers. Never had self-pleasure felt so good.

Her body tensed as small tremors started in her pussy and traveled out over her entire length. Breathing heavily, Paige closed her eyes, letting the relaxation settle into her muscles. Her legs fell limp to release her hand.

"Aidan," she whispered, awash in pleasure.

---

Aidan looked down at the trencher of food he had prepared for his new bride. Strips of meat piled in the center surrounded by the last of his vegetables. With the house left empty most of the time, there'd been little need to see to the planting and storage. He had let the villagers who took care of his home use the garden space. When he had been a boy the larder had been overflowing with food and the house always smelled of his mother's cooking.

"Soon we will fill this house with a family," he said to himself. "Now is the time for patience. I have had more of her than any man could ask. It was wise of the ancestors to assign women separate bedchambers." The reasonable sound of his own voice did not ease the ache in his loins. He wanted nothing more than to grab her, hold her close and spend the rest of his time at home in her arms.

Carrying the tray in one hand and a jug of ale in the other, he began walking toward the bathing room only to hesitate. They had been together all day. Was it too much? She had gone outside to be alone and he had interrupted her. No matter how eager he was to see her naked in his bath, he wondered if he shouldn't give her some time alone.

Thinking of the warm blue water clinging to her delectable nipples caused him to bite his lip and moan. He started for the bathing room door. Then, remembering how she had looked out in the rain, her face turned to the sky with a look of complete and open rapture when she didn't know he watched her, he stopped and went back to the dining table.

"Ach! What are you doing, boy? Leaving my door open to invite the storm in?"

Aidan turned, pushing up from the table before he had a chance to sit down. A smile broke across his face at the voice. "Mother. You're back."

"Just this eve. The gods are angry tonight. They finally chased me off the sea," Carrina of Fallenrock answered her son. Lines of age had been smoothed by the salt of the open sea air. A rasp resounded in her voice, a sound that had not been there when he was younger.

Aidan gave her a hug, affectionately patting her short gray hair. "And I imagine Martin will chase you back onto the waves come sunup."

"It's safer ashore while the blugin run the next couple of days." She chuckled. Time and loss had taken their toll and he saw that toll in her serious eyes. Even when she laughed the sadness was there. Unlike most women of Staria, she wore the white tunic and breeches of a sailor. The clothes had been yellowed by years on the sea and worn to the point no one would suspect her to be a woman from such a prestigious family. Aidan was pretty sure that was why she looked the way she did. The disguise hid her identity and, if she mentioned having a "husband" or two, very few men would try to claim her without first seeking permission from her nonexistent spouses. "Ah, food."

Aidan glanced toward the bathing room. Paige was too far away to hear them.

As Carrina reached for the tray of cooked meat, she continued, "I skirted the edge of town on my way here. There's talk of a new oracle in the area. It was a little hard to make out everything, but I hear she is beautiful and has come through the fairy rings." Taking a bite, she grinned meaningfully at him. "As the highest-ranking man in the village and a sacred protector of the oracles, you should lay claim to her before any others."

"Here two seconds and you're already scheming to see me wed. Hm, should I return the favor? Martin would be very pleased to receive a missive as to your joyous return and unclaimed status. I am sure the whole village would rejoice in celebration."

Carrina grabbed another meat strip and gestured it toward him with a suppressed laugh. "And that would make him the master of this house and your new father."

"Point taken." Aidan grabbed a strip and bit into it.

"Aidan, my clothes are wet and I didn't see anything to dry off with." Paige emerged from the hall, dripping with water and wearing nothing but an arm across her chest and a hand splayed over her sex to mimic clothing. "Do you have—oh, blessed forest!" Paige's loud scream and pounding footfall were only outdone by Carrina's shout of surprised laughter.

A door slammed, encouraging Aidan to go after his bride. To his mother he said, "The oracle has already been claimed."

Carrina's squeal of delight followed him down the hall.

Tracking the wet footsteps to the room he had laid Paige in when he first brought her home, he pushed open the door without knocking. He couldn't help the smile that curled on his lips to see her naked ass pointing in his direction as she dug through the trunk of clothing. She gasped, twirling around with a tunic pressed to her chest to hide her wet body.

"I'm taking the food to my room!" his mother yelled through the door. "I want grandchildren!"

Paige flinched. Aidan tried to give her what he hoped was an apologetic look. "That's my mother. Apparently, your storm chased her from the sea."

"It's not my storm." Paige stiffened. "I didn't make it rain. I told you already. I can't control the weather or what it does to—"

"Paige, calm yourself. I did not mean to imply you had aught to do with—"

"Calm myself? Calm myself!" She gave a wry laugh. Then to herself, she mumbled, "What am I doing here?"

Aidan hated to see the look on her face, lost and perhaps a bit frightened. He had expected modesty and embarrassment, but not that.

"It has been a long day for you." He resisted the urge to go to her. He was a warrior and wasn't sure what to say to comfort her. Yelling at her as he would a fresh knight scared of the battlefield hardly seemed appropriate. "I will leave you to rest. Please, let me know if you have needs."

She didn't answer, only continued to stare at him with her wide, confused eyes. Aidan slowly backed away, leaving her alone in the room.

---

"This is much more appropriate for a woman of your position. I cannot believe my son let you run around the village in his old clothes." Carrina nodded her head in approval, studying the gown she had forced Paige to wear. Well, "forced" might be a little harsh. It's not as if the woman pinned her down and held a knife to her throat. Instead, Carrina had used something even more fear-provoking—her determined stare, a stare that started the moment Paige opened her eyes to see the woman leaning over her.

Paige eyed the woman in return, taking in her yellowed, ill-fitted clothing. "A woman of my position?"

"As Lady Paige of Fallenrock, wife to Sir Aidan," the woman answered, as if it shouldn't have needed clarification.

Paige turned from the woman to look down at herself. Diffused, morning light shone through the narrow window, shadowed by falling rain. It created a strange streaking light across her exposed cleavage. The light green undertunic gown flowed around her hips and legs only to be pressed tight against her waist by the darker green corset. The tight bodice of the corset covered her bared nipples, but did little to hide the fact that her breasts had been pushed together and up like some sort of trophy display. The wide neckline exposed her shoulders and fell loose upon her upper arms before forming long, flowing sleeves. Reaching into the top of her bodice, she tried to fish the undertunic's neckline up and out to cover her chest. It was no use. There wasn't enough material.

"Ah, I knew this gown would fit you. Just don't let the townsfolk see it. I got it off Lixie's clean laundry pile last night." Carrina chuckled. "I have a bit of amusing gossip for you, Paige."

Paige didn't answer, only half listening as she tugged the laces binding her waist tight.

Carrina, completely oblivious to her companion's mood, continued, "Lixie wanted one of my sons for herself, but Aidan and his brothers were always off to war. Before she had a chance to work her wiles on them, her own first husband claimed her. Now you wear one of her best gowns. Though I doubt Lixie would find much amusement in the fact that her gown succeeded where she had not."

Paige had "borrowed" plenty of items when living on her own and didn't so much as blink at wearing the stolen gown. What did bother her was the lack of movement the gown allowed and the fact she could barely breathe with the corset pulled so tight. How could she make a run to the forest if she needed to get away?

"The larder is empty so Aidan is hunting this morning. He should have gone before the rains started, but then I suppose he has been preoccupied." Carrina gave another small laugh, seeming to entertain herself more than anything.

"Are you sure you're his mother?" Paige asked before she could stop herself. She wasn't used to mothers speaking so freely about their sons. All was known, but her people never spoke of such things in full detail.

Carrina laughed harder, the gruff sound booming in the room. "I suspect the sea might have swallowed my manners. It's been awhile since I have talked to people who are really there."

Paige turned, really looking into the woman's eyes for the first time. She saw Carrina's gaze shift, moving from Paige's face and gown to the fire box only to land on the narrow window. Paige understood that look, had felt it herself during those long, cold, isolated winters in the forest.

"I understand," Paige said. "I have heard the invisible conversations too. I believe the mind creates the insane to keep us sane. It will pass."

Carrina's inner wildness calmed and she nodded once. "This house is too quiet. You should have heard the sounds it made when all my boys were home. Now the walls echo silence. You must get pregnant and fill it with noise. I had six sons, you should have more. Eleven, no twelve, methinks, or a lucky thirteen. We could build more rooms at the end of the house, and with so many children it will be easy to replant the garden."

Paige tried to smile politely, but the urge to run filled her. Perhaps Carrina's sanity wasn't rooted in mild insanity. Perhaps she had really just gone mad alone on the sea. Perhaps losing five sons and a husband to war had done it.

"Aidan takes family very seriously and will agree, so it is settled. Thirteen children." Carrina grinned, spinning around the room. "And we shall name the first for my husband and five for Aidan's brothers." Hitting the wall, she stopped and placed her cheek to the stone. "This house will sing again." She petted the wall, as if it were a living thing. "Won't you, house, you will sing. Won't you whisper to me now? What do you think of our plan?"

Paige didn't move. Carrina blocked the only exit. Thinking to change the subject, she said, "If you have a bow, I can hunt."

Carrina blinked in surprise, as if coming out of a stupor. "You are a woman. You are to be protected and provided for. Did they not tell you your role?"

"Just because I'm a woman doesn't mean I need to be protected," Paige argued. "I have lived on my own for a very long time."

"There are rules," Carrina insisted. "Rules and ways and traditions."

"They are not my ways. I don't need to be taken care of. I don't even know if I want a husband and children." Why was she arguing with Aidan's mother? All Paige knew was that she would not be giving birth to thirteen boys—no matter how much this woman wanted her to.

"The gods chose you for my son," Carrina snapped. "You are his reward for bravery in battle. It is your duty to be a wife, to give him children and to keep his home. If you fail and my son dies in battle because you do not see to his needs, then his blood will be on your hands and I will make sure everyone knows it."

---

Aidan's body ached with the haul of a successful hunt and the chill of the wet, unpleasant day. Still, he couldn't help but smile as he saw his wife waiting for him in the doorway. It didn't matter what she wore—the belt of the fairies, his old tunic, nothing at all—she always looked beautiful to him. But to see her in the gown of his people, to see her as a true Starian woman should appear, caused his stomach to tighten with pleasure.

He would be blind to miss the way her breasts thrust up along the bodice, or the way the skirt clung to the curves of her hips to tease his senses. The length of her hair had been brushed back and bound at the nape of her slender neck. A few wisps of red had come loose and fell about her shoulders.

"Your mother left," she stated. "Something about spying on the town to make sure it's safe."

"A favorite pastime of hers, though I do not think it's the town's safety she is after as much as the town's gossip." He stopped near her, aware of what he must look like after a day of crawling around in the mud. Rain hit his back, the droplets not quite making it to where she stood beyond the stone doorstep. Shrugging a crossbow from his shoulder, he caught the strap with his hand. "What she won't tell you is that she is ultimately spying on Martin. Every time she comes back she leaves him a little hint that she was here. I'd almost feel sorry for the poor man, but since he can no longer fight in battle, I suspect it's her teasing that keeps him going. Even an old warrior enjoys the fight and intrigue."

He couldn't resist touching her and lifted his free hand to loop a finger around the soft red strands stirring closer to her face. Her lips parted ever so slightly and he imagined he could feel her breath against his wrist. A fine shiver worked over him, causing strange sensations to course through him. Ignoring the sudden rush of feeling, he turned his attention to where they touched and noticed the dirt marring his fingers as it contrasted her clean hair and face.

"I regret that you were embarrassed last night," Aidan said softly, loath to let her go. Every time he looked at her, he wanted to pull her close and kiss her. "I did not know we were to have a visitor."

"This gown is stolen." Paige gave a nervous laugh and looked down. Aidan followed her gaze, his attention stopping at her breasts. He licked his lips, wondering if she would protest being pulled out into the sprinkling rain so he could hold her.

"I should have provided gowns for you. We'll go to the village tomorrow to see the seamstress. You can have as many as you like." His eyes met hers and an intensity passed between them.

"You should come out of the rain." Paige took his hand, leading him into the house. Once inside, she let go and shut the door.

# CHAPTER 6

Paige took Aidan's hand, leading him down the hall toward the bathing room. She had thought of running when Carrina left her alone, but her legs wouldn't seem to move and she found herself waiting for him in the uncomfortable Starian gown. He had said he had family, but five dead brothers, a lost father and a mother whose brains had abandoned her? Paige's heart broke a little at the thought. No wonder he seemed overeager to have a wife. He was lonely.

When she opened the bathing room door, she wasn't sure what to say to him. So, instead, she went to the hand pump and began filling the bath with water. Finishing, she knelt by the edge, dipped her hand just below the surface and observed, "Water is clear in my homeland and we don't have it running indoors."

"From what I understand, it's clear in most planes. Here it's only the underground, blue mineral springs that flow this color. It stays warm no matter how long it is away from a heat source. There have been many winters that the springs have saved us from a cold death." Aidan placed his bow on the floor and untied his sword scabbard. After placing his sword by the bow, he added two knifes to the pile. "Aboveground, our water flows clear, or mostly clear."

With the tight bodice pushing into her stomach, Paige shifted her position to sit next to the water. She dipped her fingertips, lifting them so they rained sapphires. "Can you drink it?"

"Only if the circumstances are dire and you will die without. Too much will make you sick, but will keep you from dying of thirst."

She kept her eyes on the water, but from the corner of her vision she saw him pulling his tunic over his head. The sound of material dropping against stone caused her to stiffen. Paige dipped her hand again, watching the blue tint her long sleeve as it got too close to the surface. A warm hand skimmed the back of her neck and she turned to find Aidan's naked arousal before her. She looked up the length of his body, meeting his gaze.

"You are worth fighting an eternity of battles for, my oracle," he whispered, so soft she barely heard him. "And yet, when I look at you, I do not think of wars."

Paige tried to answer, but no one had ever said such a thing to her and she wasn't sure how to answer. Aidan stepped past her, into the water. She followed him with her eyes, watching the strong, flexing muscles of his ass as he moved. Blue water swallowed him into its depths, until even his head disappeared under the rippling surface.

When he reappeared, he leaned along the edge and sighed. "What is it you think when you look at me?"

"I think that you, ah..." Paige's hand shook as she skated her fingers along the surface, imagining them like two tiny legs on a wintery pond. She bit her bottom lip, saying thoughtfully, "I think you carry yourself like a warrior and I think you have a lot of scars."

He grinned, pleased with the compliment. Paige tried not to laugh.

"What else?" Aidan prompted, reaching for soap.

Instead of going deeper, Paige flicked water at him. "You look like you've been crawling around in mud."

Aidan roughly rubbed his hands over his face, cleaning it before surging across the bath to reach her. Wet hands gripped her hips. "It is my honor to provide for you. I would not have you starve when I am away. I have asked some of the women from the village to help you plant the garden. It should be a good year for crops for a large portion of the land has been resting."

"I can feed myself," she assured him. "There is no need for them to come."

"It helps the villagers to have a joint garden. They'll get extra vegetables for their families and a portion will be sent to the soldiers." His hands tightened and his voice lowered. "Take down your hair."

Not waiting for her to obey, he pushed up from the bath and tugged at the pins holding her hair, taking his time as he found all of them. Finally free, the locks spilled over her shoulders. Paige ran her hands over her head, detecting how his fingers had wet strands of her hair. She pulled the bulk of it off her shoulder, moving it aside to allow him access.

Aidan nuzzled her neck from behind, moaning softly into her skin. The warmth of his breath fanned over her, causing her to shiver. Heat radiated off him, his flesh warmed by the blue water. She closed her eyes, feeling his hands on her stomach, working to free her from the tight hold of the corset. As the laces loosened, she breathed a deep sigh of relief.

Aidan's lips brushed along her shoulder, skimming so lightly she barely felt the touch. Her mind focused on him, the shifts of his body, the kiss of his breath, the sound of a water droplet hitting the surface of the bath when he moved. The bodice loosened more, allowing his roaming hands access beneath the stiff material. He skimmed the bottom curve of her breasts, but couldn't do much more with the bodice hampering his movements.

"Come into the bath," he whispered, pausing to nip at her earlobe. Paige trembled, lifting her arms to reach behind her head. She touched his hair, keeping his lips close to her neck. He kissed her hard, sucking and licking along her throat. Her heart beat fast, thumping uncontrollably in her chest.

Aidan broke the contact of his lips and tugged the corset over her lifted arms. He tossed it aside. The tunic dress's neckline slung low, baring her breasts and shoulders. Without the aid of the corset, the green material slid easy from her arms to pool around her waist.

Aidan's warmth encircled her once more and Paige couldn't help but wonder if the fairies had known they were giving her such a man when they tossed her through the portal. Did the little creatures realize that a land such as Staria seemed like a paradise to a woman like her? Paige was a Forestter and this land was forest and earth and she understood it. Fallenrock's constant rain calmed her thoughts. Its people understood her curse and called it a blessing. Here she could do good deeds, save lives, have friends, be happy. For the first time in her life, she felt as if she could belong to a society, not cast out onto its edges.

Then there was Aidan, whose hands tried to protect and worship at the same time. He cupped her breasts, massaging gently with heated, wet hands. His lips resumed their kisses against her shoulder and throat. Slowly, he pulled her back. Her gown caught beneath her, tangling in her legs. Aidan caught her against him, slipping a hand under her ass to support her weight. With one gentle motion, he drew her into the bath completely, sinking into the water. Paige sat on his lap, her naked back pressed to his chest.

Aidan moaned, his hips arching beneath her, pressing his heavy cock along the cleft of her ass. The tips of her hair floated in the water around them, sticking to the sides of her breasts when she lifted up. Using the advantage of his position, Aidan explored her body. He pinched her nipples. Paige reached behind her, touching his hips briefly before gliding her hands over his. Bronzed tattooed flesh contrasted with her skin. His fingers worked beneath hers. Water lapped her skin, an erotic caress that enhanced the moment. She squirmed, restlessly working against his arousal, an arousal that grew larger with each press of her cheeks.

He hugged her tight, wrapping his arms around her to touch her stomach, hips, upper thighs and back to her breasts. Paige moaned, enjoying the firm sensation of his touch. With each passing second, his movements became more eager. The room faded away until all that existed was the thin space separating their bodies.

She needed him, needed his touch, needed to feel the strength of him inside her. Paige tried to lift up and angle her body, but Aidan stopped her. Instead, he reached between her thighs to torture the clit he found buried in the folds of her sex. Fire shot through her senses, centering over her breasts and pussy. Stroking her pussy with the full length of his hand, he kept her ass tight to his cock. Harsh breathing hit her neck as he rubbed himself against her. A finger slipped past her folds, pushing up into her wet sex only to wiggle back and forth.

Paige rode his hand, gasping at how good the position felt. Aidan bit at her shoulder, not hurting but definitely hard enough to let her know how he anguished for release.

"Argh," he groaned roughly, the sound impassioned and raw. His body jerked hard and she knew he spilled his seed into the water.

Paige let go, joining him in his pleasure. Tremors racked her, weakening her limbs. She collapsed against him, letting her head fall back onto his shoulder. He held her, his hand resting possessively on her breast.

"I did not mean to find release so fast," he admitted, "but you are too beautiful to resist."

Paige turned on his lap, straddling his legs to get more comfortable. The evidence of his desire had lessened somewhat, though his cock still remained partially lifted. Aidan looked deep into her eyes, as he pushed her hair back to better see her face. His intensity forced her to meet his gaze.

Within moments, the heat of his cock grew between them. Paige moaned, her pussy answering his primal call with a rush of moisture. She breathed deeply, holding onto his shoulders. The blunt tip of his erection drew along her sex, thick and hard. Paige impaled herself on him, unable to help the smile that spread over her features.

Aidan held her hips beneath the water, lifting her up only to let go so she slid onto his full length. His eyes stayed focused on her, silently commanding her to keep her eyes open. Paige held onto his neck, keeping a slow, deep rhythm. It felt too good to let the waves of release take her and she tried to hold back. But Aidan forced her up and down faster and harder. His breathing became a deep, harsh echo all around her. She tensed, unable to stave off the trembling rush of pleasure her climax wrought. His hands slid over her back.

"Ah," she panted weakly. His cry of passion answered her in a loud, conquering shout of release.

For a long, sweet moment she stayed on his lap, their bodies joined. She rested her forehead to his, still looking into his eyes, though her lids were heavy. When the pounding of her heart slowed, she lifted off his cock.

"The gods have truly rewarded me." He didn't look away. Even when she turned her gaze to the water, she could feel him studying her. "Together we will fill this house and..."

Paige stiffened, unable to keep the thought of thirteen children out of her head.

"What is it?" Aidan's eyes narrowed and the open expression on his face died a little beneath a hardened mask. She had been so caught up in his touch that she hadn't noticed the unusually affectionate look until it was gone.

"Can't we just be?" Paige bit her lip and tried to scoot off his lap. He held tight. "Can't we just make sure we're going to last before we start talking about children? There is no reason to rush into a union. We can just be..." She gestured helplessly, unable to think of the right words. "We can just be."

"Why would you deny we are joined? The gods have sent—"

"Your gods," she broke in.

"I don't understand. You said yourself the fairies sent you here. They do the bidding of my gods. I have acted as a man should act. I am a soldier, a knight, I have proven myself in battle. I have done my duty." He still didn't let go of her. If anything, his hands tightened on her hips, gripping so hard his fingers hurt her. "Why do you doubt my honor?"

"Ow, stop." She squirmed violently, trying to shake him off.

He instantly let go of her and drew his hands back, appearing horrified at what he had done. "Paige, I did not mean to harm you."

She slipped off his lap into the depths of the water to hide her nakedness. With the sudden tension between them, she felt too exposed. "My desire to make sure we will last before making a big commitment has nothing to do with your honor and everything to do with prudence and good sense."

"I trust that you will be a good wife." He looked as if she had stabbed him in the chest. "You believe I will not uphold my end of the marriage. That is the only reason you would say such a thing to me. What is it? You do not think I will protect you? Feed you? Treat you well?"

"You can't trust me, Aidan, you don't know me." Why was this so hard to explain? Why couldn't he just let their relationship unfold with time? Why did it have to be marriage and children from the very first instant?

"I know you are an oracle, come to me from the Forestter people," he said. "I know that you are my blessing. Why would I question anything else? Why would I worry about things that have not happened, will not happen?"

"Yes, and I suppose you know I'm a woman and I have red hair," she answered wryly. "That is not who I am. Those things are superficial. They do not matter."

"Then I will spend the years getting to know who you are." He clenched his hand into a tight fist and his features tightened on his face. "You are my wife."

"Are you telling me that there is never an unhappy marriage in Staria? That every claimed woman is happy and true to her husband?" Paige swiped her hair from her face, peeling the wet locks off her shoulders.

"Of course not, but I have faith that our marriage will be blessed. I have done everything I was supposed to do." He slammed his fist onto the edge of the bathing pool with a heavy thud. "Why are you making this complicated?"

"Why are you yelling at me?" She surged to her feet, not caring that she had begun screaming. "Because I don't want to have thirteen children? Because I'd like to learn a little bit more about the man who has claimed me? Because I want to learn more about this new world? You cannot fault me for that, Aidan."

"I will tell you what you need to know."

"Well, kiss my toes!" She snorted sarcastically, lifting her arms to the side in a wide, mocking gesture of relief. "Why didn't you say so? Had I known there was no need to think and decide for myself, I wouldn't have put up a fight. By all the trees, impregnate me, oh divine master. I am here to serve as the happy little house maiden."

"I do not like what you are saying. I never asked you to be—"

"Well, then maybe you should tell me what I need to say. However will I know what to do without your guidance, Sir Aidan?" The aftermath pleasure of their encounter drained from her limbs, replaced by anger. She needed to walk. She needed the forest. She needed out of his presence before she challenged him to battle.

"You misunderstood my meaning, my lady." Aidan stood, facing her. She couldn't help herself as her eyes dipped down over his spectacular form.

"I'm going for a walk." She pulled her tunic dress from the ground, not caring that it was damp in spots as she pulled it on her damp body. "Do not follow me."

"You are my bride, Paige," Aidan said in warning.

"So you keep saying," she grumbled. Slamming out of the bathing room, she marched down the hall, fighting the gown. Why wouldn't he just listen? Why couldn't he understand? Finally giving up, she tossed it aside and went to raid the trunk for the male clothing she had altered.

"Daughter!" Carrina called, her voice booming. The happy tone didn't last long. "What happened to your new gown? I told you to be careful with it. I only found you one."

"I'll be outside. So if you and your son wish to continue planning my life, I won't get in the way." She didn't stop as she met with the moonlight-tinted rain.

---

The storm regained strength and raged for three days, barely lifting as the gods seemed to rain down some unknown vengeance upon the people of Fallenrock. The foul weather kept Paige inside with Aidan and his mother. No amount of rooms could help her escape Carrina's scrutiny or Aidan's probing gaze. He looked as if he might speak, but held back, showing none of the affection he had before their argument.

Paige assumed the euphoria of her "marriage" to Aidan would have eventually faded, but after only one fight and a few days? It only proved her instinct was right. He pushed for them to be together too hard and fast. The moment she expressed doubt, he shoved a stone wall between them. Apparently, the knights of Staria did not like to be questioned. It only confirmed she was not the wife for him. Paige would always question.

The rain would not stop her from navigating the forest. Though it wasn't ideal scouting weather, it would hide her tracks. If she could manage to get far enough from the suffocating house, there would be no way Aidan could find her. Any thoughts she had entertained about any other alternative to her situation were just a fantasy. Whether it be in her homeland or in Staria, she belonged in the forest, friend to the trees, sister to the very life and death of the seasons. Even now she felt nature's draw.

Paige pulled the front door open, hoping to slip out of the house undetected. This was the first time since Carrina's arrival that she'd been left unattended in the front room. Gentle drops beat along her shoulder, the sprinkles cool in the evening breeze. Dark magenta light caressed the landscape, giving it an eerie glow.

"I wondered how long it would take you to run," Carrina's voice drifted to her from the side of the house. "I have watched you. I know you have been thinking of leaving us."

Paige stopped, not stepping fully into the rain. Lying, she answered, "You're imagining things. Who said I was running? I just like the rain and wanted fresh air."

"I have watched you. I see what you are thinking," Carrina repeated. She came to Paige's side, staring out over the yard.

"Did the house tell you that?" she mumbled wryly.

"It has been quiet." Then, giving her daughter-by-marriage an accusing look, she added, "I blame you for that. I do not understand why you must resist your fate."

"Of course it is all my fault," Paige muttered, not losing her sarcastic tone. She looked to the heavens, wishing one of the rods of lightning would strike her in the head. From experience, these accusations would last as long as Carrina lacked distraction. "How long until you take to the sea again? I am sure you miss the waves."

"Trying to send me to my death? All in town speak of how you predicted Callum's last moments. Is that what you're doing out here. Watching my death in your visions?"

"Did you say last moments?" A deep sadness stabbed Paige in the chest, causing a sharp pain near her heart. She felt the hints of her dream world falling about her. "Callum died?"

"You saw it in your vision. It happened just as you foretold. The gods swallowed his boat beneath the waves and him with it." Carrina nodded. "It is a very good death for a fisherman. Honorable. Right. His body is where it belongs—in the sea. He would have wanted such an end."

"I don't believe you. There is no way you could know what happened to Callum. You can't go into the village. You don't want to be claimed." Paige wanted the knowing look on Carrina's face to be another one of the woman's wild imaginings.

"With the right disguise I can slip through the streets undetected." Carrina waved her hand in dismissal. "And I do have friends. I was born in Fallenrock Village."

"I failed," Paige whispered, horrified. "Why didn't he listen to me? I told him to stay out of the water. All he had to do was stay home for one storm."

First, Aidan emotionally abandoned her because she dared to question him, dared to ask for time. Now, her prediction did not help anyone. Maybe the fairies hadn't sent her to the perfect world. Perhaps that was the little creatures' ultimate punishment—to give her hope and take it away.

"You gave him time to arrange what he needed to," Carrina said. "It was a true blessing. He had a chance to make right those things that would have otherwise been undone."

"Blessing?" Paige shook her head in denial, slowly backing away from the woman into the stormy night. The Forestters hadn't wanted to hear about her visions, didn't want her help. The Starians listened, but if they didn't heed her warnings then how was that better? Callum was still dead. She had failed. And with that failure combined with Aidan's distance, she saw all reason for her to be part of this society slipping away.

"Where are you going?" Carrina demanded.

"I need to meditate," Paige lied, smiling in what she hoped was a convincing expression. "Alone."

"Callum had time to say what he needed to," Carrina said, her voice loud so as to be heard in the storm. "His family is grateful. It is a good death."

Paige kept walking, barely noticing the cold rain soaking her clothes.

"You know, the gods did choose you for him. I am surprised you do not see it. The other oracles foresaw it. If he didn't claim someone soon, it was predicted he would have no children. If you walk away from here, everyone will learn of your betrayal and no one in Staria will help you."

"The Caniba..."

"Those beasts?" Carrina laughed. "They would devour you rather than help you. They are not called man-eaters without reason. You would be better off seeking aid from a mammoth wolf."

"I do not need the Starian or the Caniba people." Paige crossed her arms over her chest.

"Come, let us eat," Carrina dismissed the claim. "Your clothes are wet and it is time for the evening meal. You can dishonor the family and run like a coward tomorrow."

Paige frowned and considered her options before marching back to the house in irritation. As she passed the older woman, she mumbled under her breath, "You should know about running, Carrina."

*I failed. Callum is dead. I'm a failure.*

The thought swirled around her brain in an endless chant.

*Failure. Failure. Failure.*

Paige had dared to hope that Fallenrock would be different, that here her curse would have meaning. To have that hope taken away with such finality left her all the more bitter and alone. And Aidan's moodiness did little to convince her to stay.

# CHAPTER 7

"I must go."

Paige looked up in surprise. Aidan stood across the main room, clutching a missive in his hand. He was dressed for riding in a short, plain tunic and breeches. A weapon hung at his waist. His lips pressed together in a long, grim line, a trait that carried itself to his narrowed eyes. She tried to read the emotion in his hard gaze, but only saw anger.

"Where did that come from?" She looked at his hand.

His grip tightened, crumpling the parchment in his fist. "A boy delivered it this morning before you awoke."

"Is it...?" Paige pushed up from where she sat at the table, abandoning the half-eaten bowl of boiled grains. "War?"

"No." His face gave nothing away.

"Then...?" She took a step toward him, closing the distance.

"It is no concern of yours. I will be gone a day or two." He turned from her, as he had every time she came near him since their fight in the bathing room. "My mother has gone for supplies and will be back later."

A strange sensation prickled the back of Paige's neck but she nodded in understanding. Realizing he didn't see her, she tugged his arm to get his attention. "What is happening?"

Aidan studied her face, his expression searing, as if he might tug her into his arms and kiss her. Her lips tingled expectantly, waiting for more. Instead, he patted her shoulder and stepped around her. "Actually, I may be longer. You should have sufficient supplies until I get back."

With that, he marched from the house. Paige stared for a long moment in confusion. A pat on the shoulder? Like she was some sort of distant acquaintance? And why wouldn't he tell her where he was going? It was clear that wherever he went, it was urgent and important to him.

Paige waited until she heard the sound of horse hooves before rushing to change out of the red and cream gown Carrina stole for her. She slipped into one of the several old tunic shirts and pants she had managed to alter out of Aidan's old trunk. Pulling on a pair of short boots, she armed herself with a knife from the weapons wall.

She didn't bother to stop for food supplies. The forest would supply anything she needed. Outside the weather had cleared, leaving blue, peaceful skies. Jogging through the mushy grass toward the tree line, she headed in the same direction she'd heard Aidan's horse travel. She found the animal's tracks easily in the muddy ground surrounding the forest and took off into a sprint right behind it. The horse would outrun her, but it couldn't hide from her.

As she ran past thick brush and dense trees, leaping over fallen logs and dodging low branches, Paige smiled. The stress of being trapped inside a home began to melt. She hadn't realized how much she missed being encompassed by nature. The thump of her feet hitting the ground mingled with the strange, distant noises of birds and insects. The sounds were a reminder of how much she needed to learn about the creatures of this land.

Paige soared through the air, grabbing a branch to swing over a particularly rough patch of earth. She skidded to a stop, listening past the beat of her heart for a sign of Aidan's horse. He would have to slow on this treacherous path if he valued the animal's legs.

Detecting a distant sound, she turned course, leaving the tracks to cut across the forest.

Aidan stared at the small cottage, noting how the once happy home seemed to have become a sad echo of the past. Where once laughter carried on the breeze marked by childish stick fights and Ileen's sweet hold over her brothers, now stood a palpably thick silence.

His horse neighed lightly, drawing his attention to the fact he had been standing for a long time. Forcing his feet to move, he didn't want to face the other side of the cottage door. Until he looked, it wouldn't be real.

The door moved before he reached it and Ileen's face appeared in the small opening. It was real. He saw it in her big brown eyes, glassy and red from tears. Peeter was dead, killed in battle by the Caniba. First he lost his brothers and now his childhood friend. With Paige's declaration of not wanting his children and her doubts as to his worth as a husband, he had never felt so alone. Pain forced its way into every inch of his body, until his muscles ached and his stomach churned. A throbbing settled in his temples, straining the back of his stiff neck. Nothing was as it should be.

*The gods curse me. What have I done to deserve such a punishment?*

"Dandan," Ileen suddenly wailed, running for him as fast as her small legs would carry her. Automatically, he lifted her up into his arms. A lifetime of training kept him strong and his eyes dry, but inside he wanted to crumple to the ground and scream until his throat was raw.

"Beautiful Leenie," he whispered.

"Papa," she said, that one word revealing her full comprehension of her loss.

"Your father is with the gods. He is a hero who honored you," he murmured. The words only caused the child to gasp shakily before crying once more.

Seeing Shana looking out at him, he walked into the home and quietly shut the door. She reached for her daughter, but Aidan bore the child's weight to the ground since Shana was pregnant. Shana urged Ileen toward the back of the cottage. When they were alone, she said, "They called him to track scouts in the southern marshes."

"Peeter could track a single boar fly in a herd of wild boars." Aidan touched her shoulder lightly and felt her shudder.

"The missive said he found Sorceress Magda's scouts. He and Richard of Daggerpoint were killed taking the Caniba beasts." Shana's lips tightened. He could see the worry and sadness in her face. She cared deeply for her husband.

Aidan knew everything she said and more. His letter from the king would have been more detailed. Even in matters such as these, women were to be protected. Shana didn't need to know Peeter suffered, or that he bled for hours before the gods took him to a warrior's paradise. "His actions will do great things in defeating the Sorceress. Songs will be sung for him. I was told he died well, with great honor."

"I do not need to be told." Her eyes trailed to the back of the cottage, to where her children's low voices could be heard. Her face tightened and her breathing deepened. She rubbed her stomach. "I know their father was honorable. He was a Starian warrior."

"You will have everything you need," he assured her. "Your children will be cared for and your larder full. My mother will help you bring this child when your time comes. I will send her to help you both now and after."

Shana took a step back from him. "Please, do not, Sir Aidan. Not today. Not now." She rubbed her belly protectively. "I know the oracles said you must find a bride, but please, I beg you not today. Not now. I know it is not done in Staria, but my heart is Peeter's. I am still his wife..." She closed her eyes tight and slowly shook her head as if she could erase what was happening.

Aidan frowned, staring at her for a long moment before he finally understood her meaning. "You misunderstand. I only seek to take care of my friend's family. I am not claiming you."

Shana gave a strange laugh of relief, though the sound was filled with a wry grimness and deep sorrow. She surged forth, falling into

Aidan's chest as she gripped his tunic. He stiffened at the show of emotion before awkwardly patting her on the shoulder.

"I cannot tell you how you have eased my mind, Aidan." She trembled so hard that the rest of her words were lost.

---

Paige took a deep breath, then another, unable to calm herself. The run through the forest had been fast and hard, but that wasn't what set her world to spinning. Aidan's horse pawed the ground behind her, but she ignored the creature. He had tied it to a low branch near the forest line.

Staring through the narrow slit in the wall, she saw Aidan's hand stroking the back of a woman as he held her close. The woman laughed, the sound odd and distorted by the way her head presumably pressed into Aidan's chest. Angling her body, Paige tried to get a better view of his face. She knew Aidan was in there, saw his hand.

Who was this woman? Another wife? A lover? A whore? This was why he was in such a rush to leave her?

Paige frowned. It had been days since Aidan found release with her and he was a man of insatiable appetites. Did his abrupt departure mean he was seeking release with this woman? Why else would he hold the woman like that, stroking her back?

Blind jealousy filled Paige and she stumbled back from the narrow window. Her foot bumped into a stick and it landed on the ground with a loud thud. Without thought, she grabbed it and held it tight. The smooth wood had been carved into the shape of a sword with the end curved to the side.

He claimed her without her permission, brought her to his home, and forced her to tell her vision to a village full of people who would do nothing to stop Callum's death. He made her feel something for him, touched her, kissed her and made her hope. And now, he was here with that woman in his arms.

Paige's heart felt as if it squeezed inside her chest. Hearing a noise behind her, she turned, wielding the stick sword in front of her. Aidan stared at her from the doorway, the woman close to his back.

"Paige?" Aidan began.

Paige growled to stop whatever it was he had to say, but her anger was partially directed at herself for still caring. Even now he took her breath away. Forcing her eyes from him, her gaze traveled down to the very obvious growth at the woman's midsection.

"Paige." This time his tone warned.

She noted the protective way he leaned to the side, hiding the woman behind him. A deep pain radiated in her chest, settling over her heart. Every hope she had allowed herself crumbled around her when she looked at him. Spurred into action, she screamed and swung at the same time. The stick hit him in the side of the leg, catching him by surprise. Aidan tumbled to the ground. The woman yelped, hopping back on unsteady feet.

"Thirteen children!" Paige yelled, fighting her urge to go to him on the ground, but more so the urge not to hit him again. She saw the passion in the other woman's face, so much emotion and feeling. "I'm agonizing over the fact that your crazy mother insists I'm supposed to give you thirteen children and you're well on your way to a family right here."

Holding his calf, he tried to hobble to his feet. "Paige, halt. Give me the weapon. There is a—"

Paige threw the stick at his head. "You forced me to be your wife. You put me in your home and fill my head with lies about what life is here. Did you think I would not discover what it really is? Did you think me a fool who did not know the ways of men? We have one fight and you run off to—*argh*! And to think I did believe you when you said men here were faithful because the gods demanded it of them. Faithful to yourselves is what you meant. Yourselves and your pricks!"

"Dandan?" A little girl appeared next to the woman and behind her Paige saw several boys. Tears stained the child's cheeks and Paige instantly regretted scaring her.

"Aidan?" the woman asked in shock. "Did she say she was your wife?"

"Dandan, make her go away!" the little girl demanded loudly.

"No," Paige interrupted, answering the woman. She was unable to look at the girl's watery brown eyes. Paige hadn't meant to terrorize the child. "I am not his wife. I am no one. This has all been a big mistake."

Aidan made it to his feet, but Paige didn't give him a chance to stop her. She ran for the forest, cursing the Faerians, the fairies, the entire land of Staria, Aidan, but most of all cursing herself for daring to believe things could be different here.

Aidan's shouts followed her, but they only made her run faster. Maybe the fairies had successfully punished her after all.

"Paige!" Aidan shouted in an effort to run after his wife. He didn't know what she had heard or thought, but her anger had been clear. His ankle gave out when he tried to sprint and he stumbled.

"Mama!" Ileen shouted. "You are leaking. Dandan, help Mama!"

Chaos erupted, forcing his attention to Shana and her children. The woman grasped her stomach and the ground around her feet was damp.

"Help your mother inside to her bed," Aidan ordered the boys, hobbling toward his horse. "I ride to get help."

As he swung onto the animal's back, he ignored the pain in his leg. The limb wasn't broken and would heal. Aidan urged the beast to hurry, but not in the direction he wanted to go. Hopefully Paige knew the forest as well as she claimed. He tried not to think of the wild beasts that roamed the woods. Mammoth wolves, the monstrous cousins of the smaller prairie wolves, were particularly vicious. Some of the older ones were nearly as tall as a man with the predatory skills to take out a whole group of Starian knights. For the most part, they stayed in the mountain range far to the north, but it wasn't uncommon for them to migrate down when hunting, making their way along the coastline before cutting over to Fallenrock's forestland. Thankfully, he hadn't seen any recent tracks.

Turning his concern to Peeter's wife, he rode to find his mother, knowing she would be outside Martin's house, tormenting the man.

After six sons, she would be better equipped to help a woman giving birth than a knight wielding an axe and sword.

---

Hiding was easier than she had ever imagined. Aidan didn't even try to come after her. It only proved her point more—he only wanted her when she put up little fight. Apparently, he had a steady woman, and by the looks of her she would soon be back in commission to tend to his needs. She had seen it before—forest liaisons when a man's wife was large with child.

"I just didn't think Aidan was like that," she had whispered to herself more than once. Everything was crumbling, all her hopes for his land. "How could I have been such a fool?"

Evening was darker in the dense part of the forest and she nestled in for the night next to a large tree trunk. The surrounding silence allowed her mind to roam and her thoughts instantly went to Aidan. They started with remembering his face, the tilt of his lips, the open expression he had carried in the bath before they fought. One idea led to another and she found herself moving slowly against the earth. Tree bark scratched at her back, but she pretended it was Aidan's nails raking along her spine. For all his faults and betrayals, the man was an excellent lover.

Then why did he have to pretend there was more? He could have just let it be sex. He didn't have to lie. He didn't have to make her feel something for him.

Paige moaned. Aidan had wonderful hands, rough with calluses from years of weapons training. When he touched her, his fingers molding possessively into her flesh, her skin felt as if it were on fire.

Aidan was man enough to stir any woman's desires and the thought caused a wave of rage and passion to consume Paige. She didn't want him claiming another woman or his strong, large body fucking someone else. Who wouldn't want such a perfect warrior in their bed?

She closed her eyes tight, thrusting her hands between her thighs to ease the ache. Even now she could feel the sensation of his cock slipping along her folds, pressing and probing. Losing herself, Paige let go of all control, letting the half-dream, half-fantasy take root, just like when the fairies dosed her with their sexual ambrosia.

"Must have more," she whispered, desperate to have him. "More."

She loved the animalistic sounds he made when he entered her. Paige slipped a finger inside her sex, moving it to mimic Aidan's touch. A blade of grass tickled her shoulder, like his long blond hair did when he thrust above her.

"Aidan," she cried softly, wishing she had the power to make things different between them. Her pussy was wet for him and the bittersweet stroking of her finger didn't replace the feel of solid cock. Her hand brushed along her clit and she met with a gentle release.

Righting her clothes, she turned on her side. The meager pleasure didn't last long as a wave of loneliness washed through her, worse than ever before.

Aidan wanted nothing more than to run from the house, from the sound of the newborn baby girl crying. Unfortunately, the midwife threatened to pin him down if he did so much as move. The elderly woman tugged at a bandage, tightly wrapping his leg.

"Do not look so worried, sir," Helen said, coming to the end of her bandage only to grab another one. "I hit my husbands much harder than this and we are still blessed. Today is a day for rejoicing. A girl is born. The prophecy of Shana's children has come true."

Aidan didn't feel like rejoicing, not with Peeter fresh in the ground, not with Paige missing in the forest.

"Peeter should have been here." Carrina appeared in the cottage doorway, carrying a pail of water. "He would have found much pride in the lungs of his new daughter." As she made her way toward the back of the house, past the eyes of the older children, she added, "And the oracle I sent to help you has arrived."

"Oracle?" Aidan's head snapped up and he tried to stand. Helen pushed on his sore leg, making him fall back. Aidan ignored the twinge of pain. "Who? Not...?"

At Carrina's short laugh, he groaned.

"Yea, Sir Aidan, it is I, Oracle Teena." The oracle swept into the room, her long white robes fluttering with her excitable movements. "Oh, look at your poor leg. I suppose I cannot make you perform for me. I will just have to think of another reward for what I've seen."

Out of all the oracles, he could tolerate Teena the least. Aidan glanced at the tattooed bands on his arms—as a guardian of the oracles he couldn't avoid her. Teena's visions were clear, which gave her a kind of queenlike status in the convent she lived in, and the woman used her position to her amusement. The last time he saw her, she made him dance before she would tell him what was in her visions.

"Oh, there now, why don't you smile for me, sir? Or I might not decide to help you." Teena arched a brow. The youthful expression belied her true age. When Aidan managed to pull his tight lips upward into a strained grin, she laughed harder. He wanted to cover her mouth and force her to be quiet. "Oh, very well. I suppose you still blame me for my last prediction. Though I am very pleased you took my words so seriously, methinks you might have gone too far. You only had a few weeks to wait before the breeding ceremony. There was no need to grab the first woman who crossed your path."

"What do you care?" Aidan grumbled. "You said to take a bride quickly or be forever alone. And the old crones agreed with you. I found a bride, I took her. I did what you said. There is no need for me to attend the breeding ceremony to look at bartered brides."

"That is where you are wrong, my dear sir." Teena twirled about the room, pausing to randomly touch this item or that. She hummed to herself, as carefree as a girl child and just as impish. The crying from the backroom lessened, but Teena pretended not to hear the insistent sound. "You will attend the ceremony at Battlewar as you were commanded to do by your king."

"Married men cannot attend," he argued. "I cannot take another wife."

"You question me? Perhaps I will make you dance after all despite your ankle." Teena frowned at him, clearly not liking the fact that he dared to question her.

"And perhaps the next time you are in need of my protection I won't be there." He glared back at her.

Helen gasped, quickly walking from the room as if he had just set it on fire.

Teena watched the elderly woman and chuckled. "I always did love your defiance. I find it quite to my amusement."

"You were saying about Battlewar? How can a married man be a part of the ceremony?"

"Besides the fact the king ordered you to go?"

"Oracle," he warned. "I am very short on patience today."

"Very well." Teena looked at him, but she didn't see him. The dark brown of her eyes began to lighten, slowly turning to a milky white as she peered into his future. Her body shook, her expression fading into a blank mask. Even her voice lost its buoyancy, as she spoke, "Your misfortune is not of my doing, but yours. The gods sent you a bride but you claimed her too eagerly in your haste to get out of the ordained ceremony. You should have taken her with you to Battlewar and set her before the hall so all may hear your claiming. Right now, it is only your word that you staked your claim. The gods demand more from you. They demand that you go to the breeding ceremony and make your intentions known to all. You are a great knight of Staria, a man who is known to honor the gods, and your support of the new brides, even if you do not choose one for yourself, is what the gods wish."

Aidan didn't move, every part of him focused on Teena's words.

"But you ignore the king's order to go to the breeding ceremony and you upset the gods by not claiming a bride during the ceremony. Now it is not known if your marriage will be blessed or if you will have children." Teena stopped shivering and her eyes cleared. The haphazard smile returned to her lips. "Why is it so hard for you to believe that the gods reward our men with these women? Do you really think they care how we marry? Your bride's reluctance proves their anger toward you. If I were you, I would send another to find her and bring her to the ceremony where you will reclaim her for all to see. It is your only chance of appeasing the gods, though I do not know if it will be too late for you." Teena began to turn from him only to pause, "And from now on, as a reminder of the gods blessing on the ceremony, all brides must be bound by the hands to signify the binding of the marriage. What is done cannot be undone. It will help these new women understand."

When Aidan didn't readily speak, she arched a brow.

"Rejoice," he mumbled, saying the traditional words, "the oracle has spoken."

"Thank you, Sir Aidan." With that, she turned her attention to the back of the cottage. Walking toward the sound of the crying baby, she began to hum a soft blessing on the home. She did not look at him again.

"Meat."

Paige blinked, screaming as her foot was jerked and her body pulled from her place on the thick branch. She had been sleeping, dreaming again of Aidan's hands when the rough sound forced her from her bittersweet fantasy.

Her arms flailed as she searched for hold, finally finding it on a cluster of leaves. She managed to stop her fall temporarily, but another hard jerk forced her to the ground. She yelped upon impact, before knocking her head. Her vision wavered as she fought to stay conscious. A hand caught her jaw, the fingernails biting into her flesh.

An awful smell wafted over her, stinking like the long-rotted flesh of a fallen deer left in the forest by careless hunters. Her vision cleared by small degrees, but she couldn't be sure what she saw was real. Wild, sunken eyes peered into hers from a nest of uncombed hair. The gaze was cold and mocking, yet too intelligent to be a mere creature of the forest. It was a man, but nothing like the men of Staria she had seen. This guy was primitive, unbathed, draped in matted fur pelts.

He began to laugh, showing a mouthful of sharpened, yellowed teeth. "I found meat."

"Caniba," she whispered, the idea hitting her hard. Every nightmarish word Aidan and Carrina told her about their enemy to the south filtered through her mind—*man-eaters, snake people who live in the ground, born of the unholy fornications of people and wolves, the lowest thing a man can become.*

"Meat," the creature-man grunted, the word drawing Paige's attention to the fact that others moved to join him.

*We are far north of the borderlands,* Aidan had once told her, *and I promise you I will protect you with my life.*

But Paige had run straight south, traveling for days in the hopes of discovering another of Aidan's lies. She had searched for the Caniba, sought them out. For if Aidan lied about Paige being his only woman, then he had to have lied about the man-beasts.

"Meat," another voice repeated, the sound barely recognizable as a word.

Too late, Paige tried to wriggle free. Her bumped head made it hard to concentrate. Then there was too many of them, hands pressed down upon her, grabbing and clawing, their grips much more painful than the Faerians' had been. She screamed, but the man-beasts only laughed.

They dragged her across the earth before finally heaving her up into a wood and rope cage. They lifted two long sticks off the ground, forcing a strap to tighten and lock her only exit. The cage swung in the air. Paige held on, trying to pull at the wooden bars and twined rope. It was no use. She was trapped.

# CHAPTER 8

"You should be proud," Sir Edward said, looking up at him from where he knelt on the ground. The words were hardly pleased. "She runs well and covers her tracks."

Aidan shifted on his horse, scanning the trees. "We must find her. We're too close to the borders. I don't like her being so near the Caniba's homeland."

"Gregory's encampment is near, we could stop for supplies and ask if any have seen signs of her." Edward motioned to the east as he strode toward his waiting horse.

"No, she will not go near the camps. She is heading south." Aidan wasn't foolish enough to ignore Oracle Teena's words, but neither could he stand by while he sent Edward after his runaway bride. It was not in his soldier's nature to do nothing. How could the gods expect him to go to Battlewar Castle to await the ceremony? Everything about his beliefs demanded he act, everything in his soul demanded he find his wife.

"Does she not know the dangers?" Edward asked.

"She knows." Aidan refused to say more. How could he admit that Paige didn't listen to him? That she didn't believe him? He absently rubbed his thigh, as if doing so would ease his ankle.

"These tracks are fresher. They head west but it could be a trick." Edward was a fine warrior, one Aidan had fought next to on several occasions. He lacked refinement and had a coarse manner that often bristled the nerves of those around him.

Peeter would have made a better choice to help Aidan in his search, but his friend was gone and Edward was the closest scout available. Despite his rough and rude nature, he was the perfect choice for tracking Paige. Edward would never physically hurt her, he already had a wife and he knew the southern forests and marches along the borderlands. If anyone could navigate into the Caniba territory, it was Edward. And, unfortunately, it seemed that was exactly where Paige headed. "If you are sure she is headed south, we will be better off riding hard for the borders. From there we can sweep back up and try to force her northward."

"I would rather catch her," Aidan whispered so Edward wouldn't hear. "I need her safe."

Edward was right. Paige was good at hiding her tracks, taking to the trees at times, doubling back to throw them off the trail. What she didn't count on was how well Aidan knew the forest. He had tracked his brothers in childhood, endless hours of endless days spent training for their warriors' future. And where his intimate knowledge of the terrain ended, Edward's began.

"It will not be long now," Edward assured him, sighing heavily, as if the chase was barely worth his time. "If she's avoiding the camps, there are only so many directions she can go."

"South," Aidan agreed, falling behind Edward's horse. "As soon as we find her, I'll ride ahead to Battlewar. Tie her up, but only if you have to, just make sure she gets there in time for the ceremony."

---

"Really, I can hunt. I'll bring you food," Paige struggled, desperate to be free of the tight ropes binding her arms to her side. Her legs were tied together, trapping her like a cocooned worm. She almost preferred the sickening swing of her former cage. At least then she had use of her limbs.

Paige's head throbbed, a testament to just how hard she had hit it when the man-beast pulled her from the tree. Heat from a nearby fire inflamed her flesh, not enough to sear, but miserably close. The more she struggled, the tighter the binds became.

Four Caniba men shuffled around the small, makeshift encampment. The firelight cast their ghoulish form with a terrifying light, making them appear bigger and taller. They grunted, their words to each other more animal than man. Bits of flesh clung to their cloaks, the untanned leather the cause of their awful stench. They spoke amongst themselves, whispering and grunting, only deigning to say to her the occasional, "Meat."

She, apparently, was the meat.

"Please," Paige pleaded, knowing that her words would make little difference. Why had she run so far? She could have been happy in the forest. Safe. She had been so angry, seeing Aidan with that other woman. Now she would do anything to be able to see him again, to talk to him, to hit him with another stick for daring to go to another woman after making her feel something for him. Murmuring to herself, she said, "There is no hope. The fairies have won for this is a cruel and heartless punishment and the Faerians are indeed evil for worshiping such tiny monsters."

She never imagined the little winged creatures would be so cruel as this. Mischievous, yes, even so far as to cause heartache, but to have her end up as the main course in a Caniba feast? Or perhaps this was just fate and the fairies had no idea where they sent her.

Her hands ached and so she did the only thing she could, she began to scream, using all the power in her constricted lungs. The sound caused chaos amongst her captors, but she didn't care. She screamed louder.

---

Aidan's heart lurched in his chest and he slowed his horse. Reining it to the side, he lifted his hand for Edward to be quiet as he listened. The faint echo of a scream sounded.

"This way," he ordered, spurring his mount past Edward's as he cut west through the forest. From such a distance, he couldn't be sure if the woman was Paige, but his heart beat an erratic rhythm nonetheless. No Starian woman would have come so close to the borders willingly for they knew the dangers and Starian men would have forbidden it. The knights had seen what the Caniba did to their victims and the idea of them doing such to a woman was unspeakable.

The screams became louder, but so did the unmistakable stench of the Caniba. Aidan's stomach curled at the pungent odor wafting downwind. As the tone of the voice became discernible, his heart nearly stopped.

Paige.

*By all the swords, accursed woman, why did you run from me?*

Forgetting all about the oracle's warning, he drew his sword. His wife needed him to be a warrior. Sweat beaded along his temple as tension filled every muscle. Years of training forced all emotions from his body until his thoughts became a stream of silent orders to his body and all he could do was act.

*Dodge tree. Swing blade. Leap onto the good ankle. Save wife.*

Before he landed, he had assessed the situation. Paige lay on the ground, squirming. Though they had her bound tight, she screamed at them in rage, thrashing so the Caniba soldier above her couldn't get a good hold. The dirty man held a knife, his crazed eyes torn between finishing what he was about and turning to fight the new intruder. Finally determining Aidan to be the bigger threat, he kicked Paige hard in the gut. Her screaming stopped with an audible cry of pain.

He flicked his sword in one swift motion and turned to challenge the man. There was no need to speak. The Caniba could not be reasoned with for their minds were not like a normal man's. Aidan swung, making contact with one of the soldier's stomachs. Behind him, he heard Edward join the fight, a battle cry on his lips. Metal clanged against metal, echoing over the forest. Determined, Aidan fought his way toward Paige.

Paige watched Aidan through tear-filled eyes. Her stomach hurt from where she had been kicked, but the tightly bound cocoon around her body kept her from curling up into a ball. His expression was filled with brutality, his eyes narrowed, his sword moved with swift and deadly force. One of her Caniba captors had fallen to the ground before she could see what was happening.

Relief warred with fear as Aidan descended on the man who'd kicked her. She fought to free her arms but her ties were too tight. Another Starian erupted from the forest behind Aidan, dressed in a hard leather jerkin and dark breeches. Metal diamonds plated the leather, creating a symmetrical pattern over his thick chest.

"You cannot have what is mine," Aidan growled, drawing Paige's attention back to him. A chill raced through her veins at the harsh sound. "You will die for daring to touch her."

The Caniba man circled around Aidan, wielding a chipped knife. There was no fear in the man-beast, no hesitance or prudence. The Caniba warrior thrust his weapon, howling as he charged first. Aidan held himself with confidence, holding firm as he studied his opponent.

The clang of metal hitting metal rang over her. Aidan's friend managed to slit the throat of the man he fought. He strode to where Paige lay on the ground. She expected him to free her, but he merely stood over her to watch Aidan.

She flinched as another loud clash echoed through the forest alcove. A scream of terror built inside her but she swallowed it back. In her struggle to be free, she had inched too close to the fire. The heat from the flames began to burn her flesh and she wiggled away.

The Caniba fighter slashed at Aidan's arm, drawing blood. Crimson wetted his tunic shirt but he didn't stop. Paige looked to the motionless Starian knight standing above her.

"Help him," she pleaded. Two against one would be better odds. Why was the knight just standing there?

The man looked down at her with a snort of disgust. "Keep quiet, woman. You are the cause of this."

She glared at the knight, but he didn't appear to care. Paige's head fell to the ground and she watched, helpless and trapped, as

Aidan took another wound to his arm. The Caniba man charged again. She thrashed on the ground, desperate to help Aidan. Her heart leapt in her chest as the man swung. Paige couldn't help her scream of concern, "Aidan!"

Deftly, Aidan dodged the blow, surging forward. He knocked the Caniba's knife aside and drove his sword through his enemy's stomach. Next to her, the knight howled victoriously, thrusting his sword into the air. Paige barely heard it as Aidan's eyes found hers. Blood dripped over his hand as he walked toward her.

"Edward, your knife," Aidan said, holding his hand out to the man. The knight at her side gave over the blade from his waist.

"We should ride," Edward said. "There may be others in the forest."

"I have only seen these four," Paige said.

Both men looked at her as if she were an imbecile.

"I suppose there could be more." Paige flexed her hands as Aidan cut her free. She tried to read his expression. He didn't smile at her, but neither was he frowning. Instead, he seemed to look past her, as if he didn't trust himself to address her directly.

Paige rubbed her legs, noting where drops of his blood landed on her breeches. When she tried to stand, she wobbled and almost fell. Aidan's strong hand shot out, steadying her as his fingers curled firmly around her upper arm. Shock waves of heat washed over her at the touch. Her lips parted and she breathed deeply. She tried to speak, but when she looked up into his eyes, he was staring at her. His lips tightened. For a long moment, no one moved.

"I will tend to the horses," Edward said at last, sounding more exasperated than polite.

Paige's heart raced and she realized she held her breath. She forced the air from her lungs, panting as she pried her gaze away from his. A rush of memory came over her, of his hands on her body, his lips kissing her mouth, the way he moved against her. The man was emblazoned on her mind. He had captured her soul and she knew in that moment she would never have run far enough away from him.

"Aidan," she began, licking her lips. "I—"

"Did they injure you?" he asked, inspecting her with his eyes.

Paige shook her head in denial. "No. Nothing I won't recover from."

Edward rudely snorted in the distance and muttered to himself.

Aidan ignored the man. Without further comment, he walked her into a dense, private area of the forest. He favored one leg as he limped, but he didn't let on that he felt any pain. His hand on her arm kept her from dropping to the ground but not from tripping as he led her over fallen branches, slippery leaves and wet grass.

When he finally stopped, his handsome face turned to her. She detected lines of anger marring his tight lips. His eyes narrowed and he looked as if he might speak. His breathing noticeably deepened and she wondered at it.

Paige stiffened. All of a sudden, Aidan leaned into her. She tried to pull away, unsure if he would strike her. Instead, his lips found hers, hard and passionate. He swallowed her cry of surprise. A thrill coursed through her, seeming to jump off his skin onto hers. Her cry turned into a moan and she grabbed onto his biceps.

His kiss claimed and conquered. He became forceful, clawing at her shirt, jerking it over her head only to toss it aside. Chilly air hit her flesh only to be instantly replaced by his heat. He drew his fingers along her waistband before shoving an insistent hand down the front to cup her sex. Her pants pooled around her ankles. Her pussy was damp, and instantly flooded him with her cream.

Growling, he said, "I burn for you."

Dizzy from the feel of his bold fingers stroking against her, she convulsed against him. Her pussy tightened. Aidan's lips slid down her jaw to devour her neck before moving down her chest. He sucked her nipple, hardening it into a bundle of nerves.

Paige forced all thoughts from her mind. Right now she wanted nothing more than to make love to him in every way imaginable. She rocked her hips against his palm, wanting what she knew he could give her. Massaging her breast, he drew his mouth back up her throat to bite at her earlobe. Small sounds of submission left her throat.

Paige reached for his large arousal, stroking him through his breeches. She unlaced his breeches, pushing them down to expose his cock. Caressing his erection, she kissed his throat before making her way lower. Aidan tossed his shirt aside, finally naked before her. She licked his chest, his nipples, and the indention between his abs.

Sinking to her knees, she kissed the smooth, mushroomed head of his cock. His breath hitched and his hands found hold on her head. She licked him several times, flicking her tongue over his flesh as she sampled his taste. Aidan moaned and his hips jerked ever so lightly. Parting her lips, she kissed the head. His moans turned to pants as she took him deeper with each passing kiss of her lips.

The cold, wet ground cushioned her knees, but she didn't move to stand. His cock was too big to take all the way in her mouth, so she stroked him with her hand, cupping his balls underneath. She sucked him deep only to pull back and do it again.

Aidan jerked. Whatever tension and anger that had taken hold in him soon disappeared under her administering mouth. He rocked in rhythm to her sucking and his fingers tightened.

"My lady, hold. I cannot..." He groaned.

Paige pulled off of his cock at his insistent tug at her head and grinned up at him, licking her lips. Aidan joined her on the ground. He trailed hot kisses down her parted thighs, moving his tongue in small flicks as he neared her clit. His penetrating gaze bore up into hers as he lowered onto her moist slit. She jerked, crying out in pleasure.

He licked her in long strokes as his fingers delved into her wet passage, sliding in the cream that coated his fingers. When she pushed at his shoulder, he only sucked her deeper, thrusting his tongue into the moist cavern of her body. He nibbled and sucked her to the brink of release, only to pull back, denying her.

Aidan crawled over her body, the weight of him pressing her into the ground. She watched him move, mesmerized by the precision of his form. He was a man who knew how to use his body and did so to perfection. Then, suddenly, she saw his cut arm. The wounds no longer bled but crimson trails had dried on his flesh as a testament of his recent injuries.

"Your arm," she said, reaching toward the cuts.

"Is fine," he told her, before she could show too much concern. "But my body is not." He ground his hips into her, as if to prove how badly he ached. His hard cock glided along her slit without penetrating. "Turn around."

She blinked in surprise, unsure she had heard him correctly.

"I want you on your hands and knees," he ordered, the words hoarse. Some of the anger had come back to his gaze and Paige realized too late her mistake in pointing out the wounds. Surely, they only reminded him that she had run away from him, that she had struck him in the leg.

"Aidan, I—"

"Turn around," he insisted, his tone warming.

How could she resist him? Paige turned around, secretly glad to have her back off the colder earth. She looked down to a patch of flattened grass in the shape of her head. Aidan groaned. His cock probed her from behind, pressing along her slit until he found what he was looking for.

Paige thrust her hips back to swallow him inside her. She gasped as he filled her completely. Aidan began to move, thrusting wildly inside her tight pussy, as if he sought to both punish and please her with the force of his claiming. Paige didn't mind. She liked him wild and strong, liked the way he fucked her faster and harder and deeper.

Aidan took her hips, controlling with his hands as he rode her. Loud grunts of pleasure sounded from him, punctuating each forward thrust. Her own harsh breathing echoed back to her from the ground. She dug her fingers into the earth. Tension built and she stiffened in anticipation, praying he wouldn't stop before she met her release.

Then, finally, she found what she had been looking for. Euphoria erupted inside her sex, spreading throughout her limbs like fire to tinder. Aidan kept riding, forcing her climax to continue. Her pussy clenched him hard. With a resounding yell, he jerked roughly, joining her in their violent release.

Paige's heart beat so hard she feared it might pop out of her chest. Her limbs shook, more so now that Aidan's weight pressed her from behind. When he pulled out and away, she looked over her shoulder to find him limping toward their discarded clothing. She waited for a sign of affection from him, something, a hint of the man he had been with her before. Instead, he began to dress, pulling his tunic over his head.

Paige turned, unable to force her body to move as fast as his. She found her shirt, trembling as she put it on. Aidan tugged on his pants and boots. “Aidan?”

“Get dressed, my lady. Edward will escort you to Battlewar Castle for the breeding ceremony. I advise you to be careful with him. He is not so gracious as me.” With that, he left her to stare after him.

Only fear of Edward finding her naked motivated her to hurry with her clothes. There was nothing to be done about the mud in her hair and on her skin. She tried to brush it off, but it did little good.

After a time she heard footfall on squishy leaves coming in her direction. Edward appeared, a frown etched on his features as he looked her over. “Move it, my lady. I do not send gilded invitations and I am not your mate. Make me come after you again and I will cleave you with my sword and take your head to Battlewar on a pike.”

# CHAPTER 9

"You still do not understand, do you, my lady?" Edward spat in her direction. Though he called her "my lady" the words held no respect. Not once in their travels had he showed her kindness, often going so far as to tie her up at night so she couldn't run. "Your husband is your master."

"So I should just bow to my husband, without question?" She snorted, purposefully goading his ill humor. Her body was sore, her heart broken and her patience gone. How could Aidan have left her like that? With Edward?

"Yea. When you are chosen at the ceremony by your husband, it is an honor," he paused, looking down at her, "for *you*."

"Good thing Aidan is nothing like you, sir," she mumbled. "I feel very bad for any woman who you would choose."

"Who said Aidan would choose you at the ceremony? He would be well advised to claim one of the Divinity otherworlders. Their place will have been explained to them. They will know their duty is to submit to their master. They will be good wives."

Paige stopped walking. Aidan would choose another? Didn't he already have another? What of the pregnant woman? Not for the first time since she ran she thought that maybe, just maybe, she had been hasty in her assumptions about the pregnant woman. But that wasn't her whole reason for leaving Aidan. She'd needed to see the Caniba, foolish as that idea was now. She'd needed to know he told the truth and she'd needed time to think about what had happened since being pushed through the fairy ring.

At first, she hadn't thought she would miss her old world. It wasn't like the Forestters were going to mourn her going. But small things began to creep into her mind—the taste of the *gaha* herb in her water, the distinctive smell of the trees that grew near her home, the comfort of the sparse, yet familiar objects that documented her life, being able to visit her parents' gravesites.

"Aidan said that once the claiming was done, it couldn't be undone," she said, searching Edward's face for a sign he was jesting.

"Normally, yea, but the oracles have proclaimed that, to be official in the eyes of the gods, he must claim you at the breeding ceremony at Battlewar." Edward touched the hilt of his sword and arched a threatening brow. "They gave him the perfect way out and methinks he'll take it."

Paige sighed heavily and began walking again, focusing on hiding her true feelings. Her legs were tired, but she would much rather walk than ride pressed up against the surly knight. On more than one occasion, she had considered hitting him upside the head with a rock. "I cannot believe that all Starian men wish for their women to submit blindly. They cannot all be swine like you."

Edward growled, instantly swinging off his horse. "You will learn respect, woman! Aidan has no reason to choose you, and with his denial you will lose all hope of having status in this world. You'll be poor, at the whim of whoever will take you. But don't look so worried. I will recommend men with a strong hand to silence your tongue. You will learn that your place as a woman is to be subservient—from rubbing your husbands' feet to spreading your legs when any of them demand it, even if they command you to stay on your back all day as they take turns hopping on for a ride. A well-fucked woman is a silent, obedient one."

"You insult Aidan now?" Paige bristled in affront.

"Hardly. No single man, no matter how much of a man he may

be, can keep a woman fucked into silence." He looked her over and snorted in disgust.

"I do not need a husband to control my moods, let alone many, Eddie," she protested and taunted at the same time. She knew by the look on his face that he despised the nickname. "And I think that is what bothers you the most. You know my will is stronger than yours. You know that I'm not scared of you."

Edward leaned into her face, his harsh breath hitting her skin and making her sick to her stomach. Paige stumbled back, tripping. She fell to the ground with a hard thud.

"We'll see about that. Mark my warning, my lady. You will be chosen and you will bend to their desires. You won't have a choice. It's either fuck 'em and suck 'em or be cast as a demon spawn incarnate who will be shunned from society, spat on in the streets, locked up and starved like the bottom rung of woman that you are."

"Blazes take you!" she cursed.

"The choice is not yours, lady." Edward spat at her as he spoke the words. She swiped her cheek in disgust. He chuckled, a dark sound that made her want to knock the teeth from his head. "Resign yourself to spreading your legs."

"Is that a threat?" She didn't like the way Edward was looking at her.

"I have a wife," Edward said, as if that made any sexual threat from him impossible. "But should anything happen to her, you can bet I will not be taking you as my next bride."

Paige felt around on the ground, stopping when her fingers encircled a heavy stone. Gripping it tight, she screamed, surging up from the ground to swing at the unsuspecting man. Her reinforced fist hit his face. Paige jumped back in surprise, not really expecting to make contact with the seasoned warrior. Edward's head snapped back and blood flew in tiny droplets over the side of his horse. Howling in pain, he grabbed his nose as blood began to gush over his lips.

"You cursed whore!" Edward yelled. He grabbed for his sword, partly drawing it as he glared at her. She knew he wanted nothing more than to run her through. To her great surprise, he let the hilt go and the sword slid back into its hold. “The castle is just beyond those trees.” He grabbed her arm and threw her toward the horse. “Mount up. I wish to be rid of you.”

---

Days blended until Aidan couldn’t even count how much time had passed since seeing Paige. All he knew was the ceremony was the following morning and he had prayed to his gods endlessly for a better marriage, a blessed marriage. He had been given the unheard-of option of refusing to take her a second time, but how could he say no? All hope of his future depended on her, of children and of a happy life. The oracles foretold it. His soul wanted it.

Paige was his only chance at happiness in his war-torn life. How could he not claim her again? Even as she dishonored him by leaving him, he wanted her. She could make him go through a thousand levels of Caniba pits and he would still want her, need her, long for her.

Forever. He was bound to her, more surely than a few simple words spoken at a breeding ceremony. When he had been forced to do his duty by Peeter’s wife, he had wanted nothing more than to forget duty and honor and run after her. He knew he would find her. Not once had he doubted it. But the idea that he would never see her again caused a fear he had never felt in all his years of battle.

Now Aidan stood alone in the stone worship chamber. Outside wood surrounded the ancient building and inside each sound echoed, amplified so the gods may hear a worshiper in their temple. Columns lined each side, creating an aisle to the front slab table. He had limped the half-day’s distance from Battlewar Castle, taking first to the underground passageways then to the dense forest trails, hoping the gods would better hear him in the old place. A horse would have been faster, but he wanted to prove he was humble in his pleading.

*Your bride’s reluctance proves their anger*, Oracle Teena’s words filled his head, tormenting him with their certainty.

Aidan forced his feet to move and placed his favorite knife on the slab.

*If I were you, I would send another to find her and bring her to the ceremony where you will reclaim her for all to see.*

Even now Edward traveled with Lady Paige to Battlewar. He should never have left her alone with the ill-tempered man. But Aidan knew Edward's lack of charms would keep Paige from sweet-talking an escape. For all his roughness, Edward would not physically hurt her.

Aidan frowned, sighing in frustration. He shouldn't have gone to her. He should have slain the Caniba and left without a word like he'd originally planned. But she had looked so scared and he wanted her so much. How could the gods expect him to leave her when she needed him? It was hard enough not demanding to know why she ran, why she struck him.

*It is the only chance at appeasing the gods, though I do not know if it will be too late for you.*

Why couldn't he have just walked away? Why did he have to risk angering the gods just to kiss her? To touch her? Seeing her tied up like a meal for the Caniba had made him want to hold her, feel her, assure himself that she was unharmed. But he had let it go too far and now he could have possibly cursed himself and his future life.

*You upset the gods by not claiming a bride during the ceremony. Now it is not known if your marriage will be blessed or if you will have children.*

And so, Aidan bowed his head to his gods, hoping they'd forgive his weak flesh and knowing that he had dishonored himself. Taking the knife, he sliced his inner palm. The pain was superficial compared to the turmoil inside his chest. He then placed his bloodied hand on the slab, letting his blood smear as he began to whisper the ancient plea given to the Starians by their gods when the world was first made.

Paige didn't know what was going to happen to her. Edward didn't speak as he rode hard across a prairie beyond the forest toward a city bigger than any she had ever seen. A large wall encircled the giant village and castle. Soldiers walked along the top, guarding those within. Paige didn't know who'd be foolish enough to try to invade such a fortress. Then, remembering the few Caniba she had seen, she shivered. That race seemed crazy enough to try.

A balding knight watched them approach from above the main gate, the only entrance she could see. Only after Edward called up to the man in greeting did he move out of sight. Moments later they were let in. Paige looked up as they passed under, shivering to see the iron-reinforced giant spikes, which made up the bottom of the gate, looming over her head.

Edward led his horse through the narrow streets. Paige searched for Aidan, expecting to see him at every turn. Instead, she found a constant stream of movement as men and women took to the crowded streets. First, there were the peasants' homes, tightly set buildings with no room between houses. She would suffocate in such a place. Remembering Edward's words about her having several husbands to keep her in line, she glanced behind her. Dried blood stained the man's face. Edward growled low in his throat and she quickly looked away.

Paige couldn't help studying her surroundings. There were a couple of barns, many workshops, small breweries and a large marketplace where the commoners sold their wares. Beyond the market, in the center of the city, a second, shorter wall encircled the inner bailey and castle. Contained within were the exercise yard where the knights trained, a small chapel and the stables.

The further they got the more dismal she felt. How could she run and hide in a place filled with so many people? Already she found it hard to breathe. The smells choked her throat and made her lips curl.

Once inside the large castle, Paige began her search for Aidan anew. He was nowhere to be seen, and the more she looked the more her heart ached. Edward had gotten great pleasure in telling her of her duty at the ceremony, of the men who would be there.

Edward grabbed her arm, leading her through a crowded hall. The light came from a large fire box along a far side of the room. Like most things in this place, it was immense and towering. Woven tapestries lined the walls in strips of material, showcasing coats-of-arms and various symbols.

Warriors watched her with interest, gruffly calling greetings to her keeper. Some wore lightweight tunics, others leather jerkins like the guards, others light chainmail and pieces of armor, and still others wore no shirt at all. Muscles bulged, littered with puckered scars and tattooed designs.

Paige tried to maintain a sense of decorum and bravery, but the idea of any of these men claiming her as a wife terrified her—let alone several. As if sensing her fear, Edward told a group of men, "If Aidan does not make claim, she is most willing to be the bride of many. So long as you don't mind sharing, this is the lady for you!"

The words were met with loud cheering. Paige opened her mouth to protest, but Edward jerked her hard and strode with her through the rows of tables, leading her by her arm. Before they made it across the hall, he announced her "availability" several more times, each announcement lewder than the one before it. By the time they left the main hall, she could practically feel the sexual energy in the eyes watching her.

"Aidan," she whispered, willing him to appear.

Edward laughed coldly. "Sir Aidan won't help you. You'll be lucky if he lays claim to you a second time. The man has a chance to be free of you. He saved you from the Caniba and his duty to you is done. Why would he not take it? A soldier like him deserves much more than a whore like you."

"A whore who broke your nose, Eddie," Paige spat. "How about I tell your fellow knights about that? You will not sound so tough having been overcome by a woman."

He growled and his hand tightened. "Come, Lady Paige, let's find you a bath. You will want to be presentable for your new husbands. And if I were you, I'd start praying that they don't tear you apart, because they won't be the gentleman Aidan is. They will fuck you until they have had their fill. Welcome to Battlewar Castle, my lady."

---

"The faster you make them come, the less time you must spend in their presence."

Paige didn't move, didn't let on that she heard the serving woman, Sera. The tight fit of the woman's white corset top squeezed her healthy waist and thrust up two very generous breasts. Long blue skirts billowed around the servant's legs.

After being stripped of her clothing, scrubbed clean by maids with probing hands and not enough sense, scented and dressed, Paige had been indecently questioned by a man named Brock. The man marked her attributes off in his little book like she was an animal to be sold at market. Apparently, if Aidan refused to take her, the others wanted to know why and it was Brock's job to find out. And when she didn't readily answer his questions, he threatened to drag her naked into the hall so the knights could see for themselves that she was "well-formed".

Afterward, she was pushed into a small prison cell with several other women. She had spent the night half awake, trying to drown out their whimpering cries. But how could she blame the other prisoners for their fear? They too were going to be brought out before the Starian men to be claimed. From what she could tell, Edward's assumptions about the other potential brides had been a lie. These women had no idea what they were doing in Battlewar and even less idea of what was going to be expected of them by their new husband or husbands.

Paige was glad that she had at least been afforded a long, shapeless white robe to hide her figure. With luck, these other prisoners would attract the men long before they looked at Paige. It didn't take long for her to realize Aidan was a veritable prince amongst his people. He treated her with respect and honor. She wasn't so sure the others would do the same. Sera's words didn't help to change her mind. Edward had been right when he said she was to be her husband's whore.

"That is all they want—a vessel to find release in," Sera continued, repeating word for word what she had lectured to Paige the night before. The servant eyed the half-dozen girls in the cell as she handed them loaves of bread. "Do not expect tenderness, but if you don't deny them, if you don't resist, you'll be treated fairly enough. And if you give them sons, you'll be greatly rewarded. Life here is not so bad."

It always seemed to come down to children. Paige thought of the men in the hall, her potential "husbands", and shivered. She wrapped her arms around her stomach, trying not to be sick.

"This isn't happening, this isn't happening," a dark-haired prisoner repeated, over and over. "Wake up, Edith, wake up."

"I'm telling you how to best survive this place, please, listen. Spreading your thighs is easy enough a task for a decent life. Don't bring trouble upon yourself. Let them find release. They are not such boars when they get what they want," Sera insisted.

*Aidan, don't leave me here. I don't belong here. These women are not like me. They're...*

Paige glanced back to the bars, staring past those around her while trying to think of the best word to describe the women. Their mannerisms and speech were so far from her world and what she had seen of the Starian one.

As if to prove Paige's assumptions right, the blonde tried to explain their situation to the crying Edith, "This is another plane of existence you've stepped into. Looking at a foreign dimension is like looking at your world if had it evolved in a different way. To a point there are many similarities. Languages, generally, are relatively similar. Some people will look the same, but not be the same people. Certain events like natural disasters will be shared. Weather is the same and this is still Earth. These people are still human-ish."

"You're as crazy as they are," Edith answered, backing away.

While the blonde-haired prisoner tried to soothe Edith's fears, a tall, dark-skinned, black-haired woman gracefully paced in front of the bars as if she might pounce on a second sniveler. Paige turned her eyes back to the bars, absently picking at her wool sleeve. She wondered if the blonde was some sort of fairy. How else was it she knew so much about the other worlds?

The last prisoner, a well-endowed brunette, tried to work a thin metal hair ornament into the prison lock. Suddenly, the woman jerked her hand back and Paige stiffened, hearing the sound of steps coming for them.

"Aidan," she whispered, biting the inside of her lip while she peered to see who came. "Please, Aidan. Come for me."

Paige swore her heart stopped beating when it wasn't him. Why wouldn't he come? Visit her? Talk to her? Let her explain? Let her ask questions? Let her beg him to take her away from this castle.

"Please, Aidan," she whispered, "I don't belong here. Come for me."

A burly man dressed in a hard leather jerkin and dark breeches approached the cells, standing between the bars and the blue-gray stone wall on the other side of the narrow hall. The guard crossed his thick arms, creating a veritable blockade more effective than the iron.

"The flaxen one and the crying one," the man ordered his fellow guards. "They do not carry themselves well. Take them and give them the philter."

Paige sighed in disappointment. The men carted away the two whimpering women, much to the protest of Edith, who pathetically begged, "No, wait! I'll be good. I swear I'll be good. Please, don't hurt me. Please, I'll do anything you want. Do you want me to make you come? I will. I swear I will. I'll do you all!"

"Careful what you wish for," Paige said under her breath, her fingers working even faster to pick imaginary specks from her sleeve.

As soon as the men were gone, the brunette went back to work, her face set as she tried to feel around in the lock with her hairpin.

"You won't be able to open it," Paige said, letting the dejection overtake her. Aidan was not coming. There was no hope. She had been a fool. Staring at the lock picker, she continued, "Even if you did, there would be no escape. You'd have to fight through the warriors' hall, out of the guarded castle gates and run three strikes over open prairie until you reach the forest. Should you survive the wild beasts that live there, you'd soon find yourself prisoner to an even more vicious race of creatures—monsters so fierce and depraved they'll make you beg for death. Trust me, with the war going on in this forsaken place, we're in the better of the two sides."

"Who are you that we should trust what you say?" the brunette asked.

"Name's Paige," Paige answered. These women still had hope. That much was clear. Part of her wanted to dash that hope so she wouldn't have to be alone in her misery.

"Lilith," the blonde interrupted.

"What do they want with us?" The black-haired woman stopped pacing. All eyes turned to her. "Oh, I'm called Jayne."

"They want us to be their whores," Paige answered, bitterness seeping into her hard tone as she remembered Edward's words. "They don't call it that, but that is what they want—a subservient woman to rub their feet and spread her legs. If you don't, they get pissed and the whole lot of them will stare at you like you are the demon spawn incarnate and will blame you for your chosen warrior's bad mood. It's either fuck them and suck them, or you're treated like the bottom rung of Starian society."

"Again, I ask, why should we trust you? We don't know you," the brunette said as she continued to try to pick the lock. "You could be a plant sent here to make us behave, with horror stories of what's beyond the tree line."

"I don't care if you trust me, but I know what I'm talking about. This isn't my first time in a cage." Paige tilted her head back and sighed. At least this cage was big compared to the small wood and rope contraption the Caniba had used to trap her. Closing her eyes, she whispered, "They'll be coming to get us soon."

"What's your name, locksmith?" Jayne asked.

"Karre."

"Well, Karre," Jayne said. "I don't think we have much of a choice. If we all work together, maybe we stand a chance. Now, I don't know how we all got here and at this point I don't think it matters, but I do know I'm not staying to spend the rest of my life as some guy's sex toy."

"I agree." Lilith stood. "We need a plan."

"Fine," Karre grumbled.

Paige opened her eyes and shook her head. "Don't look to me to join your little band. You're only fooling yourselves. I've been to the Hanging Forest. I made it all the way to the Starian borders and I've seen the creatures that wait beyond."

"What about a dimension jump?" Lilith asked. "Does anyone know if this place has inter-dimensional travel technology?"

"A what?" Paige furrowed her brow in confusion. *Inter-dimensional travel technology?*

The women ignored her question.

"Staria? It's too primitive. They don't have the technology here," Karre said. "I got a glimpse of the castle when they brought me to this cell. Through a door I saw servants cart water from a well in buckets and the drive wasn't paved. No artificial lights or motorized vehicles. Though there were several large horses."

"I've never been here," Jayne contributed, "but I'm inclined to agree from what I've observed. These prisons don't use lasers or shocks."

*Lasers? Shocks? Artificial lights?*

Paige had no idea what these women were talking about.

"Someone's coming." Karre's words kept Paige from asking more. The locksmith pulled her arms out from between the bars. She thrust her lock-picking tool back into her upswept hair.

Paige grimaced to see Edward approaching. He frowned. "Only three new ones?"

"It's all they sent us," the guard answered.

"How's it going, Edward?" Paige queried, keeping her face hard and emotionless. "I see the nose is healing nicely."

"Lady Paige," Edward growled, glaring at her as if he wanted to pull the sword from his waist and run her through.

"Open the door, Eddie," Paige taunted. Maybe if she was disagreeable enough, they'd send her away like the other two. "Let me break it again."

Edward grumbled but didn't answer.

"I thought there were five new." Brock joined his fellow guards. His dress reminded her of Edward, but his personality was less offensive—albeit by a very small degree.

"What's wrong, Brock? Don't I count anymore in your little ledger?" Paige asked.

"You are not new," Brock stated, frowning at her in disapproval. "Your lord is waiting for you and I do hope his punishment is harsh."

Paige's smirk faltered. Aidan waited for her? Mistaking her silence, Brock grinned victoriously. Edward's eyes narrowed and he gave her a smug look, as if to remind her that it wasn't likely Aidan would take her back.

"You already have one of these guys?" Karre whispered, jerking Paige's arm.

"Yes, but..." Paige began.

Karre growled under her breath. "I should have known."

The men left. Accusing eyes turned toward Paige. She shrugged, saying the only thing she could think of. "Ladies, welcome to Battlewar Castle."

---

"I say we make a fight of it," Jayne put forth, twisting her arms in an effort to be free of the ropes around her wrists. She had already put up a good fight as the men came to restrain them in the prison cell. Karre had been no less defiant, though her moves seemed more calculated and her eyes ever watchful. Lilith clearly wasn't the fighter Jayne was, but reminded Paige more of Karre, watchful and waiting.

Paige simply held out her hands and let them bind her. There was nowhere to run and little reason to fight at this juncture. Four women could not overpower the warrior-filled hall Edward had led her through earlier. Besides, the breeding ceremony was starting soon. And as much as Paige wanted to entertain the idea of joining forces with the others and making a run for the forest, something inside her begged her to try to find Aidan. The ceremony was her best bet for talking to him again, to begging him to choose her. Even though she feared he might reject her, a part of her had to believe that he would take care of her as he had often promised.

"Paige already tried fighting and running," Lilith whispered, automatically testing the tight ropes around her wrists. The women made no move to follow the guard out of the prison area. "The way I see it, we don't have any choice but to join forces and pool our knowledge. I think we should gather intelligence. None of us seem to be from this world, so that means they had to get us all here somehow. If we keep our ears open, we'll find out how. There might be a way out of here yet."

Feeling somewhat guilty for her earlier speech of hopelessness and doom, Paige tried to be helpful. Even if she wasn't running, it didn't mean she couldn't help the others. "I've already looked for fairy rings when I was in the forest. I didn't even find evidence of fairies. Though, I'm not surprised. Fairies don't like wars and this place is nothing but one giant battlefield. I think my journey here was a one-way trip."

"Fairy rings?" Karre snorted with soft laughter.

"What?" Paige asked, looking around at the others. "Isn't that how you all got here?"

"No more talking. They're ready for you," the guard announced, motioning his fist forward. "Let's go. March."

Lilith refused to move, no matter how many times the guard demanded it.

"Let me help." Paige tugged on the woman's arm, feeling her shake beneath her hands. Trying to give Lilith the will to take those first steps, she purposefully tried to scare the woman into walking, "Brock's ill-tempered and in the end you'll still be marching out there. Just be glad he's letting you keep the clothes. This is one group you don't want to greet naked."

The other women didn't speak, instead choosing to stay in ominous silence. Paige walked in line out of the prison corridor into the blue-gray passageway. Her heart beat so hard she didn't see her surroundings and barely felt the cold stone on her bare feet.

The sound of the main hall penetrated her thoughts and Paige glanced up to the arched doorway that would take them inside before the eager men. She bit the inside of her lip. How could she let any of these men touch her as Aidan had?

*Aidan. Please, choose me again. Don't leave me to many husbands.*

Warriors watched the women as they walked in. Paige refused to meet their eyes for fear they might take an interest in her. A slight blush warmed her cheeks and she wondered exactly what kind of rumors Edward had spread about her.

"Come on," the guard muttered when the women didn't move fast enough. His voice did not boom as it had in the prison corridor as he led the brides through a path made between the tables.

Hearing a low growl, Paige glanced quickly to her side. A man reached for her skirt and she quickly sidestepped him. Her actions caused a round of laughter. Realizing averting her eyes wasn't the best plan of action, she glanced over the crowd. She held herself tense and ready to fight off anyone who tried to touch her.

The eagerness in the men's gazes made her uneasy. Those men who had a woman were being pleasured by them in various ways—a stroking hand over their thighs, lips to a neck, a wiggling ass between a man's legs. Tension filled the hall and the talking quieted by small degrees.

"Stand here," Brock ordered, pointing. Paige followed the others to the front of the hall. They stopped before an empty table. It was raised above them on a high platform—a place of honor. Then, yelling, he announced, "Bring in the firsts so they may make their choice."

Noise erupted once more. Paige jolted in surprise at the sudden sound. Then she saw him. Aidan limped in, leading a group of men to the table. She couldn't take her eyes away, willing him to look at her, to smile, to give her a sign that he was going to pick her.

---

Aidan clenched his fist, looking down over the main hall from the high table. Metal goblets and pitchers of mead and ale spread out before him. Like the rest of the castle, the hall had been designed over centuries of careful planning and fine tuning.

Aidan was one of the six "firsts" given the privilege of first choice. For him, there was no choice. Paige was his. A fact his stiff cock was now very aware of.

Each man wore a different-colored long tunic, reaching to the knees, over tight brown breeches. Woven belts wound their waists, the end straps hanging along the right thighs. Aidan was glad for the long shirt, as it hid just how painfully he needed his wife.

Seeing Paige, her hands bound like the oracle commanded, he had to force his eyes away and turned to the large fireplace on the other side of the room. It radiated enough heat to warm the hall. The firelight shone through the white of Paige's gown, outlining her slender form in silhouetted detail. His cock stirred, ready to forget everything that had happened if only to plunge into her wet sex once more.

*Please, someone claim the shifty brunette so I may take Paige and go*, he thought. Because of what he had done, he knew he must wait to choose last. The more he suffered, the better his chances for a happy future were.

Battlewar Castle always made him uneasy. The walls seemed to close in on him and everywhere he went people surrounded him. This time was worse. His fellow countrymen looked at him with a touch of pity and many had already said they supported his decision to not claim the Lady Paige a second time.

A crescendo of laughter and cheering sounded over the hall. The women wore tight corset tops, much lower cut than the women of Fallenrock Village. All of them had husbands who they wiggled enticingly for, some going so far as to sink beneath the tables to give them oral pleasure. Sex was a natural part of life and no one noticed the behavior. What bothered Aidan was the way the unattached men were staring at Paige—as if they could already picture her naked in their beds. He resisted the urge to jump up and challenge them all to a fight to the death.

After seeing some of the more sexual acts happening behind her, he imagined taking her and hauling her away as Ronen had done his new bride, forcibly leading her to his bed where she could service him in any way he chose—taking him into her mouth as she had in the forest, sucking him, pleasing him. And after he came, he would lick her sweet pussy until it was so moist his cock would harden again just for the chance to play inside the tight hold of her cavern.

Lord Ronen and his brother, Sorin of Firewall, had already chosen the first two women, leaving Aidan with Sir Rian, Sir Vidar and Lord Serik. The Divinity otherworlders were to have sent more brides—a lot more—but rumor had it many of the women who'd walked through the inter-dimensional portal had been sent back. It left Paige and a brunette open for claiming.

Aidan looked down the line at the three other men, waiting for one of them to speak. None readily did.

"Oh, all right, I'll start," the brunette said, grinning saucily at the head table. "My name is Karre. I like jewels, riches, power, servants, fine clothes and to be worshiped daily. I also like to get my way. Any takers?"

Sir Rian looked horrified by her announcement and recoiled in his seat. He ran his fingers through his short brown-blond hair before scratching the scar on his cheek.

"Come on, gentlemen, don't be shy." Karre strode before them, carrying her bound arms as if she had been in this position before. "I only bite when I want to."

Sir Vidar cleared his throat and adjusted in his seat. Karre winked at him.

Lord Serik shared a glance with Aidan before shaking his hand. Standing, he said, "I have no wish for a bride. Excuse me."

If Karre was insulted by his sudden departure, she didn't let on. Instead, she started laughing. "Here I am in a room full of warriors and not a one of them is man enough to handle me. I must say this sets a personal record."

"I can handle you." Sir Vidar stood. "Mine."

Karre arched a brow in challenge. "We'll see about that, soldier."

"Rejoice, Sir Vidar has chosen!" the herald announced, trying to hide his laugh.

---

Paige watched Karre follow her new husband from the rowdy hall. She was the only one left. With each second, she waited for Aidan to claim her, to take her out of there. He barely looked at her.

Battlewar was nothing like her home. Everything was too big, too loud and she didn't understand much of what the other brides had to say.

*Contact Divinity Headquarters on dimensional plane 269. My employee number is 54367D,* Lilith had yelled when her new husband forcibly dragged her from the room. And when Paige mentioned fairy rings, they'd laughed at her. Inter-dimensional travel technology. Lasers. Shocks. Artificial lights.

Paige curled her bare toes against the cool stone floor. She couldn't stay there. She couldn't live anywhere without Aidan. She wanted to go home, to Fallenrock.

Why wouldn't he look at her?

Why wouldn't he claim her?

Paige's lips trembled. She glanced to the side, seeing a pair of narrowed brown eyes on her. The burly knight stared at her chest.

"Mine."

Paige gasped, blinking hard as she looked toward the head table. Aidan stood, limping past the chairs to come around the table. Unsure she had heard him right, she didn't move.

"Rejoice, Sir Aidan has chosen!" the herald said. Audible groans sounded behind her. "Let us drink in celebration. The brides are claimed!"

Cheering erupted and a loud round of toasting commenced, each shout more bawdy and suggestive than the last.

As Aidan came down the platform, she tried to smile. Relief flooded through her. "Aidan," she began, but his look stopped her. A firm line pressed along his lips, casting his features with harsh disapproval. Without a word, he limped out of the hall.

# CHAPTER 10

Paige hurried after him. Torches along the walls illuminated their path. She ignored the burn of the rope against her skin. The more she moved, the tighter the bindings became. Once they were out of the main hall and away from prying eyes, she hurried through the blue-gray stone passageway, past the wooden doors with thick metal handles spread out on either side. Mazelike tunnels and passages wound around the central hall, each one filled with minimal decorations and landmarks that made them hard to navigate. She had been led through several of them earlier and still didn't know where she was going.

A moan caught her attention and she glanced to the side to where an inlet led to a door. Seeing a knight with his breeches around his ankles, aggressively thrusting between the thighs of the woman he pinned against the wall. Paige stumbled but didn't stop. She quickly averted her eyes, hurrying past. Now that was something she had yet to see in the halls.

For a man who limped, Aidan managed to set a fast pace. She jogged to catch up to him, her bare feet making soft noises on the floor. Paige's bound hands made her movements awkward. "Aidan, wait."

To her surprise, he stopped walking. The noise from the hall had faded, surrounding them in silence.

"You must have something to say to me." Paige studied his back, willing him to turn around. She inched closer, aware of the couple behind her.

"No, I do not, my lady." Aidan tried to walk away. Paige grabbed his arm, lifting her bound wrists to force him to stop. He gave a small hop, changing feet when his weight fell on his sore ankle.

Paige looked down at his foot. "I did not mean to..." She took a deep breath. "Did I do that to you?"

Aidan appeared as if he might not answer. Then he took a deep breath and relaxed. "It was not so bad. It would have healed if I would have kept my weight off it as the midwife suggested."

"I wanted to thank you for coming after me. I should have listened to you when you told me of the Caniba." Paige heard a loud moan and she glanced back to the inlet where the couple hid.

"You should have," he agreed, drawing her attention back.

Paige's breathing deepened. Aidan's masculine scent drifted over her, as did his warmth. Did he lean closer? Suddenly, her cheeks felt flushed and her heartbeat quickened. Another, lighter moan sounded and she realized it came from her own throat.

"Do you have more than one wife?" Paige asked, thinking of the pregnant woman. "I saw the way you held her, the way you looked at her and the way she looked at you. And the children. Are they...?"

"Shana is without husband," he answered, his voice lowering.

Paige nodded in understanding. A pain took hold in her chest. "She's your mistress."

"She is my friend," he corrected, not denying his connection to Shana.

Friend. Mistress. To Paige there wasn't much difference. Her nose began to burn, but she blinked back her tears. The pain spread, sending a dull ache over her chest and stomach. She wanted him so badly, wanted to touch and hold him, but how did she come to terms with Shana?

Was a little bit of him better than nothing?

Unable to resist, she kissed him, pressing her mouth tightly to his. Maybe she could convince Aidan that she was the only woman for him. She pushed all thoughts of Shana and the children from her mind. If Shana didn't care about the arrangement she had with Aidan, how could Paige feel sorry for the other woman? Paige only felt sorry for herself, for the way her heart broke. Yet, being without Aidan was worse. She had been a fool to think she could leave him.

Instantly, his hands were on her body, gripping the small of her back as he drew her into him. Her tied hands made it impossible to properly touch him back. The light, brushing weight of his cock teased her stomach, easily detectable through the material of her white gown. Her body jolted with desire, warmth and moisture flooding her pussy. Her nipples ached, hardening.

Aidan turned her around so her back was against the wall. She gasped to feel the hard, cold stone. A torch burned over her head, casting his face with a bright orange glow. He tugged at her skirt, insistently urging it up.

"Your ankle," she protested weakly.

"Will be fine," he answered, his words hoarse as he gripped her naked ass. Rocking his hips into her, he let loose a growl. He reached between them, tugging frantically at his laces. "I have more pressing needs, my lady."

It was all the urging Paige needed. She lifted her arms, hooking her bound wrists behind his head. "I didn't think you would choose me again."

"How could I not?"

"Edward said—"

"No, I do not wish to talk of him right now." He sighed heavily before claiming her lips. "All I wish right now is to be in the slick warmth of your body."

Aidan managed to free his heavy arousal. Aggressively he pinned her tighter to the stone wall, angling his cock to strike.

"It would seem the Lady Paige is not so averse to Sir Aidan as we had heard."

Paige stiffened. Her eyes rounding as she turned to look past Aidan's shoulder. He had stopped kissing her, but didn't move.

Paige saw the woman from the inlet and her man. The woman stared at them, licking her lips even as she chuckled.

"Aidan." Paige lightly lifted her hands, but kept them around his neck, using his body to shield hers. She urged him to let go of her leg. He did and her gown fell to hide her body.

"You disturb us," Aidan shouted gruffly.

The woman laughed, but the man nodded his head once and grabbed the woman's arm, taking her in the opposite direction.

Paige pushed up on her toes, managing to pull her wrists over his head. Her fingers ached, the numbing pain becoming more prevalent now that the pleasure had been put to a halt. She looked down, flexing her fingers.

"You are bound too tight." He brought her hands to his lips and kissed them gently. "Come with me." Aidan tugged his pants and held them at the waist with one hand and gently pulled her behind him with the other.

Stopping at a door, he knocked, paused, and then walked in when no one answered. Inside, the decorations were sparse, just like Aidan's home. A large bed covered in a big fur pelt caught her attention. Aidan let her go, walking over to a weapons wall to take down a knife. The fire box was barren, leaving the room dark but for a stream of light coming from a narrow slit in the wall. After the bright passageway, she had to blink several times.

"There are animals like that here?" She gestured to the pelt.

Aidan glanced over, nodding. "The mammoth wolf. They come down from the mountains." He sawed the knife against her wrists, deftly freeing her.

She sighed, flexing her fingers to draw the blood back into them. Going to the pelt, she touched the fur. "Do you hunt them?"

"Yea."

"Will you take me to see them sometime?"

"Perhaps." The sound of Aidan sitting on a cushioned seat caused her to turn. The laces at his waist were still unfastened from their time in the hall. He tugged on his boots, tossing them aside. Her eyes strayed to the bulging cock still hard and ready.

“I’m sorry I ran. I’m sorry I hit you.” She took a step closer, lowering her jaw as she studied him.

“You said that already.”

“No, I said I wanted to thank you for coming after me and I should have listened to you when you told me of the Caniba.” Paige gave him a small smile.

He dropped the second boot and leaned back. His arms rested at his sides. “Why did you run?”

“How could I not?” It wasn’t an answer but she didn’t know what else to say. I’m sorry? You should be sorry? I saw you with her and I couldn’t think beyond it? After days spent worrying that he may not want her again, she was in no mood to have her heart broken by discussing it in detail. “May we speak of it later?

“If you wish.”

Paige bit her lip as she went to him. “Where were we before we were interrupted?”

Aidan lifted his hand, lightly tracing over her red-tinted wrist where the rope had rubbed into her flesh. “Take off your gown.”

Paige lifted the simple garment over her head and dropped it aside. She stood naked before him as his narrowed eyes slid over her body. A slow smile curled his lips and Aidan reached for his tunic shirt, pulling it off and tossing it aside so his chest was also bared.

She shivered, kneeling before him. He watched her with narrowed eyes. Inching forward between his thighs, she let her fingers skate up the muscles of his legs toward the thick arousal straining against his breeches. Paige licked her lips, slowly drawing her tongue to wet the flesh. His gaze roamed to her breasts and soon his hands followed, cupping them, teasing the nipples. She closed her eyes and sighed, as she leaned into him.

The laces were still undone and it didn’t take much to pull his pants from his hips. He lifted off the seat, letting her undress him as she slid the warm material down his legs and off his feet. When she had him naked, she kissed his knee, leisurely moving to his hip, pausing to bite at his side. Aidan moaned, stiffening slightly.

Paige moved her mouth to take his cock between her lips. She kissed the tip before tracing her tongue along the ridge. Slowly rolling her mouth forward, she sucked gently. Aidan brushed his fingertips along the back of her ear as he lifted his hips to thrust deeper into her mouth.

With a deep groan, Aidan hooked her beneath her arms and lifted her up onto his lap. His chest rubbed along her nipples. His strong hands moved over her back, protective yet masterful. The blond length of his hair tickled her shoulders.

He explored her ass as she ground against him. The words strained, he said, "Take me inside you."

Paige lifted over him only to plunge down, impaling her body on his cock. She inhaled sharply, letting his hands guide her as he lifted her up and down, up and down, in an endless progression of perfect movement. Her legs hit the arms of the chair, keeping her body from taking him as deeply as she wanted to, but the friction felt too good to stop and reposition.

She let her head fall back on her shoulders as Aidan drew her breasts to his mouth. He sucked a nipple between his lips, moaning into her. The tension built, causing her to increase her pace. He grabbed her ass, rolling her forward on each down thrust. His lips slid from her breast and he groaned heavily so that the noise echoed all around her.

Suddenly, he pushed up from the chair, taking her with him. Paige wrapped her legs around his waist to keep from falling as he carried her toward the bed. Almost roughly, he dropped her on her back. Her legs hung over the side, still hooked to his waist. Aidan came over her, eagerly searching to reenter her slick passage. His hands pressed along her sides. Bracing his feet on the floor, he took her hard, rocking forward into her ready body.

Paige kept her legs around him, spurring him on. The tight muscles of her pussy clenched him, holding him deep. He withdrew to the opening of her sex, only to thrust once more. She tightened her legs, keeping him deep. Aidan began to stroke her core in shallow thrusts. She jerked in pleasure, clawing at his arms to urge him on.

Soft fur cushioned her back as his heavy weight held her down. Aidan caught her nipple between his teeth, biting lightly before letting go. Then, reaching between them, he massaged her clit in tiny circles.

"Ah, please," Paige begged, needing the wonderful torment to end. She became trapped in a mindless web of ecstasy and thought her mind might explode with the intensity of it. Then, finally, she met with blessed release. Tremors raked across her entire frame, until her hand weakly dropped down his arms, barely able to keep a hold of him. Inside, it felt as if her bones melted.

Aidan's climax soon followed and he shuddered above her. With a light moan, he dropped down on his elbows, pressing his forehead to hers. For a long moment, they didn't move, only shared in harsh breaths. He moaned lightly, rubbing his lips to hers in a gentle kiss before pushing off her.

Aidan crawled onto the bed, lying naked on top of the fur coverlet. He wound his hands behind his head, closing his eyes. Paige joined him, stretching out next to him. He sighed heavily, saying, "This is not your world. No matter how much I want it to be, it is not."

Paige thought of Battlewar—overcrowded, overbearing and filled with strange unpleasant smells. "No, this place is not."

When he looked at her, a deep sadness filled his eyes. He turned on his side and caressed her face. "What if I told you there was a way for you to go home to your world? To rejoin the Forestter people?"

"You know of a fairy ring? I found none in the forest."

"I know of an inter-dimensional portal, a strange machine that will somehow take you home to your plane. All you have to do is walk through it." Aidan glanced away from her and back again. "It is beneath the old dungeons of this very castle. I can take you to it. I will contact the Divinity otherworlders and ask them for the directions to your home world. We can remain here until they find which plane is yours. If that is what you wish."

Paige sat up on the bed, curling her arms around her knees. Her fingers worked against her flesh as she hugged herself tightly to keep from shaking. "You want me to leave? You claimed me so you could send me home?"

"No. I will admit, sending you home was never my intent. I

truly believe the gods sent you to me, to be mine. I would hold on to you forever if you agreed to stay as my wife. But I have come to realize that I cannot force you." He ran his hand up her back, following her spine. "You chose an unknown life in the forest over being my wife and faced nearly being devoured by the Caniba beasts. If you are truly so unhappy, I cannot make you stay with me."

"Those other women in the cell talked about an inter-dimensional portal, but I didn't understand most of what they said. They acted as though they stepped through fairy rings all the time."

"It is how they came to be here. The people who sent them call themselves Divinity Corporation. They made their own fairy ring to travel through. They do not wait for fairies to bring them to the right world. They travel like we would jump across the room, leaping from one world to another with ease."

"Why?" Paige frowned, unable to think of any practical reason to hop through worlds like that. "Did they lose someone through a real fairy ring? Do they need hunting land?"

"I believe they are traders. They wish to give us women in exchange for water." Aidan furrowed his brow in thought.

"Then, they have no water on their land." Paige nodded. That would make sense. "They try to save their people."

"Methinks their missions are not so noble. They only wanted samples of the blue mineral water, not drinking water, and not enough to save a whole world of people." He drew his fingers along her back, as if writing on her like she was a piece of parchment and his finger the pen. "Their logic is flawed, their reasoning faulted. You saw the women they brought to us. Two had to be given a philter to knock them unconscious before being sent back to Divinity."

"I saw them." Paige thought of her night in the prison cell, trapped with the terrified women.

"It is as I've told my countrymen from the first. Brides cannot be brought to this land by force just because we want them. They must be blessed and sent by the gods in reward for a man doing his duty."

"Those two cried all through the night and one even started yelling." She rubbed her ear, remembering the high-pitched, incessant screams. "I'm inclined to agree with you. Brides should not be forced."

"I understand what you are saying." Aidan's hand stopped and he withdrew it. "I will make arrangements to send you home."

"It might be best if I did," Paige answered, unsure how she managed to get the words past her lips. Part of her wanted to run, part of her wanted to stay. Here was her chance to go home, but she found she wasn't ready. But how could she stay knowing what she did about Aidan and Shana? Just thinking the woman's name brought back that expression on her face—the agony, desperation, love, so much raw emotion as she clung to Aidan. When he didn't say anything, she added weakly, "I do miss a few things."

Aidan merely nodded, not speaking. When she looked into his eyes she couldn't think of what those things might be.

"I miss the tastes and smells. I miss listening to festival music from the trees." Small things, all things that she could live without.

He looked down at his hand, studying the edge of his fingernails. "Is there a man waiting for you? You never said."

Paige gave a cheerless chuckle, shaking her head in denial as she thought of how she scared off any suitors merely by being alive. "No. There is no one."

"Then you won't consider staying, of seeing if you enjoy being my wife? I promise to honor you. I will take care of—"

"Aidan, it's not that. I know you're honorable by all the standards set by your people, but I cannot share you with your friend. I saw the way she looked at you, the way they all looked at you."

"All?"

"The children. A father should be with his children."

Aidan began to chuckle. At first it was small, but it quickly grew into a hearty laugh. "You think you have to share me with Shana?"

Paige studied him. "Shana isn't your lover, is she?"

"Lover? No." Aidan sobered some, his smile dropping. "She is the wife of a friend who died following Caniba scouts. It is my duty to help her and Peeter's children."

"That was the reason why she looked at you like that, with so much emotion. She lost her husband. I thought…" Paige closed her eyes. "I thought that emotion was for you."

"And that is why you ran." It was more of a statement than a question.

"Yes. I saw you with her and—"

"You struck me." Aidan lifted his ankle, showing her a fading bruise.

Paige leaned forward, crawling so she could lightly kiss his leg where she had hit him. Then, lying on her stomach, she skated her fingertips along his shin. "I don't want to stay here."

"I understand. Tomorrow I will send word to Divinity."

Paige dropped her hand and glanced over her shoulder. "I mean, I don't want to stay at Battlewar. The village is too big. I find it oppressive."

"Where do you wish to go?" He sat up on the bed, touching the back of her thigh.

"Back to Fallenrock." She concentrated on drawing random patterns on his calf, careful not to touch the bruise.

"You wish to stay as my wife?" His hand moved higher.

"I wish to stay," Paige said carefully, "and see what happens between us. Why must we rush into marriage?"

"You wish for two fortnights filled with intention courting?" Aidan massaged her ass, deeply rubbing the muscles.

Paige closed her eyes, enjoying the intimate attention. "You remember?"

"I remember everything you say," Aidan said. "Your people have two fortnights filled with intention courting and then exchange blood to seal a union. We have satisfied my people's rituals. If I must satisfy yours to prove to you that I am your fate, then so be it. I will gladly face the challenge."

Paige licked her lips, smiling. It touched her that he would honor her traditions.

"My first intention is to kiss you here." He leaned over, pressing his lips to the back of her thighs. His fingers continued to massage. "And here."

Paige jerked when his lips brushed lightly over her ass cheek.

"That is not how intention courting is done." She turned to look at his face. "You have to state your intentions."

"I am." He grinned. "I intend to kiss you here." He kissed her hip. "And I intend to kiss you here."

"Those were not the intentions I speak of. You have to come to my doorstep every day with a gift. Normally, you would speak to my parents first, but since they have passed and I have no guardian..."

"Then I can kiss you here?" Aidan nipped at her ass cheek.

"You are not allowed to kiss me at all."

At that, he frowned and sat up. "You jest."

"No." She shook her head. "It's a time when you state your intentions."

"But, we can still...?" Aidan lifted a brow meaningfully and glanced at her hips. "Yea?"

"No." Paige couldn't help laughing at his look. As much as she wanted to lean over and kiss him, she knew that she needed him to face this challenge to prove he really did want her for more than easy sex. She pushed up on the bed.

"But, I will not use my lips," he swore. Covering his mouth, he said from beneath his fingers. "No kissing."

"Come, Aidan, take me back to Fallenrock." She reached for her white bridal gown and slipped it over her head.

He grumbled, pushing up from the bed. "Fine, but only because we can do nothing else."

# CHAPTER 11

"I will tell everyone what you are doing," Carrina said, pointing a bony finger at Paige. By the look on her face, one would think Paige was a traitor to Staria. "How do you expect to have thirteen children if you do not let your husband touch you? There is something very wrong with you. Very wrong."

"Blessed morning, Carrina." Paige yawned in greeting, stretching her arms over her head as she walked past Aidan's mother. The warm glow of morning sunlight called to her and she headed outside. Well, if she was perfectly honest, the warm glow of Aidan's naked chest as he did his morn exercises called to her more.

"Very wrong!" Carrina yelled after her. No matter how many times they explained their arrangement to the woman, Aidan and Paige could not convince her there was nothing wrong in their marriage.

"All right," Paige said absently over her shoulder, not really paying attention. She wore a new gown, made for her by a seamstress from the village. The cream-colored linen underdress with a brown and tan striped corset bodice was her favorite.

The first fortnight of intention courting had been rough. They rode on separate horses from Battlewar Castle to Aidan's home.

With the aftermath of their coupling so fresh in their minds, they were able to resist that first night. The next couple of days were harder. Aidan's hot gaze made her almost give in, but he respected her and kept his distance. The days after that, he started gravitating closer to her, sometimes to the point she could feel the heat of his body looming close.

It was pure torture.

The second fortnight began with Paige biting her lips to keep from crying out as she pleasured herself in her lonely bed. Her fingers felt good, but they weren't Aidan. She missed his touch.

Yet, for all its torment, not touching had its advantages and she began to see the logic of her Forestter ancestors. Staying apart forced them to find other ways of spending their time together. They could speak without falling into passionate kisses. Aidan told her of his brothers, of Peeter, of the pranks they pulled on each other while waiting for battle. He brought her gifts—mostly throwing knives and daggers. Though, he did bring her a bow and quiver of arrows. Paige still got giddy thinking about the fine quality of the weapon, even if he never gave her a straight answer about taking her to hunt one of the mammoth wolves.

"I believe your mother plans on feeding us her special food again. She has that look on her face," Paige said, coming around the side of the house. "How anyone can be in the mood to do anything after eating such a horrible concoction is beyond me. It is about as tantalizing as talking about bearing thirteen children. Do you know she told me the other day that she thought nineteen would be better?"

"She only says such things to get a rise out of you," Aidan dismissed. He swung his sword before him several times, thrusting and twisting as he took on an imaginary opponent. He began moving with more vigor than usual, his face tight. "I will speak to her and tell her you do not wish for children."

"Who said I do not want children?" Paige frowned.

"You did. Often. I told you I listen to what you have to say."

He was right, he did listen, but clearly he had misheard. "I said I did not wish for thirteen children. Why must it be none or many? In my world two is considered acceptable, four many. Thirteen is unheard of."

Aidan stopped, lowering his sword while he studied her. Sweat glistened on his neck and chest, gluing strands of his hair to his back and shoulders. He breathed deeply from his exertions. "Four?"

Paige laughed at his hopeful look. "We'll see."

"So, does this mean you are agreeing to stay here as my wife?" He dropped his sword on the ground, striding toward her. Lifting his hand, he made a move to caress her cheek, but stopped midair. Paige turned her cheek into his palm, but he drew it aside. "We still have one more day."

"Are you sure your count is not off?"

"It is your custom, not mine," he said.

"I say we are properly courted." She tried to lean into his hand again, but again he pulled it away.

"It is my custom to prove to the gods I am worthy." He dropped his hand and stepped back. His eyes held liquid promise as he licked his lips. She shivered, the rush of denial overwhelming her senses. "I will not fail so close to my goal, no matter how hard it is to not touch you."

Paige lifted her hand, letting it hover close to his face. She felt his breath on her palm. Heat radiated from his chest. "I do not think I can wait."

Aidan glanced around. "Come with me." He led her toward the stables, going behind the building. A dense overhang of trees brushed up against the back of the building, creating a private alcove. Aidan kicked off his boots and turned to her, keeping distance between them. He tugged at his waistband, unfastening the laces. "Disrobe."

Paige glanced behind her.

"Take off your gown. Let me see you," he insisted.

Paige slowly tugged at her laces, wondering what he had in mind. She smiled, thinking he meant to claim her here and now. The thought made her fingers quicken their task as she jerked the corset over her head. The linen underdress soon followed. Warm air tickled her naked flesh, arousing her already taut nerves. Her nipples hardened, puckering into needy buds. She tossed the gown over a tree limb before facing him.

When she tried to go to him, he held up his hand to stop her progress. Aidan stood naked before her, his gorgeous, flushed body tight with muscles. Spots of light shone on him through the trees. His cock lifted, full and thick from the long, seemingly endless days of denial. He ran his hand down the center of his chest. His eyes focused on her breasts.

"Touch them," he said, the words low. "Let me watch."

Paige, understanding his meaning, reached for her chest. She rubbed her breasts in slow, pleasurable movements. Her breathing deepened as arousal focused where she touched. Aidan's hot gaze and panting mouth captured her eyes. He touched his own nipples, mimicking her movements.

Paige pinched her nipples and gave a low moan. Aidan's hand instantly went to his arousal to fist the length of his cock. She watched him stroke it, never having seen anything quite so erotic or arousing in her life. Her hand seemed to have a mind of its own as her fingers glided down to her sex. She parted the folds, jolting visibly as she brushed her clit. Gasping, she did it again.

"Aidan, please," she begged mindlessly. "Let me touch you."

"Touch yourself for me," he commanded hoarsely. "Let me watch you come."

Paige stared at his cock, licking her lips. She continued to finger her clit and fondle her breasts. Her head became light with desire and she wobbled on her legs. "Please, Aidan, I need you inside me. I need it. I cannot take any more torture."

He looked like he wanted to give in, but instead said, "We cannot. We have one more day."

"It's been so long," she cried. Rocking her hips against her hand, she massaged her clit. "At least give me your hand. Let me ride your fingers. Or your mouth. I want to ride your tongue. Oh please, kiss me, suck on my pussy."

"Get on the ground," he panted, pumping his fist hard and fast.

"Oh yes!" She licked her lips, getting on her knees. "I'll go first. I'll suck your cock." Paige opened her mouth, ready to taste him.

"You know how to tempt a man, my lady," Aidan growled. He took a step for her.

"Yes, come here. Give it to me. Give me your cock."

"Lie on your back," he said in a rush, each word more frantic than the last. "Spread your legs so I can see your fingers going inside you. Let me see what I have suffered for."

Paige groaned, realizing he didn't mean to touch her. However, she obeyed and got on her back, opening her legs wide as she slipped her finger into her wet, aching pussy. Suddenly, her body could take no more and she came. Her muscles seized with pleasure and she could barely move as she let the pleasure rack through her.

Aidan stood over her, pumping his cock. "Oh yea, so beautiful, so wet. I want to fuck you so badly. I want to taste your cream. Let me see you taste it."

Paige brought her fingers to her lips and tasted herself. Aidan jerked, spilling his seed on the ground between her thighs. He sunk weakly to his knees.

Paige turned her knees inward, staying on her back as her heart began to slow. Aidan drew his hand along her calf, keeping it from touching as he pretended to caress it. She rolled her head back on her shoulders, looking up at her dress hanging on the limb. The breeze pushed it gently over her head only to let it drop back on the branch. "I'm not sure if I feel better or worse."

"Perhaps I should go hunting today," Aidan said, eyeing her naked form. "Alone."

"Perhaps you should," she agreed, sure she'd not stop herself from attacking him should he try to initiate another no-touch sexual encounter. Standing, she tugged her gown off the tree and began shaking out the long folds so she could redress. Absently, she considered her day and said, "And perhaps I will try to get Carrina to visit Martin. I might drag her in front of him so he can finally claim her."

"She does not wish to be claimed," Aidan said, a little defensively. He tugged on his pants.

*Ah, men and their mothers,* Paige thought wryly. "Since when has that fact stopped a Starian man?"

Aidan frowned and Paige instantly wished she could take the

words back. She didn't mean them as harshly as they sounded. "It is not the same thing."

Paige pulled the gown over her head to keep him from reading her doubtful thoughts. She had plenty of room to make argument, but refrained. "Perhaps she wants to be caught."

"Do you wish to be caught?" He arched a brow.

Glad to see his playful mood, she said, "It depends on what you bring me tomorrow, mighty hunter. Ask me again then."

"So you are the new oracle." Oracle Teena's dark brown eyes focused on Paige, sweeping up and down. Aidan had told her stories of the woman. At the time she thought he exaggerated about the woman's sanctimonious attitude. "We are quite insulted that you have not been to the temple to visit."

"I was not aware I needed to go to a temple." Paige crossed her arms over her chest. The woman had been waiting inside with Carrina when she came back from her semi-tryst with Aidan. Outside, she heard the sound of his horse riding away. He already left to hunt.

"A new oracle comes to join us and you do not think it warrants a visit?" Teena clicked her teeth. She walked around the room, holding her arms away from her body so her long white robes fluttered behind her.

"I did not come to join you. I was sent here by mad fairies." Paige turned her full attention to Carrina. "You arranged this meeting, didn't you?"

"Methought you could use Oracle Teena's help," Carrina said. "If you will not be a wife, you can be an oracle."

Paige gasped at the bold words in front of a stranger. "Who says I'm a wife? How many times do I have to explain it to you?"

"So you prefer to be a camp follower?" Oracle Teena asked, smiling mischievously. "I am afraid the oracle council will not allow that. You have been claimed and by a guardian. There are worse husbands to have."

"You should listen to her," Carrina said. "Her visions are some of the clearest."

"It is my pleasure to help," Teena preened at the compliment. "But, it is true. I predicted your coming for Sir Aidan. The fact that you have problems in your marriage is no fault of mine. He was instructed to go to the breeding ceremony but he claimed you too soon. I had a feeling he would."

"Sure you did," Paige drawled. She really wanted to grab a chair and throw it at Aidan's mother. With a deep breath, she refrained.

"I know what you're doing. Of your custom." Teena gave a small, condescending laugh. Looking at Carrina, she said, "Could you leave us, lady? Perhaps you should take to the forest. Methinks Martin comes looking for you."

"Thank you, Oracle Teena," Carrina said, interest lighting on her face as she ran outside.

"He's not," Teena said when they were alone, "but Carrina enjoys the game."

"What do you want with me?" Paige asked, not liking the condescending way the woman presumed to know her and her life.

"Me?" Teena waved her hand in dismissal. "Nothing."

"Well then, it was a pleasure to meet you. Safe journey home." Paige made a move to leave.

"Wait." Teena frowned, her tone becoming dark and irritated. "I can see you are one to talk of points."

"I do not even know what that means."

"Let me be direct. We want to know what your gifts are." Teena crossed her arms, losing the graceful fluttering she'd shown before. "How did you know of Callum's death on the sea? No one else saw it."

Paige took in the woman's expression. "You want to know if I'm better than you."

Teena's face reddened. "This is about Staria, not me."

"Sure, it is." Paige shook her head. "I see it all over your face. Let me guess. You are the type who is used to people acting like Carrina, never questioning you. But, me, I do not know you. I am not scared of you or your predictions. It's easy to say you saw me coming and you knew this would happen, but if you really want to impress me, tell me something that is not old news."

"Very well." Teena closed her eyes briefly. When she opened them the brown had faded to milky white.

Paige took a step back in surprise. "What are you doing?"

Teena's expression faded and her body shook. Blankly, she droned, "You should not be angry at me for your mistakes."

"My mistakes?" Paige demanded. "What gives you the right to—?"

"Aidan has proved his worth to the gods, but you have not. This marriage is blessed, but the gods may have more trials for you."

Paige arched a brow. Teena stopped shaking and her eyes cleared.

"That's it?" Paige asked, snorting with laughter. "What in the green of the forest am I doing listening to this? That's the best you have? A vague premonition that the future might hold trouble for Aidan and me? You could say that about anyone. You call that impressive?"

Teena's forehead wrinkled in anger. "Well, I-I-I—"

"Let me help." Paige let go of all control, allowing the rush of feelings and images into her soul. She let the wind carry her through the forest, past trees with broad leaves and fat trunks, by red-tinted shrubs, over trickling brooks lined with rocks and the acorn-littered ground. Then, like a burst of sunlight, she felt warmth overtake her entire body. She saw Aidan looking at her, reaching for her, smiling at her as if the expression was permanently etched on his features. But it wasn't his face. It was the face of an old man who had his eyes and his smile. Gray had overtaken his blond hair, now shortly cropped, and wrinkles carved his face.

"You have always had my heart, my lady," Aidan whispered, his voice raspier than she knew it to be. The breeze swept her mind around him until he overwhelmed her senses and in that moment she knew that all would be well. Paige breathed heavily as she was jerked from the moment. Never had a vision been so vivid and real.

"What?" Teena demanded. "What did you see?"

"The gods may have trials for us," Paige answered, grinning, "but we are definitely blessed."

"That is what I said!" Teena protested. Paige took her by the elbow and escorted her toward the door. "But you did not say anything that I did not see—"

"Good journey, Oracle Teena," Paige replied. "I'm sure I will see you again."

"But, your gifts? You have not told me of your—"

Paige shut the door, cutting off the oracle's words. She didn't know about the Starian gods' blessing or her family curse. She didn't know if Teena spoke the truth or was completely mad. All she knew is that she had seen into the future and it was more than she could have ever hoped for.

Sweet feelings of hope and excitement flowed through her. She looked around the home with new eyes, feeling as if she had finally found the place where she truly belonged.

## CHAPTER 12

Paige nervously fingered the blade of the knife she had taken down from the weapons wall in her bedchambers. The double-edged dagger had finely carved scrolls down the center ridge of the blade, which led to a pointed tip. A silver pommel carried the same fine carving and black leather strips wound around the hilt.

All day, nervous excitement coursed through her veins and time seemed to go so slowly she thought she'd go mad from having to wait. She had even gone so far as to help Carrina clean the long line of rooms along the hall. They were the old bedchambers of Aidan's brothers and covered with a fine layer of dust.

Not even Carrina's sour looks and disappointed grimaces could mar Paige's happiness. She had seen her future and it looked wonderful. Even old, with wrinkled skin and grayed hair, Aidan made her heartbeat quicken. And his words. Oh, those wonderful words.

*You have always had my heart, my lady.*

She wanted to jump up and down every time they echoed through her mind. He'd never said anything like that to her before. But then, why would he?

*You have always had my heart, my lady.*

Paige winced, accidently cutting her fingertip on the sharp blade. Sucking on her hurt finger, she walked from the room.

"Paige?"

Her heartbeat sped to hear Aidan's voice. She hurried down the hall toward him. The soft glow of orange light from the fire box illuminated his face as moonlight silhouetted him from the opened front door.

"A new gown?" He motioned at her green dress. The bodice was a darker shade than the under tunic.

"It came today from the village," she answered.

"Hm." He nodded in approval.

"How was hunting? Did you bring me something?" She pressed the pommel of the knife into her palm, rubbing it in small circles as she was careful not to cut herself again.

"I did, but I do not think you want to see it, at least not in that gown." When he came closer, she saw his hair had been washed and slicked back from his head. Seeing her attention, he ran his hand over his hair, explaining, "I stopped at the creek."

"Your mother asked Oracle Teena to stop by," Paige said, trying to lead the conversation toward her vision. She looked at his face, trying to contain the eager hope she felt at remembering her vision.

*You have always had my heart, my lady.*

"I must apologize for that, my lady. Oracle Teena is, ah..."

"Exactly as you described her," Paige said. Aidan didn't reach to touch her. Paige couldn't take it. She dropped the knife and surged forward, throwing her arms around his neck.

Aidan stiffened in surprise, but didn't stop her as her lips crushed into his. He returned the kiss briefly before pulling away. "It is not time for—"

Moaning, Paige pressed forward again. She didn't care that they had a few hours left before the official ending of the intention courting time. She drank in the taste of his lips, wanting to devour him. It had been too long and his taste was too good. The warm contours of his firm body rubbed into her chest until her breasts ached for more contact.

Aidan groaned. His hands gripped her ass tight, lifting her from the floor to keep them together. He kissed her so hard his teeth cut into her mouth and she made a small noise of surprise. "Ow."

"My apolo—"

"I love you," she said, the words flowing out of her.

"You, ah..." He blinked in obvious surprise. Not letting go of her ass, he kept her pressed against him. However, the swaying of his body had stopped and she got the impression he gripped her more because he was taken by surprise by her declaration than anything else.

"I realize what you said, that Starian men do not put much stock in love, but I love you and I think you love me. Actually, I know it even if you do not." Paige caressed his cheek, brushing cool, wet hair from his face. The fingers digging into her ass cheeks flexed but didn't let go. She felt the unmistakable press of his cock to her stomach. "I can wait for you to say it because I know that someday you will know it too."

"What? How? Did Oracle Teena say such a thing? Because this does not sound like something a Starian oracle would say. We are not trained to give credence to such sentiments."

"I hardly found Oracle Teena's predictions impressive. She will have to do more than mumble a few words and change her eye color to impress me." Paige arched a brow. "You forget, Sir Aidan, you are with an oracle right now. I know things."

"But, you see death from the weather. That is hardly the same as seeing what you claim."

"Yes, I do see death. But it would seem I also see life now. Perhaps you were right. This is the right place for me with my curse." Paige grinned. Her feet dangled and she wrapped her arms around his neck.

"And you saw that I love you?"

"Yes." She nodded, waiting for his stunned expression to fill in. Two fortnights ago his hesitance in this situation would have hurt her. Then, she wouldn't have thought him capable of loving her as she had come to love him. Now she understood him and his ways. He'd been raised a warrior, a soldier, a man of honor and duty. The notion of love was going to be new to someone like that. But her vision gave her hope, and his future words tore down the last of her hesitance and defenses. He might not be able to say the words today, or even understand them, but someday he would and that was good enough for Paige.

"And you saw me tell you this?"

"Yes." Nodding again, she added, "You were quite old with short, gray hair and very handsome lines in your face. And you said to me, 'You have always had my heart, my lady.' I heard it as clear as I hear you now. You love me."

"And this pleases you?" He finally began to move, adjusting her against him without setting her on the floor.

"It pleases me very much." Paige licked her lips. His body felt so good, so right.

"If you are pleased, my lady, then I am pleased." Aidan took her mouth, as if pouring into her all the unspent passions that had built up inside him.

"Oh wait," Paige pushed on him. "We cannot. Not yet."

Aidan groaned. "Please, by all the bloody battle axes in Staria, do not tell me we have to go another two fortnights. I cannot take denying myself of you."

Paige laughed, pushing at his chest so he let her go. Aidan groaned loudly before making small, pouting noises behind her. She found the knife on the floor and picked it up. "I need to cut you first."

Completely unconcerned, he said, "I have not played this game before."

"The exchanging of blood," Paige answered. "Roll up your sleeve."

Instead of listening, he pulled his tunic over his head and threw it onto the table. He loomed over her with stalking grace, lowering his chin and narrowing his eyes. Paige trembled. He came to her and lifted her knife hand. His fist wrapped hers, controlling the blade. He brought the tip to the center of his chest and traced the flat of the blade downward, not drawing blood.

"Where would you like to cut, my lady?" His words were low

and seductive. When he reached his stomach, he lifted the blade to his lips and licked the pointed tip.

"I, ah..." Paige swallowed, fascinated by the movements of his tongue.

"Yea, Lady Paige?" he whispered.

"Arm," she answered, the word hardly audible.

Aidan let go of her hand and held out his arm.

"The other one."

His seductive grin widened and he offered his opposite arm. "Here. Cut. Take what you need of me. It all belongs to you anyway."

Her hand trembled nervously as she took the blade and put it to his forearm. The sharp dagger moved over him, but didn't cut. Aidan laughed. "You will have to push harder than that, my lady. My skin is not as soft as yours."

Paige tried it again, making a light wound. He kept his eyes on her, not flinching, not showing any pain. When blood beaded on his flesh, she gave him the blade and turned her arm so the palm of her hand faced upward.

"Shouldn't you remove your tunic as well?" Aidan grinned hopefully. She gave a small laugh, but didn't move to undress.

"Please make it fast," Paige said, holding out her arm. She bit the inside of her lip and narrowed her eyes, waiting for the pain. Aidan drew the blade so fast it took her a moment to realize he'd finished. A small trail lined her arm and she turned it over, pressing her wound to his.

"I will never harm you again, Sir Aidan, this union is sealed. We are one," she whispered.

Aidan leaned into her. "I cannot hear you, my lady. You are too quiet."

Paige cleared her throat, repeating louder, "I will never harm you again, Sir Aidan, this union is sealed. We are one." Then she continued the traditional words, "Our blood now flows through each other and as I live for you, you now live for me."

"I will never harm you, sweet Lady Paige, this union is sealed. We are one." He brushed his lips along the corner of her mouth.

"Our blood now flows through each other and as you live for me, I live for you." Aidan paused. "Is that how it is done? Are we finished? Or should I say you are claimed?"

Paige shook her head in denial. "Finished? Oh no, my husband. We are just getting started."

---

Aidan watched his wife's ass as she led him down the hall, past the chamber she'd been using. She paused by his bedchamber door, pushing it open to lead him inside. He found the way she'd hesitated to cut him adorable, though the wound she inflicted hardly hurt. It wouldn't even leave a scar. Already, it had stopped bleeding, as had hers. Aidan had found he didn't want to mar her pretty flesh, though if it was what she needed to know he was serious, that she was his, then he'd obey her wish.

Her words had shocked him with their certainty, *I realize what you said, that Starian men do not put much stock in love, but I love you and I think you love me. Actually, I know it even if you do not.*

Paige believed what she said. He saw it in her eyes when she said she loved him. The words, though startling, did something to him. They made him consider more—more beyond duty and responsibility.

His room looked much like the chambers at Battlewar, bigger than other rooms in the house, but sparse in décor. The large bed next to a cushioned dressing chair held his attention through the corner of his eyes. Before he could push her down onto it and fall on top of her, Paige pulled him into her and began kissing him. Her hands ran all over his body, touching everywhere she could reach as he tugged the laces of her corset bodice. With eager precision, he stripped her of her clothes before setting to work on his pants. Before his breeches fell to the ground, he had his lips on her breasts, sucking and licking the hard nipples.

Turning him, she pushed him down on a chair, forcing him to sit. He reached for her, but she slowly spun so her ass was to him. She backed up, lifting her arms behind her head while she rubbed her ass along his cock. Aidan grabbed her chest, squeezing as she moved along him. His cock ached with need. It had been too long since he felt the close heat of her body, the wet clamp of her pussy. Even their wanton encounter behind the stables didn't calm his ardor.

"Ah, Paige, methinks we should discuss—" Aidan tried to force her more fully onto his lap. He rocked his hips into her, molding it to the soft cleft of her ass.

"Shh," she hushed. "This is our wedding night. Let's just enjoy it."

She massaged his cock with her ass, circling her hips. He grabbed her breasts, holding her down against him to keep the pressure tight as he rubbed against the warm, dry flesh. Pushing up, she finally faced him, only she didn't climb on his lap as he wanted. Instead, she got to her knees and parted her lips. Paige flipped her hair over her shoulder, out of her way. He jerked before she even touched him with her wet mouth.

Paige sucked him between her lips, her whole body working erotically as she moved over him. He kept his hands at his sides, letting her have complete control. She reached up his chest, scratching him as she moved up and down, up and down, sucking and licking and biting. Every glide and pull caused his body to tense and shudder. He gripped the arms of the chair. He closed his eyes and bit his lip, trying to hold back, but her suctioning lips demanded he give her everything. Aidan came between her lips, mesmerized by the lapping way she enthusiastically drank him in.

She stopped, smiling at him as she licked his juices from her lips. "I like your taste."

He groaned, reaching for her, but she swatted his hand.

"I know you like watching me." She wiggled her body in front of him, leisurely swaying and spinning in a seductive dance. Her hand moved, forcing his eyes to follow them as she touched her thighs, her breasts, her glistening pussy. "I want you hard again."

It was a desire he would have no problem granting. Already he felt his shaft stirring. "I want *you* again."

* * *

Paige felt no inhibition in knowing Aidan watched her. She knew he cared for her, saw the desire in his eyes. The feeling was empowering, as was the knowledge she could control the warrior with just one look or touch.

Aidan shot up from his chair, grabbing her from behind. Strong, calloused hands slid over her tingling flesh, exploring where her hands had just roamed. The growing evidence of his renewed desire brushed the back of her hip. Aidan swept her hair aside, kissing her throat, the nape of her neck, the long line of her spine. He traveled, kneeling behind her. Teeth nipped her ass cheek as hands roamed her thighs. She had yet to find her release and each sensation was amplified twentyfold.

Aidan slipped his finger along her wet slit, parting her sex. He probed her pussy, thrusting his finger inside her only to wiggle it around. He moaned against the side of her hip. Paige touched his head, massaging his scalp.

Aidan rose to his feet and his finger slid from inside her. Gently, he lifted her into his arms and laid her on the bed. Starting at her toes, he massaged his way up her legs until she worked her feet against the mattress.

"Aidan, please," she begged, trying to sit up so she could pull him up. "Please, I need you."

Aidan crawled over her, forcing her onto her back. He licked her breasts, devouring them as he sucked her nipples deep into his mouth. Her legs worked against him as she tried to force him up. Finally, he pushed her thighs open with his. Her hips searched for him.

Aidan touched her again with his hand and she was certain he was trying to torture her. Steamy eyes watched her thrash about. He rubbed her, circling her swollen lips and clit with precision. She panted and cried out, sighing and moaning at the feel of him. When he felt her body begin to tremble, he pulled back.

"I need you," Paige whispered, reaching for him.

Aidan groaned, not hesitating as he brought his cock to her

willing body. He was so handsome, his bronzed body so perfect. He thrust forward, filling her, taking away the ache of their fortnights of being apart. Nothing mattered, nothing existed beyond the look in his eyes, the feel of his tongue, the sound of his harsh breath.

Unyielding hardness mixed with scalding heat. He braced his weight with one hand while roaming her body with the other, moving it smoothly over her flesh. He kept his movements deep and small, exerting pressure in all the right places. Paige moaned, overcome with raw, unrefined emotions.

Paige caressed his neck and jaw before pulling his face down to hers for a kiss. Aidan quickened his pace as her tongue slid past his lips. She squirmed beneath him, her knees lifting to tighten along his waist.

"Aidan, ah," she tried to speak into his lips, wanting to say all the things swimming around inside her. All that came out was a series of moans and pants. Logical thought and reason left her. Her heart hammered so loud she heard it thundering in her ears.

Aidan broke the kiss, lifting up for better leverage. He rocked against her core, moving faster and harder. Paige watched his muscles rippling in his chest, fascinated by the way the shadowed light appeared to dance over him.

Tension built low in her belly, the agonizing pleasure almost more than she could bear. Paige cried out, not caring who heard her. She held on tight to his biceps, digging her fingernails into the thick muscles as she quaked uncontrollably. Seconds later, Aidan's cry joined hers. He buried himself hard and so deep she was sure he touched her very soul.

Paige's moan turned into a soft pant before fading into an incoherent whimper. Her limbs fell weakly to the bed. Aidan rolled next to her and pulled her into his arms. Holding her tight, he said, "I would like for you to stay with me tonight."

"You'll sleep with me every night. I plan on staying forever." Paige sighed, smiling happily as she let the softness of sleep lull her into its depths.

# Epilogue

"I do not wish to go to a fire ceremony at Battlewar," Paige protested, dragging her feet as Aidan tried to lead her to her horse. Behind her, Carrina laughed. She wasn't sure if the woman chuckled at the young couple fighting over a man's duty to attend the ceremony and Paige's abhorrence for any town bigger than Fallenrock Village, or the antics of Shana's boys as they stick-fought across the yard. The children visited often to train with Aidan. Paige found she didn't mind their company at all.

"I have already told you, my sweet lady, there is nothing you can say to make me sway my course. We were invited and, as honored guests who are new to marriage, we should attend. The king gave me leave from my duties to make an appearance."

"But, I must go to visit the other oracles. They told me I had to go back to them if I saw a vision." Paige put her hand dramatically to her forehead and moaned. "I'm seeing falling trees. The Hanging Forest is on fire. Animals stampeding. People screaming. Your horse—"

"A good effort," he laughed, "but I can tell when you have a real vision. And you have had several visions since visiting with the other oracles, Oracle Paige, and have not once gone back since your first visit."

"I would be there every day. I have no desire to tell them I can predict the daily weather. If they found out, they would probably try to give me a white robe and make me practice those moves Teena does." Paige held her arms to the side and began to mimic Oracle Teena's walk, the gliding self-importance combined with wide, over-dramatic movements.

Aidan chuckled.

Paige let her lashes fall over her eyes as she tugged a suddenly pliable Aidan toward her. Licking her lips, she said in a breathy whisper, "Are you sure there is nothing I can do to convince you?"

"We may," Aidan cleared his throat, "do *that* when we get to Battlewar." He gave her a meaningful once-over. "Perhaps on the way as well, my lady."

Aidan kissed the tip of her nose, tugging her insistently behind him. "You have your new gown. Most ladies would be pleased to show it off."

"I'd be pleased to take it off," Paige said, glancing down at the green gown with the gold corset. It was a beautiful gown, one of several her husband bought for her. "Please let's not go."

"We must. Now, no more argument." He continued to walk toward the stables. "Besides, we have reason to celebrate."

"Oh?" she arched a brow. "And what reason is that?"

"I received a missive from the king this morn."

Her heart nearly stopped beating and this time no amount of pulling could make her move. "You have been ordered back to the battlefront, haven't you? I knew this day would come, that you would have to go, but so soon? How long? Can I go with you?"

"I'm ordered to a new battlefront," Aidan said. Then, frowning, he commanded, "And no, you cannot go to the battlefront."

"New?" Paige began to pace. "King Wilhelm is sending you over the borders, isn't he? I have had a feeling someone will be going over the borders. I never thought it would be—"

"Paige, calm yourself. I will not die in battle."

"Oh, I know." She nodded in agreement. "I already saw you as an old man. But that doesn't mean you cannot be hurt, or gone for years."

"I'm to guard something very precious." He held onto his wrist, putting his hand over the tattoo.

"Well, I hope it's a rock in the middle of the forest." She refused to smile, even as he gave her the most adorable look.

Aidan tilted his head to the side and began looking her over. "A rock? No, that is not how I would describe it."

Paige glanced behind her before chuckling. "Why don't you tell me?"

"The king ordered me to stay in Fallenrock. Caniba spies were found in the forest north of the border. They have been stopped, but it has been decided that the oracles need more protection. So, I'm in charge of the new encampment outside Fallenrock Castle. It is less than an hour's ride from here." He reached for her, pulling her into his arms.

"So, you're saying you will always be around? That I will never be rid of you?" she asked, trying to maintain a straight face.

"Unless you had other plans for your life, my lady." He kissed the tip of her nose.

"Well, Baker Fredrick from the village is in need of a wife and Merrit says a minimum of ten husbands are ideal to run a proper household." Paige barely got the words out before Aidan had her tight to his chest. He lifted her feet off the ground with a growl. She laughed, squealing as he spun her around in a circle. "I jest, I jest!"

He set her back down. "Good, because I will never approve of a second husband. You are mine. Only mine."

Paige wrapped her arms around his neck, letting her body fall into his. "Only yours, Aidan. I love you."

Then, to her surprise, he answered, "And you will always have my heart, my lady."

Unsure she'd heard him right, she asked, "Did you just say…?"

"I love you too, Paige. I see your face and my chest tightens. I think of you and my lips smile. I might not understand it, or why the gods would wish it to be so, I only know that you are the greatest reward a warrior could ever receive. I love you. I should have said it sooner, but..."

"But you are a warrior and warriors are not taught about love," she finished for him. "I understand, my love."

"Now, come. We really must ride." He swept her up into his arms, carrying her toward the stables. "There is nothing you can say to—"

"I'm with child," Paige announced. Behind her the boys began to giggle. Carrina screamed, happily clapping her hands.

Aidan finally stopped moving. His eyes widened in shock but he didn't set her back down. "You are certain?"

"The midwife is." Paige gave a small grin. Then, louder, she yelled over her shoulder, "It's either that or your mother has been cooking marriage potions into her food again."

"I have not!" Carrina protested. "Not since you two made your marriage right."

"I hope you kept the recipe." Paige winked at Aidan so Carrina couldn't see. "I have invited Martin over to dine tonight."

Aidan hurried to the stables, passing the main door as he carried her behind the building to the private alcove. Setting her down, he knelt before and put his ear to her stomach. "My son." Then, looking up at Paige, his face filled with happiness, he whispered, "My heart."

Paige ran her hand into his hair, stroking him gently as he continued to listen to her stomach. Everything was perfect.

*You will always have my heart, my lady.*

The End

# *Taking Karre*

BOOK FOUR BY MICHELLE M. PILLOW

Second Electronic Printing April 2012, The Raven Books

First Electronic Printing August 2009

ISBN 9781452412979

# *About Taking Karre*

## DIVINITY WARRIORS BOOK FOUR

**In a land forever at war, meeting women is the last thing they can think about, so what's a lonely alpha warrior to do?**

Warrior Sir Vidar of Spearhead is too busy guarding the borderlands of his war torn country to bother with the headache of selecting a bride. Ordered to marry by the king, he plans to grab a woman and get back to the warfront, never to think of it again. That is until he meets the alluring Lady Karre with her teasing eyes, lush lips, and irresistible ways.

Known by many names, inter-dimensional thief Karre, has only one purpose—take down the company that ruined her life. When her luck runs out and she's caught, Divinity Corporation condemns her to matrimony on a primitive, warrior-filled alternate reality where Karre soon discovers there are worse fates than being prisoner to an insatiable alpha male.

Before long, days and nights filled with bliss becomes something neither expected, and when Karre is taken, Vidar is forced to confront emotions a battle-hardened soldier never expected to feel.

# *Prologue*

## THREE WEEKS AGO, DIMENSIONAL PLANE 395, ADULT PLEASURE CENTRE VWH

*Because right now, in this moment, she was their fantasy.*

Karre marched out on stage in red stiletto heels, a slinky dress, big grin and nothing else. She kept tempo with the hard, drumming beat of music. Men hollered, whooping their excitement just to see her. She smiled at them, looking over the crowd of heads. She could make them do anything—beg, buy, steal, kill—because right now, in this moment, she was their fantasy.

Blonde hair piled high on her head, garnished with a string of diamonds and rubies some suitor had given her. It was a sweet trinket, one she might even keep, not that she would remember where the jewels came from. She traveled too much and had more important things on her mind.

Karre turned slowly with her arms raised above her head. The hem of her short dress lifted to just below the curve of her ass. When her back was to the crowd, she bent forward. The cheering grew as the men got a peek of the naked treasure hidden beneath the clinging silver. What did she care if they saw her ass? Her pussy? Her breasts? They were just skin, flesh, a tool like any other. No matter how much they wanted her, they would never be able to touch her.

On this dimensional plane of existence, humans cohabitated with humanoid creatures. The first time Karre saw a vampire sucking on the neck of a shifted werewolf, she'd nearly sprinted out of the room to find her wrist portal to flash out of there to another plane. The portable device looked like a large bracelet to most, but to Karre it was her sole means of survival.

Necessity made her stay where she was. This plane was the easiest to get jewels on without resorting to thievery and the hard, shiny rocks were good for trade in nearly every dimension. Besides, not counting the dancing, being in Dimensional Plane 395 was like taking a vacation. With so many strange and different creatures, they never questioned anything she said and most were focused more on blood-drinking and pleasure-seeking.

Being in a new dimensional plane was like being in your world, but only if had it evolved in a different way. To a point, there were many similarities. Languages, generally, were relatively similar, though for some reason the written word consisted of unfamiliar symbols. Some people looked the same, but were not the same people. Natural disasters and major human events were shared. Weather was the same and each place was still Earth.

"I adore you, Sparkle!" a man yelled. "Marry me!"

Karre turned to look over her shoulder at the crowd and winked. A plethora of large green horns, red flesh, reptile skin, webbed fingers, sharp fangs, and ridged flesh stretched out before her until the mass became a single entity flowing back and forth like a wave.

"I'll take that as a yes," the same voice answered her playful flirting. A rush of similar proposals followed the first, showering her in declarations of love. But she wasn't fool enough to believe them. What they felt wasn't love. It was lust.

Karre knew their adoration for what it was and used it to fuel her dance. She twirled and wiggled, thrust her ass toward them, drew her hips in seductive circles, only to pause in a sexy pose in time with the music. Slowly, she undressed, peeling the slinky gown off her body. Several lights flashed, illuminating her from various angles, leaving no curve unseen.

Just flesh. Just a means. Just another job. Just another plane and soon a distant memory.

Her smile widened, as she knew this was her last dance, at least for this trip. The cheering rose, but she stopped listening. And then it was over. Karre held still, letting the dying notes find their silence before walking naked from the stage.

"You were wonderful tonight, Sparkle," a new dancer fawned. "The crowd loves you. I was wondering if you'd show me how to—"

"Is he here?" Karre asked, stopping the woman from starting a conversation Karre didn't have time for. It's not like she could tell the truth—that all her dancing skill was someone else's memories uploaded into her brain by a device she'd bartered for on another plane.

"He's in your room," the woman answered, frowning slightly at having her question dismissed. "And he brought a large case. I think it's full of gifts so you'll consider his suit."

"Perfect," Karre grinned. Taking a long robe the woman held out, she slipped it over her shoulders. "I don't want to be disturbed."

---

*Two weeks ago, Dimensional Plane 154, Stac Lesh Mansion*
*Because right now, in this moment, she was the help.*

Karre stared at her red, curly hair in the liquid-silver reflection wall. It had been pulled into a bun at the nape of her neck. The long skirt of the plain uniform and padded body suit did much to hide her figure under the thick gray wool. An apron, changed every time so much as a spot marred the pristine white, covered high over her chest and low to her knees. With the clothes and makeup to pale her face into an unimpressive mask, no one would look twice in her direction because right now, in this moment, she was the help.

She had expected to keep her head down and do her job for months before coming back into this room. But in putting on the uniform, she became invisible. The rich people she worked for didn't look in her direction twice. Well, that wasn't necessarily true. When the wife was gone, the husband had looked at her more than twice. A big grin showcasing blacked-out teeth and a very inappropriately timed belch had changed his interest quickly.

Karre reached to touch her reflection. Behind her, the rich baby's room spread out like the entrance to a palace. Gilded ceilings etched with clouds, golden rays of light and ridiculously cheerful fat angels stretched above as white marble stretched below. It was cold and unwelcoming and more than any one person deserved.

"Oh, wonderful, finally, help," the rich wife said, sweeping into the room. Karre didn't bother to learn the lady's name. "Rich wife" was much easier to remember. The woman held her child under the arms, away from her chest, as if contact with the baby would somehow ruin her carefully planned outfit. "Which one are you?"

"Brigitte, ma'am."

"Take Cinny," the woman ordered. "Mommy needs time to collect herself."

Karre suppressed her groan of frustration at being interrupted and stood to dutifully take the child. She cradled the poor creature close and walked it toward the crib.

"Sing to Cinny before you put her down," rich wife ordered, standing before the liquid silver as she brushed at her clothes.

Karre stopped walking. Sing? To the gurgling, wiggling mass in her arms?

"Well, Brigitte?"

"Mistress, mistress, let me come in," Karre sang the only child-like-sounding song she could think of at the moment, pausing to clear her throat. "I have the pence if you have a quim."

"What a pretty tune," the woman said. "I've never heard it. What does it mean?"

"My dad sang it to my mom," Karre answered, letting the memories she had uploaded into her mind take over her personality —Brigitte of the Fallen Women, a whore's daughter raised in a brothel, adept at blending into new environments. She left off the word "once" before adding the lie, "I'm not sure what it means."

"Carry on."

"Mistress, mistress, I'm stiff as a pin. I need your..." Karre continued, lowering her voice as the woman left her alone with the gurgling, oblivious child. Stopping, she laid the baby down and said, "Sorry, kid, it's the only song I knew the words to. But I guess it's all right. I turned out just fine with lots of jewels and pretty things and you're too little to understand what any of it means. You should be more worried about growing up in this place with that mom of yours. Now, if you just be good," she paused and tucked a blanket around the infant's body, "I've got a job to do."

Going back to the wall, Karre again reached for her reflection. She stepped forward, letting the liquid hit her hand. It stung, freezing cold in the warm room. For a moment, she hesitated, glancing back at the gurgling child. She thought about grabbing Cinny and taking the baby with her.

"Sorry, kid," she whispered, "even with that mother, you're better off here."

It was a delicate balance—keeping her purpose in her mind while living out the personality and quirks of another—almost like having two people in her head. Karre's hand met with the wall as she felt around, searching for the device she'd hidden. When her fingers met with a smooth, flat surface, she frowned. Putting a second hand to the wall she became frantic, sliding her palms in wide, searching arcs. Perhaps the adhesive she used had come loose. She bent her knees, crouching as she searched the bottom corner of the liquid reflecting wall. Her fingers were so cold it became hard to feel, but the molecular structure of the liquid kept the silver from trickling down her arms as it remained bonded to itself.

Then, to her great surprise, warmth gripped her. A hand wrapped her wrist and jerked her forward. She was pulled through the wall, feeling the sting of silver before landing on a hard, stone floor. Gasping and shivering, she looked around the secret room. A wall of computing towers lined one side, next to three technicians silently typing away on their holographic keypads.

"Lose something, Brigitte?" a man asked, coming close.

Karre glanced up from the floor, "No, sir. I have nothing to lose."

"You are extraordinary." The man laughed. Her eyes instantly took in the familiar insignia of the Divinity Corporation. "Finally, we meet."

Karre forced a grin she didn't feel, letting him see her blackened teeth. Knowing what she looked like, she couldn't help but wonder at his choice of words. Extraordinary? "I wasn't aware we were destined to meet, sir. How lucky for me."

"I can assure you when I'm done with you, you won't feel lucky." The man leaned down, studying her face. He had the militant rigidity of a soldier, from the purposeful jerks of his body to the engraved frown lines around his mouth and eyes. His hard gaze bored into her, filling her with cold dread. She, or rather Brigitte, had seen that look in men's eyes before. They were usually the kind to beat a prostitute the second they couldn't get their pricks hard.

"I've heard that one before," she mumbled, pretending to be unimpressed.

"I'm Director Tomes and..." He paused, lifting the small, wrist-wrapping device she'd been searching the liquid-silver wall for. Divinity had the only known source of top-secret inter-dimensional travel technology and they wouldn't like the fact that someone had stolen it. "I have a feeling you know where I am from. It was very naughty of you to borrow our only portable jump prototype. Our scientists will be very interested in seeing how you got it to work. This device will make traveling to uncharted worlds much easier. No more carting around temporary portals. No more perfectly timed pickups from headquarters. No more rescue parties."

*Less supervision so you can do more dark deeds,* Karre silently added.

"We'll be able to explore planes at a much faster rate," Tomes continued, as if it was a good thing.

Just like an infectious disease.

"Sorry, I'm not available for science lessons, but if you'd like to make an appointment, I'm sure I can fit you in," Karre hummed in pretend thought, "uh, never."

"Oh, you're going to be fun to break, my dear," Tomes promised. "Talbert. Get her ready to go."

*One week ago, Dimensional Plane 25, Divinity Prison Hold*
*Because right now, in this moment, she was in deep shit.*

"Sabina, Frannie, Marget, Sulon, Lo Li, Sparkle, Sunset, Twinkles, Saren, Mariska, Marisa, Ms. Pentafore, Lady Pentafore, Madam Pentafore, Domma Pentafore, Prima Pentaf—ugh." Director Tomes sighed heavily, setting down his electronic clipboard. He leaned over, pressing his face close to hers to look into her eyes.

The dank stone room surrounded her, smelling of stale air and dust and now the distinct odor of Tomes' cologne—gun oil and sweat. Her throat tickled, had tickled for the last several hours, but she couldn't cough, couldn't swallow. Karre didn't move. She couldn't. All she could do was to try to block her thoughts from the director's probing questions. Because right now, in this moment, she was in deep shit.

"I'd be here for hours reading all your aliases. There are twenty-three Pentafores alone," Tomes said quietly. Her eyes stayed fixed on him. Short black hair had been cut tight and neat to his head. Though wrinkles fanned from his eyes, his healthy physique gave him the appearance of youth and power.

Director Tomes had her immobilized. Her arms had been tied, her legs cuffed with chains and a truth box affixed to her head. The device worked by inserting microscopic blades into her brain, causing the sensation of fire to explode into her skull. Internally connected to the machine, she knew exactly which images it pried from her thoughts. She heard and saw everything as it tried to project her secrets into holographic reality for the whole room to see.

In theory, the box would project memories in response to the questions Tomes asked her. It tried to force the truth from the wearer's mouth. In most cases, the device worked. In Karre's case, she had told so many lies, lived so many lives, it couldn't decipher her thoughts from her imagination.

"Why don't you just tell me who you are? End this suffering. We already know your real face, your real eyes, your real hair." Tomes tucked a strand of her brunette hair behind her ear. "You're such a pretty thing, too pretty to be caught up in this mess. Why don't you end this? I'm really not a bad guy when you get to know me."

The last thing Karre wanted was to get to know Director Tomes.

"You know most people have a seizure after having this," he paused meaningfully and tapped the box, painfully jolting her head as he punctuated his words, "on for so long."

Karre forced herself to remember the time she'd roundhouse kicked an attacker in the side of the head. The image played out for Tomes. It was as close to a threat as she could manage without the ability to move or speak.

Tomes stood, sighing heavily. "Fine, don't give us a real name. Don't tell us how you got the prototype to work. It doesn't matter."

Karre repeated the memory.

A tech arrived next to Tomes holding a clipboard and whispered into the director's ear.

Tomes turned a sharpened gaze on her and smiled wryly. "Clever, clever girl. I see you've been to Plane 23. No wonder our truth box doesn't work on you. You do realize you are dangerously close to scrambling your brains each time you implant someone else's stolen memories into your head." He grabbed her face, squeezing it in his palms. "How often do you use it? Do you even remember who you are?"

Karre fought the answer to that question as it tried to crawl out of the darkened corner of her brain. Yes, she used the memory implantation device, but only to help her stay in character when she went undercover. When she changed herself like that, the truth of her goals stayed, but it became buried in the thoughts and speech and look of another's life.

*Mistress, mistress, let me come in. I have the pence if you have a quim.*

Brigitte's bawdy, childhood song echoed through her mind and she knew the box played it for her captors. The memory of being a child, hidden in the closet while yet another man sang that song shot through her. The technician looked shocked. Tomes chuckled. Karre knew that it wasn't really her childhood, but she felt the deadness of Brigitte inside her.

"Where you're going, you won't need a name or a past," Tomes said. "You'll just be some man's property. Where you are going, we'll always be able to come and get you, but you will never be able to leave. Have fun in Staria, sweetheart. They're going to love a feisty little thing like you and I guarantee they will put you up for a role you've never played."

# CHAPTER 1

## UNDESIGNATED PLANE NUMBER, OUTSIDE BATTLEWAR CASTLE, STARIA

*Because right now, in this moment, she was a little cramped for space.*

Play dead or fight her way out? As feeling slowly came back to her limbs, Karre tried to discreetly stretch her legs. Her thoughts ran rampant, some her own, some implanted. This part of the process, the coming down from the virtual drug of another person's life, always made her feel a little crazy. She found it best to concentrate on the present during these times. It looked like playing dead was her best option. Running away might be a bit hard, because right now, in this moment, she was a little cramped for space.

Two of Divinity's henchmen dragged her behind them on the ground, carting her in a canvas sack on what felt like a flat board with two small, crooked wheels near her feet. Her body jolted painfully as she bumped over the rutted earth.

Before they left, Karre had watched as Talbert and a couple of others dressed in primitive clothing—long, loose, threadbare tunic shirts over tighter brown pants and boots. Tomes' team of scientists had time to study the prototype she had stolen from them, figuring out how to make it work, while she was busy playing maid.

*Sure, I do all the calibrations and they'll claim it as their achievement. Too bad they don't know the little secret about it yet.*

Their first unofficial, unsanctioned Divinity Corporation trip had been to take her to this strange, primitive plane—Staria. Out of the four-hundred-thirty-six dimensions on Divinity's corporate-approved chart, she didn't recognize this one as one of them. And Karre had pretty much seen them all and more. Unfortunately, she didn't remember the jump since they'd knocked her unconscious.

She wondered how human this reality was. Karre had seen a lot of things in her travels—crazed worshippers bent on human sacrifice, a tribe of women who only ate bugs, people who danced in circles at every sunrise. She'd even seen men who alternated wives daily, moving from home to home until no one knew who fathered a child. Each generation, the offspring would move to different villages to prevent gene contamination.

Logically, she could assume most of the people in her current plane of reality had never even heard of dimensional travel or portals. Divinity wouldn't want her dead in case they decided later that they needed her—whether it was to get her help with the portal device or to try her for crimes not yet known. And what they didn't know about her activities was quite a lot.

Karre bit her lip. Just to see if it would work, she rocked her body as she hit a hard bump, trying to fall off the makeshift cart. She barely made it a quarter turn before a rope jerked her back into position.

So much for escape.

Watching yet another large horse pass by the small hole she had managed to work into the canvas sack, she frowned. Servants carted water along unpaved roads. The sound of voices mixed with the clomping of hooves and the squeaking of carts. Natural light and even more natural smells surrounded her. No motors ran, no flying machines squealed, no electrical hums resounded constantly in the background. Staria was as primitive as could be imagined.

*Well, that's not exactly true. There was that one plane that had nothing but furry monkey men throwing dung at me. What a mistake in dialing that one was.*

Karre snorted at the memory before she could think to stop herself.

"She's awake." She recognized the whine of Talbert's voice.

"She's not going anywhere, not strapped down like that," the other captor answered. She couldn't be sure who he was, but her best guess it was Talbert's leering buddy, Winston. "We're almost there."

"What if she screams?" Talbert inquired.

"Let her. Look around. No one here will care. Why do you think they chose this place?" A boot nudged her hard in the back and low words hissed through the sack. "You hear that, thief? Scream all you want. We have papers here that will land you in Starian prisons for the rest of your life. Behave and you just may be allowed to roam free."

These men didn't know her very well. Karre was not a scream-for-help kind of girl. She had gotten caught and she would get herself out of it. She didn't need a do-gooder trying to save her. Besides, asking for help only meant you ended up owing someone. She would be beholden to none. Though being allowed to roam free sounded much better than being in a prison.

Karre angled her head, inhaling deeply through the hole. The air was fresher than what she had in the bag and she took several breaths before again looking at her surroundings. The motion of her body stopped as her carriers halted in their progress.

Two legs passed close by her peephole. She heard part of a conversation, said in a man's laughing voice, "...your bride. You should be happy."

When she could again see, it was a full view of a masculine hip. Sunlight hit his crotch, outlining the gentle bulge in his tight black breeches. Instantly, she took in the details. Thick hand-stitching ran along the side of his thigh, ending at his narrow waist in tightly knotted laces. The muscles of his thigh flexed as his weight shifted. A strong hand fell down, revealing a scar over the back of his wrist, only to lift back up.

"Duty demands I be here," a deep, resonate voice answered the first. The sound sent a tiny quiver of chills over her body and she wondered if she was remembering someone else's feelings. "I would much rather the king chose a wife of even temperament for me. Then she could be delivered to Spearhead and I would not have to leave my post. These ceremonies are a waste of valuable time."

"Why would you not seek to choose your own bride?" the laughing voice asked.

"If the—" the deep, sexy voice answered. Karre's body was jolted as the two henchmen began to walk once more.

"Ah," she whispered, curiously trying to listen to and watch the conversation. It was of no use. Her captors quickened their pace. She managed to get a fleeting glimpse of the man's chest, but he turned his back to her and his face remained just out of view.

---

"I do not know why you look as if someone is forcing you by knifepoint to claim your bride. You should be happy." Sir Oskar laughed, lifting his hand to wave at a merchant selling racks of dried meat near the edge of the marketplace. The merchant pointed at a slab of dark meat. Oskar waved again, holding up five fingers to indicate the quantity of his purchase without actually talking to the seller.

Sir Vidar of Spearhead sighed, absently watching his friend order supplies for Spearhead Fortress. He placed his hands on his hips and glanced at a couple of men carting a pile of canvas on a slab of wood. They had ridden all the way to Battlewar Castle from the southern borderlands and Vidar determined that they might as well make full use of the trip. He gave a rueful smile, not repeating his thoughts out loud. Many of his people might disagree with him that fetching a bride didn't make full use of a trip.

Bright sunlight mixed with a warm breeze. It was a fine day to walk through the market. Permanent booths of the local tradesmen butted against the inner bailey wall, packed tight with merchandise. Off the main road through town, traveling merchants had set up horse-drawn carts side by side, and sold wares out of the back. They decorated them with brightly colored strips of material to draw the eye. The booths were clustered together to form narrow walkways impossible to pass through on horse, which was why Oskar and Vidar had abandoned their mounts within the inner gates to be stabled near Battlewar Castle.

"If I appear cross it is only because I do not like the wasted time. Alas, duty demands I be here," Vidar answered after a long pause.

He dropped his hands, twisting to watch a woman with flowers dance and sing her way around them. She winked at first Vidar and then Oskar in invitation. Vidar smiled back automatically. Women were scarce in his world. Males became a necessity for battle and their natural evolution seemed to answer the call with more sons than daughters—when they did have children. Their low birthrate wasn't from lack of trying when the warriors were home, but war took them away all too often. Sometimes forever.

By the look of the woman's escorts trailing behind her, she already had at least a couple husbands. If necessity demanded it, he would allow his wife to take another husband, but he would definitely be the first. Sighing, Vidar continued, "I would much rather the king chose a wife of even temperament for me. Then she could be delivered to Spearhead and I would not have to leave my post. These ceremonies are a waste of valuable time."

"Why would you not seek to choose your own bride?" Oskar asked, the humor still thick in his voice. His friend found much amusement in Vidar's orders to find a wife and bring her back to Spearhead Fortress. Vidar had been one of the six chosen for the ceremony because of his position of power at Spearhead. To see their commander married would give hope to the people of his keep. To see a Starian leader married to the first batch of traded Divinity brides would give all Starians hope in the future.

"If the Caniba attack while we are away, I might miss my chance to discover what Sorceress Magda is up to. We are so close. I can feel it in my bones." He absently watched the cart being pulled away. The canvas moved and he frowned, wondering what it was they carted. He wasn't really worried, just curious. All of Battlewar Castle had been designed for war, just like everything else in their land. If these men didn't belong past Battlewar Town's outer bailey wall, they would never have made it past the heavily guarded front gate.

"I will have the supplies loaded and on the way back to the borderlands before you are done with the breeding ceremony," Oskar assured him. "We can ride out as soon as you claim your woman."

"Good." Vidar nodded. "Send some of the men a half-day's ride from here to put up a tent for my bride. With such a quick departure, I will give her whatever comfort I can while we travel—at least the first night."

"Do you think these otherworld women will understand our ways?" Oskar asked.

"A woman is a woman," Vidar answered indifferently. "The gods will give me what they give me. The king showed me the trade agreement. The women must be able to bear children, be in good health, able to do their duty and will know their place. What do I care if they are born in Staria, or are brought through the fairy rings from distant lands, or are traded for with Divinity aliens from another plane of existence? So long as she is not our enemy..." He shrugged, waving his hand in dismissal of the subject.

Okay, so a part of him wanted a bride, but for purely sexual reasons—someone soft and sweet, someone strong and silent, not too pretty, not too bold, not too needy and not too demanding of his time. He had maids to clean his home, cook his food, sew his clothes, but they were all married and off-limits. What he didn't have was a woman to warm his bed.

Vidar had much to give a wife. He was a strong warrior, a capable provider. He had the skills and means to protect his woman, and he lived close to the battlefront with many opportunities to bring honor to his name. "You order the supplies and pay the coin. I'm going to the castle to ready myself for the ceremony."

"It is not until tomorrow," Oskar teased. "How much readiness does a man need?"

"Off with you," Vidar grumbled good-naturedly. With that, he left the market and made his way toward the center of the city to a shorter inner wall that encircled the castle, including the exercise yard where the knights trained, a small chapel, and the stables. Several of the soldiers lifted their hands in greeting but didn't stop him. He didn't want to talk to anyone right now. Seeing the two strange men with the cart hauling their sack toward the servants' entrance, he turned in the other direction.

---

The moment Karre sensed the busy streets were well behind them, she began to squirm inside the sack. She reached for the peephole, tearing it open with a loud rip. She had heard their plan to take her into the servants' entrance of a castle and knew that if she wanted to escape, now would be her chance. Who knew what kinds of horrors awaited her inside this Battlewar Castle? It wasn't like Divinity had to operate under any kind of humanity laws. Her first thought was she was being sold as a sex slave. She never really made it to a second thought.

"Stop her," Talbert yelled to his companion. His red face looked more like a natural condition than the result of the excursion to the castle. Karre bucked up from the cart, ignoring her pained muscles. Like a feral cat, she leapt, striking out with her fingernails. The crashing weight of her body had more effect on him than her hands as he fell back in surprise. Her limbs ached and she didn't get up as fast as she would have liked. Spinning, she found the thick-jowled Winston fumbling with a vial and injector. They'd planned on drugging her again to keep her compliant.

With the cart between them, he could not stop her as she darted into the narrow castle door. Not stopping to consider her route, she ran, turning corner after corner. The long white, shapeless gown covering her body hampered her legs and she jerked the skirt up. At first, she heard the henchmen behind her. It only made her run faster.

It was dumb luck that she managed to run unseen through the maze-like halls. As the sound of pursuit faded, she slowed, trying to get her bearings. Her bare foot stepped on a stone and she gasped, half hopping, half jogging as pain radiated up from her arch. The blue-gray stone walls and minimal decorations made it hard to track where she was going. Wooden doors were spaced evenly on each side with lit torches burning brightly in between.

When the pain didn't lessen, she was finally forced to stop and lean against the wall to check on the injury. The stone had punctured the delicate flesh. Frowning, she realized she had left a blood trail on the cold stone behind her.

Careless. Very Careless. Shit.

Unexpected movement caught her eye and she gasped, dropping her foot. It was too late. A man walked around the corner, crashing into her. Initially, she thought it was one of the guards and made a move to strike. The man grabbed her wrist with lightning fast reflexes, stopping her blow before it even began.

"Hold," he ordered.

Karre blinked in surprise. That voice, a stranger's yet oddly familiar. It was the man she had watched through the peephole. Her breathing deepened and her heart quickened. She wasn't prepared for the reaction and she found herself staring at his broad chest. The smell of him captured her senses. He was earthy, fresh, like the wind through a forest. Heat radiated up her arm from the firm grasp. Her eyes trailed down to that hand, seeing the scar along his wrist. It confirmed what she already knew.

His simple linen over-tunic fell loose to his hips, not covering the pants she had admired earlier. His arms were left bare—thick, muscular arms. A black tattoo wrapped around his upper bicep, the lines bold and confident just like she imagined the man to be.

She bit her lip and pressed her legs tightly together. Firelight danced over his flesh, illuminating every dip, curve and puckered scar. She found her gaze going to the bulge between his thighs—strong thighs surrounded a thickening cock. A woven belt wrapped loosely around his waist, holding a sheathed knife. Her hand flexed and she forcibly stopped herself from taking the belt in hand. Opposite the short blade, his sword hung from a shoulder scabbard that crossed his chest.

"You are dressed as a bride." The statement was simple and matter-of-fact.

Karre blinked, looking up at his face, almost afraid to see the man who went with the voice. Hazel brown eyes met hers. Yellow flecks ringed the iris and spread out like little starbursts in his eyes. Lids lowered in an almost animalistic way.

"I'm dressed as a..." Karre frowned, comprehending the word. "Bride?"

Did he say bride?

"I thought you were to stay in the..."

*Blend in, Karre. Do not draw attention to yourself. Be what you need to be.*

Karre cut off his words, placing her hand over his scarred wrist as the sound of running feet came from behind. "Please, hide me." The words were purposefully breathy and meek. Big strong men usually liked their women mild-mannered and controllable, so she went with it. She lowered her eyes, letting her lashes fall and her lips tremble. "Please, don't let them hurt me."

The hand on her tightened. The man glanced back and forth down the hall. "Come with me." He ushered her into a nearby room, quietly closing the door behind them.

Karre leaned her ear to the door, unable to help smiling at the sound of two henchmen running past. Pushing away from the wood, she turned. "Thank you."

His narrowed eyes watched her for a moment before turning his attention to the door. "Are you in trouble? Who are those men? Are they—?"

"We should stay here," Karre interrupted. She took quick inventory of the room. It was a sleeping chamber complete with trunk, small bed and a disturbing amount of weaponry hanging on the wall. "Just for a little bit until they're gone."

"Who are—"

"You were saying something about a bride? You're here to get married, right?" She kept her eyes wide and innocent, all the time taking in every detail of his reaction. Pulling at her waist, she discreetly drew the material so it pulled snug to her chest and hips. The motion had the desired effect. The man's eyes went to her breasts.

"Yea, I am one of the firsts. The king has ordered me to the ceremony to choose a bride." His breathing deepened.

"Choose? You don't know who you will pick?" How peculiar.

"No. I do not." He shook his head in denial as the tip of his tongue appeared along the bottom edge of his mouth. "I do not have an understanding with a woman. I will choose who the gods will me to."

"Who the gods will you to?"

"Yea. I am told that those men who do not have an understanding with a woman are filled with an urge by the gods during the ceremony. In that moment, they know who to choose."

*An urge? Is that what they're calling it nowadays?*

She tried not to laugh. Karre found herself looking at his mouth with lips so full and firm. She bet he could kiss a woman breathless. How long had it been since she'd been kissed? Two months? Five? Ten? Twenty? Days ran together, blending into months and years. Logic and reason told her now was not the time to fulfill her neglected lust. Now was the time to keep a level head and make good an escape. Now was the time to find a portal out of there.

Logic and reason were very poor defenses against lust.

"So tonight is your last night as a free man?" She licked her lips so they would glisten.

"No, I am not to be imprisoned." He frowned, confused.

Karre did laugh that time. She took a bold step for him. Why not give in to her base desires—if the desires were really hers and not some residual impulse from someone else's implanted emotion. Remembering how Brigitte wasn't really interested in men, she pushed all echoing thoughts from her mind. Tonight was hers, no one else's.

Karre needed to bide her time before going back out into the hall and what better way than with a virile hunk of a man? It wasn't like she would see him again. It wasn't like sex with him would compromise any objective. "I meant your last night free from the bonds of an arranged marriage."

"Then tonight is your last night free as well," he returned. "Your clothing indicates that you are to be a chosen bride."

Karre didn't care what her outfit said. She would be no man's bride. "Perhaps no one will choose me."

He laughed. His entire body shook with the force of it. "No bride has ever gone unchosen."

"Hm." She kept her expression steady, not finding the same humor he did in the idea of her future as a Starian wife. "Then we should not waste our last night of freedom talking."

"You are part of Divinity's trade agreement," he said, as if suddenly understanding her strangeness. "Forgive me, I should have realized since only women from the trade agreement are going to be at this ceremony. That is why you speak so strangely. You are not from Staria."

"Trade agreement?" Interesting. Very interesting. Though hardly surprising. Nothing about the corporation surprised her anymore. With an actual Divinity trade agreement in place there would have to be portal travel to and from this world. Director Tomes might want her to believe she was dumped on a primitive plane to be forgotten, but where there was a portal, there was a way out.

"Yea." He nodded. "You are here in trade for the blue mineral water that runs in our underground springs."

"Am I?" She arched a brow, listening closely. Perhaps a quick romp wouldn't be the only thing she got from his warrior man.

"I am happy to see you do not look pale and weak like the first of your people to arrive. I have heard stories from the men who were there that day when the Divinity aliens first approached us in the midst of battle. We almost slaughtered them where they stood for being allies to the Caniba."

"The Caniba?" She licked her lips again, surprised by his forthcoming conversation.

"Our enemy. They are a dishonorable, disgusting people who eat the flesh of men and think only of pleasing their overlords. The most deadly of which is Sorceress Magda. Her army drinks the poison of snakes and would follow her orders into a pit of fire to be burned alive." His face darkened into a temperate rage and he looked past her.

Karre grimaced. The man surely knew how to kill a seductive mood. Didn't he realize she was flirting with him? "Surely they are not so bad as all that."

"And worse," he swore. His eyes practically sparkled with the passion of his convictions. "There is no peace with the Caniba, only war. It is my self-given task to discover where the sorceress' encampment lies and I will gladly die for that information, for it will be a great victory for my people. I believe I am getting closer. We suspect she is in the Hanging Forest, very near Spearhead Fortress. That is where I live."

"Well," Karre tried to sound cheerful, "good for you. It is always nice to have a purpose to fight for."

Crazy barbarian.

"Thank you, Lady, ah...?"

Karre ignored the prompt for her name and hurriedly said, "So, how did this war of yours start?"

"It has been that way from the beginning of time and will always be so long as they live. That is the role our gods have given us."

*Wow, and the foreplay just keeps coming,* she thought sarcastically. *Well, I did ask.*

He crossed his arms over his chest, dominating the room with his stance. "Methinks we get on quite well, my lady."

"Yes." She forced a wide smile. "Quite."

"This is good." He smiled, as a tentative, searching expression crossed his features.

*Blend in, Karre. Be what he needs to see. That's it. Smile wider. Lower your lashes.*

"What is your name, soldier?" Karre broke their eye contact, not liking his probing gaze. He looked at her as if he were trying to read her soul. She had a feeling he'd be very talented at prying secrets out of someone, should he set his mind to it.

"Sir Vidar of Spearhead."

Karre tried not to chuckle. She gravitated toward him, not taking a direct path as she made her way closer to the bed. Her heart beat faster and she felt a little dizzy. Why did he have to look at her like that, like he could peel away all her armor? All her defenses?

She touched the bed. Everything in her told her to run. Karre normally trusted her instincts. They had served her so well in the past.

But his smell was inside her head and his gold-flecked eyes wouldn't stop looking at her as if he could see within her soul. She ran her fingers through her messily upswept hair, pulling a dark strand forward, trying to get some measure of comfort by seeing which character she was playing now. Her fingers bumped the special, hidden hairpin tangled up in the locks, only recognizing it because she knew it was there. Otherwise, it felt like real hair until twisted straight. Not even Tomes had detected it.

It was her hair—long, brunette, wavy. No wig. No dye. No drug-altered state. She touched her face. No fake pustules. No thick foundation makeup. She bumped her fingernail against her front teeth. No blackened smudges. Maybe that was why she felt so exposed and nothing had even happened. The picture she showed him was all her.

"Methinks your pursuers are gone. If you give me their names, I will see they are punished for scaring you. I am sure they saw your clothes and thought to press their suit should you not be chosen at the ceremony by the firsts."

"I don't want to go out quite yet." This might be her closest chance to feel normal, to see what it was like to be with a man as Karre—not James or Linnie or Sparkle or Brigitte. Then again, she could just stop making excuses for wanting Vidar and could do what her body had been urging her to do from the first moment she'd heard his deep, sexy voice.

*None of this matters. None of it. Reality is merely a perception. Each plane flows into another until nothing is real. Nothing is permanent. Nothing matters.*

Karre had seen many planes, many existences, and only a few things stayed the same. She could only depend on herself. No matter how noble a person appeared, they would ultimately do the selfish thing and nothing ever lasted.

"Did they injure you, my lady?" Vidar reached as if to examine her and stopped mid-motion. He furrowed his brow, doubtful.

"Starian men respect women—we do not hurt them. If someone..."

Karre looked up at him and his words trailed off. "Vidar." She let his name roll off her tongue on a purr.

"Y-yea?"

"You sound like a very honorable man." Karre lifted her hand, letting her fingers glide up the center of his chest. He stiffened beneath her touch, his piercing eyes darting down to where they touched. Animalistic fire radiated off him, jumping from his nerves to hers. She swayed toward him. "And you look like a very strong warrior."

Karre bit her lip, pressing her fingers more fully into him. The contours of his chest molded into her palm, unyielding and hard beneath his tunic. His heart beat a steady rhythm, urging hers to join in.

"And this pleases you?"

"Oh, yes, very much." She nodded. "It pleases me very, very much."

If ever there was a sign from the gods, this had to be it—a bride finding him the day before the ceremony, appearing meek, asking him for help so that he might protect her. She was much more beautiful than he would have asked for. In his experience, women...

Vidar tried not to let his thoughtful frown show. Well, in his experience watching other men's experiences, beautiful women were more trouble and more demanding.

As she took a deep breath, he found his eyes moving from the hand on his chest to where her breasts molded the white material. The generous globes would fill his hands to overflowing. His already half-interested cock twitched and he felt all logical thoughts draining with the blood from his brain to fill his member.

Shiny, brunette waves framed her face, showcasing the brown of her eyes and the fullness of her pink lips. Perhaps a bit of beauty was not so bad—if that's what the gods wanted for him. Who was he to question when she looked up at him like that? When she licked her mouth? When she leaned closer, knotting her fingers in his shirt?

What else was this encounter if not an inspection of him as a potential husband? Could he blame a woman for campaigning beforehand? For actively searching for a man with honor and a valiant war record? In fact, Vidar respected it greatly. Decisions such as marriage should not be taken lightly. It was important to be assured that your partner was of good stock. That was why men made the final choice, because women sometimes got too emotional—at least according to his late father.

She tugged up on his shirt playfully. "Let me see you, warrior. Let me see how strong you are."

Vidar did not hesitate as he pulled his shirt over his head. His kind had never been shy about sex, but still a little guilt nagged the back of his mind. He was to choose a bride and he didn't know if it would be this woman. Though hardly unheard of, what he was doing right now, in this moment on this day, wasn't encouraged. His stomach tightened and his cock lifted to the point it ached. The woman could belong to another on the morrow.

But not today.

"Mm," she moaned low in her throat, letting her delicately long fingers trail on his chest. "You are a warrior, aren't you? Thick, big," she paused and her fingers skated down to his waistband, haphazardly following battle scars, "solid." Her breathing visibly deepened and she moved around him, as if inspecting him for her own personal army. "I'll bet you know how to move, hmm?"

"Would my lady care to examine my weapon?" Unashamed, he reached for the laces at his hip while kicking out of his short boots. He pushed his breeches from his hips before lifting his feet out of them. Vidar kicked them aside, liking of the feel of air on his flesh as he stood naked for her. She came fully around him, pausing as she looked at his towering cock.

"I see that it's not just the height and breadth of your people that are big, my lord," she said.

"I am sir," he corrected, "not a lord, though I do manage my own manor. It is very prosperous."

"Do you now?" She gave him a secretive smile.

Before he could inquire about it, she took his cock in her hand

and stroked. He inhaled sharply. The woman pressed her mouth to his chest, brushing light kisses along the contours of his muscles. Moaning lightly, she licked at his nipples.

"You are so warm," she said, moving up to nip at his collarbone. She tightened her fist on his shaft. "Why don't you lie down on the bed?"

It wasn't a question. Like a knight untried in battle, he quickly made his way to the bed and flipped onto his back. His eyes devoured her, wondering what she would do next. He'd been with women, but they were always camp followers, respected whores who pleased the soldiers they followed. Unfortunately, their numbers were few and the soldiers many. Often, after they chose a partner for the night, they would get straight to the matter. It seemed it was the men who always wanted to take things slow, to make it last.

She started to crawl toward him, but he stopped her before her second knee hit the bed. "Take off the gown."

The woman brought her foot back down to the floor and grabbed the gown. Slowly, almost teasingly, she pulled it up. Inch by glorious inch, she uncovered her shapely legs. Vidar gripped the fur pelt beneath him on the bed. Next came her thighs, agonizing in their leisurely reveal. Then, finally, the heart of her sex guarded by a strip of soft, dark curls. Vidar began to grab his cock only to stop. He didn't want to come too fast. He wanted her to do it.

Mm, hips, round and soft and unscarred. Her flesh was so smooth and tan, so perfectly shaped. His mouth became dry as he waited to see her generous breasts. Their size was unmistakable under her gown. He wanted to grab them, bury his face in them until he couldn't breathe. He wanted to fuck her pussy while he sucked her nipples. Some of the knights talked of legs or eyes or a woman's fine backside. Vidar had always been partial to great pair of breasts. His grip tightened on the bed.

Oh, the bottom curves. If he could have moved, he'd have surged forward to rip the gown from her body like a madman. Then, finally, the wait was over. She tugged the gown over her head and threw it aside. The motion tousled her hair around her shoulders, but he barely noticed. His eyes were fixed on the large, dark nipples on two very round globes. They were bigger than he'd thought, if that was even possible.

All thoughts left him as she leaned to crawl onto the bed. He watched them bounce and move, mesmerized. "You are...mm."

"I will take that to mean you like what you see, my sir."

"Oh, yea." He didn't correct her misuse of his title. At this moment, she could call him anything she wanted. By all the bloody swords in battle, she could demand of him anything she wanted. The woman straddled his knees, swaying gently as she reached her hands over her head to stretch. He licked his lips, hungry to test the soft texture of the globes in his mouth. "I wish for you to finish me now."

"You do, do you?" She gave him a slow, controlling grin. Raking her nails up his thighs, she stopped when she reached his hips. His cock stood tall and she leaned over him. Opening her mouth as she looked up at him, she stretched her neck long so he could watch as his cock was swallowed in the valley of her breasts. It was the most erotic, most arousing thing he'd ever seen. The soft mounds caressed him gently and his hips jerked. Her weighted hands pressed him down so he couldn't press up.

Vidar's gaze narrowed in on what she was doing. He was completely captivated. His stomach tightened as he rolled forward to reach for her chest. He pushed her breast into his cock, squeezing it as he rubbed the softness to his turgid length. It was unlike anything he'd ever felt—soft like a pussy, but dry and enveloping.

"You're a naughty warrior, aren't you?" she whispered. He began to deny it when she shifted her weight and pressed her arms to make her breasts surround his penis. "Aren't you a bad one? Do you like it when I do this?"

"Yea." He could barely speak. Vidar fell back, too immersed in sensations as she worked her pliable flesh over him. Thrusting up, he fucked her like he'd never fucked anyone else, would never have thought to try.

"Does the bad man warrior need to be punished?" She squeezed him tighter.

"Yea, my lady. Punish me." He didn't know what he was saying, only that he needed her to continue. His balls tightened and he felt like he was close to coming. Suddenly, she pulled off him and he nearly lurched off the bed at the sudden lack of contact. He'd been so close and now his cock throbbed with the need to squirt his seed all over her.

"I agree," she purred like some sort of feral cat. She scratched his hips, avoiding the one piece of him that desperately needed to feel her. "You do need to be punished."

"What is my crime?" he demanded, almost desperate.

"Here it is the night before you're to take a wife and you're in here with me. I'd say that's very bad of you, my sir." She thrust a finger into her mouth, licking it as he watched.

"Please..." He started to reach for her. Something about the way she spoke didn't evoke shame, but a forbidden sense of desire.

"Good, I like it when you beg me." She scratched him harder. He nearly came undone.

"Please, finish me," he instantly begged.

She sucked her finger, thrusting it in and out of her mouth several times.

"Please, lean over once more," he panted. His heart hammered in his chest.

Releasing the finger with a loud *pop*, she leaned over. This time, she licked the mushroomed tip of his penis to taste him. The thought of those full lips around his shaft made him lurch up. He grabbed her head and thrust at the same time, bringing her roughly down on his cock. When he hit the back of her throat, he moaned, only half way inside.

"Suck me like you did your finger," he commanded. Sweat beaded his flesh and he felt as if he ran the whole of Staria.

She began to and he loosened his hold. But the satisfied smile died on his mouth as she knocked his hands aside and pulled off. She artfully avoided his attempt to pull her mouth back down. "Tsk, tsk. Naughty, naughty, eager knight trying to bruise my delicate mouth with his big weapon."

"Woman," he warned, the threatening tone ripping from his

throat. He couldn't think, couldn't see beyond the bounce of her chest, the fullness of her lips.

"What are you going to do, my sir? You going to pin me down and fuck me? You going to teach me a lesson? Show me just how naughty you are?"

Before the last word left her mouth, he had her flipping through the air to land on her back. Her breath left her in a big rush of air. He fumbled between her legs, pushing her thighs open to make room for his hips as he angled his cock toward the glistening heat of her pussy.

The second the tip of his cock felt moisture, he shoved forward. She gasped, closing her eyes as he fitted himself deep. He didn't expect her cavern to be so tight on him, clamping him as he stormed her keep. He groaned, rocking very slightly as he felt the hard grip.

"I have never had a woman feel so..." He moved his hips in a small circle. "It is as if you have never been stretched by a man. I find it very pleasurable."

She held on to his neck, kneading the muscles. He continued with his shallow thrusts, enjoying the pleasure of her body. Bracing his weight with one hand, he cupped a breast. Her eyes stayed closed, but she was panting and shivering as he moved.

"Give me your name," he said, captivated by the woman beneath him.

"Karre," she answered with a gasp. Her eyes flew open as she looked at him, but she didn't say more as her climax hit her hard.

Vidar moaned, finally letting his body spill over. He jerked out of her, spilling his seed onto the bed. With an exhausted sigh, he rolled next to her on the small bed. The fur stuck to his hot, sweaty back but he didn't care.

"Lady Karre," he said, smiling. "I will remember that."

# CHAPTER 2

*Because right now, in this moment, she was...Lady Karre?*

Karre? Did she actually tell him her name was Karre? What in the idiotic, brain-dead, body-numbing, pleasure-laden hell had she been thinking? Karre?!

Clearly, she had been taken aback by the way he moved his body. Or perhaps it was the way he looked at her, rather her breasts, with liquid heat in his hazel gaze. The gold flecks tried to lure her in with their animalistic charm. There had to be a reason for her lunacy. Because right now, in this moment, she was...Lady Karre?

Shit!

*Relax, Karre. No one will ever know it's your real name. They'll think it a lie like all the others. Divinity would never believe you were stupid enough to use a real name on their "prison realm".*

*Why couldn't I have just said Suzetta? Or Majie?*

*Shit, shit, shit!*

"Tell me of your world, Lady Karre," Vidar said, his voice filled with the leisured, sated drawl of a satisfied man. His finger trailed over her arm. "I'm curious to hear of the other realms. Is yours like this one?"

*Shit!*

She pushed up off the bed with an energy she didn't feel. Survival instinct gave her the fuel she needed to fake nonchalance. Her first idea had been to control him, to make him want her, desire her. That had worked all too well. Why did she have to go and say her real name? Each time he said it, she felt a little sick to her stomach because his voice was low and delicious and rumbled the syllable just right. That word was more intimate than any other because no one knew it.

"My home world is a plane like any other," she answered, reaching into her hair to ensure the hidden hairpin was still artfully tangled in the locks. She set to work pulling the locks up off her neck to cool off. "You know how it is. Every plane is just the same world with a different conclusion. People pretty much talk the same—sometimes they look the same. Weather is the same."

"But I have heard of some wondrous devices—boxes that talk, fire that does not burn. I've even heard tales of how one plane has these contraptions that heat your food within seconds."

"You don't say." She had stopped listening. Grabbing her gown, she pulled it over her head and made her way hastily for the door. "I think the halls should be clear now. Thanks for entertaining me. It's been, ah, yeah."

"But, wait—" Vidar demanded behind her. She heard him move on the bed. "Where are you going?"

"Ah, now, let's not get all sentimental, warrior man." She pulled the large metal handle. "Have a nice life and a wonderful wedding. May your bride be...yeah."

With that half-hearted wish, she slipped from the room.

"Getting to know the locals, are you?" Winston asked.

Karre turned, ready to fight, only to run face-to-chest into her henchman captor. The man stood a head above her but had the broad, medically enhanced physique any thug would be proud of. He grabbed her arms tightly. Her eyes rounded. How had they found her? As if to answer her, the bottom of her foot throbbed.

She glanced at the floor. Spots of dried blood led to where they stood. How could she have been so careless?

She opened her mouth to call for Vidar for help. If anything, he'd provide a distraction so she could get away. Winston grunted. Talbert shoved the needle into her leg. The sharp pain was followed by an almost immediate numbness.

"He-lp," she whispered, the plea hissing from her parted lips as she dropped into blackness.

---

What exactly just happened? Vidar frowned at the door as he jerked on his clothing. Grabbing his boots, he tucked them under his arm as followed Lady Karre to demand some answers.

The hall was empty and he went to look around the closest turn. She wasn't there. Vidar growled and threw his boot against the passageway wall. It thudded hard before falling to the stone.

*You're a naughty warrior, aren't you?*

Now, with her disappearance, the once playful words seemed mocking to him. She had demanded he turn over an ounce of control to her and he'd done it—thoughtlessly, eagerly, willingly.

*Naughty, naughty, eager knight trying to bruise my delicate mouth with his big weapon.*

She had definitely mocked him. Was this a game to her? Or perhaps a test that he had failed?

*Here it is the night before you're to take a wife and you're in here with me. I'd say that's very bad of you, my sir.*

Did she consider his succumbing to her to signify lack of honor and faithfulness on his part? But what of her? She was to be married and she had seduced him within moments of running into him.

Irritation completely overrode the pleasure he'd experienced with release. When she walked out, her eyes had been distant, calculating, nothing like the seductive woman who'd enticed him to her bed.

Thinking of it, he groaned. He couldn't get her breasts out of his mind—full, soft, wickedly perfect.

*Naughty, naughty, eager knight.*

---

"The faster you make them come, the less time you must spend in their presence," the servant whispered.

Karre tried not to chuckle. The woman didn't know how true that was. Or did running out on a man after sex count as an example of what the woman was implying?

Sera's white corset top squeezed her healthy waist and thrust up two very generous breasts. Long blue skirts billowed around her legs. She stared at Karre before turning her consideration to the half-dozen other women in the prison cell. The smell of freshly baked bread caught Karre's attention as she took a loaf and bit into it. Director Tomes hadn't been big on the feeding of his prisoner.

"That is all they want—a vessel to find release," Sera continued with her advice. "Do not expect tenderness, but if you don't deny them, if you don't resist, you'll be treated fairly enough. And if you give them sons, you'll be greatly rewarded. Life here is not so bad."

Karre tuned everyone out, eyeing the guards with Sera. They barely seemed to notice her. She really had no interest in life here, or in the other women in her cell, or in providing sons for warrior men. What she did have an interest in was escape. And, as past experience taught her, she would need to get ahold of some valuables to do it.

A loaf of bread was shoved through the bars, close to Karre's head. She blinked, glaring at Sera, as the woman talked over her. "I'm telling you how to best survive this place, please, listen. Spreading your thighs is easy enough a task for a decent life. Don't bring trouble upon yourself. Let them find release. They are not such boars when they get what they want."

One of the guards sniffed in amusement. The sound was so soft that Karre didn't think the others heard it. Apparently, he was well aware of the scam the guys had going in this place. Tell all the women that if they didn't have sex, the men would become overrun with fierce emotions they couldn't control.

Very clever of them in a primitive, completely predictable male kind of way.

Sera finally left, taking the guards with her. Karre reached into her hair, finding the small hairpin in the upswept mess. A few strands pulled from her scalp as she released it. Giving the other women a once-over, she set her half-eaten loaf on the floor and didn't hesitate to kneel beside the bars. She reached through them, turned the hairpin so it became a hard lock pick, closed her eyes, and inserted the end of the hairpin into the lock and began feeling her way around to see how the mechanism worked.

One of the prisoners whimpered and Karre willed her to keep her mouth shut. They'd already been warned about annoying the guards. Someone leaned close and Karre peeked to see the tall, black-haired lady at her side. The woman carried herself well, as if used to fighting. Like Karre, each prisoner slash assumed bride wore the white, shapeless dress with bare feet. Behind the fighter, a redhead picked at the sleeve of her gown like it contained buried treasure within the thick weave.

"Put it up," the black-haired beauty warned under her breath.

Karre thrust the hairpin back into her hair seconds before a burly man in a hard leather jerkin and dark breeches appeared before them. A long, thin scar traced down the side of his cheek, giving him the increasingly familiar battle-worn look all the other men seemed to favor. She forced the image of a naked Vidar out of her mind. She wouldn't be able to concentrate if she allowed fantasies of the knight to penetrate her brain.

Metal diamonds plated the leather, creating a symmetrical pattern over the guard's thick chest. Karre considered kicking him through the bars so he would be knocked unconscious on the blue-gray stone behind him. The pattern made such a nice target, after all. The man crossed his arms over his chest. "The flaxen one and the crying one. They do not carry themselves well. Take them and give them the philter."

"What?" one of the prisoners screamed. "No, wait! I'll be good. I swear I'll be good. Please, don't hurt me. Please, I'll do anything you want. Do you want me to make you come? I will. I swear I will.

I'll do you all!" To disprove her point, her body began to shake and she started bawling anew.

"Oh, please." Karre rolled her eyes. Like having sex with a big, handsome man was anything to be afraid of.

*Oh no, please stop, Vidar,* her thoughts mocked, mimicking the pleading woman's high-pitched voice in her head, *I don't want to have an orgasm.*

The barred door opened and four men filed inside. Karre stepped back, out of their way. Two grabbed the now sobbing woman and dragged her out. A blonde screamed, kicking and fighting as tears streamed down her face.

As soon as the men were gone, Karre went back to work, her face set as she tried to feel around the lock with her hairpin.

"You won't be able to open it," the redhead said, looking up from her preoccupation with her sleeve. "Even if you did, there would be no escape. You'd have to fight through the warriors' hall, out of the guarded castle gates and run three strikes over open prairie until you reach the forest. Should you survive the wild beasts that live there, you'd soon find yourself prisoner to an even more vicious race of creatures—monsters so fierce and depraved they'll make you beg for death. Trust me. With the war going on in this forsaken place, we're in the better of the two sides."

"Who are you that we should trust what you say?" Karre inquired. Just a little bit longer and she would have it. If they would all just shut up and let her concentrate.

"Name's Paige," the redhead answered.

"Lilith," another said.

"What do they want with us?" the black-haired fighter added. "Oh, I'm called Jayne."

"They want us to be their whores," Paige said. "They don't call it that, but that's what they want—a subservient woman to rub their feet and spread her legs. If you don't, they get pissed and the whole lot of them stares at you like you are demon spawn incarnate and blames you for your chosen warrior's bad mood. It's either fuck them and suck them, or you're treated like the bottom rung of Starian society."

"Again, I ask, why should we trust you? We don't know you." Karre didn't need some stranger giving her advice. "You could be a plant sent here to make us behave with horror stories of what's beyond the tree line."

*Perhaps the portal out of here is beyond the tree line.*

"I don't care if you trust me, but I know what I'm talking about. This isn't my first time in a cage." Paige tilted her head back and sighed. "They'll be coming to get us soon."

"What's your name, locksmith?" Jayne inquired.

Karre had a rule, one she'd learned the hard way. Never give two names when on a plane. All too often, paths would cross and lies would be found out. "Karre."

It sounded strange to say the name out loud.

*Lady Karre, I will remember that.*

An involuntary chill worked along her spine, settling uncomfortably hot near her pussy. The man did have a sexy voice.

"Well, Karre," Jayne said. "I don't think we have much of a choice. If we all work together, maybe we stand a chance. Now, I don't know how we all got here and at this point I don't think it matters, but I do know I'm not staying to spend the rest of my life as some guy's sex toy."

"I agree." Lilith stood, as if hoping Jayne would have a logical solution they could use. "We need a plan."

"Fine," Karre grumbled, still thinking of Vidar and wondering how she could manage to get him back into her bed for one more go. Seconds wasn't usually her style, but there was something about the big warrior man that sent moisture flooding out of her pussy.

Paige shook her head in denial. "Don't look to me to join your little band. You're only fooling yourselves. I've been to the Hanging Forest. I made it all the way to the Starian borders and I've seen the creatures that wait beyond."

"What about a dimension jump?" Lilith asked. "Does anyone know if this place has inter-dimensional travel technology?"

Karre stiffened, pausing in her lock picking.

"A what?" Paige furrowed her brow in confusion.

When it became apparent no one knew, Karre answered, "Staria?

It's too primitive. They don't have the technology here. I got a glimpse of the castle when they brought me to this cell. Through a door I saw servants cart water from a well in buckets and the drive wasn't paved. No artificial lights or motorized vehicles. Though there were several large horses."

"I've never been here," Jayne contributed, "but I'm inclined to agree from what I've observed. These prisons don't use lasers or shocks."

"Someone's coming." Karre pulled her arms out from between the bars. She thrust her lock-picking tool back into her upswept hair.

A new guard arrived dressed similarly to the other men she had seen. His nose had a crook across the bridge. He frowned. "Only three new ones?"

"It's all they sent us," said the man who'd ordered the other two women away.

"How's it going, Edward?" Paige taunted, her face hardening to hide all emotion. Karre looked at her in surprise. Maybe little red had some spunk after all. "I see the nose is healing nicely."

"Lady Paige," Edward growled, glaring at her as if he wanted to pull the sword from his waist and run her through.

"Open the door, Eddie," Paige ordered. "Let me break it again."

Edward grumbled but didn't answer.

"I thought there were five new." Another of Edward's fellow barbarians joined them, completely ignoring Paige's comment.

"What's wrong, Brock? Don't I count anymore in your little ledger?" Paige sneered.

"You are not new," Brock stated, frowning at her in disapproval. "Your lord is waiting for you and I do hope his punishment is harsh."

Paige's smirk faltered. Brock grinned victoriously.

"You already have one of these guys?" Karre hissed, grabbing Paige's arm. The woman didn't look at her.

"Two were not suitable. They were taken away," Edward answered. "Too weak."

"Three will have to do." Brock sighed. Karre arched a brow,

slightly offended by his downtrodden tone. As the two men walked off, he added, "I'll tell my Sera to make ready."

A long silence filled the cell, broken only when Paige whispered, "Ladies, welcome to Battlewar Castle."

---

Vidar pumped his hand over his cock, biting his lip. He couldn't help it. Images of Lady Karre danced in his thoughts, driving him mad. He wanted to kiss her. He wanted to strangle her. He wanted to throw her up against a wall and fuck her.

By all the bloody battleaxes in Staria, he just wanted her.

One taste wasn't enough. He leaned against the wall, bracing his weight with one hand as he pleasured himself with the other. His guest chambers were sparse, like most of the rooms in Battlewar, containing a trunk, a table, an adequate bed, a cushioned chair, a lit fireplace and a wall filled with weapons. There was no need for finery. He wouldn't be staying long.

Vidar knew the necessity of the breeding ceremony for their people, but, as the esteemed Lord Sorin often said, "Nothing in the process of prancing women before the warriors, who pick them based on an urge, guarantees a well-made match." He was inclined to agree. If he chose a bride based on an urge, he'd be taking Lady Karre home with him this night.

The longer his kind went without the exhausting pleasure of the bed, the more their moods were said to be altered—or so their women complained. He pumped his calloused hand harder and faster, trying to get rid of that base urge. Every logical part told him claiming Karre would be a mistake. She was beautiful, dangerous, manipulative. The more he lay awake the night before thinking of her, analyzing every second of their time together, the more he knew she wouldn't be the type of mate he sought.

Vidar switched hands, adjusting his weight. After coming three times that morning, his body wasn't finishing as quickly. He planned on ridding himself of all desire so he'd not be swayed by her pretty face.

He felt the end coming and turned, pressing his back into the wall as he went at it with both hands. Vidar cupped his balls, pumping his tight fist harder and faster. Oh, but how her pussy gripped him. And those soft breasts. Moist, sucking lips. So wet. So sweet. So hot.

The muscles in his stomach tightened. "*Agh*," he cried out roughly as he came. Breathing hard, he looked at the bed where the silken garments had been laid out by a maid. Tradition demanded grooms dress in the shiny clothing. Vidar sighed heavily. It was an odd reminder of what was coming—silk where he was used to seeing armor.

Crossing over to a basin of water, he washed his hands and swore he heard Lady Karre's mocking laughter. He hit the water surface hard with the flat of his palm, making it splash over the sides and onto his knee. The trail tickled as it brushed against him, just like her hair had done when she crawled over his thighs.

Vidar braced his hands on the small table before forcibly pushing up. His cock stirred, as if mindlessly searching for Lady Karre to comfort it. With a growl, he grabbed the shaft almost angrily. It looked as if he'd be coming for a fifth time before the ceremony began.

# CHAPTER 3

*Because right now, in this moment, she was getting married.*

Marriage. It was never something Karre had considered. Well, she had considered a fake engagement once, but that really didn't count since she would have gotten off the plane before saying her vows. Here, now, standing in the main hall of Battlewar Castle, she realized there was no way out—no matter how often she searched her rope-bound wrists looking for the portable jump prototype—because right now, in this moment, she was getting married.

A crescendo of laughter and cheering resounded over the hall. The boisterous uproar had been going on for some time, as excitement pumped through the crowd. Women wiggled and pranced in their tight corset tops and billowing skirts, trying to entice the men. Some of the gigantic knights wore lightweight tunics, others leather jerkins like the guards, others light chainmail and pieces of armor, and still others wore no shirt at all. Big metal goblets had been set before them, next to matching pitchers, on the long rows of rectangular tables. Muscles bulged, littered with puckered scars and tattooed designs.

The light came from a large fireplace on the far side of the room. Like most things in this place, it was immense and towering. Woven tapestries lined the walls in strips of material, showcasing coats-of-arms and various symbols. Karre looked around, studying the artifacts, wondering how much they'd be worth in trade.

*Not now. Blend in.*

Karre turned her attention to the head table, set high above the hall at the end of the room as a place of honor for the bridegrooms. Out of all the ceremonies on all the planes, she had never seen something as simple as the Starian marriage. Already two of the women had been claimed. Karre frowned, trying to remember their names —Jayne and Lilith. She hadn't really been paying close attention from the moment it became evident they wouldn't be able to help her escape. The women had discussed fighting, but nothing came of it.

An oversized, ill-tempered man they called Lord Sorin pointed at Lilith, stating the single word, "Mine," and, with that, they'd been married. Next, Lord Ronen, Sorin's brother, pointed at Jayne. "Mine." And so, too, was Jayne wed.

In a way, Karre respected it. No pretense, no lies, just a simple point of the finger, a single uttered word and it was done. There were no promises of never-ending love, of happily-ever-after, of enduring whatever.

She looked at Vidar, meeting his guarded gaze. Karre tried to smile at him, but he quickly turned his eyes away. Her smile fell. It wasn't like she wanted to be married to him, she assured herself. Why should she care who chose her? All the men appeared to be well-built and made of muscles. Sir Vidar wasn't so special. He just happened to be the first one of them she'd run into. Besides, it wasn't like she was going to actually honor vows she didn't agree to.

Karre watched him carefully, taking in his every movement while trying to appear as if she wasn't. Vidar looked at her again and she pointedly ignored him. Two could play his game. She glanced at Paige before turning to look over her shoulder at the watching crowd. A grinning redhead in bright green sank beneath a long table filled with knights. By the way her man's head rolled back and his hand slipped under the table, it was clear the woman was indiscreetly sucking the guy's cock. Karre saw a couple of others do the same around the hall. Oddly enough, no one seemed to notice the bold behavior.

When no one spoke to claim Paige or herself, she turned back to the table. Four men remained, presumably one had already chosen Paige. If she wasn't mistaken, it had to be the man who stood first in line by the way he tried too hard not to look directly at the woman. Each bridegroom wore a different-colored long tunic, reaching to the knees, over tight brown breeches. Woven belts were knotted at their waists, the end straps hanging along the right thighs. All were strong, with proud eyes and humorless expressions. The first limped when he walked, but by the way he stared at the other bride, Karre easily assumed he belonged to Paige. Remaining were Sir Vidar, a brown-blond man with a pronounced scar on his cheek, and a bearded knight with irritated eyes.

*Blend in, Karre. Right now you are a bride.*

If bold behavior was what these men wanted, then that was exactly what she would give them.

"Oh, all right, I'll start," Karre announced, drawing attention to herself. Paige seemed almost relieved. She grinned at the bridegrooms and batted her lashes, doing her best not to look too long at Vidar as she gave the others equal attention. "My name is Karre. I like jewels, riches, power, servants, fine clothes and to be worshiped daily." She paused and arched a challenging brow, "I also like to get my way. Any takers?"

The brown-blond warrior looked horrified by her announcement and recoiled in his seat. He ran his fingers through his short hair before scratching the scar on his cheek.

"Come on, gentlemen, don't be shy," Karre strode before them, feeling very much like an auctioneer selling herself. She carried her bound arms like the situation was an everyday occurrence. "I only bite when I want to."

Sir Vidar cleared his throat and adjusted in his seat. Karre winked at him, unable to help herself as she witnessed his obvious discomfort.

The irritated man snorted and shook his head in denial. Standing, he said, "I have no wish for a bride. Excuse me."

Karre laughed, highly amused by the way he practically ran to get away from her. Perhaps she'd be the first woman in their history to not be claimed. She supposed if no one married her, she would be free to leave. Ignoring the slight ping to her ego, she dropped her arms in front of her. "Here I am in a room full of warriors and not a one of them is man enough to handle me. I must say this sets a personal record."

"I can handle you." Sir Vidar stood. "Mine."

Karre arched a brow in challenge. Inside, she trembled, unsure if it was fear or excitement that took hold of her at his words. "We'll see about that, soldier."

"Rejoice, Sir Vidar has chosen!" a herald announced their match, trying to hide his laugh. Wild calls sounded behind her, encouraging Vidar and teasing her.

Vidar bowed slightly in her direction before walking toward a side entrance near the head table. She followed behind him, her body eager to feel his, even as a sense of foreboding unraveled in her brain. A strange instinct told her to run, to not follow him even though he led to inevitable pleasure and great sex.

*I want him too much. I should run.*

She swallowed, suddenly nervous at the realization. How could she keep herself detached when she couldn't stop staring at his firm ass beneath the drape of his long tunic? She listened for his low, seductive voice, liking the way it made her stomach tense in instant arousal. The farther they walked from the main hall, the more she began to ache. Cream gathered between her thighs, wetting her pussy in anticipation. Logic didn't stand a chance.

Vidar wasn't sure if he should be happy or angry that Karre's challenge had goaded him to take her as a wife. After finding release five times, he had seriously thought he was up to resisting her. Instead, his cock had gotten hard at the first look of her in her white gown. The fireplace lit her from behind, showcasing shadowed curves—lush, soft, perfect curves. His hands flexed, his heart raced, and he knew he couldn't let any other man have her.

However illogical the decision might be, what was done was done and it could not be changed now. He was a man after all and a man needed a wife. Karre was more beautiful than he'd wanted, but he couldn't deny the terrible ache in his loins and the desperate need he felt to have her again. The rest would come in time. With Starian marriages, it always did. He just had to trust that the gods knew what was best and had given him the urge to choose his bride.

Pushing open the door to his assigned chamber, he knew that his belongings—all but a change of clothes—were already packed and on their way back to Spearhead Fortress along with the rest of the supplies. He waited for her to walk in, wondering at the expression on her face. It didn't match the almost frightened look in her eyes.

Was she scared? Of him?

"Why did you run from me?" he asked, resisting the urge to pull her into his arms. It seemed strange to ask her that, when there were so many things he should think to ask of his new bride. He opened his mouth but stopped himself from adding, *Did I do something wrong? Did I fail your test for me?* The questions would make him seem weak.

"I had some place to be," she answered. How easily she dismissed him with her easy voice and light toss of her hand, as if his question was nothing. Then, giving a wry laugh, she said, "Apparently, I had to get ready for my wedding day."

"You did not wish to be chosen." Vidar tried to understand. Perhaps time would help him translate her moods, but right now they frustrated him beyond all recognizable belief. "But you said...?"

She stepped close to his chest, looking up at him with steady eyes. The nearness cut off his words. "I believe you claimed to be man enough to handle me, my sir."

"Sir," he corrected.

Her mouth tightened at one corner. "I said sir."

"You said, 'my sir'," he said. "It is just sir. Or you may call me husband." Vidar found it difficult to say the last word aloud to her. It seemed too new, too strange.

Her eyes dipped to settle on the middle of his chest and did not lift back up. "Yes, I suppose I could call you that, warrior man."

She didn't call him "husband". Vidar didn't make her.

Sexual tension held tight in his body, but still he hesitated. This wasn't like before. Now she was his bride, his wife, his mate. The moment seemed to call for more intimacy than before, but as she had said, he was a warrior. What did warriors know of intimacy? Should he say something nice to her? A compliment, perhaps? Ladies seemed to like those. "You appear to be very strong."

Her eyes shot back up with a small laugh. He looked into their brown depths, willing her thoughts to enter his mind, to answer all his unasked and un-thought-of questions without his having to ask them. Those accursed eyes kept their secrets well hidden.

"And you appear to be very strong, as well, warrior." She touched the spot on his chest that had held her notice moments before. Running her finger down a direct path to his navel, she added, "And warm." The fingertip rimmed his belly button through the soft tunic before skimming over the thin trail of hair hidden beneath the cloth. "And firm." Her touch danced in such a way as to bring his shirt up inch by slow inch. "And you smell nice, of herbs and fresh air." As if to prove her point, she swayed closer, breathing deeply. Her eyes closed and she licked her lips. Her fingers found naked flesh on his stomach, but instead of trailing back up, she skimmed his waistband searching for his laces. "And I seem to remember your taste being..."

Vidar's breathing deepened. His hands flexed. This was not how he would have envisioned this night to be, with a bride doing the seduction, yet he couldn't bring himself to interfere with her plans. She wanted him. That was a very good start. Perhaps the gods knew what they were doing. They had given him a woman to slake his desires.

Then what was the little nagging feeling in the back of his soul?

She blinked, her lashes dipping slowly over her eyes. He fell under her complete spell. Those lips parted with a breath that hit his neck, soft and warm. She moaned, so light that he wasn't sure he didn't just merely feel it. He took a deep breath, wondering when the suspension of time would be over and they would again move toward each other. The scent of her flesh, a new memory, but a strong one, wafted over him.

Vidar stayed entranced in her gaze as he lifted his hand to touch her arm. Her fingers loosened the ties at his waist. He shifted his weight, lifting his foot to pull off one boot and then the other. As his bare feet hit the floor, he again touched her arm.

"What do I taste like?" he asked.

She hesitated. "There's an ocean on another plane and when I stand on the cliffs, face to the crashing surf, it splashes very lightly on my face to make my lips taste like a gentle salt and sweet air. You skin reminds me of that. But your mouth is a different thing altogether. Your lips taste like..."

Vidar kissed her tenderly. He gripped her arm, drawing her near. Her breasts grazed his chest, a tease of more to come. Karre's fingers stopped working on the laces as they slid around his waist to his back. She held him to her. Tiny jolting sensations raced over his skin where flesh touched flesh, exploding in his lips, radiating over his back and stomach. His cock reached for her, begging for its own aggressive contact, but Vidar held back, enjoying the taste of her mouth.

"Like a man who should be kissed," she whispered, when they parted to share a joined, shaky breath.

A fine haze clouded her eyes. She kept her mouth close to his so that they breathed the same air. Her hand stayed on his back, keeping him to her. Her lashes fluttered violently and she pulled back, as if stunned by her own admission.

This time the words were harder, not as vulnerable. "Like a man who should be kissed everywhere." Aggressively, she pushed at his stomach, forcing him up against a wall. "Take off the shirt."

Vidar pulled at his tunic and tossed it aside.

"Mm, good warrior," she murmured. Karre leaned in to nip at his chest, biting only to lick at the insignificant wound. Hands slid over his chest, palms flat and exploring. Her lips wrapped around a nipple, pursing for a kiss. He shivered and closed his eyes as she trailed warm kisses along the folds of his muscles. She touched his sides, his chest, his neck and jaw, all the while continuing the exploration with her mouth.

Vidar massaged her back, crushing her white gown in his hands. He maneuvered it up to reveal her legs. "Take off your gown."

Karre laughed. "You're not in charge, warrior." She bit him harder.

"I am—"

She bit him again, harder still. A small gasp escaped him and the pleasure the tiny pain caused. Karre raked her nails over his stomach, causing the muscles of his abdomen to contract.

"You are not in charge here, warrior," she insisted, digging her nails just a little deeper. "I am."

"Yea," he whispered, finding himself mindlessly agreeing with her. "You are."

"Very good, warrior." The pressure of her nails lightened. She pushed back. "Unlace your pants."

He glanced down to where she'd tried to untie his breeches. The knots had been loosened and retightened in her fumbling to get them undone. He smiled, grabbed a single strand and tugged. She watched as the knot pulled apart.

"Turn around," she ordered. He arched a questioning brow but did not deny her. Karre ran her hands down his back like claws. The cold sensation of the uneven stone hit hard against his chest and stomach. She rubbed his back, exploring every inch with her firm caress. Then taking his wrists, she lifted his hands up so they pressed near his head. His forehead pressed forward and he closed his eyes.

Karre pushed the breeches down on his hips, letting them hang low. She scratched his ass, fondling it with hard, deep presses of her hands. Her tongue ran up his spine. His hips flexed forward, bumping his covered cock into the unforgiving stone.

"Ah," he gasped, his hands dropping somewhat at the involuntary movement. She pushed at his elbows, forcing them back to their original position.

"So many scars." She traced haphazard patterns over his back where he'd been struck with weapons in battle. "Move your arms again and I'll give you another one."

He clenched his teeth.

"Say you understand," she ordered.

"Yea," he panted.

"Good, warrior." She rewarded his obedience with another deep caress, this time along his hips. Her fingers curled around the hipbone, nearing the impossibly hard heat of his cock. Pushing his pants down around his ankles, she said, "Don't move. I wish to look at you."

Rustling sounded behind him and he wondered what she was doing. His breathing deepened and he was sure he'd not be able to take her game. Every nerve tingled with anticipation, as if wondering where and how she would touch him again.

"Kick off the pants."

He did.

"Spread your legs."

Again he obeyed, placing his feet shoulder-width apart.

Her touch came, causing him to tense as it ran as a single finger up his inner thigh to the underside of his ass cheek. Warmth replaced her finger as she kissed him. He gasped, realizing she knelt behind him. A woman had never touched him there, like that, taking so much control. No woman had ever wanted to, not that he knew.

Every part of him focused on her, the whisper of her breath, the bite of her teeth, the lick of her tongue, the bold caress of her fingers as they moved ever closer to his cock. Unable to help it, he angled his hips in her direction.

The unmistakably soft globes of her breasts pressed into his ass. Taut nipples drew a path up as she stood, keeping her body to his. Her hand moved around, cupping his balls. Vidar groaned, leaning his head back. Another hand snaked around to grab his cock. She rocked against his ass, forcing his hips to move, forcing his cock to slide in her fisted hand.

"I've never been taken like this," he said, panting. He balled his hands into tight fists.

"I like watching you move, muscles beneath flesh." She bit his back hard. "Contracting and releasing." She licked the wound. "Lower your hands to mine. Show me how you will move for me."

He hesitated at the command. "You wish for me to..."

"Yes. I wish for you to..." She drew her hands away, placing them on either side of his shoulders as she kept her body to his.

His cock ached even worse now that the pressure of her hand was gone. He pushed back from the wall, not turning as he grabbed himself. She continued to rock along his body, keeping him moving. Slowly, she pulled away. He couldn't hear her feet but he knew from the sudden abandonment of her heat that she had put distance between them.

"Mm, yes, keep going," she ordered. "Show me how well you move, warrior."

The bed behind him made a small creak. He glanced back. She crawled onto the bed completely naked. With her lush ass to him, she didn't see that he watched. Karre maneuvered onto her back and he glanced back to the uneven stone of the wall. But he had to peek again, had to see. She had lain down and parted her thighs. Her hand touched her mound as she rocked against it. A finger slipped into the wet folds of her sex only to come out glistening. Her eyes lifted, meeting his. Her free hand moved up her stomach to her breast to tease the hard nipple.

He pumped his hips harder, so close to coming, so aroused by the very presence of her. His face tightened and he bit his lip. So close. So close. So...

"Don't finish," she ordered. "If you do, I won't fuck you."

A terrible physical pain racked his stomach at the very thought, but his desire to claim her forced him to obey. A little bit of his seed managed to escape on a tremor but he tensed, forcing it not to happen completely. He swiped the tip to remove the evidence and wiped his hand on the stone wall before turning to face her. "Your warrior is ready, my lady."

Karre knew she had to take control of their affair from the start or else she would be forever at a disadvantage. What she didn't expect was to enjoy the game so thoroughly or to be able to bend him to her sexual will so completely. As he stood, so near completion, cock so full that veins ran up the sides to the flushed tip, she took a deep, steadying breath. Oh, but he'd been gorgeous to watch —firm ass, tight hips, rippling back.

She tried to pull her hand off her pussy, but neither her hips nor her fingers would stop what they were doing. Without waiting to be commanded, he came to her. Karre knew she should demand he stop but consoled herself with the knowledge that she had beckoned him with her eyes, thus not ruining her game.

"Fuck me," she ordered belatedly. He was already crawling onto the bed to do just that. He smiled, a small curling twist of his lips that said he noticed the lateness of her command as well. His eyes narrowed, as if to say he intended to do just that.

He came between her legs, not stopping his crawl until the head of his cock was at her slick entrance. With a perfect thrust of his hips, he filled her with his thick length. She gasped at the size of him, even as she'd been expecting it.

No testing thrust. No time to adjust. Vidar pulled back only to strike. Keeping his hands on the mattress, he stayed above her, riding her hard and deep. A low, pained growl escaped him as she grabbed onto his shoulders.

It felt so good, being pounded by the thick warrior and his amazing weapon. Her breasts bounced, drawing his eyes, and he fucked harder. Sweat spread over his face and she realized he was holding back his release, waiting for her to come with him.

He leaned back, drawing her body up so that she sat somewhat on his bended knees as he continued to thrust. She braced back on her hands. Vidar took hold of her hips. The new position pressed his cock tight to the sweet spot of her sex and she jerked in warning of what was coming.

"Ah," Karre cried, tensing so hard she couldn't control herself.

"That's it, my lady," he urged. "Finish for your warrior. Give me my prize."

The intimate words more than anything forced her to come as he wanted her to. She gripped the coverlet beneath her. Ripple after pleasure-laced ripple coursed over her. Vidar grunted, suddenly stopping with a victorious yell of his own. He came inside her, their bodies pressed tight as he trembled and released.

Seconds later, he dropped her hips and fell forward, nearly crushing her with his weight before he rolled next to her on the bed. Minutes more and the heavy breathing slowly subsided. Neither one of them moved to separate their tangled limbs. Karre was sure she might never move again.

"I believe I will enjoy having you often, Lady Karre," he said, slipping a hand up to rest on her exposed breast. "Yea, oft indeed."

Karre wondered why the bold promise both exhilarated and frightened her.

"Mm, we should get dressed. We ride out tonight toward home. The knights will be waiting for us to catch up to the supply carts."

"Tonight?" She could barely move, let alone ride. She had seen the big horses and knew exactly what he meant. "But I thought we would sleep here tonight. Do we really need to run off so soon?"

"If it is another go at my cock you are after, I'll gladly make sure we find the time." He licked at her cheek playfully, stroking close to her ear. Slapping her ass cheek, he ordered, "Now, come."

She suppressed a groan. So much for controlling him.

Karre would just have to try harder.

# CHAPTER 4

*Because right now, in this moment, she needed to stop staring at his finely tuned ass and figure out her next move.*

Karre could take many things with a fake smile, a pretty pout or a well-played blink of her lashes. Riding a galloping animal that bounced her into Vidar's back as she was forced to hold onto him wasn't one of them. If her nerves weren't stinging with wicked purpose, her backside was being spanked by the constant movement until, even several minutes after she had gotten off the horse, her ass was numb.

Glad to have an excuse to walk around, she heeded Vidar's warning not to wander too far from the makeshift campground. It wasn't as if she had anywhere to go. A fire burned in a small forest clearing, attended to by a handful of knights. The orange, flickering glow danced seductively along Vidar's back as he stood, arms crossed, talking to a new rider who'd just joined them. He shifted his weight, instantly bringing to mind the way she had ordered him to turn his back to her. What in the stars was she doing? Because right now, in this moment, she needed to stop staring at his finely tuned ass and figure out her next move.

Oh, but his ass was so nice to watch. He shifted again and she forced her eyes away. Noticing that several of the men around the fire studied her, she gave them a smile she didn't feel and made her way toward the tree line for a closer look into the depths of the forest.

All traces of Brigitte had faded from the forefront of her mind until the memories felt more like a book she'd read long ago. She knew the story, but the vivid details and feelings it evoked were gone. The mild headache and state of confusion she was left with would pass soon as well. Tomes had no idea how right he was when he mentioned the brain scramble. The implantation device was useful and made staying in character easier, but she wasn't sure how many more times she would be able to use it.

Looking at the campfire, she thought, *Not that I'll have reason to use it here.*

The full moon shone bright over the clearing, illuminating that which wasn't orange with firelight. Beyond, though, inside the denser trees, only speckles managed to pass through to move softly over the forest floor. A stout breeze whipped her hair into her face and she tugged it back, absently pulling the long strands onto the back of her head to pin them into place.

"Your friend, Lady Jayne, has run away from her husband." The low resonance of Vidar's tone warmed her and she turned to look at him. A few of the men moved from around the fire to mount their horses and join the rider who'd come to the camp. "I fear it is not a good omen, considering Lady Paige also ran from her mate."

"She's not my friend," Karre said distractedly, all the while thinking, *Good for you, Jayne. I didn't think any of you would have the guts to resist them.*

And the truth was, Karre hadn't believed it. She'd really thought the other brides were all talk.

"Where are they going?" She nodded to the departing men. The sounds of hooves beat over the night.

"To help Lord Ronen search. I can spare Sir Oskar and the

others for a few days. We are away from the battlefront and no Caniba will harm us during this part of the journey." He glanced around the encampment. Motioning to a low tent, he said, "If you would like to get out of the wind, we could—"

"Wait," she broke in, "do you mean to imply that the Caniba might attack when we get to Spearhead?"

"Yea, it is possible." He nodded. The strange combination of distant firelight silhouetted him while the moonlight contrasted his face into a ghostly pool of irregular shadows. "The borderlands are not as tamed as Battlewar Castle, but I will protect you. It is my duty."

Karre brushed his comment aside. She could take care of herself. Then, as a cold chill crept over her, she shivered. Why hadn't she considered his home before? "What manner of people are the Caniba again?"

"I do not wish to speak of such things to you," he answered. "Not on this night."

Even as he said it, his words from the day before unfurled in her head.

*They are a dishonorable, disgusting people who eat the flesh of men and think only of pleasing their overlords.*

"I would have you speak of such things to me," she countered. "If I'm going to be put into danger, I have a right to know what it is I'm facing. Are they really as bad as you said before? Or is the whole man-eating thing just a story to scare tourists?"

"Tourists?" A heavy sigh left him and he instantly dismissed the question. "You have nothing to fear from the Caniba. You will not be running like the others and I will protect you."

He seemed so sure of the fact. Not really lying, she agreed, "No, I have no plans to run away from you." It was true. At this moment, she had no real plans of running away. Her plans consisted of finding something of value she could trade so that she might *possibly* later run away.

"Good. I do not know how much or how little Divinity told you about our world, but you otherworlders do not know this land or the dangers in it." He looked as if he would lift his hand to beckon her to him, but she subtly shifted, letting the heavier shadows of nearby trees fall across her face. She hoped it hid her expressions.

"Do we need to look for Jayne?" Karre asked. She tried to never get emotionally invested with people from the planes she visited, but she couldn't see leaving someone to die a horrible death by cannibals.

"I have promised to keep an eye out for the missing bride, but it looks as though she's gone in a different direction. I need to get these supplies back to the fortress. There are matters there that await me."

"What matters?" She curled her toes in the oversized boots she wore.

"They are matters of war," he dismissed, as if that answer should have sufficed.

"Are you going to try to find where that Maggie's encampment is?"

"Sorceress Magda."

"Are you going to try to find where Sorceress Magda's encampment is?" She crossed her arms over her chest, not liking the way he spoke to her—as if she were some silly woman who couldn't possibly understand.

"There is no need to discuss it."

"I want to discuss it," she insisted in frustration.

This time the denial was firm, flat, final. Vidar crossed the distance to join her in the deep shadows. "I do not think you should worry yourself with—"

"Then I don't think you should worry yourself with ever sleeping with me again. If you are going to treat me like a child, I'll act like one. This is me pouting." She dodged his hand, not bothering to uncross her arms as she skirted past him toward the fire.

Vidar watched her leave, frowning after her in confusion. He'd been told women had strange moods, but this was unexpected. Women were to be protected. Why would she wish to hear of the atrocities of the Caniba tonight, their wedding night? Surely, Divinity had told her everything she was required to know.

*Perhaps this is another test?*

The firelight outlined her as it had in Battlewar's main hall, showing the shadow of her figure beneath her gown. His body stirred. She had less brains than a tree stump if she thought of never coming to his bed again. Then, hearing the laughter of the knights as she approached, he tensed. They couldn't see what he did from their position, because the flames would cast her in orange light, but that didn't stop him from stalking after her.

"My lady, please, join us by—" Lother, one of his warriors, said. The man shared a wife with three others and never showed a moment's regret in the decision. Though the man was married and would not seek another, Vidar didn't like the way Lother smiled at Lady Karre.

Vidar grabbed her arm tightly from behind and jerked her with him toward his tent. She gasped, her eyes widening as she looked at him in surprise. He thrust her in front of him and shielded her body from the view of the others. Sudden silence turned to a burst of noise as the men laughed at his supposed eagerness.

After several paces, he pushed open the front flap, pausing so she could lower her head and duck inside. Once they were alone, she ripped her arm from him. At first he couldn't see her expression, but as his eyes adjusted to the dim light, he found her glaring angrily in his direction.

"Lay a rough hand on me again and I will bite it off." The words came from behind her gritted teeth, as if she didn't trust herself not to make good on the threat.

The venom in her words surprised him.

"You had better say you understand or Lady Jayne will not be the only woman running tonight."

Surprise turned into a scowl. He stepped menacingly forward to tower over her. "I do not know where you come from, but in Staria we do not make threats we cannot carry out."

"Do not presume to know me or what I am capable of. Oh, I assure you, the threats I speak out loud are the ones you should be least worried about." A new passion came to her eyes. He knew he'd just met her and he shouldn't be surprised by any of her expressions, but this one concerned him. First meek, almost innocently sweet, then giving, then calculatingly cold, then an outspoken bride, challenging him, controlling him, softly agreeing to stay with him only to now threaten abandonment and much worse. Who was this woman? Which of the temperaments was truly hers? Or were they all her, a mingling of mixed messages and teeming emotions inside one person, changing her as constantly as waves changed the ocean surface?

Then a thought unfurled in his brain, one he could not stop once it started. Lord Sorin had chosen his second wife this night, but the first, Lady Bianka, had tried to play Sorin false, throwing herself at every man who'd look at her. She had burned down Sorin's family home of Firewall before seeking her carnal pleasures at the hands of the Caniba. Those monstrous beasts took what Bianka offered before ultimately taking her life. The tale was whispered amongst the people—a warning to young girls of the price of dishonor, a warning to men of the price of defying the gods.

"Perhaps you did not understand when your place in our world was explained to you." He craned his neck, purposefully trying to scare her. "I will explain again. Marriages are unions, unbreakable, ending only in death. Women are to be protected and cared for. You will not run from me for I will do my duty and protect you, even if I must protect you from yourself. Women are to be provided for. I will provide for you. I will be a generous husband and you will not want for anything that is in my power to give you, so long as you do your duty. Threaten me again and I will punish you. Run from me and I will come for you. You are mine, my lady, and I do not let go of what is mine."

He'd expected feminine outrage at his words, some kind of feverish denial. Instead, her face calmed and her eyes deadened of their angry passions. Vidar did not like the change in her. He did not like the anger, but this coldness was much worse.

*So be it,* he resigned himself. *I cannot take back my words for I did not lie to her.*

"Death, you say?" She arched a brow and leaned back to study his face. She touched where he'd grabbed her and began to rub. The motion was brief, as if she caught herself and changed her mind. His hand flexed with the urge to reach out and check to see if he had hurt her. He did not think his hold too firm, but then again, he was used to ordering about knights, not women. "So there is a way out."

"I'll pretend you meant to humor me with your wit."

"Anything I want, huh?" Her eyes lit at the prospect. "What exactly is my duty? Because the only explanation I received was from the maid, Sera, insisting I sleep with you in order calm your bad temper."

"Divinity—" he began.

"Knocked me unconscious and dragged me here as a prisoner. That is what I was doing in the hall," she broke in. "I was escaping my captors."

"Prisoner? What have you done?"

"I don't suppose you would believe that I am innocent?" Karre chuckled. She didn't meet his gaze as she began to walk around the tent. The one-room enclosure had been put up in a hurry as the men made camp. Usually, they would only bother with a tent if there was to be rain, instead choosing to sleep outside by the fire. However, considering the quickness of their departure on Vidar's wedding night, he'd ordered the small comfort for his wife. All right, he'd ordered it for himself as well—for the privacy it would afford him with his bride. How was he to know she would fulfill his desires before leaving Battlewar?

He licked his lips, remembering just how good she'd felt. The tight grip of her quivering sex as she came, flooding him with her cream. A low groan sounded in the back of his throat and he fought to suppress it, remembering the feel of her breasts, the look of her parted thighs—thighs that welcomed him to slip inside.

Her feet absently kicked at the fur pelt on the ground, flipping it over before smoothing it right again with the tip of her toe. The words low, distant, she said, "I did nothing wrong."

"Then the gods must have their reasons. They brought you to me. That is the only explanation. I regret that you did not travel here under the greatest of comfort, but if this is your destiny, then there was no stopping your arrival. This is our joined fate."

She gave a soft laugh. "Will you tell me your expectations of my duties, or will you make me guess? Or is giving you untold pleasures in bed to be my only role?"

His cock jerked, completely satisfied with those terms. His head forced him to speak. "Women tend to a man's home, though at Spearhead you will have to merely direct the servants to see to our needs."

"All of our needs?" She gave him a playful smile. "Do you use the servants to—?"

"No, not those needs." Vidar's gut tightened at the thought of any other in her bed. After he'd met her, the idea of his bride taking more than one husband left him feeling a little cold. He did not want to share her talents with other men. The possessiveness took him by surprise. "The gods smile at Starian unions and, once we marry, we do not seek another. We stay faithful because the gods demand discipline. War demands discipline."

"Marriage and war." She laughed harder, though the sound was barely audible. Her shoulders shook. "That sounds about right."

"Sera was correct in her advice to you." His words lowered into a husky murmur. "If you please your husband, he will be of better temperament."

"Out of all the planes, I have never heard that line used in such a way before. Though several times I have been told the penis will implode or explode if it is not massaged. Sorry, warrior, but you're going to have to come up with a better line than that."

He grimaced. "It is not a line. It is true."

"If you insist." She turned fully to him, giving up on kicking the furs. "So sex and housekeeping in exchange for anything I want? It sounds like being a kept woman."

"Yea, I will keep you." He nodded in agreement. "It is the will of the gods."

Karre tried not laugh, as he misunderstood her meaning. But truly, what he proposed sounded more like a mistress than a wife—at least according to many of the planes she had been on.

When he had grabbed her arm in his bruising grip, dragging her like some piece of chattel into his tent, she'd snapped. The cool resolve of her façade had disappeared. Her arm ached, but she couldn't be sure if it was the memory or an actual pain that stung the nerves.

*Foolish, foolish, Karre,* she admonished. *No game is won without thinking, without control. Take back the control.*

Funny how, in all her travels, she had never been put in this position. Sure, she'd had the chance to be a mistress. The course of action would even have been easier than, say, becoming the maid with blackened teeth and frizzy hair, but she always felt she was above using sex to get what she wanted. Okay, so as Sparkle, she had used her sex appeal, but it was hardly the same thing. A pang of guilt wrapped around her heart. That was exactly the arrangement she was making now. At least she was attracted to Vidar. He would make a fine lover.

Yes, lover, not keeper. That is how she would think of him. Lovers gave gifts to their mistresses all the time. It was not the same thing as stealing from him.

*It's all about perception.*

"You do not speak of love," she observed, "only of protection and sex."

"Unions are made of necessity, not love," he said.

"I'm glad to hear it. I would not have believed you if you said you loved me." Karre ignored the small ache the admission caused, refusing to give the tightening inside her chest any credence.

"Starians love their country, their people, the sanctity of life, but there is no room for romantic love in our world."

She coughed, pressing against the center of her chest. The knot didn't loosen. At his concerned look, she explained, "Dust from the ride. I'm fine."

"Would you like me to get you a drink?"

"Yes, please." She nodded. He disappeared out of the tent.

*Get control, Karre. Keep it together.*

Karre absently pulled the clips from her hair, fluffing the locks in an effort to enhance her appearance. She looked down at the shapeless gown and frowned. With nothing else to replace it with, she pulled the material over her head and tossed it aside. Then, lying on the fur, she positioned her body carefully, tugging a wayward strand over her shoulder to curl around her breast.

"My lady, your—"

"Ah!" Karre gasped, covering her chest as a young knight walked in with a goblet. He made a strange noise, dropping it on the dirt floor. Red liquor flew across the tent making a slash over her stomach. "Watch it!"

It all happened in an instant. The young man stood, gaping at her waist where the liquor stained her flesh. She tried to push up, but with her arms over her chest, she wobbled and had to brace herself. The gesture exposed a breast. The man made a strange strangling sound before running from the tent as if the fires of hell were after him. Karre let out a burst of laughter.

"I brought food," Vidar said as his hand appeared inside the flap. "What did you do to Groff? He ran into the forest looking like —" Vidar skidded to a stop, looking at her on the fur. He began to smile, but the look faded as he glanced behind him, back to her naked form, behind him once more. "I will string that boy up by his toes."

"Wait." Karre pushed up to stop him. "Leave him be. I think the fear of what you might do was enough. It's not like he knew what he was walking into." When he looked as if he might protest, she hurried to add, "What have you brought me?"

"Oh." He looked at the trencher he carried. "Meat. The men roasted it on the fire."

Karre lay back down, letting her fingers dance along the fur, as she purposefully drew attention to her naked waist. "Bring it to me."

"Did Groff...?"

"Did he look?" Karre laughed, stretching along the fur. "A naked woman was lying on the floor in an otherwise sparsely decorated tent. Yes, he looked and then he ran for his life. Let him be."

Vidar's foot hit the goblet as he stepped forward. It spun and skidded to the edge of the tent. Karre leaned upon her elbow, cradling her head in her hand.

"You're not scared of me, are you, warrior? You won't run away to the forest, will you?" She turned, angling her shoulder back as he neared, giving him free view of her chest.

He knelt, shaking his head in denial as he set the plate near her chest. Karre reached forward to run the back of her hand against his cock, massaging him through his clothing. Already he was eager and hard. Vidar groaned.

"That knight got me wet," she said. His groan turned into a scowl of rage, until she pointed at her hip. "He spilled wine." She trailed a finger along her waist where the liquor was beginning to dry and stick.

Vidar moaned softly. Warm lips brushed her flesh and he began to lick her clean, sucking and biting at her flesh. She kept her hand on his cock, light and teasing. He slid his hand over her ass, cupping her cheek. When he slid his fingers along the back of her thigh, inching them to enter her pussy from behind, she stopped him.

"I'm hungry, warrior. I wish for you to feed me." Karre knew she had her practical reasons for wanting to control him, but as her plan formed in her head, she found she liked their game. If she let him explore her as he'd been intent on doing, she wouldn't be able to keep a straight head.

Vidar lifted a piece of meat from the trencher. Karre pursed her lips and shook her head, refusing to take it. She rubbed his cock harder, rolling forward just enough to reach his balls.

"Take off your clothes so that I may feast." She licked her lips.

Instantly, the shirt was pulled off his chest and thrown at the side of the tent. In his eagerness, he shook as he jerked at the laces. Standing, he kicked his feet to rid himself of his boots as he pushed off the pants. Karre put her head on her hand again, resting against it.

"Feed me," she ordered, not moving as she opened her mouth wide.

Vidar grabbed his cock, stroking it a few times as he knelt back down. The towering shaft bobbed near her face. She reached out with her tongue, licking the smooth tip. He touched her breast, lifting it in his palm, smashing the nipple with his palm until it hardened against him. Walking forward on his knees, he brought his erection closer. Karre sucked him a little deeper, taking the full head into her mouth. Her lips hooked on the ridge as she sucked.

He groaned, reaching over her head. Vidar crawled on top of her, straddling her shoulders as he rested on all fours. The motion turned her onto her back and angled his cock toward her face. Karre gasped in surprise and he took advantage, thrusting his cock deeper into her mouth, nearly choking her on its thick length.

She took hold of his hips to control the depth. His hips worked, fucking her mouth, gliding along her lips and teeth. When he learned the limits of her mouth, she took hold of his balls, rolling them as she sucked hard.

"I enjoy feeding you," he whispered, the admission harsh as it came from above her head. Karre's lungs burned and she was forced to push his hips, taking his cock from her mouth. Protesting, he groaned. "I am not finished. I wish for you to drink me as well."

Gasping for breath, she pushed her large breasts together and looked up at him. His eyes glinted as he got her meaning. All thoughts of her sucking him to completion must have left him because he hungrily lowered his body along hers until his cock fit in the crease of her breasts.

"Now you may come," she said, as if granting him permission.

"Oh," he grunted, pumping so his inner thighs pinned her body down. The intimate smell of his erection filled her senses as the wide tip bumped into her chin. "I enjoy your breasts. So warm and soft and full." He began to find release, the movement of his hips becoming jerky. As he came, he kept moving, spilling his seed over her throat to form a warm necklace before drawing the moisture between her tightly pressed breasts to make his cock slide in his own juices.

He stopped, breathing hard and not moving to take his cock from between her breasts, even as she released their hold on him. Karre raked her nails up his hips and moaned. He might have come, but her body's arousal was merely heightened by the display.

He crawled down, staying above her as he kept her against the floor with the canopy of his body. Bending at the elbows, he leaned down to kiss her mouth.

"I am wet again, warrior," she said before his lips could find their mark.

He furrowed his brow as he looked at the cum he'd squirted around her neck. She saw the moment realization dawned on him. Karre laughed as he reached for a discarded piece of clothing to wipe her clean. The rough material scratched her skin. When he finished, he grinned as if he thought himself very clever. He leaned to kiss her again.

"It is your turn to dine," she said, stopping his mouth once more. She pushed at his shoulder and spread her legs until they bumped the barrier of his body. When he didn't move fast enough, she slipped her hand between them and began rubbing her clit in tiny circles. "Fuck me with your tongue."

He followed her gaze down to where she masturbated. "You wish for me...? I have never dined on a woman there."

As if fascinated and hesitant at the same time, he crawled down her body. She threaded her legs along the outside of his. He licked his lips and she nearly screamed at the seductive agony of his contemplation. Slipping two fingers along the folds, she parted the soft lips. Then, reaching for his hair, she pulled him to her pussy before falling back onto the furs.

Hot breath fanned the parted folds and she pushed on her heels to lift her ass off the ground. His tongue reached slowly to her clit to flick the bud, as if tasting a foreign dish for the first time. He drew his tongue back, as if sampling her intimate taste. A low moan escaped him as he did it again. Then, with increasing eagerness, he ran the flat of his tongue up her folds, over her fingers.

Vidar adjusted his weight to lie more comfortably between her legs. He grabbed her wrist and tossed her hand out of his way. Like a starving man at a fresh spring, he began sucking and drinking her pussy. His hands grabbed hold of her legs, keeping her firm to his mouth as he smothered his face into her folds. His nose stroked her clit as he shoved his tongue inside her cavern. He moaned, vibrating her with the sound. Never had she had such an enthusiastic partner.

Karre bit her lip as she came against his face, shaking and trembling as her moisture coated him. He didn't stop and the sensations became too much. She pushed at his head, gasping, "Enough, Vidar, enough."

He pulled back with a self-satisfied grin. "I will be doing that again, my lady, but for now your taste has made me hard." He crawled up her body and she felt the heat of his cock brush her thigh. The velvety smooth shaft was heavy with desire. "I would like to ride you."

Still weak from release, she opened her mouth to speak, but he was already set on his course. He brought his cock to her still slick opening and thrust inside. Vidar made a primitive noise of satisfaction as her pussy accepted him.

Wildly, he fucked her, biting his lips as he watched her breasts bounce around with each thrust. The hard sex caused little jolts of pain deep inside her sex, but the instant pleasure following it more than made up for any discomfort. His gorgeous muscles tightened and flexed, captivating her as her breasts did him.

He grabbed a breast and squeezed, pinching the nipple between two fingers. Tension shot throughout her entire being. His mouth opened wide and she knew he held back. "Finish for me," he demanded. "Give me my prize."

Karre came, hitting her zenith with a gentle cry of relief. Seconds later he froze over her, staying buried as he met with release. With a deep, almost pained sigh, he collapsed next to her and pulled her hot body against his even hotter chest. Grabbing a breast in his palm, he closed his eyes. "I am well satisfied. My lady may have whatever she desires."

The pleasure of release diminished some at his words. He'd meant it as a compliment, but it left her feeling a little bit like a whore being paid for services. She thought about inching away from him but she was too tired to move.

# CHAPTER 5

*Because right now, in this moment, her ass hurt too much.*

Karre gritted her teeth, trying to think of anything but the endless rocking of the horse beneath her. Dissatisfied with her white gown, Vidar had given her a man's tunic and breeches. It suited her just fine, as she bunched the gown beneath her butt to cushion the ride.

Their morning started early, before the sun even deigned to shine down upon the waking soldiers. Vidar awoke before her, eating his breakfast before coming to massage her awake with his hands on her naked breasts. But there had been no time to finish what he started as the sound of cart wheels squeaked outside. For the first mile or so, the feel of his body tempted her desires, but now she just wanted to slip off the horse and never move again because right now, in this moment, her ass hurt too much. The sensation in her backside went from numb to burning to sharp jolts of pain to a combination of all three.

"You said I could have whatever I wanted." Karre leaned forward to whisper up into Vidar's ear. She had told herself she wasn't going to cash in on his sexual "payment" but she couldn't take anymore.

"Are you hungry?" he asked, reaching down to his leg where a satchel hung.

"No, I wish to walk."

"We are very close to—"

"Please, Vidar. I am not used to riding."

"Of course, my lady." He shouted a command to one of his men, urging them to continue on. Their horse stopped. When they were alone, Vidar swung down and reached up to help her to the ground. Her legs wobbled and she placed her hand on the horse's side to steady herself. Vidar took her by her arm. "Can you walk?"

Karre nodded, trying not to limp as she stretched her legs.

Vidar made a small clicking noise and led her forward on the worn path. The horse followed behind them.

"You said before that Divinity traded the brides," Karre said, wanting to take her mind off her aches. Learning of yet another Divinity crime might make this detour worth it.

"Yea."

"What for?" She threaded her hand on his arm, but only because she needed to steady herself. As the cart squeaked and horse hooves softened with distance, the surrounding forest's gentle noises became apparent. The light hum of insects mingled with the slightly louder call of distant birds. In the illumination of late day, the new spring leaves seemed to glow. Tiny veins threaded them in imperfect symmetry as they crashed and danced above in the trees, taunting their fallen, brown brethren on the forest floor below.

"Water," he stated simply.

Karre stopped walking and dropped his arm. "Water? I was traded for water? Are you joking?"

"No. The Divinity aliens wanted some of the blue mineral water and offered us brides in return." He gave a small laugh. "They had great talks about the matter until finally King Wilhelm agreed to give them one small vial per bride."

As he moved on, the horse's head neared her back. She took several fast steps before falling into a leisurely pace beside him. "A vial of water. I am worth a small vial of water. That's insulting. Is it at least a cure for age? Or some kind of miracle water? Is it an elixir that makes you men big and strong when you drink it?"

"No, most would not say it is magic and we do not drink it unless desperate. It can make you sick. Though, it is blue."

"Oh great, you can't drink it but at least it's a pretty color. Decorators and spa owners everywhere will be so happy." She gave a wry laugh. The insult was too much. She remembered the henchmen had given her a bowl of such water to clean up with at Battlewar. She had thought it was mixed with some kind of soap for cleaning.

*Brides for bathing water. Wonderful.* Even her thoughts dripped with sarcasm.

"If it cheers you, the water is special. It stays warm no matter how long it stays away from heat. It has saved men from the cold." He swung his hand over his head and smacked a low branch.

Karre laughed dryly, stating, "Oh yes, that makes me feel much better."

They walked in silence and slowly the feeling returned to her backside. She breathed deeply, taking in the fresh forest air. It had been so long since she'd had time to relax and enjoy a simple walk. Reaching a fallen log across the path, she started to step over it. Vidar's hand was instantly on her arm, helping her over.

"Have you ever traveled to another plane?" She'd originally meant the question as a way to start a conversation, but as she said the words she realized the strategic cunningness of it. If he had traveled, she'd find out how.

"No. Before Divinity, people only came through the fairy rings. Since we're always at war, fairies do not like our land and they do not leave rings for us to travel through." He didn't let go of her as they cleared the log. "But since I was a boy, I've been fascinated by the idea of other worlds. I love hearing the stories of such strange places."

"Where is the Divinity portal?" she asked. "Perhaps I could take you to another world? I know of some nice ones. We wouldn't be gone long. Think of it as a vacation."

"No." The answer was flat and the lightness of his tone faded. "I cannot leave the borderlands. There is much to be done."

"Oh?"

"How about you? How many planes have you traveled to?" he asked instead of elaborating.

Countless. Hundreds. Hundreds of hundreds.

"A few." Karre pulled her arm from his grasp under the pretense of stretching. When she finished, she dropped her arm to the side, putting distance between their bodies. The ground squished beneath her feet and she grimaced as cold, wet earth clung to her short boot. "Ew."

"And the world you are from?" He offered his arm so she might steady herself as she swiped at her foot. "Is it like this one?"

"No. It's nothing like this one." Karre gave up on the mud and wiped her hands on the ends of her borrowed tunic shirt. Dirt smudged over the red.

"Is it—?"

"I don't hear the knights," she interrupted so he couldn't probe more into her home plane. Turning her full attention to him, she stepped into his path, forcing him to stop walking. "We have the forest to ourselves."

"Are you not sore from the ride?" Vidar's words might have held a hint of denial, but his eyes lit with interest.

"Come with me," she pulled him off the path into the trees, gripping his tunic in her fist. The horse began to follow, but Vidar made a noise and the beast stopped, instead grazing alongside the path.

"I wish to speak—"

"Here is good." Karre slid the hand on his chest up, pulling the material to expose the laces at his waist. With a deft tug, she untied them.

He looked as if he might protest the quickness of her advances. "My lady, I—*ah!*"

Karre tugged his pants down to his knees, letting them slide the rest of the way to trap his ankles. His cock had started to rise with interest and she cupped the shaft, stroking the length until it firmed against her palm. She licked her lips, dragging her tongue leisurely as he watched.

All questions left his eyes as he gave in. Karre smiled, took the hem of his tunic and bunched it by his chest, out of her way. "Hold this."

His hand pressed flat, holding it up. Karre sank to her knees, scratching her nails against his hips. He tensed, threading his fingers into her hair, rubbing along her temple insistently. Looking up at him, she kept her eyes on his as she leaned forward. Her lips parted, slipping around the wide tip of his erection. Vidar's breathing deepened.

Karre worked her mouth down his length, sucking gently. He groaned in satisfaction. His eyes closed as he tilted his head back in rapture. She rolled her tongue along his shaft, all the while running her nails down the backs of his thighs. His strong abdomen muscles rippled beneath his flesh. He rocked in time with her mouth. She felt him quiver and reached for his balls. Almost instantly, he jerked, coming inside her mouth. Swallowing, she let his cock slide from her lips.

Vidar breathed heavily, his hand dropping from her hair. He lowered to the ground, joining her. Crawling forward, he forced her onto her back. He brushed his lips against hers. "My turn."

He tugged at her laces, pulling her breeches free. Then, eagerly, he dipped his head between her thighs, as if he'd been waiting all day to taste her. He moaned, the sound vibrating her clit. He licked along her pussy, sucking, biting, thrusting his tongue inside her.

Her ass pressed into dry leaves and the crunching sound of their destruction punctuated each movement. Vidar massaged her hips with his hands, rocking them up toward his mouth. Karre gripped his head. Tension built, filling her with a bittersweet agony. She wanted the sensations to last forever, but she couldn't stop the rough jerk of release that washed over her.

When the last tremors subsided, Vidar looked up and gave her a satisfied grin. "The fortress is close." His pants still bound his ankles and he pulled them up as he stood. "There, we can bathe and dine." He reached to pull her up. "And find you an appropriate gown."

"You said the fortress was close, I had no idea it was only a hundred-pace walk. Why didn't you insist we finish the ride?"

Vidar watched his wife from the corner of his eye. Behind them, his horse walked a lazy pace without having to be led. "Because you asked me to stop and it was within my power to grant you the simple request. Oskar will see that everything is taken care of in my stead."

Though small compared to the great city of Battlewar, Spearhead had a symmetrical charm—for a fortress on the brink of a vicious Caniba attack. A single watchtower lifted high into the sky, lording over the square-shaped castle beneath. Thorn hedges formed a perimeter around the outside wall, surrounded by the murky waters of a moat. Vidar kept an eye on Karre, wondering what she thought of her new home. Surely, the sight would impress her.

"Sir Vidar!" yelled a knight from atop the battlements, announcing Vidar's arrival to those behind the stronghold's wall. "And Lady Karre!"

"Rejoice, Sir Vidar has chosen!" a woman near the front gate shouted, prompting a chorus of others to join her. "Rejoice! Rejoice, Sir Vidar has chosen!"

Karre stiffened at the words, her face tightening. He watched a strange expression filter over her, first shock, then resolve, fading to determination. Glancing in his direction, her determination was replaced by a light smile. But he studied her eyes and their intensity was nowhere near the lighthearted emotion she wanted him to believe.

Taking her arm, he led her over the bridge and through the opened front gates. The raised stone of the bailey wall surrounded the courtyard, looping about from one side of the main castle to the other in an oval shape. Atop the wall that stood several feet wide was the walkway surrounded by battlements with corner spiral stairwells leading from the ground to the battlements. Next to the tower, the main part of Spearhead Fortress sprawled along the backside of the wall.

The wide courtyard teemed with activity, just like Battlewar

City but on a smaller scale. Unlike Battlewar, Spearhead had no market, no tightly pressed homes filling tiny streets, but there was a self-sustaining brewery and gardens for food. Livestock was tended in the north, the meat part of the supplies they brought back with them.

Now, the movement stopped as those gathered cheered the new couple. Two guards pushed the oversized doors of the main gate closed and secured them with a thick timber. Karre whistled lightly. When Vidar looked at her, she said, "This will do."

He grinned with pride and excitement. "Welcome to your home, my lady."

---

"Welcome home indeed." Karre gave a wry laugh as she looked around her new bedchamber. It was adequate in size with pale stone walls, a smoothed stone floor, large stone fireplace and a stone bench carved beneath a narrow stone window. "This is exactly like the time I spent a month trapped in a cave because Lopa-lis were after me."

Okay, so it wasn't *exactly* like the cave. It did have furnishings.

"My lady?"

Karre turned to Jordinne, the maid Vidar assigned to assist her while he left for some mysterious duty. She was a pretty girl, youthful in appearance and temperament. She suited Karre just fine. Youth was easier to manipulate. "I asked if it would be possible to have a bath. You do bathe here, right? They gave me a bowl of water at Battlewar when I would much prefer a tub or shower. Even a waterfall would do."

"Yea, my lady, we bathe," Jordinne giggled. "But here in Spearhead we do not dress as men—not like those heathen ladies of a Battlewar."

Like every other woman Karre had seen in Spearhead, the servant wore a long flowing dress cinched tight with a corset top that dipped low to lay bare a fair amount of cleavage. Karre wondered if Jordinne had ever seen a woman from Battlewar, because when

Karre had been there she'd not seen a single lady there dressed as a man.

*Well,* she thought, looking at her own clothes, *no one but myself.*

"Yes, they do seem a barbaric lot compared to this place," Karre agreed to win the woman over. It worked. Jordinne's smile widened. "And with your great enemy so close, it is a great accomplishment to remain so civil."

Jordinne nodded enthusiastically. "Yea, my lady."

"I require a bath," Karre said, slipping comfortably into her new role. If this plane demanded she play the part of Lady Karre of Spearhead, so be it. She had pretended to be a lady of means before. "I will also need gowns and shoes worthy of Spearhead as well as sturdy clothes for riding. Food and drink."

Karre again looked around the stone tomb of her chamber. One door led out of the room, opening up to Vidar's bedchambers. She'd been informed that noble women did not sleep with their husband throughout the night. The large bed dominated Karre's room and had been covered with a decorative fur, but the muted browns and grays of the sewn squares only added to the overall drabness.

"And, if possible," she continued, "I need some material samples, some lightweight chain or rope, someone who can sew, a couple swords, a knife or dagger. Hmm, actually, you'd better have several weapons sent up for my inspection."

Jordinne watched her, not moving.

Karre sighed. "See to it, please."

"Yea, my lady." Jordinne nodded and hurried from the room, her eyes deep in concentration.

Karre relaxed and tugged at her clothing, stripping out of the traveling garb. Completely naked, she crawled onto the bed and under the fur covers. The soft mattress molded to her body, cushioning her sore muscles. She moaned, content for the moment. Maybe the chamber wasn't so bad after all.

Karre awoke hours later, rested and incredibly aroused from endless dreams filled with the wicked temptation of Vidar's masculine body. In her sleep, she had pulled the covers off her chest, revealing her naked breasts. Sitting up, she found that someone had been in to light the fire.

Karre pulled the blanket up to quickly hide herself as she looked around. The room was empty. The clothing she had discarded earlier was gone, replaced by a neatly folded gown on the end of her bed. A tray carrying a trencher of meats and bread was left on a low table next to a goblet. Leaning from the bed, she grabbed the goblet and took a long drink of the sweet liquor before setting the empty goblet back down with a sigh.

She didn't like the fact that someone had come in while she slept —let alone spent enough time to light a fire, deliver laundry and bring in food. It wasn't like her mind to let down its guard. She would have to take more care in the future.

By the light coming through the window, she knew the hour was late. Karre kicked off the fur. The room was warm and her flushed skin nearly glowed in the firelight. A bath had been left near the fire, the blue water warm and inviting when she skimmed her fingers over the surface. Instead of stepping into the metal tub, she went to the door. The tub was small, but she would find a way to fit Vidar in there with her, even if she had to sit on his lap—*especially* if she had to sit on his lap.

His room was empty. Glancing over the sparse décor just to be sure, she frowned. Shouldn't he have come back from his duties by now? She had a hard time believing that a man of his passions would have checked in on her and left her to sleep.

Disappointed, she left the door open and went to her bath. Heat caressed every inch beneath the surface of the mineral water. She lifted her arm, watching the blue droplets rain down from her fingers like liquid sapphires. On the floor next to her, she found sweet smelling soaps. She took her time, watching the open door, waiting for Vidar to come in and catch her naked in the tub.

Karre soaped her breasts before standing to wash her stomach and thighs. The lather caused her hands to slip pleasurably over her form and she bit her lip. Images of Vidar invaded her senses—strong, sexy, erotic, masturbating as he faced the wall. She smiled, her knees weakening as she sank back into the water.

Karre leaned her head back, rubbing her soapy breasts while reaching between her thighs. She massaged her clit, rubbing it in small circles. Lazy eyes stayed fixed on the door, willing him to come to her. She pressed harder. He didn't come to her and she couldn't hold off the tremors of release.

"Lord Ronen's man has arrived. He informs me that they have recovered Lady Jayne from the forest. She was abducted by Caniba scouts," Sir Oskar said, joining Vidar along the low ridge. Moss-covered trees lined the wetlands, beyond the shallow waters that surrounded the island hill of their new encampment. Patches of vegetation grew in the water, forming a random pattern in the surface. It was the perfect location, almost pretty but for the stale air of the surrounding marshlands that settled thickly in their lungs, carrying the faint scent of death. "He brings a missive from the king."

Vidar looked from the mossy trees to Oskar's hand, taking the letter. "She made it to the borderlands, then?"

"No. They were discovered near Widowsrock." Oskar's frown mirrored Vidar's.

"That far north? In the forest?" He broke the wax seal, not looking at the letter as he stared at Oskar for confirmation.

"Yea, but that is all I know. The man would tell me no more, only insisted on my honor that I bring this to you."

Vidar hurriedly unfolded the parchment to find two pages. He read over them quickly. "King Wilhelm says Sorceress Magda's men were caught with maps of Staria. They are charting routes through the forest originating at Spearhead and heading north toward Battlewar and Fallenrock. The king urges me to renew efforts to find the sorceress. Everything he has is at our disposal. He sends troops to reinforce the borderlands and the forests."

"Sorceress Magda has yet to show herself. All we have are rumors that she is even near here." Oscar took the first page of the missive when Vidar offered it to him. They had shared much and owed each other their lives more than either of them could count. "For all we know she could be five miles underground and fifty miles from the border."

"She must be close. I feel it like an oncoming sickness—close but not quite within reach." Vidar turned, looking in the direction of his fortress. It was impossible to see it from where he was, but he imagined it perfectly. Lady Karre would be there, settling into her new home, her new life. He thought of writing her but had not found the time to put pen to paper. Now, with news of Magda's daring, he would have even less time for it.

Besides, what would he say with no news of battle to speak of? Should anything happen to him, she'd be informed by one of his men so simply saying "I'm alive" seemed pointless. Perhaps she wasn't concerned. Perhaps she was. Perhaps she didn't think of him at all.

*She is probably too busy to give me more than a passing thought.* Though the most likely scenario, he found the idea bothered him somewhat.

Shaking his bride from his thoughts with great effort, he sighed and turned to the rectangular tents outlined by firelight in the coming dusk. Tiny sparks from the flames danced in the evening sky before dying out. The tents, varying in sizes, spread out over the high clearing on an orderly grid to create pathways. The larger tents were in the middle with progressively smaller ones fanning round them. Banners hung from the tent flaps, pinned to the opened entryways. Their brilliant colors stuck out against the light caramel of the canvas.

"It says here that the map did not go too far into the forest. They could not have been spying long," Oskar pointed out. "He wants a report as to our progress. What will you tell him?"

"What can I tell him?" Vidar muttered, feeling a little bitter. "That his sending me to Battlewar for a bride left Spearhead open? That Caniba spies broke through the forest near my fortress? I can't even be certain when they snuck through. This is the first I've heard of it."

Oskar did not offer any words of comfort and Vidar did not expect any. "You needed a bride and now you've got one. There will be no need to leave Spearhead again. You followed the king's orders."

"Read the rest of it." Vidar handed him the second page.

"Sir Vidar," Oskar read aloud, "I have been informed that the Divinity brides might not have known about coming to our land. Already Lord Sorin and Lord Ronen have expressed discontentment from their wives. Let us hope it is nervousness from traveling to a new land, but if it is more than that, we must do all in our power to ensure these first marriages stand. I do not want marital chaos in my kingdom, especially amongst my noblemen. We need this trade agreement with the foreigners to work. More brides means more children. Within a generation we will have more knights to defend this kingdom. Already the Caniba outnumber us by at least three-fold. Then, gods willing, maybe this war will end and we will wipe the beastly scourge from existence. I should like to be remembered as the king whose actions started the downfall of our enemy."

Vidar's stomach tightened with worry. How was he to look after a woman and see to his warrior duties? Marriage was supposed to ease the stress of life, not add to it.

"You are a man of great honor, sir," Oskar continued reading, his voice lowering. "I expect you to find happiness in your marriage. I will not have the trade agreement tarnished by rumors of the gods being angered with us for trying to take more brides than they readily bestow. The knights need a reason to fight and the hope of a lady always seems to be the best motivation. I am not ready to give up on this alliance. Do whatever you must and learn what you can of your wife's presence at the breeding ceremony. Keep this news to yourself. I have no wish to dampen the spirits of the men with Sorceress Magda threatening our borders."

Oskar handed the letter back and Vidar folded it only to clutch it in his hand. He knew his orders, contradicting as they were. He needed to stop Magda and ensure his wife's happiness. Though, the last shouldn't be hard. It was unfortunate Sorin and Ronen had not found peace in their marriages, but Karre seemed happy to be with him.

"Do we ride for Spearhead?" Oskar asked.

"Not yet." No. No matter how badly he wanted to go to his wife, to feel her against him, he was needed at the marsh encampment. "I have left orders to be informed should my wife need anything. There is nothing to worry about. The maids will see to Lady Karre and ensure she is taken care of. Besides, I have prisoners to interrogate."

Two warriors had fallen, Richard of Daggerpoint and Peeter of Fallenrock, while capturing some of Sorceress Magda's scouts in the southern marshes. With her people popping up everywhere, something big was close. He could feel it in his bones. The fallen Starian men could have killed the Caniba warriors and lived, but both men knew their duty and knew that they needed live prisoners for information. They died well and were not taken by the cannibals. After several weeks without their queen, Vidar hoped the scouts would be ready to talk. Caniba warriors became erratic and unpredictably mad when withdrawn from their idol.

"Let us hope that tonight is the night we discover where the sorceress' encampment lies." Vidar led the way up the incline toward the tent village.

# CHAPTER 6

*Because right now, in this moment, she didn't care if she found anything worthy of hawking for a portal ride, she needed to get the hell out of Spearhead Fortress.*

"It is whispered that Sorceress Magda studies the black arts. Her followers dance with the serpent and are made to endure its poison before joining her army. Only those who live, the toughest of the Caniba, are allowed into her ranks." Jordinne paused in her story, looking at the other two maids gathered in Karre's bedchamber. The maids sat in thickly cushioned chairs, newly padded as per Karre's design. Richly colored fabrics hung from the walls to hide the stone underneath, flowing red and golds. Matching fabric hung around the bed, creating opulent curtains, held open with corded ropes. Firelight shone from the fireplace, contrasting their faces, exaggerating their expressions.

Karre took a deep breath, trying not to shiver. She hadn't moved for some time from her place lounging on the bed. Vidar had been gone for weeks, leaving her to make her way in Spearhead alone. He'd just dropped her off and left. The fact stung, but she refused to dwell on it as she busied herself with familiarizing herself with the fortress and the people in it. She played the role they demanded, though it was tougher than other identities she had taken. They all called her Karre and she wasn't sure what kind of character to be under her real name. She didn't even know how to be her real self. Characters were much easier.

Karre had searched for valuables, something portable she could carry with her when she discovered a way off this plane. The weapons inspection brought little more than sharp blades and used swords. Bolts of material were nice, but they wouldn't travel easily. And, as far as she could see, the fortress had no treasury. However, that was beginning to matter less and less as the women spoke. Because right now, in this moment, she didn't care if she found anything worthy of hawking for a portal ride, she needed to get the hell out of Spearhead Fortress.

"And these Caniba are close to Spearhead even now?" Karre asked, thinking of the man-eaters the Starian people described in morbid detail—hairy, foul-smelling, beast-warriors with eyes pitted deep into their faces, sharpened teeth to bite into their awful meals and flesh covered with so many dirty pelts it looked as if they had fur.

"Yea," Jordinne nodded. "Right on the border. Over the last four years, Magda has been getting very close to Spearhead and her warriors more aggressive in battle. Or at least that is what our men tell us."

"And you stay here willingly?" Karre searched every one of their faces. Each set of eyes looked back at her as if she'd just asked them the stupidest possible question. "Why not move north where it is safer?"

"Our men will protect us," Jordinne said calmly.

"And if they don't?" Karre gasped in disbelief. "Or if they can't? What will you do then?"

"To say such a thing is..." Jordinne's weak voice trailed off.

"It's dishonorable," the redheaded Bratene answered, her green eyes wide in her round head.

"It was just a question," Karre whispered, seeing their mounting irritation at her doubtful words. She didn't need to make enemies of the women.

"Those men, the strongest of the beasts, live only to serve her, obsessively doing the sorceress' biding," Jordinne said quickly, as if trying to gloss over Karre's improper question. Her words filled with the drama of her tale. "They go mad when they can't see her. I've seen it happen to a prisoner once. They cry and yell and pull out their hair."

Karre had asked them to tell her of the Caniba but did not expect the tales of horror and depravity that they spun for her like youngsters around a campfire.

"The Caniba rise from the earth and disappear like ghosts," Bratene added.

"It's impossible to tell Magda's numbers," Synna said, her words as soft as her sweet demeanor. She tugged shyly at her brown curly hair. "Her armies sleep beneath the earth, in the ground."

"They hibernate like snakes," Bratene broke in, "but are the children of men and wolves. Wolf-men."

Dancing as Sparkle, Karre had seen several wolf-men. Sure they drank blood, but they'd been harmless enough. But had they turned evil and attacked, she could see how claws and fangs would make for a fearsome opponent.

"My first husband, Sir Fredrick, was one of the men who tried to infiltrate her camp," Synna continued as if Bratene hadn't interrupted. "He came back, but was never the same since being held as her prisoner. They have him locked away in a room lined with mattresses to keep him from bashing his own skull against the stone walls as he cries for the presence of the sorceress. I don't know what she did to him, but he is no longer my husband. He eats without utensils or plate and a man must watch him at all times to be sure he does not hurt himself or escape." Synna gave a small sniff and rubbed at her eyes. "I shall never see him again."

Jordinne leaned over to pat Synna's leg gently. "The gods will reward him well in the afterlife. Take comfort that you have other husbands."

Synna nodded but said no more.

"The Caniba are beasts, a race born of the unholy fornications of people and wolves," Bratene insisted, repeating her earlier words. This time she stared at Karre, as if to make sure she heard.

"Those are just children's stories," Jordinne denied. "You know better than to scare Lady Karre with those tales. Our men have fought and killed many in battle. They are flesh and blood."

"They are the lowest form a man can become," Bratene said.

"Be that as it may." Jordinne sighed heavily.

"It is why we all carry a knife," Bratene said lifting her skirts to show her upper thigh. A sheathed blade had been strapped tightly to her leg. "For if we are ever taken, we know what needs to be done."

"But I thought you said the men would protect us," Karre couldn't help saying, testing their earlier logic.

"They will," Bratene inserted quickly. "Of course they will."

"We trust our men to be honorable," Jordinne added.

*Then why carry the knife at all?*

Karre gave a nervous laugh, one she didn't feel.

"But if the gods so choose," Bratene said carefully, lightly touching her throat.

"Yea, if the gods so choose," Jordinne reiterated.

"You should carry one as well," Synna said, "just in case the gods so choose."

Karre studied them each in turn, taking in their earnest expression, reading more there than they would ever say. At their expectancy, she nodded once.

*Yeah,* Karre thought derisively, *if the gods so choose.*

---

It was time to get out of Spearhead Fortress and head north. Usually Karre wasn't one for taking off into an alien plane's wilderness on her own, but desperate times called for a desperate Karre to grab whatever she could find and run far away from the people-eating monsters. This wasn't her fight. She already had a great adversary—Divinity Corporation—and it was an all-consuming, vile foe. She didn't battle beasts with a simple blade for protection. Even a forest filled with mammoth wolves, wild boar and charging bucks was preferable to wolf-men cannibals.

Karre felt her thigh, where the maids insisted she keep a knife hidden. They'd given her a sheath that tied around her waist on top and around her thigh on the bottom to hold the knife in place. The weight was a constant reminder of what was out there.

*Our men will protect us.*

Jordinne had been so certain. That was well and good for them, but Karre's man hadn't been seen or heard from in weeks—and she did not count Sir Oskar's few mumbled sentences when he'd stopped by the fortress as word from her husband. Apparently, Vidar was at a marshland encampment seeing to his "duty". No wife, on any plane, would put up with the duty excuse.

*Good thing I'm not really a wife.*

Striding through Vidar's chambers, she didn't bother to look around. She had already snooped through his belongings. Aside from clothes and weapons, there was nothing noteworthy.

Outside the chamber, she slowed her steps, keeping her feet soft on the stone. She'd had the seamstress sew her a bag. Its strap fitted over her chest and the large bag hung alongside her hip. Inside, trinkets she had collected were padded with bits of material to keep them from clanking as she walked. She'd also wrapped foodstuffs for the journey.

She wasn't scared, not of this, not of stealing out of a castle in the middle of the night. Over the last week, activity seemed to increase in the fortress. Knights came and went, always armed and sometimes covered in blood as they rode into the castle, always grim-faced and determined when they rode out. Tension tightened the lines of those who stayed behind.

Karre had been in some pretty rough situations, but wolf-men who ate their victims? The images it conjured made her stomach curl and the nightmares were even worse.

*Our men will protect us.*

"Then where the hell is my great protector?" Karre took a deep breath, trying to convince herself she didn't care that Vidar was gone. Why should she? They had only known each other a short time before he left. So what if her body still desired him? So what if in her nightmares it was always him coming to save her? So what if in the dreams that followed they made love—tender and sweet, hard and rough, bent over tables, pressed against trees, in the dining hall at his place of honor, on the battlements, in the brewery... Okay, so there wasn't a place in the fortress she hadn't dreamed of being with him in.

She forced her mind to clear until only the task at hand filtered through her thoughts. Walking down the darkened hall, she ran the back of her hand over the stone to keep on path. Twenty steps would take her to her turn, then another twenty-three until she reached the main hall. Hopefully, with the late hour, no one would be there.

Karre quickened her pace, going through the arched doorway to the main hall where everyone gathered to dine during the day and drink generous amounts of liquor in the evening. Drinking would lead to fornicating and the people of Spearhead didn't always retire to their chambers when it came time to "play".

Scanning the long rows of tables littered with goblets, she found one couple sleeping on top of one at the far side of the room near the large fireplace. Karre walked to the head table, where she dined with a few of the honored knights, and grabbed an etched metal goblet. Shoving it in her bag, she reached for another one, dumping the remaining liquor on the floor. When she'd taken all five of the etched ones, she made her way toward the entrance with her hand on the bag to keep the goblets from clanking.

Her foot stepped on something in the dim light. She gasped, looking down to find a retracting hand disappearing beneath a table.

"Hold, watch it," someone mumbled.

She stiffened, waiting several seconds before moving. The person's hand did not reappear. Letting out her captured breath, she renewed her pace.

The chill of early morning brought with it a strange silence. The courtyard normally bustled with activity, but now it was abandoned and desolate. Faint shafts of light streaked the sky, but it was still too early for the sun to rise. Stars shone bright and she looked up to get her bearings. On most planes the constellations remained the same and once you could read them, it was possible to navigate no matter where you were—so long as you could see the sky.

She neared the front gate, looking up at the battlements. The guards walked the length four times an hour throughout the night, circling back behind the castle. With no man guarding the gate, she took the steps leading up the outer bailey wall. She couldn't unlatch the gate without drawing attention, but she could climb down the side of the wall onto the pathway from the gate to beyond the moat. With luck, no one would spot her escape.

Karre took off the bag and lifted it up, ready to swing it over the side. The sound of approaching hooves caused her to draw back her hand at the last moment, clanging the goblets as she clutched the bag to her stomach.

"Ho! Open the gate!"

*Vidar!*

*Shit!*

"Identify yourself!" Vidar demanded when she didn't move. She could see by the silhouette of his body that he was looking up at her. Karre ducked down, hiding from view as she went to the narrow stairs to climb off the wall. The sound of running feet came as a guard made his way to investigate.

Vidar came home now? After weeks of being gone? It was a cruel twist of irony that he arrived the exact moment she tried to leave him. A shiver worked over her at the thought and she looked at the sky. It couldn't be...

*If the gods so choose.*

Vidar shouted behind her as she ran from the wall, but the words were distorted. The gate creaked open behind her and Vidar rode in. "Karre?"

She stopped moving. There was no point in running now. Slowly, she turned, watching the horse come to a stop. A knight closed the main gate behind him as another from atop the wall watched the scene below. As the man by the gate came to take Vidar's horse, Vidar strode the remaining distance toward her.

*Think, Karre, think. Come up with an excuse. Smile at him.*

"What are you doing on the wall, my lady?" he asked, his handsome brow furrowed.

She had forgotten how good he looked. The golden flecks in his hazel eyes caught up the moonlight, casting an animalistic, primal charm about him. Memories of his hands, how they felt, of his warm lips running over her flesh filled her. Her nerves tingled, as if reaching out to him.

"Looking," she managed to answer after some time.

"Looking for what?"

Think of something.

She hugged the bag tighter. Weakly, she said, "For the Caniba."

His questioning expression turned hard. "Caniba? Have they been spotted near the gate? Why wasn't I informed? Get inside at once!" He reached for the sword at his waist and began to turn around to chase after the guard.

"No, they haven't," Karre said, stopping him. "The maids told me stories and I... It's silly. I think I scared myself and I just had to see the countryside for myself to make sure they weren't out there."

He looked at her again with piercing intensity and she lost her breath. Her eyes traveled down over his form—moving over his broad chest to his waist. Seeing the knife hanging near his hip, her eyes moved back up.

"I couldn't sleep," she finished, patting the blade hidden by her skirts.

At that, he relaxed. "There is no reason to be scared. Every man here would lay down his life to protect you, my lady."

*And if they fail?*

Vidar reached to cup her cheek. "You look worried."

"Sleepy," she mumbled. An awkward moment passed between them. He withdrew his hand and averted his eyes to the entrance behind her. The breeze shifted and she smelled the dried perspiration on his body, mingled with horse and dirt. "Should we go in?"

Vidar nodded. Karre looked at the wall, thinking of how close she'd come to escaping this place. But with Vidar there, the urge to run dissipated, replaced by the need to touch him, hear him, taste him. When he touched her, she felt safe, as if that brief contact could melt away all her worry.

"Will you wake a servant to bring me a bath?" he asked, falling into step beside her.

"Yes." Her breathing deepened. Vidar in a bath, naked, wet.

"Thank you, my lady. I am weary from the ride." He reached to take her satchel. "Let me take this to your chamber for you."

Karre snatched it back in surprise. The goblets banged together. Vidar stopped walking and arched a brow. Panicking, she dropped the bag and lifted her arms around his neck, kissing him hard. His lips tensed and he gasped in surprise, but her insistent tongue to his mouth forced him to relax.

She let her body mold to his, feeling a tingling pressure where they touched. Karre moaned, momentarily forgetting herself. Vidar placed his hands on her hips and pushed her firmly back. "Let us go inside."

Karre grabbed her bag and used his words as an excuse to carry it herself. "I'll see to your bath."

---

After waking a servant and putting her stolen goblets back on the table, Karre hurried back to the chambers she shared with Vidar. Her heart beat fast, with both the idea of almost being caught and the promise of Vidar's seduction. By the time she reached his bedchamber door, she was breathing heavily.

Without knocking, she went inside. To her surprise, she found Bratene leaning over Vidar in the metal tub, scrubbing his naked back. Vidar moaned, a low, throaty sound of pleasure.

Karre skidded to a stop, her mouth opening. For a long moment, she didn't say anything as she waited for them to notice her. The servant lifted his arm, washing his side. Karre crossed her arms over chest, still waiting to be noticed. Bratene's hands dipped beneath the water, following the indent of his spine down, down, down...

"Stop right there," Karre demanded loudly.

Bratene gasped and jerked away from Vidar. The maid's eyes were wide when she turned to Karre. Vidar glanced back, his movements slow. She expected remorse or guilt, instead he just looked.

"Out," she ordered Bratene.

"But I have not finished," the maid protested.

"Out," Karre repeated with more force. "Now."

Vidar's brows lowered over his gorgeous eyes.

"My lady," Bratene mumbled, rushing out of the door.

When it slammed closed, Vidar said, "She wasn't finished."

"What? Washing you?" Karre stormed across the room to her door, going into her chambers to hide her bag before coming back to face him. "I thought men of Staria did not sleep with other women once they were married."

"What are you talking about?" Vidar frowned.

"Perhaps the word sleep was too vague," she answered, pacing past his tub only to turn around and pace back so she could face him. Hands on hips, she continued, "You said that your gods smile upon your marriages and that you do not seek to fuck other women because you have to be faithful or warlike or disciplined. War, marriage..." She slashed her hand at him, not even coming close to touching him.

"We stay faithful because the gods demand discipline," he corrected. "Just as war demands discipline. It is our way."

"Whatever," she grumbled.

"You are angry?" He made no move to get out of the bath and the firelight reflection on the glistening water that beaded on his soap-trailed flesh made her mouth go dry.

"What do I care if the maid tries to..." She gestured at his chest. A thought whispered in the back of her mind that she needed to stop talking, needed to walk away, needed to rethink what she was doing. This conversation wasn't calculated or planned and it definitely was not advantageous. "I mean, you've been gone. You..." She hesitated at his piercing look. "You didn't tell me you were going."

The argument seemed silly now that it was said.

"You are upset because I left without speaking with you first?"

He straightened. "I told you I had duties to attend to and I sent word with Sir Oskar."

*Oh, yes, the mumbling Sir Oskar. How did the knight put it? "My lady, Sir Vidar sends his respect. He is detained at the marshland encampment. Have you a message for him?"*

"I was not told you needed me while I was away," he added.

Why was he looking at her like that?

"What do I care if you leave? You don't owe me an explanation. We only knew each other a few days before you left." Karre frowned. And that was it. The truth of it. The whole of their relationship. A few short days, a ceremony and a small trip. She had no reason to say the things coming out of her mouth. She had no reason to be jealous of Bratene.

Oh, but she was jealous. Her entire body seethed with it. The emotion struck her hard, forcing her to act without thought. And it was not only jealousy, but anger and frustration that he left her, his bride, alone in a strange fortress threatened by cannibals. She didn't ask to marry him, didn't plan to stay married to him, for such a thing would never work, but he didn't know that.

"Then you are jealous that Bratene bathed me? There is no reason. It is a servant's job to bathe—"

"Well, I made some changes while you were gone," Karre interrupted, well aware of how she sounded but unable to stop. "I can work, too, you know."

He smiled and there was a definite challenge in his gold-flecked gaze. "Changes to bathing?"

"Yes. No. I mean we still bathe. Of course there will still be bathing. But maids don't bathe married men." Karre knelt by the tub and reached her hand behind him. Finding the washcloth the maid had dropped, she pushed it onto his back. The warm heat radiating off him and the subtle smell of Starian soap caused her to inhale deeply. "I can bathe you and, if I'm not around, you can do it yourself."

"But servants—"

"Yourself." Karre pushed at his back. Bathing servants weren't unheard of in her travels, but neither were the "happy endings" they included with the deal. "No maids are to be massaging any part of you while I'm around."

"Very well, my lady, it will be as you wish."

"Good." She nodded, moving to methodically scrub his back. "I'm glad we understand each other."

# CHAPTER 7

*Because right now, in this moment, she didn't want to think.*

Karre massaged Vidar's neck, having discarded the washcloth to use her hands. Soap made her fingers glide over the solid ridge of muscles and she took full advantage of his wet, naked state. She explored every inch under the guise of washing him. Her thighs tightened and her pussy ached to be filled as moisture gathered along the soft folds.

She pulled, urging him to lean back in the metal tub. Small protests erupted in her mind, but she willfully refused to heed them because right now, in this moment, she didn't want to think. Karre rubbed his chest, pressing her hands firmly in the center and massaging them outward. She skimmed his nipples and his breath caught.

She kept exploring, moving leisurely down until her hands dipped beneath the water. The tight hold of her green corset pulled tight to her chest, forcing her breasts up and together to create deep cleavage. Vidar stared at her breasts as she leaned over him and gripped the edge of the tub.

She found his navel and the back of her hand brushed his solid cock. Vidar groaned. Wet fingertips found her breasts and thrust between them. She wrapped her massaging fingers around his erection, gliding down to his balls, then up.

"Take off your gown," he ordered.

Karre made no move to obey. She twisted her hands on his cock, lacing her fingers as she worked her hands over him beneath the blue water.

"I wish to take you now," he said, not as commanding as before. "Lift your skirts and climb on top of me."

Karre ignored the request. She pumped harder, gripping him tighter. "No, I'm bathing you."

Water splashed on her sleeves and shoulders. She thrust one hand down to grab his balls and the root of his shaft while the other continued to move along the smooth arousal. The hand between her breasts tried to tug the mounds from the corset, but without loosening the laces, they were bound too tightly.

Vidar tensed, his body jerking beautifully as he came beneath the water. She kept pumping, milking his cock of every last drop. When his head fell back, she stopped, grinning. Running a finger down the center of his chest, she said, "There's a good warrior."

"Yea," Vidar breathed, his limp body hers to command. He didn't know why the maid's presence had upset her, as it was common for servants to attend a leader's bath, but he found he liked the spark of jealousy he saw in her. Besides, no maid had ever given him a bath like the one he'd just had.

Lids fell heavy over his eyes as he watched Karre stand. She began pulling at her corset and he licked his lips in eager anticipation. Glorious breasts spilled forward and the bodice dropped to the ground. The underdress had been cut low in the front, open to her waist. She pushed the wet sleeves aside, unveiling her naked form.

Vidar pushed up from the bath, stepping out. He'd missed the feel of her body. Even as his cock lay limp and satisfied, he knew it would easily be roused to go again.

Instead of dropping her gown, she walked to him, holding it

before her. She used it to dry him off. He couldn't resist cupping a breast as it came within reach. He groaned, squeezing it.

Karre covered his hand with hers and pulled him with her toward his bed. She sat on the end and spread her thighs. "Kneel, warrior."

He did as she commanded, kneeling between her legs. The pink folds were parted, showcasing the hidden bud of her clit surrounded by the glistening cream of her body. Her pussy welcomed his mouth and he moaned as her taste filled him. He thrust his tongue into her before licking up her slit. She squirmed, thrusting into him. He gripped her thighs.

His cock lifted, jealous of his mouth's pleasure. He reached to pump the shaft, helping it to full capacity. Feeling how wet she was, how open, he surged to his feet. She looked at him in surprise, but he didn't wait. Bringing his arousal to her pussy, he thrust hard, pulling her body into his so they slammed together. He had to bend his knees to make their position work, but he ignored the burn in his thighs and calves as he propelled his hips back and forth.

"Oh, oh, oh," Karre gasped over and over, punctuating his thrusts with the feminine sounds. Her large breasts bobbed as she reached her hands over her head to grab the fur coverlet on his bed. He fucked her harder, just to watch them move. Oh, how he wanted to bury his face between them. How he wanted to lick them, bite them, fuck them until they were covered in his cum.

He knew he had missed being with her, but he hadn't realized how much until this moment. Her pussy trembled around his erection and her back arched off the bed. Vidar couldn't resist her body's call as she came. He jerked, meeting his climax as her muscles clamped down. With a great sigh, he collapsed to his knees and rested his head on the edge of the mattress. Her legs were still open, unmoving against his arms.

When he regained his strength, he crawled up onto the bed and lay down next to her. "Would you like me to carry you to your chamber?"

Karre gave a soft laugh. "I heard that Starian men and women don't sleep in the same bed." She pulled her legs up over the side and inched higher so their faces were close. Stroking his cheek, she said, "That's another change I'm going to make. There's no reason to sleep in separate beds. You can carry me back to my room, but only if you plan on staying there with me."

---

What had she been thinking? Sleep in the same room? The Starian setup had been perfect, affording her privacy. Even as she knew her staunch control was slipping, she couldn't help snuggling closer to Vidar's side. The man was a machine in bed, going for hours, and incredibly enthusiastic.

After carrying her to her bed, he'd taken his time exploring her breasts—nipping, kissing, licking, fucking. He pulled her on top of him to straddle his face as he lay on his back. He'd buried his mouth and chin in her sex, only turning her around as she began to climax so she could ride his cock to completion. He bent her on her hands and knees and took her from behind, pounding into her until sweat slicked their bodies and she couldn't breathe from the sheer pleasure of it. He then turned in the bed and lay on his side, leisurely licking her pussy as she sucked his marvelous cock.

Karre believed he would have kept going had she not protested and begged to sleep. Now, as morning light streamed into the room, she felt his hard cock nudging her naked thigh. She lay on her stomach, her head turned from him. Vidar lifted her hair before brushing his lips along the back of her neck.

"I will have to thank Sir Jacque for his words. I find I enjoyed implementing his advice." Vidar nipped at her flesh while his hand skimmed over her naked ass.

Karre chuckled. "Who's he?"

"A soldier from the marsh encampment. I felt how you enjoyed such things." Fingers followed down the cleft, nearing her pussy. "There are more positions that I would like to try."

"Haven't you had enough?" She moaned in protest, only partially meaning it. Her muscles ached with the dull fatigue only a night of sex could bring.

"Of you? Not even close, my lady." Vidar pressed his hips into her. "I wish to finish you again before going to break our fast."

"Do you have to leave again?" She turned her face into the bed.

Vidar's finger wiggled its way to her clit. "Only when word from the marshland encampment calls me away."

"Why would they call you?" She parted her legs slightly to ease his way.

"I do not wish—" he began.

"How is it you wanted to take me?" She turned to him, eyeing him through her lashes.

Instantly, he pushed up. "Sit on my lap."

Karre did, straddling his legs. She smiled when his eyes instantly went to her breasts. "You were saying? Why would they call you away?"

"I do—" Vidar gasped as she pushed her breasts into his face only to withdraw. "I interrogated Magda's spies while I was there." Karre did it again, twisting so her nipple hit his mouth. He sucked it into his mouth and groaned. She pulled back and the nipple slipped from his grasp with a loud *smack*.

"What did you find out?" Karre reached between them and took hold of his shaft, intent on carrying out her own interrogation. She rubbed the tip along her folds.

Vidar closed his eyes. "Sorceress Magda plans to lead her minions against Spearhead. I've discovered her plot and alerted the king. He sends us reinforcements."

Karre hesitated at the news.

"Mm." He pulled her hips down, managing to get the tip of his cock inside her before she caught herself. "It will be a glorious battle."

Glorious? She hesitated again.

Vidar pulled her down on his cock and she gasped as he filled her, stretching her sore muscles. "I will bring you much honor, my lady." He lifted her up. "You will find much pride in my sword." He jerked her onto his shaft.

Karre lost her train of thought. Vidar pushed his hand up between her breasts, urging her to lean back while on his cock. She braced her weight on her hands. The position put pressure along the sweet spot in her pussy. They thrust in a leisured rhythm and when her release washed over her it was perfect.

Vidar took her upper arm and pulled her to his chest. He groaned, stiffening as he came. He kept her impaled on him as he adjusted himself on the bed to lie down. He held her to his chest, rubbing along the small of her back.

"Perhaps it is too early to dine. We should stay right here," he whispered moments before his chest rose and fell in even breaths.

---

Karre's arrival at Spearhead couldn't have had worse timing. Apparently, they had gone decades without an attack on the fortress, but by Vidar's own words, a siege was imminent. She saw the evidence of his concern on the faces of the knights, in the way their rigid security became even more so. They drank less, brooded more and the number of guards patrolling the wall doubled.

Escape would not be easy, but how could she stay, knowing what she did?

"Who are you?"

Karre blinked, so lost in thought she didn't hear Vidar's approach. "What do you mean?"

*Did Divinity say something to you?*

In the last few days, cast under the rapturous spell of Vidar's touch, she had almost let herself forget that the corporation was out there. How could she think of evil deeds when his touch was so heavenly? An easy rapport developed, making for lighthearted banter but never serious conversation. It wasn't a perfect marriage, but it was the best relationship she'd ever been in. Well, to be honest, it was pretty much the only real relationship she'd ever been in.

If he tried to get serious, she'd distract him with sexual advances and invitations. His hand brushed her thigh under the table when they dined. His eyes met hers over the distance when he exercised with the men. He took her in their bedchambers, in hidden alcoves, in abandoned rooms, and once near the stables in a tight corner near the courtyard. He met her body's every demand, giving in to her whenever she wanted him, whenever she needed to stop his questions. But now, as he looked at her, she knew there was going to be no stopping the questions he'd been trying so hard to ask.

The passageway they stood in was unremarkable, other than the fact it had become Karre's sanctuary. With an old, locked door and dead end, only the maids came to the far end of the castle and not much at that. She'd already picked the old lock, only finding a dismal run of empty, old iron bar prison cells.

Her breath caught and she felt as if the surrounding castle closed in on her. Somehow, in the isolated almost primitive world of Staria, she'd managed to forget who she was. Maybe that's why she didn't try harder to leave. With so many knights, in the middle of nowhere on a low traffic plane, she had felt hidden, safe. Only after she learned of the Caniba had the urge to run filled her.

Karre glanced behind her, but it was the dead end. Vidar blocked her only escape. Her mind raced for her next move. "Is this a game? Did Sir Jacque give you more ideas?"

"It is a simple question," he said. "Who are you?"

*Sandie, Faith, Temperance, Hope, Devil, Sparkle.*

"I'm Karre." She forced a smile. "Your wife."

"Who were you before you came here?" he asked, leaning against the wall. He had an animalistic grace, even in his leisured pose.

*Mazi, Ms. Lara Pentafore, Lady Pentafore, Madam Pentafore, Domma Pentafore.*

"I was Karre." She widened her smile. "Not your wife."

Vidar didn't move for a moment, but then suddenly tilted his head back and laughed. "You once told me that there was an ocean on another plane and that you liked to stand on the cliffs so the water would splash on your face when the tides came in. Was that your homeland?"

"I also said that your skin reminded me of it." She reached to touch the side of his face, but he caught her wrist. "What is it?"

*What did Divinity tell you?*

"What are you hiding?" He didn't let go of her.

"Nothing." It took all her power to keep the innocent look on her face and she wasn't sure she was even successful. "There is nothing to tell."

Vidar studied Karre's blank expression. The king had ordered him to learn of his wife, but every time he tried, she distracted him with her amazing kisses and lush body. Now, as she artfully avoided his direct questions, he became concerned. Perhaps there was something she wasn't telling him. The faint hints he had were disconcerting—such as how she claimed to have been delivered against her will.

"I know you planned a trip," he stated. A maid had found her bag filled with trinkets from the fortress. All were things he'd freely give her, had she but asked. "Your bag had supplies for travel."

"You went through my room?" She frowned, narrowing her eyes as all pretense of the smile left her.

"Tell me why you chose to come here." He didn't let go and she didn't fight him.

"Who said I chose it? You picked me, remember?" She didn't move from her spot, didn't cringe or back away.

"Why will you not answer me? Who are you, Karre? One minute you're meek, the next bold. You never speak of your homeland or how you've come to be with me." It took all his willpower not to kiss her, not to let her tempt him with her perfect mouth and pleasing ways.

"I thought you said it was the gods who brought me here." She tried jerking her hand away. He kept her in his grasp, afraid she might run if he let go. "Apparently, it's as simple as that. Perhaps you should ask them how I've come to be here, for I don't know the answer."

"Who are you?" Vidar yelled in frustration. His words echoed around them.

"I don't know anymore," she answered, just as loudly.

That surprised him. "You lost your memories?"

"No." Her pull on her wrist weakened as she stopped fighting his restraint. She studied his face, as if trying to decide her next words. "I-I scrambled my memories."

He tilted his head, studying her in confusion.

"But I still know which are mine. I know who I am. I just don't know *who* I am in the larger sense of the word. I've been..." She made a weak noise and shrugged, still not making any sense to him.

"You are my wife, Karre. I do not know if you understand fully what that means. Whatever it is you are running from cannot hurt you." Lifting his hand to her cheek, he ran his fingers along her jaw. "I will protect you."

Her gaze fell at his touch. "And what if you fall by the Caniba's hand? What then? Will you come back from the grave to protect me?"

"Then I will die with honor and make you proud."

"Proud?" Her eyes shot back up to meet his. "How is your death supposed to make me proud? I'm not a monster."

"The pride should come in my honor and in a good death."

"That brings me back to—how the hell are you supposed to protect me when you're dead?" She jerked her hand. He gripped harder until she stopped.

"Should that day come, another will take you under his protection." He hated to think it and refused to imagine her with another man.

"Passed to another husband? You mean I have to go back to the ceremony?"

"There are other ways. You could take..." He couldn't say it.

"Another husband while you're still around?" she finished astutely. "No, thanks, warrior. I think one is more than enough. I would hate to see the havoc two of you would wreak on my life."

He relaxed. Without realizing it, a knot had formed in his stomach. It now eased its hold, allowing him to breathe. "The Caniba will not harm you. Every man in Staria would give his life to make sure of it. I understand that you do not know our ways, but you are Starian now. We do not run from danger."

"All I do is run." She sighed. "Let go of my arm."

"Only if you promise to tell me how you came to be here."

"That's simple." She laughed, though the sound didn't hold any pleasure. Then, as if coming to a decision, she said, "I got caught and Divinity sent me here as my punishment."

"Caught? Doing what?" As promised, he let her go. She rubbed her wrist as she backed away from him. He widened his stance to block any retreat out of the dead-end hall.

Her mouth trembled before she answered, "Stealing documents from one of their safe houses."

Vidar's hand flexed. It was as if he could still feel her pressed into his palm. "A thief?"

"A very good thief," she corrected, "despite being caught."

He studied her face, waiting for her to smile, to laugh, to indicate she was joking. Instead, she merely looked at him, her expression guarded and closed. A thief? His wife?

"Honestly, my getting caught was dumb luck on Divinity's part."

"How so?"

Again she looked at him as if she decided whether or not she could trust him. "I knew the security risk was great, but how could I pass it up? It was a safe house."

"And?" he prompted.

"I went in smart. I met someone who brought me a briefcase full of security codes and a map. Getting in was easy. My only mistake was not having the right layout of the mansion. The architects forgot to mention the secret Divinity tech room behind the nursery mirror. Figures the one place I think to hide my wrist portal is on the door to a secret room. My misfortune and Divinity's dumb luck." She sighed, running her hands into her hair and shaking the locks. Muttering, she said, "I don't even know why we're talking about this."

He opened his mouth, but he didn't know how to answer. His wife was talking about infiltrating enemy territory. Such things were not easy or for the weak of heart. As if seeing her for the first time, he looked at her face, her cunning eyes.

"Sorry you pried? It's not the answer you were looking for, was it?" She walked past him, turning her shoulders so they didn't touch. "Too bad. It's the only answer I have." She made it around the corner before he could even think to stop her.

No, it wasn't the answer he looked for.

Karre hurried away from Vidar. What had she been thinking? Did she really expect him to react any differently? He tried to hide it, but she saw the disappointment in his eyes, the silent retreat of his emotions. She had tested him, not telling him anything Divinity didn't already know until she knew how he would react. Well, she'd gotten her answer. It was right there in his beautiful eyes.

*Fool. Stupid idiot. I should have kept my mouth shut.*

She didn't know where she was going, only that she had to keep moving, had to keep taking turn after turn, through endless passageways until she was sure to be lost—which was hard to do when she knew her way around. When she finally stopped moving, her hands shook and her knees wobbled, forcing her to the ground. She pushed into a small alcove, pressing her back to the hard stone as she drew her limbs into her chest. Her eyes stung and she realized that tears ran down her cheeks.

*Stupid fool!*

The hall was eerily quiet as Karre made her way up to the head table to dine. The knights studied their meals, muttering in low tones that blended together to make one giant murmur of incoherent sounds. Nervously, she found Vidar. He'd sent a maid to command her to the hall to join the meal, which seemed strange since he'd not really spoken to her for the last couple of days. They didn't even share the same bed. She never thought she'd miss the feel of someone next to her as much as she did.

Karre's blue linen skirts felt abnormally heavy as she made her way to the head table. The darker blue of the corset pressed her stomach into her spine, but Jordinne had insisted on tightening it—something about bolstering the recently low morale of their leader.

Maybe if she passed out from lack of air, Karre wouldn't have to see his questioning gaze.

"What has happened?" Karre asked, taking a seat by Vidar. His hand paused in the process of lifting a two-pronged fork to his mouth. "Is it the Caniba? Do they attack?"

"I wished for you to join us, as is your duty." He placed the meat into his mouth, chewing thoughtfully. "Your absence has been felt."

"Oh?" She watched his face.

"By the hall," he added. "The people have asked after you."

"Did you tell them?" Karre looked over the hall, to the rows of long tables filled with knights and their women. Several stared back at her. "About me?"

"I saw no need to announce it," he answered, frowning as he stabbed a vegetable with a little too much force. His words didn't really bring her any comfort.

"Then why is everyone so..." She paused, trying to think of the right word. "Tame?"

"Magda's scouts were killed near the border, not far from here. It is beginning." He didn't even try to shield her from it, not like before when she had to pry information out of him with her seduction.

"Are you leaving to fight?"

"Not yet, but soon. The king promises reinforcements. I'm to wait here for them to arrive prior to riding out to engage the sorceress before she and her armies pass into our borders." He didn't look at her as he continued to dine.

A maid brought her a trencher of food, causing Karre to jolt in surprise as it was set in front of her. She nodded her thanks and forced herself to eat, though in the end she rearranged the food more than consumed it. All her attention focused on Vidar. A cold chill worked over her from him. She hated him for it and hated herself for having told him even the smallest grain of truth. Lies always suited her purpose so much better.

"Have I made a long enough appearance?" Karre placed her fork on the trencher and reached for her goblet. The food might sit on her stomach like a rock, but the liquor would calm her nerves and hopefully numb her brain.

"If you're ready to go, I will escort you." Vidar took his goblet and finished off his drink.

"Why don't you just have the maids and knights trail me?" Karre muttered bitterly. "Or did you think I would not notice they have been keeping an eye on me the last couple of days?"

"You're paranoid."

"Uh-huh," she said dryly.

"The maids serve you and this castle. The knights are protection," he elaborated. "There is a threat nearby. I would think you liked the extra security. You seem to doubt my ability to protect you."

Feeling bitter, she let her hand brush up against the knife along her thigh and mumbled, "Don't worry about me. I will see to myself. Stay here in your hall." Karre stood, wondering if he would follow her but unsure if she wanted him to.

Vidar waited until Karre disappeared through the arched doorway before standing to follow her. It had taken all he had not to go to her the last couple of days, but he needed time to process what she'd said. She admitted to being a thief. He resented her for it, even as he was drawn to her. A thief? Why had the gods tempted him with a thief? His family honor reeled at the injustice of it. What if the others discovered the truth? What if she left him, as she was surely going to do the night he came home from the marshlands?

Walking faster, he let his feet hit hard upon the floor. He shouldn't have to occupy his mind with Karre, not when there were more pressing matters of war. The people of Spearhead depended on him to protect them. The people of Staria needed him to maintain the borders. Magda was one of the most formidable foes they'd seen in a long time and she was planning an attack in his territory.

*A woman is a woman,* Vidar had told Oskar the day before his wedding. *The gods will give me what they give me. The king showed me the trade agreement. The women must be able to bear children, be in good health, able to do their duty and will know their place. What do I care if they are born in Staria, are brought through the fairy rings from distant lands or are traded for with Divinity aliens from another plane of existence? So long as she is not our enemy.*

Now he knew his mistake. Vidar should have demanded the king be more specific with his future, like the brides should not have a criminal past. Instead, all he could think about was finding a bride for sexual release, a soft, sweet body to slake his desires in. Karre did do that for him. His breathing deepened and his cock hardened until his pride warred with desire.

When he caught up to her, he wasn't sure if he would pleasure her or punish her. His hand wrapped around the back of her arm and he tugged her with him to the nearest door. With the hour being so late, no one occupied the sewing chamber. He let go of her and shut the door.

"Afraid I would run off?" She arched a brow, the sourness of her mood still apparent in her tone.

By all the bloody swords, she was still beautiful—even angry.

He didn't answer, at least not with words. Vidar grabbed the sides of her face and crushed his lips to hers. He needed to taste her, feel her. Her soft lips parted and he slid his tongue between them. In that moment, he didn't care what she had been before coming to him. Right now, she was his.

The pressures of his life faded, replaced by her mead-laden kiss. She moved against him, running her fingers into his hair, pulling him closer as if she needed him as badly as he needed her. What was it about this woman that made all logic fade?

He turned her, walking her past the large weaving loom toward the long sewing table. When the back of her thighs hit the tabletop, he kept kissing her, leaning her back until she was forced to crawl on top. Bolts of material cushioned her head as she stretched out before him like a feast of the flesh just waiting to be unraveled and eaten. Vidar fully intended to dine.

Karre moaned softly, wet with anticipation as he slowly undressed her—loosening her corset, pulling her garments over her head. No torches burned in the sewing chamber. Blue moonlight shone over them, streaming in from narrow windows to illuminate his face with an unearthly glow.

Vidar leaned over the table as he stood beside her, looking down at her naked form stretched out before him. He ran his hand over her breasts, brushing the nipples lightly so they peaked into hard buds. Not answering their aching call, he instead ran his hand along her ribs. She reached for him, but he pushed her arms away. Understanding his game, she lifted her arms over her head and didn't move.

Karre closed her eyes, following his playful touch with her mind, wondering at the change in him. It was as if he tried to learn her for the first time. The nerves tingled wherever he touched, sending out signals to her pussy until cream nearly dripped from her sex. Sensations skimmed along her toes, her calves, up her outer thighs and hips. He crossed her waist, circling her breasts before tracing the line of her arms. By small degrees his touch became firm as he retraced his original path, endlessly traveling over her body. By the time he made it back to her breasts and squeezed them in his palms, she was writhing on the hard wood.

She couldn't take waiting any longer and reached between her thighs to rub her swollen clit. It felt so good she cried out softly. Vidar took her breast in his mouth, aggressively sucking the nipple. His hand covered hers over her pussy. As she worked her clit, he slipped a thick finger into her slick sex and wiggled it around. Another of his fingers pressed down between the cleft of her ass, rubbing along the rosette of her anus. She rode their combined hands, sliding her finger into her pussy to join his. He went much deeper and the pressure of their fingers worked pleasurably against the sweet spot hidden inside her cavern.

Karre met with release, rewarding their efforts with a flood of cream. Breathing hard, Vidar crawled onto the table, drawing up between her thighs. Her ass rubbed against the hard wood as his weight held her hips down. He'd loosened his pants and now brought his thick, hard cock to claim his prize.

He thrust his hips forward, filling her to the brink. Wildly, he rode her, pounding and gliding in her wet pussy. Lighter tremors worked over her and she climaxed once more. Vidar grunted, suddenly stopping as he, too, found release.

Pinning her to the table with his weight, he pressed his nose to hers. Karre's legs fell along his sides. Their breathing mingled as he looked deep into her eyes. She waited for him to speak, but instead he pushed up and crawled off the table. Karre was slower to get up, sitting naked on the table as he dressed. When he finished, he turned to her and sighed heavily.

"Is this goodbye?" Her jaw tightened. Why else would he look at her like that?

"I had hoped you would come back to our chambers with me," he answered. "A bed would be much more comfortable."

Karre exhaled in relief. Giving him a small smile, she said, "Then hand me my gown. I have no wish to run naked through the halls."

# CHAPTER 8

*Because right now, in this moment, Karre needed to confess everything, even if it was to a sleeping man.*

For the first time since she had left her home world, Karre felt as if she might actually stop running. Sure, she knew the feeling might be fleeting, knew that tomorrow she might not be able to stop herself from going, but right now, as she looked at Vidar's sleeping face, she could actually imagine what it would be like to never jump to another plane. The idea terrified and exhilarated her because right now, in this moment, Karre needed to confess everything, even if it was to a sleeping man.

Karre sat on the bed, her legs crossed as she leaned her elbows onto her knees. Her sated body should have forced her to sleep, but her racing mind refueled her with a nervous energy. If she decided to stay, then the Caniba would become her enemy. She would have to face the fear and learn to live with their constant threat. However, before that, she would have to convince Vidar that she should stay for something other than duty and the will of the gods. Maybe she even needed to convince herself. Or maybe there were gods watching them, moving people around at will because of some great, incomprehensible plan.

Confusion filled her, causing her thoughts to swim around in her head.

"I have been searching for a plane like this," Karre whispered, reaching to push a lock of hair off Vidar's forehead. "A low-tech place off the grid with very little inter-dimensional traffic. A person could disappear here. You have no idea how valuable that is. Divinity only wants your mineral water and perhaps to use you as a dumping ground for those they want to keep out of the main system—like me. They don't even have this world listed in their primary database. I have been thinking about that a lot. I memorized all four-hundred-thirty-six so-called known dimensions so I would know which ones to avoid and which to be careful on. Even that other prisoner bride at the ceremony said this place was uncharted. It means they don't have any use for it beyond what they're already trading. Once they have their fill of the water, they'll most likely never come back. I've seen it many times. With infinite worlds, they don't pay attention to all of them. They take what they can use and then they go."

He didn't answer, not that she expected him to as she watched his even breathing.

"It would be nice to have the PJP back. Um, that's the portable jump prototype that I had to travel to different planes without their main portal." She rubbed her wrist, thinking of the device. "You know, just to have it. Just in case I ever needed it." Karre laughed softly. "Just to get to my stash one last time to do what I need to."

Still, he slept.

"You should see some of the things I've collected. I have notes about missions Divinity wouldn't want anyone knowing about. I have pictures and video files and confessions. I have their office policies and contract copies that show obvious moral codes violations. I think that is why they want me alive, but where I can do no harm. They think by analyzing the PJP they will find out everywhere I have gone. What they don't know is that I have reset the history. They will never find what they're looking for."

She ran her hand lightly over his cheek and down his throat. His pulse beat steadily under her fingers. The fur blanket covered his stomach but left his chest bare. She drew her hand down to feel his heart beneath her fingers.

"Divinity is not the company you think it to be. They present themselves well, but they are not noble. They do things. Horrible things." She took a deep breath. "They make people do things, become things."

"What did they force you to do?"

Karre gasped, jumping back at Vidar's calm words. Apparently, he wasn't as asleep as she'd thought. How much had he heard? "You're awake."

His eyes opened, meeting hers. "Of course."

"You should have said something. You should have stopped me."

"Why would I interrupt? I was listening to you speak." He turned on his side, resting on his arm as he touched her naked thigh. "Please continue."

Karre hesitated. It was different now with him looking at her.

"Please," he insisted.

"Divinity's actions made me a thief. They changed the entire course of my life." Karre pulled away from him, turning to stand on the floor. She felt too exposed as she strode naked to his trunk. Pulling up the lid, she grabbed the first tunic she found and pulled it over her head. "I've spent many years trying to prove what I know of the corporation, but they have covered their tracks very efficiently. I foolishly thought I might be able to stop them, but there are too many planes for them to hide."

"What is it you know?"

"That they stole lives. My land was called Grenlay Islah. I lived with my father near the water. He had retired from our country's military. I wanted to be a scientist and build better technology to be used in astronomical research. Astronomy is what we call the study of the universe beyond the earth's atmosphere—stars, sun, moon, planets. It seems so far away now, so small in importance to what I know now. My world isn't anywhere near close to discovering inter-dimensional travel. Normally such ideas were the thing of entertainment novels and holographic plays." Karre continued to pace, not meeting his eyes but very aware that they were on her. It seemed strange telling this story, perhaps because it was the truth. It had been a long time since she had told her truth to anyone.

"Come, my lady," he urged, patting the bed. "Sit. Please."

Karre refused, continuing to pace. "But you see, just because we weren't close to actually discovering parallel plane travel, it doesn't mean we didn't understand the concept. I think that's why Divinity came to us. We were primitive enough not to know how to chase after them but advanced enough to understand what had happened when they took us to a new plane."

"They stole your people?"

Karre stopped at his words and nodded, wondering if he could possibly believe her. No one else had. "Yes. Kidnapped them. Plucked them up and carted them away like they were picking flowers for their table. They took my father. They pulled him right off the street when he was out for a run. I would have never known what had happened, but I happened to be coming home at the time. I saw their uniforms, their alien equipment. No one would believe me. The police, um, enforcers of the law, thought I was distraught. They wanted me to seek medical help and have myself committed into a grief asylum. A few months later I saw the uniformed men again."

"What did you do?" he prompted when she paused.

"I followed them through their portal. It was like nothing I'd ever felt or seen. It's like being pulled apart on a molecular level and put back together. I thought I was dying. But then I showed up in their science facility. They were so arrogant, they didn't even have guards, like they knew no one could touch them or stop them. I grabbed one of their jackets, slipped it on and walked undetected through their facility. Someone asked me if I was from some place I had never heard of. I said yes. From there I integrated and learned, going from base to base, changing my appearance and my name until I found myself working for the science and technology department."

"And you sought the truth of what had happened?"

"There is no proof. I've looked. When the rest of the company, also known as those people not in charge, started to spread rumors about it, the executives terminated the project. That included permanently terminating those involved."

Vidar arched a brow.

"They killed everyone who knew anything," Karre clarified. "As for my father, I never saw him again."

"What did they take him for?"

"Gladiator fights," she said, "in some Romanesque plane. They took soldiers from my world and sold them to masters who forced them to fight to the death. The plane loved it because they felt all other planes were inferior to them. Otherworlders didn't have rights and were considered a subspecies."

"Were they at war? Not that such a thing would excuse forcing men from other worlds to fight a war that was not theirs to fight."

"No. It was for entertainment."

Vidar frowned in disgust. "To waste life for the sake of passing amusement. Shameful."

"When I finally got to the gladiator plane, I found my father's portrait painted on an arena wall." She paused, letting the pain of the memory roll through her. Karre had sat by that wall, weeping for hours, only leaving when one of the plane's residents came by trying to sell her loaves of green-tinted bread. "Apparently, he did really well before they decided to make him battle three wild beasts with his bare hands in celebration of their ruler's birth anniversary."

"I am sorry to hear this. My father died in battle, as well."

"At least it was a battle he chose to fight and not because some pompous rich master wanted to be entertained," Karre said, feeling bitter from the memory. "I might be a thief, but I only steal from Divinity and their allies for the purpose of stopping them."

"Why are you telling me this now?" Vidar frowned and pulled the fur covers from his hips to swing his legs around. Her eyes instantly turned to his waist before glancing away. "Do you think to leave me to continue your pursuits?"

"I had no intention of ever telling you any of this," she admitted with a humorless laugh. "I thought you were sleeping."

"Then I suppose it is good that I have been trained to sleep lightly." His hand shot forward and he grabbed her wrist. Gently, he pulled her toward him.

Karre resisted briefly but then gave up, needing to feel something other than pain and uncertainty. "I'm tired of running. I want to stay here, but I'm terrified of the Caniba. If I could just see them for myself, I'm sure I could put my mind at ease. The images of them that have been described to me are—"

"You have nothing to fear. We will protect you." Vidar cupped her cheek, running his thumb over her lips. "I will protect you."

"I know better than anyone there are no guarantees in life. Rules and ideas that work on one plane do not on another. You can't promise that I will be safe. You can't promise that I will be protected. All you can do is promise you will do your best." Karre put her fingers over his lips to keep him from answering. "And all I ask is that you try."

His eyes narrowed, the intensity of the look all the more effective by the way the gold flecks picked up the firelight. "You have my word, my lady."

Karre was struck with the full impact of what she had revealed to him. More or less, it had been her life story. No one, not on any of the planes, knew so much about her.

She grabbed his face, pulling his lips to hers in a deep kiss. Moaning, she thrust her tongue between his lips. Vidar's hands roamed the backs of her thighs to push up the tunic she wore. He cupped her ass, rocking her hips forward.

Karre put her knee between his legs and crawled over him, urging him onto his back. When her lungs burned for need of air, she pulled back, panting as she looked down at him. This time there would be no games between them. She was too tired of pretending, of being someone else. "I don't want to run anymore."

Vidar pulled at the tunic shirt, helping her to lift it over her head. His hands skimmed over her breasts and ribs before settling on her hips. "You don't have to run. You are home."

Karre smiled. "But I do need to fight. If the Caniba are as bad as everyone says they are, then I wish to help in the battle to be rid of them. I can't sit here inside a fortress and do nothing. I need to focus on fighting so the fear doesn't overtake me. And if I could just get to my stash, I have things there that can help."

"There is no reason for you to go to battle." Vidar ran a lazy fingertip over her stomach, tracing the lines of her muscles. "Your presence in Spearhead helps greatly, my lady. Your beauty gives the men hope." He pushed his hips up, drawing attention to the ever-growing strength of his arousal.

She laughed, feeling giddy as she lightly scratched his chest. His cock brushed her stomach as she straddled his thighs. Karre kissed his neck, trailing her tongue over his flesh. His pulse beat against her lips.

Vidar wrapped his arms around her, caressing the small of her back and curve of her ass. Her breasts rubbed his chest until her nipples peaked against him. He moaned, his breath tickling her shoulder.

She laid her body fully to his, their legs twining, their flesh pressed together, hands exploring, hips rocking, moving in harmony. Parting her lips wide, she took in his breath as her mouth hovered over his. He flicked his tongue, enticing her to close the distance. She did, pouring all the passion she felt into her kiss.

Vidar groaned, rolling her onto her back. He shoved her thighs open with his, becoming more aggressive in his need. The tip of his cock brushed her folds, parting her with its firm persistence.

Karre closed her eyes and bit her lip. She arched her hips into him while pulling on his ass, silently begging him to take her. Every inch sang with pleasure and awareness. The mattress shifted with their weight, but he didn't thrust inside.

Breathing hard, she opened her eyes to study his face. He stared down at her, his narrowed eyes sweeping along her chest, up her neck to her lips. She worked her legs along his and reached between them to stroke his cock. A soft moan escaped him as she massaged the velvet length.

Muscles flexed and tensed along his chest as she drew his cock along her moist folds, enticing and teasing at the same time. The thick tip bumped her clit. She jolted in pleasure and did it again.

Vidar entered her slowly, taking his time, letting her feel every sliding inch. She let go of his cock. Her hands explored everywhere she could reach. She wanted to touch all of him, taste all of him. When she drew him into her kiss, she moaned, sucking his tongue past the borders of her lips.

Karre angled her hips, meeting his thrust, urging him deeper into her pussy. A light sheen of sweat covered their bodies. She squirmed beneath him, her head rolling on the mattress as she broke their kiss to gasp for breath. Delightful sensations coursed through her body, radiating everywhere at once until she felt as if her body might explode into flames.

Vidar pushed up for leverage and he thrust harder, deeper. Her body tensed, her entire length going rigid as she met with release. The tremors racked over her. Vidar grunted, his hips jerking as he emptied himself into her. He collapsed against her, bracing his weight on his elbows to keep from crushing her.

After a long moment, he crawled off her. They readjusted on the bed and Karre burrowed under the covers, stretching out next to him. Suppressing a yawn, she said, "I really do want to help in the fight against the Caniba. If I am going to stay, I need to help. I have skills, ones that could be put to good use."

"Your desire to fight is understandable," he answered, closing his eyes and pulling her tight against him. "But your presence is enough. It gives us pride and a sense of duty to see what it is we are fighting for. A beautiful lady, a symbol of family and hope, is what you are to the warriors."

Karre's expression dropped some as she looked at him. He was serious. She stiffened in disbelief. "A pretty face to fight for?"

That wasn't exactly what she had in mind.

Vidar closed his eyes and nodded. "Yea. Very pretty."

---

"I'll show him pretty," Karre grumbled as she shoved the lock-picking pin into her upswept hair. The once-locked door swung open on silent hinges. She grinned, glancing down the long corridor to make sure she wasn't followed.

Karre had been into most of the rooms at Spearhead Fortress, but there were still a few locked doors she needed to get behind. The first one she'd visited that morning had been a weapons chamber, filled with rows of swords and shields, spiked maces and sharp daggers, spears and arrows. There had even been a few potion bottles and strange contraptions she had never seen before.

She shut the door behind her. Dust stirred as she walked. Unlike the rest of the fortress, the chamber had not been cleaned for some time. It made her search easier. She lifted her skirt, pulling it between her legs and tucking the end into the bottom of her corset so it wouldn't drag on the ground and give evidence of her being there. Stepping lightly, she placed her foot in the markings of larger footprints, following them across the room to a wall of shelves stuffed full of rolled parchments.

Karre pulled one from the shelf, noting its lack of dust. The wax seal had been broken and she unrolled it. The tight script was impossible to read. Although the words were probably ones she knew, apparently the Starian alphabet wasn't, because she couldn't read it. Without something to compare it to, it could take months for her to decipher what it said.

Putting the document back where she'd found it, she slowly retraced her steps to the door. She secured the room and straightened her gown before making her way down the corridor in search of the next locked door. Under her breath, she muttered, "I'll show him pretty."

---

Nothing. In the past, documents had always been one of the surefire ways of discovering fast information. Only, with no key to read the Starian language, she had no hope of learning anything from that method. She had searched every locked room in Spearhead and found no clue as to how she could help against the Caniba.

However, never one to give up, Karre decided to try the next best thing—gossipers.

"What are you mumbling about?" Jordinne asked, frowning as she looked up from her sewing. "Show him pretty?"

"I didn't say anything," Karre answered, grimacing.

"You've been saying it over and over." Bratene appeared more interested in poking her finger with the tip of her needle than applying it to her task. She didn't draw blood, but it seemed to alleviate her boredom. Then, mimicking, the woman said, "I'll show him pretty. How dare he say I'm just supposed to be pretty."

Jordinne laughed. "Got a taste of the Starian warrior, did you?"

"I got a giant bite of him," Karre grumbled, inciting laughter. Even Synna giggled from her place in the corner of the room.

"What did he do?" Jordinne cut her short thread and immediately began threading the needle with a new one. She worked fast, as if she'd sewn her whole life.

"He told me I was to be an inspiration for the warriors," Karre said. It seemed strange talking to the women, almost as if they were... friends. She hid her frown, uncomfortable with the word, unable to trust it completely.

"Ah, the 'something for the men to fight for' speech," Bratene said. "Methinks they want us to wear our best dresses every day."

"You mean our tightest corsets," Jordinne teased.

"They want us to scrub the floors and look like goddesses while doing it," Synna inserted.

"Well, to be fair, I like mine to be shirtless and silent." Bratene laughed. "And with a big sword to take into battle."

"Shameless," Synna murmured. "Utterly shameless."

Bratene threw a scrap of cloth at the woman. "I dare you to tell me you don't like a man with a big spear."

"I just like him to know how to wield it," Jordinne said, drawing Bratene's attention away from Synna. Karre noticed the woman tended to do that a lot, saving the more timid servant from Bratene's cruder barbs.

"I know you all said that we were supposed to let the men protect us, but who protects the men from themselves?" Karre studied them carefully.

"Every woman knows a man cannot take care of himself," Synna answered, reaching toward Jordinne to grab a small knife to cut her thread. "If not for women, they'd be running about naked and covered in dirt."

"Starving," Jordinne inserted.

"Stinking," Bratene added.

"And, according to Vidar, with nothing to fight for," Karre mused.

"Women bring civility to men." Synna had managed to rethread her needle and continued to sew.

"They need it with Sorceress Magda so close. We have never seen such a formidable foe in my lifetime, or my mother's." Jordinne put her work down and stretched her arms over her head. "I will gladly celebrate the day she is no more."

"I think I can get to Magda," Karre announced, her hand shaking. Bratene and Jordinne gasped in unison and Synna dropped her sewing on the floor. When no one spoke, she continued, "I've been listening to the men, hearing their stories of how she comes up from the ground. So, it can be concluded that they live in caves. I have a skill for blending in. It will be easier if I can get my equipment from off-world, but if you all—"

"No," Jordinne shook her head, interrupting. "Vidar would never allow it. The men would never allow it."

"We will never allow it." Synna slowly reached to the floor to pick up her sewing.

"Just consider for a moment," Karre said. "I've been to some of the most advanced planes in the parallel universes and to some of the most primitive. I don't want to live in fear of Magda and I don't want to risk..." Karre paused.

*I don't want to risk losing my husband, my new life, to some crazy cannibal queen. I don't want to be taken by another husband should Vidar fall in battle.*

A sharp pain radiated in her chest and she pressed her hand between her breasts to try to stop it.

"We don't doubt your skills, my lady, but—" Synna began, her tone placating.

"Then help me," Karre pleaded. "Tell me everything you know

about her encampment. Surely your men talk. If I can go there, if I can gain some kind of intelligence that will help us conquer—"

"And what if you are captured? What happens to Vidar when he loses a wife who has left him without children?" Synna demanded.

Karre eyed the woman, surprised at the passion in her normally mild voice. "I haven't given children much thought."

What else could she say? Children? She had barely given herself time to adjust to the idea of not running away, of staying as a wife.

"Well, perhaps you should give it thought," Synna quipped.

"Children here? With Magda at our door?" Karre studied her hands, twining and untwining her fingers. Come to think of it, she hadn't seen too many children around the fortress.

"What would you have us do?" Jordinne inquired. "March alongside the men into battle? Wield a sword and pray for an honorable death?"

"I have no wish to fight in battle," Bratene said. "I am content with my place."

"Neither do I," Karre admitted. "I'm not talking about fighting in combat. But if I could find how Divinity brought the other brides here, I know I could find a way to help. I could gather information. I could tell the knights where to find the sorceress."

The women stared at her, their expressions blank.

"You don't know where the Divinity portal is, do you?" Karre sighed. If she could get to her stash, she would have a better chance of infiltrating the sorceress' encampment. "It's not in my nature to do nothing."

"Here," Synna thrust a piece of cloth at her. "Busy your hands. Then you will be doing something."

# CHAPTER 9

*Because right now, in this moment, Karre had no idea who she was supposed to be.*

Strategizing and talking and thinking about fighting the Caniba sorceress was a lot different than actually finding the means to implement her plan. Since Karre's father had been abducted, she'd run toward danger, faced unknown planes, traveled to other dimensions until there were times she could barely remember her own name, let alone her own land. She had learned how to set aside her fears, and facing a Caniba queen, once she'd decided to do so, wasn't something she would back away from. When Karre invented a role, she became that person—the maid, the dancer, the noblewoman, the pedestrian, the baker. Whatever the job called for, that was who she was—with or without the damned memory implanter.

But now? What role was Lady Karre, wife of Sir Vidar of Spearhead?

She hadn't lied to Vidar when she said she didn't want to run anymore. At that moment, it had been the truth. As she looked at his firelight-caressed face, she had wanted to sit on that bed forever, staring at him, breathing him in. However, now as she looked over the main hall filled with knights, hearing the coarse banter as she sat alone at the head table, she wasn't so sure she wanted this to be her everyday normal. Because right now, in this moment, Karre had no idea who she was supposed to be.

Vidar had sent word that he rode out with some of the men. A strange feeling overwhelmed her, but she couldn't figure out what it was. Apathy? Regret? Frustration? Confusion? Resolution? Desperation? Enclosure?

How could she wait and do nothing? The maids refused to discuss any further plan of action. So was this it? Was this her life? Would she sit at her throne-like place above the main hall, staring out at the many knightly faces, watching them eat, hearing them talk, worrying about the Caniba? Day after day?

"Worrying about Vidar?" she whispered, frowning into her lap. No one heard the soft question and she was left without an answer.

How had she become so invested? How could she let her guard slip? How had he wormed his way into her emotions?

Karre found it hard to breathe and reached to grab the stout liquor. She gulped it down, feeling it burn its way to her stomach. Then, as realization dawned on her, she choked, coughing it back up so that it sprayed over her trencher of food, onto the table and floor.

"My lady?" Jordinne's voice penetrated the fog that settled over Karre's senses. The hall became quiet, or perhaps she couldn't hear it over the heavy beat of her heart. A hand pulled at her sleeve, forcing her around. Jordinne stared at her in concern. "My lady?"

"I think I love my husband," Karre whispered, unable to work her mind out of the daze. She pulled her arm from Jordinne's hold and stumbled away from the table.

"Karre?" Vidar's heart hammered in his chest as he rushed toward her bedchamber. "My lady, are you well? What's happened? Karre, are you in here?"

Strange reports of her stumbling from the main hall had been carried to him on his way to scout the marshlands. Jordinne assured him that his wife had not been poisoned, but after riding hard to get to her, he had to see her for himself. An unseen hand squeezed his heart in his chest at the thought of losing her. He didn't care to analyze the feeling too closely.

As he walked into her bedchamber, he noted, not for the first time, the décor Karre had added to the room. It looked like nothing he had ever seen. The warrior in him wanted to retreat, away from the lush environment into the familiar world of stone and steel. The man in him wanted to lie on the bed and let the thoughts slip from his mind as his wife attended him in lavish comfort.

Seeing her resting on the bed, he slowed. Karre lay on her stomach, her back rising in even breaths as she slept. Her face was turned to him, shadowed by the way her shoulder blocked the firelight. He smiled, his eyes moving down over her naked back. Silken covers molded over her ass and hips, outlining the shape of her legs.

He leaned against the bed and brushed her hair from her face. Then, not wanting to disturb such a beautiful sight, he made a move to leave. Karre grabbed his wrist, stopping him from turning away. She opened her sleepy eyes, blinking heavily.

"You're not the only light sleeper." Her words were thick and a little husky. "I thought you had to leave."

Reaching for her, he touched her forehead, feeling it for heat. "I got word that you were ill."

"Ill?" She didn't move from her stomach. "No. Not ill."

"Then?"

"Just tired." As if to prove her point, she stifled a yawn and straightened in a stiff stretch. "Has something happened? Why are you back?"

"Are you so eager to see me gone?" A small smile curled on his lips as he teased her.

"I'm glad to see you safe." Finally she turned, keeping her body hidden beneath the covers as she lay on her side.

The smile turned into a wide grin. "I am glad to see you well."

"I'm glad to see you here." She reached for his tunic, pulling him toward her. Her eyes fixed on his lips as she brought him into her kiss. Warmth radiated from her sleep-flushed skin. She kept the kiss brief, only slightly parting her lips.

"I am glad to see you naked." He chuckled softly and slid his hand over her covered hip. Her lashes dipped low over her eyes, shading them. Her breathing deepened. "And I am glad to hear that you have grown feelings for me."

She stiffened under his hand. "W-what? Who, ah, where did you get that impression? I didn't say... What?"

"Is it not true? Did you not say you loved me?"

"Jordinne," she whispered in realization. "She heard me." She grimaced slightly. "She told you."

He'd not dared to fully believe the maid's words until that moment, when he saw the uncertainty in her eyes. A strange feeling unfurled in his chest, warm, new, uncertain. Everything about his training as a warrior spoke against such feelings. Men had to be hard and in complete control. Friendship was expected in a marriage. Caring was encouraged. But love? How did he even know what that meant? How would he even know if he felt it? The idea was as foreign as peace. Sure, they knew about the concept but never expected to see it implemented in their lifetimes.

"Yes," she whispered, her breathing deepening. "I have grown feelings for you."

The words pleased him. How could they not? Strange emotions filtered through him but he wasn't equipped to decipher their meaning. He needed more time to think and analyze. He refused to lie to her. He respected her too much for that. "You are a fine wife, my lady."

Karre's lashes lowered over her eyes and for a moment she didn't move. Then, giving him a small smile, she said, "Come to bed. It's late."

"Yea." He kissed her temple. "Let me hang my weapons. I'll be back in a moment."

*You are a fine wife, my lady.*

Karre watched Vidar leave, forcing all emotions from her expression. When he disappeared out of the door, she turned in the bed and faced the wall. A fine wife? She told him about her feelings and he called her a fine wife? She wasn't sure if she should cry or punch him in the nose. No one liked their feelings to go unrequited, but she couldn't force him to love her.

But a fine wife? Fine? Surely he could have managed a much better compliment. Then again, he was Starian. It was quite possible he couldn't manage a better compliment.

She took a shaky breath and then another, trying to exhale the pain building in her chest. Closing her eyes, she focused on keeping her breathing even, pretending to sleep. Vidar came back into the room. She heard him moving behind her, the whisper of his clothes as he undressed, the stirring of the fire as he tended the flames.

The mattress moved under his weight as he climbed into bed. She rocked gently before he settled next to her. His hand slid along her hip before coming to rest. He merely held her, didn't try to wake her with kisses or insistent desires. Within moments, he slept. Karre opened her eyes to peek at him. He lay naked beside her, as perfect in form as any finely carved statue. Her heart pounded, as if begging him to wake up and look at her, to say something other than she made a fine wife. He didn't stir and she knew deep sleep would not find her again that night.

---

Light filtered through the narrow slit, casting the bedchamber in a sleepy light. Karre yawned, not feeling rested. She adjusted her limbs on the bed, stretching along Vidar's side. Her movement roused him and he blinked heavily, suppressing a yawn.

"Good morn, lady wife," he said, instantly pulling her close. His arms felt so good and protective. For a moment she forgot why her heart ached so badly. "I much prefer waking up next to you than surrounded by soldiers in the marsh encampment. You are much prettier." He paused, brushing his lips against her temple. "And you smell better, much sweeter."

Surprised at the gentleness in him, she waited to see what he would do next.

"You do not speak." Vidar placed his knuckle under her chin and turned her face toward his. "Did you not rest well? I tried not to disturb you."

"Mm," she moaned softly, snuggling closer to him. "It's too early to speak."

He glanced at the window. "But it is daylight."

"Early daylight," she corrected.

"I am not tired." His hand glided down her back, pressing her stomach against his. Since they'd slept naked, there was nothing to hinder their meeting flesh. The unmistakable interest of his arousal formed along her hip. His voice lowered into a husky murmur. "And yet I cannot seem to force myself out of bed to tend the morn exercise."

"Exercise," she purred, running her hand up his chest. Everything about him stirred her passions—his look, his feel, his smell. She detected the whisper of his breath against her cheek, tickling her flesh. His eyes pierced her with their intensity. The exhaustion drained from her limbs, replaced by the restless energy of desire.

Vidar kissed her briefly before drawing his mouth along her jaw to her neck. She wanted him so badly, always wanted him. Strong hands ran along her body, along her hip to the outside of her thigh. Fingers skated over her knee before finding the path between her legs that would lead them to her center heat. Her sex welcomed his touch with a flood of cream.

His lips moved over the heavy pulse in her neck. Taking his time, he pressed measured kisses along her collarbone to her shoulder. He angled her onto her back to give his mouth better access to her breasts. A tremble worked over her needy flesh. Every nerve focused on where they touched. Soft noises left her, joining his longer moans.

Vidar wrapped his lips around a taut nipple, sucking gently. He massaged the other breast, mimicking the movements of his circling tongue with his fingers. Karre caressed everywhere she could reach, following the defined contours of his muscles. Sensations overwhelmed her, drowning out all thoughts.

When he came above her, parting her legs with his, his mouth joined her once more. This time the kiss deepened until their tongues waged a war in their mouths. With the intensity of pleasure exploding between them, they both were equally victorious. Her lungs burned for air and she had to pull away. Lips parted, she panted against his mouth.

Vidar brought his body to hers. The tease of his cock slid over her pussy, pressing into the wet hold of her slit. There was a gentleness in him that she hadn't seen before as he delved forward, filling her with his strength. They rocked together in perfect unison, breathing each other in with every thrust.

His eyes held hers in their grasp as effectively as his body pinned her to the bed. Tension built, so sweet and pure it made her heart ache with the intensity of its promise. As her body climaxed, racked with pleasure, she wished she could hold on to the moment and never let it go.

Vidar jerked, stopping movement as he came inside her. Grinning, he rolled to his side. His arms fell limp in complete relaxation. "A man could die happily in your arms, my lady."

It wasn't "I love you" but she decided it would do for now. Smiling sleepily, she answered, "Death is not something I'd ask of you, Sir Vidar."

---

Vidar couldn't stop grinning as he sauntered through the courtyard. Everything seemed more pleasing than normal—the sky was a wonderful shade of blue, the air was sweet, exercise enjoyable, his fortress proud and strong, his people smiling despite the threat lurking at their gate. He couldn't name what it was that had changed. Maybe the sun shone with a different light. Maybe the cook used a new herb in the porridge and it altered his perspective. Or maybe it had something to do with the invisible thread he felt connecting him to his wife.

Invisible thread? It made no logical sense and yet there the thought was.

He passed through the fortress entrance into the hall. Servants wiped the empty tabletops, finishing up their cleaning of the morn meal.

"Sir Vidar, I must speak with you."

Vidar stopped walking as he heard his name. Seeing the maid Synna approaching him, he nodded at her, encouraging her to speak.

"It is about Lady Karre," the servant said.

His smile faltered. He glanced around. Everyone else was far enough away the conversation wouldn't be overheard. "What about my lady?"

Synna opened her mouth and hesitated, as if rethinking her decision to come to him. "You know what happened to Sir Fredrick after he infiltrated Magda's camp."

"He is a hero," Vidar placed a steady hand on her arm. "He was very brave to try. None doubt that."

The woman glanced to the floor. "He is locked away in a room lined with mattresses to keep him from bashing his own skull against the stone walls, forever changed by what that witch did to him. I would not see your wife face the same hero's fate."

"My wife?" Vidar stiffened, feeling as if he'd been kicked. He pushed Synna aside, ready to surge past her. "Has she been taken?"

"Hold." Synna grabbed his wrist before he could run out of the fortress. "She is yet unharmed. I believe she still sleeps. But I feel I must warn you of what she plans. It is my duty."

Vidar crossed his arms over his chest. The pleasure of his day drained into a hard knot of stress in his stomach.

"She thinks she can get to the sorceress by infiltrating the Caniba's world." Synna grabbed his crossed arms and squeezed so hard her nails dug into his flesh. He barely noticed the sting it caused. "Please, Sir Vidar, stop her. Do not let her face the madness. Do not let her end up like my husband. Death is better than such insanity."

He sighed, trying to calm the woman even as he fought the urge to run to Karre and demand she give up such foolish thoughts. "I would never allow it, Synna. Thank you for coming to me, but I swear Lady Karre is not going to face the Caniba."

"You are not to leave the fortress without supervision."

Karre looked at her bedchamber door in surprise, unable to believe her ears. She had heard Vidar come into his room but hadn't expected him to barge through her door making stern demands before she even managed to get out a greeting. Endeavoring to remain calm, she asked, "And why not?"

"I know of your plan to face the Caniba queen. I forbid you from leaving this fortress without my permission." Vidar breathed so hard his shoulders lifted with each breath, giving him the air of a predatory beast who had just run down his prey.

Karre pulled the laces of her blue corset bodice tight and tied them with a slipknot to hold them in place. She smoothed the long skirts of the cream-colored underdress while keeping a steady eye on him. "I see."

"Then it is settled." The stiffness of his shoulders began to relax.

Instead of agreeing, she said, "I have traveled to some of the most advanced planes in all of the parallel universes and I have been to some of the most primitive. I have been put into situations you cannot imagine, tortured, chased—"

"That has nothing—" he began.

"Sought after," she continued, raising her voice to drown out his. "I'm not some weak, delicate flower that you have to water and protect. I know you do not want to hear it, but you can't plant me in the ground and tell me to look pretty and not to move. I have thorns and—"

"Are saying you want to farm?" His arched a brow.

"I'm saying that you cannot tell me what to do. I stay because I want to stay, not because anyone told me to." A dull ache started in her chest at his arrogant expression. "You said you had prisoners. If I can get to the Divinity portal, I can get this device that will help me read the prisoners' minds. I can get to Magda. I can—"

"I will not listen to this."

"I'm the perfect spy with my talent and skills," she yelled louder. "The way you all protect women around here no one would ever suspect me. Your problem is that you sent in warriors when you should have sent in someone more subtle. Just consider—"

"No." The denial was flat, hard.

"Then consider your people and how stopping Magda would save many lives. I've seen the men present the sword of the fallen knights to their wives. Those women might nod and accept the death token, but I see their eyes. Something dies inside of them." Realizing she screamed, she took a deep breath and eased her tone. "I do not want to be presented your sword."

"Karre." Her name came out on a sigh as he closed his eyes and ran his hands through his hair.

"What of children? I know you want them, but you can't want them to grow up with Magda. All I'm saying is I'll go in, find out where she's hiding and I'll get out. I'll report the layout. I'll—"

"No."

"You can't stop me. If you don't tell me how to get to the Divinity portal, I'll go on my own."

"Do not test me," he warned. "Give me your word of honor that you will forget this foolish plan."

Karre bristled at his decree, not liking this demanding side of him. Anger bubbled inside her, flooding every nerve. "If you want to keep me here, you're going to have to tie me up in the courtyard and put me under guard because that is the only way you're going to make me do what you want me to."

With that, she marched toward the bedchamber door, storming out on her husband, intent on getting away from him.

"Karre!" he yelled, chasing after her. "I have not finished discussing this."

Thinking more of defying him than what they fought over, Karre ran, going faster as he followed behind her. Words flew between them, growing in heat and intensity. By the time they reached the main hall, they were yelling at the top of their lungs, making a spectacle. "Leave me alone!"

"You will do what I say," he demanded.

"I will not have you dictate orders to me," she returned. Those gathered in the hall turned to watch the argument. "I am not yours to command."

Vidar stiffened and she knew he was acutely aware of their audience. "I am your husband. I have every right to command."

Karre didn't care who heard them. To her thinking, it was best everyone knew her position. Refusing to back down, she balled her fists. "Oh, yeah? And you think you're man enough to make me?"

# CHAPTER 10

*Because right now, in this moment, she was tied up and put under guard.*

Shadows fell heavy over the wide courtyard, cooling the heat of the day as a gentle breeze swept over the open yard. Women carted buckets of water from the well into the fortress. They did their best not to look at Karre, but she saw them peeking from the corner of their eyes. She couldn't blame them, because right now, in this moment, she was tied up and put under guard.

Damn him.

Karre grimaced, thinking of Vidar as she stood, tied to a T-shaped post, in the middle of the courtyard. A chain ran along the top, binding her wrists over her head and a large shackle held her waist to the post, leaving her feet free to kick at the dirt. Her ties didn't hurt, merely annoyed.

Somehow their argument had spiraled out of control and she'd ended up in the courtyard by her own taunting. The anger felt good, the release, the passion, the heavy breathing. Still, how could she back down? She wasn't his to command, not like that.

If he could protect *her*, then she could return the favor and protect *him*. She loved him, but she wouldn't be controlled by him.

"Way to take a stand," she mumbled, more bored than annoyed. "I could have told him to lock me in my chamber. Or chain me to the head table with a bottle of liquor."

Karre kicked at the ground with her toes, trying to find someone, anyone, who would look directly at her so she could call them over to keep her company. Maybe she could convince them to let her go. It could be a diverting game—making Vidar catch her. The idea caused her body to tingle and her mind to swirl with deliciously wicked thoughts.

"Focus, Karre," she admonished, pushing aside all sexual desires. This was bigger than a mere sexual game. This was her life, her future. She needed to concentrate.

"Have you reconsidered?"

Karre struggled to turn. Vidar's voice came from behind her. She wondered how long he'd been standing there. With the breeze hitting her face, she hadn't detected him. When she couldn't see more than the side of his arm, she said, "Have you?"

"I have no wish to leave you out here, but you challenged my authority in the great hall in front of my men." The heat of his breath brushed over the back of her neck as he leaned close. "Simply promise me you won't try to spy on the Caniba and we can end this. I only seek to keep you safe."

"I don't know. I'm rather comfortable right here." She lightly swung her hands back and forth, taking what little movement she could. "It's a beautiful day."

"You are a frustrating—*grrr*." With that growl, he marched off. His steps stopped and he came back. Very softly, he said, "If you change your mind or become uncomfortable, signal the knight on the battlement. Just say the word and we can forget this...*misunderstanding*. I have no wish to keep you prisoner like this. Please, my lady."

"Do you reconsider? Because the way I see it, if you can protect me, I can try to protect you. I will not make you a promise I do not intend to keep. I may be many things, Vidar, but I will not lie to you."

"I cannot reconsider."

"Then, I'm sorry, but I'm quite comfortable remaining right here," she answered.

"As my lady wishes." He touched her hip before leaving once more.

Her mind focused on her hip where he'd touched her. Sexual thoughts tried to invade, taking over her reason, trying to make the whole captive scenario a game. Arousal warred with logic and for a moment she let arousal win. Her breathing deepened, causing her bodice to feel tight against her breasts. She closed her eyes, imagining Vidar dressed all in black, stalking around her as if ready to pounce—potent, sexual, animalistic...

The creaking of the front gate snapped her out of her budding fantasy. She tensed, watching to see who came through. Was it more soldiers carrying the blades of the fallen to new widows? Even knowing Vidar wouldn't be among them, she felt her stomach tighten at the mere thought of it.

*I cannot back down.*

First knights entered, filing in two by two. She searched them for fresh wounds but didn't see any. Synna and Jordinne hauled baskets heaped with laundry, pausing to watch the visitors. Synna glanced at Karre, looking incredibly guilty. Karre sighed. So that was how Vidar discovered her plan. She should have known. Synna had tried a couple times to point out how foolish Karre's words were.

As a man entered, clearly the leader if not by his carriage then definitely by his massive size, she narrowed her gaze in recognition. He was one of the bridegrooms from the ceremony at Battlewar. What was his name? Lord Big Moody Knight?

Behind the large knight, horses pulled a cart. Seeing the blonde bride who had been a part of the marriage ceremony, Karre forced her expression to go blank. Spearhead guards pushed the oversized doors of the main gate closed and latched them with a thick timber.

The cart stopped and the blonde emerged, rubbing her back and wobbling on shaky legs. Wondering what, if anything, the woman had learned, Karre whistled loudly and yelled, "I see you've survived." Then, before she could stop herself, she added, "I had my doubts."

Karre cringed inwardly as the blonde jerked in surprise and looked over. The comment was true, but she hadn't meant to say it. The blonde seemed weaker than the others and not at all suited to handling the giant man who had claimed her.

*Lilith.* The name hit her, crawling out of her memory. *Her name is Lilith. He is Lord Sorin of Firewall.*

Karre smiled, wiggling her fingers in greeting. Her chains jingled at the movement. Hurrying on before Lilith could think about her last comment, Karre said conversationally, "Great weather we're having."

Lilith glanced around the yard. Sorin stood near his dirt-covered knights and equally caked horses. With her husband occupied, Lilith cautiously walked to where Karre waited. Under her breath, she asked, "Karre? Are you all right? What's happened here?"

"Small misunderstanding," Karre answered with a short, dismissing laugh. "Nothing to be concerned about. How's your guy been treating you?" Karre leaned to the side and pretended to study the newcomers. "Which one was he again? The big guy?"

"I found the way out." Lilith whispered urgently. Karre's easy smile dropped and her eyes narrowed at the information. Maybe Lilith wasn't as weak as she had first thought. "It's at Battlewar Castle in the dungeons. I tried to leave to bring back help, but it's too guarded."

Karre didn't answer. Her mind raced. Battlewar? She was sure she could find her way back there, but how would she make it undetected? Even if she managed to get past the guarded gate and through Battlewar Village unnoticed, she would have to face the crowd of knights who roamed the castle. The place was a palace compared to Spearhead Fortress in both size and population.

Lilith continued, "Have you seen Jayne or Paige?"

Karre's smile lifted with great effort, though her mind stayed focused on the conversation. "No. You're the first."

"I promised Jayne I'd try to get word to everyone." Lilith bit her lip, checking to make sure they weren't overheard.

Young boys who worked in the stables led the horses away. Servants welcomed the men, ushering them inside. Friends greeted friends.

"I'll draw you a map and write down the code to my home dimension." As Lilith spoke, Lord Sorin turned his attention to them. "I'll find a way to get it to you, just check your chambers. Someone at Divinity headquarters should help anyone who comes through the portal if you tell them what happened."

*Yeah, right. Divinity would just love to help me escape them. Thanks for the offer, but I think I'll pass.*

"If you see Jay—" Lilith continued.

"Sh." Karre shushed the woman. Sorin was too close. To cover what Lilith had revealed, she announced, "Yep, beautiful weather for a ride into battle."

"My lady," Sorin said, joining them. He nodded at Karre, as if acknowledging her statement as fact.

"My lord." Karre bowed her head, the action not as respectful when done with rattling chains. Lilith opened her mouth to speak, as if to reassure Karre in her tied up state. Karre could care less about her ties. She wasn't scared of Vidar hurting her. To cut off any sentiment, Karre began to hum playfully as if she hadn't a care in all the dimensional planes.

Sorin led his wife away. Karre watched the knee-length flaps of his black long tunic hit purposefully against his legs. Lilith stumbled next to him, causing the big warrior to stop. Curious, Karre stared as he gently placed his finger beneath Lilith's chin and lifted her eyes to look at him. Though she strained, she couldn't hear their words. Sorin's motions were gentle when he finally led Lilith away.

"Hm. It would seem she has tamed her beast," Karre said to herself, somewhat impressed. "Now, if only I could win this battle with mine."

Aggravating wench!

Vidar paced his chambers, hating that Karre was tied up in the courtyard, hating that he'd ordered it done to her, hating that she had publically goaded him to do just that. And for what? Because he had laughed at the incredibly ridiculous idea of his wife infiltrating an evil sorceress' lair as a spy? Okay, so he could have held his temper in the great hall, but she'd been yelling too.

Contrary to her obvious lack of faith in his ability to protect her, he did have a plan. Already his men informed him Lord Sorin was close, just as the king promised. Once reinforcements arrived, they would handle Magda and her followers.

"Sir Vidar," a maid said from the door. "Lord Sorin has arrived."

"Thank you, Calla." Vidar tugged his tunic over his head, tossed it on the bed and grabbed a fresh one from his trunk before heading toward the main hall to greet his guest. Pulling it over his head as he walked, he let the long sides of the black tunic fall around his knees.

His guests were seating themselves at the head table when he arrived. Lady Lilith clutched her husband's arm and Vidar heard her whisper, "What's happening to Karre? Why is she tied up?"

Vidar frowned. His fellow Starians would never question such a thing. It wasn't her concern, but the business of a man and his wife. Had Karre actually been abused, the people of Spearhead would have revolted against their leader in protest. To stop further questioning in wake of graver concerns, he answered before Sorin could, simply stating, "A misunderstanding."

"Oh," Lilith made a soft noise and had the decency to glance away.

Vidar bowed toward Sorin, acknowledging him before doing the same to Lilith. The lady had an angelic face and the coloring to match. Vidar much preferred his darker temptress.

Aggravating seductress!

"Lady Lilith, may I introduce Sir Vidar," Sorin said. "This is his home."

"Only until the king assigns it to another," Vidar answered politely. He tried not to think of Karre, even as he glanced over the hall in hopes that one of his men came to inform him of her contrition. "My lord, if you would come with me?"

He didn't wait for a response as he made his way to the old scroll room. Reaching to his waist, he pulled at a small pouch near his knife to take out a key. Because of the nature of the documents stored inside, the chamber had not been cleaned for a few years. Ignoring the dust, he strode across the room to a wall of shelves filled with rolled parchments.

"What news?" Sorin inquired, shutting the door behind him.

"Sorceress Magda has yet to show herself, but they found tracks near the marshes and we uncovered plans too. I've sent word to the marshes that we ride at dawn to join them." Vidar unrolled a map of the land surrounding Spearhead Fortress and laid it on the table, holding it open. "Lady Lilith is welcome to stay here. Her every comfort will be met and I will leave a small contingency of soldiers to guard the fortress."

Even though Sorin was higher ranking by birth, Spearhead Fortress was entrusted to Vidar, as was the nearby borderlands. These were his decisions to make and Sorin did not dispute them. Once on the battlefield, they would each lead their own armies.

Sorin nodded. "I agree. It is not safe at the encampment and my lady is delicate to the ways of war. She will remain here."

Vidar thought of his wife. She was far from delicate. "Lady Karre wishes to join the war."

"These women they send us." Sorin chuckled, clearly thinking Vidar jested. Leaning over the map, he asked, "Where is your army positioned? I will send orders to my men. By the grace of the gods, we'll have Magda's head."

---

Karre grinned as the lock binding her wrists opened with a soft click. It hadn't been easy in her position, but she managed to get the lock-picking tool untangled from her hair. She found she much enjoyed the challenge, freeing herself in a courtyard filled with Starian knights. Clearly they underestimated her. Even her guards kept a lax eye on her as they talked with the newly arrived guests. Though, to be fair, since Vidar told her he didn't want to keep her prisoner, they probably weren't too concerned with making sure she stayed bound. And really, if she got caught, it's not as if anything would happen.

As the courtyard quieted and guests filtered in for the eve meal, Karre slipped out of her ties and made her way through the back passageways to her bedchamber. Her muscles were a bit sore, but she didn't mind. She found herself smiling as she thought of the look that would cross over Vidar's face when he discovered she had escaped. That image led to others—him running after her, barging into her chambers, finding her on the bed, the captor after his naughty captive.

Ugh! *Quiet, brain,* Karre scolded her wayward thoughts. *This isn't a game. It's not about sex. I'm making a point. He needs to know he can trust me. He needs to know I can take care of myself.*

Seeing a basin of water, she slowly bathed, running a wet cloth over her flesh. The fire dried her as she paced naked through her chamber, stretching her muscles and restlessly plotting. How to get to Battlewar to the portal? Or would her "daring" escape from the courtyard be enough to convince Vidar that she knew what she was doing?

She stopped. A chill crept up her spine, filling her with dread. Karre slowly turned.

"I knew that locator we implanted would come in handy." Director Tomes lounged against the wall as if he'd always been there, watching, waiting. The tight black of his Divinity uniform molded to his body like a second skin and the wrist portal wrapped his wrist. He was alone. His cold eyes dipped over her naked body and he smiled. "You're looking well."

Karre fought the urge to run and hide. Forcing her limbs to remain steady, she went to her trunk to pull out her most conservative tunic.

"There is no need to cover up for me. In fact, Sparkles," he paused and arched a brow. "May I call you Sparkles?" When she didn't answer, he continued, "Why don't you put the gown on the bed?"

Karre made a move to pull it over her head.

"I insist." He tapped a laser pistol as it rested in a side holster next to his leg.

Karre tossed the gown on the bed. "What do you want?"

"Perhaps I should call you Lady Karre." Tomes laughed, pushing off the wall. "That is what they call you here, isn't it?"

"Call me what you wish. I'm used to many names." She shrugged a shoulder. "What do you want, Tomes?"

"I must say you have done quite nicely for yourself. I'm not surprised. Women like you tend to make your way to the top no matter where you go. Though, I will admit, I had hoped you would end up the wife of a mucker, but then this place," Tomes gave a disdainful look around, "is hardly civilized. Even the lords and ladies are primitive, living by fire and sword. How hard it must be for you knowing of the worlds you have seen, knowing of the things you done. I could never live here."

"What do you want, Tomes?" she repeated.

"Want?" He chuckled. "I will give these Starians one thing. They do know how to dress their women." His eyes dipped over her. Karre didn't move. "The men are a little too muscled for my taste, but I saw a few skirts I wouldn't mind plundering. There is nothing sexier than a lush woman forced to bend to my will."

"I'm really not interested in your sex life, so I will ask one last time, what do you want, Tomes?"

His cold gaze grew colder still. "What have you done with the information you have stolen? We've traced every jump in your history. You never go to the same place twice, but we know you have documents. Where are they? Are you working with someone?"

"What reason would I possibly have to tell you?" she asked. Her eyes roamed to the wrist device and her fingers flexed, eager to touch it, to possess it. They would never find where she had gone or how she hid her tracks.

Tomes followed her attention down his arm. "Interestingly enough, when we traveled to where you had been, we noticed something. This device rewrites itself. There is no way of telling where it's gone without the code to reset it. We realized the only way we're going to find our documents is if you take us. Ingenious of you, really. I'm impressed. But then again, I am smarter."

"Modest, too," she mumbled sarcastically.

"I knew there was a reason to keep you alive, a reason far greater than trading for warm water." Tomes drew near, too near for her liking. He looked, but he made no move to touch her.

"You say you're smart, but you keep making me repeat myself," Karre mumbled, before saying very slowly, "What reason would I possibly have to tell you? What is in it for me?"

"Help me and I'll get you off this plane."

"One plane is as good as any other," she said, nonchalantly. "You would have to do better than that."

"Then help me or I'll kill everyone on this plane and leave you to rot here alone or at the mercy of anyone I choose to send here to join you." His slow smile and narrowed gaze made more promises than his words ever could. "Is that better?"

"You've had your look." Karre reached for her gown and stepped back. She tugged it on. The loose material billowed around her without the aid of a corset. "What exactly do you propose? I know I can't trust you."

"Oh, I'm hurt," he said in feigned shock. When she didn't react, he smiled. "It's simple. You don't have a choice in the matter. Come with me, be a good girl and I let you live."

"An offer I can't refuse," she muttered, knowing his words weren't an idle threat.

Tomes reached for his wrist. "Get ready to travel, Lady Sparkles. You have one last job to do. Save this world or I will destroy it."

---

Vidar could barely breathe. The guilt and worry ate a constant knot in his stomach and settled a permanent weight over his heart. Karre was gone, vanished like a wood spirit into the night forest. He had looked everywhere, questioned everyone. Beyond a few people saying they saw her walking alone from the courtyard to the castle, there was no sign of her—no tracks, no fairy rings she could have slipped through, nothing. He would have yelled at the knights manning the wall, but he had only ordered them to make sure Karre was well, not to keep her prisoner. For all they knew, she had been participating in some otherworlder ritual.

One conclusion could be drawn. His stubborn wife had talked about infiltrating Magda's encampment and she must have put her plan into motion. But how did she escape the chains? How did she escape an armed fortress full of his knights without being seen?

Already rumors surfaced about Karre's disappearance. The maids claimed she'd been moved to the dungeons. The knights thought the newly married couple played games. Only Synna seemed to have come to the same conclusion as Vidar—Karre went to battle.

He wanted to look for her. His heart ached to do so, but duty demanded he fight. Magda was close. Sorin and his men were ready for battle. The king's orders were clear. His duty to protect his countrymen weighed heavily on him. And in doing his duty perhaps he could somehow find Karre and bring her home. In the end, Vidar spread the rumor throughout Spearhead Fortress that his wife rode out with him to war, to support his efforts and show the Caniba she was not afraid. After what Karre told Synna and the others was spread about, his claim would be believed.

*Gods curse her! How could she run off? How could she leave me now? Before such an important battle?*

Maybe the king's fears were founded and these otherworld women would bring them nothing but trouble. Maybe he worried for naught. Maybe Karre was safe and had merely run away from him. Maybe she was in Magda's clutches right now only feet away from him underground.

Maybe, maybe, maybe!

"Argh!" Vidar screamed, charging his horse forward as the ground began to shake beneath him. The not-knowing ate at him and he turned his frustration to the only thing he could—the battle before him.

He lifted his sword, hacking his way through the surrounding enemy. More Caniba emerged from the ground, covered in dirt as they clawed their way up like a mound of spreading ants. The hairy beasts all looked the same to him—smelly, pelt-covered monsters with sunken eyes and sharpened teeth. Their hair hadn't seen a comb, ever, and he highly doubted any of them had heard of bathing.

Three days earlier, Sorceress Magda's army had come up from the ground right through the middle of their encampment. Like a giant serpent of dirt snaking through the ground, the topsoil had sucked into a pit taking a few of their men with it. Caniba warriors rose up, splitting Vidar and Sorin's armies in two. Sorin's men were surrounded, fighting with little reprieve an army twice the dwindling size of theirs.

Vidar ordered his men to hold their ground, as they worked their way deeper into Magda's territory. If they found the sorceress, they could end this. The Caniba felt nothing beyond a driving need to please their queen. Without Magda, her minions would become a scattered mess.

With each thrust of his sword, he heard Karre's name whispering through his head. He slayed his enemy, thrusting his sword into flesh, trying not to watch the Canibas' distorted faces, faces that were impassioned even in death. The smell of sweat, blood and dirt filled each gulping breath. Metal hit upon metal, clanging and clashing over the rough terrain of the battlefield. Starians shouted and moaned, the Caniba growled and grunted and all around them men died.

*Karre. Karre. Karre*, his mind chanted, tormenting him with the knowledge that he didn't know where she was.

Vidar fought harder, yelling an ancient battle cry to the gods. Then a cry sounded, carried on the wind, "To Lord Sorin! He's going for the sorceress!"

Blinking hard as sweat stung his eyes, Vidar took his focus from the immediate area to look at the large picture. He'd been so intent on the fight he hadn't realized they'd met their goal. They'd rejoined with Sorin's men. Vidar swiped his brow, watching as Sorin made his way toward the makeshift throne of Sorceress Magda.

Eerily pristine in her gown of sparkling white, Magda sat on a carved wood platform, lifted up so that she might watch the carnage she had created with the pride of a goddess. Her evil children swarmed around her, a thick, living wall of protection. Dark, smooth hair fell about her shoulders to her waist and the inky depths of her eyes became even more so by the black lines drawn thick around them.

"To Sorin!" Vidar shouted, seeing how close the lord was. If Sorin could get to her, he could end this. Burning, white heat radiated over his stomach as sharp, metal-tipped nails clawed through his tunic to rake his flesh. He grunted, too consumed by the battle to stop and notice the cut, even as he felt blood trickling down his waist.

"To Sorin!" the men caught up his cry. "To a good death!"

"Help him!" Vidar ordered. A blade cut his arm and then his thigh, as he pushed harder and faster. "Fight to Lord Sorin!"

Sorin had broken rank, leaving a tightly formed unit of knights behind him. Caniba soldiers turned their attentions to him. No Starian had ever made it so close to her in battle.

"To Sorin!" the men shouted.

Caniba warriors surrounded the man, bearing down on him. There was no way Sorin could fight his way through the crowd alone. In a bold move, the lord threw his main line of defense, launching his sword through the air at Magda. The swarm took him down before the blade hit its mark.

Vidar pushed forward, feeling his men at his back. Magda screeched, slumping in her throne. Instantly, her men panicked, turning the tide of the battle as they retreated. The battlefield cleared and the Starians gave chase. Finding Sorin on the ground, wounded with claw and teeth marks, Vidar dropped to his knees to check the man.

"He lives," Vidar said. "Find Lance to tend his wounds and then get him to the marsh encampment." To a nearby group, he ordered, "Search the fallen."

Vidar stood as his orders were carried out. He breathed hard and gripped his sword in frustration. With a violent scream, he threw the weapon after the Caniba warriors. The enemy was too far and the blade embedded into the dirt.

*Karre. Karre. Karre.*

"I've lost her," he whispered, sure he'd never felt anything as painful as the helplessness the idea caused.

*Uncharted Dimension, The Dead Plane*

Blood trickled down Karre's chin, but she refused to swipe it away. Hot wind would dry it soon enough and she wouldn't give Director Tomes the pleasure of seeing her discomfort. The beginning ache of a bruise stretched over her jaw.

The desolate plains of the uncharted dimension went on for what Karre imagined would be the whole planet. Here Earth was nothing but sand and rock and wind. Nothing grew on the surface and by extension no animals lived. It's why she called it the dead plane. It's why it was the perfect hideout. She had never seen another person there until now.

"I need assurances that you won't leave me here," she said, keeping her emotionless gaze fixed on his face. A man like the director wouldn't expect her to give in too easily. Tomes had brought her himself, not going to a Divinity base for assistance. She wondered which piece of information she had that made him worried enough to come here alone.

Karre wasn't surprised when he hit her again, this time in the ribs. Growling, he waved his laser pistol in her direction. "I said move it."

Karre tried to take a deep breath and coughed. Holding her injured ribs, she stumbled up the side of the rock incline at the base of a lonely mountain in the sandy sea. Her feet slipped on a bed of sand.

"Move," he growled. "No tricks or I will leave you here."

"Yeah, yeah, I'm moving. Next time you want your prisoner to move faster, try not hitting her in the ribs." On the top of the incline, the ground leveled out and she limped toward a small opening in the rock face.

"Oh, you'd be surprised at what I could do with a female prisoner." He chuckled, the dark sound causing a creepy sensation in her stomach. "Or perhaps you wouldn't be surprised, since you already know. Did you like watching my files? Do you know how much men are willing to give to visit my mansion of pleasure? They won't be pleased that you have the contact list."

Karre kept her back to him so he couldn't see her face. She didn't have any idea what he was talking about. But then, to be fair, she hadn't looked at all her stolen files. She just collected them to be analyzed later when she had enough gemstones saved to set up her own personal research base somewhere.

"Are we close?" he asked, when she refused to answer him.

"It's in the cave." She leaned against a boulder and motioned to the entrance. It was evident by this chatty mood that he didn't plan on letting her leave. If he didn't kill her first, he'd leave her here to die. It wouldn't take long, not in the plane's horrible elements.

Tomes motioned for her to go first. "No tricks."

The stone was warm to the touch, almost hot. Come nightfall the temperature would drop drastically. Very mindful of her footing, she inched inside, turning sideways in the narrower space. Reaching forward into the darkness, her hand hit a tarp. She pulled it aside.

"Wait," Tomes ordered.

"I'm not going anywhere. You have the portal." She stiffened as the tip of his gun pressed into the small of her back. "There's light just inside."

Karre inched forward, reaching around the corner for the old lantern. Finding it, she reached along the side, grabbing a small knife she kept there for situations just like this. Director Tomes truly underestimated her or truly overestimated himself.

Holding the lantern, she turned the knob several times to light it while keeping the small folded knife in her hand. The sharpened side of the blade bent over toward the handle, keeping it from cutting her palm.

A soft glow illuminated her cave. The dingy brown-and-gray rock had been more home to her over the years than any other place. Now, when she thought of home, she thought of piercing eyes flecked with gold, of swords and knives, of castles and thick forests. She thought of strong hands, toe-curling kisses and a deep voice that made her heart thump wildly in her chest.

The cave fanned out in an oval, carved with jagged walls and natural shelves. A stuffed mat had been rolled and stuck in the corner, just in case she ever needed to stay the night. Freeze-dried foodstuffs were buried in a sealed container, as were medical supplies.

"You're going to kill me, aren't you?" Karre frowned and set the light on the ground. Stark, ghoulish shadows formed on his face, but she read the truth in his eyes. "There is no point in denying it. We both know how this game is played."

"Indeed," he agreed.

"What about the Starians? Will you let them live?"

"There's no reason to hurt the Starians. They have proven to be quite useful for a dumping ground. You, Jayne Hart, Lilith Grian." He chuckled. "It worked better than I could have ever hoped. Marriage as a prison. You have to admire the serendipity."

"You are the reason we...?" She frowned. "What did they do?" When he looked like he would refuse to answer, she added, "What does it matter if you tell me? I'm dead anyway."

"Jayne 'The Sweet' Hart lost a fight and in the process lost me a substantial bet. Lilith Grian was a foolish data analyst, logging her little historical notes. She was easily expendable." Tomes looked over Karre. "The other two we sent saw some of our men coming through a portal. Funny how the Starians sent them back. Even if they do talk about what happened to them, no one on their plane will believe them." He started laughing, his eyes tearing up with mirth. "We once kidnapped a bunch of people from some half-developed plane dressed as these gray, big-eyed, big-headed creatures, probed them anally and then set them down naked in random fields.

They told the other inhabitants on their plane they were taken by aliens. They still don't know what all that anal probing was about. I swear, we were so drunk. Now that was a video file you should have stolen. It is unforgettable."

"You've got issues, you know that, right?" Karre didn't find the same amusement in his sick games as he did.

"You still don't get it. When we discovered how to jump to new planes, we discovered the potential to become gods. We can go anywhere, do anything and they can't stop us. Sure, some of the corporation tries to install rules and moral codes, but those of us willing to claim our right as gods are truly free."

"I was wrong. You don't have issues—you're just insane." She backed away from him, toward the jagged stone of the cave wall.

His laughter died and he frowned. "Now it's your turn. What made you think you could fight us?"

"You kidnapped people and took them to the gladiator rings," she stated. "You took the wrong person."

"The fights?" His eyes swept over her in new consideration. "We wouldn't have taken you for the rings. I never sent women to that plane. Someone else, perhaps? A friend? A lover?"

"My father." Her hand gripped so tight she wondered if she would be able to make her fingers work. She felt the tears in her eyes, tears of anger, tears for the past.

"Your father?" His initial shock turned to disbelief. "You've caused me all this trouble because I ordered your father taken to the gladiator plane? How did you know it was me? Those files were destroyed."

He'd ordered it? Karre couldn't move.

"Enough small talk." His gun hand jerked, as if holding back his barely contained urge to shoot. "Where's the stuff?"

"Why should I tell you? I'm dead anyway."

"Do we really need to do this?" He scowled. Then, almost bored, he said, "If you cooperate you die fast. If you don't you die slow and painful. Either way I get what I want." He sighed heavily. "I always get what I want. I'm a god."

Karre fingered the knife in her closed fist, ready to unfold the blade as soon as he turned his back. Her throat dry, she whispered, "Behind that rock."

Keeping his gun trained on her, he moved to look where she pointed. Karre held her breath. Without realizing it, she had begun to shake. Tomes smiled and she knew he must have seen the glint of light coming from a small hole. He reached in to grab it.

A loud pop sounded and she jerked, knowing he had touched the device. The knife dropped from her fingers. Tomes screamed, his body convulsing as it electrocuted him. The portal device on his wrist sparked and smoked. His finger tightened on the trigger and a pulse of light shot out. Karre jumped to the side, but it grazed her flesh, searing her arm. She fell to the ground with a moan, her whole body sore from his earlier beating.

The gun went off a second and third time and she closed her eyes tight, curling into a ball. She jerked with each shot, knowing it'd be over soon. The electrical charge would not only kill Tomes but it would fry the portal on his wrist. No one knew where she was or where to look for her. She would be trapped there. Alone. Her husband would never know what happened to her.

*Vidar, I'm sorry.*

Tomes stopped moving and the cave became as silent as a tomb. After a long moment, she crawled toward the rock Tomes had reached behind. She avoided looking at his still face. He had been an arrogant fool. Karre had security protocols set up all over the cave. Did he really think she would risk losing everything she had worked so hard for?

Pulling out a small box shoved in the back, she held it close and went for the key on the other side of the cave. She leaned against the wall, ignoring the pain radiating over her body, and opened it. A single button waited inside. She hesitated before pressing it.

It was done. Her father was avenged. Every piece of information she'd collected over the years went out through a tiny portal, duplicated and sent to predestined planes. There would be no hiding Divinity's secrets now. It was not how she wanted to disperse the information. She had intended to extract a slow, thought-out revenge. This box was her last-option button. And now that it was pressed, everything she'd worked so hard for was done.

"Vidar," she whispered, knowing the plea was hopeless. She dropped the box as a burning light began to flood the cave. Closing her eyes tight, she tried not to cry. "Come get me. I want to come home."

# CHAPTER 11

*But he could not save her and all the pleasure of brief release was replaced by his sense of failure.*

She did not return.

Vidar welcomed the hardness that slowly crept over him. It radiated from his broken heart. Hopefully, given time, stone would replace the organ and he'd be free of the pain that now followed him wherever he went. Questions dogged his every moment—both in wake and restless sleep. Where had she gone? What happened to her? Was she alive? Dead? Why did she leave him? Why wouldn't she send word? What should he do? How could he find the unfindable?

Not knowing was slowly killing him. Not having a plan of action to make it right was killing his soul. Warriors needed to act, to fight. He didn't know how to deal with his helplessness. Nothing in his life had prepared him for it.

The only reprieve he got from his torment were those brief moments in his dreams where Karre would come back to him—smiling, naked, soft and warm. She would wake him with her kiss, the caress of her hand, the brush of her body. The dream was so real, he could feel the press of her pussy against him, wet and inviting. He felt her breasts in his palms. He saw her rising over him, taking him in, crying out for more. As the dreams faded, he heard her voice whispering from far away, "Vidar. Vidar. Come for me. Save me." Then he'd come, spilling his seed in his bed.

But he could not save her and all the pleasure of brief release was replaced by his sense of failure.

---

"Don't you think you should report it to the king?" Oskar asked, joining Vidar on the battlements.

Vidar stiffened at the man's words, knowing what his friend spoke of—the missing Lady Karre. He'd spent hours on the fortress wall, looking out over the surrounding countryside, watching the far trails for a hint of Karre walking home to him.

"No," Vidar stated flatly.

"We have searched everywhere for her. It's as if she disappeared off this plane, even though we know it's impossible. The only way she can leave is through a fairy ring—and we don't have fairies—or through one of those alien portals. There are no tracks in the forest, no word of her at Battlewar Castle, no sign of her since she walked away from the courtyard. I've been discreet, but people are beginning to talk. The servants whisper about the lady, saying she's run off and that she's been taken." Oskar said. "You cannot bury the truth forever. Something must be said. It's been weeks since—"

Vidar growled, turning on the knight. He grabbed Oskar's tunic and forced him back against the low wall. "What is the truth? I care not what people say." He let go and stepped back. "We will say nothing."

"As you wish." Oskar straightened, not retaliating. Vidar wished he would. He could have used the fight more than the look of pity in the man's eyes.

"I wish for you to do as I say and saddle the horses." Vidar strode away from him, calling over his shoulder, "If a battle does not come to us, I will go to it."

*Perhaps in a good death is where I will find you, my lady. For I have looked everywhere else.*

Karre could barely move, yet she somehow managed to crawl on top of the uncomfortable pile she had made from all her treasures. She had to use the tarp over the cave entrance to secure it, so now sand blew in to choke her lungs. Hugging her limbs around her treasures, she tried not to breathe too deeply. It had been days since she had eaten—a fact that her stomach wouldn't let her forget—and she had drunk the last of her water the evening before.

Tomes' body lay outside, buried by sand. She found it fitting to leave him where no one would come looking, eternally alone. Once concluding he was in charge of the gladiators, she could connect him to other crimes.

But she couldn't think of any of that now. She had to concentrate. The wrist portal hung loose around her arm. There was no guarantee that she had gotten it to work. Or if it did work that it would even send her to the right dimension and space. She could end up in a boiling river or stuck inside one of Spearhead Fortress' walls. Regardless, she had to try. It was her only chance.

"Vidar, I'm coming home," she whispered, activating the device. Light radiated from the wrist portal and a fire burned into her flesh. Defensively, she tightened her arms around herself and closed her eyes. Every cell in her body felt heavy. She couldn't move. No matter how many times she went through, she would never get used to the sensation of being pulled apart at a molecular level. But this time it was worse. The device was unstable and she felt as if her limbs were being ripped off. "Oh please, let me go home."

Vidar strode across his chambers to grab a sword. Oskar waited for him outside with a small contingency of men. Taking it from atop his trunk, he slid the sheath over his shoulder with practiced ease.

He would fight every Caniba he came across until he found his wife or died trying.

As he turned, a strange blue light caught his attention. He frowned, watching the bottom edge of Karre's chamber door. Blue shifted to pale green and he rushed toward it. Throwing open the door, he found the source of the glow at the foot of Karre's bed.

Vidar lifted his hand, shading his eyes from the brightness. On instinct, he gripped the hilt of his sword. Suddenly, a solid mass formed in the light, hovering over the ground before dropping a couple inches to thud onto the floor.

As the light faded, he dropped his arm. "Karre?"

Could it really be her? His heartbeat quickened in relief and worry. Confusion made it hard to move, but he still found the will to step forward.

She didn't answer, didn't move or make a sound. Her face was turned from him and she lay on top of a strange, uneven mass. Smoke curled from a bracelet on her arm and he smelled the unmistakable stench of seared flesh. He hurried to her side, pulling the hot metal from her skin. It had burned its shape into her arm, blistering the flesh.

"Karre?" Vidar pulled her toward him, cradling her in his arms. He brushed the hair from her face. She was thin, her skin tight against her face. His heart beat hard and his fingers shook as he lifted them to her throat. He felt her pulse. "Karre, look at me. Open your eyes."

Lashes fluttered but then settled. Without opening her eyes, she moaned. He gasped to hear it, relieved that she lived. Nothing else mattered.

She asked weakly, "Did I make it? Am I home?"

"You're home, love, you're home," he murmured, holding her tighter.

*You're home, love, you're home.*

Karre heard his voice, as it came from far away. Another dream? Or was he real? Vidar would never call her "love", but she was too weak to fight the small grain of hope. If she were dying, then why not let the warmth of his arms and the sound of his loving voice be the last thing she felt? It beat pain and starvation.

Her body ached, her arm burned and the rough trip through the portal made every inch of her insides feel as if they had been ripped apart. She was lifted up and cradled into safety and warmth. Her mind slipped, content to fall into darkness.

Vidar did not leave Karre's side, not when he carried her toward the hall, ordering a servant to find a medic and bring food, not when he laid her on his bed, not when he gently bathed her, not when her eyes opened and they forced broth into her, not when she whimpered throughout the night. Between burns, cuts, bruises and starvation, she had been through a terrible ordeal.

It wasn't until the second night that she managed to keep her eyes open and her thoughts coherent. Seeing her looking up at him as he stroked her cheek, he couldn't help but smile. "You're alive."

"I don't feel very alive." She chuckled. Her hand landed gently on his, holding it to her cheek. "Tell me I'm not dreaming. Tell me you're really here and that I'm really home."

Pleasure erupted inside him when he heard her voice. It filled him with a joy he had never known. It was hard to be demanding and angry about her leaving when she was in his arms, looking at him with those seductively beautiful eyes.

"You're not dreaming. I'm here. You're here. We're together," he assured her. "Where did you go, Karre? I looked for you. I searched everywhere, but we couldn't find any tracks. Why didn't you tell me you were leaving? Was it because I tried to stop you from going?"

"No. It's not your fault. It had nothing to do with our argument or that stupid incident in the courtyard. I'm almost embarrassed thinking of how ridiculous we were being. I just wanted so bad to help you, help the people of Staria, help make Spearhead safe."

Vidar leaned his forehead against her temple. "Can you understand that I can't allow you to fight the Caniba? Everything I've ever learned says I have to protect you. If something happens to you, I will have failed in my duty as a warrior. My honor demands I do not fail you. But it's more than that. I couldn't bear it if something happened to you. I'd rather fight to the death a thousand times than let you walk within a hundred yards of Sorceress Magda."

"I understand." She nodded. "But it is not in my nature to do nothing. I won't try to infiltrate her encampment. However, I would like to help."

"My lady, I—"

"I won't do anything without coordinating with you first," she assured him.

"There is time to discuss this later. Right now I would hear where you went. What happened?" He didn't want to let her go so he held on tighter.

"There was no time. I didn't have a choice. I had to go," Karre sighed, dropping her hand from his to rest on the bed. "There was something I had to take care of."

"Because of Magda?"

"No, I had to go to another plane. I needed to finish what I started. I sent files detailing several of Divinity's underhanded deals to my contacts and various media centers on numerous planes. I gave the dimensions proof. Now it is up to them to do something about it." She closed her eyes. Vidar listened as she told him of Divinity's Director Tomes, of how he'd come for her and forced her to go to the dead plane where she'd kept the hidden treasures now in her room. She told him of how she'd avenged her father by causing the death of the man responsible. "The portable jump prototype was fried when Tomes' sins came back to him. I managed to fix it for one last jump by scavenging parts from the other devices I've collected."

"The thing on your wrist?" He lifted her arm to kiss near the healing burn.

"Yes. I wasn't sure it would work." She caressed his face. "I cannot believe it did work. I really thought I would never see you again. The odds of my ending up here," she coughed, her eyes watering. "I should have gone to another dimension. I should have ended up trapped in a stone wall. I wasn't even sure I had the directions inputted right."

"I told you the gods have their reasons. They brought you to me a second time. They know that you belong with me." Vidar kissed her forehead. "And I belong with you. None of those other things could have happened because we are fate."

"Fate?" She moaned softly. "I like the sound of that."

"So do I." Vidar brought his lips to hers.

Karre drew strength from his presence. She was still sore from her ordeal, but it didn't matter. The wounds would heal. By some miracle, she had made it home to him and that's all that mattered. She dug her fingers into his hair, gripping tight, as if he might slip away into a dream and she would wake up alone.

"I thought I'd never see you again." She pushed at him, drawing strength from his nearness. Rolling him on his back, she tugged at his tunic, needing to feel his flesh.

"As did I." Vidar leaned up and lifted his arms, letting her undress him. "I have never felt such fear."

Passion and need filled her, fueled by the fear she had carried while stuck on the dead plane. She kissed him, devouring his mouth with hers. Every moment they were together had filtered through her thoughts while she was away and they now poured into their kiss. She loved everything about him—his smell, his taste, the way his brow furrowed when he was arguing with her, the way his eyes smiled when he looked at her from across a room.

Urgency filled them. They tore at each other's clothing, ripping the material in their haste. Karre gasped as her breasts rubbed against his firm chest. His masculine scent surrounded her and she breathed deeply. She straddled his thighs, leaning into his rising cock. It pressed into her stomach.

Karre eagerly explored his body, trying to touch every ounce of flesh. Anticipation washed over her, centering on her pussy and breasts. She wanted to feel him and needed him to feel her. He pushed her up to give himself better access to her chest.

Vidar groaned, rolling her over. Strong fingers rubbed her

breasts in firm strokes, budding her nipples into his palms. Their legs tangled in the covers. She worked her feet along his calves in an effort to free their limbs. Once free, Karre hooked her legs around his waist. She reached between them, taking his cock to stroke the turgid length. Her hand bumped into her sex, giving herself pleasure as she touched him. She arched her hips upward, letting her clit rub against her hand. A jolt of pleasure racked through her with each pass.

He licked the corner of her mouth, trailing wet kisses over her jaw from her chin to her earlobe. He thrust a finger into her sex, wiggling it until she panted in desperation for more. She spread her legs wider, inviting more.

He bit her lobe. "I want to be inside you. I burn for you."

"Then take me." She took her hand from him, moaning in encouragement. "Take all of me. I never want to be without you again, Vidar. I love you."

He looked as if he would speak, but he'd already slid his cock along her slick folds. She thrust up, urging him inside her. His hips propelled forward, fitting himself to the hilt. Vidar rocked on top of her, taking her slow and easy, as if he was afraid of breaking her. He braced his arms on either side of her, keeping his perfect rhythm as he thrust in and out, in and out.

Karre held on tight, unable to take her eyes off him. Firelight danced on his tight flesh but was nothing compared to the inner fire in his eyes. His name left her lips with a pleasured groan. Seconds later, she came, trembling in violent release. He stiffened, jerking as he too met his end.

When the climatic tremors receded, he fell to her side and gathered her against him. He kissed her temple, keeping her close. "I don't know when or how, but I love you, too, my lady. When you were gone I felt as if my whole world no longer mattered. I will give anything to make you happy, just don't leave me again. All I have is yours. I love you, Karre, forever."

No words could describe the feelings that erupted inside her at his admission. Turning to face him, she grinned, "Now I know I didn't make it through the portal. This is too perfect to be real."

Karre laughed as she pulled a piece of torn parchment out of her shoe. For the first time in weeks, she felt great. The bruises and cuts had healed. Even the burn on her arm no longer ached, though it had formed into a scar around her wrist. Oddly enough, the mark only seemed to draw the esteem and compliments of the Starian knights. Rolling the parchment in her fingers, she said, "I know where the Divinity portal is hidden."

Behind her place on the floor, Vidar stopped moving. An easiness had developed between them, an understanding that didn't always need words. But it was more than that. There was trust. She glanced over her shoulder, seeing him near the bed. Slowly, he pulled his tunic over his head. "Oh?"

Karre closed her eyes and pretended to concentrate. "It's true. I saw it. It is to the north." She peeked at him, trying not to laugh at his confused expression. "Yes, north. Battlewar Castle. Dungeon." She again peeked at him. Confusion turned to worry. "No, hold on a moment, it's the old dungeons." Worry faded into concern. "And," Karre paused, lifting the piece of paper to read, "Last door, down stairs..." She started laughing, unable to continue as realization replaced his small frown. Shaking the small note, she said, "Lilith left me directions to Divinity's headquarters so I could escape you."

Vidar strode to her and reached to help her to her feet. "Escape, my lady? Never."

"Never," she agreed, standing next to him. She wrapped her arms around his neck. Meeting his lips, she kissed him briefly. "We should go. The device is ready."

"Are you sure this is what you want to do? I still do not like taking you over the border." He placed his hands along her hips, sliding them back to rest on the small of her back. "I'd rather keep you here."

"We've discussed this," Karre said, "at length."

Vidar nodded. She knew he didn't like it, but at least he wasn't forbidding her to go with him. "Gather what you need. I will ready the horses."

# CHAPTER 12

*Because right now, in this moment, Karre no longer had a role to play.*

The stagnant air as they traveled through the marshes made it hard to breathe. Moss-covered trees surrounded them, creating a curtain along the narrow trail of dry land. Karre let the horse make its own way as it walked behind Vidar's mount and before Oskar's. Both men had assured her that the Caniba would not rise up from the water. Even with their reassurances, she found herself constantly tense and straining to see peeks of landscape beyond the mossy veil.

"Are we close?" Karre asked, wishing she'd shared a horse with Vidar. She could use the comfort of his body. He'd refused, saying he'd be better able to protect her if his limbs were free to fight.

"One minute closer from when you asked a minute ago," Vidar said, looking back. Concern shone through his handsome eyes and she knew with one word she could make him forget this course of action.

A nervous tension rolled through her. Never had the stakes been so high. Everything she loved depended on her abilities and the idea of failing Vidar terrified her more than being trapped on a dead plane, more than capture by Divinity, more than death itself. Because right now, in this moment, Karre no longer had a role to play. This wasn't an act. She wasn't in character. This was her life. Everything she could ever want. If she failed...

*It will not fail,* she told herself, refusing to think of it again.

---

The horses splashed through the shallow marsh waters, past small patches of earth sticking up in random patterns. Vidar's horse led hers to higher ground, to the town of rectangular tents bathed in moonlight and firelight. The smell of burning wood from the bonfires dominated the evening. Tiny, orange sparks from the flames danced in the evening sky before dying out.

Karre reached behind her, patting the satchel that hung against her horse. It bounced with each movement, but she'd padded the contents inside to keep them safe. As the ground leveled and they entered the camp, Vidar reined his mount next to hers.

The tents, varying in sizes, spread out over the high clearing on an orderly grid to create pathways. The larger tents were in the middle with progressively smaller ones fanning round them. Banners hung from the tent flaps, pinned to the opened entryways. Their brilliant colors stuck out against the light caramel of the canvas.

"The Caniba prisoner is here?" she asked.

"He is," Vidar acknowledged.

"Then let's get started. I don't want to wait." Karre let go of the satchel.

Vidar dismounted and moved to help her down. "This way, my lady."

Vidar did not like his wife's presence in the encampment, but he was proud of her for coming. He knew how important it was for her to belong in her new world—to help, to prove herself worthy. She was worthy—he tried to tell her as much but she needed to feel it.

Oskar stayed behind with the horses as Vidar grabbed the satchel and walked her toward a nearby tent. Two men guarded the front flap, with more around the sides.

"Careful, Sir Vidar, the madness is deepening in him," one of the guards said. "He cries for his queen."

Vidar nodded. Karre appeared brave, but he knew the truth. He saw her hands tremble ever so slightly, saw the hesitance in her eyes as he opened the front flap to the holding tent. Dirt floors stretched along the entire length, worn smooth by the constant brush of feet over the earth. In the center, their Caniba prisoner was tied to a thick wooden chair, which had been weighted by lead shoes bolted to each leg. The light was dim, kept purposefully so. Bright lights seemed to aggravate their prisoner. Not that the harsh, rapid breath resounding over the space could be considered relaxed. It sounded more like a rabid dog caught in a trap. Perhaps that was exactly what their prisoner was.

As his eyes adjusted to the dim light, he saw Karre make a move to step past him. He held out his arm, stopping her. "Tell me what needs to be done and I will do it."

"Hand me my bag," she said. He did and she knelt on the floor to rummage through it. She kept glancing toward the center chair.

The Caniba stared back at her with ravenous eyes. His jaw moved in slow bites, working open and closed. A deep scar ran along the man's cheek, down across his chin and back up the other side. His hair bunched around his head in tight knots and frayed strands. He didn't smell as bad as the others because one of the Starian knights had doused him with soapy water.

Vidar stepped in front of his wife, blocking her from view as she busied herself putting together her device. She'd been working on it since she'd gotten back, spending endless hours adjusting and readjusting. Vidar had built catapults, forged weapons and strategized battles, but he'd never seen anything as confusing as the inner workings of her contraptions.

"Ready." Karre stood and handed him an alien device. It looked like a metal helmet with strange carvings and protrusions all over it. "Put it on his head. I'll do the rest."

As Karre tried to put a matching device on her own head, he

ordered, "No. I thought we agreed that I would take on the prisoner's memories. I do not wish for you to see such things."

"I never said that specifically," Karre denied. "Put it on him. I know how to navigate to find the memories we need. I can do it faster."

"But you said they happen as visions. I know this land. I know where the visions will lead," Vidar argued.

The Caniba growled at Karre, "I will feed you to my queen."

"Charming." She dismissed the prisoner, still not getting too close. To Vidar, she said, "I'll describe it in full detail. Put it on him."

Instead of instantly obeying, he leaned into her and kissed the corner of her mouth. "If it becomes too much..."

"I know. I'll stop. I promise." Karre slipped the helmet on her head, adjusting it.

Karre couldn't stop, no matter how depraved she felt on the inside. She felt the Caniba's hunger. It built up inside of him like a disease, festering, oozing, consuming the soul like a demonic poison. When he was away from his queen, a physical pain came over him.

"He doesn't have a name. None of them have names. Not anymore, not that they can remember, not that they care to. Magda drugs them," Karre said, keeping her eyes closed and her thoughts focused on traveling through the enemy's brain. She saw the Caniba queen in a large stone cavern. Torchlight surrounded her throne, shining off her white gown like a million tiny stars. Oddly clean amongst the dirty obsession of her followers, Magda carried herself like royalty.

"Karre?" Vidar's voice penetrated the heavy fog.

"She puts the drug into her cup and offers it to her warriors as a reward. One taste and they are addicted. It keeps them loyal," Karre continued. She smacked her lips, as her mouth filled with a salty-metal memory of the sacred Caniba wine coated her tongue. "She serves it in blood." A rush of pleasure filled Karre, streaming over her entire body. "It feels wonderfully euphoric. It's in my blood. It feels like I'm flying and spinning and dancing. The pull is too strong. There is no cure for it. We must obey my queen."

Karre felt the press of the other followers against her arms. She would give her life for the bloodthirsty sorceress, commit any deed.

"Try to find where she's hidden," Vidar instructed.

The prisoner growled from his place on the chair and tried to fight Karre's mental probing. She pulled her thoughts from the ceremony, not having realized just how far she'd slipped into the sorceress' spell.

"I'm coming from the mouth of a cave. She's ordered me to the borderlands. Already the fear and hunger grow in my stomach. I must please her so she will reward me." Karre clenched her fists tight. Her head began to throb. She'd modified the memory implanter to let her access his mind. The device wasn't supposed to work like this—keeping people connected for so long. It was supposed to upload memories and then quickly implant them.

"I hear water. It's the queen's bathing pool. We're not allowed to use it, but we can watch." A sharp pain shot through her head and she cried out.

"End it," Vidar demanded.

"I almost have it," Karre gasped. "It's a waterfall. Big. There's a crooked tree several miles away."

Karre screamed and clawed at her head, fumbling for the button to turn the device off. Vidar's hands were on the helmet, lifting it off as soon as it deactivated. Chanting filled her, echoing from the prisoner's mind. Her vision swam, causing her world to teeter out of control.

"Karre? Karre?" Vidar sounded so worried. His arms were around her—safe, secure, forever.

The pain was too much. It radiated all over her. She answered the only thing she could. "I will feed you to my queen."

Vidar gathered Karre into his arms and carried her from the tent. A trail of blood streaked down her cheek from her nose. She didn't move, but he'd heard her last words clearly.

*I will feed you to my queen.*

The words chilled him. He'd seen the blank look in her eyes, heard the desperate pain in her voice. Why had he let her convince him to do this? What if the Caniba's thoughts didn't leave her? What if she went crazy? He should have asked more questions about the device. She'd made it seem so harmless, as if she'd done it a thousand times.

"Grab the lady's bag," Vidar ordered the guard. "Send Lance to my tent."

As Vidar carried his wife toward his usual tent, he saw a couple of men coming out of it. He nodded, knowing they hadn't been given much warning about their leader's arrival. Rushing her inside, he laid her down on the narrow bed.

The redheaded Lance appeared holding a device much like the ones Karre had. "Step back, Sir Vidar. I will scan her."

Vidar hesitated, but finally stepped back to let the medic work. "What is that thing?"

"Lady Lilith retrieved this handheld scanner for us from a medical plane and gave it to me at the Fire Ceremony. It was used on Lord Sorin's battle injuries and even his scars were removed. Lady Lilith trained me how to use it. If my report to the king is favorable, we'll be able to trade for more. Already it has saved lives, mended bones, broken fevers." Lance lifted the unit over his unmoving wife. "What happened?"

"She was injured by alien technology." Vidar's gut tightened. "Let us hope she can be saved by it."

---

*My queen!*

Karre gasped, pressing her temple. The echoing demands of the Caniba prisoner's memories screamed in her head, filling her with a desperate ache, and she'd only glimpsed into the man's brain. She couldn't imagine what it would be like to actually be drugged into submitting to Sorceress Magda's will.

"Karre?" Vidar whispered, concerned.

She blinked, trying to push the feelings aside. Her eyes focused on his handsome face. "I'm all right." Karre reached for him, holding onto his shoulders. "Come here. I need to feel something warm." After the coldness of the Caniba, it was true. "I need you."

She barely registered their surroundings, not caring that the voices of knights sounded outside their tent. Vidar captured and held her attention. Cream instantly pooled along her folds, wetting her sex.

Karre took a deep breath, realizing her corset had been loosened while she was passed out. She moved on the bed, liking the way the stiff material brushed her nipples, caressing them with each hurried breath.

"You had me worried," he said, his hand on her hip inching up her skirt. His eyes drifted over her length to briefly pause on her chest before again meeting her gaze. "Promise me you are done and that you will leave the fighting to me from now on."

"I promise no such thing," she whispered. Karre smiled at him, moving gently along his body as he settled against her. She reached for her skirt, pulling it up faster so that she could freely move her legs. Desire and passion built, coursing through her until she thought she might explode with the intensity of it. Then she set to work on his breeches, tugging the laces at his waist. Her hand slid next to his arousal. "Mm, you're so warm. I ache for you. Come here."

"Are you sure you're well?" Vidar glanced at the tent flap, as if he expected someone to walk in.

"No. I know I am not." Karre squirmed, parting her legs. Her body tingled, each nerve alive. "I need you inside me, warrior. Now." She licked her lips, keeping them parted.

"Whatever my lady wishes." His body shifted and he lifted over her, settling between her thighs. She shoved his breeches down his hips, freeing him enough to allow their bodies access. He slid his hand down her side. "I am powerless against you."

The thick tip of his cock probed her pussy, gliding along her slit before finding aim. He thrust into her. Her heartbeat quickened, pounding in her chest. She inhaled deeply.

He took her slow and sweet, letting her feel every agonizing moment. When she was with him, everything else faded away. She breathed in his scent, felt the press of his body, the warmth of his nearness, the taste of his kiss.

Karre angled her hips, silently urging him to go faster. He gave her what she wanted, driving forward, sliding, pounding, harder and faster. She gasped, desperate to find her release.

She bit her lip, moaning loudly as she reached her climax. The muscles of her pussy quivered, gripping his cock as he buried himself deep. Vidar shuddered, letting loose a loud groan as he came. Karre giggled, not caring who heard them.

"I love you, my lady," Vidar whispered, lying next to her on the small bed.

Karre smiled and closed her eyes. A sudden shot of pain went through her and she gasped, grabbing her head. Flashes came to her, dark and twisted. Vidar's voice was far away, but she heard his panic. She felt the brush of stone against her hand, damp and cold. Blinking hard, she said, "I know where the queen lives."

---

Vidar didn't like taking his wife with him past the borderlands into Caniba land, but they needed her implanted visions to find their way through the twisted maze of stone and forest. And navigate she did, leading them through the countryside as if she were native to the land. He worried about her, saw the faded light in her eyes right before she told them where to go.

"This is it," Karre whispered, pointing toward the sound of running water. She lay on the ground next to him and the small contingency of knights with them. Thick shrubs hid them from the Caniba. Aside from the plant life, the forest seemed dead, devoid of even the smallest of animals. The only sound beyond the wind was the low hum of insects. "She lives behind the waterfall. I don't know what's past there, but she'll be there."

Vidar nodded. "You have done well, my lady. Now it is time for you to go."

"What?" Her rounded eyes looked into his. "I'm not going anywhere."

"I won't fight about this now. You've done well and brought great honor to our name. You showed us the way. Now I need you back in the safety of the encampment." Vidar knew before she even opened her mouth that she would argue with him. He nodded to Oskar. The man, having his orders, took Lance's handheld medic unit and pressed it against Karre's arm. Her mouth opened but only a soft wheeze sounded as she passed out.

"My lady will not be happy when she wakes up," Oskar said.

"But she'll be safe," Vidar answered. "I'm entrusting you to take her to the marsh encampment."

Oskar nodded, gathering Karre into his arms. Vidar waited several minutes, giving them time to get away before turning his attention back to the waterfall. He'd miss Oskar's sword and knew the man gave up much in turning away from the battle to protect a lady. But Oskar, like all Starians, knew the importance of such a task. To the three remaining knights he said, "At the ready, men. In there lies a great victory to this war."

---

Two dead and one injured out of four. Vidar looked down at his bloody arm and frowned as he flexed his tingling hand. Next to him, Luca remained unharmed. The two fallen were laid along the narrow cave next to their killers.

Green light shone over the cave, emanating from worms in a trench along either side of the natural pathway. A sickeningly strange combination of flowers and unwashed bodies filled the cave air, as if someone used heavy perfume to cover the need for a bath. Steadying his breath, he motioned Luca to continue.

Without hesitation, the man surged forward, sword held high. The passageway opened up into a large cavern. Luca lifted his hand. Vidar crept forward and stopped. Inside the sparse room, Magda crouched alone in the center of a circle. Her back was to them, but

Vidar recognized the pristine white of her gown—strange in such a dirty home. He could see her bare feet firmly planted.

Luca moved forward, stealthily placing his feet on the ground. Vidar joined him, circling the sorceress in the opposite direction. She stiffened. The knights stopped. Luca pulled a knife from his waist and threw it at the woman. Magda screeched, surging to her feet. As she stood, the sorceress revealed the front of her gown. The white was stained crimson, as were the woman's face and hands. She caught the knife's hilt with lightning speed, spinning it around in her hand before launching it back at Luca. The knife embedded in his shoulder and he stumbled back.

Magda screeched again, the sound high and long, baring four perfect fangs amidst her teeth. When she looked at him, her eyes shifted color, filling with eerie golden threads. Her hands spread out to her sides, as if daring him to try. Vidar grabbed his knife and threw. Instead of waiting for it to hit its target, he charged the queen while her attention was focused on catching the blade. As the knife landed against her palm, she turned. Vidar thrust his sword. His blade missed, slicing through her dark hair. He saw Luca stand, the man's arm limp.

There was an odd grace to the way Magda fought, as if she had no fear of death or pain. It was very unlike the brute style of the Caniba. She leapt and spun, landing with ease on her bare feet only to twirl in the opposite direction. Vidar tried to chase after her, but she was too fast, dodging his best swings. No human he'd ever seen could move like that.

Luca growled, jerking the knife from his shoulder to throw at the woman as she sped past. It hit her arm, but she kept going. She jumped, screeching as she sprang off the cave wall before landing behind Luca. Grabbing Luca's head, she bit into his neck with a vicious rip. Vidar ran. Luca dropped to the ground, unmoving.

Magda flew at him, bloody mouth wide open. With inhuman strength, she flung him across the room. When she came at him again, he lifted his sword and embedded it in her stomach. Even stabbed, she didn't stop. Vidar grabbed her throat, holding her fangs back seconds before they sank into his flesh. They rolled over the stone floor. As his back hit, the sword blade slid up her stomach. Her strength waned. Vidar grabbed the hilt and jerked. Her eyes widened as it hit her heart. She stopped moving. Then, as if she'd never been there, her body turned to ash, which rained down on top of him. The sorceress was dead.

Coughing, he grabbed his arm and struggled to his feet. He reached for his neck, feeling the sticky blood where her teeth had scraped. He could barely lift his sword as he stumbled toward the entrance. If he didn't get out of there soon, he'd be dead too.

---

*I'll kill him!*

Karre pushed up from the fur rug on the ground, ready to storm out of the encampment tent and back over the borderlands. She knew the way now. It was imprinted in her head. At least the insistent screaming of the Caniba's pain had left her mind. As she made her way to the door, she skidded to a stop. Vidar was there, lying on the bed. He looked bloodied and bruised.

"Vidar!" She hurried to him, all anger replaced by the sight of him. He didn't move, as his chest rose in shallow breaths. How long had she been out? What happened? She remembered being shot with the handheld medical unit. Had they been attacked? She briefly felt his forehead, noting the intense heat. Frowning, she hurried for the tent flap. Seeing Oskar next to several riders, she beckoned the man over.

Oskar ordered the riders to go and they took off in different directions.

"What's happened?" Karre demanded. "Another attack?"

Oskar grinned. It was a look she'd never seen on the man. "I sent word to the castles. Magda is dead. Vidar has done it. You have done it, my lady." Those who heard the knight began to cheer in excitement. The wave washed over the entire encampment. "Her spell is broken. The prisoner in the tent has calmed. He had no idea where he is or what happened to him. It is the same for those in Magda's camp. They don't know who they are. Vidar crawled out of the queen's cave and they simply laid down their arms. Magda's spell is broken. I've even sent word to have Fredrick released. Synna will be very happy to have him home."

Karre stood in shock before turning to look at the tent. "Where is Lance? Vidar needs help. He needs—"

"Lance is on his way. Vidar will live. Go, be with him. I'll send the medic as soon as he arrives." Oskar turned, shouting in victory to again make a wave of sound over the encampment as others joined him.

Karre went back to the tent and to Vidar's side. She brushed the hair back from his forehead. "I can't believe you drugged me to face her alone."

"I wasn't alone," he mumbled, not opening his eyes. "I had three good men with me who gave their lives for the fight."

She let loose a long breath to hear his voice, even if it was hoarse. Frowning, she saw punctures at his neck and gently turned his head to the side. "Who bit you?"

"Magda tried." This time he did open his eyes, weakly reaching to grab her hand and pull it from his jaw. "She was very strong. She kept fighting even after I ran her through. I have never seen anything like it. Then she just stopped."

"Did she stop after you stabbed her in the heart?" Karre rested her palm against his chest, feeling his heart beat.

Vidar nodded. "I saw the death in her eyes and then she turned to dust."

"Vampire," Karre said. "It makes complete sense. She must have come here through a fairy ring just like others. She used her blood to enslave the Caniba to her will. That is why they've gone crazy and can't remember who they are now that her hold over them is broken. Her power was in her blood. When you killed her, you ended that power."

"Vampire?"

Karre sighed thoughtfully. "I've only met a few on Plane 395, but they were in the Adult Pleasure Center VWH—that's vampires, werewolves, humans. They were relatively harmless, but I've heard stories of other, darker creatures. They're undead, supernatural beings, nearly impossible to kill and they survive by drinking the blood of the living. She could have been here for centuries, ruling the Caniba, asserting her hold over them, making them bring her live food offerings. It makes sense that she's in the earth, too. That kind prefers to live in the ground."

"They let our men pass to pick up our dead without a fight. They seemed more confused than anything." Vidar tried to sit up, but she pressed on his chest to keep him down.

"Sir Vidar," Lance interrupted, coming into the tent. Seeing Karre, he added, "My lady."

Karre stepped away, hovering as Lance set to work mending Vidar's wounds. When the man had finished and left, she stopped him from getting up by crawling on top of him and pinning him to the bed. "I'm not happy with your decision to drug me and cart me back here."

"I did what I had to. I needed to know you were safe." He ran his hands along her hips. Though still visible, his wounds no longer looked as bad as they had been.

"Oh, I'll forgive you eventually, but you're going to have to work for it." She laughed as he quickly flung her onto her back.

"As you wish, my love," he said before he kissed her. "As you wish."

# *Epilogue*

*Because right now, in this moment...*

Karre smiled in pride as she watched her husband being granted a lordship by the Starian king. He'd fought well and bravely and deserved the honor and the permanent bequeathment of Spearhead.

Battlewar Castle overflowed with those who'd come to celebrate Magda's demise. The war was over, a thing not all of the Starians were prepared to accept. But with Magda's hold over the Caniba gone, the enemy had lost their will to fight. It was more than could have been hoped for. They all knew how important and formidable the sorceress was, but no one had known what she was or that she'd come from another plane. With her death came peace and a whole race of warriors with no idea what to make of their lives without a battle.

"I've been authorized by the king to begin renegotiating bridal trade," Lilith said, glancing across the low table at Karre. Jayne and an obviously pregnant Paige had joined them at the table. "With Director Tomes missing and some sort of disruption at the company, I think we can pretty much get anything we want."

Karre hid her smile.

"Just make sure the women know what they're getting themselves into," Jayne said, subtly wiggling her fingers in her husband, Lord Ronen's direction. Five young boys stood next to him. They were Jayne and Ronen's adopted children.

"Impossibly stubborn men who no longer have a war, so they turn their attentions to their wives." Paige laughed, gently rubbing her stomach. "Not that I complain at Aidan's attentions."

"I might even open up trade with other dimensions, if anyone here has any requests or ideas," Lilith added.

"I might have a few," Karre answered, trying not to show her amusement. "More medic units, food synthesizers, massage booths, oh, and there is this great shoemaker on Plane 45 who makes wonderful boots. They fit the foot like a second skin. I always meant to do more shopping when I was there."

"I'll put it on my list," Lilith drawled.

"Warriors without a war," Jayne mused, standing. "Whatever will we do with them?"

"I'm going to go lie down," Paige said, waving over Aidan to join her.

Karre turned her full attention forward, smiling at Vidar as he made his way toward her. The main hall faded away as she looked at him. Her breathing deepened and her heart quickened, just like the first time she'd seen him in this very castle. His eyes narrowed and firelight reflected off the yellow flecks that ringed his irises. Everything about him captured her senses.

"Well done, my sir." She bit her lip and pressed her legs tightly together, trying to tame the sexual desire she felt for him. It was no use. She found her gaze going to the bulge between his thighs—strong, muscular thighs surrounded a thickening cock.

"Actually, that would be my lord," he corrected. She took his hand and followed him as he led her through the hall. Once there, he swept her into his arms.

"You know, I've never slept with a lord before." Karre kissed his neck.

"We'll have to rectify that, my lady. After tonight, you will never sleep without a lord again." And with that he whisked her down the hall.

The End

# About Michelle

**Michelle M. Pillow**
***New York Times* & *USA TODAY***
**Bestselling Author**

Michelle loves to travel and try new things, whether it's a paranormal investigation of an old Vaudeville Theatre or climbing Mayan temples in Belize. She believes life is an adventure fueled by copious amounts of coffee.

Newly relocated to the American South, Michelle is involved in various film and documentary projects with her talented director husband. She is mom to a fantastic artist. And she's managed by a dog and cat who make sure she's meeting her deadlines.

For the most part she can be found wearing pajama pants and working in her office. There may or may not be dancing. It's all part of the creative process.

**Michelle loves talking with readers on social media!**

www.MichellePillow.com

facebook.com/AuthorMichellePillow
x.com/michellepillow
instagram.com/michellempillow
bookbub.com/authors/michelle-m-pillow
goodreads.com/Michelle_Pillow
amazon.com/author/michellepillow
youtube.com/michellepillow
pinterest.com/michellepillow

# *Ariella's Keeper*

## THE SERIES CONTINUES...

Divinity Healers
by Michelle M. Pillow

*Alternate Reality Romance*

When his father threatens to take away his research facility's funding if he doesn't come home, Dr. Sebastjan Walter has no choice but to do so. This isn't just a family reunion. It seems his father has arranged a marriage—Sebastjan's. Seeing his chance to make one last final deal to get his father out of his life, he agrees to marry the off-plane woman. After seeing her, he can't help but think he's made the better bargain.

Ariella has been held prisoner by the Medical Supreme since he cured her of a childhood illness. Forced to stay in his home as his ward, she has no choice but to do whatever he wants. When he demands she marry his son, Ariella finds this is one order she might not mind obeying.

## Chapter One Excerpt

*City of Asclepius, Country of Chiron, Dimensional Plane 187*

There was little worse than being stuck in a medical dimension as the undeserving prisoner of an overbearing doctor. And, since that doctor happened to be the Medical Supreme, by all rights the most powerful man on dimensional plane 187, Ariella was even more out of luck. For who would go up against such a powerful man in order to save an off-plane woman from an alternate reality? A woman with nothing and no one to make her rescue worthwhile?

Supreme Walter didn't trap her in with chains or lock her away with iron bars. No, his plan was much simpler and much more diabolical. He had injected her with a virus, specifically engineered by him to keep her within his home and forever under his control. Her body became her jailer, the boundaries of her flesh her prison walls. She couldn't run, couldn't escape. If she wasn't so tormented by what was done to her, she might actually admire the sick perfection in which the Medical Supreme kept her.

Then again, probably not.

Only the chemical antidote he pumped into the mansion's air vents kept her alive. Sure, she had an inhaler so she could walk the grounds or for when he wished to take her out and show her off as his ward. But if she were out for longer than six hours, she'd die a horrifically painful death.

If Ariella disobeyed him, he took away her cure. If she vexed him or refused his orders, he took away her cure. If she didn't make certain the servants had his evening sustenance on the table on time, he took away her cure. If she didn't log in at least an hour of exercise a day and keep her food intake down, he took away her cure.

Yep, a definite pattern.

"And when he tires of me or demands more than I can give, he'll take away my cure," Ariella whispered, staring at her reflection in the mirror. Sometimes she barely recognized herself. It wasn't just the toning of her daily exercise, though that did take away the softness from the figure prized in her youth. Her clothes were the height of

Chiron fashion consisting of a pair of loose black slacks and a long gray shirt with a stripe of green down the front to match her eyes. She'd been forced to grow out her blonde hair, letting the waves fall down over back. Running her finger over her lips, she watched the color stain smear only to regroup exactly where it belonged.

One of the benefits of living on one of the most medically advanced planes of existence was the constant monitoring of health. She'd never felt better in her life—unless her cure was taken away, of course. Every meal, though bland, was perfectly balanced with her body's dietary needs for the day. If she became overly stressed, one of the maids appeared to give her a shot in the neck to take the symptoms away. Her heartbeat was monitored by the mansion's central computer, as was her location.

*Captive. Prisoner. No escape.*

The words filtered through her mind in a constant stream, repeating over and over throughout her day. She wondered if she were to run and never come back if she'd even be allowed to die. It was possible Supreme Walter would save her and force her back, after a sufficient amount of punishment of course.

Ironically, she'd come to this dimension for a cure, but while she was getting treatment there was a rebellion on her home dimension and her family was killed. Without her father's political position, Divinity Corporation had little use in demanding the Medical Supreme send her back to her home reality. Besides, there was nothing on her home dimension to go back to but certain death. She'd be murdered the moment she appeared through the portal.

Though the viability of alternate realities was well known and accepted on her home dimensional plane, Divinity Corporation had the only known source of inter-dimensional travel technology. They were her only hope, for no one in the Chiron capitol city of Asclepius would take her word over the Medical Supreme, and Divinity was not coming to save her.

Out of the four hundred thirty-six known dimensions, Ariella had only been to three alternate realities—home, a Divinity base and this one. Each foreign dimension was like looking at a copy of her home world, if history had evolved in a different way. To a point there were many similarities. Languages were relatively similar. Some people appeared the same, but were not the same people. Certain events, like natural disasters, were shared, and the planet was still basically the same planet.

"But this is not home." She looked at the ceiling of her bedroom. The longer she stared, the smaller the great room felt. Like all places on this plane, the room was overly sterile, each surface hard and unwelcoming but for a few engraved curls and wisps decorating the edges. Marble and metal blended together with great square columns to form self-sterilizing walls. The gray and green chairs and bedding matched her clothing. By Chiron standards, it was the most lavish of places.

Swallowing nervously, she again turned her attention to the long mirror. Supreme Walter had been acting strange, becoming more possessive of her time and ordering a full array of checkups—tests that centered a little too intimately on her private regions, as if confirming she was a virgin yet again. The man was obsessed ever since he'd discovered her maidenly status at her first medical appointment. Where she came from, it wasn't such a rare thing. People were expected to wait, though she knew not everyone did.

Ariella was no fool. She knew what men wanted with their leering eyes and lustful bodies. She had seen the educational films, read the forbidden manuals, whispered girlish secrets to her now-passed sisters. She had seen the way Supreme Walter stared at her stomach and hips, as if calculating the children she would have. It left her feeling cold and empty.

"Tonight wear the new clothes I bought for you and wash your body well," he had said as she stood from the dining table. "I have put scented lotion on your dressing table. Use it. Everywhere."

Lifting her fingers, she smelled the herbal concoction on her hands. It was pleasantly sweet and a horrible omen of what was to come. If she thought it would do any good, she would jump from her second-story window. Though, the last time she tried to end her life, the mansion's security devices activated and caught her in an invisible net. Walter had not been pleased.

"If I must do this, I beg the goddesses that he should find his release quickly." Her thighs tightened, clamping together. The very idea of him coming over her naked body made her stomach ache. "Or perhaps his heart will seize before the time comes and I will be free."

Who was she kidding? The other doctors would only save him.

# *Join the Exclusive Club!*

Join the Pillow Fighters' Reader Club to stay informed about new books, sales, contests, giveaways, exclusive content, preorders and more!

michellepillow.com/author-updates

# *Please Leave a Review*

THANK YOU FOR READING!